CRUSADE

Book Three of the Paladin Trilogy

CRUSADE

Book Three of the Paladin Trilogy

DANIEL M. FORD

sfwp.com

Library of Congress Cataloging-in-Publication Data

Names: Ford, Daniel M., 1978- author.
Title: Crusade / Daniel M. Ford.
Description: Santa Fe, NM : SFWP, [2018] | Series: The Paladin trilogy ; book 3
Identifiers: LCCN 2017059142 (print) | LCCN 2018001072 (ebook) |
   ISBN 9781939650771 (epub) | ISBN 9781939650788 (mobi) |
   ISBN 9781939650764 (e-pdf) | ISBN 9781939650757 (softcover : acid-free paper)
Subjects: | GSAFD: Fantasy fiction.
Classification: LCC PS3606.O728 (ebook) | LCC PS3606.O728 C78 2018 (print) |
   DDC 813/.6—dc23
LC record available at https://lccn.loc.gov/2017059142

Published by SFWP
369 Montezuma Ave. #350
Santa Fe, NM 87501
(505) 428-9045
www.sfwp.com

Find the author at www.danielmford.com

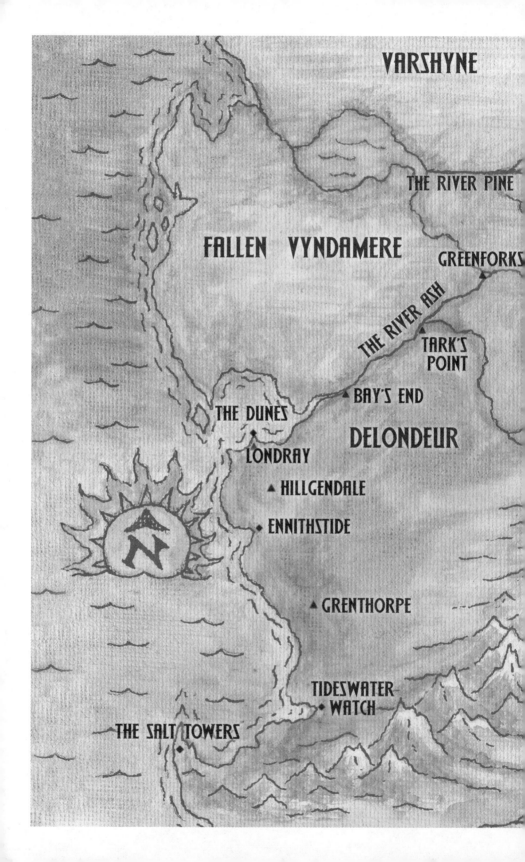

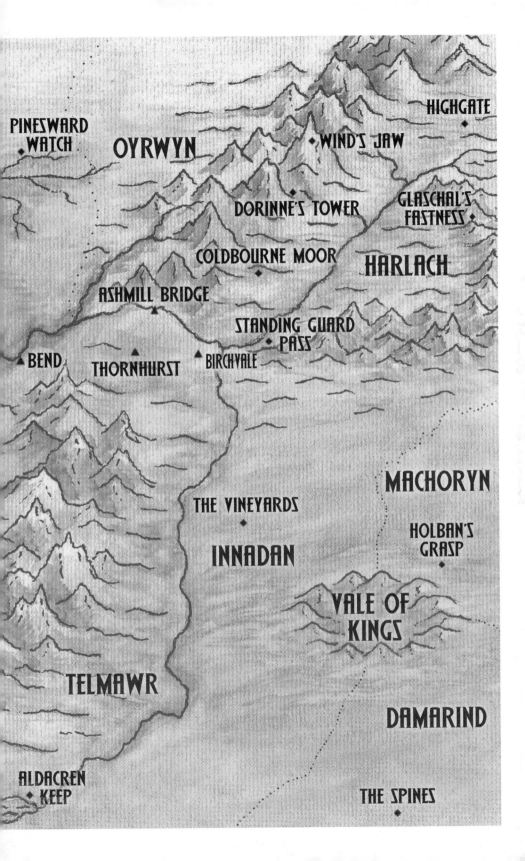

To Lara,
For more reasons than there are words in this book.

Table of Contents

"In Keersvast and the Concordat, we think
of the Barony folk habit of swearing by an
afterlife of torment known as 'the Cold'
to be a barbaric and superstitious notion.
That opinion is shared only by those who
have never, in fact, experienced a winter
in the Baronies or beyond."

—an excerpt from *A Bard Abroad,*
by Andus Carek

Prologue

The winter sky over Londray and its icy harbor was hard and bright. Not quite gray, not quite white, and certainly not blue, it lacked sun and clouds both. On this particular day, it looked, some might say, like it felt.

Cold.

No snow fell, which was a small blessing. But the cold was felt by everyone, from the fur-robed lordlings at lessons in tower rooms studded with braziers, to their tutors, the priests of Braech and Fortune who fumbled at their books with gloved hands. It was felt by the greenhats who patrolled the city streets and walls, huddled under fur mantles and carrying horns full of coals as close to their skin as they dared. It was felt by shop-boys running errands, taking orders, or making deliveries for their masters, who ran as fast as they could in as many layers of clothing as they could stand.

The boys who hoped to be taken into a trade in the spring prayed, as they did every winter, to be taken by bakers, blacksmiths, or cooks, who were said to be the only folk who stayed warm in winter.

The fishermen, boats docked and tied for the winter, huddled in shacks, burned whatever fuel they could afford, and tried to move enough warmth into their fingers to mend nets and splice lines, or carve trinkets for sale from likely pieces of bone they'd collected throughout the other seasons.

The men and women who haunted the streets felt it the worst. But then, they felt everything the worst. And there were more of them in the wake of the riots and the unrest that had gripped the city in the short weeks of fall.

One such man, who felt a certain burden of guilt over those riots, still couldn't contain the energy that sent him knocking around the walls of Londray.

Though he felt the cold, felt it sear his lungs with every breath he drew, it was nothing compared to the fear that clutched at his chest while he wandered his city's streets with a much slighter limp than he'd once had.

It was nearly a month since Baron Delondeur himself had ridden out of Londray at the head of a small army. He had lurked by the gates then, along with other wounded veterans, clutching their usual signs and bowls.

Even a man with the legendary, fearless flair of Lionel Delondeur didn't go to war in the midst of winter, on the cusp of The Longest Night.

Tibult had kept his head down when the Baron's natural son had taken over, kept it down further when the Baron's daughter had sailed back from Keersvast just before the harbor would face the real danger of freezing over. Once it did that, no one sailed in or out without paying hefty considerations to Braech's clergy. There'd been a lot of fighting then, between the greybands who followed Chaddin, the Delondeur bastard, and those loyal to Landen. Landen—with sorcerous aid, some said—had made quick work of the pretender, freed her father, and restored him to the seat.

When that happened, Tibult cursed himself for not having left before the winter settled in. And it was leaving he meant to do.

Somewhere out there in Barony Delondeur, in a village he'd never heard of till the autumn past, on the wrong side of the Thasryach and hard against the Oyrwyn border, there was a man who could finish what he'd started when it came to Tibult's leg.

A paladin.

Tibult had spent the fall and the early winter telling anyone who would listen about what had happened, what he'd felt, and where he meant to go as soon as the snows melted.

Winter would put up a long fight, he knew. It always did. Snow could blanket the valleys and the plains, not to mention the mountains, for months at a time, and when it would start and stop was anyone's guess, which was why the lords and Barons tried to end their campaigns soon after autumn came.

Which made Lionel Delondeur's move at the onset of deep winter all the more puzzling, and all the more frightening. So Tibult, along with a lot of other lamed soldiers-turned-beggars, had gone to watch the army march off.

Soldiers, more than other folk, could be counted on to drop links or food or even a blanket or a wineskin now and then.

They could also be counted on to gossip.

This lot, as Tibult had watched them, had done plenty of the latter but little of the former. They were, he realized while they marched out boasting and singing, not veteran men. They were the sons of merchants and tradesmen and sailors playing at soldiering after a pitiful fortnight's training.

But there were still three hundred of them, and they were still headed to the place Tibult had most wanted to be, according to how they gossiped.

Thornhurst.

It had almost been enough to drive him back to despair. Almost enough to make him waste the weight he'd hoarded on bottles of spirits, enough to send him reeling off down a pier.

Three hundred unblooded boys still made it three hundred to one, as far as Tibult knew. Three hundred to three if he counted the dwarf and the woman who saved him when he'd tried to give himself to the bay.

She should count, he had chastised himself. Probably twice.

So he'd held on to some shred of hope. Of faith. Why, he couldn't have said. It was more than just the shred of healing that had gone to his leg. It was the thing he couldn't name that lay behind the healing. Something vast and powerful and loving, that saw him and all his faults and failings and offered him love in spite—or because—of them.

So now, nearly a fortnight after the Baron had marched off, he found himself inside a veteran's tavern, drawn up close around a mug of wine, cheap and hot, and wincing as a heavy hand pounded his shoulder with a mix of soldierly affection and real force.

"You still hangin' on to that Freezin' story o' yers?"

Tibult looked up into the face of the newcomer. He had the shoulders of a blacksmith and looked healthy to Tibult's eyes, but he carried a sign and a bowl like the rest of them. Tibult had never figured out why.

"Aye, Mattar, I am."

"Well," Mattar said, dropping heavily onto the bench next to Tibult, "if yer man was ever out at this Thornhurst, he's gone t'the Cold by now."

"We've all gone t'the Cold," muttered a figure seated across the table, tugging at old brown bandages that covered half her face. Mottled white flesh, burned and twisted, descended her neck.

"Don't mind Teague," Tibult muttered. "And I don't b'lieve ya, Mattar. I just can't."

"Well I don't believe you either, Tibult," the big man replied with a laugh, which he followed by smacking the table and calling for wine.

"I walk more easily than I have since I took my wound."

"Since a horse sat on ya, ya mean?"

"The horse had its leg broke by a mace, Mattar," Tibult replied. "It were a good horse, fast and strong and eager t'please. I never even got t'name him. Deserved better than dyin' the way it did." The heat in Tibult's answer surprised even him. He'd found that with the edge of his pain taken away by the paladin, he had more time and energy to think on things like that, to remember that he once had thoughts.

Mattar slurped his wine noisily. "Could be ya just started t'get better. S'been known t'happen."

"I know what I saw and felt," Tibult replied. He sought out his wine cup and had a deep drink. He didn't want to say much more about that night, the riots, the woman who'd gotten him to start them. "I have t'think it took more'n a few score unblooded shop-boys to do for a paladin."

"There were two, three hundred of 'em, and a number o'knights who wanted to show their loyalty to Delondeur, given it had just been in question, as it were. He had the Long Knives with him too," Mattar added. "Those boys'll slit anything's throat, and then have its purse empty before the body hits the ground."

Tibult threw back the rest of his wine and pushed himself to his feet. Moving too fast still put an ache in his hip, but he didn't care. He wanted away from Mattar's nagging voice of doubt.

Mattar stood up with him, frowning. "Look, Tibult," he said, "I don't mean anythin' by it. Brother o'Battle and all that," he added, fumbling in his belt for links. "Let me buy."

Tibult had just reached the door then, and made to open it, when it swung open of its own accord. A man he didn't recognize had thrown it open. "To the nearest crier's stand," the man yelled. "They've news of the Baron and a battle!"

Just as quickly as he'd come the man disappeared, leaving a stunned tavern crowd in its wake.

There was a moment of pause, then, as one, they surged for the door, none faster than Tibult.

* * *

By the time they'd reached the stand, the crier had already mounted. Silence but for the swirling of the wind reigned as the speaker, a corpulent figure made more so by heavy layers of fur, drew in his breath from the same searing cold as the rest of them.

"The Baron Lionel Delondeur," he proclaimed, "the fifteenth Baron of his line, Elf-Friend, Giantsbane, who defeated the Island Alliance, Conqueror of Barony Tarynth…" The crier drew the pause out, gathering more wind into his fat red cheeks. "Is. DEAD."

The mound of fur-clad crier held up an unrolled scroll, blue ribbons dangling from it. "This news is confirmed for us by the Temple of Braech," he went on. "That the Baron was most foully murdered by a renegade Oyrwyn lord."

The crier's voice was cut off by a shout, as another, younger man pushed himself to the platform, much to the shock and consternation of the fat crier. "I have it from Fortune," the man yelled, holding up a similar scroll bound in white cloth. "The Baron was not murdered! He fell in single combat against a paladin!" He put a great deal of shout into the last word. "One Allystaire Stillbright, resident of the Delondeur village of Thornhurst." The man thrust his scroll into the air. "What's more, the paladin holds both the Lady Heir Landen Delondeur and the Baron's natural son, Chaddin, as hostages!"

"As prisoners," the fat man yelled back. "To be tortured!"

"That's a Freezing lie," the younger crier said.

Their voices dissolved into a babble that Tibult couldn't be bothered listening to; he turned to the crowd that had followed him out from the tavern. Mattar stared at him, hard, wide-eyed.

With a snap to his voice, Tibult said, "I'm leavin' as soon as there's a break in the cold. Mayhap before. Any man wants to come wi' me is welcome, no matter what his hurt. I'll do my best t'get him there. You with me?"

Mattar extended a hand. "Aye. I'm with ya. Brother of Battle?"

Tibult thought on it as he shook Mattar's hand. "Let's try to be brothers o' somethin' better than that."

CHAPTER 1

Reunions and Reconciliations

"Audreyn?"

Allystaire's half-gasped word hung in the air a moment, while he and his sister stared at one another. He braced himself as if for a fight.

She flung her arms around his neck. After a moment of dumbfounded stillness, he wrapped his arms around her back as hesitantly and carefully as he could.

Behind him on the stairs, he heard Idgen Marte snort. "It's been nine days. Pretty sure the Mother's strength is gone, Allystaire. You needn't worry about crushing everything you touch."

He laughed at himself and wrapped his arms around his sister for a moment, inhaling the scent she wore, expensive but subtle. It reminded him of different times, halls full of knights and ladies in fur-lined silk. He stepped back, rooting himself back in the present: a drafty stone-walled Inn full of folk dressed in leather and wool.

Allystaire opened his mouth to begin asking the questions that filled his mind. His voice was halting, his throat dry, and Audreyn was faster.

"You look like the Cold incarnate, brother," she said, studying his face with eyes that were a match for his, dark blue, unlikely to miss much. "Or at the very least like one who has been detained there for some time."

Allystaire's thoughts turned to the more immediate past. To the Goddess. Lying on some silken bed straight out of a minstrel's song, broken and defeated. Dead. Believing he had failed, when he saw the Goddess weep, only to be granted the vision of Gideon defeating the sorcerers, and cleansing the skies over Thornhurst of its unnatural darkness.

"For once," he said, his voice still an uncharacteristically slight croak, "I do not feel it." He placed a hand on Audreyn's hand and said, "A moment, sister." He turned to the table at which Gideon, Torvul, and Mol sat. The boy watched him quietly, his brown eyes as wide and knowing as ever. The dwarf smoked and grinned, his bald pate gleaming in the light of the lantern he'd hung over the table, the smoke of his huge covered pipe curling up into the darkness above them in widening rings.

"Gideon," he said, waving a hand. "Come here, please." The boy stood up. He was not tall for his age, which Allystaire guessed to be roughly thirteen summers, was built slightly, had a light tan shade to his skin, and his scalp was shaved more cleanly even than Torvul's. As the lad approached, hesitantly, Allystaire took a step towards him and wrapped one arm around the boy's shoulder, surprising him with the force of the embrace.

I am sorry. The boy's voice sounded in Allystaire's head. *I almost cost us everything with my—*

"Hush," Allystaire said aloud. "You saved us. I thought I had failed you, Gideon. I thought I had lost you."

The boy was silent, his face impassive. For a moment, though, his thin arms clung as tightly to Allystaire as Allystaire did to him. Then he stepped away, casting his eyes to the ground, and adjusting the robe he wore self-consciously.

Allystaire surveyed the rest of the room. Ivar, the mercenary captain, in black mail and black leathers, wouldn't meet his eyes. One set of intense eyes he did meet, to his surprise, were those of Rede. The paladin extended a hand and a finger at the former Urdarite monk.

"I know not why you are here, but if Idgen Marte has not killed you yet, there must be a good reason. I would like to be made aware of it in the next few moments, or I will rectify her mistake."

"He is the reason we are here," Audreyn said, cutting him off and stepping between him and Rede, pushing Allystaire's arm gently down. She extended her other hand to indicate the blond man who'd also risen when Allystaire entered the room, who finally stepped forward to speak.

"Rede came to us, alone, in the depths of Oyrwyn's winter. On foot. He said you would need our aid," Garth said slowly. "Convinced us to ride out and seek you on Delondeur's border."

"He made it to Highgate? In winter?" Allystaire looked to Rede, still silent, who met his gaze without challenge.

"Coldbourne Hall," Audreyn said. "The young Baron was convinced to cede possession of it back to me, and thus to Garth."

"Still impressive to make it that far into Oyrwyn on foot this late in the year," Allystaire allowed, looking from Rede to Garth, and then back again.

Rede finally spoke, slowly at first, choosing his words carefully and enunciating them as if he had chewed them a little first. "I would not have come back to this place if the Shadow's curse had not truly haunted me. I need to atone; I know it. I will beg your mercy, Arm. I don't deserve your forgiveness." His voice sped up as he went, the last words tumbling out in his quiet, tense voice.

"He's been right helpful since he got here," Torvul put in. "Hoppin' to it at every turn." And then in Allystaire's head, the dwarf's voice added, *And I trust him only as long as he stays where I can see him and Idgen Marte can kill him. Mind him.*

"So the two of you came riding from Coldbourne to Thornhurst in the midst of winter, and you arrived when, exactly?"

"Not the two of us," Garth said. "Not quite. He said you would need aid, but he did not know in what way."

Allystaire felt an ache gathering behind his eyes and he reached up to the bridge of his nose. "How many did you bring with you, Garth?"

"As many knights and household guards as I could muster," the knight answered, with a shrug. "Fifty lances, of which mayhap half a dozen are knights. Two hundred foot."

"Garth, does the Young Baron know that you have *invaded* Barony Delondeur?" Allystaire moved to the table where Torvul sat and joined the dwarf on his bench, slumping against the table, feeling the ramifications begin to pile up on his shoulders, interlacing his fingers behind his head.

"Allystaire," Idgen Marte's voice snapped. "Worry about the consequences later. There were plenty of the Baron's men who needed containing. Not to mention

Landen and Chaddin, who were ready to set about killing each other as soon as the battle ended. If Audreyn hadn't shown up and taken them in hand, I don't know where we'd be right now. None of us were in any position to stop them."

"I am sorry," Allystaire allowed. "If someone could please, for the love of the Mother, get me something to drink—and I do not Freezing mean water—then I will speak to everyone, one at a time, and sort out what is to be done." He lifted his head and found Cerisia eyeing him from across the table, her face slightly shadowed and impossible to read. "Archioness," he acknowledged, nodding. "Please excuse my manners. What are you doing here?"

"Observing—and acknowledging, formally, on behalf of my Goddess—the foundation of a new faith," she said, a faint smile playing at her lips.

"Anathemata?"

"Rescinded," she said. "As far as my authority extends."

"Which is how far?"

"Delondeur, Oywryn, and Innadan. Telmawr as well I suppose, for all that it matters."

"Will Braech's Temple do the same?"

"I doubt it very much," Cerisia replied. "The Sea Dragon's representatives fled before the battle even ended. Something about this place terrified them. They were on edge the entire time, and couldn't wait to be off."

Gideon, Allystaire thought, but didn't say. "Halfway is a start. It will do the folk good to hear that, at least."

Cerisia laughed very lightly and leaned forward so that her features were no longer concealed by the edge of the lantern's light. "Barely awake after convalescing from from injuries that would have killed any three normal men, and you are already thinking ahead, planning, trying to understand where this will move next, and what it means for the people under your guard."

"What are you saying, Archioness?" Mol, who'd slipped away, returned to Allystaire's side with a bottle in hand, pulled the cork from it, and set it next to his elbow. He felt the cool glass of it through his sleeve. Meanwhile, the young priestess slipped onto the bench next to him, on the very edge of it, and leaned against his shoulder.

"That you, Allystaire Stillbright, are truly as much a paladin as has ever walked this world. Mayhap more so."

"Stillbright?" An echo of two voices, Garth's and Audreyn's. Allystaire was shocked, momentarily, to hear himself called that, then he found himself nodding his thanks to Cerisia and turning to his sister and brother-in-law.

"Aye. That is what they were calling me." He turned to eye Torvul, who simply grinned around his pipe, maddeningly. "That is what I called myself," he added absently, remembering the moment he'd done so, facing down the ensorcelled Lionel Delondeur, his enemy given a grim and terrible strength, armed and armored by the very bones of his own men. "That is who I am. If you had any thought that your coming here would result in me returning to Oyrwyn, or to Coldbourne, I will disappoint you."

Audreyn frowned. Garth sighed and looked away. His sister said, "Have your drink. I brought as much of the better part of Coldbourne's cellar with me as I could," she said. "And the lass fetched your favorite."

Allystaire finally looked to the bottle at his elbow, already open, and without bothering to look or ask for a flagon, raised it to his lips. His intended quaff became a sip as soon as the red passed his lips.

"That is old Innadan stuff. From before the Strife," he said, lifting the bottle and staring at it in wonder. "I never thought to see its like again." He looked to Audreyn, and said, "How much did you bring?"

"As much as they could pack. All told, it is better than six score bottles," she said, beaming.

"It was a mighty pain to pack and carry along with the supplies for the men in the midst of winter, let me tell you," Garth added.

He took another careful sip, and said, "Good that there is so much. The people of Thornhurst will enjoy the celebration all the more," as he set the bottle down.

Mol laughed next to him, then beamed a smile up at Audreyn's shocked face, and for once, Allystaire saw his sister at a loss for words.

"It is time we retired, Garth," she said. "It is late and my brother is going to insist on being foolish," she finally muttered. The blond knight looked over her shoulder apologetically at Allystaire, but was swept out in her wake, a burst of cold air billowing into the Inn as they left.

"They've got Freezin' huge pavilions set up just outside the wall," Torvul put in. "And they brought half a bog's worth of those little moss bricks your folk like for fuel with them. They'll manage in the weather." The dwarf set down his pipe, knocking the dottle out onto a tiny bowl set on the table with the heel of his hand.

"What of our people? Enough buildings standing?"

"Most sleep in the Temple," Mol said. "It stays warm through the night. Thanks to Gideon," she added. The boy shrugged dismissively.

Allystaire looked to the opposite table, to Cerisia and Rede, and said, "I mean no offense to either of you, but I will be straightforward. I will speak with you both when I have the time. Yet I think it is time that we five, and we alone, speak of what has happened."

Cerisia stood gracefully, her mantle of silver fox fur flowing around her as she moved. "As you once told me, you are not a subtle man. No offense taken."

For his part, Rede simply left the Inn wordlessly, without a backward glance.

"Where does he sleep," Allystaire asked as he watched the door shut.

"Not sure he does," Torvul replied. "Got a lot of energy, that one. I'd start worryin' about where I'd sleep, were I you, if she finds out there's no bars on the doors," he added, pointing a thumb towards the stairs Cerisia had recently ascended.

"I think the Archioness has got competition even she can't live up to," Idgen Marte said, dragging a stool to the edge of their table and plopping on it. She stuck one boot atop the table, grabbed the wine bottle, and took a pull.

"What d'ya mean by that," Torvul said, eyeing Allystaire.

"Not my place t'say," Idgen Marte said, handing the bottle off to Mol and wiping the back of her hand.

Allystaire felt his cheeks betraying him as he plucked the bottle from Mol's hands, earning an indignant stare from the priestess. Torvul's scrutiny was like a physical weight. Finally, the dwarf slapped the table lightly.

"You dog," the dwarf exclaimed. "You sly dog."

"Enough," Allystaire said, setting the bottle down. "That is between me and…and Her. Where do we stand?"

"Landen and Chaddin are hostages. Garth and Audreyn disarmed all their remaining men. We're keeping them warm and fed and clothed," Idgen Marte said. "I know Chaddin was on our side in the battle, but he was ready to start pressing his claim the instant you fell. I don't know how long Gideon could've kept them in check had Oyrwyn arms not suddenly arrived."

"I could've stopped them from fighting," the boy said quietly.

"Aye, I think just by showing up and walking around you'd keep them quiet during the day," Torvul allowed. "But I'm not sure that would've kept them from going at it with daggers in the night. We've got them separated, opposite ends of the town. They're looked after, I promise you."

"I will want to speak to…" Allystaire stopped himself in mid-sentence, and lowered his head. An image of Renard, the reliable old soldier who'd followed him out of Bend so many months ago, charging to his aid to the last, torn apart by Battle-Wights. "Dammit," he muttered, feeling, for the first time in more years than he cared to count, hot tears gather at the corner of his eyes.

Silence reigned a moment, all of them with their heads bowed.

"He died a hero, Allystaire," Idgen Marte finally said, breaking the quiet.

"He still died. I asked him to leave, to take Leah and go…"Allystaire trailed off with a sigh.

"And he refused," Idgen Marte replied. "He knew what we faced, and he chose to face it. Honor that choice," she said.

Allystaire nodded, blinked away the tears gathering in his eyes. "One more thing to do. The list grows by the minute." Struck by a sudden thought, he looked to Mol. "What of Ardent? The other horses?"

She looked up at him, her eyes distant for just a moment. "Fine. Beyond the northern gate, in the valley."

He sighed. "Good. I know where I am headed in the morning, then." He felt weariness suddenly spring upon him, as the list of tasks began to draw itself up in his mind. "And I must sleep. So should all of you."

He stood, looking at the four of them as they stood with him, Mol finally snatching the bottle and helping herself to a swig, then setting it down. "We made it," he said. "Past the Longest Night. I do not know what the world will have in store for us next. I know we can meet it together. Aye?"

"Don't go gettin' all teary on us now, boy," Torvul said gruffly. "You're not suited to it."

"I mean it," Allystaire said solemnly. "How could I not? We have only just begun our work," he said. "And I pity those who will align to impede us."

CHAPTER 2

Horseflesh and Attachment

"The brother I remember would not go to so much trouble for a particular horse."

Audreyn picked her way along the frozen track, keeping pace with Allystaire, Garth, Gideon, Mol, and Idgen Marte despite being the only one in a dress, and wearing boots finer than the day called for. She seemed to take three steps for every one of Allystaire's, but they were short, contained, determined, and she never looked likely to fall or slow. All of their breath steamed in the air, billowing in clouds. Thankfully the wind was low, but dead grass crunched underfoot, frozen even under the risen sun.

"Not just any horse," Allystaire replied, trying to watch both Garth and Gideon as they walked to either side of him. The latter seemed unwilling to go too far from Allystaire's side this morning, but hadn't spoken, and had mostly avoided looking him in the eye. The former maintained a wary distance, constantly, Allystaire thought, trying to stand between him and Audreyn.

"Well, that's just it," Audreyn countered. "Most Oyrwyn men are mad for horseflesh. They can discuss the bloodlines and books of lineage with a precision that would wear well on an Urdaran monk arguing points of theology. You, on the other hand, cursed the expense of the stables and said you'd prefer to save the weight and fight on foot if the rest of them would just be sensible and do the same."

"She isn't wrong, Allystaire," Garth put in mildly. "You practiced riding with the same devotion you practiced all the rest of the craft, but you never seemed to enjoy it much. And as I recall, when you bought the grey in question, all you wanted to know was about his training."

Allystaire stopped on a small rise on the road, hitching at one side of his belt, tugging at an empty loop. "The horse's name is Ardent," he said.

"So you said," Audreyn replied warily.

"Never known you to name a horse. Always said it was no use to get attached, all that mattered was that they were healthy and trained," Garth said.

"Well, in the first place, I did not name him," Allystaire said. "She did," he added, gesturing to Mol.

Despite the cold, the girl priestess who ambled along beside them wore only her blue robe, and no shoes. Allystaire had frowned at her bare feet when they set off, and opened his mouth, ready to deliver a lecture, until the girl had smiled at him, reached up to pat his hand, and walked away. As they walked, Mol occasionally wandered a few paces away, knelt to the ground and pressed her hand to it, cocking her head as if listening for something.

When Allystaire waved a hand at her, she quickly shook her head. "I didn't name him. I only told ya what his name was."

"That sounds like a lot of rot," Garth replied.

"You should be used to hearing a lot of rot, Garth. Goddess knows I talked enough of it in my time," Allystaire replied. He took in a deep breath, relishing the way the air seared his lungs. *There's something sweet in it, being out of doors again under a clear sky, under the sun, with no Battle-Wights, sorcerers, or Delondeur spears trying to kill me*, he thought.

"Still do," Idgen Marte added.

Allystaire ignored her as he went on. "Still, I know now why I said the things I did when I was training you, and all the others." He set off again, sparing a glance to Gideon. Unused to the cold, the boy held his cloak tightly around him, huddled miserably under it as if he could make himself disappear beneath the fur collar. "And that is what is wrong with the whole business."

"What business?" Puzzled, Garth stepped closer to Allystaire. The blond knight was taller, rangier, his strides eating up more ground, so he had to rein himself in to keep from passing the shorter but heavier Allystaire.

"War," Allystaire replied. "And knighthood."

"Am I going t'have t'hear about how knighthood is an *idea* again," Idgen Marte asked. "Because if so I'd just as soon turn around. I like my horse as much as I like anyone, but I'm not getting lectured *and* freezing my tits off at the same time. One or the other," she declared, to Audreyn's laughter and Garth's shock.

"No. Because I do not know just how to say what I mean yet," Allystaire replied. "About knighthood, anyway. As to becoming attached?" The road took them up a small hillock. As they crested it, the small herd of horses that had escaped Thornhurst a week prior, sent away by the Voice of the Mother, came into view. Most of them nosed among the grass, but one stood apart, staring straight at them.

"The reason I spoke that way, the reason I taught you not to become attached to your mount, the reason I turned boys into hard men while calling them knights, Garth, is because the more a man is attached to the world—the more of it he loves—the harder it is to tear it to pieces," Allystaire said.

He turned away from the rest of them then and strode forward, letting out a piercing whistle as he went. The destrier broke into a light trot; while the rest stood and watched, man and horse met each other.

Allystaire wrapped his arms around Ardent's thickly muscled neck, lowering his head into the horse's shoulder. Ardent lowered his head, pressing so hard into Allystaire that he was nearly knocked from his feet. He stepped away then, rubbing one gloved hand along the horse's neck. Mol, meanwhile, had raced forward to meet the herd, such as it was, and simply waved a hand at them.

"Come on, then," the girl yelled. "It's safe now."

To the gasping astonishment of Audreyn and Garth, the two dozen or so animals turned as one and began walking in the direction the girl indicated. All of them but Ardent, who stood by Allystaire's side and only began walking when he did.

"That's not canny," Garth half muttered.

"You'll get used to it," Idgen Marte said flatly.

"So all of you are bestowed with these Gifts, I believed you called them?" Audreyn, after her initial shock, pursed her lips and adjusted the hood of her cloak. "Even the girl and the boy?"

"My name is Mol, and his is Gideon," the priestess called out, as she walked unworried amidst the scramble of horse's hooves. Idgen Marte, meanwhile, picked out her own lean brown courser from the crowd and moved to its side, running her hands along its flanks.

"That was our grandfather's name," Audreyn said, turning to Gideon. "Did you know that?"

"Yes," Gideon slowly turned his eyes to Audreyn's face. "Allystaire told me as much when he offered it to me."

She frowned, one delicate eyebrow pointing downward. "My brother named you?"

"Yes," the boy replied. "I had not yet earned one, so Allystaire and Torvul took it upon themselves to offer them to me. Gideon appealed to me."

"And what is the nature of your Gift then, Gideon? Are you to be a knight like my brother?"

"Knighthood is a foolish and stultifying tradition," Gideon replied. "And I will have no part of it. As to your first question, I do not know if you would understand the answer."

Audreyn's back suddenly stiffened and her mouth drew into a thin line. By that point, though, Allystaire had approached and couldn't stifle his laughter at Gideon's answer.

"Please do not be offended, sister," he said. "I promise you he does not mean to speak down to you or to imply that you are stupid. I have known the boy for months now and I do not understand half of what he says. And our Gifts," he added, catching Audreyn's eyes, "are not something we discuss. The time may come that you see them."

"I've seen yours," Garth replied. "When you broke my leg."

"And then healed it," Allystaire added quickly.

"Not before you grabbed ahold of my voice and forced me to speak," the blond knight said, a bit of heat creeping into his words.

"To speak the truth," Allystaire replied calmly. "I could not force you to do otherwise. And I am sorry about the leg. For what it is worth, Garth, that was the first time Her strength came over me. I did not know what to expect."

"You did horrid things that day, Allystaire. Terrible things," Garth said. "I have seen as many battlefields as any man alive, but what you did to Casamir? I turn as green as a squire seeing his first blood to think of it."

"Casamir had wanted killing for years. Since he had grown old enough to realize how he could use his strength and his station, really," Allystaire replied. "I am not going to lie—Cold, I cannot—and say I did not take some satisfaction in being the instrument of his death."

"You cut him in half with the blow of a hammer! With him in good Oyrwyn plate!"

"I know precisely what I did, Garth," Allystaire replied. He looked from the knight to his sister and said, "You wanted to discuss our Gifts? Fine, then. That strength that came upon me that day, Garth, when did it happen?"

"When we put the fetters on you."

"Wrong," Allystaire said, his voice still calm and even. "Think closely. When did it happen?"

"I remember taking your hammer from your belt, and then suddenly everything went to the Cold."

"When Casamir ordered Miles to ride the boy down," Allystaire replied. "The strength comes on me when I know, beyond any doubt, that innocent folk are endangered, and when I must put my life at risk to save them. Are the results of that strength pretty? No. But they are necessary. *Terrible to behold.* Those were the Mother's words to me. And it was. And I would do it again without a second thought. Now," he said, looking to the destrier behind him, "we are done speaking of it. I want to get my horse to a stable and spend some time with the comb and the brush, make sure he is fed and watered and ready to be ridden. And to make sure he knows I appreciate all that he has done and risked for me."

As if he understood Allystaire's words, Ardent stamped at the ground and let out a quiet chuff, breath streaming into the cold air.

"It's just a horse, Allystaire," Audreyn said dismissively, moving right back to her earlier theme.

"He might be. Or he might be a miracle, or being a horse and a miracle are one and the same. Nevertheless, I will do precisely as I said, because this horse has been a truer friend to me than all but the four who serve Her with me, and has risked his life for me time and again."

"You don't sound like the man who taught me," Garth said then, shaking his head, as the party turned to head back for Thornhurst.

"You would do well to forget much of what that man said."

CHAPTER 3

Negotiations

"**M**y thanks for retrieving our horses," Chaddin said, standing over a hissing brazier, holding his hands near the flames. His tent did little to keep the wind out, but standing near any of the three iron braziers spaced around it made it tolerable. "I thought we'd never see them again."

Allystaire and Idgen Marte stood a few paces away from him near a brazier of their own. "They did just as Mol told them to," Allystaire said with a shrug. "They should have been brought back in immediately after the battle, honestly. My apologies that it took so long."

"We would've gone to get them ourselves if we'd the liberty of leaving the village," Chaddin muttered. He'd grown a patchy blond beard since Allystaire had last seen him, highlighting the features and light coloration that marked him as Lionel Delondeur's son. Unacknowledged or not, the history of the soldier's parentage was there for anyone who'd known the Baron well to see. "Weren't we your allies in the fight? Why aren't we being treated as such?"

"Because you were ready to murder surrendered enemies the instant he was indisposed," Idgen Marte said grimly, pointing at Allystaire. "And there'd been enough Freezing death by then."

"I was ready to do what must be done," Chaddin insisted. "Landen was at the Baron's side. Have you forgotten that? With him through the assault, the sorcerers—"

Allystaire raised a hand to halt Chaddin and spoke once he fell silent. "That Landen supported her father and ousted you is evident. I believe it is less than certain as to whether she shares blame for the actions of the sorcerers, the creation of the Battle-Wights, or for what your father had done at the end."

Chaddin shivered at the memory of it, and not from the biting cold. "Do not call him my father," he said. "He may have gotten me on my mother, and taken me into his service when she presented me, but he hadn't much choice in the matter. I was just another soldier to him."

"Fine," Allystaire agreed. "My point remains. I do not know how much Landen knew."

"She is her father's daughter. That ought to be enough."

"That ought never be enough."

"How do you plan to sort it out, then?"

Allystaire smiled. "I will simply ask her what she knew, and when."

"And when she lies?"

Idgen Marte laughed and Allystaire sighed. "Come here, Chaddin. Please. I will do no harm to you." As he spoke, he pulled a thick glove off his hand and held it out. When Chaddin approached, he laid it lightly on the man's neck. "I am going to ask a simple question. Try to dissemble, to lie to me about the answer. Now, who was your mother?"

Chaddin tilted his head and started to shrug Allystaire's hand off, but the paladin wouldn't budge. Finally the man blurted out, "A camp follower named Esme." Then he did break away from Allystaire's touch, shoving his hand away and stepping back.

"I tell no one that! How did you do that?"

"I am a paladin, Chaddin," Allystaire said. "You have seen me do it before, to Lionel. I thought simply showing you would be faster than explaining."

Chaddin's high cheekbones were colored red with shame. "Why that?"

"It seemed a harmless enough question. And it is a harmless enough answer."

"It is a shameful one."

Idgen Marte snorted then, looking away in disgust.

"Why?" Allystaire narrowed his eyes slightly as he asked the question.

"To be the son of a whore? How could it not be shameful?"

"I'd rather be the son of an honest whore than find pride in bein' the spawn of a man like Lionel Delondeur," Idgen Marte spat. "And before you go condemning your mother think about what choices she had. Fewer than you did, no doubt."

"Chaddin, I have known many camp followers and many Barons. I prefer the company of the former. And I promise you the latter have far more reason to be ashamed," Allystaire said. "If you wish to speak about it more, we can. For now, I want to know what you and your men need, and what you are willing to do."

"Our mounts are a good start. Our arms, liberty of the town, Landen's head."

"The last you will not get," Allystaire said. "And given that you ask, I am not inclined to release your arms. Liberty, though, you shall have. In parties no greater than three at a time, I am afraid." Chaddin glowered, but Allystaire pressed on. "I do not seek to punish you. I would reward you for your aid against the Baron if I could, and I still might find a way, but these are poor folk, and my purse has long since grown thin. The situation remains tense. If I were to let all of you out at once, I could not stop you from butchering Landen's lot without a bloodbath. I do not want any more blood shed on this ground. Do you understand?"

Chaddin nodded, then turned away, swiping a hand aimlessly through the air, the fingers curling into a fist for a moment.

"Chaddin," Allystaire said, "when we met you in Londray, I was impressed by your calm, the way you carried yourself, your assurance and composure. You seemed everything I would have wanted in a sergeant, or an officer. And now your head is hotter than I remember. Why is that? Is it simply the ambition of a Baron's seat? Has it worked on you so quickly? Do not answer. Think on it, aye? I will go to see Landen now, but I will stop and have orders given about your liberty. I will also have wine and ale brought, decent stuff. If you want for any necessity, I will do what I can. We will talk again later." Then he extended his hand.

Chaddin watched Allystaire carefully as he spoke and took the offered hand, shook firmly and heartily, but remained silent as Allystaire and Idgen Marte took their leave.

Outside the flaps of the tent, two soldiers, their grey Oyrwyn livery padded beneath with many layers of wool and fur, snapped to attention as Allystaire appeared. He gave them a simple wave and they relaxed almost imperceptibly.

After a few paces distance, Idgen Marte said, "You have a way with those sorts of men. Soldiers, I mean. At his core, that's what Chaddin is."

"I ought to. I had the charge of thousands of them," Allystaire replied.

"Plenty of men are given rank and status. Doesn't mean they know what to do with it," Idgen Marte pointed out.

"But with Chaddin, it is not hard to see, is it?" Allystaire asked as they began traversing the village. Few folk moved out of doors, though here and there were small parties clearing away the rubble of the battle. Allystaire was glad that he'd missed the task of dealing with the bodies.

He thought, if he breathed deeply, beneath the overpowering cold he could detect just a bit of the rotten stench he'd known for more than a score of years. He tried not to.

"What isn't?"

Allystaire sighed. "That he is a good man, trustworthy, brave, composed. You threatened to kill him, remember, when he arrested me. Put the point of your sword right before his eye. Did he blink?"

Idgen Marte shook her head. "He didn't."

"Precisely. We left him holding a bag of shit. The Baron in chains, a weak foundation of power based on a few loyal soldiers, and a riot at his walls as the professional army scrambled to get home."

Idgen Marte winced. "I was hoping you'd forgotten that part."

Allystaire eyed her a moment, and then sighed. "You did what you needed to do. I made my peace with it." He paused on the track and looked back to the cluster of tents that held Chaddin and his men. "And yet, despite all that was arrayed against him, he held it together. At least until a woman with more loyal swords, a better legal claim, and sorcerers showed up to take it from him. And still, he did not panic. He came seeking allies. He was not ready to give up the fight. And that," Allystaire said, raising a finger, "tells us some important things."

He turned and they resumed walking, Idgen Marte matching pace with him easily. He walked fast, trying to build up warmth in his limbs. "Unfortunately, I am worried about what sitting in the Baron's chair for a few weeks has done to his ambition. Is the idea of Baron Chaddin Delondeur fixed so firmly in his mind that he cannot let it go?"

"So what if it is? You've said yourself we aren't out to meddle in politics."

"I am not thinking of meddling, precisely," Allystaire replied. "But what else are we to do? Turn them loose into the village? They will murder each other and our folk are caught between them. And if we can find a way to avoid the Barony tearing itself apart in blood, so much the better."

"What d'ya have in mind, then?"

"I am not sure yet. I have to talk to Landen. I have some ideas."

"You do know that hanging the Baron's daughter is likely to be looked on sourly, aye?"

Allystaire stopped, fixing a curious look at Idgen Marte. "What makes you think I mean to hang her?"

Idgen Marte stared. "I remember Sir Miles."

"If Landen proves to have dabbled in the same waters as her father, then yes," Allystaire said, "she probably dies. As far as I am concerned, we have the right. I do not know enough to hang her yet."

"Didn't Lionel have other children? Sons?"

"Aye, but Landen is the one who matters."

"Oldest?"

Allystaire shook his head. "Not how Barony Delondeur decides the matter. Cold, Lionel himself was the youngest of three. Delondeurs go into the world and make something of themselves, then return and claim the seat. That Landen is the only one who returned in Lionel's moment of need might mean that she is the only one who still lives."

"So what is your plan?"

"I told you, I do not know. But I am not leading with the noose." He paused. "I am not ruling it out, either."

"That's an improvement, anyway."

They managed the rest of the walk in relative silence until they passed swaths of scorched earth past the Temple.

"Where the sorcerers died," Idgen Marte said. "That was an ugly business."

"I know," Allystaire said. "I saw it. From…elsewhere," he added, as he sensed her forming the question.

"I can only hold off asking you about all that for so long," Idgen Marte said.

"Hold off a while longer," Allystaire said. A few minutes more of walking, and, spread out just beyond the east gate, they found where Landen and the remnants of the Delondeur host were guarded, tucked into a tent at center of the Oyrwyn camp that sprawled eastward.

Allystaire noted with some pride the way Garth had laid the camp out. Tents were staggered, not laid out in neat rows, all the better to confuse an attacker. Horses were picketed in different locations to make striking at them more difficult, and guard patrols moved along in groups of three, their armor bright and their weapons—mattocks or long, two-handed axes on shoulders, short swords on belts—well cared for, clean and deadly looking.

"Coldbourne men," Allystaire muttered as he saw the weapons and the livery they wore, a hawk in the rising position, brown on a dark green field.

"What's the bird?"

"A harrier, also called a marsh hawk," Allystaire replied. "It had long been the device of Coldbourne, but my grandfather changed the posture when granted the fief from the close to the rising, to symbolize how he had risen in life." He pause. "It is an ugly thing, is it not?"

"No more or less than most," Idgen Marte replied. "I would wager that once upon a time it mattered to you very much."

"Aye," Allystaire agreed. "It did." He avoided looking at the standards flying over the pavilion in the middle of the camp, both the Coldbourne Hawk and the Highgate Towered Wall, and avoided the stares of the men in dark green surcoats as he passed, conscious of the weight of their eyes as he moved among them. Not one of them said a word.

Allystaire twitched aside the flap into the prisoner's tent and was shocked, both at what he saw and what he didn't see.

What he saw was a knot of figures clinging miserably together, barely dressed for a Barony indoors, much less in a tent. A few blankets were stretched across the outer ring of them, but none wore cloaks or coats.

What he didn't see were braziers, a firepit, fuel, or furniture of any kind.

"This," he lightly growled, "will not do." He turned on a heel and flung open the tent again. His voice cracked like a whip when he called out. "BAN-NERMAN!"

A passing soldier whose dark green surcoat bore three brown stripes beneath the Hawk badge stopped and snapped to attention. "M'lord!"

"Fetch the Lord of Highgate, if you would. With all speed." Allystaire paused. "Please. Tell him that I wish to discuss the disposition of his hostages."

The man saluted by clicking his heels and thumping a closed fist on his chest, then moved off at a run.

Allystaire headed back inside the tent, slipping his own cloak, a heavy brown fur he'd never tried to identify, off his back and handing it to the nearest Delondeur prisoner.

"Landen?" He peered among the knot of shivering prisoners. Blonde, tall, with pale skin stretched taut over strong cheekbones that made her resemble her father, Landen stood and picked her way past her men, grimacing.

"Is this how you treat your hostages, *paladin?* You're still an Oyrwyn running dog. I knew it."

Allystaire sighed, and shook his head, ignoring the fact that Idgen Marte had stepped to his side and shifted her stance, preparing to shove her away. *Expecting me to lead with my fists?*

"Landen," he said quietly, "I had nothing to do with how you are being treated. I have been unconscious for more than a week, and only awoke last eve. I assumed that Lord Garth of Highgate would know better than this. Tell me everything about how they have treated you."

That took some of the wind out of Landen, who blinked several times, before gathering herself again and answering sourly. "They give us naught but stale bread, gristle, and blocks of ice. They give us a brazier at night, one, and almost enough fuel to keep it warm till dawn. For better than a score of men."

"A wonder none of you have frozen to death. It ends today," Allystaire said. "You have my word. Either Garth will remedy things or I will take you inside the village."

As Allystaire spoke, the tent flap was thrown aside by Garth himself, wearing bear fur over his green-enameled scale armor. Allystaire turned on him and let some heat into his voice.

"My Lord of Highgate, please explain your treatment of my hostages."

Garth took in the tent, his mouth wrinkling at the scent that pervaded the air. His eyes widened in shock. "I left the details to Sir—"

"The details? What command did you give him, precisely?"

"That the prisoners were to be treated appropriately…" Garth trailed off as Allystaire simply stared hard at him.

"Fix it," Allystaire said. "Immediately."

It was Garth's turn to harden his face and draw himself up. "Do you wish to reclaim the Lordship of Coldbourne, which would entitle you to give orders in this camp?"

"Do not be ridiculous, Garth," Allystaire snorted. "These people are my responsibility, and I will not have them treated this way."

There was a tense moment as Garth stared Allystaire down; the latter seemed more calm about it, until the taller, fairer man turned away with a grunt, threw open the tent, and called, "BANNERMAN!" in a passable imitation of the same whip-crack tone Allystaire had used moments earlier.

Garth stepped out and beyond the tent, they could hear him delivering a rapid series of orders to fetch blankets, bread, hot drink, fuel and something to burn it in. The stamp of feet was unmistakable.

Allystaire listened carefully, nodding along faintly, till he turned to Landen, satisfied for the moment. "Have your men untreated wounds? Any cold-death in the hands or feet?"

Landen shook her head. "Your folk saw to our wounds before the Oyrwyn men arrived. The dwarf boiled something to clean them out and others sewed, under her guidance," she said, nodding to Idgen Marte.

"Does any man feel ill? Feverish?" Allystaire looked among the crowd for any signs. One man, who looked a few years older and grayer than Allystaire, with scars crossing his balding head, stepped forward and held out one hand.

"Seemed foolish t'complain t'you, m'lord," he said. "No sense addin' to the misery." He pulled back his sleeve and held out his hand. Three of the fingers had the unmistakable purple and black blisters everyone living in the Baronies knew and dreaded.

Allystaire frowned and took the man's hand carefully. "This has taken days, man. It must have been agony."

The old soldier only shrugged.

Allystaire laid his left hand directly over the man's dying fingers and let his eyes close. His senses gradually came to incorporate the other man, the frozen and dying tissue in his hand. And along with it, the many other small and large hurts he'd taken in a soldier's life. Uneven shoulders. Scars on his scalp from a helm that had been beaten into it. A knee that ached from morning till night, and sometimes woke him up.

He felt all of it, knew all of it, shared many of the same ailments. They were both intimate with pain, with ignoring it and shoving it aside when need be.

That common bond, the shared experience, allowed Allystaire to more easily draw from the Goddess's Gift to heal him. The blisters began to dissolve; the man gasped in pain as blood flowed normally in his fingers again, and shuddered as life returned to the waxy skin.

Everyone in the tent gasped with him.

Allystaire dropped the old soldier's hand, said, "What is your name, man?"

"Harrys, m'lord," the man answered while flexing his fingers and prodding them with his other hand.

"My name is Allystaire. Not m'lord."

The man looked up, his expression suddenly halfway between a smile and a sneer. "I know your name."

"What unit do you serve in, Harrys?"

A pause. "Baron's Own."

Allystaire let out a low whistle. "Good horsemen. Did not know they were here."

"Aye," Harrys replied, his tone still a bit reserved. He hesitated, then added, "We were. Just not in strength." Another pause. "Not the first time we'd gone up again' ya, either."

Allystaire nodded. "I know."

"I almost had you once."

A sudden shock rippled through the tent. Silence followed it. Idgen Marte was suddenly at Allystaire's side. He looked to her sidelong, saw her hands resting on her belt, not far from the long knives sheathed at either end of it.

Landen cleared her throat. "I think that's quite enough, Harrys."

Allystaire held up a hand to Landen, chuckling faintly. "I would like to hear what the man has to say, with your leave."

Landen shrugged. Allystaire turned back to the old soldier.

"Almost had me, eh?"

"Aye." Harrys chuckled as well. "The Vineyards."

"Pretty name for an awful pile of rock, eh?"

Harrys laughed at that, more genuinely. Some of the tension went out of the tent. By now, Coldbourne soldiers had started to pour into the tent carrying thick wool blankets, braziers, stones for a fire pit, baskets of peat bricks. Most of them paused in their tasks as they caught the conversation.

"Too pretty for the work was done there," Harrys offered.

"Too true," Allystaire replied. "What happened? When you almost had me?"

The man grinned as he remembered. "Wasn't Baron's Own, then—hadn't the training for the lance and the armor yet. I was an outrider with Cantle's light horse. Screening the edges of our siegeworks and camp when your lot caught us with our pants down comin' to Innadan's aid." He paused again, seemed to chew his words. "Cantle was an idiot. It wasn't a job for light horse. Should've been scouting so we'd've known you were comin'. Still, we put up a fight."

"I remember," Allystaire replied. "I was unhorsed."

"Was your nose broken," Idgen Marte couldn't help but mutter, to which he answered, "Probably."

"True, and nobody wanted t'come Freezin' near ya, swingin' that hammer. Ya'd your back to me, though, and I laid on the boot to my mount, ready t'brain ya with my axe. We all knew who ya were already. Not the invincible Lord Coldbourne yet, just the Oyrwyn knight whose shield hit like an anvil, whose lance was the breath of Braech itself. Knights and lords used to boast they'd kill or take you; common men wanted no part of ya. But I saw ya on foot and there was my chance. Out of throwing spears, damn the luck. I was one heartbeat away, and ya still didn't know I was comin'. Some damned Oyrwyn knight put his shield right in my face at the last moment, near knocked me senseless. One of my troopers grabbed my reins and pulled me clear."

Allystaire listened carefully, nodding as he remembered the day, the Old Baron Oyrwyn's decision to come to Innadan's aid. Delondeur had split his besiegers into two separate camps, smartly. Allystaire had chosen to attack the smaller, given his first command, to try and draw a response from the larger. It hadn't, but it had allowed the arriving Oyrwyn host to roll up the smaller camp against the walls of Innadan's Keep, the Vineyards, and force a Delondeur retreat.

The old soldier's words brought it all back.

"Well, Harrys, I am glad you did not manage it," Allystaire said.

Harrys held up his newly healed hand and put on a bent, brown-toothed smile. "Think I am as well."

Allystaire extended his right hand then, and Harrys took it in a warrior's shake. The Oyrwyn men, muttering to themselves, suddenly found themselves very busy again.

"Landen, see to the needs of your soldiers, eat, get yourself warm, then send a messenger for me—I will ask the Lord of Highgate to put one at your disposal—and we can discuss what is next."

Landen paused with a bulging wineskin lifted towards her lips, opened her mouth to speak, and then simply nodded. "Aye. And…thank you for seeing to our treatment."

Allystaire nodded and ducked out of the tent, Idgen Marte behind him.

"What is next," she muttered for only him to hear.

"I have no idea," Allystaire admitted.

Idgen Marte looked towards the pavilion at the center of the camp, its pennants listless in the still of the day. "I think I know what's next for me. If you need help with Landen, seek out Torvul or Mol. I have business."

"I know how to handle Landen." He followed her gaze towards the command pavilion, eyes narrowing. "What business?"

"My own," Idgen Marte said, as she tugged on her own cloak and headed for the center of the Oyrwyn camp.

CHAPTER 4

Asking Questions

A turn later, Allystaire found himself sitting at a table across from Landen. She was more warmly dressed than before, in an old grey woolen cloak, and a matching muffler tucked around her collar.

She stank, but Allystaire was too used to such to let it bother him. He set two cups on the table along with one of the bottles Audreyn had brought, pulling it open and pouring into both. Landen eyed her wine suspiciously.

Allystaire sat down, laid his hands on the table in front of him, and frowned, an expression that made his face, not fair at the best of times, even more grim. "Landen, I do not flatter myself if I suggest that you have heard talk of me for most of your life. Has it ever been suggested I would poison someone?"

Landen shrugged faintly, and reached for her goblet. "I suppose not." She had a sip, sighed deeply in appreciation, set the cup back down but kept her hand curled around it. "Your reputation had more to do with the noose."

"When I felt it necessary to kill outside the bounds of battle, I saw no reason to hide the deed," Allystaire replied.

"Most of those you hung were under your command, so you had no need to."

"Most," Allystaire replied. "Not all."

"I do not like the turn of this conversation," Landen admitted. "In short, if you do mean to hang us all, then get on with it."

"I do not wish to hang any of you," Allystaire replied. "But I am not ruling it out."

"You've no legal right—"

"Landen," Allystaire replied, "I am a landless exile in a renegade Temple, and I just killed the ruling Baron of the most powerful western Barony." He leaned forward across the table, locking his eyes on hers. "Do I look like a man who is interested in his *legal* rights?"

"You do not," Landen agreed, but she met Allystaire stare for stare. "Yet at some point you will have to justify your actions here, in the aftermath. Yes, you were attacked and defended yourselves. Anyone can see the moral point, though whether they will agree that rebellion against a Baron is justified—"

"Of what 'they' are we speaking?"

"The other Barons," Landen said. "Surely you understand that Barons Oyrwyn, Telmawr, and Innadan will learn of what took place here and be forced to react."

"Landen," Allystaire said, "your father was embroiled in slavery inside his own borders. He profited from the sale of his own people into bondage, then turned some of them over to a sorcerer to be murdered as a tool of divination. This is to say nothing of what he did outside these very walls, having one of his own knights murdered to grant him power to match mine. There are dozens of witnesses that heard his admission to the first charge. I rescued a woman from the table of the sorcerer myself, and she now resides in this village. Scores saw our duel, heard his admission there. If the other Barons come seeking evidence of his crimes, I will have it to give and you know it."

Landen absorbed Allystaire's litany in silence, finally lowering her eyes to the table. "I saw the sorcerers in their camp when we attacked. Spoke with them. I am glad they are dead."

"Not any more than I am," Allystaire replied. "I found an entire family once, butchered by one of them, to empower his magic. I swore that day I would find him, and end him."

Landen was silent for another moment, and met Allystaire's eyes again. "Very impressive. What does it have to do with our talks?"

"I need to know how much you knew, and what you thought of it all," Allystaire said.

"Knew of what?"

"The slaving, the sorcerers, all of it."

"I have been at sea these past two years," Landen protested, "chasing pirates off Keersvast."

"All well and good," Allystaire said, extending a hand. "Now give me your hand and answer my questions."

Landen kept her gloved hands flat on the table, made no move to take Allystaire's hand. "And if I refuse?"

"I cannot allow you to," Allystaire replied. "I would like you to volunteer, though."

"Volunteer for what?"

"To give me your hand and answer my questions."

"What will happen?"

Allystaire felt himself struggling not to answer, but the Goddess's gift cut both ways and the words came whether he willed them to or not. "You will tell me the truth, because the Goddess has made it so. No one can lie to me. Neither," he added, of his own volition, "may I speak a lie."

She extended one hand halfway towards Allystaire's, hesitant, curious. "Truly?"

The paladin nodded faintly and reached for Landen's wrist.

"Did you know your father profited from slavery?"

"No."

"Suspect?"

"Not for profit, but there were rumors that some of the convict oarsmen on his warships were not convicts. I never investigated."

"Why not?"

"I feared the truth."

"What of the sorcerers?"

"I believed them like any other swords-at-hire."

"And what of the necromancy they employed? The Battle-Wights?"

Landen swallowed hard. "It seemed…practical, to assault a wall."

"Would you seek to use them in battle again?"

That question seemed suddenly harder to answer; Allystaire felt Landen straining against it, and tightened his grip.

"Not if I could avoid at. At utmost need, in defense of Londray itself, I might if I had the means. But I would feel myself damned for it."

"If I were to let you leave Thornhurst, with your men, what would you do?" Allystaire sought Landen's eyes again, but she turned them to the side, staring hard at the carefully swept stone floor of the Inn.

"Return to Londray and assume my seat."

"What actions would you take regarding Thornhurst?"

Another pause; Allystaire concentrated, willing the answer from her.

"I do not know," Landen admitted, a quaver in her voice.

"Do you want revenge for your father's death?"

"Wouldn't anyone?"

"And Chaddin?"

"He is a traitor to his Baron, and should answer for that."

Allystaire sat back, taking in a deep breath and letting go of her hand. Landen stuck both hands beneath the table.

"I dislike your last answers," Allystaire replied. "Your father wanted killing. Surely you saw as much."

Landen shrugged, but couldn't keep a trace of anger from her eyes. "He was still my father. Surely even you understand that."

"I had a father once, too," Allystaire said. "And when I was your age, had someone killed him, I would have wanted vengeance. But one of the things my father and the Old Baron Oyrwyn taught me, perhaps the most important thing they taught me, was that a leader must look straight at the things in front of him. Your father had been making himself into a monster for years and became one in truth at the end. The world is a better place without that Lionel Delondeur in it. Look straight at that fact, Landen, and tell me I am wrong."

"You are not wrong," Landen admitted. "May a daughter not mourn her father?"

"Mourn the man he was," Allystaire said. "There was a time I believed that Lionel Delondeur was a good man. A man I wished I did not have to fight. Gerard Oyrwyn shared that belief till the end of his life."

"My father often said the same of Old Oyrwyn. I wonder why they fought at all, then?"

"Keep asking that same question of all of us, Landen," Allystaire said, reaching for his wine and throwing back a healthy mouthful. "Why have any of us fought? Do not repeat the history to me. Do not even answer the question, not now. Just keep asking it."

Landen drained her wine and eyed the bottle questioningly. Allystaire nodded, so she refilled her cup, set the bottle down carefully.

"Have I passed your interrogation? Will I hang?"

"I will not hang you, Landen Delondeur," Allystaire said slowly. "But I am not yet sure what I will do. What do I tell the people under my guard, if I release you, you become the new Baroness, and return with a larger army in the summer?"

"That is what some of the lords would counsel me to do, what they'd expect me to do."

"A good Baroness listens to the advice of her lords, but must bear the responsibility of her decisions alone."

"Aye," Landen agreed. "Perhaps we can come to an arrangement?"

"It is possible," Allystaire allowed. "I would need to converse with the other servants of the Mother."

"I need to return to my men, take their measure. Some are convinced they'll hang if you so much as look at them. What news can I bring to them?"

"You can tell them anything we spoke of here," Allystaire said. "And tell them to expect further visits from us; I will see that they are properly treated."

"Hanging weighs heavy on their minds."

"The Mother can be merciful, Landen. Mercy is a kind of strength," Allystaire said. "Your father was beyond my capacity to grant it, as were the sorcerers. Your men need not be. I have very little stomach for more death just now. If any of them wish to know how such mercy may be granted, tell them to speak to the Voice."

"The barefoot girl?"

"Her name is Mol."

Landen stood. Allystaire did the same. They walked towards the door of the Inn, Landen extending a hand that Allystaire shook. The Baron's daughter made to open the door, then stopped. "Has any mention been made of a knight named Darrus Cartin? Anyone identified his body or kept him prisoner elsewhere?"

The name pricked at Allystaire's memory, though he couldn't quite place it. Suddenly it snapped into place, Delondeur, wearing his ghastly armor, swinging his massive sword, spitting the name out in contempt.

"Your father had him killed to provide him his strength, Landen," Allystaire finally said. "He told me as much, when we dueled. I am sorry. Was he a friend?"

"Aye," Landen said. "A friend." Her lips pressed into a thin line. "You are right about my father. About looking straight at the thing. He needed to die."

Allystaire nodded, clapped her on the shoulder. "That is a hard thing to admit. Keep asking yourself that other question."

Landen nodded, then headed out into the cold, a pair of Oyrwyn soldiers having stood by the door to the Inn the entire time peeling away and following her in lockstep.

Keeping asking yourself that question and you'll be a better ruler than your father was, Allystaire thought, but did not say, as he watched Landen leave.

CHAPTER 5

Power in the Shadows

Idgen Marte was impressed that Audreyn hardly started when she appeared in the corner of her pavilion. The noblewoman straightened in her chair, carefully balancing the wooden lap desk perched on her legs. Audreyn wore a dress of practical cut, skirts divided to allow her to sit a saddle, but far more richly made than any other garment Idgen Marte had seen in some time, and finely tooled sealskin boots with fur lining.

"Why did you not simply ask to enter?"

"First, I didn't know if your guards would allow me," Idgen Marte replied, staying, for the time being, in the shadows cast by the flickering brazier that was warming the tent. "And second, it is probably best for both of us if no one sees us talking."

Audreyn opened the hinged lid of the desk and set the sheet of parchment she'd been writing upon inside it, shut the lid, set the desk on a folding table to her left, and stood. "My husband might return. The men outside will hear us talking."

Idgen Marte smiled faintly. "I expect your brother will keep your husband busy for a while, if I know Allystaire at all. The guards won't hear me. And if you're willing to listen to what I have to say, well, I have to wager you'll not speak of it to them."

"And if I do? Is there an ultimatum implied?"

"'Course not," Idgen Marte replied with a dismissive shrug. "I'm not here to threaten you. I want to get to know you. Ask you some questions."

"I should like to do the same," Audreyn replied. "What exactly is your relationship with my brother?"

Idgen Marte walked around the edge of the brazier, putting its warmth—and its shadow, her means of instant exit—at her back. "Eh?"

"You sat at his bedside during his convalescence, like a troll guarding a cub. You love him?"

Idgen Marte laughed faintly. "You're being protective, aren't you?"

"Of course I am. Now answer my question."

"I will. It just seems odd. And no, not the way you mean."

"Then why? Why the fierce devotion?"

Idgen Marte sighed, dropping her eyes to the ground for a moment. "It is one of my tasks."

"What do you mean? Tasks from this Goddess?"

"Aye," Idgen Marte said. "The Mother, the Goddess, the Lady. She's not particular about what we call Her. When She Ordained me, to use Allystaire's term, told me what I was to become, She also laid duties upon me. And one of them is to keep your brother alive when his own inclinations would kill him."

"Are you his shield bearer, then?"

Idgen Marte smiled at the question. "Carrying a shield would give them a target. No. There are dangers he does not see. And those enemies never see *me*."

"An assassin, then? A strange companion for a self-proclaimed paladin."

"If I had to be. I would've killed Lionel Delondeur in his sleep in the Dunes, eaten a hearty dinner and slept well that night. But you err," Idgen Marte added pointedly. "He is not self-proclaimed."

"Then why did you not?" Audreyn ignored Idgen Marte's correction, opting instead to press a new inquiry. "It would have saved lives."

"No," Idgen Marte said, shaking her head. "It wouldn't. The consequences would've been dire. Instant chaos. Recriminations and wars that would still be raging. There would be no future for the Mother's Temple if we announced it by assassinating a sitting Baron."

"No doubt that was my brother's objection," she said, moving to a table that held decanters of wine as well as goblets, all glass, expensive to own and to transport. She selected a decanter of white, poured two goblets full, and brought one to Idgen Marte. "He is prone to looking so far ahead, or so intently, that he does not see what is around him, dangerous or otherwise."

"That I will drink to, Lady…" Idgen Marte paused, then ventured uncertainly on. "Coldbourne? Or Lady of Highgate?"

"Either is true," Audreyn replied with a light shrug, then reached out to nudge the edge of her glass against Idgen Marte's, and sip.

For her part, Idgen Marte drank significantly more deeply, nearly emptying the goblet, then gasped appreciatively. "Cold, even this far north you people make some damn fine wine. Innadan?"

"Damarind," Audreyn corrected, taking another delicate sip. "Innadan's primary rival in Baronial wine production." She tilted her head over her glass. "You are southern."

"Concordat," Idgen Marte confirmed.

"Precisely what sort of a nation is that?"

"A massive one," Idgen Marte answered, pressing her lips thinly as she finished. *Damn. She is better at this than I am.* She corrected herself. *More in practice.*

"Then what brought you this far north?"

"I am a warrior. Was a blade-at-hire for a long time. We go where the work is, and for a long time the work has been here."

Audreyn was already opening her mouth to launch another query, but Idgen Marte cut her off by extending her goblet with a smile.

Smiling in return, Audreyn took the goblet and moved to the table to refill it. *Damn, that smile is much like Allystaire's. It never touched her eyes.*

"The two of you have such a strong resemblance. Is it your father you favor or your mother?" Idgen Marte moved forward to accept the goblet.

"Our father, for he is the only parent we share. My mother was Anthelme Coldbourne's second wife." She smiled wryly. "You know, in Oyrwyn, being said to share my brother's features is not a compliment."

Idgen Marte snorted. "I'd wager he did well enough with the ladies."

"Well," Audreyn admitted, "win enough tourneys and heads will turn. He was, perhaps, fairer in his youth."

"And what of your head, Lady Coldbourne and Highgate? Did it turn for a tourney winner?"

Audreyn smiled, a faint blush moving along her smooth, pale, tastefully powdered cheeks. "I will admit that it did. There is something grand in all the foolishness, after all, the horses, the magnificent tourney plate, and he wears it well. But there is more to Garth than that, I assure you."

"Is there?" Idgen Marte said. "He still thinks Allystaire is going to ride north with him and claim Oyrwyn for his own, doesn't he?"

Audreyn frowned. "He won't admit it in the light of day, but I'm afraid he shelters that hope, yes."

"If there is something grand in all the foolishness, the crashing of lances and fine armor atop finer horseflesh, why does that grandeur give them the right to turn your entire country into their Freezing melee ground?"

Audreyn considered the question, eyes hardening again. "How do you suggest I stop them? Don armor myself and beat them all at their game?"

"Armor just makes one a big slow target anyway. Better to never be there when they try to hit you. But there are things all of us can do. Before I elaborate, I need to know. How badly do you want to see the world change, Lady Coldbourne?"

"See the world change? How, exactly?"

"Your brother wants to end the wars, the Succession Strife, whatever you people prefer to call it. Foolish an aim as that seems, I've learned not to get in his way, just to cover his flanks while he does what he's said he'll do. And I could use your help."

Audreyn's lips were a thin line, her eyes narrowed. It wasn't that she looked like her brother so much as her mannerisms put one in mind of him: the deliberation, the care, the gravity.

"Answer me one question."

Idgen Marte shrugged. "If I can."

"You followed him before he was ordained. Why?"

"He hired me to guard Mol while he killed a warehouse full of slavers."

Idgen Marte was hoping that her frankness might cause Audreyn to stumble. There was no such luck as she didn't even blink. "He must owe you quite a bit of weight at this point."

Idgen Marte laughed as lightly as she could. "We're well past counting links, Ally and me."

"And then you were, what, immediately drawn into this new faith? You don't seem the zealous type."

"I took some convincing."

"Then why'd you stay? A true sword-at-hire is only as good as the daily weight. I know this. You haven't the connection to him that the Ravens do, so why?"

"Suppose I could sense the story gathering around him."

"And you're a collector of tales, then? A jongleur?"

That brought Idgen Marte up short, glass halfway to her lips. "That's three questions now, Lady of Highgate. Time to answer mine."

Audreyn inclined her head very faintly, hiding a smile behind her lifted wineglass.

"What are you willing to do for your brother?"

"I have convinced my husband to invade a neighboring Barony in small numbers in the dead of winter. I don't think that's a question that needs answering."

"Then what can you do to help him end the war?"

Audreyn took a seat on one of the folding camp chairs, composing herself carefully. "I am not the sort to put on armor and go to battle. That is not unknown, of course; you've met Landen. And it is more common in the eastern Baronies. However," she went on, raising one hand, and one elegant finger. " Do you know what we're taught in Oyrwyn, after things etiquette and needlework and music?"

"Dancing," Idgen Marte guessed, her tone flat.

"Well, yes," Audreyn admitted, flushing a bit. "Yet after all that, we are taught to manage the gold, the silver, the gemmary, the household stores. The lady of a fief takes charge of its supplies and its links."

Idgen Marte set her wine down and licked her lips. "And?"

"I can make the weight disappear," Audreyn said flatly. "No links to hire warbands, to pay the smiths and farriers, or to buy the horses. I can't stop them from calling up the soldiery, or from culling the harvests to feed them. I can't stop the knights, who must pay for their own arms. But I can damn well make it harder for Oyrwyn to carry on a war I don't want it to fight. The weight of two of the largest fiefs are under my control."

"And would you? Make the weight disappear?"

"If I have to, to keep it from Gilrayan Oyrwyn's hands."

"You know I am asking a dangerous thing from you, Audreyn."

"I told you. If my brother would see it done, then so would I."

"I would not have taken him for the kind to inspire that sort of filial affection."

Audreyn smiled, but in a way that didn't reach her eyes. "And yet, *you* follow him, for a reason as vague as 'chasing stories.' I will tell you why, and shed some light on who my brother is, Idgen Marte. But you must do the same for me."

In for a bent copper half, in for a chain of gold. "What would you ask, Lady Coldbourne?"

"When I asked if you were a jongleur, you flinched." Audreyn paused. "You are not a fearful woman, but that word hit you like a blow. Why?"

Idgen Marte sighed. "If I'm going to tell you this, I'm going to need more wine." She started to move for the table and the decanters it held, but Audreyn stood and beat her to it.

She poured, passed, and sat on the bed while Idgen Marte took the chair.

"So. Jongleur. Minstrel. Bard. Call it what you like. I was bound to be one," Idgen Marte said, suddenly conscious of the low, grating rasp of her voice. "Apprenticed to one of the finest in all of the Concordat. Deitering Thale." The name brought a palpable longing to her mind and body, her heart beating louder. "In the Concordat a minstrel is a glorious thing to be. It brings freedom, even power. In the right hands, a song is a devastating weapon. None were better at it than my master, until the day he came too close to a line. He was too well known to attack, but his student?"

Idgen Marte reached to the collar of her cloak and shirt, hooked her fingers on them and pulled the garments down, exposing the scar that started at the side of her chin and drew a fissured white line well down the side of her neck. "The hired men knew what they were doing, with a blade so thin and fine and a knowledge of the body that most chirurgeons wouldn't equal. In the Concordat's greatest city, gold can buy any knowledge, no matter how obscure."

"They did what? Damaged your voice?"

"Destroyed it."

"What did you do?"

"Killed the men who did it, and the man who hired them, and a whole lot of people in between. And *I* was the one called an outlaw for it." Idgen Marte pulled her collar back into place. "What end did this questioning serve, Lady Coldbourne?"

"If we are to work together, I have to know who you are."

"Fair enough," Idgen Marte said. Self-consciously, she tugged at her collar again, pulled the right side of it a touch higher. "Now. Enlighten me about your brother. Show me that he's not just a blunt instrument."

"Our father died when I was very young, my mother soon after. Both carried away by a particularly bad flux. I was barely five years old and I hardly knew my brother except as a man who always smelled of horses and steel and sweat and was never home. When he came back to Coldbourne Hall that autumn, I was terrified of him. I hid in a wardrobe. Do you know what he did?"

"Hammered it open and lectured you on your responsibilities?"

Audreyn laughed. "No. He just told me that he would be in the courtyard with a new pony he'd just brought home and needed to exercise. The riding lessons that followed earned my trust. He spent the entire autumn earning my affection. Allystaire knew if he didn't take charge of me, no one else would. He made sure I had tutors, took me with him to Wind's Jaw in the winter. He promised that whenever he could be near me, he would be. And he was as good as his word. When he returned from campaign, he would bring presents, speak to me of what my tutors had taught me, and he always brought me with him to Wind's Jaw for the winters," Audreyn said, finally pausing to reach for her wine to wet her lips and tongue.

"He was your father as much as your brother."

"Some combination of the two. Anthelme was not terribly interested in me, and my mother was ineffectual. Almost everything I learned, I owe to him."

Idgen Marte paused for a moment, sipped at her wine. "An autumn flux after your father's death, is that the same flux that killed Allystaire's…" She paused, searching for a word.

"Love? Dorinne. Yes, it was," Audreyn said. "I never met her, or if I did, I do not recall. I didn't even know about her until years later." She smiled. "You know he is secretly a romantic, yes?"

"Allystaire? Cold, he only told me about her because he thought we were going to die within the turn. Said that plenty of time had passed, enough to heal the wound."

"He would say that," Audreyn replied. "Do you know what he did?" When Idgen Marte shook her head, Audreyn continued. "He had her remains moved to a guard tower just outside Wind's Jaw, on a southerly approach. It sounds a bit morbid, yes, but he did it so he could visit her grave when he was there, for her home was a long, impassable journey in the winter. You'd never see it unless you knew to look for it, as it sort of hangs off one side of the tower, hidden by the battlements. He kept it planted with her favorite flowers. Mountain veitch and loosestrife, as I recall. He never rode that trail, to or from Wind's Jaw, without stopping, climbing the tower stairs, and slipping down to the graveside. Not once."

"Cold," Idgen Marte breathed, sitting up straighter. "There's a song in that," she half whispered.

"There probably would be songs if more folk knew," Audreyn replied quietly. "The men who do know, like Garth, keep it to themselves. To tell the truth, Idgen Marte, I think if Oyrwyn faced invasion, there are knights who'd die to defend that tower. Not because it guards a trail. Because of what it means to my brother."

"To guard a grave?" Disbelief was clear in Idgen Marte's tone, in the twist of her mouth.

Audreyn shrugged. "What can I say? Symbols mean so much to men like that."

"He does inspire loyalty," Idgen Marte said. "And yes, those things do mean a great deal to men. What about to you?"

"Women in Oyrwyn are more practical," Audreyn said. "If someone were to make a ballad out of the story of Allystaire and Dorinne, we would sigh and dab our eyes when it was well sung. But I don't think I'd die for a grave."

"Then why let them do it?"

Silence reigned for a moment.

"I can reach out, discreetly, to other Oyrwyn ladies. If Oyrwyn cannot arm itself, and Delondeur cannot march because there is no Baron or Baroness in the Dunes, then who is left to go to war?"

There was another pause, then Audreyn stood. "Before I do this, I have to know what my brother plans to do with the Delondeur claimants. Leaving the seat unoccupied is a recipe for chaos."

"I don't know," Idgen Marte said. "I will tell you as soon as I do."

CHAPTER 6

The Rules of Battle

Allystaire watched Landen walk off with her Coldbourne guards in tow, then pulled his own cloak tightly about him and ventured back out into the cold of the day. He left the village square and turned up the road towards the Temple, swinging his arms and legs as he went, flexing his fingers inside his studded gloves.

Feels a little like carrying a weapon, he admitted to himself, balling his right hand into a fist and running the other hand over the iron studs sewn into the leather, the rings around each joint. *Got to make sure to ask Torvul about getting something fixed up when he has the time,* he reminded himself. The thought of one task, or even of one task he needed to ask someone else to perform, was enough to start a list. *Must speak to Mol about the Delondeur prisoners. To Idgen Marte about what my sister wants. To Garth? Mayhap. I need to see to the people, see if there are wounded,* he thought. *Though surely if the wounds were bad Mol would have brought me to them. I must speak with Gideon.*

That last thought brought him up short. The boy's unusual reticence the previous night weighed on Allystaire's mind. *I need to speak to him as soon as I might.*

Luck, apparently, was with him, for when he came in sight of the Temple, Gideon and Torvul were busily seeing to the dwarf's boxy wagon, scrubbing soot off of it with long-handled brushes.

"You are going to need more than dry brushes and arms the likes of yours to get that wagon clean," Allystaire called out as he approached.

Torvul didn't stop brushing, merely turned his head and spat. The alchemist once again wore his dark green traveling jerkin, trousers, and hobnailed boots, with no extra fur or wool in evidence, no gloves or muffler or hat to cover his gleaming bald pate.

"As if you'd even know how to clean your own ass," the dwarf rumbled. "Growing up Lord of Coldbourne, probably had servants for it."

"In point of fact, my father, and the rest of the men who trained me, were rather severe on points of cleanliness and hygiene," Allystaire said. "Of course, most of that applied to armor and weapons."

"Pfah! Typical," the dwarf said. "Keep all the implements of war bright and shiny."

"What else is there to do in the winter?" Allystaire had wandered to their side, and cast a glance sidelong at Gideon, who was brushing studiously and ignoring Allystaire.

The surface of the dwarf's wagon was intricately carved in repeating geometric patterns that Allystaire hadn't noticed before. As he tried to follow them with his eyes and make sense of them, he slowly found his focus slipping.

"Watch it now, boy," Torvul said, stepping to Allystaire's side and giving his sleeve a hard tug. "That won't do."

Allystaire shook his head clear and looked down at the dwarf. "What just happened?"

"Discourages thieves. Tell the truth, I thought it'd worn off years ago. Along with many another thing," he muttered. Then the dwarf held out a spare brush that resided in one of the many pockets of the jerkin that hung down over his thighs. "Make yourself useful."

Allystaire took the brush with a mild chuckle, briefly examining it. Like all the dwarf's tools, it was simply but exquisitely made, with stiff bristles that looked like boar to his eye, and a smooth handle his hand fit snugly around. "Torvul, again, it is soot. How is a simple brush—"

Wordlessly smug, Torvul held up a small bottle from another pouch.

"Ah." Allystaire extended his brush, Torvul dropped some liquid onto it, and Allystaire began scrubbing. Soot vanished beneath the brush with the slightest pressure.

"Once again," Gideon spoke up, "I could simply wipe the entire thing clean for you."

"No," Torvul said. "Firstly, you don't trivialize your Gifts that way. You don't see Allystaire here terrorizing some poor gamblers at cards or dice by compelling the truth of them."

"Actually," Allystaire began, but Torvul's deep and powerful voice rumbled right onward.

"Secondly, this wagon is my home, and it does a dwarf's hands and heart good to interact with it. Thirdly, it does *you* no harm to engage in a little physical labor out of doors. And last, and really this is the most important bit, this wagon is stuffed so full of my trinkets, potions, elixirs, philtres, gear, and equipment that I am terrified beyond reason of what might happen if you swept your power over it."

"I have enough control to avoid that," Gideon protested, though Allystaire was uncertain how much confidence was in the boy's tone.

"To avoid a cataclysmic explosion, I've no doubt. To avoid changing the properties of even a single stored ingredient? What happens if one of my memory stones captures the energy you—" Torvul stopped, his brush hand dropping to his side. "Wait. That is brilliant. Let me go—"

"No experiments, please," Allystaire said. "At least not until I can get a safe distance away. Besides, I need to speak with you both."

Torvul grumbled and lifted his brush again, carefully digging its tufts into a corner. "What about, then?"

Allystaire looked sidelong at Gideon again; the boy kept brushing studiously.

"What do the two of you think of Chaddin and Landen?"

"Landen," Gideon said, "is a product of her class and station."

"Meaning?"

"Could mean a lot of things," Torvul said. "Could mean she's a drooling inbred, a warmonger, a zealot, or a garden variety idiot—"

"Those are independent of class and rank," Gideon said. "What I mean is, she is educated, she has been held to a set of standards all her life. By those standards she is probably a good person, or a good representative of her class values. By ours? I don't know. She fought against us, and the Mother."

"I spoke to her on some of those points. She knows, in the end, that her father had to be destroyed, and the sorcerers with him. She is under no illusions on that score."

Torvul rumbled contemplatively. "Politics may force her to come seeking revenge."

"Our victory weakened the Delondeur family," Gideon noted. "Many of the lords were already wavering in their support because of Chaddin's coup. Some might seek to widen those fissures and seize more power for themselves."

"Assess our priorities, Gideon," Allystaire said. "What do we want out of what comes next for Barony Delondeur?"

"Peace," Gideon said, "for the Mother's folk. The chance for Her Temple to grow, for our message to reach more people. Stability."

"And an end to the war," Allystaire added. "I have not forgotten the pledge I made. We have a chance here to begin to see that come within our grasp."

"We also said we weren't goin' t"play politics," Torvul pointed out. "Gideon had the right of it then. If we dirty our hands in it once, we are forever stained."

"I do not mean to play politics, exactly. I am not going to war for the son or daughter of Lionel Delondeur. Yet if they refuse to see sense, neither can force me to release them to take up the seat."

"You can't imprison them forever," Gideon said.

By now, the wagon was mostly clear, with Torvul vigorously scrubbing at some spot of dirt only he could see.

"No," the dwarf offered, squinting for a moment at a spot on a wheel's hub. "But if they think we mean to…"

"I cannot lie to them, Torvul," Allystaire reminded him. "I cannot even bluff."

"Which is why you should let me do the talking, among other reasons too numerous to list," the dwarf shot back.

"I will not imprison them forever, nor will I play hangman with those who do not deserve it because it would be expedient. However, if I were to let them go, on their own, released from my protection, Garth would never let either of them get farther than out of sight of the village."

"You would not turn them over to their enemy," Gideon protested. "That's choosing sides, taking part."

"No, it is not," Allystaire said. "If Garth wanted to seize them now *we could not stop him*. That he has not done so is, well, it is for complicated reasons. But if I were to simply wash my hands of them, he *will* snatch them up, and from where he sits he would be right to do it. The opportunity is too great. He could put himself on the Baronial seat, or offer Delondeur up on a platter to Gilrayan Oyrwyn," Allystaire said, his mouth wrinkling distastefully at the name.

"And how would that bring peace?" Gideon asked.

"A stable Barony is a stable Barony," Torvul said faintly. "Doesn't matter to us whose ass is in the seat. Within boundaries, of course."

"You have it right. I care nothing for the fate or the future of the Delondeur family. I do care what becomes of the people of the Barony. One way or another, I will have peace."

"How would allowing Oyrwyn to conquer the Barony bring peace," Gideon asked.

"It would not have to be a conquest if they had the two most likely heirs in their hands. And Cold, Delondeur is in such a weak position now, Garth could probably conquer them a month after the thaw, if he wished."

"What's to stop Oyrwyn from rolling over us, then? What's to stop Garth from just seizing Landen and Chaddin anyway?"

"I am. Not because I can fight off all the men he brought, but—"

"Because of who you are t'them," Torvul finished. "This Garth really put himself and hundreds of men and the balance of power all at risk because of how he admires you."

"Do not," Allystaire said, "discount my sister's role in their coming south. Or her ability to restrain him. If it came to it, though, he is as much a product of his class and station as Landen Delondeur. He will act like an Oyrwn knight and lord."

"That's what you taught him to be," Gideon said.

Allystaire frowned. "I was a product of it all, too, Gideon. Yes, Garth will act as I taught him to. He already tried, once. Before we found either of you, Garth offered me the Barony. Said the men would rise for me. I have no intention of asking them to, but Baron Oyrwyn does not know that, and he must fear it. Assassins we may need to fear, but not an open fight."

"Stones Above, you have thought this out," Torvul said. "I'm almost impressed."

Allystaire held his brush out to the dwarf. "It is past time to get indoors by a fire," he said.

"And outside of something warm, red, and spiced," the dwarf agreed, taking the brush and drying it off against the frozen grass. "So what is it that you do intend?"

"We will discuss that with Mol and Idgen Marte," Allystaire said. "Oh, I need—"

"Your hammer." Torvul looked up at Allystaire, frowned. "It's lost, Allystaire. You didn't just shatter the haft; you split the head. I can use the steel to make something new out of it, but I can't simply give you the old one back. It'll take some time."

Allystaire absorbed the knowledge with his head bowed, jaw set firmly. "It was only a tool," he said. "See to Idgen Marte's sword first, if you could. She has been without much longer."

The dwarf grinned. "It's ready. I mean to make a gift of it to her when the moment's right."

"And burial parties?"

Gideon cleared his throat. "I have preserved the bodies and we have them resting in a shed. The folk wanted you to say words."

"And I will," Allystaire said, "as soon as I can find them. Tomorrow morning."

"Graves are gonna be a chore to dig," Torvul said. "We could wait for the thaw."

"I will dig them myself," Allystaire said. "I will not shy away from a task because it is difficult."

"Well, that's why Her Ladyship named you the Arm," Torvul said. "Let me fetch some things from the wagon. You two go ahead. You've things to speak on, and y'know it."

Torvul disappeared into his boxy home, leaving Allystaire and Gideon face to face. Or so they would be, if the boy met his gaze, but still he cast his eyes to the ground.

"Gideon." Allystaire searched for the words, finally settling on, "Why?"

"Why what? Be specific or I can't answer you." The boy's answer was too fast, too annoyed. Allystaire tried to keep a frown from creeping across his face.

"Why are you being petulant? Why will you not look me in the eye or speak to me?"

Gideon twisted halfway away from Allystaire, wrapping his thin arms around himself somewhat awkwardly. He forced himself into a more relaxed posture, hands at his sides, and finally looked straight at Allystaire's eyes.

"Because I failed you all," the boy said, working hard to keep his face blank, stoic. Allystaire could see that he was on the verge of breaking down, with tears gathering in the corners of his eyes.

Stunned, Allystaire could only manage, "What?"

"I failed you," Gideon repeated. "You. Renard. Everyone else who died. I could've destroyed the Battle-Wights with a wave of a hand. I could have defeated Gethmasanar and Iriphet with a *thought*. I did, but too late! The damage was done then!" With every word his composure shattered a little more. By the end he was shouting, with tears rolling down his cheeks. "I almost cost us the entire battle because I was prideful and shortsighted and not strong enough..."

Allystaire sighed and walked to the boy's side, wrapping his arm around his thin shoulders, feeling their sobbing quake. "Walk with me, Gideon."

"Why?"

"Because," Allystaire said weakly, then added, "it will be easier to explain to you why you are being foolish as we walk."

"That makes no sense."

"Neither does anything you said. Tell me something; when it comes to sorcerous conflict, how many years of experience did the two sorcerers have that you did not?"

Gideon considered the question a moment as he tried to surreptitiously dab at his eyes with the back of a gloved hand. "It could probably be measured in centuries."

"Experience matters, Gideon. Not just raw power. The strongest or fastest or best armed man does not win every fight," Allystaire said. "And in the end, you are here. They are not."

"Neither is Renard," Gideon said. "Neither are the men who died fighting the Wights, or the men the Baron had killed to make more of them, or to make his arms."

"Gideon, stop." He slid his arm from around the boy's shoulders, and turned to face him, placing one hand on each shoulder. "Look at me."

Allystaire waited till the boy's wet eyes met his own again. "Gerard Oyrwyn once told me that there were two rules to battle that can never be broken. Rules so old, they were made by the gods, not by men. Can you guess at what they are?"

The boy thought a moment. "You don't mean rules in the conventional sense, about how to position men or how noncombatants should be treated?"

"No."

"Then I can't guess," Gideon admitted.

"The first rule is that in battle, people die. The second is that nothing you do can change the first rule."

The boy's face started to wrinkle up in distaste till Allystaire held up a hand. "I do not doubt that you find it foolish on its face. And I have heard many a man say it flippantly, to make light of deaths recently and cruelly dealt. That is not how I intend it. Remember this: even power such as yours cannot change the basic facts of war. People die. People we want to protect, people under our care. We will feel Renard's loss every day. All of Thornhurst will. Leah and their child, especially. Yet he chose to be where he was, to do what he did. Honor his choice; do not blame yourself. That way lies a pit of grief so wide and deep it will swallow you whole. Trust me."

Gideon nodded, lowered his eyes for a moment as he considered. "You ought to say that at his funeral. The first bit, at any rate."

Allystaire sighed. "I will. As soon as I can make a moment to arrange it." He dropped his hands from Gideon's shoulders then and the two resumed walking. They were silent a moment

before Allystaire spoke again.

"That the other sorcerers managed to trap you is not something to be ashamed of. You overcame it."

"To your first point, it is. I should have seen it. I should not have been so arrogant as to assume I could overpower them. Gethmasanar in particular could be subtle. And I didn't," Gideon said. "I wasn't trapped, exactly. I was lost. The spell that Gethmasanar laid upon the Wight I destroyed—it may have been on all in that first wave—it was a swift and powerful thing. Do you remember the trap they laid for you along the road, The Grip of Despair?"

"Till the end of my days," Allystaire replied, jaw tensing at the memory of feeling his will to live, not sapped, but crushed so thoroughly that he nearly died, of the world going grey.

"It is somewhat like that, but it does not have a name, so far as I know. It planted an urge to live free of mortal constraint, to become a being of pure intention. The seed fell on fertile soil. At the same time, it pulled me loose from my body. And it made me forget everything that tied me to this place, to the world itself, to the people around me. I forgot about you, Mol, Idgen Marte, Torvul, and all the people under our protection, about the battle itself. I was pure Will without limit, but that meant I was also without definition, without cause, without any reason to enact my Will upon the world. Without such anchors, I was powerless. This is actually a bit of a breakthrough in magical theory," he added, almost apologetically.

"Torvul would be interested to hear some of this, I expect," Allystaire said. "How did you remember?"

"I don't think I would have if your voice hadn't reached me."

"Mol said she had been calling for you, that she could no longer feel you."

"I don't know Mol as well as I do you. I am not as connected to her. It wasn't just that your mind reached for me," Gideon added, choosing his words slowly and carefully. "It was what you said." He paused and pursed his lips tightly for a moment. "You called me son."

Silence fell again, with neither Allystaire nor Gideon looking directly at each other.

Finally, after chewing for a moment on his bottom lip, Allystaire said quietly, "I have no natural children, Gideon. I had charge of Audreyn for some time, it is true. But it seems likely that you are the closest I will come to a son. I was dying, and that was my honest thought at the time."

"What does it mean, to be a father and son? I have no memory of my parents, only sorcerous masters. Bhimanzir was not paternal."

"A father teaches his son the things he believes a man needs to know."

"That is what you've done since the moment we escaped the dungeons of the Dunes," Gideon said. "Isn't it? The lessons, from knives to horses to the problems you'd set me to solve, all the discussions."

"It is what I have tried to do," Allystaire said. Finally he looked down at the boy by his side, instead of the frozen grass and mud beneath his boots. "It is what I will try to do so long as we are together."

"And yet I think they are not always the things you were taught by your father," Gideon said.

"Much of what I know, I learned from Gerard Oyrwyn. More than from my father. Some I learned on my own. Mostly in the past six months." He paused. "Some of it, from you. If I have taught you anything, so much the better. But I know I have learned. I could not be more proud of you if you were my own flesh, Gideon."

Uncharacteristically, Gideon stepped forward and flung his arms around Allystaire. He responded in kind and the pair of them embraced for a moment.

"I am still sorry that I was gone for so much of the battle," Gideon mumbled into Allystaire's side. "It was a mistake, whatever you say."

"You are allowed them, Gideon. Mistakes make a man. No, forget that. *Overcoming them* makes a man."

The boy stepped back and looked up at Allystaire, smiling, an unusual expression on his typically reserved features. "Even now you don't stop trying to teach."

"And I will not," Allystaire said, "until I know that you know everything I can teach you." He paused. "Except the lance, I suppose."

Gideon laughed and the two resumed their walk. "Do you promise? To both."

"I promise."

Allystaire clapped the boy on the shoulder. Instead of shrugging his hand away, Gideon leaned into his arm for a moment. Then they walked on, till the Green and the Inn were before them.

"What is your plan for Landen and Chaddin?" the boy asked as he hopped a few quick steps ahead to pull the door open. Once inside, he hastened to the hearth and the fire burning inside it.

"I would rather explain it the once," Allystaire said. "Let us wait for the rest of them." He glanced behind the bar, where Timmar was busy cleaning. For a moment, Allystaire considered, then he pointed to a jar on a shelf behind the counter that he knew held the best brandy the village had, and held up two fingers.

Timmar glanced to the boy at the hearth, tilting his head questioningly.

Allystaire smiled faintly and nodded.

Timmar reached for the bottle.

CHAPTER 7

Graves

Sweating and flushed, having removed cloak, hat, gloves, and pulled open his jacket, Allystaire finally allowed himself the luxury of sitting upon an old stump-seat, one with a patina of long use. His muscles protested as he set the mattock, still grimy with clay, down beside him. Gideon did the same, practically falling to the floor, shovel at his side.

"The cool feels good for now, lad," Allystaire said, "but we cannot go too long in it. Dangerous."

"I know," Gideon puffed out. Neither of them wanted to look at the occupants that shared the cowshed with them, the sheet-wrapped bodies, deadly wounds taken from Battle-Wight or mortal soldier mercifully covered with homespun, the shrouds secured with links of hempen cord.

"How many more do we have?" Gideon said.

"Too many," Allystaire replied. "I will see about getting help after we rest." He forced himself to look at the rows of bodies. With the anonymity of the shrouds, he was able to avoid putting names to them. He saw that slips of parchment were stuck into the cordage, and couldn't quite summon the will to get up and look at them.

Gideon stood up and murmured to him. "Look straight at a thing, Allystaire. Whatever it is."

Allystaire nodded and stood, looking over the first row. Among the first three, he saw the strip of parchment that read "Renard," and hung his head and closed his eyes. Gideon stood awkwardly at his side; even with his eyes tightly shut, Allystaire could feel that the boy was searching for something to say.

"You need not speak, Gideon. Sometimes there is nothing to say."

The boy sighed in relief.

"The last I spoke to him that was not an order or a request," Allystaire said. "I told him that of all the knights I had known, with all their glorious armor and weapons made to their own hands, steeds with lineages prouder than any Baron, there were none I would rather have at my side than him."

"He was not a knight," Gideon pointed out quietly.

Allystaire was silent a moment, then bent to pick up his mattock and his winter gear. Laying the mattock against his legs, he began pulling his warmer clothes back into place.

"Where are we going?"

"To ask Torvul an important favor," Allystaire said.

Gideon sighed and picked up his shovel, levering it onto his shoulder with a grunt of effort. "He is stretching himself very thin. He'll grumble about another task."

"The day he does not grumble about a task is the day I will begin worrying about him," Allystaire said.

* * *

"Another job, another task for the master alchemist, smith, stonecutter, armorer, gemmarer, scribe, horticulturalist, priest, necrobane." Torvul paused in his rant, rolling his eyes towards the sky. "Did I miss anything?" He paused, snapped his fingers. "Cook! Of course." The dwarf wore a thick leather apron over his jerkin, standing over the small forge Thornhurst boasted. It wasn't a proper smithy, mostly used for shoeing horses, but Torvul had managed to get a hot enough fire blazing in it. Several cloth-wrapped bundles waited on a table nearby with a pile of tools.

"I am not sure what a few of those words mean," Allystaire said. "And I would not ask if it was not important," he added.

"Necrobane might not be entirely warranted," Gideon offered quietly.

Torvul glared at him. "Well, when you get to my age, you can start tellin' folk what titles they may or may not append to themselves." Then he sighed, and said to Allystaire, "I know it is. But are you sure you need it tomorrow? I may finally have what I need for your hammer after putting some finishing touches on Idgen Marte's blade."

"This needs to be done. They have waited long enough, need to move on. First the mourning, then a celebration."

"How do you mean to get all the graves dug?"

"Ask for help," Allystaire said. "The Delondeur prisoners might be willing to lend a hand. I know if I had spent a week stuck in a barely heated tent, I would be glad of the chance to get out of doors and do some physical work."

"Well, not all of them were too happy to talk to the lass in the past couple of turns," Torvul said.

"Any in particular I should speak with?" Allystaire's voice was calm, but subtle shifts in his stance, in the way his right hand started to curl up, caught the dwarf's attention.

"Stones Above, boy, the last thing you need to do is go in there swinging that rock-cracking fist of yours," he said. "They just weren't sure what it was all about. A few of them took to it. I think one or two were trying to have us on, but Mol was having none of it. I couldn't hear the words she was saying, but I knew, once or twice, it just *felt* different."

"I trust her to know what she is doing. Stop trying to change the subject," Allystaire said. "I do need it, if you can manage it."

The dwarf looked to the fire he'd stoked, and plucked at the apron he was wearing. "How big do you need it?"

"Just big enough to be legible."

Torvul grumbled, let out a harsh Dwarfish curse. "You'll need to bring me the stone. There is a pile out behind the temple from when they raised it up."

"Have you a rope?"

"So that you can what, drag it here like an ox dragging a plow? There's a sledge, too. Stones, but you're dense." Torvul paused. "Well you might be developing a certain political savvy, but otherwise you'll go straight through the walls if you have to."

"Is that a yes?"

Torvul breathed another guttural Dwarfish curse. "Aye. But hurry."

Allystaire turned to leave, then stopped. "Torvul, a question."

The dwarf turned a baleful eye upwards at him.

"What became of Delondeur's arms? Those that the sorcerers constructed for him."

"I said I had a project of my own," Torvul replied flatly.

"Torvul." Allystaire's eyes widened, as did Gideon's.

"I *unmade* them," Torvul said, raising his hands, palms out, conciliating. "Figured if I could learn to do that, I might come up with better ideas how to fight the things."

"Did you?"

The dwarf shrugged, tapped the side of his bald head. "Still letting it rattle around. I think so."

"Promise me you will use caution, Torvul."

"I," the dwarf said, laying one long-fingered hand on his chest, "am the very *soul* of prudence, caution, wisdom, and careful planning, Allystaire."

"You should have let me destroy them," Gideon said. "They were dangerous, even to you."

"We may face Wights again. What he learned now may save lives then."

"Fair enough," Gideon said. "If you do any more work with the material, please ask me for help."

"I will. Now go fetch a stone before I change my mind. And you," he said, pointing a finger at Gideon, "if you would be so kind, head to my wagon and fetch chisels one through four, my three smallest hammers, and a good handful of acid vials. Please?"

It was only then that Allystaire noticed the dwarf was leaning rather heavily on the anvil.

"Go on, Gideon," Allystaire said, "I can manage a bit of stone and a sledge myself."

The boy nodded, and he and Allystaire moved off in separate directions.

* * *

The stone proved heavy, but manageable, but Allystaire appreciated the opportunity to work up another good sweat. His muscles yearned for exertion after a week in bed.

When he thought of that week, some muscles yearned a little more forcefully than others. He had to stop, pause, lower his head and search for his breath. It was the first time since he'd woken that he'd thought of it.

Of Her.

Her hands. The many and varied and indescribable tastes of Her lips and Her mouth.

Allystaire felt his knees going weak and his breath becoming harder and harder to find. He fell to one knee, felt the cold seep up through his trousers and then the wool of his pants, and was able to center himself. He resettled the rope upon his shoulders and began pulling again.

The sledge didn't quite fly over the frozen ground, but he made good time.

What ought the stone say, he thought to himself, as he pulled the sledge up the slight incline to the smithy, where he saw Torvul and Gideon bustling about with handfuls of tools.

Must ask Leah, he told himself. A hard cold pit opened in his stomach when he thought of speaking to her. He forced it aside. *Look straight at it. Go speak to her after you drop off the stone.*

When he finally let the rope drop from his shoulders, he found Torvul waiting with a stack of parchment and a handful of charcoal sticks.

"What is it that you want the stone to say, exactly? And how do you want the lettering to look?"

"Torvul, do as you think best with the lettering. I need to speak to Leah, so leave some room," Allystaire said. "As for what I want?" He held out a hand for a stick and a piece of parchment, which Torvul reluctantly gave over.

Allystaire hastily scratched out a few words, and handed the sheet over. Torvul eyed it warily.

"Doesn't even make sense to me," Torvul said. "Order of the—"

"Faith, Torvul. It will make sense tomorrow," Allystaire replied.

"Fine," the dwarf muttered. "Off you go. I've got work to do."

"We all do," Allystaire said, taking a deep and steadying breath as he started working his way towards the Temple.

It wasn't a long walk, and Allystaire found himself wishing for more time as he pushed open the doors of the Temple and entered into its surprising warmth. He found himself shedding gloves and hat and cloak almost immediately as he swept his eyes about the building. Hardly any residue of the battle remained within the walls.

The Temple was well populated, with folk moving around, sweeping, speaking quietly in small groups, and some waiting to pray at the Pillars of the Will and the Voice. He smiled when he saw an old, lean hound, her muzzle grey, sleeping just behind the Pillar of the Voice. The dog didn't even open her eyes as one of the supplicants leaned forward to stroke her side, but she did shift and make a soft contented-dog sound.

There was one woman sitting on a bench about halfway between entrance and altar, shoulders slumped, a palpable air of loneliness about her.

Allystaire didn't even really need to see her honey-blonde hair to know it must be Leah. He could feel it like a wound in his chest.

He took yet another steadying breath, and more carefully peeled away his outer garments. Tables had been set on either side of the entrance, and they held various hats, mittens, scarves and the like. He added his to the pile, and then, walking quickly, made his way to her side.

Leah sat on the edge of the bench. Rather than ask her to move or slide around her, Allystaire knelt at her side.

Her hands curled around her belly; she was more obviously with child now. Her head was downcast, and he expected to see the signs of tears or red around her eyes, and was surprised when he did not.

For a moment, he could only lower his head. Part of him hoped she would speak the first word, but he cursed himself for a coward.

"Leah," he said, and though he had aimed for quiet, in the relative silence around them his voice sounded as loud to his ears as a mace hitting a shield.

She looked to him, but said nothing. Her face was not empty, but worn with sorrow. Tired, too tired from grief to weep or yell or, he suspected, even to speak. Lines were wearing into her skin, which had lost much of the farm girl glow he had remembered.

"Leah," he tried again. "I cannot say…" He stopped again. "I am sorry it took me so long to come speak to you."

"What words of yours'll matter, Allystaire," she said faintly. "What d'ya have t'tell me that I couldna waited for?"

Allystaire winced, shut his eyes. "There are no words that can matter, really," he admitted. "Yet I should have come to you as soon as I was able."

"Ya've great matters t'attend to," she muttered.

"No matter is greater than my duties to you and your child. Nor greater than the debt I owe Renard."

"Dead men can't collect."

"I know. But I…these things need to be said, Leah. If you do not want to listen, I cannot blame you. In the morning, I hope we can gather and say the final words, give him to his rest."

"He's gone to it days ago. The rest is just words and nonsense."

"No," Allystaire said. "There you are wrong. This village, all who inhabit it, as long as it stands, will know that your husband died a hero in its defense. He deserves that. Your child deserves to see it, and to grow up knowing it. I am going to see to it."

She was silent, had turned her face towards the altar, so he pressed on. "Since this all started, since Bend, Renard was my right hand. Half of what got done around here did because he made it get done. And in the end, before the end, his courage and his determination shamed me."

"Shamed ya? How?" Leah turned her face back to him, her hazel eyes narrowing and focusing more clearly.

"I told him he should leave. Should take you and try to escape with as many other folk as could manage. He refused, and he was right to do it," Allystaire said. "He told me that for the first time in a life spent carrying a spear, he knew *why* he was fighting. And that it was on the right side."

"What…" She paused, took a quick breath. "What was it he said he was…"

"You, Leah," Allystaire replied. "And your child. All the things he said he would not have had if it were not for the Mother. He told me I had no right to tell him he could not or should not choose the fight, that it would take more than lords and heroes to win it. That other folk had to be willing to face the darkness in men like Lionel Delondeur, and defend what it meant to take from them. And he was right."

She bit her bottom lip, and small tears welled in the corners of her eyes. "That sounds like him," she said, the words halted by the tears that threatened to fall, the mouth that wanted to betray her and wail and grief. "The old fool." She started to sob, briefly, and Allystaire stood as if to embrace her, but she halted him with an outflung hand, forced her tears away, took a deep and shuddering breath. "The old fool," she repeated, though with the tiniest, fleeting smile breaking across his face. "Do…will I have to speak?"

"Only if you wish," Allystaire said. "If there are things you wish to be said, but do not feel you can say them, write them down—"

"I'm not lettered, Allystaire," she said.

"We will remedy that in the coming months," he said softly. "Then tell anything you wish said to Mol, or to me. Fair?"

She nodded, wiping at her eyes with the back of a sleeve.

"Leah, I promise you I will give your husband the legacy he deserves. And that you, and your daughter, will want for nothing that we can provide."

"We'll work for our share," Leah said, quiet but insistent. "I don't know at what, yet."

"Worry about that later," Allystaire said.

She nodded and was silent a moment. "Who's seein' to the grave?"

"I already have, with Gideon's help."

Another, longer silence. "Did…when he was hurt, could ya not heal him? I've seen the gift y'have for it…"

Allystaire shut his eyes at the memory of the Battle-Wights, too many for even him to fight, swarming over him, stabbing into his side. His calf twinged as he remembered one driving its bladed hand straight through his leg, pinning it to the ground. Of how he'd watched, enraged and helpless to stop it as Renard was torn apart. "I could not reach him, Leah," he said. "They had overcome me by then."

"Did ya try? T'heal him, anyway, even now…the Goddess has worked miracles."

"It is not given, even to Her, to snatch someone back from beyond their death," Allystaire said. "So She has told me. To attempt it is forbidden to me."

"D'ya know what lies in death, then? Folk speak of the Cold, but surely my Renard can't deserve that. Fortune's priests don't speak t'folk like me. Braech's neither, though I heard one goin' on about drinkin' and fightin' and sailin' forever."

Allystaire swallowed, turning the question over. He though of his time spent with the Goddess as he recovered from his wounds.

"I do not know what lies in the next world, Leah," he admitted. "Yet I do think the Mother greets us there and eases our passage into it. If rest is to be found there, or solace, or happiness, Renard has earned it as surely as any man I have ever known."

She merely nodded, wiping at her eyes again.

Allystaire stood, painfully. Though the stones beneath his feet were unnaturally warm, given the weather, kneeling on them had stiffened his knee. It might have become a torment had he spared it any attention. "I must go. Think on whether you wish to speak, or want anything said. Is there anything you want on the stone? Anything about Renard's home or kin?"

"Thornhurst was his home, and me and our babe to be his only kin, or so he said. Put that," Leah replied, resting a hand atop her belly. "Say he was husband t'me and father t'her...I've not decided on her name yet. Can y'leave space?"

"I will tell Torvul to do so," he said.

She turned in her seat to look up at him. "What else will be written on it?"

"Sir Renard," Allystaire replied. "First of the Order of the Arm."

Her brows knit close in the center of her forehead. "Order o' the Arm? Sir? Renard was no sir."

"He will be. It is time, Leah," Allystaire said, "for knights to serve people, rather than tread upon them. Renard will serve, forever, as the example of what I mean."

"Is that what y'meant by givin' him a legacy?"

Allystaire nodded lightly, studying her face carefully from above.

She thought a moment. "I'd rather have him," she said, almost inaudibly.

"I know," Allystaire said, tightening the muscles of his stomach as if he'd just been punched. "As would I. But I cannot give you that. Mayhap I can give the world something in his name."

Leah folded her hands in her lap and looked down to them. Allystaire laid one of his hands upon her shoulder and gave it a gentle squeeze, then turned and headed for the Temple doors.

As he went, he ducked his head and swiped quickly at the corners of his eyes.

CHAPTER 8

Volunteers

Allystaire saw Mol approaching the Temple as soon as he stepped outside, so he paused to wait for her and watch her approach. Her feet were still bare beneath her sky-blue robe, a fact he had learned not to question. Her face did not carry its usual unruffled calm; instead a frown, bordering on a grimace, creased her small features.

"What troubles you, Mol?" Allystaire asked.

She wasn't startled by his question, though she'd made no sign that she'd seen him, but she answered his question without even averting her gaze. "It is a problem for the Shadow," she said, and made to continue past him into the Temple.

Startled by her response, Allystaire moved into her view. "Mol! What is the matter?"

She lifted her eyes to him. The inquisitive brown eyes he remembered, bright and quick, had long since been mingled with something vastly old and knowing. Now, it was almost as if the girl he had known had been entirely erased by the presence of the Goddess. Mol's gaze carried nothing like the impact of speaking to the Goddess directly. Less a hammer blow and more of a slap, but still a shock.

"Do not impede me, Arm. If I say it is a task for the Shadow, then it is," Mol said, with a note in her voice that demanded obedience. Allystaire suddenly dropped to a knee on the steps of the temple, balancing himself awkwardly, cold seeping from the stone into his bad knee.

"I am sorry, Voice," he found himself saying, before he knew it. "I did not mean—" He found his words being cut off as Mol stepped close to him and hung an arm around his shoulder, leaning against him for a moment.

"I'm sorry, Allystaire," she said, more of Mol's country accent in the words. "I…it's not you I'm angry at. I'm sorry," she repeated. "I've not always got m'gifts as well in hand as I should," she muttered, then shuffled away from him. "Stand. Ya look right foolish. Ya've no need t'kneel t'me."

Drawing a sharp, lung-stinging breath, Allystaire stood up. "Think nothing of it, Mol," he muttered, patting her on the shoulder before moving off.

Have to ask Idgen Marte what that was about, he thought. *Not that she'll tell me.*

The searing cold air began to drive into his lungs, and Allystaire became suddenly and intensely aware that he'd not eaten for turns. "There will be food later," he muttered. "Torvul will see to it."

Assuring himself did nothing to calm the rumblings of his stomach as he made his way out to the Oyrwyn camp once more.

The sentries and men moving about the camp still stared, but perhaps a little less intently than before. Allystaire ignored the occasional click of a heel or clatter of armor as a man he passed snapped halfway to attention, then relaxed.

Inside the tent, conditions, and morale, had improved. It was warmer, the men were all better dressed, and the aromas of better food still lingered.

"Gentlemen," Allystaire said, and all the heads turned in his direction. "If any of you crave exercise, a walk, a change of scenery, I could use volunteers."

"Volunteers for what?" The man asking the question was the old veteran Harrys.

Allystaire swallowed. "There are bodies, from the battle. I mean to lay them to rest tomorrow. I cannot dig a large enough grave myself. I will put beer in the hand of any who come to help, when the job is done. Full flagons," he added.

"Gotta be better than sittin' in here," Harrys said. "I'm your man."

"We could all use the air," Landen said then, suddenly. "Every man will come if you have the tools."

"Tools we can find," Allystaire said, and the Delondeur men began to shuffle out around him, herded by Landen.

"Most o' this lot gonna be as much use as tits on a fish," Harrys muttered, just barely loud enough for Allystaire to hear, as he passed out of the tent.

"Why do you say that?" Allystaire asked.

"Bunch of thieves, layabouts, and merchant's sons," Harrys said. "As used to workin' a shovel as they were a spear."

The two men fell in step together after Allystaire called out directions towards the Temple, and its adjacent graveyard; one mass grave holding the victims of the slaver raid, and one single, freshly dug for Renard. Landen had them moving in something resembling a solid line.

"You say that with implications of regret about the outcome of the battle," Allystaire offered.

The other man shrugged and grunted noncommittally. "Professional soldier in me talkin'. Don't like bein' on the losin' side."

"None of us do," Allystaire replied. "If I may ask, though, if the men Lionel brought here were mostly untrained, how did a veteran of the Baron's Own wind up with them?"

"A dozen of us on winter garrison," he said with a shrug. "It's a shit duty, but makes extra weight in your pay. And it's mostly for show, anyway. Assembly and drill once or twice a week, keep your horse in trim, wall duty every other week. Plenty o'time to drink, and, ah…carouse," he finished uncertainly.

"You need not curb your language around me, man," Allystaire said. "Whatever the differences between us, I am as much a soldier as you are."

"There, you're wrong," Harrys said. "You were a knight and a lord and now you're a knight and a lord whose fists shatter things made o'steel and bone and dark magics."

"Spent a score of years on campaign, Harrys. Ate the same food, slept in the same camps, fought in the same battles," Allystaire said. "And I am no lord now."

"Slept on a cot and not on the ground, I'd wager," Harrys said. "Had all that cunning foldin' furniture, and squires and servants around t'pack it for ya. Better women, better wine."

Allystaire sighed. "Some of what you say is true. The servants, the wine, the furniture. Not the cot, though. I never lost the knack of sleeping in preparation for a stand-to."

Harrys turned his flat brown eyes to Allystaire. "I've heard you Oyrwyn lot are hard. Old mountain ice, they say. Seems mad t'me for a man not to stretch out when he can."

They walked in silence for a while longer, till Allystaire filled the air with a cloud of breath in a sigh, and asked, "What were your thoughts on the Baron, Harrys?"

"A showman. Wanted us all t'love him, like in stories and songs."

"And did you?"

"Once, maybe," the soldier snorted. "Ordering a village full o'yer own folk put t'the torch will put paid to love."

"And what of slaving? What of hiring sorcerers? Of giving his own people to them for their divinations, of giving his own wounded men to be made into monstrosities."

Harrys shifted uncomfortably, rubbing at his left shoulder. "That all true? That upstart's lot were puttin' those things about."

"It is true," Allystaire said. "Every word of it. You *saw* the Battle-Wights, Harrys. Those were the Baron's men. Your Brothers of Battle."

Harrys frowned, biting at the inside of his lower lip. "That weren't right. A badly wounded man, a man ya know is bound for the Cold and has only shriekin' agony between here and there, maybe you ease that man along. Can't be soldierin' long as I have without doin' it or seein' it done, and prayin' that the men you're with'd do it for you." He shook his mostly bald head. "But sendin' a man who's a few days away from walkin' home to sorcerers to be butchered. That's..." The old soldier sputtered, looking for a word.

"It is evil, Harrys. That is the word you are looking for," Allystaire said. "I know it is a word that soldiers do not consider much. Any man who survives a few years campaigning knows the men on the other side are probably good and evil in equal measure to himself and his comrades. But Lionel Delondeur can be rendered that simply. He was evil, and he needed to be stopped, and that is why the Goddess gave me the strength you saw in the battle. It is why She gave me the power that healed your frostbite."

"Because you're a good man, is that it?"

"Because I had come to understand that I was not," Allystaire said. "And because someone needs to stand against the Lionel Delondeurs of this world."

"Kill 'em, you mean."

Allystaire nodded. "I suppose I do."

By now the small column of men had reached the field Allystaire had directed them to, and they stood about, stamping their feet against the frozen ground, rubbing hands over their arms. He gave Harrys a nod and walked towards Landen, feeling the old soldier's eyes on his back as he went.

* * *

Once tools were fetched and the space marked off, the work went quickly, with many of the Delondeur men putting their backs into it eagerly, if for no other reason than working made them warm. Many of them lacked experience with mattock and shovel, but when long deprived of the chance at exertion, a man comes to crave it, or so Allystaire reasoned, given how quickly they dug.

"Remarkable loose earth in this village," he'd overheard one man say, as he'd hacked up the ground with a mattock.

Allystaire had to admit, it had seemed unusual how easily the earth gave way to the mattocks, how light the piles of frozen earth were in the shovels. Finally, after clearing more ground than should've been feasible with men who'd had one good meal in a week, he turned towards the nearby Temple.

Gideon stood on its steps, casually gesturing with a hand held low at his side. Allystaire smiled and lifted his shovel in a brief salute.

When the work was done, the men leaned on their tools and then looked to him expectantly.

"Give me a moment," he said. "Beer will be forthcoming. I promise." He cleared his throat, closed his eyes, and concentrated a moment. He could, if he focused hard enough, determine where, relative to him, Gideon, Torvul, Mol, and Idgen Marte were.

Gideon was within the Temple, as was Mol. Idgen Marte proved a bit harder to locate.

In…the middle of the Oyrwyn camp, he thought, curiously. *What is she about?*

That left the dwarf, who was closest, by the smithy, likely still hard at work.

Torvul, Allystaire thought, pushing the words in his mind towards the dwarf.

A sour answer came back almost immediately. *Ya can't rush craftsmanship. What is it now?*

The Delondeur men helped me dig the graves for the promise of beer and hot food. I cannot take them to the Inn and let them mingle with the villagers.

Allystaire's mind was filled, briefly, with the stone-on-stone grinding sound of Dwarfish cursing, only to have it quickly shoved aside by Mol's voice.

They may have to mingle with the folk this night. Snow is coming. Badly enough that even in an evenly heated tent, some men will freeze.

Allystaire was briefly taken aback by Mol's intrusion. *Could we not have Gideon heat their tent?*

There are some men among them who need to spend a night in the Mother's Temple, and our people need to see them do it. We cannot be enemies any longer, Allystaire. Time to start proving that. Take them to the Inn.

As you say, he thought, but not without a ball of doubt building in his gut.

He turned to the men, most of whom stared at him, their expectation turned to curiosity, even fear.

"Beer is that way," he said, pointing to the road that led back down into the village and the "And food."

Landen's eyes were narrowed. "What did you just do?"

Dammit, Allystaire thought. *Should not have done that in front of them.* He shrugged. "One of the gifts of the Goddess. I was speaking with Her other servants," he admitted.

"You were standin' there with your eyes closed like a man about to have a fit," one man observed.

Murmurs ran through the crowd, with Landen eyeing him carefully and Harrys edging up behind her to watch Allystaire with the same intensity.

"Believe me or do not," Allystaire said. "Talking does not get you any closer to your reward for the work." And with that, he set off.

Harrys was the first of the crowd to follow after him, then Landen. The rest followed their Baroness.

CHAPTER 9

Enemies No More

Allystaire stood against the wall of the Inn, watching the Delondeur men huddle around the long table, the village folk clustered around the other end, and Chaddin's knot muttering darkly to each other in the corner.

"Well. This has all the makings of a bar fight men'll sing of for years."

By now, he was so used to Idgen Marte simply appearing at his elbow he chuckled without even starting or flinching at the sudden intrusion of her voice on his thoughts.

"Mol told me to bring them here," he muttered. "Said we have to start living as though we are no longer enemies." He sighed, lowered his head, and pinched the bridge of his nose. "She also told me that snow is on the way. A good deal of it, and that I need to herd them into the Temple to-night."

Idgen Marte frowned. "What of the two hundred some Oyrwyn men? We can't get them inside."

"They have doubled tents, seal skin, furs, and a lifetime of knowing how to survive the cold around a peat fire. They will be fine. These men have wool blankets, old scarves, and three braziers. It is a wonder they had not frozen to death by the time I came to them."

"Going to speak to Garth of that?"

"If I get the chance. I have no authority over him any longer, but as his teacher, I hate to see standards slip that far," Allystaire said.

His attention was suddenly drawn by the movement of chairs and of two men standing up. His eyes sought them out, his gut tightening, fists starting to clench anxiously. He relaxed when he saw that they approached him, and who they were.

Henri and Giraud, farmer and stonemason turned militiamen, came to him, hands extended.

Allystaire took first one, then the other's forearm, and pulled them by turns into a backslapping embrace; they returned his greetings and did the same with Idgen Marte. "You gentlemen look none the worse for wear and I am glad to see it," he said.

"We're happy t'see you up again," Henri admitted, smiling. "Somethin' we wanted t'speak of, though." Without waiting for a response, he turned and pointed the tables where the village men sat and drank. "Him," he said, singling out one of them, a tall and rangy youth with a long red scar creasing his cheek. Allystaire leaned forward, focusing on him.

"Is that Norbert?" he said, disbelieving. He knew it was, but the gangly youth who'd once set out to be a reaver had put meat on his frame. Between growing into his body and the scar that stood out on his cheek, he looked far older than he had when Idgen Marte had caught him skulking around Thornhurst in the summer.

"Aye," Giraud replied. "He fought like a man possessed at the battle."

"Lad is a good archer," Henri admitted. "And I saw him crush one o'them Battle-Wights with a stone he levered up out o'the ground, then pull the mace wired to its arm free and set about him like a reg'lar hero."

"What is it that you wanted to speak of, then? It sounds like the boy did well."

"Aye," Henri said. "And we think he deserves t'have his sentence lifted."

Allystaire raised an eyebrow. "Lifted?"

Giraud nodded. "We talked with the other militiamen. We all agreed that no amount of fetchin' water or feedin' stock could be asked of the lad anymore. He fought as well and as brave as any man save you and…" The mason's gentle, bearded face fell and his voice trailed away.

"And Renard," Allystaire muttered, the two men nodding. He watched Norbert for a long moment then, the way he spoke and laughed with the men around him, jibed and was jibed at. It was an easy comradeship, so natural to those who had been through danger together and were happy to have come through it that he could never have missed it. "Send him over to me."

Giraud and Henri nodded and walked off.

"Well," Idgen Marte muttered, as they watched the men speak to Norbert and point towards Allystaire, "looks like that was a bit of genius on your part."

"Not genius," Allystaire said. "Just hope. And a good guess."

"I was waiting for you to say 'Faith,' in that way of yours, you know, where you lean forward a bit and your draw the word out for profundity."

He chuckled, but by then Norbert was in front of them.

Allystaire extended his hand. The tall youth looked at it like he wasn't sure if it was a trick of some kind.

"From what they tell me, Norbert," Allystaire said, "we are Brothers of Battle now. Do you know what that means?"

Haltingly, Norbert took Allystaire's forearm in his hand, and they shook.

Idgen Marte cleared her throat, and extended her own hand, repeating the embrace. Still, the lad said nothing, his eyes wide, a bit fearful.

"It means," Idgen Marte said, "that we kicked the piss out of Battle-Wights together. We're bound by that now. Obligated."

Norbert's eyes went wide. "Truly? I heard the men, the blackguards I rode with, speak of such a thing, o' bein' brothers o'battle. They told me I would be once I was blooded with them, but never explained…"

"Tell me, Norbert," Idgen Marte went on, holding up a palm towards Allystaire, "what do you think of battle now that you've seen it?"

"I didn't like it much," the boy replied. "I was scared half the time and confused the rest. But it felt like somethin' I needed t'do. So I did it."

"Is it something you want to do again," Allystaire asked.

Norbert swallowed and looked to Allystaire, setting his shoulders. "If I have to."

Allystaire nodded. "Good." He lifted a hand to point to the scar. "You want me to see if I can heal that?"

The boy lifted a hand to the livid red line, smiling a little. "No. Ah…" He colored a little. "The lasses like it."

"That they do," Idgen Marte said. "Just mind that you don't take any blows closer to your eyes, eh? Because they probably like them, too."

The boy flushed more, stammering, till the swordswoman slapped him on the shoulder and turned him around. "Go on. Back to your mates."

Flustered but clearly bursting with pride, Norbert shuffled off back to the table and sat between Giraud and Henri.

Allystaire turned to face Idgen Marte, lifting an eyebrow and saying nothing.

She shrugged. "Does no one any harm to hear a bit o' praise now and then," she said.

"Fine. Do you think we should erase his sentence?"

"I think if we don't the folk'll do it for us," she replied. "So it's probably just a formality."

Allystiare nodded. "Aye."

Their attention was quickly drawn to the sound of a mug slamming against a table. The quiet rumble of talk dropped away and heads turned.

Chaddin was rising from his table, a fist clenched, shoving aside the restraining hand of one of the knights that sat near him. The object of his ire was easy to surmise, as he glared daggers across the room at his half-sister, who returned Chaddin's look with pride, but not hostility.

Shoving his chair away, Chaddin broke away from his men and headed for the door. Slowly the four who'd been sitting with him got up and followed him.

"I had better see to that," Allystaire muttered. He pushed himself away from the wall, pulling gloves from his belt and pulling his cloak more tightly around his neck.

The cold of the evening still hit him like a blow. His eyes stung and his breath burned in his throat.

Worse, snow was beginning to fall in light and powdery flakes that dusted the ground, a picturesque warning of what was likely to come.

He spotted the shapes of Chaddin and his men moving back towards their camp, and called out. "Chaddin! I would speak with you if you have a moment."

The men stopped, turned as one, with Chaddin in their center. The former sergeant hastened towards Allystaire angrily, his pale face reddened by the cold.

"About what," he called out, the heat and force of his voice lessened by the wind that started to whip up.

"About Landen. About the future of the Barony," Allystaire said.

"If you had stayed and supported my uprising, the future of the Barony would be assured," Chaddin yelled. "If you had agreed to my terms we could be making plans for how to hold it. Instead you sit in council with a woman who tried to destroy this village and your temple. You break bread with those who came here to kill you."

"If I had supported your uprising, the Temples of Braech and Fortune would have moved against us in strength," Allystaire said. "Imagine the Choiron calling on the berserkers, whipping the Islandmen into a frenzy at the chance to revenge themselves on the Barony that broke them. Imagine the havoc Fortune's whispers, not to mention Fortune's gold, would have wrought among the rich. Nothing would be assured. The Barony would be burning."

Chaddin was taken aback by Allystaire's response, but rallied quickly. "So? For supporting you, what do I get in return? Landen and her men apparently get the finest treatment, seats by the fire—"

"Landen and her men had volunteered to dig a grave for those lost in the battle," Allystaire said. "I promised them beer and a hot meal in return. Have you wanted for anything this village could provide you since you arrived?"

Once again, Chaddin faltered, while his men murmured among themselves, stamped their feet, rubbed their arms. To his credit, Chaddin eventually shook his head no, as did the rest of them.

"I am taking an easy hand with Landen because I want no more enemies than I already have," Allystaire said. "If what we have begun here is to survive, I cannot afford them. Surely you can understand that."

"You mean her to keep the Baronial seat," Chaddin said, flatly. "Don't deny it. You do not want to dirty your hands, so you'll do the easier thing."

"Chaddin," Allystaire said, "if you think I seek the easy way to do a thing, you have not been paying attention. What I mean to do is have *peace*. I want you and Landen to come to an agreement, and I have some ideas about what it could say. The Barony *cannot* have the two of you at odds."

"And what if we disagree?"

"Then I will let the Lord of Highgate do as he sees fit with the putative Baronial Heir and the Pretender," Allystaire replied coldly.

Chaddin's eyes went wide with anger. "You wouldn't." The men behind him bristled, hands curling into fists.

Allystaire ignored the men and focused on Chaddin.

"Do not test me," Allystaire said. "An agreement would benefit the both of you. Most importantly it would benefit the *people of this Barony*," he shouted. Impulsively, Allystaire took a half-step forward, looming over Chaddin.

To his credit, Chaddin didn't move, and he kept his eyes steady. The men behind him took an involuntary half-step back.

Allystaire was able to keep a smile off of his face at their reaction. Barely.

"It is the people, Chaddin, I am here to help. They deserve peace. They are *owed* peace. I will see that they get it, and preferably you and Landen will help me do it. But one way or another, I cannot allow you to be enemies any longer."

By now the snow had begun to swirl in a rising wind, and all of the men standing in the midst of it were feeling the cold. Allystaire looked from the Inn, to the dark, moonless sky above, and said, "Learning not to be enemies begins tonight. With snow coming, you are going to want to pack into the Temple with the villagers. Landen's men will be there as well. Use the time to speak to her, at least a little. Please."

Chaddin's face started to turn sour, but he looked back to his men, then turned to Allystaire and nodded. "We've no wish to freeze to death. We'll be there."

"Unarmed." Allystaire's tone brooked no dissent. Chaddin nodded in agreement and turned to lead his men away, their breath steaming above them in the night air.

* * *

With the benches stacked up against the walls and most of the stone floor covered in furs, blankets, cloaks, and jackets, the Temple was able to accommodate the bulk of the village folk, all of Landen and Chaddin's knights and soldiers, and a good sampling of village dogs.

Barely.

It was also just this side of too warm, though no fires burned in it. Just after folk had started to arrive, Gideon knelt to the floor and set a hand upon it. Instantly it had started to radiate a warmth that rose up and filled the space. Add to that the press of bodies, and it was warm enough that occasionally, a sleeping form sat up and tossed away one of its piled covers.

Not everyone slept, though. A few petitioners knelt by the altar, praying, their shadowed forms unrecognizable at any distance. Some sat at the edges, talking quietly.

Allystaire sat against a wall just inside the doors, watching the altar. The five-pillared oval seemed to glow indistinctly in the otherwise dark Temple, giving off enough light to see that petitioners knelt at a couple of places, offering prayers. A dark shape disengaged from the sleeping mass of people and crept up to the altar, kneeling in front of the pillar that was just to the left of the center.

Pillar of the Arm, Allystaire thought. *My pillar.* Then aloud, he murmured, "Not that anyone is praying to me. Or should."

He shouldn't have been surprised when Idgen Marte answered him. "No. Someday though, maybe."

"How long have you been sitting there?" He looked to his left as he realized she was seated with her back to the wall, the same as him.

She shrugged. "Long enough. Too warm in here, though. Going to stumble my way back to the Inn and sleep in a bed if I can. Wanted to give it all a look, see if it stayed peaceful in here."

"It will," Allystaire said confidently. "Everyone is too tired to fight." He peered some more at the figure kneeling at the pillar of the Arm.

"Want to know who that is?" Idgen Marte leaned forward.

Allystaire turned towards her again. "You can make it out in this dark, this distance?"

She snorted. "If he held up a letter by the light the altar gives, I could probably read it. And it's that Delondeur man-at-arms whose hand you healed."

"Harrys," Allystaire muttered. "Interesting."

They went quiet, listening to the backdrop of the all the sleepers, the quiet whuffling of the dogs that slept among them, the faint murmur of talk and prayer.

"Torvul showed me the stone. Order of the Arm?"

"Knighthood," Allystaire said, "as an idea, has merit. It is time to prove that."

"Where will you find the knights?"

"Give me the right people and I will make them knights."

"Harrys one of them? Landen, Chaddin?"

"He might be," Allystaire admitted. "But the latter two, I doubt very much."

"Village folk? What if Norbert decides he wants to be a knight?"

"Let us hope it will not come to that."

"I'd say you're mad, but I've seen you solemnly promise to do things twice as mad as this, and you're still here. But what about armor, horses, arms?"

"Some of it we can provide, having captured a deal of it during the battle," Allystaire said. "But the knights I mean to make might mount a charger and carry a lance or wear an armsman's jack and carry a spear. It will not matter to me."

"Might matter to the world," Idgen Marte pointed out. "Hard to take a man seriously who calls himself a knight if he's wearing leather n'not steel."

"When you met me, I wore no steel," Allystaire said. "Was it hard to take me seriously?"

"Cold, Ally, I think a court fool would be forced to take *you* seriously," Idgen Marte answered. "Norbert might need to work a little harder."

He laughed lightly, mindful of those who slept nearby. "I think we all need to begin thinking about how this can move on beyond us. After us," he said.

"It's been less than a year and you're planning for the years after our death."

He shrugged. "I think forward, Idgen Marte. I always have. Made me a good warlord."

"Well," she said, "you're right. There ought, maybe, to be an Order of the Shadow as well."

"Thought on it, have you?"

"Thought? Cold, who says I haven't already been recruiting?"

Allystaire was silent a moment as he thought. Suddenly he recalled where his Goddess-given senses had told him Idgen Marte had been earlier that day. "Audreyn?"

"An interesting woman, your sister. Devoted to you, you know. Shares a lot of your traits, some of your ideals," Idgen Marte answered.

"Do not put her in danger, Idgen Marte."

"Does she have less of a right to make that choice than you or me? Than Renard did?"

Allystaire didn't answer.

"She told me some more about you, you know. It's like pieces of a lost song falling into place," Idgen Marte said. "How you brought her up, what the wars demanded of you. About Dorinne."

"I told you that time had healed that—"

"No, Allystaire, you didn't, because if you had, that would've been a lie. And we both know you can't speak a lie. What you said, and I note now you were watching your words carefully, was that there had been a lot of time for it to heal. Not that it had."

He was silent a moment, then said, "I was a fool, then. A fool for listening to my father and to Gerard Oyrwyn. We should have done as we wished. They would have done nothing; my father had no other sons and the Old Baron had been grooming me for command since I was eight summers old. He would not have cast me aside."

"What was it you said to Garth this morning? The more of the world you love, the harder it is to tear it to pieces?"

"Aye. And I let them hammer love out of me. Hammered it out of myself."

"You tried," Idgen Marte said, "but you couldn't quite do it. That's why the grave and the flowers. Mountain vetch and loosestrife, was it?"

"And heather."

"There's a song in this."

"Then make one."

Idgen Marte shook her head fiercely. "No. I…no. Not that."

"The more you love the world and what is in it, Idgen Marte, the easier it will be to defend."

Allystaire stood up, moving slowly to ease the aches he felt as he did, leaning heavily against the wall with one hand. He reached the other towards Idgen Marte. She took it and he pulled her easily to her feet.

"You have a point, Ally. Which is amazing enough in itself," she added. But then she shook her head, and one hand unconsciously stroked the side of her throat. "But you don't know what you're saying when you tell me to make music."

"As you would have it," he said with a slight shrug. "I will speak on it no more."

"See that you don't," she teased. "Now let's see if we can't slog through the snow back to our beds."

"I mean to stay," Allystaire said, shaking his head lightly. "There is space and much to do in the morning. And the folk still bear watching."

"Have it your way. Stone floors or a wall to sleep against; you fear comfort the way other men fear pain." She turned and disappeared from his view before he could offer a warning about the snow that she probably didn't need.

CHAPTER 10

Rest and Foundation

The Temple was still quite warm when the hard light of a winter dawn broke through the windows that surrounded the altar.

Allystaire snapped awake when that light reached his eyelids, sat up, and stretched.

The popping of joints in his arms and back awoke at least two people sleeping a few feet away.

With a sigh he pushed himself to his feet, and began tightly rolling the furs that had made up his bed. He looked to a pile a few feet away that had already been left neatly stacked.

What is that boy after, Allystaire wondered. He headed for the door. There was no need to pick through the crowd, as he'd slept at the very edges.

He put his hands on the wood of the door, expecting to have it open through a good deal of snow, though he hoped it hadn't drifted. He gave it a quick hard shove, and nearly fell forward as it opened without resistance.

Allystaire gawped for a moment; whatever snow had fallen on the steps was gone. The path leading deeper into the village was likewise clear, as was the Temple field and the recently dug grave.

"You hadn't really thought that through," Gideon said. Allystaire turned to find him leaning against the wall. "The grave, I mean. It filled up with snow. I took care of it. And you are letting the heat out of the Temple."

Quickly, Allystaire shut the door and stepped outside completely, shivering and wishing for the cloak, gloves, and hat he'd left inside. "What did you do, exactly?"

"I cleared the snow away so the folk could move about the village. So that the burials could happen. It would've taken turns to do it otherwise, even if everyone worked at it together."

"How…" Allystaire's surprise drew the word out far past its single syllable.

"I moved some, melted some," Gideon said.

Allystaire stared at the boy, trying to gather his thoughts. "I hoped you would avoid obvious displays."

"It was the practical thing to do," Gideon protested. "And it was easy." He looked out over the partially snow-covered landscape. "It is harder, sometimes, *not* to change things."

"What do you mean?"

Gideon frowned. "I have come to see the world differently. I…all of it is in flux, all is change. You probably see things as fixed. Immutable. Even the snow, well, it can be moved, but until the weather warms, it is here. A fact. Like the walls of the Temple are a fact." He looked back up to Allystaire, shaking his head, eyes a little unfocused. "There are no such facts for me. All I see is change. The potential of it, the possibilities. I could melt all the snow that fell in the Barony if I had the right vantage point."

"And you would flood villages situated on rivers that could not take so much melt so fast," Allystaire said. "You are frightening me, lad."

Gideon lowered his eyes and sighed. "I don't mean to. I won't take rash or thoughtless action simply because I can," he said. "I promise. But to clear the snow this morning seemed too practical not to do. I was trying to help."

"I know. I am not angry, Gideon. Impressed. Awed, mayhap, by the scale of what you say you might do."

"There are limits," the boy added quickly. "I can't, I don't think, transmute metals, which will please Torvul, as he has said that turning lead into gold would be blasphemous."

"Is that not what alchemists do?"

"Base human superstition. Rampant ignorance," Gideon said, dropping his voice as low as he could and practically gargling the words, doing a passable impression of Torvul's rock-grinding voice.

Allystaire laughed. "Do not mock him. He is a good friend, for all his grumbling."

"He is brilliant," Gideon said earnestly. "I'm not sure everyone realizes it." The boy knotted his brows. "Have you stopped to think on how many crafts he has mastered? It is unusual even for a dwarf."

"And then at the battle there was…" Allystaire frowned, trying to find the memory from when the world was going dim and dark as the Battle-Wights overcame him. "Stonesinging. That is what the sorcerer called it."

Gideon's eyes widened. "I hadn't heard that. The Dwarfish Stonesingers were something the sorcerers truly feared. Perhaps their only fear. But the art was lost, or so I had read."

"Well, mayhap he found it again. Ask him later, if you could. I should like to know."

"He needs to be allowed some rest. He drove himself too hard during the battle. He didn't allow himself to sleep for over a week, kept dosing himself. He'll keep doing that if we keep asking it of him."

"We all need a rest," Allystaire said. "And after today, we can have it. Come on, lad. I am cold and there is work to do."

* * *

In truth there was less work to do than Allystaire had expected, since Gideon had also taken the time to move the bodies into place.

Gideon also offered to move Renard's stone. Allystaire refused. Which is how he now found himself staring hard at it where it lay outside the smithy, wrapped in a blanket secured with thin rope, and the sledge he'd used to haul it there nowhere in sight.

Gideon stood next to him, bottom lip curled uncertainly.

"Remember to lift with your legs," Allystaire said, as he squatted and wrapped his hands under the edge of stone.

"Would you feel better if I made you an invisible sledge and you could drag it that way?" Gideon offered quietly.

"No," Allystaire muttered darkly, as his arms and legs began to strain against it. Slowly, groaning, he pulled it clear of the ground.

By a few inches.

He took a tottering step forward, unable to fully extend his legs, face set in a rictus of absolute exertion. He took another step, and another.

And then the stone floated out of his arms.

Allystaire nearly fell face-first, caught himself with an outflung arm. As he stood he turned angrily to Gideon, only to find the boy looking at him with stern disapproval.

"You can't help anyone or get any work done if you injure yourself trying to engage in a foolish gesture, the symbolic nature of which would be lost on most anyone but you," Gideon said. "And while I realize that any injury you do yourself may be temporary, given your Goddess-given Gifts, I would also suggest that this is a task you cannot manage yourself. She created five of us for a reason, Allystaire. Would you stand by and watch me labor at a task that endangered me when you could help?"

"No," Allystaire said. "I suppose I would not." His face stung with anger, though he knew the hand of wounded pride when he felt it. And he knew well how to ignore it.

"Then let us put this in place," Gideon said, "and get dressed for the ceremony."

* * *

"Does it not get terribly cold in that in this weather?" Gideon asked, as he watched Torvul help Allystaire put on his gleaming armor. The lad sat on Allystaire's bed in the Inn, while the alchemist and the paladin stood in the center of the room.

"Not if the man wearing it knows what he is about," Allystaire said, as he pulled a buckle tight. "And I do. Make sure there is no contact of skin and steel, make sure your gambeson or arming clothes are warm. And do not, no matter how much the elder boys in training dare you, lick your armor."

Torvul chortled as he adjusted the greaves. "A classic! I once got an old rival's tongue stuck to a wagon wheel for the better part of a turn. Stones Above, he swore the worst kinds of vengeance, that he'd find everything crafted by my family and destroy it, that kind of thing."

"Odd sort of vengeance, that," Allystaire said. A last buckled was pulled tight, and he sighed. "I feel wrong without shield, hammer, or sword. Unbalanced."

"I'm working on it," Torvul said, his voice taking on an aggrieved tone. "You'll not be happy till I invent an elixir that does away with sleep altogether."

Allystaire eyed the dwarf as he stood up. "Everyone needs a rest after today. You most especially, Torvul. I have an inkling of how far and how hard you pushed yourself during the battle, and I suspect you continue to do it. A new hammer and a new shield are trifles now. If I need a sword or another weapon, then doubtless I can take one from those we have captured. Goddess send that I will not, till spring. Beyond. Forever, if we can manage it."

"We can't," Torvul said. "And you know it. And I'll push myself precisely as far as I need to. If I haven't got half a dozen projects going I'll get bored anyway," the dwarf said, waving his hands dismissively. "I've got to go find my robes and figure out what I can wear under them so I don't freeze."

"The Temple in half a turn," Allystaire said.

"Yes, yes," the dwarf said as he stumped off.

Allystaire took a look at the helm that sat on a table, decided better of it. He did grab the long woolen scarf he'd found among his things when he'd woken up. "Gideon, who made this?"

He shrugged. "One of the villagers? I don't know. They seemed to have stores of the things as soon as winter really came upon us, and they've taken it upon themselves to see that we do not lack such things."

"Remind me to thank them," Allystaire said. "I have not done that enough," he murmured.

He clattered down the stairs, Gideon in his wake. When the Arm and the Will, the former in his mirror-bright armor, the latter in his blue robes, began their walk towards the Temple, they drew attention. Some folk were already gathering, but many found themselves swept up in the wake of two of the Goddess's servants.

When Allystaire and Gideon arrived, they found Mol, Idgen Marte, and Torvul arrayed on the steps of the Temple and a crowd gathering around them. Some knots were instantly identifiable. The Thornhurst militia had turned out in what passed for uniforms. Mostly arming jackets supplemented by bits of armor, with golden sunburst badges sewn on or worn around the arm, and numbering not quite two dozen now, they shouldered spears or bows with a precision that would've done credit to many more professional soldiers.

A knot of Oyrwyn soldiers, armored but not armed, stood apart. Garth stood out amongst them, not only for his blond braids and his height, but for the green-enameled scale armor he wore. Audreyn stood at his side, swathed in a too large bear-fur cloak that Allystaire instantly recognized; it had belonged to their father.

Landen's men, and Chaddin's too, were all in attendance, but, by design or inclination, the militiamen and the Oyrwyn soldiers both stood between them.

And the rest, in one large crowd, lining the path and milling about the field, were the people of Thornhurst. The people Allystaire and Idgen Marte had saved from slavery, the people who had flocked to the village in the fall when word of the Mother had been spread by their deeds.

As Gideon and Allystaire passed them as they lined the road, murmurs ran amongst them. Gloved and mittened hands reached out to touch them. Not to impede them, or to take anything—just to press a hand to his armor, or the boy's robes, and then move away. No one shoved, no one yelled.

He strained to hear the murmurs, caught only fragments. *Stillbright. The Will. Dragon. Giant. Saved us. Sorcerers.*

The murmuring melted away as he and Gideon reached the edge of the Temple's steps. Torvul, Mol, and Idgen Marte descended to meet them. Allystaire felt a moment of necessity drawing near, felt the stares of the crowd behind him. He closed his eyes and had a deep breath and briefly, intensely prayed.

Goddess, let me be the man they deserve. Let all of us be the heroes they believe we are. Let me find the words today. Let my hopes for peace, and for those who will follow after me, not be in vain.

Allystaire felt a hand slip into his, on the bare skin of his left palm where Torvul had modified his gauntlet. He looked down at Mol, who smiled solemnly up at him.

"You have long since proven yourself, Allystaire," she murmured. "You, most of all, are precisely what we believe you are."

Allystaire started to shake his head slightly, but Mol frowned and held up a hand. "I know what you would say. You're wrong. What you think is asked of you alone is asked of all of us *together*. Together we will be what the people of this village—and beyond—need."

"They will look to you," she went on. "They will always look to you, and the four of us shall always stand with you. Years from now, when all of us have gone to our rest with the Mother, men will still look to you. They will sing songs and tell stories, and measure themselves against Sir Allystaire Stillbright. They will remember you, Paladin; they will call you the Hammer of the Sun."

"The people need more than a weapon and a name to shout, Mol," Allystaire started to protest, when Idgen Marte cut in, laying her gloved hand on his pauldron and leaning her head close to his.

"A hammer can build as easily as it can destroy, Allystaire. Your words," she said. "Go. Serve them in grief once more, and then build your knightly idea, Sir Stillbright."

Mol gestured, the five of them turned. Behind them, the crowd had gone utterly silent, the collective weight of their expectation hanging in the air like their clouding breath.

Allystaire stepped forward, and began walking to the graves. The other four filed along behind him. Once again, the people parted for them, hands extended, whispering and murmuring.

He stopped when he could see the shroud-wrapped bodies lying in the opened graves, the one by itself, covered stone at its head, the others laying in a common grave.

"Brothers and sisters," he began. "People of Thornhurst and the Mother. And guests," he said, eyeing for a moment the different factions of Delondeur men, the Oyrwyn, and catching sight of the white-silks, silverfox-fur, and gold that marked the Archioness of Fortune, lurking at the far edge of the crowd. "I come before you once more to grieve with you. We have laid too many folk in the ground together. I hope, Goddess do I hope, that this is the last time we send so many to the next world at once."

He stopped and stared at the graves again, at the prone, stiff forms filling them. "I wish I could give all of them back to you. I would trade my life for any of those who lie before us. Words like this ring hollow to those mourning. There is little I can do to ease that sting. Grief is forever. I know this as well as most, I think.

"Yet the grief and the pain we carry must not weigh upon us, crush the resolve out of us. We will let it carry us forward into the work that still needs to be done. Thornhurst is safe, for now. And I would see us make it a haven for any who want refuge from the fighting that will resume when the snows melt."

Allystaire paused, trying to gauge reactions. He saw some heads bent, shoulders rocking in quiet sobs, saw some bleak faces turn grim when he mentioned the fighting.

"I promised you when we consecrated the Temple that the fighting I speak of, the wars of pointless succession, the mindless pursuit of space on a map, were over for you. I meant it. We have here, as our guests, those who will begin to help us make it so," Allystaire said. When he did, he looked pointedly to Landen, Chaddin, and Garth. The latter was too distant to make out his expression. Landen seemed impassive. Chaddin frowned.

There was a murmur in the crowd, an angry ripple, when he said "guests." Some in the crowd turned towards Landen and her men; one of the militiamen took a step in their direction.

Allystaire raised a hand. "Hold. Please, listen to me. Yes, many of you do not like hearing them called guests. I know. They came here under arms, sought to destroy your home and raze your Temple. And in another life I would see all of them hanged.

"But the Mother calls us to *mercy*. The Mother offers us *redemption*. They were badly led, blinded by bonds of blood and ancient loyalty. I would offer them mercy in the hope that they can earn redemption."

That ripple got briefly louder, angrier. Cries of "my husband" or "my son."

"Landen and her men," Allystaire said, "were led here by a man they trusted wrongly, a man they loved. Love itself can never be a sin. You have heard this, from me, from Mol. I have heard it from the Goddess Herself. We know it to be true. Yet when that love, when that faith is used wrongly by its object, who is at fault? The man who led them here told them that a false Goddess and foul sorcery sought to overthrow everything they thought was right, proper, and natural in the world. The Baron Lionel Delondeur did that. And he has paid for it. Should those who followed him out of love continue to pay for his sins? I say no. The Mother calls us to be *better* to one another than that. To kill in earnest defense of our homes and families cannot be a sin, but to hang men who are willing to repent would stain our hands with blood. And there has been enough death. Too much. On that, my friends, please tell me that we agree."

Allystaire could feel the anger drain out of them slowly, like wine trickling from a nearly-empty skin. *These folk are too spent to be too much of anything for very long*, he thought.

"That is not all I have come before you to say." He strode to the edge of Renard's single grave, pausing to take in a lungful of searingly cold air. "Everyone who fell in the defense of Thornhurst will be remembered. As long as the Temple stands, so will their memory. All of them deserve better than the words I could give them. But among that company there was one man I will speak of now.

"Renard." He stopped, swallowed hard. "Renard was my right hand. Since we came back from Bend to rebuild this village, he was ever-present. He guarded us, guided us, trained us for the fight that the Baron brought to our door. He was one of nature's own sergeants and as brave and true a friend and soldier as any man has ever had in this or any world. And before the battle concluded, Renard…he shamed me," Allystaire said. "I told him he should leave, flee, take Leah and their unborn babe and as many other folk as could or would flee, and go. And he told me then that such battles as we faced could not be fought only by those of us with Goddess-given gifts. He told me that ordinary folk, like him, needed to be willing to stand up to the Lionel Delondeurs of the world, those who have everything and want more, and tell them no. He said that such a battle needed more than heroes."

Allystaire looked up from the grave and the stone above it to face the crowd again. "His only mistake was in not counting himself among the heroes. For he was, people of Thornhurst. And now, forever, we will remember him that way."

He stepped to the head of the grave and tore away the cloth bound around the headstone.

"For those who cannot see," Allystaire said, "I will read it to you."

"Sir Renard, of Thornhurst. Beloved of Leah of Thornhurst. Forever the First of the Order of the Arm."

Allystaire reached carefully to the straps of his left bracer along his forearm, and tugged free a folded piece of dark blue cloth. He held it up, let the breeze catch it and let it unfurl from his fingers. It was the lance-pennant the folk of Thornhurst had given him when he'd ridden away in the early fall, a golden sunburst on dark blue.

"Too many of you know knights as the men in steel who take your children or your husbands away to die. Too many of us know knighthood as the line between rich and poor, between those who can do as they wish, and those who must do as they are told. I mean to change that.

"I have a different idea of knighthood, and the man who lies here embodied it. An idea of knights who will place themselves between the hearthfire of beloved home and the darkness that would snuff it out. Who will bear any burden, no matter how great, for those they love. Today, in front of you all, in front of my fellow servants of the Mother, in front of the Goddess Herself, I declare the founding of an order of knighthood based upon the ideas that Renard died for. He may not have worn a title in his life, but he proved himself a better man than any knight I have ever known. The Order of the Arm will strive to match him."

Allystaire knelt at the graveside then, and lowered the pennant onto the shrouded form within.

"I am sorry I could not save you, Renard," he whispered. "Leah and your daughter will want for nothing. No harm will befall them so long as I live. Goodbye and good rest in the mercy of the Mother."

Allystaire picked up a handful of the earth Gideon had cleared of snow, finding it surprisingly soft and warm to the touch, having expected it to be frozen. He scattered it over the shroud-wrapped corpse, then pushed himself slowly to his feet.

Then he moved to the side of the larger grave and bowed his head a moment. *Too many*, he thought. *I don't even have all the names.*

He looked back up the crowd. "We will erect a stone in memory of everyone else here. I promise you that. I do not mean to honor Renard at the cost of those who fought with him, or those he died to defend. We will honor all of them, forever. Renard would have had it no other way."

Then, once more, Allystaire knelt at a graveside and took a handful of earth and tossed it among the bodies and stood. He wanted, badly, for that to be the last time he ever stood at a graveside, ever spoke words over the bodies of folk he led or protected. He knew it wouldn't be.

Allystaire shut his eyes tightly as a spasm of despair surged up his throat. He only just managed to blink away the wetness that gathered at the corner of his eyes.

"If anyone else wishes to come forward to speak of those we lost," he called out, "now is the time."

Allystaire searched the faces. He saw Leah take a hesitant step forward, then stop and turn away, lowering her head and wrapping her arms around her belly. The crowd moved to surround her, and he heard, in the reigning silence, her choked sobs. He took half a step forward, but saw Idgen Marte taking long, determined strides and reaching Leah's side long before he could have. The dark-skinned swordswoman stood taller than almost everyone in the crowd, and could see her bend her head to Leah's ear.

Idgen Marte nodded as she listened to words that Renard's widow appeared to choke out through her sobs, leaned close to murmur replies. Finally, after wrapped her long arms around the girl, Idgen Marte stood away and came to stand by Renard's grave, clearing her throat.

"Leah wanted everyone to know how gentle Renard was behind closed doors. To us, he was the sergeant, the drillmaster, barking orders and offering none-too-gentle correction. She never heard his voice that way. She said he knew he was no kind of farmer any longer, but he wanted to try his hand at a bit of gardening come spring. That he would want everyone to know how happy he was the months he lived here, that he felt he was finally living a worthwhile life. And that he had the Goddess and Her Servants to thank for it."

Then she knelt and took a handful of earth, tossing it into the open grave. Most of what she muttered, Allystaire could not hear, but he knew he caught the words "Brother of Battle."

Leah had gone quiet as the folk listened to Idgen Marte pass her message on, had stopped sobbing. Village women to either side of her had their arms around her back, supporting her.

Idgen Marte stepped away to a general susurration in the crowd. She came to stand next to Allystaire, and he heard and felt her take a deep breath, the kind with a hitch or a shudder in it.

Henri stepped to the grave. The farmer turned militiaman looked almost absurd in his uniform of ill-fitting mail taken from a soldier of Fortune's Temple, pauldrons buckled to his shoulders that didn't match the mail, and a single battered bracer on his right forearm. The Sunburst was tied around his right arm, while the bracer had two thick lines of blue paint splashed across it, marking him as a Chosen Man, Allystaire supposed.

Henri considered his words, chewing at the inside of his cheek. "Dunno any other way t'say it. If it weren't for Renard tryin' his damndest to make what soldiers he could out of us, I think a lot more folk'd be dead. Could be all of us'd be dead. I know I would be. I'd rather be a farmer than a soldier. Cold, Renard'd say I'm only half a soldier at best. But if I hafta use what he taught me t'defend this place again, I will. And if anyone comes here meanin' 'arm to Leah, or to the daughter Renard din't live t'see, he'll 'ave to reckon with e'ry one o'us."

As Henri bent to the ground to take his handful of earth, Allystaire found his thoughts wandering to the moment he'd first met the man they were burying, guarding an absurd gate in a miniature joke of a castle in Bend. There had been a professionalism in the old soldier that was hard to miss, and Allystaire found himself wondering why Renard had left the Baron to follow him in the first place. *You traded paid work for a shorter life, my friend,* Allystaire thought. *And I am sorry.*

He traded the bright metal too many men value for the things they venerate it above: love, family, and purpose. He chose freely, My Knight. Mourn him, but do not diminish his choice.

Allystaire felt the voice in his mind. It was much fainter than usual. She felt distant, strained. Even so, he shivered for reasons other than the cold winter air.

Idgen Marte turned to eye him then, the barest hint of her typical smirk twisting her lips, but no mirth in her eyes. "He followed you, Allystaire," she muttered, "because he saw something worth following. Same things I saw. Cold, same things the Goddess saw, I expect. He wasn't the first and he'll not be the last."

"Does not make it easier to bury him."

"It shouldn't," Idgen Marte agreed.

They fell silent as more of the militiamen and villagers came forward to speak about Renard, his rough wit, his crafty lessons, his love for his wife. Allystaire stood stock still, his back straight, but let his mind drift. If he hadn't, he felt surely he would've gone a bit mad with the grief. *I mourn him and yet I knew him so little compared to these men*, he thought, as silence finally fell as the last villager stepped away.

He was drawing breath to speak up when Mol stepped forward, and the crowd hushed itself entirely.

"There is little I can add to what has been spoken in memory of Sir Renard." As always, Mol seemed to make no effort at projecting her voice, no deep lungfuls of air before she spoke. And yet her voice filled the air around them inescapably. "He wanted to give all of us the life of peace he'd never had. He loved his wife in a kind of daze, as if he couldn't believe that such love was even possible, as if every moment that he was in a world that also contained Leah was a wondrous thing he could not quite believe was real. Love like this was new to him, and yet, I think if he lived another score of years he would have loved just the same. And that," she said, pausing for emphasis, "is the quality we should most seek to emulate. Love the world, people of the Mother. Love each other. Renard did."

She bent, scooped, and threw a tiny handful of dirt, then said, "Renard *also* loved his beer, and he would be cross to see us mourning and tearful all the light turns of the day. Through the week, the month, the winter, I will come to the gravesides here three turns after dawn and again three turns after noon, and I will listen to any who wish to speak of their dead. Any who wish to come and listen with me are welcome.

"Go," Mol finished. "Remember Renard and the others in your own ways, with song or tears or laughter or stories as you will."

* * *

Late that evening, with the public mourning gone and the wine mostly gone with it, Allystaire sat at the head of a table dragged near the hearth, with Landen and Chaddin to either side and Cerisia across from him at the other end. She wore her mask, its glint giving the room an air of formality.

A pile of parchment sat at Allystaire's elbow, and while it seemed as though the taproom was otherwise empty, he knew that Idgen Marte lurked invisibly in the shadows of a corner. Lamps had been hung from braces on the beams above the table they sat at, putting the four of them into a pool of light bright enough to read and to make out each other's expressions. Beyond the Inn's oilcloth and fur-covered windows, the winter wind drove snow up against the stone walls.

Both would-be rulers of Barony Delondeur were eyeing each other over winecups. Allystaire felt badly the desire to fill his own. *You need to be clearheaded*, he told himself, not without some resentment.

"I think that is enough of trying to measure one another with our eyes," he said. "And if you had any doubts, that is my way of announcing that these talks are now beginning."

"Talks?" Landen looked to him, raising one dark blonde eyebrow gracefully. "I wasn't aware these were talks."

"When I say 'talks,'" Allystaire cut her off, "you should interpret it as *listening*. I will give the both of you a chance to have your say, but Cold-dammit, I am not going to brook any nonsense, interruptions, or attacks of pride. Is that clear?"

"Then why is she here?" Landen nodded towards the Archioness.

"Because Allystaire asked me to be," Cerisia said, voice muffled by the mask.

"Which I did because she has shown considerable courage and foresight, and because she could be wise counsel to either or both of you, if you will allow her to be."

"Once again, I recall you saying you weren't going to dirty your hands with politics," Chaddin said, through an expression that was half-smirk, half-grimace.

"I do not wish to play politics, but the stage is set, the players are upon it, and the moment is not giving me much of a choice. With the two of you and Garth in the same camp, if I do not take steps things will only get worse."

"If these matters concern The Lord of Highgate, should he not be here?" Landen put in. "He will want a say if his name is being bandied about, I am sure."

"The Lord of Highgate has been accustomed to doing what I say since his eighth summer. The habit will not have left him quite yet."

"Doing as you say is what this is all about, isn't it, Allystaire?" Chaddin set his cup down and looked ready to stand, planting his hands flat on the edge of the table.

Allystaire took a deep breath and let it out slowly, eyes closing. "All I mean to do, Chaddin, is make suggestions. Whether you follow them is up to you. It is my sincere hope that you do. If you do not, well, you have that right. You will also have to deal with the consequences."

"What consequences would those be?" Landen asked, leaning forward.

"Me allowing The Lord of Highgate to do as he damn well pleases with the pair of you," Allystiare replied. "And with an easy path into the interior of your Barony."

Silence reigned for a moment. Landen sat back, her face grim in the lamplight. Chaddin, in turn, looked at Allystaire in disbelief.

"This is how you would repay my aid to you? Threats of imprisonment, of allowing a foreign warlord to do as he likes with me?" His hands once more on the table, Chaddin was half out of his seat.

"I am doing what I must do for the people I am responsible for," Allystaire shot back. "You are alive because I gave you shelter here. Yes, Chaddin, you aided us, but it was a matter of mutual survival. This does not obligate me to hand you the Baronial Seat. Now sit down."

Reluctantly, Chaddin sank back into his seat, but kept his eyes downcast and his face bitterly twisted.

Allystaire watched him for a moment, then turned his eyes back to Landen. He felt again the warm and inviting call of the winecup at his elbow. "Both of you might as well know what my goal here is. The end of the Succession Strife, or whatever it is we are calling this ridiculous war."

Landen and Chaddin both drew in deep breaths. Without giving them time to interrupt, Allystaire plowed ahead, still eyeing the legitimate Delondeur. "I would prefer to see someone in the Seat who will not have to fight a *further* war to gain it or to keep it. Surely, Chaddin, you can see what will happen if I had taken your offer to raise and lead an army to put you in the Dunes. Even if it were successful, your own liegemen would test you at best and prey upon you at worst. Oyrwyn will see an opportunity. Old Innadan might even rouse himself. Telmawr would goad him to it. If there are any remnants of Barony Tarynth left, Cold, they will have at it as well. This is not to mention what the Islandmen and Gravek who infest the wreck of Vyndamere would do if they smelled weakness. The presence of Lionel Delondeur is about all that kept them away in the first place. Do you concede that some or *all* of that would happen?" He turned to Chaddin.

Chaddin's face fell as Allystaire spoke. Finally, hiding reddened cheeks behind a quickly emptied cup, he nodded.

"Good. That will make this easier." His eyes on the table, the edges of his hands resting on the rough planks, palms towards each other, he plowed ahead.

"Landen, had I encountered you in the battle for Thornhurst, I would have killed you. I will not guess if it is luck or providence or some part of the Goddess's plan that you survived. By all custom, law, and right of this Barony, its Seat belongs to you. Agree to my suggestions, and I will not impede you ascending it. Nor will I aid you. Much."

Landen let out a small sigh. She eyed Chaddin, and Allystaire took a moment to study the former's face. It was in so many ways her father's, with a reddish glow of health about the cheekbones and jaw that a week's short rations and bad sleep hadn't much diminished. There was, Allystaire noted, no sign of gloating in her eyes.

"As for my suggestions," Allystaire went on, "first, you should legitimize Chaddin, and position him as your heir for the time being. I would hope that you might see fit to dispense with Delondeur's antiquated rules of passing on the Seat by right of deed and derring-do, but that is of little matter here today," he added, tapping the table with a pointed finger. "For a moment, put yourself in his position those months ago and realize that he showed remarkable poise, leadership, and initiative in doing what he did. And remember that I advised him to hang your father from the highest tower available, and that he refused because he wanted to see things done legally, for his crimes to be exposed and aired to the world."

To Chaddin, he said, "This might be a moment for you to reflect on Landen's position. Like as not, you would have done as she did if the situations were reversed, knowing little save that her father was deposed and imprisoned, and sailing at great peril and speed to his rescue.

"It may seem daft that I will ask you to work together now. What I am counting on is that courage is more important to both of you than finally killing one another."

Landen looked to him as if asking permission to speak. Allystaire nodded, and she addressed her remarks to Chaddin.

"Chaddin, think on what Allystaire said about being tested by liege lords and pressed on the borders. Delondeur will need all its strength. I would not keep you idle, either—"

Allystaire lifted a hand. "I was not finished making suggestions. In fact, there is a position I would like to see Chaddin appointed to. He impressed me when he insisted on using the mechanism of the law, slow and clumsy though it may be, to bring your father to justice. Make him a magistrate, a justiciar, a minister of the law. Call it what you will. But I suggest this be a new post for this part of the world; make his writ or warrant or what have you *directly* applicable to knights and nobility. Allow the poorest and weakest folk to plead their cases with him, and see to it that his fair judgment carries the Baron's own word, no matter who it is brought against."

"The lords will never accept it," Landen breathed, half-astonished. "They have always had direct recourse to the Baron, or to an Assize overseen by a priest of sufficient rank."

"And how often has a Baron's judgment gone against them?" Chaddin spoke up now. "I served in the city for two winters, and in the field with the Londray spears for three campaigns. I was always near our father, and you know how soldiers gossip. Not once, not *once* have I heard of harsh judgment passed on a knight or a nobleman, especially if our father found him useful. At most he levied fines, for theft, wanton destruction, even murder. And he'd keep half the piddling handful of silver links for rendering his judgment and pass the rest onto the aggrieved. As for pressing? He *encouraged* it."

"That does not change the basic fact. They will not countenance it."

"They will if you make them," Allystaire said. "It is remarkable what men will adjust to when you give them no choice. Besides," he added, "they will have extra incentive to comply with the magistrate's judgments."

"Indeed," Cerisia put in, before Chaddin or Landen could interrupt. "For on this score at least, lords and knights will no longer have recourse to a Temple Assize. Not with Fortune."

Both Delondeurs whipped their heads towards the priestess, as if they'd be able to read anything behind her mask. In the dimness of the room, even her eyes were hidden.

"That," Landen began delicately, "is quite a step for Fortune's Temple to take."

"It is. But it will be worth it if it brings us a step closer to a peace."

"Are you quite prepared to forfeit the payments lords provided your priests for favorable judgments?" said Chaddin, more blunt than his half-sister.

"I am prepared to forfeit those priests," Cerisia said.

"You cannot speak for Braech in this," Landen said.

"We will not concern ourselves with Braech or his church just now," Allystaire said. "I think we are not done with them, but I am not going to pretend we can control or anticipate what they will do. What should concern you both—and the lords you think will not abide judgments made fairly by independent courts—is me.

"If the destitute cannot have the recourse of the law, they can turn to the paladin. And I will see justice done, no matter how little you or your liegemen like it."

Landen frowned, reached out, and tapped a finger against her winecup. "Why are you so interested in the law at all, then, if you intend to flout it?"

"I do not give a Frozen damn for most laws of the Baronies," Allystaire admitted flatly. "Not as they are now. If we can make the least powerful served by the law, rather than scourged by it? Then I will care for the *law*."

"How do I make them fall in line?" Landen began.

"We do it," Chaddin said. "I hang the first one brought before me that deserves hanging. Swiftly. You maintain my right to do it."

Allystaire nodded. "Precisely as I would have said."

Landen sighed. "That will not be an easy transition, especially given that the man being placed over them is a former rebel."

Allystaire waved a hand dismissively. "Ruling families engage in that kind of nonsense all the time. It only takes your word, and your willingness to back it."

Landen looked across the table at her half-brother and extended a hand. "Our father was a monster who would've destroyed this Barony to preserve himself. I see that now; you saw it months ago. Help me put his sins right."

Chaddin stood and took Landen's hand. The two shook in a quick but powerful embrace of forearms.

Allystaire and Cerisia stood with them. "There is parchment, ink, and pen here with which to make all of this official. No doubt a set of Baronial seals came here with your father. The Archioness can provide her own seal and signature as witness."

Cerisia was already drawing a heavy, curved silver handle from a pocket in her cloak.

Landen smiled wryly. "In point of fact, the Baronial ring and seals were missing when I came back to the Dunes."

Chaddin colored and dug into a pouch, producing the thick gold ring, set with a disc of jade bearing diamonds forming the Delondeur Tower, as well as two seals, carved from ivory forming a stamp of the same device.

"Good. Have at it," Allystaire said. "I intend to read it in the morning. Not that I believe either of you capable of outwitting the Archioness in some way, but I mean to have the Wit and Will of the Mother read it as well."

"Have you more suggestions?" Landen asked, eyeing the ring that lay heavy on her palm.

"Aye, two. The first we will discuss in the morning. As for the second, not a suggestion as much as a reminder."

Allystaire remained on his feet. While he did not have height on either Landen or Chaddin, he did have size and he knew how to command attention. He leaned forward lightly over the table, pressing his fists into it, hunching his shoulders and looming over them.

"Power can change a person. Often, it draws out the worst. It did to your father, whether slowly over the many years or quickly over these past few, I cannot say, but he became a monster." Allystaire stood halfway out of his chair, pressing his knuckles to the table so that he loomed over it. "I am here, in this world, to *destroy* monsters like Lionel Delondeur. If I have a hand in creating more like him, I would not rest until they were so thoroughly destroyed that when they went to the Cold, the vilest of the dead there would recoil in shock and horror and fear at what I had done to them."

He pushed away from the table. "Good night. Write fast. And legibly."

CHAPTER 11

A Crusade for Peace

When Allystaire awoke, he stared at the wooden beams of the ceiling above him. *Wonder if my breath will be visible if I let it out.* Such was the cold that had seeped through the walls. Quilts and bedclothes had been tossed aside in the night, and a fire barely stirred in the small hearth.

"Damn," he muttered, "did not bank it properly. Not sure I remember how."

He shrugged, then rolled his shoulders and winced as the joints crackled. He moved to the window, pushing aside the hide that covered it and tugging at the edge of the oilcloth. The cold air of the outdoors slapped him across the face while thin sunlight needled his eyes. He hurriedly shut it.

"Cold rooms encourage wakefulness and activity," he muttered, repeating it like some long-lost mantra.

He pulled on long underclothes, woolen socks and trousers that had been on the stones of the small fireplace, finding them only barely warmer than the air. He tugged on his boots and gathered his other clothes, then stumped downstairs.

To Allystaire's surprise, he found Chaddin and Landen both stretched out upon benches pulled near the hearth. Timmar was moving quietly around the room, sweeping. Allystaire moved towards him, nodding at the sleeping pair and murmuring, "Found them this way when you awoke?"

Timmar nodded. "Aye," he said back, though not as quietly. "Don't think they've been sleepin' long." He pointed to the table and the stack of parchment upon it, pages thickly covered with precise writing. "Lamps were near out o' oil," he added.

Allystaire nodded, considering them. "I will wake them in a moment." He bit at his upper lip. "Timmar, as to the oil, and to all we have been eating and drinking, I am afraid I have not given much thought to your expenses."

Timmar waved a hand dismissively. "There're no expenses for you, or the other servants o'the Mother. Not now nor ever. I'll make allowances where I can for guests o'yours as well."

"You have to make a living."

"I'd have no life and no Inn and no family weren't for you," Timmar said, shaking his head. "This Inn'll not collect a link from you while I live."

"You have to get links from somewhere."

"Do I? So far I can trade for what I need with the rest o'the folk," the innkeep countered, with a shrug. "Ever'one wants beer and my brother and I brewed it best, had the knowin' of it from our da. Still do. I need bread t'serve, aye. So I trade in kind w' who'ers got some t'spare. Come spring sure I'll be needin' thatch, but I can get help for work like that."

"That cannot last forever. There will be things you need that the village will not be able to provide. Peddlers and the like."

"Torvul can fix anythin'. No need for tinkers. Links will come when we need 'em an' the Mother allows it."

"That is dangerous thinking," Allystaire murmured quietly. "The Mother surely wants you to live and work sensibly."

"And isn't that what we're doin'?" Timmar smiled, revealing gaps and browned teeth. "Barter does for the Mother's folk for now. If I'm needin' silver, I'll present your friend the Lord O'Highgate with his bill. And tha priestess. Links will come," he muttered, smiling wider, before turning back to his morning chores.

Allystaire chuckled. "Very well. I see you have it well in hand, but Timmar, if you will not take silver from me, at least take my thanks. I have not always spoken them to the people of this village. Things appear in my room or my tent: food, scarves, warm clothes, wine, lamps and oil, and I think nothing of it, because all my life, servants have been there to provide such things. Yet you are not my servant. I am yours. And I fear I have not always said so."

"Cold but you use a lot o'words t'say a little," Timmar said, grinning. Then with the grin melting into a more serious expression, he added, "Just offer a thanks now'n'then if ya feel the need. All o'us 'ave seen ya bleedin' for our very lives. Three times now I've seen ya fall, and e'ery time thought you'd died. Seems t'me most men would be dead, what you've been through, and you been through it for us. Thanks go both ways."

"Three times?" Allystaire's brow furrowed.

"The warehouse, the knights who come t'take ya away, the…" He trailed off, shivering. "The dead things."

"Battle-Wights," Allystaire said. "Name a thing and we fear it less, or so I hope," he added. "At any rate, Timmar, thank you. Now I am off to go break the ice in the water barrel."

"Got a mallet back here for that," Timmar said.

Allystaire lifted up his right hand, curled loosely into a fist. "If I am to found a knightly order it is time to be back in knightly training."

Timmar snorted. "Holler when ya pass out the fourth time so's I can drag you t'the fire 'fore you die o'the cold."

Allystaire laughed, then he was out the door and, bare chested and bare headed, his breath was stolen from him as surely as if he'd been punched in the gut by a Gravekmir.

Still yourself. Master it. Count slowly to ten. He made it to eight before he began pulling clothes on over his head. Though the cold was already inside them, and he felt only a little warmer than before, he fought off the urge to duck back inside and stand as close to the hearth as Timmar would let him. Instead, he went around the corner to the barrel.

As expected, ice had gathered thickly on the top. He pushed past his elbow the shirts he'd awkwardly tugged on and took a deep breath, curling his hand into a fist.

Allystaire drew his arm back and then hurled it, knuckles first, against the ice. It rebounded. Pain blossomed from his knuckles, up to his wrist.

He grunted, moved his feet to take a better stance, bent over the barrel, and punched again.

Cracks appeared in the ice.

A third time, then rapidly a fourth and fifth, and his hand plunged down into the frigid water. Hastily he scooped it up, splashed his face. Then, holding his arm gingerly at his side but walking at a carefully measured pace, he re-entered the Inn.

He found Timmar placing hooking a large kettle over the hearth, and Cerisia, dressed in spotless white furs, sitting at a table where she could watch the door.

Her lips turned upwards into a faint grin. She murmured, "Really, Sir Stillbright? At your age?"

Allystaire hoped his cheeks were already reddened enough by the cold to hide any flush. "It seemed appropriate, Archioness. It is how every Oyrwyn squire begins his winter mornings."

"You've not been a squire for many long years," Cerisia said, her mouth still quirked. "Still, I would imagine that five blows is a respectable number for a rain barrel so deeply frozen."

"Once upon a time it would have been two," Allystaire said, smiling faintly himself. "But you are correct to think it a foolish gesture."

"One would imagine," Cerisia said, "that you of all men should have no need to prove anything to yourself."

Allystaire shrugged awkwardly, feeling exposed as he stood a few feet from the door, feeling the wafts of cold air that edged around it. "Winter encourages idleness. I only wish to guard against it."

"Idleness? Have you slept more than a handful of turns any night since you recovered? Have you rested a moment when you when had it?" Cerisia looked to the sleeping Chaddin and Landen. "You've more than fifteen years on both of them, and the labors you pushed upon them have laid them low. You are up with the dawn, breaking ice. I should think, Allystaire Stillbright, if there is any man who could do with a bit more idleness, it is you."

Allystaire wasn't entirely sure, since the light inside was still dim, but he didn't think he liked the way her eyes flashed when Cerisia said idleness. Or the set of her mouth.

Or perhaps you do like it, you idiot, he thought.

Cerisia lifted a brow. "Break fast with me, Allystaire? We probably have matters to discuss and I have found it difficult to find time in your schedule."

Allystaire nodded and took a seat opposite the priestess. "Why did you stay? Surely you could have escaped near the end of the battle."

"Straight to business then," Cerisia said, with a faint fall in her voice. She brightened as she resettled in her set and went on. "By then I had a vested interest in your survival," she replied. "And in you knowing that I was on your side."

"Why did you come to the battle, anyway? Your Temple did not commit significant troops. Nor did Braech's. Was the Anathemata less of a threat than you had promised?"

"After the Anathemata was proclaimed but *before* the former Baron Delondeur gathered his men to march, Braech's Temple suddenly had less stomach for the fight. I refused to participate any further in the battle than they did. So far as they knew, anyway," she added, leaning forward almost conspiratorially.

"Are you trying to tell me that you somehow aided in our..." Allystaire hesitated over the word victory. "Survival?"

Cerisia straightened. "Did it not occur to you wonder why Delondeur's bowmen played so poor a part in his attack? Did you not wonder why he didn't simply bury you in missiles?"

"Too little time to train proper bowmen. The men he brought were, in the main, not real soldiers. A real archer is at his craft for a lifetime. A man without that kind of time with the bow is more of a danger to his fellows than his foes. Not to mention," Allystaire added, "the ruthlessly practical was never Lionel's style. Not where others would see, at any rate."

"While that may have been true, surely he would have engaged in more practical strategies as he was foiled. As it happens, orders were given to arm every man with crossbows for an assault. Someone had the sense to test the weapons before marching the men off only to find that every single one was flawed beyond repair. The strings, especially, were broken. And the spares had all rotted."

Allystaire was momentarily puzzled, till he remembered a contemptuous flick of the Archioness's hand snapping the string of a crossbow that had been aimed at her. "Your doing?"

"The initially broken strings, occasionally rotted stock or fouled mechanism, yes," Cerisia replied. "I will admit that I was unaware of the cache of replacement strings. That, you can blame on Delondeur's amateur soldiers; they weren't packed well and the weather took care of it. But I would have done what I could."

"Why? Your own Temple had proclaimed us outlaws along with the Baron," Allystaire said. "I do not think I understand you, Archioness. You rode with an army to our gates, an army that your own Temple helped bring into being, and then sabotaged them from within." He shook his head slowly, repeated, "Why?"

"Can you not credit that I meant what I said in the letter I left you about my sympathy for the people of this village?" Cerisia shifted uncomfortably, her eyes sliding away from his. "When I saw that the Baron had enlisted sorcerers to aid him, when I realized what that meant, I could not stand idle. I hadn't the men nor the military knowledge to affect the battle directly. I did have the powers my Goddess grants to me, slight though they may seem to you, and I employed them as best I could."

Allystaire was silent a moment. "Thank you, Cerisia. You risked a great deal in aiding us, especially, as I understand it, with sorcerers present. I am in your debt."

Timmar bustled past their table, heading for the kettle that had begun to sing. As he carefully slid it from its pole, Chaddin and Landen began to stir, groggily sitting up and knuckling sleep away from their eyes, or the pain of having slept on a bare wooden bench from their backs.

"All I would ask of you is to do what I wanted when I came here in the autumn," Cerisia said. She let that hang in the air a moment, and Allystaire felt the intensity of her stare, till it was broken by her delicate laugh. "Not that. What I want, Allystaire, is much the same as what you want: to avoid blood-shed."

Allystaire swallowed, looked down at his hands on the table, noticed the slight swelling of the knuckles of his right hand, frowned. "What is it that you think I mean to do, Cerisia? Burn all Temples of the Sea Dragon to the ground? Tear Londray apart? Install myself as Baron in a bloody march to the Dunes?"

"The first had crossed my mind," Cerisia noted. "I doubt very much that you seek a Baron's seat, for if you did you'd be at Wind's Jaw right now and none of this would've happened. But surely you cannot mean to rest here, confident that your victory against one foe will keep your people safe. You will have to take arms again. I had assumed, knowing you and your reputation, that you would not sit and wait. That you would carry the fight to your enemies while they reeled."

"I have not yet decided what I will do with my enemies," Allystaire said, then he waved a hand. "No, that is not true. I have not yet decided *how* I will do it. If more arise, I will fend them off, kill them as necessary to defend those I am called to defend. If you think I mean to lead a crusade, I would say that you are not wrong, Archioness. Yet I mean, as far as I am able, to make it a crusade of peace."

"Those words do not go together, Sir Allystaire," Cerisia said quietly.

"The Goddess did not call me to Her service to do the merely difficult."

Cerisia studied his face for a moment, and was about to speak when Timmar interrupted, setting a teapot on their table and filling it with water from the kettle he'd taken off the fire. Almost immediately the scent of tea began to filter into the air, though to Allystaire's nose it smelled dishearteningly weak. Landen and Chaddin had wandered over, standing nearby, shuffling, yawning, adjusting their sleep-rumpled clothing.

Allystaire turned to them, and Landen pointed to the stack of parchment. "We wrote out an agreement as you asked."

"Suggested," Allystaire corrected quickly.

"As you suggested. With all your suggestions intact as well as some of our own design," Landen finished as if she'd never been interrupted. "Last eve you hinted that there was a further suggestion. We cannot put the seal to it if we don't know what it is."

"True," Allystaire said. "Have you overheard my conversation with the Archioness?"

"I try not to eavesdrop," Landen said.

For his part, Chaddin shrugged. "A few months ago I was a sergeant of foot. Eavesdropping is in my bones."

That, Allystaire suddenly thought, *is more of the man I thought I liked*. Hiding a smile, he said, "What did you hear?"

"Something about a crusade for peace, which sounds like a lot of nonsense to me," Chaddin said bluntly.

"I find myself in agreement with the Archioness as well," Landen admitted. "It seems unlikely."

"Well," Allystaire said, crossing his arms over his chest, and wincing a bit as he pressed his right hand against his left arm, "the two of you are going to help me bring it about. No," he said, raising a hand as their mouths opened, "I do not mean raising a banner and arming masses of men to tear down another Temple or destroy a Barony. Not Delondeur or any neighbor. I am going to ask you," he said, pointing a finger at Landen, "to hold a peace council with Baron Innadan."

"Innadan has been our primary antagonist every season when Oyrwyn was not for the past decade or more!" Landen's protest was at volume and sharp with surprise. Timmar, effortlessly gliding around those who stood or sat at the table, cleared his throat as he set mugs down and began pouring.

"There're folk sleepin' upstairs m'lady, includin' a lass with child and mournin' her husband. I'd appreciate if you kept it a bit quieter." He paused. "If you'd be so kind. M'lady"

Allystaire seized upon Landen's slight shock at the innkeep's frank address to press his point. "And how often has Innadan done more than defend his own borders, or what remains of Barony Telmawr, from your father's incursions? Oyrwyn was his ally, never his enemy. I know the man, have since I was a child. He wants peace. He sued for it, years ago, and most of us laughed at him while we drank his best wine."

"I have met Hamadrian Innadan as well," Cerisia put in. Timmar stood solicitously at her shoulder, the remnants of a cone of sugar and a small pair of snips in a bowl. "He is as weary of war as any man could be. Some men thrive on it, even if it slowly strangles the land they claim to fight for. Gerard Oyrwyn was such a man. So was Lionel Delondeur, till his need for victory drove him to the extremes that led us to this moment. Baron Innadan is drained by it. He is a few years younger than your father was," she said, one hand opening to include both Landen and Chaddin, even as she held her mug out for Timmar to ease crushed sugar into, "and yet he seems a score of years older. Every blow done to his beloved land inches him closer to death. If you would speak to him of peace, I promise you he will listen."

"How would I even get him a message? I have no access to the birds or the couriers at the Dunes."

"We will manage that in time," Allystaire said. "We have some, after all. No one will campaign till the snows begin to melt. I just want to know if you will do it."

Landen swallowed hard. "Fighting my father's war is what I was brought up to do."

"As I was brought up to fight Oyrwyn's," Allystaire replied. "It is time we stopped doing what we were taught to do. Time to learn new trades."

"Why stop at Innadan?" Chaddin looked almost startled to have spoken. Allystaire furrowed his brow, gestured at him to go on.

"Surely Baron Innadan can influence Oyrwyn," Chaddin said, a little more tentatively. "Telmawr is little more than his vassal as it is. That's two. Why stop there? Harlach. Varshyne. Go farther east: Damarind. Machoryn." The words rolled faster off his tongue as he went.

"I am all for sending envoys to them," Allystaire said. "Varshyne may take some doing, surrounded as it is by giantkin and Islandmen. But Innadan is the key, both his personality, and his Barony's geography."

"The bridge between the western and eastern Baronies," Cerisia agreed. "And respected by all of his neighbors."

"Sounds like you want to make him king," Landen muttered. Allystaire shot her a dark look, and to the young woman's credit, she winced and shook her head. "Not what I meant."

"Good," Allystaire said. "I think perhaps the problems the Baronies have had is not due to the lack of a king. I have no intention of making one."

"Well, I suppose I shall start drafting, then," Landen said, frowning a bit as she turned towards the writing implements arrayed on the nearby table. "All this ink and parchment is enough to make me wish my father had given me tutors who were the match of my armsmasters."

"You have time," Allystaire said. "You need not start it this moment. If you wish to return to your men and share with them what has gone on, I would not begrudge you the time." His eyes flicked to Chaddin. "You as well."

Landen sighed and shook her head. "The sooner we start the sooner we finish."

"While I appreciate the sentiment," Allystaire said, "and in the main, agree with it, whatever begins here will not be quick to finish. At *best* it will take months to secure any kind of agreement to meet with more than just Innadan himself. In truth it will take many years of moving relentlessly forward to secure anything lasting. I want you to understand what you are in for."

Landen eyed Allystaire a moment before she replied, her tone slightly clipped. "At the least, you might not speak to me as if I am choosing this uncoerced."

"I have leverage at the moment, Baroness Delondeur," Allystaire said. "I would be a fool not to apply it."

"And what responsibility will you bear if it turns to water in my hands and falls entirely out of them? What if Innadan, Harlach, and Oyrwyn decide to settle old grudges and invade Delondeur in a concerted effort?"

"I will bear the same responsibilities I do now," Allystaire said. "Ending the war. However I must."

Landen sighed and lowered her eyes. "You had best be right about Baron Innadan. I've only ever known him as an enemy. I don't know how well he will take a message from me. And I doubt that Oyrwyn will take a message at all."

"Leave Oyrwyn and its armies to me," Allystaire said.

"Oh? And Harlach? Telmawr? The eastern Baronies whose heraldry I barely remember?"

Allystaire sighed. "We cannot control what all of them will do, Landen. We can control what we do. If you wish to be remembered as a greater ruler, a *better* ruler, than your father, then take this first step. I will help, in the ways that I can, to see that it does not tumble your people, or any other, into oblivion."

"You speak of these things all too freely," Landen said, shaking her head. "I cannot conceive what grants you your confidence."

"Not confidence, Baroness," Allystaire said, finally reaching for the mug of tea that Timmar had poured for him. "Faith."

"As to your concerns, Landen," Cerisia said, studying the woman over the rim of her cup, "many may be allayed by choosing the right messenger. Allow me to volunteer."

Allystaire sat up straighter, setting his mug down with enough force to slop some over the side. "What?"

"I wish for peace as much as you," Cerisia said. "Carrying and delivering messages are how I can serve to achieve it. We who serve Fortune are often seen as impartial in these matters. And letting me deliver the message for you, as opposed to a party of your knights riding under a flag of truce, reduces the chance of rumor moving ahead of it and muddying the waters. And last, but not least," she added, pausing for a sip of her rapidly cooling tea, then smiling over the edge of the mug, "I can be very persuasive."

I don't doubt it, Allystaire thought guiltily, as he watched her lips, artfully reddened even so early in the day, curve above her drink. He quickly looked to Landen and Chaddin. "I would listen to her, Landen. She speaks a good deal of sense." He threw down his tea in one great gulp, and stood. "Now if you will all excuse me, I have a squirehood to relive."

Chaddin snorted, Landen winced, Cerisia merely smiled a bit more broadly. "And what is that to entail, Sir Stillbright? More shattering ice with your fists? Running barefoot in the snow?"

"Running barefoot and armored in the snow," Allystaire jibed back, grinning.

"They didn't *actually* make you do any of that, did they?" Landen asked.

"Not barefoot," Allystaire said with a shrug.

"Cold, but you knightly lot are a great bunch of fools," Chaddin said, then shrugged as eyes turned to him. "It's not as if I'm the only common-born man who ever thought as much."

"If more men like you said as much, Chaddin, then things might change." Allystaire nodded to them, sketched the tiniest bow to Cerisia, and asked, "Archioness, is our business done?"

"For now," she said, pushing the words slowly, with exaggeration, past her very red lips, her pale green eyes lightly narrowed.

Allystaire nodded and was glad of the cold that hit him when he stepped out the door.

CHAPTER 12

Interlude

In a room that was less frigid than the air in Thornhurst, but only just, the Choiron Symod stood at a window and stared, hard, at the frozen water beneath it.

He heard footsteps behind him, did not turn towards them. With a jut of his sharply bearded chin, he gestured to the frozen waters of Londray Bay.

"The very sight of it ought to offend us, yes? That anything, even the winter itself, should contend with the will of the Sea Dragon."

The Marynth Evolyn Lamaliere remained silent a moment before finally, delicately saying, "The Father of Waves is surely greater than any season, Choiron."

"Is He?" Symod's jaw quivered slightly as he bit through the words.

Evolyn saw the ripple of tension along the Choiron's jaw, clasped her hands, pressed her lips into a line, and said nothing. Inwardly, she hoped that the frigid air in the chamber would keep her cheeks from paling. She did not want to show him fear.

"Even now," he went on, giving no sign that he'd expected her to respond, "winter locks His life's blood in its embrace. Ships do not move. Trade is halted. No accords are made. War and strife settles into silence, all because the world grows cold."

"The Baronies are not the world, Choiron," Evolyn suggested, careful to keep her voice cautious, but level. Servility would not do. "In Keersvast and the Concordat, the Sea Dragon's will—"

Symod turned to face her. There were signs, though slight, of disarray in his appearance. His beard grown longer, slightly less precisely kept. A suggestion of darkness under the feverishly bright eyes. A wrinkle in his richly appointed robe.

"The Baronies are all the world that matters, Marynth. If Braech's will can be defied here, it can be defied everywhere."

"Winters pass, Choiron," Evolyn said calmly.

"It is not the defiance of winter that troubles me," Symod said, his voice a knife's edge lined in ice.

"I know," Evolyn replied.

"THEN WHY IS THE PALADIN NOT BOUND AND BROKEN BEFORE ME? WHY DOES AN UPSTART TEMPLE STILL STAND?"

If Symod's voice had been the edge of a blade just a moment before, now it was a hammer, assaulting her will and her body both. Panic bloomed along her spine; Evolyn only just fought off the urge to flee. The sound of it in the chamber was painful. Her legs faltered and for a moment she feared she was going to sink to one knee.

"Forgive me, Choiron," she said, scrambling for words to defend herself as her mind reeled.

Symod raised his hand as if to strike her, and anger suddenly rose in place of her fear. Her legs stiffened and her hand shot out to catch his as the blow descended. He had a wiry strength, but Evolyn was a determined woman, and she turned his wrist aside, her fingers curled white-knuckle tight around the ropy tendons of Symod's arm. She saw the fury it sparked in his eyes, matched it with defiance in her own.

"That is more of Braech's priestess as I know her," Symod said, a measure of his control returning to his voice, smoothing and evening its edges, as he moved his hand to his side. "That is the woman to whom I entrusted Braechsworn warriors, considerable weight, and the alliance of two sorcerers in order to kill the paladin. I find myself unable to understand why *that* Marynth Evolyn did not do as she was ordered."

Evolyn swallowed hard, calling up memories of eyes that glowed a sickly, disturbing yellow, of the twisted words that emerged from the throat of the man who owned them. The husk of a man.

"I *did* prod the Baron Delondeur into action, as was the first part of your command," the Marynth replied, forcing her own iron into her voice. "And his daughter. And such men as they could gather."

"Such men as they could gather? The Baron Delondeur is the most powerful of those rotten warlords who call themselves Barons. He has thousands of men at his command. A fraction of them should have been sufficient to be certain that this Goddess remains in the realm of rumor and superstition."

"Conditions changed, Choiron," Evolyn said steadily, insistently cutting through the monologue that had been gaining wind. "Delondeur had almost no blooded troops ready to hand, and he was not clear with me why that was the case. To make up their lack, he engaged with sorcerers. They were making abominations. Murdering men and twisting their remains into indiscriminate weapons of war."

Symod's hard sea-grey eyes narrowed, glittered. "And?"

Evolyn allowed herself a steadying breath. "And it did not seem fit that Braechsworn should share a battlefield with such creatures. Or find such a fate upon their deaths."

Symod considered her words. Evolyn knew that calculations were being made at rapid speed behind those sea-colored eyes.

"Battle-Wights," he said finally. "I have heard of them. A terror on the battlefield, or so they say."

"The reports brought back to me by Ulcas would suggest as much," Evolyn said. "Yet they were not, apparently, an impediment to the paladin."

"No?"

"Accounts have suggested that he tore them apart with his hands," Evolyn said evenly.

"Accounts." His eyes flared. "You did not go to the field yourself?"

"No," Evolyn replied fiercely. "I would not expose good and faithful men to the depredations of sorcerers. And I felt confident that they would destroy Thornhurst and the Temple."

"Braech was not there to seize the glory! This is why we failed!"

Before she could think of what to say, Symod plowed on.

"And these sorcerers, did they survive the battle?"

"No," Evolyn said. "My sources were clear on that, if not on the manner of their demise, but it seems likely they were defeated by the same force that destroyed the artifact in Keersvast."

"Do you know how to contact any further sorcerers?"

Evolyn felt fear radiate outward from her spine again. "Choiron, I do not believe their ways are Braech's."

He waved a hand dismissively, turned back towards the window. "Then we will learn new ways."

"Why do we not simply confront him straightforwardly? Strength and courage—these are the pillars of our faith."

"There is subtlety to our Lord as well, or He would not be Master of Trade and Accords," Symod countered.

"Ought we not to at least try before we go seeking the alliances of such wretched creatures as sorcerers?"

Symod folded his hands behind his back. "The application of bold force will be a part of our plan. Yet not to simply strike at the paladin directly."

"What do you mean?"

"I mean," Symod said, and she could hear the smile in his words, "that instead of confronting him, we need to force him to confront us."

"He has already tried to do so once, and we could do nothing to stop him," Evolyn said, remembering the fear she'd felt when the paladin had broken into her study, the certainty that he would kill her. The feeling that she deserved his judgment, the astonishment when he had simply left.

"But if we force him to confront us in many places at once," the Choiron said, "then whatever strength he has gathered about him will wilt."

"Please, Choiron, speak plainly," Evolyn said, weariness threatening to creep into her words.

"This Allystaire will move against anything that threatens the peasantry. If villages burn, the paladin surely must ride to their aid. If towns are sacked and coastal villages are put to the sword, surely he must look to answer for it. If Gravekling and Islandmen come down in droves upon the Baronies, called to a crusade by Braech Himself, the paladin and the rabble who follow him will exhaust themselves in a noble, heroic, and *tragic* response."

"A crusade?" Evolyn felt a ball of fear in the pit of her stomach. Fear, yes, but also a sense of opportunity. Braech favored the bold. *And how bold is it to torch villages full of innocents in the hopes of drawing out one man?* "You would unleash devastation to destroy one man."

"To destroy the greatest threat the Sea Dragon has ever known, I will empty our arsenal, employ every tool at our disposal," Symod replied.

"Every tool?"

Symod whirled back to her, his face practically set in a snarl. "Would you question me, Marynth? You who have failed, not once, not twice, but thrice, to bring this man to account, would suggest there are means we ought not employ? Your band of marauders discrediting his faith failed. Your assassin failed. Your battle failed. I will destroy the Baronies entirely if I must, as one might cut off a limb to purge a rot from the body. I will purge *you* if I hear even the tiniest whisper of mutiny from your lips. Go now. Pray. Devise for yourself a suitable penance for your failure; report it to me. If it is not sufficient, I will amend it."

The catalogue of her failures shamed her, but not because they came from the Choiron, or because she feared a penance. What shamed her were the words the paladin had spoken to her in this very temple, months ago. *Such courage, such boldness. Braech must be so proud of His Church—cravens and employers of assassins,* he had said, the words falling contemptuously from his homely features.

She turned and left, making no obeisance. As she sought out the altar, the paladin's words echoing in her head, she wondered how many epithets Symod would be adding to the list in the coming months.

CHAPTER 13

Squirehood

Allystaire started every morning, the rest of the winter, by pushing himself out of bed before the sun rose, shouldering two large stones, and running from one end of the village to the other.

On the second day, he stopped by the village's armory—a storage shed near Torvul's small house and forge—in order to appropriate a chain shirt, which he wore as he ran. The weight of the stones pushed the impression of chain links into his shoulders rubbed the skin raw, but it was pain. He ignored it.

On the third day, Cerisia watched him return to the Inn, steam billowing off of him, before most other folk were yet awake. Gentle mockery was forming on her lips as he stripped off his outer garments. Her words, whatever they were about to be, faded into a flat disbelief.

"Even that," she said, extending a finger towards the lightly clinking vest.

"Even this," he said. "When I said I had a squirehood to relive, I meant it."

"Who are you reliving it for, exactly? I heard your pronouncement of a new Order. Just where do you expect the knights to come from?"

"For myself," Allystaire said, pushing wet hair back from his face as he walked to stand in front of the fire. Timmar hadn't built it up for the day yet, but it still threw enough heat to appreciate after a turn in the morning cold. "For the people I need to defend. For the Goddess. For no reason other than that I need to do *something* to occupy myself on these mornings. As to your second question?" Allystaire shrugged. "I can only hope that they will."

"There are surely other ways to occupy your time in the morning, Allystaire," Cerisia suggested.

"True. I could be waking Torvul or trying to teach Gideon something new, or being corrected by Idgen Marte. I could be visiting the Temple, praying, going among the people and hearing their grievances and problems. I will do all of these things, but I will do this first. And now, I am going to get Ardent out of his stable and have whatever kind of ride I can manage in this weather."

"You're determined to make yourself miserable," Cerisia replied, her lips curling downward into a disapproving frown.

"No, Archioness. I am determined to do the opposite," Allystaire replied as he threw open the door.

It hadn't snowed for three days, but much of the ground remained frozen. Allystaire had forbidden Gideon expending any more energy on clearing the roads. With a half sigh, Allystaire pushed himself back into a run as he made for the stables.

The cold seared his lungs. The hauberk weighed on his shoulders, and his boots, ill-suited for the wear he was putting on them, were rubbing his feet raw through two thick pairs of socks.

The pain melted away when he got to the stables and saw Ardent, saddled and waiting, Mol standing at his side. The hooded top of the girl's head barely made the huge grey's shoulder. The destrier gave his mane a toss, eyed Allystaire as if to ask, *What took so long?*

Instinct had Allystaire looking askance at Mol's bare feet and hands, but he shook it away as he reached out for the lead. "How?"

Mol smiled and lowered her hood. Much of the girlishness had melted out of her face, replaced with something ageless, something powerful. "Does it matter?"

Allystaire swung into the saddle. "I suppose it does not, but you must be cold, lass."

"I am," Mol replied, "and I'm not. No natural movement of the world or phase of the seasons can harm me here, near Her holiest place. I feel the cold, yes, as a natural part of the world and one of the challenges of our existence."

"Mol, are you telling me that within the village you cannot be hurt?"

The girl laughed. "Of course not. A blade or an arrow would do the same grievous harm to me as it would anyone. Just not the weather." She shook her head and then addressed the horse. "I know you told me all that time ago that he was slow. You were right." She made a shooing motion with one hand. "Go, ride. Enough metaphysics for one day."

Allystaire shrugged and nudged Ardent into a trot with his knees. The horse snorted and tugged on the reins, blowing out a cloud of vapor from his nostrils.

"He wants to run," Mol called out, from a few paces away. "Let him. It'll do you good."

"A moment." Allystaire turned in the saddle to look down at the girl. "Mol, am I making a fool of myself? The Order of the Arm, carrying on like a squire?"

"In the time I've known you, you've hardly been given to self doubt," Mol replied flatly, her mouth drawing from its smile into a line.

"That could not be further from the truth," Allystaire replied. "I have hardly been given to voicing it. I simply wonder. What if I found an Order and no novices, no squires, petition to join?"

"You know well it is not novices or squires you want or need, Allystaire Stillbright," Mol replied, her voice resonant with just a hint of power beneath it. "The people you need will come. Guided like ships into harbor by a beacon light, they will find you. Some may have already."

Allystaire nodded, then walked Ardent a few more steps before giving the horse his head.

The sudden forward surge shook Allystaire in his saddle. Ardent needed several moments of running to truly gather speed, but once he did, the sensation was like no other. The cold of the air was like a whip to the flesh of his face, but the pain and discomfort of it was easy to ignore in the exhilaration of speed.

He lowered himself over Ardent's neck, letting the horse run as he would, leaving doubt behind.

* * *

On the fourth day a tall figure was waiting for him out in front of the Inn, bundled up well and stamping his feet against the cold, a scarf wound around his face and a shapeless wool cap pulled down tightly over his brows.

A deep frown creased Allystaire's features. "Go home, Norbert. Go back to bed. You have earned a rest."

"How'd you know it was me?" The pitch of the lad's voice rose in protest. He cleared his throat and pulled his scarf down.

Allystaire eyed him, pulling his mouth into a flat line. "How? Boy, you are the only man in the village who is that tall and that skinny to boot."

Norbert grunted and finished pulling the scarf away from his face, swiping at the sweat it had gathered on his cheeks with the back of his sleeve. "Haven't I got a right to try and…follow you?"

Allystaire lowered his head. "Norbert, you have narrowly avoided a path that ends in tragedy. I understand why you left your home. You have more than earned a new one here. Yet now you have seen up close the blood and pain and misery that will follow me wherever I go. Is that what you want for the rest of your life?"

"No," Norbert answered, shaking his head. "But—"

"But nothing, lad," Allystaire replied, shaking his head. "Stay here, find a lass, marry her, raise your children. Tell them stories of the battle you fought, be proud of yourself, and thank the Mother you never saw but the one."

Norbert opened his mouth to protest, but Allystaire cut him off sharply, took a few steps towards him, his breath a steaming cloud of vapor in the air between them as he began to shout. "How do you want to die, Norbert? At the end of a Battle-Wight's bladed arm? On a sorcerer's table, your innards hung about the walls? In the mud of a far off Barony, crushed under the hooves of some brigand's horse? Or here, in your own bed, surrounded by children and grandchildren?"

The boy's eyes were wide, but something settled his jaw square. "I don't want to die at all. But I've got no choice o'that, right? It'll happen someday to us all. You, me, Renard. Don't I have the right t'make the same choice as him?"

"Go. Home." Allystaire poked Norbert hard in the chest with two fingers.

With that, Allystaire turned on his heel and walked to the barrel of water at the corner of the Inn's wall. He grabbed the barrel's edge with his left hand, drew back his right, rocked upwards on his feet, drawing power into his torso, and shattered the ice that had grown over the top of the water with one blow.

Norbert stood a few paces away, watching carefully. If he felt any fear at Allystaire's reproach, at the sudden display of violence, he didn't show it.

Next to the barrel was the stack of stones Allystaire had gathered. He knelt down, grabbed one and levered it onto his left shoulder, then reached down and heaved a second onto his right.

Pushing off of one knee and one heel, Allystaire stood, and without a backwards glance, began running up the path.

Norbert watched him for a moment, then darted over to the pile of stones and gathered one himself. He tried shoving it to one shoulder or the other, mimicking Allystaire, but couldn't manage the knack of it, so cradling it against his stomach, he ran after the paladin with long, ground-eating strides.

* * *

With Norbert dogging his heels, Allystaire decided to make it two lengths of the village that morning. Norbert puffed and stumbled and almost dropped his stone many times.

Almost.

As Allystaire bent down to lower the stones from his shoulders to the ground, trying not to groan as the weight vanished, he stole a glance at the gangly young man. Red-faced, sweating, steam coming off of him.

Looks about as I feel, Allystaire thought, but did not say. Instead, he said, "I aim to take a ride now, Norbert. You have not got a horse, and surely there are tasks that will need your attention. Go home."

Without waiting for the boy to answer, Allystaire started walking.

Norbert, still puffing for breath, hurried behind him. "I know how to handle a horse. I'm no lancer, but the reavers taught me some. Renard did too, a little. I could ride his horse."

"Not without Leah's permission, for it is her animal and her tack," Allystaire replied. "And I forbid you to disturb her with such a request," he added, lowering his voice and darkening his tone.

Norbert said nothing, only continued to follow him.

While Allystaire saddled and rubbed Ardent, Norbert watched from the entrance to the stables. He darted away when Allystaire led the destrier out. Without looking back, Allystaire let Ardent trot. With enough distance, he flicked the reins and let the huge grey gallop for several moments. Only then did he chance a look back.

Long legs pumping furiously, Norbert ran behind him. He lost distance as the horse sped up, but he followed doggedly.

Allystaire slowed the horse, pulled it to a stop, wheeled it around. With several dozen yards distance between them, Norbert surely saw him stop, but kept running at the best speed he could manage.

Allystaire turned his horse again and let him run.

* * *

With his ride finished and his mount seen to, Allystaire made his way to the tiny armory. From it, he borrowed a sword roughly of a size with his broken one, buckled it around his back. The armory also contained a battered dummy Renard had cobbled together out of hardwood and broken bits of armor.

Carefully, he dragged it outside, threw off his outer coat and scarf. His skin already warmed with the morning's exertions, he barely felt the cold until a stiff breeze caught some droplets of sweat on his neck. He ignored it, drew the sword, holding it with his left near the pommel and his right stacked above it.

He shifted his feet, held the blade out long, edge towards his opponent's weapon, or where it would be. He measured the distance, imagining the opponent holding a blade as long as his. He stepped, slowly at first, swinging the blade forward at half speed, controlling the weight of it carefully.

Moving in a semi-circle around the dummy, Allystaire tried variations of every attack. Slashing, chopping, swinging, high-line, low-line, middle, edge, flat, even stepping forward to strike with the pommel. Each blow stopped just short of the dummy.

From the corner of his eye, he saw Norbert holding a shorter blade, clumsily mimicking every move.

Allystaire did his best to ignore him, as he began to repeat his circuit of the dummy, and each and every attack, at a slightly faster pace. Once again, each blow still stopped as close to the dummy as he could manage to pull the strike. Once or twice the edge of the blade nicked off the wood, sending a splinter flying, uncomfortably jarring Allystaire's arms.

When he stepped back after the second circuit, Norbert was nearly tripping over his own feet, the tip of his sword dragging in the snow. Allystaire spat in disgust, stepped back, and carefully sheathed his borrowed sword.

"Dammit, Norbert!" He didn't quite bellow, but he put enough force into his words to startle the lad, who jumped a few inches clear of the ground. "You are going to stab yourself, or me, by accident."

Norbert lowered the sword, holding it limply in one hand. Allystaire stepped quickly forward, seized his bony wrist, and pulled the sword away easily. "You have no idea how little you know about using a sword." Allystaire's face was grim, his eyes narrowed and cold.

"Then teach me," Norbert protested.

"It would take years that I do not have," Allystaire said, shaking his head slowly. "You have not got the wrists and arms for it, nor do you understand the footwork, the distances, the angles."

Norbert's jaw tightened in defiance, his eyes opening wide in what Allystaire supposed might be anger. "Teach me *one thing* then," he said. "One. How do I make my wrists and my arms stronger?"

Allystaire frowned. "Work them. Rest the weight of your body on the palms of your hands and the tips of your feet, lower yourself as close to the ground as you can manage, hold there as long as you can stand, then push yourself back up. Then do it again. And again."

"How many times?"

"Till your arms tremble and then burn. Till your chest heaves and your vision darkens," Allystaire spat. "Till you decide that you will die if you attempt another, and that you would rather die than give up." He held out a hand. "Give me the scabbard."

Norbert fumbled with the swordbelt he'd buckled on, got the scabbard tangled between his legs, but eventually handed it over. Allystaire slammed the sword home, then tossed it aside, where it settled with a light puff of snow.

"Go home, Norbert. Or at least give me space."

With that, he drew his sword again, held it in a cross-body guard with his hands low by his left hip. Allystaire let his eyes focus on the last few inches of blade, watching for any wavering, any movement. He kept his arms still, his fingers firmly wrapping about the hilt, not pressing too hard.

He held it till he saw the slightest movement of the blade's tip, long enough that his arms were burning by the time it came. Then he launched into motion, careful to keep his feet under him, his balance spread unevenly between his feet, his blade moving at full speed, contacting the dummy now more often than not.

In truth, he didn't have to think of these things, only decide to do them. The movements were ingrained into his feet, his ankles, his shoulders and arms and wrists. Thousands of practices, years of training, all condensed into a few seconds of sudden movement.

Allystaire repeated the circuit again and again. Sweat steamed off his forehead. When he couldn't hold the sword straight in guard any longer, he sheathed it. Anticipating questions from Norbert, he'd assumed the boy had left.

When he turned from the dummy, he saw him a few yards away, a long, lean figure pressed against the snow, arms trembling as he pushed himself off the ground, slowly and with difficulty. A space in the snow had cleared beneath him from the repeated impressions of his body.

If he has been at this the whole time then he is stronger than I thought. He frowned, reached for the dummy to drag it back to Torvul's armory, then stopped and stomped over to the boy's side.

"Norbert," he grunted, "you are going to make yourself ill."

"No," the lad said, his voice a strangled grasp.

"Not from the exercise, fool. From the snow. Your clothes are going to get soaked. They probably already are, and you will catch your death in wet clothes. You, an Oyrwyn lad, ought to know that. Clear yourself a space."

Norbert ignored him and squeezed out three more dips. Allystaire could see, beneath his hat, the lad's face turning bright red from the exertion.

Grumbling, Allystaire bent down and seized him by the shoulder, hauling him to his feet. "Go home, Norbert. I mean it this time. I will drag you there myself if I must. Dry and warm yourself."

The boy started to protest.

"If you want to exercise, carry rocks, break ice, chop wood, and run on your own time, I cannot stop you. Do them elsewhere, where you are warm and dry. Go."

Allystaire let go of Norbert's arm, then turned on a heel and stalked off as the boy reached up to massage his arm with his other hand. He didn't look back as he made his way to the Inn.

* * *

The next morning, Norbert was standing outside the Inn when Allystaire awoke, clutching a stone in his hands.

Allystaire strode towards him in the soft pre-dawn light, but Norbert stood his ground and spoke defiantly.

"You said if I wanted t'run and carry rocks and all the rest, on my own time, you couldn't stop me. Well it's my own time and you don't own the village, so if I want t'run the same time as you, in the same places, you can't rightly stop me doin' that, either."

Allystaire frowned darkly. "I suppose I cannot." With that, he headed for the water barrel, perfunctorily broke the ice with a couple blows of his fist, then picked up his own stones, and churned his legs into motion.

Later, soaked in sweat and sheathing his sword, Allystaire looked over to find Norbert kneeling on a cleared patch of dirt, massaging his shoulders, watching his strokes at the dummy.

"How long did it take you t'become a great swordsman?" The boy looked like he wanted to swallow the words back as soon as he spoke, as Allystaire hadn't said a word to him since they'd started to run that morning.

At this question, though, Allystaire laughed. "A great swordsman? I am no such thing, Norbert. Not at all. I have a familiarity with the sword because it was required of me, nothing more."

"You seem like a master," Norbert breathed. "Who in the Baronies could be better?"

"Lionel Delondeur, for one. Gerard and Gilrayan Oyrwyn, as well, when it comes to form and technique, anyway. Many of the knights I trained. My own father, of a certainty. I could go on. The world is filled with better swordsmen than me, and Idgen Marte is probably equal or better to them all."

"Then why're you still alive after all the years o'fighting?"

"Well, I prefer the hammer and the lance to the sword, and when it comes to the latter especially, I have some small claim to renown," Allystaire said, then corrected himself. "Had."

"Renown?"

"Fame. Mastery. Call it what you like. And besides, it is not always the better swordsman who wins any fight, even man to man with no luck, good or bad, in the way."

"No? Who does then? If luck don't play a part, as you say."

"The one who is willing to risk the most hurt, to bear the most pain," Allystaire replied, quickly, instinctively. "I am not saying to be reckless in a fight, a berzerker, pay no heed to guarding yourself. Yet once you accept that any fight is going to hurt—and that you can accept that hurt, whatever it is, however great, however grievous, take it into yourself and master it and continue on—you will not often lose."

Norbert let his hands fall back to the dirt, but didn't get back into position to resume his dips yet. "When one o'those Battle-Wights slashed me," he said, lifting a hand and rubbing two fingers speculatively along the scar that ran along his cheek, "I thought it had taken my eye. Turns out blood had just splashed in it, but…I was more scared than I like to say. I thought I was done for sure. Blinded. Dead."

Allystaire drew his blade again, and simply assumed his stance, balancing carefully, shifting weight occasionally from one foot to the other. "It is not what you fear or what you feel that matters, Norbert," he said, letting his eyes focus on the edge of his blade again, arms struggling to keep it still. "It is what you do."

There was silence. The sword hung in the air, a still and deadly icicle ascending from Allystaire's hands. "What did you do?" He grated the words through clenched teeth.

"Kept swinging," Norbert replied. "I might've thought I was blinded but I knew where the cursed thing was. With Giraud and Henri we clubbed it t'the ground and kept clubbin' till it was broken."

Allystaire grunted as the sword wavered and fell. He stopped it short of the ground, pulled his arms close to his body, and then swung the heavy weapon back into its sheath. He looked over at the gangly youth, who stared a moment, then lowered himself back to the ground, stretched out his legs, and began pushing himself up and down again with jerking, quick movements.

"Slower," Allystaire said, watching critically. "Control the movement. Control every movement, always, on your feet, on the ground, on a horse, with a sword or a lance or a bow, a bottle or a woman." Then, after a pause. "Spread your hands a bit further apart. Keep your legs straight and do not let your hips sag."

Norbert did as instructed, though he let out a giggle when Allystaire said "woman." The boy was carefully spreading his hands when Allystaire leaned over him.

"Did I say something funny, lad?" There was something strong and deep in Allystaire's voice, quiet though the words were. Something of ice and iron, a tension in his jaw, a hardening of the eyes.

Norbert shook his head and began pumping his long body up and down on his skinny arms, more slowly than before. Allystaire eyed him critically, sniffed. "That will do. Only just." Then turned and walked back to the dummy, dragging it towards the armory.

Inwardly, he cursed and wondered what had just happened.

By the time he'd pushed, pulled, wrestled, and cajoled the dummy back into place, and replaced his borrowed sword, Torvul was standing outside, between the shed and the house, wearing a thick fur-lined robe and heavy boots, a steaming mug clasped in one huge hand.

"Bit o'the parade ground armsmaster in you yet, boy."

"Boy?" Allystaire replied. "I have spent more years at war than Norbert has living, and I am a boy?"

"Well," Torvul said, slurping hot liquid. "Seeing that I am much more than twice your age, and possess thrice your wisdom and experience at the most conservative estimate I can conceive, I'll go on callin' you boy." The dwarf took a couple steps and peeked around the edge of the house, taking in Norbert at his dips. "First squire, eh?"

"Norbert is no squire," Allystaire said quietly. "He is a fool boy who does not know what he wants."

"That so?" Torvul had another swallow of his tea. He leaned forward again, peering at the lad, listening to his grunts of exertion. "Seems like he knows what he wants. Stronger arms. Where'd he get that idea?"

Allystaire frowned, etching deep lines in his scarred, homely face. "He was waving a sword around like an idiot, trying to mimic me. He was like to stab himself."

Torvul snickered. "I know exactly where he got the idea. I was listenin' yesterday morning. You make a great racket early in the day, too great for a winter morning, if you ask me. But Her Ladyship's work isn't done while laying in bed, more's the pity."

"You deserve a rest, Torvul."

"More than some and less than others," the dwarf replied, shrugging. "Too much work to do to rest much. Idgen Marte's sword, that's done, finally. Had to finish it in the dead of night, but it's done. Then your hammer, a new sword, seein' what I can do with all that dross," he added, gesturing towards the armory with his tea mug, from which he took another pull. "Puttin' together what I can for the planting, come spring. Working on improving the local beer recipes. Trying to grow some decent mushrooms."

Allystaire broke in, incredulous. "Where are you growing mushrooms?"

Torvul gestured to the house. "In there. They offered it to me for a workshop, didn't say I couldn't turn a room to fungiculture if I liked. You didn't think I was sleeping in there, did you? My wagon's just around the other side. *That's* home, where I do most o'my work."

Allystaire was silent a moment then ventured, curiously. "What about Stonesinging? Doing any of that?"

Torvul turned his face towards Allystaire, eyes narrowed. "What makes you ask about that?"

"I was still conscious when you took the sorcerer on, Torvul," Allystaire replied. "I heard what he said and I heard the fear in his voice. I thought you had said that was long gone from the world."

"I did, and it is," Torvul replied. "It was a last echo, one last bit of song from the bones of my Mother. I think it is probably the last Stonesong that will ever be heard."

"Surely not," Allystaire said. "If you can do it once, you can—"

"You don't understand," Torvul said gruffly, finishing his tea and then dumping the dregs to the ground with a flick of his wrist. "The song didn't come from me, boy. It never did. The song was in the earth itself, the stones of our homes. You..." He sighed. "You can't understand, but it's gone, probably forever, or for so long as makes no difference. We used it all. Called it all forth. Used it to sink great tunnels into the earth and to work wonders of stone and metal and gemmary. We relied upon it. When we found it slacking, did we turn back to our hands, our cunning and craft? No." The dwarf spat. "We let our homes crumble and fall apart and finally, when we could stand the sight of our failures any longer, we fled." He glared up at Allystaire. "You're probably the only human alive has ever heard the truth of this."

Uncertain, hesitant, Allystaire spoke anyway. "Then where did it come from?"

"The crossbow. The singing consumed it."

"How did you know to—"

"I was apprentice to one of the last stonesingers," Torvul said. "When I was young, before your father was a glimmer in your grandfather's eye. When we still believed that the songs were there to be found, to be called forth and shaped to our need. In the homes, the stonesingers were the masters of all crafts. There was no medium they could not work in, nothing they could not shape. They had their different gifts: great weaponsmiths, or healers, armor crafters, tool-makers, alchemists…" The dwarf's voice drifted quieter and quieter till it faded into silence. "That's enough. Go stop that boy before he passes out."

Torvul peeked around the edge of the house again. "Too late. Best go wake him before he drowns in his own sweat."

* * *

For two more days, the pattern continued; Allystaire found Norbert waiting for him outside the Inn every morning and tried his best to shake the youth's determination. Finally, on the third day, as Norbert dogged him on the way to the armory, Allystaire turned on his heels.

"This is not a story, Norbert," he said suddenly.

"What? What d'ya mean?"

"You keep following me, mimicking me, trying to earn…what? My respect. You have that. Training? To become a squire, a knight, my boon companion?" Allystaire shook his head. "There is no show of perseverance or heroic deed that is going to change my mind. I am not going to set you a task, tell you to fetch some mythical flower or impossible magical trinket, rescue a maiden or slay a monster, and then agree to take you in. This is not the story where the peasant boy knelt outside the knight's tower for three days in the howling snow without eating or moving or sleeping, and moved the knight so that he took the boy in as his page and made him his heir."

Norbert eyed him defiantly. "Dunno those stories. Don't care if—"

Allystaire suddenly leaned forward and grabbed the boy around the collar. "Go. Home." The words were spoken through clenched teeth and curled, whitened lips. "If you keep dogging my steps, you are going to hurt yourself. You are not made for this. GO." With a final shout, he tried to shove the boy away.

Norbert's face scrunched up with sudden fury, his chin quivering, his eyes watering. Crying out wordlessly, he clumsily threw a balled up fist into Allystaire's face.

The blow was a good deal more shocking than it was painful. Allystaire's jaw fell open slightly, his eyes widened. From the looks of him, Norbert was just as surprised as Allystaire was, his mouth agape, lifting his hands and stammering.

Allystaire's jaw set grimly, his hands curled into fists at his sides, and he took deep breaths to calm the anger that rose inside him.

"That," he said carefully, "was foolish, Norbert. Every man does foolish things in his life and I will let this one pass with a warning."

With another loud cry, Norbert threw himself at Allystaire, swinging his fist again in a lazy, roundabout arc aimed roughly at the side of his head.

For Allystaire, it was simple instinct to bend his knees and step beneath the uncontrolled, poorly aimed blow. He shifted his feet into a proper stance, weight distributed, power pushing up from his feet and through his torso as he twisted it into the punch that traveled less than a foot into Norbert's unprotected side. He tried, at the last second, to pull some of the force from the blow.

Norbert let out a loud cry and doubled over, clutching his side, thin arms wrapped around himself. Allystaire stepped away, his hands still fisted, watching the boy carefully.

Sucking in deep, huge lungfuls of air, Norbert forced himself back upright, though he kept one hand pressed where Allystaire's blow had landed. His face was still crunched in anger, tears leaking from the corners now. He took a hesitant step towards Allystaire, raising his free hand weakly.

"I am not going to hit you again, Norbert," Allystaire said, consciously forcing his hands to his sides. "I am sorry that I did the once."

Norbert lunged towards him, throwing both hands out and trying to grapple Allystaire's collar. He was fairly easily shrugged off, pushed away.

"What…you told me," the boy wheezed, as he finally peeled his arm away from his side, and raised it ineffectually, "about pain. This is what you meant, right?" He launched another awkwardly looping blow. This time Allystaire caught it and turned the lad's wrist, used his grip to bend Norbert's arm and turn him around so Allystaire could throw his free arm around Norbert's neck, immobilizing him for a moment. Then he let go and shoved him away, hard, resisted the urge to add a kick to his seat.

Norbert went sprawling, but came right back to his feet. He balled his fists, then threw his to his sides in frustration. Tears still welled at the corner of his eyes.

"Why? Why m'I not good enough? Was it all just lies, when y'said that it weren't about noble birth and links, but about bein' willing to bear the burdens?"

The words stung a little more than Allystaire expected, but he shook his head. "It is not only about willingness, Norbert. I cannot take the time to teach you what you must know."

"Renard himself said I was the only real spearman o'the lot, and I'm a decent enough bowshot. A knight can't carry a bow and a spear?"

Allystaire had no instant answer for that. "Why do you want this, Norbert?"

"You know why!" Norbert shouted. "Ya come along and…and you change everythin' and then you can ask me why I'd want t'follow ya? How can I not want it? I told you I left the moors n'the bogs because the brigands looked better t'me than cuttin' turf all day, and you forgive me for that. But you won't forgive me for thinkin' now that followin' you looks better'n bein' a farmer? I don't like turnips and cabbages any better than I did peat. I'd rather die fightin' more Battle-Wights next summer than after two score years diggin' in the dirt."

"I can teach you some of the spear, but little of the bow," Allystaire said.

"And what is it ya think I can't fight? Battle-Wights? Armored horsemen? Footmen? I've already fought all of 'em."

"Once," Allystaire said. "And that was with all the powers of the Goddess's servants with you. You are asking me to lead you to something you are not prepared for. You are asking me to lead you to your death."

"I'm askin' you t'let me make the choice Renard made. Why won't ya let me even try?"

Allystaire narrowed his eyes. "If I am to even consider this, Norbert, there are rules you will obey."

Norbert crossed his arms and jutted his chin defiantly, expectantly.

"The moment, the very first moment that you complain, that you ask for a rest, that you say something is too difficult, or beyond you, or that you do not know how to do it, you are done."

Norbert nodded, swallowing hard. "Aye."

"I will find you someone to teach you more of the bow, which I cannot do," Allystaire continued. "I have just the man in mind. If he agrees, and I believe he will, you will spend every waking turn he allows you learning from him. You will treat his orders and instruction as though they came from me."

Norbert nodded again.

"If, if, mind," Allystaire went on, extending a finger towards the lad, "I get so far as to teach you to ride, you will take care of the horse you ride as though it were the most precious thing in this world. If a mount suffers ill care from your hand—"

"I'm done. I know a bit of horses," the boy said, shrugging. "S'the one thing the reavers taught me."

"You will be outside the Inn every morning before I am. You will begin your day by breaking the ice in the water barrel. Then we will run, with rocks. Then wrestling and boxing, the rudiments of riding, whatever work I can help you manage with the spear. You will still need to attend to whatever other chores or tasks you have, and the bow, on your own time. If you do this for the next month, every day, to my satisfaction, you may continue for a second month."

Norbert nodded again, enthusiastically. Allystaire cut him off before he could speak.

"Fine. Go into the armory and fetch two spears and the longest, heaviest sword." Norbert took a step, Allystaire bellowed, "Run!" and both of them knew that a squirehood had begun.

CHAPTER 14

A Conspiracy

Timmar's Inn was crowded with folk enjoying their midday meal together, but when Allystaire pushed open the door and brought a gust of cold inside, his eyes were drawn to the hearth. Idgen Marte occupied two chairs near it, sitting in one, her legs lifted and crossed at the ankles on the second. She nodded towards him and lifted her feet clear as he made his way over. He eased himself down, tried not to groan too loudly at the protests from his legs and his back. Idgen Marte's snickering let him know he'd failed.

"Training schedule not treatin' you too well, old man?"

Allystaire snorted, waving a hand dismissively. "Nonsense. Best I have felt in years."

"Ya know, I almost believe that," she said as she lifted a mug to her lips. "You're not happy unless you're miserable or in pain." She glanced over as Norbert made his way inside, stripping off winter clothing as he made his way to a table where a cluster of village men greeted him. Allystaire saw Giraud slip a hand into a large coat pocket and bring forth a round wrapped bundle and push it in front of Norbert, who unwrapped it to find a fresh brown loaf that he tore into with abandon. Sweat slicked his brown hair to his head, and his clothing steamed in the heat of the room.

"How goes it, then, two weeks along?"

"He is willing and he never tires, I will give him that," Allystaire admitted grudgingly, shaking his head very slightly from side to side. "I have not spoken with Keegan on his progress with the bow, and there is only so much I can teach him with a spear. He is *hopeless* with his fists, as a wrestler," he added with a sigh.

"He needs to put on weight for that," Idgen Marte said. "It'll come if Lenoir has anything t'say about it."

"Giraud's daughter?"

She nodded. She leaned close, opening her mouth to say something else, when the door swung open again, silencing the buzz of conversation and the sounds of eating and drinking. Allystaire slowly turned his eyes to find Harrys, the Delondeur horseman, standing unconcernedly in the doorway. He saw Allystaire and from across the room and called out.

"Paladin. Need t'talk to ya."

Allystaire waved him over, but the old soldier shook his head. "Private, if ya please."

Eyes flitted from the soldier to the paladin and back. Allystaire saw Giraud, Henri, and Norbert all start to rise slightly from their seats. The two older men watched Allystaire uncertainly.

With a bit of pride, Allystaire saw that Norbert stepped clear of the table, gave himself space, and never took his eyes off of Harrys.

Good for you, lad, Allystaire thought. *He'd knock you senseless faster than you could blink, but you're learning.*

With a deep sigh that Allystaire felt probably came from his knees, he pushed himself from his chair and waved the three village men away.

"I will be fine, goodmen. Go back to your lunch."

Giraud and Henri sat immediately, but Norbert continued to watch intently until Allystaire eyed him directly and pointed a finger to the bench. Then, slowly, the lad sat down, eyeing Harrys still.

The old soldier held the door open for Allystaire, who felt the shock of the outdoors like a hard slap across his face.

"Who's that boy tryin' to give me the hairy eye," Harrys asked wryly as Allystaire shut the door and tugged his cloak tightly around him.

"Just a village lad. Pay it no mind. You said you needed to talk to me, so talk."

Harrys nodded and started walking along the edge of the snow-and-frost covered green, cutting away from the wind to take at least a bit off of its edge.

"This is, ah…delicate," Harrys said. "I need to tell you somethin' so it can be stopped, but I'm thinkin' you're not gonna want to get your hands in it."

"Harrys. I am cold, and I am sore, and you have dragged me away from a fire and food and warm wine. There is a point to this, yes?"

"Aye, there's a point, your lordship," Harrys muttered, spitting out of the side of his mouth. He paused, having led Allystaire halfway around the oval of the green, and squinted off at the buildings beyond it, and the wall beyond them. "I'm thinkin' it's somethin' the Baroness needs to hear. But I can't be the one who tells her."

Allystaire's brows knitted. "This bodes ill. I cannot promise that anything you tell me will be kept in confidence. If I speak of something, I must speak the truth; I think my Goddess would look ill on lies of omission, if it came to that."

Harrys grunted. "Well, try t'keep my name out of it. What I've come t'tell ya is this. There's two Delondeur knights o'er in the prison tent who're plottin' against the Baroness. Sayin' she's lost her head, come under too much o'your influence. They're takin' issue wi' her proclamations regardin' Lord Chaddin. They don't like the idea o'a bastard born sergeant bein' set o'er them."

Allystaire felt his jaw clench, a fist tighten. "You were right; I cannot be the one to step in here. It will be up to Chaddin and Landen to do what must be done. Why did you come to me?"

Harrys continued to look off into the village, biting at his bottom lip for a moment. "If I tell the Baroness, it's my word against theirs. Chosen man against knights. Now, I'm not afraid o'any man in a straight fight," he said, turning to eye Allystaire directly, his brown eyes hard underneath heavy brows. "But I say a word against them, it's my throat cut in my sleep. I'm old, but I'm not aimin' to die just yet."

"If you bring this to Chaddin, I am sure he will see justice done."

"They say no man can lie t'ya. That true?"

"Aye."

"Then ask 'em. They'll speak the truth, and no one can deny it."

"It begins with Chaddin and Landen. If they *ask* for my aid in judging a man's guilt or innocence using the Goddess's gifts, I will consider it," Allystaire replied.

"They're aren't just talkin', mind you. They're askin' around, feelin' the men out. Could be they've got half or more o'what's left on their side by now. Two men are already missin', spirits are low."

Allystaire frowned. "Two men are missing? Since when?"

"Week now," Harrys replied. "Must be they decided t'try an' get somewhere else. Don't seem likely they made it. Point is, it doesn't do a man any good to think on that, to hear of knights talkin' open treason when the Baroness ain't around."

"Bring this to Chaddin. I will come with you."

"I do that," Harrys said, "speak out straight against my Brothers o'Battle, see 'em hung, maybe? I can't go back to Londray. Can't go back t'my life."

"Then you need to decide what it is you treasure more, Harrys. The life you have in Londray, or the future of the whole Barony."

Harrys grunted, looked away again, squinting his eyes so tightly they seemed shut. "Then what would I do?"

"Stay here. Go north, go west. I daresay that the Baroness would be happy to have you with her, no matter what you think."

"Pfah," Harrys spat. "You know what I mean. You betray a man you've fought beside, even if he deserves it, you're no man's Brother o'Battle any longer. Not so long as anyone knows what ya did."

"Some things are larger, more important, than our desires or our brothers, Harrys, whether of battle or blood. I think what Landen and Chaddin aim to do could be one of those things."

"What you aim t'do through them, ya mean," Harrys said. "Not that I disagree with ya, mind. Too much war, for too long. And for what? Spaces a man can walk in a day or two. Cold, I hardly remember the last king. I was barely in the saddle when he died in the Vale." He stopped, balled his fists and exclaimed, "Cold! Damn fool thing for an old soldier, t'start lookin' back."

"Looking back at what?" Allystaire could read the indecision in Harrys's features, the deepening lines on the sides of his face, the downward set of his lips, the twitch in his deep-set eyes. *Draw him out*, he thought. *See if you can guide him where he needs to go.*

"Score and a half o'years o'soldierin' and what have I got? Medals, ribbons, and my horse. Which is in yer stables now, along with my tack and weapons."

"Family?"

"Had," Harrys said, with a shrug. "Daughter, married, off somewhere with her sailor husband. She's not lettered and folk such as us can't afford scriveners often, so I don't hear much. Son." He swallowed hard. "Came back in a box from his first campaign on the north border, fightin' the Islandmen pushin' into Vyndamere. His ma blamed me, left."

Allystaire winced, but said, "If you have names, a place, we can help you get a letter to your daughter."

Harrys shrugged, met Allystaire's eyes again. "I could stay here, ya said? And do what?"

It was Allystaire's turn to shrug. "Help on a farm. Help at the stables."

"I'm a soldier. My only trade. Only animal I know aught about's a horse and I ain't held a shovel since I figured out how t'keep rank and find the soft jobs."

"You helped dig the graves but two weeks ago," Allystaire countered. "Regardless, we could find you something if you wished to stay."

Harrys made a small disparaging grunt. "Doin' what? Diggin' graves? Didn't say I wished t'stay. Only that if I do as y'ask I can't go back. Not the same."

"No, they are not," Allystaire agreed. "Yet you must go somewhere, and I would not have you throw your life away."

"Just stop talkin," Harrys said. "If ya would. Cold, but you like to fill up what ought t'be silent."

Allystaire felt his jaw clench. "You came to me, Harrys," he said with a quiet edge behind his voice. "You sought my counsel, and I have given it. I would not have thought you a coward."

Harry's face swung towards Allystaire, his eyes alight with anger, shouting, "No man gets t'call me coward!"

"Then why do you need to speak in circles with me to convince yourself to do what must be done," Allystaire shot back. "If you cannot look straight at this and know what it is you ought to do then no counsel I give is going to help."

Harrys clenched his jaw, nearly baring his teeth. He lifted a balled fist but forced it back to his side. "Fine. I'll go speak to Lord Freezing Chaddin, who I knew when he was trooper Chaddin and Sergeant Chaddin and I didn't much like him then. But I've a condition for my speakin' o' what I've heard."

"Name it," Allystaire said.

"After it's done, you give over my horse, tack, gear, and provisions, and ya let me leave this Freezin' village before you turn all o'it into a graveyard wi' all your suggestin' and preachin'."

"Done. Will you go see Lord Chaddin now or do you need more time to work up sufficient courage?"

Harrys spat to one side of Allystaire's boots. "I'll go now. I'll not be needin' ya." Harrys stomped off, his hands flexing at his sides.

As the old soldier stomped off, Allystaire lowered his head and sighed faintly, muttered a curse, then shook the thought away and headed back inside.

* * *

Landen and Chaddin came looking for Allystaire in the Inn less than a full turn later, finding him by the fire, looking at a stack of crudely lettered parchment. The latter was armed, sword at his side, and Allystaire could tell from the way the former kept hitching at her belt that Landen wished she were as well.

Before either could open their mouths, Allystaire held up a hand. "I know what you come to speak of. What I do not know is why you are coming to me."

His declaration met with confusion and surprise, Landen and Chaddin turning to each other. Allystaire wanted to laugh at how closely their expressions mirrored one another.

"It is a potential crisis," Landen began.

"Aye, that it is," Allystaire said. "And it is precisely the kind of crisis you have appointed him to deal with," he added, lifting a hand from the page in front of him to point it at Chaddin. "He is the instrument of your justice, not me."

"You could bring the truth from the conspirators in front of an assize," Landen pointed out.

"Aye," Allystaire said. "I can. And if I am properly petitioned to do so, I will. But I will do only that. I will not pass judgment or mete out a sentence."

"You seem unconcerned with the success or failure of the very process you have put into place," Landen muttered. Chaddin crossed his arms over his chest, lips pursing.

"Far from it. I want to see it succeed even more than the pair of you," Allystaire protested. "Which is precisely why I must not intervene except as a way of making certain that the truth is spoken before the magistrate. Do you understand?"

"If you step in, root out the conspiracy, and deal with the traitors," Chaddin said, "then you have taken sides. Other lords will believe that Landen is your puppet. No peace is made that way."

"There's a chance they will believe that anyway," Landen pointed out.

"You are not wrong," Allystaire admitted. "There is certainly that chance. Yet if I were to act directly in your interest, shield you from the work of conspirators, then surely I sow the seeds of future treachery."

"You are subtler than my father gave you credit for," Landen said after a moment's reflection.

"Not at all," Allystaire said, setting aside the parchment and standing. "I am among the least subtle men you are likely to know. I want *peace*. I do not wish it to be the peace of the graveyard. Hold that fact firmly in mind and you will understand me. Now," he said, "if you would like me present for the arrest of the men named as conspirators, allow me to dress appropriately."

"I thought you wanted no part of this," Landen said, "except at trial."

"I do not," Allystaire replied. "However, if it turns violent, I have people to protect. And the Lord of Highgate may find himself curious over events so near to his own camp." He picked up the stack of paper and walked over to another table, setting them down in front of Norbert, whose long form was folded over a sheet, a stick of charcoal clutched awkwardly in his fist. "Your lettering is more legible but remains, on the whole, atrocious," Allystaire muttered. "Though it is better than before."

Norbert looked up, blinking at the sudden shift in perspective. He straightened at the praise, faint though it was. Allystaire patted his shoulder. "Remember," he said quietly, "no man is fit to be a knight who is not lettered. Now come with me," he said. "We are off to the armory."

The boy stood quickly, smoothly. In just the two weeks of training, Norbert had changed noticeably, no longer quite as gangly, with the beginnings of muscle mass gathering on his chest. He moved more confidently, less hesitation in his steps, fidgeted less, looked even Allystaire in the eye when he talked.

"We've already gone and done—"

Allystaire met Norbert's brown eyes and waited. The boy quieted immediately and lowered his head in apology.

"We are not after practicing now, lad. I hope it will be no more than a bit of show." He flicked his eyes towards Chaddin. "Might want to consider gathering your men and arming them." *No orders,* he thought to himself, *merely suggestions.* "Landen," he went on, "if you would come with us."

Chaddin departed with a nod—towards Landen, and not himself, Allystaire noted. "We'll be ready in half a turn."

It wasn't a long walk to the armory, such as it was, but it was a cold one, forcing all three to burrow into what winter clothing they had. Allystaire heard raised voices as they approached. This quickened his steps, leaving Norbert and Landen behind him for a quick, surprised moment. They made up the distance embarrassingly fast, Allystaire thought.

They found Torvul standing in front of the shed, holding his cudgel at his side, while Harrys stood a few feet away. The dwarf lifted the metal shod end of his stick, and shouted at the old soldier in his unmistakable rumble.

"Move another hand towards me, you *tshakavitnamar,* and I'll break every bone in it," the dwarf shouted. Harrys feinted to a side and Torvul swiped at the air mere inches from Harrys's snarl-set face.

"HOLD," Allystaire bellowed.

Torvul didn't bother to turn towards him, but Harrys did, his face set in a grimace.

"Ya told me I could have m'gear and be gone, but this cursed stack o'shit won't let me near," Harrys growled.

"I did say you could have them," Allystaire admitted, "but I had no idea your cowardice would drive you to flee the village quite so soon. Before your lords could organize an assize, even."

Torvul lifted his cudgel threateningly, with one hand, while the other crept for a pouch.

Don't, Allystaire thought, knowing Torvul would hear him. *He is no real danger.*

"What is the meaning of this, Bannerman?" Landen's words were quiet. "Desertion, is it?"

"M'current time expires the start o'the new year and that can't be far. Might even be passed," Harrys spat back. "And I've no intention of stayin' around men who know I'll go behind their backs t'see 'em hung."

"You must stay for their trial, for you brought the accusation," Chaddin countered.

"And when'll that be? Long enough for all the men t'learn of it and learn t'hate me," Harrys said.

"Even if your enlistment is over, I remain your Baroness, Harrys Ejilson," Landen said. "It is not Lord Stillbright's place to give you permission to leave when I have not."

"Sir," Allystaire corrected her. "Not Lord."

Landen eyed Allystaire with a frown, then looked back to Harrys. "I mean to conduct an assize as swiftly as possible. This very day. Then if it is truly your wish, you may leave."

"Give me back my arms," Harrys said, addressing Allystaire and trying to ignore Landen. "Do that, at least, and let me see to m'horse, and I'll give your Frozen evidence. Wi'out it, you'll have t'kill me."

Landen looked to Allystaire. "Would you release his arms?"

Allystaire shrugged. "I do not see why not. I do not feel threatened by cowards."

"That's the third time you've called me coward, you Frozen bastard," Harrys said. "There won't be a fourth wi'out blood."

Allystaire ignored him, let the words roll off of him and nodded to Torvul. "Let him in the armory. We will be with him. And if you would, help Norbert pick out something fitting."

Torvul eyed Allystaire warily, then grunted, tucked his cudgel under one arm and fished in a pouch for a key. "You know where the shortbows and spears are," the dwarf muttered. "Find what suits while I look for armor."

When the dwarf had the door open, Allystaire waved everyone else in ahead of him. He tried to keep his eyes everywhere at once—on Norbert eyeing a rack of spears, on Landen and Harrys looking through stacks of swords, on Torvul moving among the piles of mail.

Finally, Allystaire simply grabbed the blade he'd been practicing with, having left it leaning in easy reach, and walked outside, strapping it around him as he went. The mail shirt he'd put on that morning was still under his outer shirt, vest, and cloak, the weight of it having long since settled into a comforting burden. *Should have brought my gloves*, he thought, visualizing the pile of armor on a table in his room back at the Inn, both the gleaming plate Torvul had used to give him his new name, and the bits of rougher things—and iron banded leather cap, his iron knuckled gloves, heavy bracers.

Landen was the first to appear, having buckled on a swordbelt of green-dyed leather chased with silver and etched with the Delondeur Tower. The scabbard and hilt were worked in the same colors and motif, though the pommel and the crossguard were plainly made for use, and not for show. The Baroness stood a little taller, it seemed to Allystaire, with her weapon back on her hip.

Harrys stumbled out next, carrying a belt and two weapons: a falchion, a savage and practical blade, and a long-handled horseman's axe with a loop for the wrist.

"I'll be back for my armor," the soldier grumbled, as he buckled the belt around himself and thrust the falchion through a frogged loop at his right and the axe through the same on his left. "If I can find it in there. Disgrace, it is, jumblin' it altogether like that."

"Most of the rotten iron you lot wore here was so inferior it's not worth sorting out," Torvul said as he emerged just ahead of Norbert. "If I want to make *armor* out of it I'll need a furnace so I can melt it down. With enough of it, I might make some steel with a chance of stopping a table fork." The dwarf sniffed.

Norbert came out with a long chain shirt pulled over his outer clothes, belted around his waist, its ends dangling to his knees. He carried an armful of weaponry and gear, set it down to strap an armguard over the inside of his left arm deftly. *Almost as if he knows what he's about*, Allystaire thought.

Torvul eyed Norbert critically as the boy hooked a sheaf of arrows on his right hip, then picked up both spear and unstrung bow in one hand. "We'll need to get you a bow case, boy," the dwarf said. "Spear and bow do you no good clutched together like that. And I've some thoughts on how t'armor you a bit better, still keep your arms free t'draw. Give me some time."

Norbert straightened up, shifted the bowstave into his left hand, shouldered the spear with his right and turned, with almost a military bearing, towards Allystaire.

"Baroness," Allystaire said, inclining his head slightly, "we await you. A word first, if you please. My squire and I are here to defend the folk of the village, or anyone else, if matters turn violent. We are not at any command but my own." *It's also possible I'll have to explain to Garth why we're coming armed into his camp, but let's leave that be for now.*

"Squire, is it?" Harrys spat again. "Thought he was just a village lad."

Norbert bristled, but Allystaire raised a calming hand and the boy relaxed visibly. Turning to Harrys, Allystaire said, "What matter is it to you?"

"Enough of all this," Landen said, snapping command into her voice. "Bannerman Ejilson, you will remain silent unless questioned or otherwise directed." With that, the Baroness turned and set a quick pace back towards the Inn.

Torvul caught Allystaire's eye. *Shall I?* The dwarf's gruff, rumbling voice sounded in his head.

Allystaire thought, but for a moment. *Gather Idgen Marte. And Gideon. Stay at a distance but keep an eye, if you would.*

Torvul nodded and stomped off. Allystaire fell into step beside Norbert, with Landen ahead and Harrys ranging reluctantly between them, as if he didn't want to come too close to any of them.

I may have botched this, Allystaire thought. Then, clearing his throat, he said, "Harrys. You need not leave as soon as all this. In this weather, traveling will be dangerous."

"It's just snow and wind," the man grunted. "Won't kill me. Stayin' will."

"We can defend you from any—"

"I can defend m'self."

Allystaire frowned. "What of your horse? A bad snowstorm will mean her death."

Harrys hunched his shoulders and ignored the question. Allystaire sighed as the Inn hove into view, with Chaddin and his men, all armed, waiting outside.

CHAPTER 15

Harrys's Choice

It was a cold march to the Oyrwyn camp, made all the colder by the foreboding that grew in Allystaire's stomach. As he'd expected, the sudden advent of armed men on its borders had the guardsmen stirring, weapons being shouldered, a runner sent towards the command tents at the center.

Dammit, Allystaire thought, *I should have been down here more these past weeks. Get the feel of the place. Soldiers mislike staying in one place for so long.*

In truth, though, with winter on, and no way to know where storms were raging or how much snow and ice they were bringing between here and anywhere else, there wasn't anywhere for the Oyrwyn soldiers to go.

They'd gotten within a few dozen yards of the large prisoner's tent when Garth came riding up on his black, a horse every bit the size of Ardent. The Lord of Highgate swung out of the saddle with practiced ease, carrying a long-handled, heavy-bladed axe as he walked.

"What is the meaning of this, Allystaire? Why do armed men come into my camp with no warning? Why do some of my prisoners go armed *at all?*"

"They are not your prisoners, Garth," Allystaire replied.

"No? Then you are taking responsibility for their care and feeding, I take it."

"As I recall, I already had to," Allystaire shot back. "Now there is danger afoot here, and men who must be brought to justice. I ask that you move aside and let these people men conduct their business."

"And if I do not?" Garth planted his longaxe in the snow and mud at his feet and stood up straighter.

Allystaire sighed. "Do not test me, Lord of Highgate," he said quietly. "I will make my arguments eloquent, if I must." Something about the inflection Allystaire put into "eloquent" caused the blond knight to start and narrow his eyes. Garth's hand flexed around the haft of the axe, and he shook his head at Allystaire.

"You wouldn't."

"Lord of Highgate," Landen butted in, stepping close to Garth—too close, Allystaire noted, for him to bring the longaxe into play, if it came to it—"I would like to take counsel with you later, if you've the time. There are conspirators among my men and they must be dealt with first. But I have important news, I hope, of the future, and I would speak to you as a representative of your Barony. Yet now, I would ask nothing more or less than to mete out the necessary discipline and justice among my own. Surely you understand that need."

Garth's face started to draw into a scowl. "You haven't authority to treat with me as a representative of Barony Delondeur. You are a prisoner."

Allystaire cleared his throat. "She is the Baroness Delondeur, by law and by custom. Nothing you say will change that fact."

"What I say has nothing to do with it," Garth answered frostily. "What I do could change quite a lot. Hard to rule a Barony as a prisoner."

Allystaire let out a long breath. "This woman is not your prisoner, and you know it, Garth."

"Do I? Seems as though my Lord Baron Gilrayan Oyrwyn might beg to differ."

"It does not become a good man to seek the favor of Gilrayan Oyrwyn."

"There's something to be said for avoiding his wrath," Garth replied, though he half swallowed the words as he spoke them.

Allystaire tilted his head slightly, narrowed his eyes. "I have known you from a boy, Lord of Highgate. You are a good man, or at least you were. A brave man. I am going to ask you to risk your Baron's wrath."

"Stop talking in circles," Garth said, suddenly flustered. "Cold, Ally, you only left a few months ago. Do you know what it's like, suddenly being looked at to take your place?" The words came in a sudden outburst. "The men who followed you now look to me. The Baron expects me to lead his campaigns, come spring. The older men wait for me to fail and the younger assume I'll be another great man, Coldbourne's protégé," he spat. "Have you any idea how much I've risked simply to come here? And I sit here waiting for what, exactly?"

"You sit because it is the deep of winter and there is nothing else you can do," Allystaire replied softly. "I was never great," he added. "But if I can ask you to trust me—"

"How can I? I spent my *life* trusting you, from the time I was eight summers old to a few months ago. And my trust, all of our trust, was thrown aside when you simply *walked away* from us."

"I deserve your anger, even your scorn, Garth. I know that. With your help, we can do something so much greater than any campaign, any battle we ever fought."

Garth turned a half step to the side, holding up a hand. "Go. Do what you must. Explain it to me later. I'm tired of trying to think how I'll live up to you. Just answer me one question," he said, adjusting his grip on the axe and looking back to Allystaire. "In my position, right now, with the numbers and the prisoners under my nose—what would the great Lord Coldbourne have done?"

"Taken them back to Wind's Jaw," Allystaire said, "to await the orders of my Baron."

"And you ask me to do the opposite?"

"Yes," Allystaire said. "I do. I told you, Garth, you ought to forget most of what you ever heard that man tell you. It is not Allystaire Coldbourne that stands before you. I am Allystaire Stillbright, and I serve no Baron, no Lord, and no King. I will fight no wars to elevate one man over another, or to raise a banner over a few miles more of scorched and salted earth. You can be a better man than I was, Garth. I think you already are."

With a sigh, the Lord of Highgate turned. "Go. Do whatever it is you must. I need to begin thinking about striking my camp."

Allystaire nodded, then took a step to the side and looked to Landen, who once again took the lead of their little procession.

A few yards shy of the tent, Allystaire put a hand out to stop Norbert. Landen saw him, gave him a questioning look.

"We are not here to do the work for you."

Landen nodded, then asked, "How would you do it?"

"Quickly, and with less talking."

Landen nodded, then conferred quietly with Chaddin for a moment. The Lord Magistrate barked quick orders to his men. Weapons were drawn, and they rushed into the tent all at once.

From outside, they heard muffled shouts, a few thuds, saw the tent shake. Harrys muttered nervously, stamped his feet as if they were cold.

It took only a few moments for Chaddin's men to appear, working in pairs to drag out two men. Allystaire recognized neither, but he turned to Harrys, raising a brow.

"Sir Donals Brinden, Sir Mathis Averyn," the man muttered, nodding. "How long till this Freezin' trial?"

"I am not the man to ask," Allystaire replied.

"Stop yer pretendin'," Harrys spat back. "You're pullin' all the strings here. Maybe those two Freezin' traitor knights are right after all."

"You do not believe that, or you would never have come to me."

Harrys had no answer for that, so they sat silently as Chaddin's men worked to bind the conspirators with lengths of rope. When they'd been dragged from the tent the two knights seemed too stunned to resist but one of them, a barrel chested, bandy-legged man suddenly found his feet and thrust off one of his captors, then drove his fist straight into the eye of the second. The renegade went for the dirk on the belt of the second man, who reeled away, one hand pressed to his eye.

There were many reactions all at once, and Allystaire saw, felt, and even heard them. Harrys drew out his falchion and charged forward, the wide, heavy blade steady in his hand. Chaddin's men drew weapons, but none of them reacted quickly enough to do anything beyond filling their hands. Landen drew her own sword, as did Chaddin, but both were too far away to bring their blades to play.

Allystaire realized later, with some small pride, that the first sound he'd heard in all the rush, even if he hadn't recognized it right away, was the distinct creak of a drawn bowstring just behind him and to his right.

While all the armed men around him stood still, the renegade knight seized the dirk, drove the pommel into the face of the man he'd already punched, and then dragged the man towards him, pressing the edge of the blade to the unprotected throat, while his other arm, thick beneath his coat, wrapped beneath the man's arm and behind his head.

Meanwhile, a forward-thinking member of Chaddin's party punched the second conspirator in the back of the head with the pommel of his sword, sending the man insensate to his knees, then kicked him over to the snow and planted a foot in his back.

"Brinden!" Landen shouted, leveling her blade at the hostage-taker. "This is beneath you, man. You plotted and were found out. Accept your fate with something resembling courage."

Allystaire turned to see Norbert with an arrow drawn, the fletching to his cheek. The shortbow in his hands bent with the tension of his draw, but the lad himself was still and silent.

Harrys had reached the knot of men ringing the hostage taker, and spat as he shouldered them out of his way none too gently.

"Donals, ya withered stump of a Frozen cock," Harrys spat. "Ya know yourself guilty and yer actions prove it."

"That is Sir Donals or Lord Brinden to such as you, Bannerman," the man shot back, momentarily pointing his dirk at Harrys. "Speak not of what you don't understand."

"I understand plenty, you arrogant shit," Harrys growled. "I know you're lookin' t'cut a man's throat 'cause yer frighted o'losin' yer license t'do as y'please."

"Bannerman," Landen began, but Harrys thrust out his hand, palm up, towards the Baroness.

"I've got this," he muttered, then remembered to add, "m'lady" without bothering to look at Landen.

Allystaire, meanwhile, muttered to Norbert, "Move to your right. Try to circle around him."

"I can always shoot the man he's threatenin'." Norbert's muttered reply was almost inaudible, spoken out of the side of his mouth, his lips barely moving. "I'the foot or the leg, I mean. And then…"

"I heal him," Allystaire replied, startled at the brutal but sensible calculus of

Norbert's suggestion. "I see it, but let this play out a bit longer. If he moves to cut the man, shoot him if you can."

Meanwhile, Harrys and Donals eyed each other warily, and none of Chaddin or Landen's men moved in on him.

"Donals," Landen's voice rang out. "You've proven your guilt. Let the Lord Magistrate's man go and you'll be granted a merciful end."

"Oh, is it Lord Magistrate now? That his idea?" The dirk suddenly pointed at Allystaire, though Donals kept his eyes on Harrys and the dark point of the falchion a few feet away. "You've sold out your father and now you make deals with his murderer, elevate bastards over good and loyal men." Sir Donals' eyes were wide in a bluff face with a curly red beard, his words half-yelled and half-spat.

"Good n'loyal men don't go tryin' t'cut throats when they're found out," Harrys said.

"As if you've never cut a throat, peasant," Donals said.

"ENOUGH," Landen tried to roar, but her voice was a tad too hoarse for it. "Let the man go."

The rangy, lightly-armored man with two bruised eyes chose that moment to struggle against the arm that levered behind his head, only to get the point of the dagger probing behind his neck.

"Be sensible, Sir Donals," Chaddin began. "There is no way out that ends well for you."

"Base-born traitor," Donals spat back, backpedaling, dragging Chaddin's soldier with him. "I'll hear nothing from you, nor from the sorcerer who calls himself a paladin."

Idgen Marte's voice sounded in Allystaire's head. *Want me to make an end of this? Plenty of shadow less than two steps from him.*

No. Let them resolve it if they can.

"Donals Brinden, lord of throat cutters n'cowards," Harrys said suddenly. "Would ya accept a blade and the circle w'me?"

Donals actually laughed. "They'll never let me have a sword, and if they did it'd only mean your death, you doting fool. I'm twice the swordsman you are."

"There will be no trial by combat," Chaddin said, and Landen echoed him with a resounding, "No."

Harrys shrugged, his eyes never leaving Brinden's. "Then let 'im kill me before he dies. Take one more to the Cold w'him."

"Oh no," Donals shouted. "If I defeat the peasant, I leave, freely."

Landen and Chaddin shared a look, with Chaddin starting to shake his head, until Landen seized the moment.

"You will get no horse, no supplies. You get your feet, and the winter will kill you," she said. "That is the only offer you'll have."

"Fine," Donals yelled. "Everyone but the peasant back away. Bring me a blade. A decent one, a knight's weapon."

Harrys finally lowered his falchion, but didn't sheath it, keeping it instead at a low guard with his left hand wrapped around his right wrist. Allystaire looked to Norbert and nodded slightly; the boy relaxed his string but kept the arrow nocked. Landen walked a few steps forward, turned her sword point down and stuck it into the ground, then backed away, saying, "Let the man go."

Donals did indeed let the man go, and Allystaire realized just a moment too late what he meant to do. The knight gave the man a shove towards Harrys, whose bare sword pointed straight at him.

Meanwhile, Donals dove for Landen's sword and snatched it from the ground, bringing it up in both hands, smiling grimly.

Harrys had two choices, as Allystaire saw it while the moment slowly unfolded before him; he could impale the hapless man hurtling towards him, or twist, try to absorb the blow, and likely be knocked off his feet.

The old soldier chose the latter, stumbled to the ground on his side and rolled away on one shoulder.

Sir Donals Brinden came on in a furious rush, but instead of raising his borrowed sword high for a dramatic killing stroke, he kept it low and aimed to drive it straight into Harrys's body from an angle the grounded soldier couldn't counter.

Harrys didn't try to move. Instead, he hurled a handful of wet snow at Brinden's face and rolled to a side, then pushed himself up by levering on an elbow. The snow distracted the knight enough that instead of planting firmly in Harrys's midsection, the sword just barely swept across his back as it was turned.

Harrys cried out, but finished rising to his feet anyway, holding his falchion out in a guard.

Brinden came on, trying a sweeping cut.

Harrys managed to knock it aside, and then another, and a third, swinging with both arms to push Brinden back and gain space.

It was clear to Allystaire that Sir Donals Brinden hadn't been lying when he'd claimed to be a better swordsman, and it was apparent to everyone there. Harrys couldn't counterattack; it was all he could do, one after another, to block the cuts and thrusts that Brinden sent at him, backing up and giving ground all the while. The length of his weapon didn't help, as the blade the knight wielded had half a span more of length than the old soldier's falchion.

"I can shoot him clean," Norbert muttered.

"Shooting a man in the back is not how we work," Allystaire replied.

Meanwhile, Harrys had thrown Brinden back with another over-exertion, then given up his two handed grip to draw the axe from the other side of his belt with his left hand, backing up yet another step, shuffling to the side, trying to present a smaller target, showing his profile to Donals, with axe and sword held low at his side, breath heaving in his chest.

"You've no idea how to fight a knight on his own terms, peasant," Donals proclaimed, his voice untroubled, rich with arrogance. "Is this the kind of man you'd elevate above me, *my lady*?" Though he didn't look at Landen, but there was no mistaking the insult in his tone.

"You talkin' or dyin'?" Harrys, by contrast, sounded like a man more than half done in, his voice hoarse, words raw.

Donals lunged forward. Harrys tried to spin away, but the tip of the sword drew a line down his left arm. Not a deep cut, but a painful one that would slow his axe-hand. The old soldier's grimace deepened; otherwise he gave no sign.

"I'm going to cut you apart slowly, peasant," Donals said, gloating again.

Harrys growled and waved his axe, beckoning the knight forward.

Donals obliged, lunging again. Harrys took a half step to his right, bringing the axe up to parry. Allystaire grasped almost instantly what the old soldier intended.

The horseman's axe he carried had a hooked balancing point. With a flick of his wrist, Harrys trapped the first few inches of Donals' point with it, allowing him to tug the man forward.

Since Brinden still had some command of his blade, and presence of mind, he was able to slow himself from moving forward, and tug his blade so that, trapped by the hook or not, its edge dug into Harry's arm again, more deeply this time.

It availed him little when Harrys pivoted, allowing the blade to gash his arm, and planted the first half span of his broad-bladed falchion straight through Sir Donal's Brinden's breastbone.

The old soldier stepped back, bleeding freely from his arm, axe falling from nerveless fingers. Brinden fell to his knees as bloody froth bubbled up around his mouth, streaming off into his red beard. He looked up at the soldier with stunned, uncomprehending eyes.

"Call me peasant again, dead man," Harrys muttered. Then he planted his booted foot in the knight's chest and ripped his falchion free. He let the body slump to the ground.

"Remember what I told you," Allystaire muttered to Norbert, as he moved towards Harrys, who paled as he cradled his wounded arm. "It is not the skill of the sword hand alone that matters."

"It's who's willin' to bear the most pain," Norbert finished, slipping his arrow back into its sheaf.

* * *

Despite Harrys's grumbling, he'd accepted Allystaire's healing in the immediate aftermath of the impromptu duel. Now, half a turn later, with something resembling a court set up inside the Delondeur tent, Chaddin stared hard at the second knight, Sir Mathis Averyn, who stood pale and watery-eyed, hands and legs hobbled with rope, in the center of the tent. Guards flanked him, with Chaddin and Landen seated on stools behind borrowed camp tables at the back of the tent.

Allystaire, Norbert, Gideon, and Harrys lingered near the drawn-back flaps, basking in both the light and the cold allowed in. The old soldier had calmed some since he'd won the duel, and kept flexing his left arm, running his fingers inside his sleeve.

"Sir Mathis Averyn," Chaddin said, with careful, almost hesitant solemnity. "You stand accused of conspiracy against your Baroness and her appointed officers. What have you to say?"

It took Sir Averyn a moment to gather himself to reply, but when he did his voice was clear. "Who accuses me?"

"Bannerman Ejilson," Chaddin said. "Come forward."

Muttering words under his breath that Allystaire didn't have to listen hard to guess at, the soldier stumped up to stand next to the bound Sir Mathis.

"Bannerman Ejilson," Chaddin continued, "please tell us what you know of the conspiracy."

"Dunno that I'd call it that," Harrys answered. "Seems more like just a pair of frighted idiots."

"Please tell us what you heard," Chaddin said, trying and failing to hide a grin, "without any opinion."

"Fine," Harrys said. "Mathis and Brinden come to me one night spent outside the Temple. Few days after ya'd done yer proclamating on magistrates and such, m'lady," he said, nodding at Landen. "Said they knew I understood how things ought t'be done. Knew how 'twas important t'keep our traditions. Told me it was foolish t'try n'elevate peasants above their proper born masters."

"He lies," Avery said haughtily, tilting his head. "And as a baseborn man, good soldier or not, his words cannot be used as evidence against one of noble blood."

"As to your latter complaint, Sir Mathis, yes they can," Chaddin replied coldly. "As to the former, we have with us a man who can determine that. Sir Stillbright, would you consent?"

"Aye, Lord Magistrate, I will," Allystaire boomed. "Yet I would make it plain that my part in this is merely as an aid to determining the truth. My presence does not imply the approval of my Goddess or Her Temple on any verdict reached or sentence meted out."

Allystaire walked a few paces forward and placed his hand on the back of Harrys's neck. Having healed the man twice already, it was no effort at all to establish that bridging connection between his senses and the other man. Harrys was anxious; his knees and lower back ached. He wanted this to be over and was uncertain of what lay beyond it.

"Please repeat your story, Bannerman Ejilson," Chaddin said. "In brief."

"Avery and Brinden came to me n'told me that I understood how things ought t'be, was a good soldier and knowed you needed killin'," he said, pointing to Chaddin. "N'that maybe tha Baroness could b'made t'see sense once we left but till then, it'd be best t' make sure he wasn't sayin' much. They may've suggested we needed t'kill Stillbright too, if we had the chance. Remember the Old Baron proper was what Donals said."

Allystaire looked to Chaddin, who nodded. Allystaire dropped his hand and took half a step back.

"How do you answer the charges, Sir Mathis Averyn?" Chaddin folded his arms across his chest.

"Lies," he began, in outrage.

"Sir Stillbright, would you please?"

Allystaire placed his hand on the back of Mathis's neck as calmly and gently as he had Harrys's. It took him a moment. Sir Mathis was afraid, edging on frantic. He was in pain from the ropes. Most of all, he was aggrieved at the injustice of it all.

"Sir Mathis Averyn," Chaddin began, as Allystaire nodded, "did you plot with Sir Donals Brinden to murder me?"

"Yes." Mathis suddenly started as the word popped out of his mouth, tried to pull himself free of Allystaire's hand, failed.

"Did you attempt to recruit Bannerman Ejilson?"

"Yes."

Chaddin leaned forward, eyes narrowing. "Why?"

"Good soldier. Knows his place. Won't question."

Allystaire felt Harrys bristle nearby, took a half step to put himself between the man on trial and the witness.

"Why did you feel it necessary to conspire for my death, for Sir Stillbright's, and possibly that of the Baroness Delondeur?"

"Can't put bastards above better blooded men! Can't have that kind of thinking." Avery began to sweat profusely. Allystaire felt his palm getting slick on the back of the man's neck. "As for Stillbright, you mean Coldbourne! Worst enemy Delondeur's ever had. Killed the Baron! Girl's not ready. Soft-headed, it's clear. Come under Coldbourne's influence."

"How many other men had you tried to recruit?"

"Just Ejilson. Thought many of the yeomanry would fall into line behind him. Useful that way." Sir Mathis's breathing was growing ragged, each word harder to hear than the last.

"Would you have killed me, given the chance?"

"Yes," Mathis practically hissed.

Allystaire dropped his hand away. Sir Mathis Averyn slumped down to one knee on the hard ground.

"If I compel him much more, he will pass out," Allystaire said, "so long as he continues to resist. I suspect he will."

"Lord Magistrate," Landen said, "I would like to test Sir Stillbright's compulsion, if you please."

Chaddin looked to Allystaire, who shrugged. "If you wish, Baroness." He crossed over to Landen's side, extended his hand. Landen pushed aside her sleeve and took Allystaire's forearm in a warrior's embrace. "Attempt to say something that is not true."

"Such as?"

"That you are really Parthalian of song and story. That you hail from the Concordat. That you have walked on water and kicked a mountain to dust. Whatever you wish."

Landen opened her mouth, but nothing came out. Sweat beaded almost instantly on her face. Finally, she relaxed, and muttered, "I am Landen Delondeur, born in Londray." She let go Allystaire's hand, nodded absently, and said, "I am satisfied, Lord Magistrate."

Chaddin nodded, and lifted a hand to point a finger at Mathis Averyn while Allystaire drifted back to the entrance of the tent.

"Sir Mathis Averyn, you are incontestably guilty of conspiring against your Baron and his appointed Magistrate. There is a new order of things, Sir Mathis. Men of station will have to accustom themselves to it. We will pause for a single turn while I contemplate your sentence. Take him away."

Two of the guards dragged the nearly insensate Sir Mathis Averyn away, lifting his feet clear of the ground as they went.

"Please clear the tent," Chaddin said. "I would confer with the Baroness." Then he lifted his head and looked hopefully at Allystaire who sighed, but nodded. Norbert started to turn away, but Allystaire shook his head very slightly, and the youth stayed put.

"Harrys," Allystaire said, catching the old soldier just as he was leaving the tent. "Do not leave yet. I would speak with you before you go."

"S'at so? Sounded like an order, t'me."

"It is not." Then, after a pause and a heavy swallow. "Please."

The old soldier shrugged and walked off.

Allystaire watched him leave and then took a few steps towards Chaddin, who'd lifted his head and turned to Landen.

"What would you have me do, Landen?"

The Baroness shook her head slowly. "I can't answer that. You're the Lord Magistrate. The sentence must come from you."

"I feared you'd say that," Chaddin muttered. Allystaire barely heard him, though, because he was taken aback by Landen's response. *Might this actually work? Might these be the right people to lead this place?*

Allystaire pushed the thought away, because Chaddin was looking to him now. He held out a hand to forestall any questions.

"I cannot tell you what to do, Chaddin. I will not. I have no part in this except to help to see that the truth is told by all parties."

"Based on the testimony of Bannerman Ejilson, and on Averyn's own words, I have to condemn him, don't I?"

Allystaire was silent; Landen looked on with pursed lips. Norbert shifted uncomfortably. For a moment, the only sound to be heard in the tent was the slight stir of its heavy cloth walls, the slight jingling creak of Norbert's mail.

"I have killed men before," Chaddin said. "In battle, or keeping the peace. I have never *ordered* a man's death. This is a different thing."

"Aye," Allystaire replied. "And it speaks well of you that it weighs on you."

"You've done it before, haven't you? Ordered a man's death for a crime."

Allystaire nodded. "I have."

"Tell me of one."

Allystaire shook his head. "No. I will not let the man I was be your example. It is a hard thing thrust upon you, Chaddin. Face it directly."

"Have I any options? Repentance?" Chaddin's eyes lit. "Doesn't your priestess have some ritual?" He came half out of his chair, his face hopeful.

Deep lines sprung up across Allystaire's forehead. "She does," he said. "But political crimes like treason are not among those she would forgive, I think, for they are not the kind of crimes the Mother proscribes."

"She would forgive a murderer or a rapist but not a traitor?" Disbelief soured Landen's usually smooth voice.

"You do not understand," Allystaire said, shaking his head. "The structures of this world such as Baronial lines, lordship, they are meaningless to Her, and to Mol, when it comes to this. If Mathis had murdered you, Chaddin, *that* would be a crime of interest to us, something I can punish and speak out against."

"He planned to do it," Chaddin said. "Is that not enough?"

"It is not that he planned it," Gideon said, breaking his long silence. He'd been standing so still that it seemed half the people in the tent had forgotten he was there. Suddenly all eyes were on him. "It is that he intended to kill you and to take the Baroness in hand because he wished to maintain his power over the people whose exploitation makes his privilege possible."

The words rolled over them all, leaving a stunned silence in their wake.

"Try again, in plainer language please, Gideon," Allystaire said, though he smiled.

"It is not a question of what he planned to do but why he planned to do it," Gideon said quickly. "He saw, to make this metaphorical, a weapon in the hands of the people he oppresses. And it was pointed at him."

"The new court is not meant to be a weapon held to the throats of my liegemen," Landen protested.

"In his eyes, and likely in many of the rest, it will be precisely that. Do not misunderstand me," the boy added hastily. "This is hardly a bad thing. As best I can tell, the nobility of this place act with total impunity."

As he spoke, he held his hands behind his back, didn't pace or fidget. Contrasted with Norbert, who constantly tugged at his belt or flicked at imaginary dust on his mail shirt, or Chaddin, who frowned and furrowed his brow with every word spoken, Gideon was a pillar of calm and control.

"That is hardly fair—"

Landen's protest was cut off as Gideon's eyes suddenly blazed, a golden light emanating from them and filling the tent for an intense moment.

It was, to Allystaire, briefly reminiscent of the sorcerers he'd faced. He feared, for a moment remembering a day of pain at Bhimanzir's hands, the crushing power of Gethmasanar's subtle will. Yet the color wasn't a sickly yellow or a blood-drip red.

It was the color of soft summer sunlight. A golden warmth, powerful but inviting.

"I spent my first two days in this Barony watching my master oversee the construction of a pen to hold the women he intended to sacrifice. I spent the next months watching that pen fill with terrified, powerless women, taken from their homes, bought and sold like cattle. Not even cattle!"

For perhaps the first time, Allystaire heard Gideon's voice rise, and felt a chill at the hint of raw power that roared beneath it.

"Like furs. Like meat, or turnips. Like *dead things*. That is how the women were treated. Dead things that the sorcerer required, and your father provided them without a second *thought*. Had most of your knights and lords the links necessary to have hired Bhimanzir, they would have done the same if he promised them the same power. Do not speak to me of what is *fair* when it comes to such men."

The light left Gideon's eyes and the boy shrank back into himself for a moment. All was silent. Chaddin and Landen both sat straight in their seats, eyes wide. Allystaire heard Norbert mumble, "Cold, m'glad he's on our side."

"The Will of the Mother speaks sense," Allystaire said, "and probably truth. I can see if the Voice would speak to Averyn. If he were willing, she probably would. But he must be willing. No man comes compelled to our Temple."

"My mind is made up," Chaddin said. He glanced at Gideon for a moment, seemed to be heartened by something he saw or thought, and nodded, confirming something to himself. "Yes. But if he wishes to speak to the priestess, I would allow it. Best go see if she will come."

"She is on her way," Gideon said, after barely any pause. "But she fears that Sir Mathis Averyn will have little to say to her."

"She may well be right," Chaddin said. Then he took in a deep breath. "Guards!"

The tent flap was tugged open by a thickly gloved hand. A ruddy cheeked face looked in, leather and iron cap slightly askew on his head. "Fetch the prisoner," Chaddin ordered.

Gideon, Allystaire, and Norbert shuffled off to the side again. Mathis was once more dragged before Chaddin, grinding his teeth in a grimace.

"Sir Mathis Averyn," Chaddin began, standing. "I have decided upon your sentence."

Avery spat, trying to sail a blob of spittle at Chaddin. It was well wide of the mark.

"I don't recognize your Freezing court, you mad bastard," he yelled.

"Gag him," Chaddin ordered. The two guards who held him looked at one another in confusion. "NOW," Chaddin thundered. One of the men pulled his glove free then and roughly stuffed it into Mathis's mouth as he continued to try to spout obscenities. Slowly he was drowned out as the glove was worked into his mouth, with the second guard squeezing his jaw open by the cheeks.

"The world is changing, Sir Mathis," Chaddin went on. "We must all learn to change with it. The mass of people have a legal voice now, in me. That you found this so appalling as to engage in intrigue and conspiracy, and would look to commit treason and murder to prevent it, does not speak well of you as a lord of men. Blood will not save you. You are to be hanged at first light tomorrow. I give you the intervening time to write out a will, any final letters, and to speak, if you wish, with the Mother's or Fortune's priestess. They may be willing to extend you a kind of mercy. I am not."

Mathis raged impotently into his improvised gag, struggled against the ropes that bound him. His face turned beet red; saliva trickled from the corners of his mouth.

"Take him away. Remove the gag when he is out of my hearing. Do not remove his bonds. Keep him under guard."

"Ah, where, m'lord?"

"There is a cowshed that will do," Allystaire said. He turned to Norbert, working hard and failing to keep a grin from his face. "I believe my squire here knows where it is."

Norbert furrowed his brow for a moment, till realization suddenly dawned. "Aye," he said slowly, frowning. "I do."

"By your leave then, Lord Magistrate?" Allystaire looked to Chaddin, who nodded.

"Follow me, then," Norbert said, hefting bowstave and spear and leaving the tent.

Chaddin and Landen stood, and Allystaire clapped Gideon on the shoulder, nodded at them, and turned to leave.

Gideon stepped away from Allystaire's hand as they left the tent, but not before Allystaire had squeezed his shoulder and muttered, "Proud of you. You saw what no one else quite did."

The boy shrugged, but Allystaire saw the ghost of a smile traced on his thin mouth. "I merely expressed it. You saw it, too." He looked up at Allystaire. "If he accepts the repentance, do we take him in, commute his sentence?"

"I do not know," Allystaire admitted. "Tell me what you think."

"I think that you will say that we haven't the legal authority to do so, and that attempting to would undercut Landen and Chaddin. And you would be right, to an extent."

"And where do you find that extends to, exactly?"

"The legal authority is not terribly important. We *could* take him away from them, protect him if he repented and accepted the Mother."

"It sets a bad precedent. Criminals will think they can come to us for sanctuary."

"Maybe they should be able to," Gideon suggested suddenly.

"I will not make Her Temple a haven for thieves, rapists, murderers, and blackguards of every description," Allystaire declared. "Even if he genuinely repents, should his sentence be commuted?"

"Of course it should. He spoke of conspiracy. Tried to set it into motion, but chose his fellows poorly and was caught. His actual crime is political; his execution will still be about power, maintaining it, shaping it, holding onto it. It will not be about handing out a just punishment."

"Did you not just explain how his crime was about clinging to his power?"

"And his punishment could be seen as Landen clinging to hers."

Allystaire sighed. "You know that someone must wield power."

Gideon looked up at him, frowning. "Of course. An absence of it would lead to chaos and strife. We are working towards the best end we can see. I know that. But it still involves compromise that rankles me."

"We do what we can—"

"Until we do what we must," Gideon finished. "I know. I wish we did not resort to 'must' so easily."

"None of it is easy." Allystaire looked towards the road leading to the timber palisade surrounding Thornhurst. Harrys was making his way towards it, though he walked more slowly than he could have. "Would you go escort Mol here? I need to speak to Harrys."

"Mol doesn't need an escort."

"For the form of the thing, Gideon. Please?"

The boy sighed lightly and quickened his pace. Though Allystaire's stride was much longer, in little time Gideon outpaced him and was off down the road, passing quickly by Harrys.

Coming up slowly behind Harrys, Allystaire cleared his throat. The old soldier didn't stop.

"Harrys," Allystaire said. "Stop, please. Speak with me."

He turned about, shrugged. "Well?"

"Why did you agree to fight Sir Donals?"

"Never liked the son of a bitch," Harrys said, shrugging.

Allystaire frowned. "It cannot be so simple."

"Never is. But he wanted killin'." Harrys sniffed. "That lad o'yours, he's a sharp one. I think he had Donals Brinden down t'the particulars. He'd've done whate'er he could t'ruin what those two're after startin'."

"And you wanted to stop him, because you want peace. As much as any man here. You risked your life, and everything it has meant, because you saw that this slim chance is better than simply accepting things as they are."

"Might be," Harrys admitted. "What was it ya said, though? What's my life weighed 'gainst peace fer the Barony? Nothin'."

"Not nothing. But you have made a choice, and a sacrifice. I know that. I would reward it."

"Not stayin' here t'dig and grub in the dirt. I didn't want t'do that when I was a lad and I don't Freezin' want t'do it now."

Allystaire said. "I saw you praying at the Pillar of the Arm weeks ago, before the funeral."

The man reached up and scratched at the webwork of scars on his grey-fringed head. "Done it a couplea times since. I..." He swallowed hard. "I never gave much thought to gods n'goddesses. I lipped what I need ta at Braech or Fortune's temple 'fore campaigns, or t'their priests 'fore battles. Never had much use for prayer or temples o'my own time."

"Yet you came to the Mother's Altar of your own free will. Why?"

"Dunno," Harrys admitted. "Just seemed a thing fer the moment."

"Then why did you go back? Why did you come to me about the conspiracy when you *knew* this would end badly for you?"

"I…" The man sighed. "I heard a voice. Think me mad if ya like, but I heard a voice, last time I prayed. Told me I'd a choice t'make. Between what I'd been and what I might be, what was easy, what was right. Lot of it I didn't understand and can't recall. But I knew when Donals come to me what the voice'd meant."

"A woman's voice?"

"Aye," Harrys confirmed.

"Why did you not tell me that to begin with?" Allystaire's mouth fell open incredulously.

"Ya'd think me mad, hearin' voices."

"Harrys," Allystaire said, "do you believe I am what I say I am?"

"Paladin? Seen it, haven't I? Been healed by ya, twice. Don't have much choice but t'believe."

"Then why in the Cold would you find a voice reaching to you in prayer hard for me to believe?"

"Well, you may have seen n'touched yer Goddess. May have tea with 'er n'talk every eve for all I know, but this is all new t'me," he said, chin lifted defiantly.

"Had you led with that, we could have saved a good deal of trouble," Allystaire pointed out.

Harrys sniffed. "Trouble over what?"

"The Order of the Arm, Harrys. I think you are meant for it."

"Knights, eh?" Harrys narrowed his eyes, spat. "I've not got the blood for it."

"It is not blood I am after."

"Didn't ya call me coward today? More'n once?"

"I did not know then what I know now," Allystaire replied. "Even so, have you never yelled such things at a trooper when trying to motivate him?"

Harrys scowled a moment, then assumed a guarded expression, brows furrowed and lips pursed. "Could be." A pause. "What would I have t'do t'prove myself?"

"Train with me, with Norbert. With others as they arrive or volunteer."

"So yer takin' anyone?"

"No," Allystaire replied. "If Mathis Averyn throws himself on the mercy of the Mother, I would still not accept him."

"Donals were a better man in a fight, anyway," Harrys said, absently rubbing his left forearm for a moment.

"Not as good as you, though."

"Known damn few knights who were, n'truth. I always thought I was as good a man as any o'them, lowborn or no. Better'n many."

"Prove that. Live it."

"I'll have no bowin' n'scrapin'."

"Neither will I," Allystaire said. "Yet if I give an order, I will expect it to be obeyed."

"Wha' else?"

"You can never lie to me."

Harrys shrugged. "Knowed that already. What d'ya offer for my service?"

"Very little. Here in Thornhurst, we will do as much as we can for the needs of as many people as we can, you included. Food, clothing, a hearth—these I can promise you, for now. I can give you the chance to prove what you said about the knights you knew. And I can promise you that I will never order you to do anything I would not do myself."

"Not much of an offer," Harrys said. "I could make more wi' a warband."

"And how would you feel about that work? Knowing what you do of war, after a lifetime practicing it."

"Piss poor, I'd say." He looked into the distance, pulled up his old scarf and wrapped it around his neck. "I've done things in my soldierin' days. Things I need scrubbed off, feels like."

"Talk to Mol. The priestess."

"The barefoot lass?"

"The same. She will know what to tell you."

"Not sure I want t'talk to a lass her age 'bout some o'what I done. I'm no murderer nor a rapist, 'fore you think that. None of that."

"Harrys, the Mother offers us a chance to begin new, fresh. Mol is the one to speak to when it comes to," Allystaire struggled for the word, "unburdening yourself."

"Thought this was about takin' 'em on. Isn't that what you said? Bear any burden?"

"Aye." Allystaire smiled. "For that, you come to me. Tomorrow, dawn. Bring a stone."

CHAPTER 16

Shadow's Work

Something nagged at Allystaire for the rest of the day, through some chores, some more light exercise with Gideon and Norbert, through pestering Torvul about when his hammer would be ready only to hear the dwarf's dismissive "soon."

Sunset found Allystaire in the armory, watching Norbert scrub at his mail shirt with a stiff brush, while the shirt itself sat in a basin full of sand. He had his borrowed blade in his lap, was carefully wiping oil from it with absent strokes of a rag.

"Might I ask a question?" Norbert grunted with the effort of lifting his shirt clear of the basin.

"That is a question," Allystaire pointed out. "But yes, you may."

"Why d'ya clean the blade even though ya didn't use it t'day? Same with the mail. How'd it have a chance t'get dirty after we cleaned it yesterday?"

"In the winter, mail will rust the moment you turn your back. Rusted armor kills the man wearing it," Allystaire said, wiping a last spot of oil from the blade and sliding it back into its scabbard, then laying it carefully against a rack. "And cleaning a weapon at day's end is a good way to center your thoughts. Tend to your arms and armor every day, Norbert, unless circumstances truly force you to do otherwise. Your life—and more importantly, the lives of others—will depend upon them. Do not take that lightly."

Allystaire watched Norbert for a moment, saw him brushing away the last bits of sand, pulverized rock, and eggshell, watched him lay the mail shirt carefully upon a table that groaned under other pieces of armor.

"That will do for another day, Norbert. Doubtless Lenoir is waiting to feed you."

Even in the darkness that was falling outside and stealing the light from the shed, Allystaire could tell Norbert was blushing and grinning both by the way he hung his head.

"Go," Allystaire said, shooing him. "Never keep a lady waiting. Eat yourself to sleep. But be ready in the morning. Harrys will probably try to test you."

Norbert took off at a rapid pace. Allystaire slid the bar down, pulled the length of chain tight, and slipped Torvul's lock through its ends, turned the key, and pocketed it.

Missing men, he thought to himself, as he walked to the Inn. *If they simply ran for it, they are likely dead. Perhaps early victims of the conspiracy? Seems unlikely.* It nagged at him, and yet he could find no thread to pull on, nothing to seriously consider.

He kept turning the idea over in his head until he found himself pushing into the Inn's welcoming warmth. The hearthfire was huge and bright, and many lamps were hung, among them Torvul's small and powerful white-beamed lantern.

Even so, there were few enough folk about. The dwarf and Gideon sat at a table together, their food and drink pushed to the side, bowls of stew half-eaten, a loaf untouched, the boy holding forth in a low but excited voice. For once, Torvul didn't interrupt, correct, or interject; he simply listened, rapt.

A few farmfolk shared tables, as did some of Chaddin's men at one. Harrys sat alone in a corner, and, as he expected, Idgen Marte sat at the hearth, a jug of wine on a small table beside her, one long leg thrown over the arm of the chair as she leaned back.

She was already pouring him a cup of wine as he, having shed cloak and hat and scarf, came to sit.

"Good stew tonight," she offered. "Keegan and his lot brought in an old doe they shot, and a long string of rabbits."

"Back to eating meat, then? I thought they had lost their taste for it."

"Some have," she said, handing him his wine. "They want to help feed the village, so they hunt."

"Are they holding up in the winter?" He took a long sip from the cup. It had been heated, and heavily spiced. Where the spices had come from, he wasn't sure, but he was grateful. It hadn't much flavor otherwise. But it sank down his throat in a slow warming roll and he felt it spread to his stomach, reminding him of his hunger, what he'd done that day to earn it.

She nodded. "Look a pack of savages, covered in stinking furs, but they're healthy. I talked to him about comin' inside the walls. They'll not do it unless things get worse."

Allystaire nodded, had a second sip of wine, let it become a large swallow. His eyes drifted into the fire, squinting, and in his head he couldn't help tugging at the problem of the missing men again.

"What?" Idgen Marte leaned forward, dropping both boots to the ground.

"Cold, you read me faster than anyone I have ever known," Allystaire said with a small laugh.

"It's my job, and you're not a subtle man, as you always remind me. You'd be a terrible card player. Come on." She nudged his knee with one finger. "Out with it."

"When he came to me this morning," Allystaire said, "Harrys let slip something about a couple of the Delondeur men gone missing. I had not the time to think on it much earlier, but…"

"Ah," Idgen Marte said, sitting back and setting down her wine. "That."

Allystaire set down his wine as well. "That?"

"Aye, that," she replied, shrugging. She dropped her voice. "If it helps, they're not missing. I know exactly where they are, but it's a bit of a walk and it's cold. They're not going anywhere."

Allystaire eyed her for a moment, brow furrowed, cheeks tensed. "I assume you had a reason."

"Of course I did," Idgen Marte replied. "You think I would've done that lightly?"

"Why?"

"It came from the Voice," Idgen Marte said. "Sit, eat, and listen."

* * *

The only part I don't like about how Cold-damned dark winter gets is how Cold-damned cold it gets, Idgen Marte thought, as she lingered in shadow along the tree line. Even wreathed in shadow, seeing the world as a blur, its only defined spaces where light and dark mingled, she could not escape the cold.

Regular skulking will do, she finally admitted to herself, and released her Gift. The world shifted instantly back into focus. Darkness swallowed her. She put her back to a tree and let her eyes drift nearly shut, waited. Eventually, from the light of the moon, stars, and the distant fires and torches of the Oyrwyn camp, her eyes adjusted and began to pick out shapes.

None of them were moving, no matter how hard she stared at the vague outline of tents and pavilions, tried to will the shadows to separate into men.

Two men. She muttered their names to herself once again. *Chosen Man Rhomand. Sir Luch Chattren. The first is heavy, jowled, grey. Wrestling and boxing champion of his unit. Known toady to the latter, a dangerous man with a sword. As his sort tend to be.*

In her mind, she heard the description in Mol's voice. Sort-of-Mol's voice. Mol had been speaking as the Voice, then, not as an eleven year-old girl. Speaking as the furious avatar of a goddess, with a timeless, powerful anger behind it, and a resignation. She closed her eyes and ran through the conversation again, every moment of it, every spoken word and nuance. She may never have become the minstrel she'd trained to be, but the recall she was taught still served her well.

"It'll look suspicious, two men disappearing at once," Idgen Marte said, when Mol had found her alone in the Temple.

"These two are well known to consort with one another," Mol countered. "It will appear as if they have struck off together. And they have hoarded supplies anyway, though not to leave, to sell dearly to their fellows."

"How do you know this?"

"They confessed to that as well and meant it even less. They will be coming to check on their cache, to add to it. Meet them."

"And do what?"

Mol had turned those large, ageless brown eyes up at her. "The Shadow's work."

"I'm not a murderer, Mol."

"I never suggested you were, Idgen Marte," the girl said, anger melting into a sad resignation. "You will ask them to surrender. To face the justice of their Lady Baroness, or the Lord of Highgate, or the Arm. They will refuse. And what will you do then?"

"The Shadow's work."

The weight of the tree brought her back to the moment. She let her breath out slowly, blowing it down the neck of her coat so no steaming cloud would give her away.

So damned cold. She moved her toes within her boots, her hands inside the sleeves, against her forearms, where she'd tucked them. Winters in Cansebour were pleasantly chilled. Flurries were a novelty. Snow that lasted more than a day in the streets was a generational event.

At least there was the weight of the sword at her side. At least there was that. She pulled her right hand free, wrapped it around the hilt, the leather-wrapped wire smooth, warm, fit to her hand like it was made for it.

It had been, after all.

Torvul had been waiting for her as she left the Temple that night, after praying. He hadn't said a word at first, just extended it to her, held almost reverently in both hands. Slightly longer than the one that had broken months ago, the curve more pronounced, even in the failing light of winter the hilt and the slim silver lines along the scabbard gleamed with deadly beauty. She'd looked at him curiously, and not a little in awe.

"You've got a lot of reach," he said. "Best to maximize it. More curve, more force. Think of it as the thinnest sliver of a crescent moon. One that you see on a night with a lot of shadow."

She had never been a woman given to tears. Less so since she'd taken to the life of a sword-at-hire. But the weight of that sword in her hands, on her hips as she had buckled it on, the mastery of craft that she could feel in its weight, in the hilt, the way it fit at her side and how she knew it would move with her as she walked or ran or blurred from shadow to shadow, what it meant—that brought tears to the corner of her eyes.

Torvul pretended not to notice, and she didn't have to hit him. It was a good decision for both of them. Solemnly, she had bent down, wrapped her arms around his barrel chest, and kissed his cheek. He'd smelled of smoldering coal and hot iron, astringent and earth.

When she stood, she muttered, "If you tell anyone I did that…"

"Too smart for that," he said, waving a huge hand in the air.

"Why now?"

He looked at her then, the weight of his dark, deep-set eyes almost palpable. "You have work to do, Shadow."

"How do you—"

"I'm the Wit. It's my place to know things. Go. May it serve you well."

She was snapped out of her reverie as two shapes broke apart from the greater mass of darkness at the camp. They were dozens of spans away yet, but the moon and starlight was enough too make out their rough form, if no detail. They were coming closer, straight for her.

They stopped. One appeared to kneel, then a light suddenly flared, was quickly dampened. A shuttered lantern.

Rather that use her gift and fade into shadow, she simply stepped, quick and graceful, to the other side of the tree, ducking nimbly under a branch as she went. She made no sound.

Stupid. Ruining their eyes. She turned her head so she saw them peripherally, trying to maintain her own. *Then, they don't have a reason to be afraid. Yet.*

She heard them stomping through the trees then, snapping branches as they went. Then muttered counting, as one of them paced from one tree to another, then to an empty spot. They knelt.

The lantern, though shuttered, leaked enough light to cast shadows around them. She waited.

Branches were shifted, and rocks. A bundle wrapped in heavy cloth was unearthed.

She reached for her Gift. The world slowed, blurred. She leaned forward, was suddenly standing in front of them.

"Good evening, Chosen Man. Sir Luch. Out for a stroll?"

To their credit, they didn't take too much fright. Both of them reached to their belts for weapons that weren't there. Luch drew himself up. He was tall, but thin, with a kind of hard, mean slenderness to him.

"We have liberty of the camp."

"This is beyond the camp. And I don't give a good Cold damn what liberty you think you've been given."

Rhomand went for the lantern, opened the shutters. That only gave her more opportunity. She spoke up again from behind them.

"I don't even care about your little hoard. Not the food you have been sneaking, at any rate. If you are hungry, ask; someone from the village would feed you. The little collection of links, though? And the brass ring with the chip of glass, the little squares of silk, and whatever other treasures you took from that farmhouse? Those I'll need back."

There was a long, guilty silence. She had her hand to her sword.

"Witch! You'll have to do better than that to frighten us." Luch again, imperious, arrogant.

Her reply came with her lips mere inches from his ear, a knife from her sleeve pressed to his neck for just a moment. "How about now?"

He jumped half a foot away, swung an arm wildly. Rhomand whirled, the lantern blurring in the night.

"Her name was Cecile," Idgen Marte said, feeling anger burrowing up in her. "We knew she died in the first attack. She was put into the ground today. She was trying to keep her farm going after her husband died back in the summer, when reavers burned this place to cinders."

"What're you on about?" Rhomand swung the lantern towards where her voice had come from. When he saw nothing, he bent down to pick up a rock. In his huge-knuckled hand, at the end of a thick arm, it would make a formidable weapon. If he had a target.

"Her name was Cecile, and she sent her son inside the walls to be protected, but she wanted to mind her house and her stock no matter what we told her. She threw down the bottle-flare the Wit had given her and then took up a crossbow and put a bolt into your horse," she said, reaching out and flicking at Luch's cloak with the tip of her sword. Finally holding it, not even aware that she'd drawn it, the sword was like a song waiting to be sung, a lute waiting to be played.

"Some peasant did shoot at us, yes," Luch replied, bending down to seize his own stone. "Shame when they involve themselves in war that way. Only one recourse."

"She shot your *horse*," Idgen Marte said, rage lowering her already scratchy voice to a hiss. "What did you do next?"

"Took proper retribution!"

"You detailed your favorite murderer to burn her house, and you killed her as she watched it burn. Not before you plundered what little of value you found in it, of course. Then you crushed her skull and moved on."

"Peasant got what was owed her," Rhomand wheezed. He never stopped moving, stone at the ready, arm cocked to throw or swing. "As will you, demon-bride!"

Circling them was effortless. Unfair. Moving to their rear, then their front, flashing from spot to spot in mid sentence, fooling their ears.

This work is not about what is fair, Idgen Marte reminded herself. She raised her sword.

"I will give you this one chance. Choose whom you'll confess to: Landen Delondeur, the Lord of Highgate, or Allystaire Stillbright. Confess your crime, accept your punishment. Die like men."

"I will not die in this shitstep village," Luch sniffed and impulsively hurled his rock. It thudded off a tree trunk, shaking snow and dead leaves to the ground, skittered off into the night.

"We confessed what'er crimes we felt like t'tha wee girl," Rhomand protested.

"You cannot repent of what you do not regret," Idgen Marte said.

"Peasant lives do not trouble me. And we are unarmed; would you make yourself a murderer as you claim we are?"

"People like Cecile have long clung to shadows to keep them safe. Their hope, their refuge, is in being invisible. If the men with the swords don't notice them, the men with the swords don't kill them," Idgen Marte replied. "I am that shadow. I cannot save them all."

She appeared between them. Her sword flashed, cut Luch's legs out from under him.

"But *I* am a Shadow with a sword."

Rhomand's rock flew at her, but she was already ducking and gliding towards him. Her sword darted out, the flat parallel to the ground. Her stroke was true; it parted his clothing like paper, speared straight through his ribs and into his heart.

She pulled it free so fast and so clean the wound had barely started to bleed. He fell to his knees, dead before they reached the ground. The lantern hit the earth, stood upright, so straight and direct was his fall. His body slumped forward.

She stood over Luch. "I gave you a chance," she said, lowering the blade to his throat.

"Were I armed," he panted, "this would be different. Is this how your Goddess metes justice, paladin?"

"Allystaire is the paladin," Idgen Marte answered him. "He is the hero, the knight, the holy man of song and story. He would have tried you, hung you. Mayhap you could have goaded him to a fight." She shook her head and said, "He would not have killed you from ambush, in the dark. But he is bound to be a legend; I am but a shadow."

The very tip of the sword took his throat, and his last words were lost in a choked gurgle.

She bent and cleaned her sword in the snow, drying it on the inside of Luch's cloak. She bent and grasped the bag they'd hidden. In it was a meager pile of brass that barely glinted with silver. Scraps of silk and other kinds of cloth. A few pieces of jewelry. Such poor treasures for men to have died for.

"And yet you died for them as well, Cecile," Idgen Marte muttered. "For them and for the life you were trying to rebuild. I am sorry I was not there for you then. I am sorry that all I can offer you and our Mother is cold and meager justice. I hope She has gathered you close in the next world."

The Shadow lowered her head as she sheathed her newly blooded sword. For the second time in a night, tears threatened the corners of her eyes.

She hefted the bag in her hand, gripped it hard.

The tears didn't fall.

* * *

Allystaire was silent for a long, drawn-out moment after she'd finished relaying the story. A tray with a bowl of stew, a fresh loaf, and a small bowl of butter sat untouched at his elbow.

"You're not usually one to let food linger," Idgen Marte said, for lack of anything better to say. "I'm sure you're thinking of all the ways this was wrong."

He held up one hand, palm out. "What did you do with the bodies?" His voice was barely above a whisper.

"All of that, and your first question—"

"Please answer me." With his voice so quiet, she couldn't quite judge how much anger was in the tone.

"I, ah, may have requested Keegan and his lads take care of it."

Allystaire nodded. "Why did you not come to me?"

"It was my task," Idgen Marte replied. "Appointed to me by the Voice. And in some ways by the Mother Herself."

"Why not force them to confess to me, or to Chaddin?"

"You hadn't gone making suggestions yet," Idgen Marte pointed out. "And their crime was the vilest, and it was against one of ours. Because she shot a horse."

"Do not mistake me," Allystaire said. "If I knew of their crimes, no matter what Landen or Chaddin said, I would have seen them dead."

"You could've known about their crimes," she pointed out. "All you'd have to do is ask."

"Think of where that leads," Allystaire said, shaking his head. "Am I to question every man that passes through Thornhurst? Interrogate every person I contact, and slay them if I deem them a black enough sinner? I cannot wield Her Gifts summarily. That would be tyranny."

"You gave Sir Miles a pretty summary judgment, if I recall."

"He had tried to kill a child, *after* I had surrendered. He was a mad dog and I suffer no lack of sleep for having put him in the ground."

"Then we ought to understand one another perfectly," Idgen Marte said.

"Why could you not tell me?"

"Had I told you that I was off to kill two of Landen's men, you'd have wanted to know why. Then you would've insisted on coming with me, calling them out and killing them properly, publicly. And what would that have done t'your plan for Landen and Chaddin?"

Allystaire sighed, turned to the plate at his elbow and absently ripped off a hunk of bread. He swiped it across the butter, stuffed it into his mouth, and chewed thoughtfully.

Good sign, Idgen Marte thought. *He's not too angry to eat.*

Finally, Allystaire nodded. "You are right. It would have ruined any chance of my suggestion working." He raised a brow. "It still may not, you know."

"We will see that it does."

"What if it all melts away with the snow, as soon as they leave?"

"You are a better judge of people than that," she assured him. "And Landen needs support if she hopes to hold her seat."

"A Baron's seat can change someone fast, and rarely for the better. Still," he said, "I think Landen saw the truth of what her father became, and it frightened her. She will sue for peace. Innadan will be willing to listen, at least. Oyrwyn, though…"

"I have taken steps in that direction," Idgen Marte said. "Oyrwyn will find campaigning difficult to manage in the coming year."

"So many unknowns linger over this. How will the Sea Dragon's Temple respond?"

"They cowered in fear during the battle. They fear Gideon."

"I do not think that the Choiron Symod cowers," Allystaire replied. "He wisely stayed out of Gideon's reach, yes. Do not doubt that he is thinking of a way to counter him, to fight back. And there may be sorcerers yet to trouble us."

"Cold," she swore. "Eat your dinner. Let us get through the winter first. Then send Landen and Chaddin back to the Dunes, and Garth and your sister off to Highgate, and Cerisia off to the Vineyards, and then we can start looking for the next blow."

"I would rather be delivering the next blow than waiting for it," Allystaire replied. "But that depends on knowing who our enemies are and where they will be, and we cannot, in truth, say that we do." He pulled the bowl of stew into his hand, cradling it in one large palm, heedless of the warmth of it. He shoveled in a few spoonfuls, eyes going distant as he chewed hastily.

"If it's guidance you need, go to the Temple. Pray," Idgen Marte said. "I can't tell you what to do next and we both know you'd not likely want t'listen even if I did."

He spooned more stew into his mouth quickly, nodding appreciatively at the bowl, then at her suggestion. "I think I may," Allystaire said. "I have not tried to speak to Her since…" He trailed off, set the bowl down.

Idgen Marte leaned forward. "Since *what?*"

Allystaire knew the flush in his cheeks was going to betray him. "Since I recovered."

"Don't be a prude, Ally." She smiled. "She surely isn't."

"It feels wrong to speak of it," Allystaire replied, a kind of wonder lighting his eyes. "And I do not think I know the words."

"That's why you haven't prayed?"

"Her presence has always been overwhelming," he said. "Even Her voice in my thoughts. And now it is compounded."

"Pull yourself together," Idgen Marte said, slapping his knee. "If you need guidance, go seek it. Be a man about it. Don't act like some squire who's just had his first tug."

He sighed, seized what remained of the bread, and took a bite, nodding. "You are right. Tonight."

"Go now," Idgen Marte said, "before the Temple fills with folk looking to sleep there." She grinned wickedly. "You'll not want to go waking them all up."

* * *

Mol was waiting for him at the top of the Temple steps. She swung the door open for him with a light touch of her hand, then stepped delicately through after him.

While a few of the village folk seemed to be preparing for sleep, or talking quietly, or even sharing food here and there, the Temple wasn't nearly as full as it would be in a few turns.

Before he knew it, Mol's hand had slipped up into his and she was guiding him forward gently.

Her steps barely made a sound on the laid stones of the Temple's floor. His sounded like a tattoo upon the rim of a great drum. When they reached the altar, Mol suddenly took his hand in both of hers, and looked up at him.

The naiveté of the girl he'd rescued so many months ago was, he thought, completely worn away. Her features still betrayed her endless curiosity and her insight, but there was a resigned sadness in her face that pained him to look upon.

"Oh, child," he started.

"Shhh." She shook her head, faintly. "I am not a child anymore, for all that I am only a few months older than when you rescued me. In truth, I am not sure what I am. There is so much I know without having *learned*. So much I simply know to say, or to do. It is confusin', sometimes."

The slight slip into her rustic accent tugged at him. He knelt, put his arm around her shoulder.

Allystaire half expected her to cry, or to go on speaking. Instead she threw her arms hard around his neck and then stepped back. With him on one knee, they were practically eye to eye, though in falling night hers were only dark pools above her cheeks.

"Much is given to us. Much must be taken," Mol said. "All of us have sacrificed. If I must give up girlhood a few years early, it is not so great a thing."

"I have gained everything," Allystaire said. "If my sacrifice is only pain and hardship."

Mol silenced him with a finger placed upon his lips. "Speak with the Mother. I cannot know if She will reply. The winter is not Her season, and She was greatly taxed by the battle. Even more so by what she did afterwards."

"Do you mean my recovery?"

"Did She not tell you Herself that it was forbidden to encroach upon Death's demesne?"

The words were like a cold shock in Allystaire's gut, but Mol was already backing away, then vanishing into the shadows that swallowed the Temple's interior.

Allystaire looked at the five pillars. He couldn't make out the symbols on any of them, except for that of the Arm, directly in front of him: a hammer.

He knelt again, on both knees this time, tried to ignore the jolt of pain that brought with it.

Goddess, he thought. *I have set into motion something I am uncertain of. I think, I believe, that if we pursue the course correctly we can bring the peace I promised to Your people. I do not know. If you have any guidance, please lend it to me.* His thought trailed off as his eyes focused intently on the hammer graven into the stone before him.

There was no answer.

He swallowed hard. *Goddess, I do not ask that you come take my fears from me, or my self doubts, or that you tell me what you would have me do. If I am wrong, if I have judged the men I chose wrongly the consequences would be staggering.*

Allystaire. Her voice was faint, like an echo coming to him across a chasm, but the sound of it in his head was like a balm. *I cannot make your choices for you, nor would I. I told you once that I would not have chosen a man of lesser conviction. I can only guide and influence you upon the path. The steps that carry you forward are yours.*

I know, Goddess. I know. I just seek that very guidance.

Allystaire. There was the suggestion of Her touch along the back of his neck, Her fingers stroking his skin. He shivered audibly.

Suddenly he was no longer in the Temple, but standing in that other place where the only factor of existence was Her presence. She filled all of his senses, all at once, so powerfully that he wanted to weep for the love of Her.

Even so, the radiance that typically surrounded Her form was softer, more muted. She was almost indistinct, fuzzy at the edges.

"The battle taxed me," She said, her voice just as thin as it had been. "As did my final Gift to you."

Before he could help himself, Allystaire swallowed hard. "Final?"

She smiled sadly. "If I were to bring you to me again, My Knight, as fully as I did, you would wish never to return." Her hand cupped his cheek; his knees nearly melted beneath him, for all that it seemed Her hand didn't quite touch him.

Allystaire nodded. He resisted the urge to turn his face into Her palm, to put his lips against Her hand. Perhaps She felt the tension in him, for Her hand dropped away.

"There are Rules that govern even Me and My Sisters and Brothers, that have always governed all of us as we rose and fell, were forgotten or revived."

Before he could even pose the question, She shook Her head, scattering diffuse beams of sunlight across Allystaire's vision.

"I cannot explain them to you. That is Forbidden."

"What can you tell me, then?"

"That My Gifts will not abandon you, never, so long as you do not abandon me. That you should speak with Gideon when you return."

He swallowed. "Am I doing your will? The Order of the Arm, the peace treaty?"

"You are doing your will in My service, Allystaire, which is what I called you to do."

He nodded. "This has become so much more than finding one band of reavers."

"And yet it is the same. The desire for justice, the anger within you at what had become of the poor and the weak, your determination—they are the same."

She stepped close to him then, enveloping Allystaire's sight so thoroughly that he had to close his eyes or be blinded.

"I wish I could bring you to me, My Knight, as I did before. If you truly wished to leave your labors behind you, if you asked that of me as some final boon, in truth, I do not think I could refuse you."

"And you know I cannot ask that," Allystaire said. "It is my fondest desire. But it would be cowardly to leave them behind because I am afraid to lead them forward. It would not be…"

"Knightly," She said, finding the word before he could. "And that, Allystaire Stillbright, is why I love you."

She leaned forward to kiss him, but the sizzling power of Her lips on his flesh was a pale imitation of what it had been after the Longest Night; still it was enough to buckle his knees and tingle his spine. "The well of my love is bottomless, My Arm," she whispered as She drew away. "And anything may be drawn from it."

With those words, the radiance around Her began to fade, and suddenly Allystaire felt stone digging painfully into his knees. He stood with a grunt, trying to force down the disappointment at finding himself back in a plain, stone-walled building, with the dark and cold of winter pressing in upon it. Along the gold-flecked red stone of the altar, there was a flicker of the radiance he longed for. A trick of the uncertain light, perhaps, but he pressed a hand down upon the stone, felt its warmth, tried to gather it into himself so that he could carry it with him into the dark.

CHAPTER 17

Theory

"**O**ne more time now," Torvul said as he and Gideon walked headed out of the Inn, their neglected dinners finally eaten, as Allystaire spoked with Mol at the altar of the distant Temple. "And go slowly. Pretend y'were explaining it to Allystaire. Use small words and not too many of 'em all at once."

His breath steamed out into the air in a great cloud, but the dwarf didn't mind the cold much. *Better the cold than the heat,* he thought absently as the silent boy beside him gathered his thoughts.

"I said I think I have discovered something about magic that no one else has."

"Well, everybody who touches it thinks that at some point, boy."

"I am not everyone, Torvul. I have contended with *gods.*" The boy let that pronouncement hang in the air for a moment, then said, "Well, with fragments of them, or what part of a god is touched by the prayer of an empowered servant."

"Ya've a point there," the dwarf admitted, rubbing at his chin. He felt the stubble there, thought of the razor and the bowl in his wagon. *Time to sharpen it.* "Come t'my wagon. We'll have a jot of *ikthaumaunavit* while we talk."

"I don't enjoy spirits, but we'll walk and talk where you will."

The dwarf set a quick pace, swinging his short legs from his hips with the ease and confidence of a man returning home. Gideon kept pace with him, taking shorter, smaller strides.

At the wagon, a simple flick of his forefinger, followed by a thumb and smallest finger squeeze at its edges, and the lock that held the door fast dropped into his hand.

Gideon had to duck to make it through the door but could stand comfortably once he passed under it. Both of them felt a small jolt as they crossed the threshold, an undeniable twinge of power that brought with it a feeling of belonging.

The wagon was pleasantly warm; a small stove at the far end of the boxy interior emitted the heat, but no smoke. Torvul puttered up to it swiped his hand across it, muttered a word. "I'm going t'work while you talk. Have some preparations t'make. Sit on the bed."

Gideon nodded and slid open a long cupboard door to his left. Crammed inside it was a tangle of blankets and pillows. He was able to wedge himself into it, but only after lifting out the folding table and stool that stacked within it.

Torvul's home was a model of efficiency that way. No space within it was wasted, and most of it had more than one use. There were cabinets and racks built all along the meeting of wall and roof, filled with glass bottles, earthenware jugs, tightly capped metal cellars, and pouches. Likewise, hooks and ties descended from the ceiling, many holding bundles of drying plants. Torvul grabbed a few here and there, and a copper-bottomed pot from a hook on the side of the stove itself, and began picking the leaves away and dropping them in, muttering to himself.

"What's that?" Gideon had to lean forward to keep his head away from the edge of the cupboard-bed.

"Ah? Oh." The dwarf coughed. "Just thinkin' on memory stone, the making of them. These," the dwarf said, testing the heat of the stove's surface with one finger, "were fired in the last working Stonesung Kiln in the Homes. I never saw it, of course, but my master had."

"It saddens me when the knowledge of something goes out of the world," Gideon offered.

"Saddens? Yes, if you're talking about the knowledge of a recipe for stew or a pretty little song, or the memory of a war, all its tragedies and indignities. When it's the knowledge my people had, it's a Freezing tragedy, Gideon. A crime. Sad doesn't…" Torvul felt his voice deepening in sudden, frustrated anger, but stopped as the boy held up one hand.

"I did not mean to stir such memory, Torvul. I am sorry." He bit his bottom lip, then said carefully, "What if the making of them was not necessarily entirely forgotten?"

"It is. There's no Stonesong left in the world, boy, or if there is, we know not where t'find it."

"Well, that's not relevant to what I mean," Gideon said. "Let me try and explain again, please."

"Fine." The dwarf set his copper pot on the stove, picked up a skin, uncorked it, and squeezed a clear stream of liquid into the pot along with the leaves he'd added. The strong smell of pure, neutral spirit filled the wagon.

"When the sorcerers trapped me during the battle, I didn't understand what had happened. I only knew I was free of physical cares, of mortal worries. I was a being of pure Will. The world fell away from me. Do you understand?"

"Aye," the dwarf said as he put the skin back on its hook, then went to a rack of tools and pulled free a tiny silver balance. He looked up at a rack of metal cellars and deftly pulled one free with his dexterous fingers. "They made ya forget yourself. It's a trick they're fond of."

"No," Gideon said. "It isn't. It was not a simple spell. They *unmoored* me. Set me adrift from the world. And in that state, while I existed, I could work nothing upon the world. No act of Will. Do you understand?"

The dwarf dipped a tiny silver spoon into the uncapped cellar, the smell of heating spirits now competing with that of rain-wet earth. "No."

"Without a connection to the world, physical, and, I expect, emotional, magic is not *possible*. It cannot be worked. Think on your own craft," Gideon said, all in a rush. "Without your home, without your songs, it began to fail you, yes?"

"We dwarfs have long known that our sense of home, of community, was the source of our power," Torvul said. "This isn't new."

"Please, bear with me. The sorcerers give themselves over to magical power. They sacrifice their very being to it. Body and soul. They literally erode, over time. Why doesn't it happen right away? And a second, related question: why do you never see a sorcerer who has taken this power into himself give himself over to research, or to a quiet life? Why do they interfere in the world?"

The dwarf carefully weighed the specks of rare earth he laid on the balance with a tiny, precisely cone-shaped ingot, peering at it through a squinted eye.

"What're ya driving at?"

"What brought me back to the world, to myself, to the mortal shell I *needed* in order to work my Will, was Allystaire reaching out towards me and," he cleared his throat, "calling me son. It forced me to remember myself. My time with him, and the rest of you. What do sorcerers cling to? Wealth is practically meaningless to them, as they can achieve almost whatever they wish without it. After the first few years in their power, the pleasures of the flesh are meaningless as well, as their bodies become effectively sexless. By the time they are Iriphet's age, not only do they not need to eat, drink, or sleep, they *can't*. So why do they not simply fade away?"

A straight-edged file of silver in one hand, Torvul scraped the flecks of powdery dirt into a mortar and pestle made of blue-veined stone. "I imagine you have some thoughts on the answer."

"I do," Gideon said. "I think power, the use of it, becomes an end in itself. Why would Bhimanzir come to the Baronies? What is to be gained by it? Only the exercise of their power. They interfere and meddle and plot because they *must*. It is a lust for power that drives them to sorcery in the first place, and once they attain the power they seek, they must keep driving after something. If they do not, their very ability to use their power will vanish. And so will they."

"Well," Torvul offered, "that doesn't help us kill them." Using a matching pestle, he gently ground away at the substance inside the mortar.

"Torvul, this swings both ways. The more one has to live for, in short, the more power they can bring into the world. And I think," Gideon said carefully, "that with Her help…we could bring *all of it* into the world."

The pestle dropped from Torvul's fingers, clattering on the worktable that folded down from the wall of the wagon, and then bouncing to the floor.

"You're mad," the dwarf said as he bent to pick it up.

Gideon's face was intense, his cheeks drawn, eyes wide, leaning forward as he went on in a rush. "The sorcerers take children from their parents. Somehow they can sense the Will within them, the ability to tap into the power. But there is no telling how powerful they might be until they start to turn pubescent. Perhaps one in five taken children is allowed to live at that point because their masters are able to determine just how strongly they can reach across the Barrier. Now imagine that there is no Barrier."

The dwarf's eyes widened. He dropped the pestle again, but at least it landed in the mortar. "Then every gifted child would—"

"Be able to tap into the magic. To exert their will. And not only children, anyone that is so gifted." Gideon swallowed once. "Allystaire put weapons into the hands of common men, who would otherwise never wield them, in order to defend themselves against their oppressors. Now imagine if folk have this? What happens to the press gang that comes for their sons? The reavers that come for their daughters? The sorcerers themselves?"

"You would loose who knows how many sorcerers upon the world."

"Would there be a risk of that? Yes, I'll admit it. But many of the manifestations of it would be minor, like the odd hedge wizard one hears of, a strange old man who tells uncanny fortunes, or a village wise woman whose poultice and compress are a bit more potent than any other. And if we could find the larger powers, we could guide them."

"The Order of the Will," Torvul breathed. His knees wobbled, and he clutched at the edge of his table. "That's what you're after."

"Perhaps," Gideon said. "Eventually. I do not think any would be gifted in precisely the way that I am. Who knows what they might be, in time?"

"This is a massive idea, lad. Are you quite sure it's possible? And if it is, are you sure it's something you ought t'do?"

Gideon thought a moment, then gave his head a quick shake, his eyes dropping to the wagon's smooth, well-aged floorboards. "I am not certain that I can do it, no." Then he lifted his head to meet the dwarf eye to eye. "But if I can, then I am certain that I must."

"Why? What makes you so certain?"

"Because we are not here to defeat some sorcerers and a single power-mad nobleman in a battle to save some few score souls," Gideon said. "We are to here to change the world." He pursed his lips for a moment, and continued on. "The Goddess has said that in this world, power is too often an accident of birth."

"The kind o'power you're talkin' about would still be an accident."

"But it would be more widely distributed," Gideon replied. "I do not know what causes someone to be born with the ability to exert their Will as magic. I doubt anyone does. A poor child is as likely to be born with it as a rich child."

"It's dangerous."

"Change always is," Gideon replied fiercely. "And what are we here to do, if not change the world?"

"For the better," Torvul said.

"And if someone was born with the gift that allowed them to recreate memory stones, Torvul—a source of heat that requires so no fuel, that'll never burn down a cottage or kill a child with smoke if a chimney is stopped up, that frees turns out of a crofter's day spent at monotonous labor—imagine it being available to the poor. Would we not then have changed the world for the better?"

Torvul lifted a hand. "It's not true that it requires no fuel. They needed fuel for the makin' of them, vast amounts of it. They don't get hot enough to work metals or other crafts. And no one's Stonesinging a Kiln ever again. But," the dwarf conceded, turning once again to his mortar and pestle, and beginning to grind again at the substance he'd tipped into it. "You've a point. It might do great good in the world. If it were possible."

"I feel that it is. I think I cannot do it myself," Gideon said. "I think it might require all of us. Maybe," he shrugged, threw a hand out uncertainly, "something else. I know not what."

"Well," Torvul said, "if the Wit and the Will can't figure it, no one can." He carefully poured the contents of his stone bowl into the pot that now boiled on his stove. The wagon's interior filled with a strong, rich scent: rain-turned earth and something powerfully herbal growing from it.

A silver whisk with a wooden handle so worn it was almost black was suddenly in Torvul's hands, laying delicately in his fingers, lightly scraping the pot as he gave it three quick revolutions. Then he lifted the pot from the stove, setting it on a small block of stone laid into the wooden foldout table.

Torvul held his hand over the steaming pot and sung, as quietly as his powerful bass rumble could manage, three quick notes. The liquid inside cooled instantly, the steam dying before its first-risen streamers disappeared against the ceiling.

"What're you making?"

"A little something for the planting. It might be months away but I like to be prepared," Torvul said. "We'll have no trouble feeding ourselves through the next year. Stones Above, we'll have no trouble feeding half the damned Barony if it comes to it." As he talked, he bent beneath the table and opened a cupboard, pulling free a long-necked, wide-bottomed glass decanter.

"I see. Is the crystal a bit ostentatious for it?"

"First, boy, if you're goin' to do things, do them with style." The dwarf's tool rack produced another silver implement, a funnel, which he set carefully in the decanter's neck. "And second, it needs to sit in glass for, oh, three days at least. Ensures potency, as the glass is more energy porous than the stoneware I'll eventually store it in."

"You're making that up," Giden said flatly.

"I never would," Torvul answered, deadpan. Then he touched a finger to the glass and sung another quiet note, held it for a long moment. The liquid inside turned a luminescent green, then darkened.

"There's no such thing as energy-porous material."

Torvul turned to Gideon, holding up a hand. "You know a great deal, especially for a boy o' tender years. But ya don't know everything, and I'm one of the last dwarfs in the wide world who studied with a Master Stonesinger."

"Fine," Gideon said, "then explain."

"I'll do that," Torvul said, setting his tools back on their rack, sweeping imaginary dust off his table. Then he picked up the balance and roped it carefully into its niche, did the same with the mortar and pestle, then folded up the table against the wall, securing it in place with quick snaps of his wrist. "After I have a drink."

He reached for a jug hung from a ceiling hook and uncorked it with the well-practiced flick of a thumb, poured a measure into his mouth.

Gideon folded his arms and waited.

"Finally," the dwarf said with a deep and satisfied sigh. "Now, we're dealing here with a domestic kind of philtre, yes? It can't do any harm, and we're tryin' to direct its energy wide and far. So we want it t'gather as much potency as it can. By putting it in well-cut glass for some time, we're allowing in as much of the energy of my *home* as it can gather. And since my home," he added, pointing to the wagon, "is set within my wider community now, it's absorbing a bit of every song, of every bit of magic worked, of all the energy that goes into making this place home. That'll leak in through the glass. Now," the dwarf went on, wetting his lips from the jug again, and assuming the tone of a lecturer. "Too long and it'll start to leak out—since the glass is porous it'll go either way, once a certain balance is reached, anyway. So after some time has passed, I'll store it in a tightly sealed earthenware crock. Less'll leak out of it that way. Very little, in fact."

"If this was true, there'd be ways to measure it. Instruments."

"There were," Torvul said. "In the homes. I don't have them and I don't know how to make them. I don't even know what they were, or what they looked like," he added. "I've only got the wisdom passed t'me by a dwarf who was damn near three hundred years old, and that was in between him drinking himself t'sleep and weeping for what he'd lost." Torvul said, stabbing a finger into the air. "*Weeping.* A dwarf possessed of tunneling wisdom and the learning and power of a thousands-year-old craft, reduced to a sobbing child. I don't take what wisdom I did manage to glean from him lightly."

"Tunneling?" Gideon cocked his head to the side.

Torvul grunted, took another swig. "Your folk build up. You say towering. What direction d'ya think we built? Besides," he added, "think about how much harder it is. What's stoppin' ya from building upwards, eh? Air and weight. Try and build down into the earth sometime. Heh." Another swig. "I think that's why Master Ochsringuthringolprine wept, really."

Gideon said nothing, only raised a brow.

"Early in his life, he literally moved mountains. The inside of 'em, at any rate. And as he died, he couldn't even make a wheel turn without horses hitched to it."

The dwarf set the jug down, sighed. "Pardon my melancholy, lad. It's of no use to anyone." He eyed Gideon, knitted his cragged brows. "We need t'tell Allystaire of your thoughts."

"I know," Gideon replied. "And Mol, and Idgen Marte. Allystaire is so caught up with his new squire."

"Don't be envious. He'll teach you anythin' he'll teach that boy, and more besides, if you let him. Go along for more of the exercise."

"I've no wish to be a knight."

"I know, and so does he. Yet some running, some work with a staff or a bow, that'll do you no harm."

"I can defend myself."

"And yet I recall some crazy bastard of an Islandman burying his axe in the back of one of the sorcerers and ending him." The dwarf quickly unfolded the stool Gideon had taken from the bed and set himself down on it. "Did we ever figure out who that was or what he was doin' there?"

Gideon shook his head. "No."

"What'd you do with the body? Bury it with the others?"

"Aye."

"Far as I know Islandmen believe they need to be buried within sight and hearing of running water," Torvul said, "if not directly in it. Allows their soul t'travel t'the sea, to Braech."

"I did not know that," Gideon said. "But I was not well versed in the superstitions of the region before being brought here."

"Ya'd still call it superstition, boy? Really? I think you'd know better than that."

Gideon nodded meekly. "The habits of my raising stay with me, Torvul. I didn't mean it dismissively. Besides," his eyes went distant as he thought, "I have been thinking over that moment. I do not think that Islandman needs to fear what awaits him in the next life. Braech's eye was upon him, but...so was the Mother's." He frowned. "I am not sure what to make of Braech's presence at the battle."

"Why?"

"His servants fear me, and they stayed well away. But I know of your encounters with them prior to finding me. Assassins? Poison? That does not seem His way, from what little I do know."

"Well," Torvul said, crossing his thick arms over his barrel chest, "a screamin' berzerker chargin' straight to his death, axe in hand, sounds a bit like the Temple o'the Sea Dragon t'me."

"That's hardly comforting," Gideon said. "Assassins come singly, or perhaps in twos and threes. But main, brute force could overwhelm us, and quickly."

"You sound just like Allystaire," Torvul grunted.

"Is that a compliment?"

"Yes and no. It is, in that for all I jibe at him, he's perceptive. Sees into things quickly. It's not, because mostly what he sees are the darkest edges of things, the ways they can go wrong, their capacity for harm and horror."

Gideon was silent a moment. "If we don't look for the darkest places, we cannot bring light to them."

"Again. Just like him."

"That doesn't make me, or him, wrong."

"No," Torvul agreed. "It doesn't." The dwarf stood. "To the Temple then, for the song of dusk. D'ya want t'lay out your idea for Allystaire alone, or have a go at all of them at once?"

"I'd rather explain it the once," Gideon said, as he stood, reaching for the coat and hat he'd taken off upon entering.

"One more thing," Torvul said as he unlatched the wagon door, letting some of the interior's gathered warmth out. "If you tell Allystaire what I said about him not bein' wrong, you'll regret it. Turn all your hair bright green."

"I shave my head."

"I can make it grow thrice as fast into the bargain, and melt your shaving knife. You'll be a shaggy green monster, the terror o'the village lasses."

Gideon quickly descended the stairs, Torvul following after, locking the wagon behind him. "Speakin' of village lasses, boy, are there any—"

"No," Gideon said quickly.

"Why not?"

"I've not time for that, and it would be too dangerous."

"Stop," the dwarf said, raising a hand. "Mind your own words to me, just this eve. The more you're connected to the world, the more of your Will you can exert upon it, eh? Didn't Allystaire say somethin' to that effect weeks ago?"

"He did," Gideon answered. "The more you love the world, the harder it is to tear it to pieces."

"Listen to him then," Torvul replied. "Learn t'love the world. He'll not thank himself if you turn into who he was before the Goddess found him. And what you just said—well I didn't know him then, but I think it likely those are the kind of thoughts Allystaire Coldbourne would've had."

"It doesn't make what I said any less true. It would be dangerous."

Torvul clapped the boy on the back with an open hand, hard enough to just knock his breath away. "World's dangerous, lad. Love it anyway. Come along then."

CHAPTER 18

Snow Melting on the Green

No matter how dark the night or how cold the winter, eventually the sun will begin to drive them away.

And so it did, slowly at first, the snow piled on village greens all over the Baronies beginning to melt. The days when the piles dwindled noticeably were often a time of small celebrations, miniature festivals where chores were eased, barrels were rolled out, and instruments recovered from dusty cases.

The celebrations focused on the passing of the most dangerous season and the joy of surviving it. A bit of fun before the backbreaking, monotonous work of spring began. Fields would need clearing, plowing, and planting. Fences, houses, sheds, and byres would need repairs.

But in the Baronies, this first hint of winter's end had long since brought with it a kind of fear, a breath held all over the countryside. For forty years, spring had brought with it one inescapable fact.

War.

* * *

"Snow's meltin' on the green," Tibult said, standing at the edge of the doorway of the large cowshed he, Mattar, and the others had made their home in for the past month and more.

Mattar lumbered up behind him. "No green here," he rumbled. "Just a farm."

Tibult turned, wincing as his weight touched down on his still-mangled hip. "It's a sayin', Mattar. Don't have to be a green n'front of us fer it t'be true, aye?" He swallowed. "I think it's time t'get movin' again."

"I'll get 'em up," Mattar said. "Ya know…we were lucky t'get Waltin this far, I don't know we'll get 'im 'round the mountains."

"We will. Let me go talk t'Jonas, see if he can be persuaded to pass us some bread or th'like." With that, Tibult swung himself out the door, leaning heavily on the stout stick he'd used as a replacement for the crutch he'd tossed into Londray Bay. His leg and hip weren't as bad as they'd been on the crutch, but as the winter had passed and he'd taxed himself doing whatever chores he could, along with Mattar and the others with them who could work, he'd felt it more and more.

Jonas was waiting for him at the door. The old soldier-turned-farmer was looking critically at the horizon, sweeping his grey eyes towards the distant peaks of the Thasryach to the north.

"'Spect ya'll be movin' on now," Jonas said. His voice was gruff, raspy, ruined by years of yelling orders and smoking from a huge bowled pipe. Even now he was pulling the latter from a pouch at his waist, absently packing it with a thumb and forefinger.

"Aye," Tibult said. "Can't thank you enough for what you done fer us, Bannerman."

"Ah, I left that behind me a long time ago. Besides, I was a footman. Never known one o'yer horse troopers t'salute me proper, not matterin' how green his arse was." He set the pipe in his mouth, sucked on it unlit. "I was happy t'take ya in. Plenty o'work needed doin'. Still will if ya've a mind t'stay."

"We've got t'be on," Tibult said, thinking of that one brief taste of healing compassion he'd once had. And in truth, Jonas had been inventing work for them ever since they'd shown up at his farm in the midst of a snowstorm, wearing ragged tabards or old signs, clutching sticks to walk with, and leading Waltin by a rope tied around his waist.

"T'Thornhurst, eh? Hope yer tales are true then. If ya come back, though, I'll find work for your hands t'do. Even the blind fella," he said. "Never seen socks n'long woolens darned so fast."

Tibult smiled. "If ya could see yer way clear t'havin' some extra bread baked—"

"I'll do more," Jonas said. "I'll give ya bread, also flour and a big side o' gammon, a small barrel of good fat and another o'brandy."

"It's too much, Jonas."

The older man tsked around his pipe. "No, it ain't. When ya get there, y'tell this paladin about m'farm and m'family and that there's good men left in the world, men willin' t'do a turn for strangers 'cause they can. And when ya done that…ask his Mother's blessin' on us. 'Specially m'sons. We've escaped the press so far…" He trailed off and shrugged as smoke gathered above his head.

"I know," Tibult said. "Every spring a father has t'wonder."

"Aye. Now go, get yerselves ready. I'll 'ave the dray n'horse ready in a bit. You'll bring it back t'me now, when your hip is better, aye?"

"I will, Jonas," Tibult said. "I promise. I swear it."

"Don't swear," the man said, rolling his lips around his pipestem. "But if ya can get word that ya made it safe, I'd appreciate it."

"That I will do." Tibult extended his hand for a shake. Jonas clasped it and said, "Brother o'Battle."

Tibult grimaced lightly, nodded, but only said, "Brother." Then he turned and began limping back to the barn on his stick. If he could've run, he would have. The snows were melting on the green and the roads were clearing, and the paladin and his healing Goddess awaited.

* * *

Allystaire, Gideon, Norbert, and Harrys were all running north along the road leading up from Thornhurst when they saw the wagon. Headed south, with a few riders alongside it, trundling slowly along the road, but making progress nonetheless.

They glided to a halt, Allystaire in the lead, and one by one, dropped the stones from their shoulders, letting them thump heavily on the road.

"Peddler?" Norbert's voice carried optimism in it.

Harrys was hitching at his belt, itching for weapons that weren't there; instead he bent and hefted the stone he'd just dropped, propping it back onto his shoulder but keeping his right hand bent under it, as if ready to hurl it.

"One way to find out," Allystaire said, privately glad of the break and trying not to show it. He forced himself to stand upright, not to lower his hands to his knees, and to try to take in the sharp air at a reasonable pace instead of gulping it. He turned to the boy at his side. "Gideon?"

The lad nodded, closed his eyes for a long moment. Then suddenly they snapped back open. "One wagon with a man on it, four riders. Some small arms, but a peddler, I think. The wagon practically groans with wares. One of the men is a minstrel. Lute case on his back."

"Well," Allystaire said, "the roads must be well, and a peddler comes to Thornhurst for the first time in months. It will do everyone good."

"Snow's melting on the green," Norbert said brightly as he bent to pick his rock back up.

"Come on, lads," Allystaire said, hefting his own rock again. "Back to Thornhurst to spread the news. Quick now."

By the time the wagon and its riders reached the village's northern wall, Allystaire, Norbert, Harrys, and Gideon were waiting to meet them on horseback.

The latter had spread the news fast by letting Mol know even as they'd run back into the village, and the Voice had shared the news far and wide. Casks were being rolled out of the Inn even as they rode past, and Timmar had a wide grin on and a prybar in his hand.

As always, Allystaire turned his hands more practically, saddling Ardent and the other mounts, including his own palfrey for Gideon, Harrys's dun courser, and the most docile gelding in the village's stables for Norbert.

Lightly armed, Allystaire had told them, and meant it, though now as a wagon and horsemen hove into view, he wished for more than the iron-studded gloves on his hands and the sword on his back. He eyed the others; Norbert had his bow and arrows cased and slung on the wrong side of his horse, and had his reins drawn across it, pinning it against the saddle. Allystaire frowned, made a note of it. Harrys had thrust his falchion into his belt. When Allystaire had offered Gideon a dagger from the armory, the boy had frowned, but taken it anyway.

"Remember," Allystaire muttered, "we are a welcoming committee, not an interrogating committee." Then he cleared his throat and addressed the slowing wagon and Ardent stamped at the ground.

"Good morning," he called out, across the few yards separating them. "Welcome to Thornhurst. What brings you?"

The driver of the wagon, a long, lean man with a close-cropped grey beard, stood up and raised a hand. "Greetings," he called out in a fine, clear voice. "The open roads bring me! Rohrich of Ashmill Bridge, Peddler, Gossip, Tale-Teller. As for these others, one I pay to accompany me, two were stuck on the wrong side o'the mountains when the snows come, and the other, I'll let him introduce himself," he said, sweeping his hand past the men who rode with him, and finally to the man with the lute case on his back.

Though the weather had started to warm, this particular fellow was heavily bundled in a fur-lined, hooded coat that was pulled tightly down over his head. He pushed it back, revealing a face that was a solid shade darker than Idgen Marte's, clearly marking him as a Concordat man.

"My name," he said, sketching a half bow from his saddle, "is Andus Carek." His voice was rich and smooth, filled the air without sounding too loud, carrying the slightest shade of an accent. "Bard, minstrel, troubadour, jongleur; choose the word that suits your tongue. The open road brings me as well, but also a woman I met some months ago whom I believe I could find here, a lady named Radys Glythe."

"There is no Radys Glythe here, I am afraid," Allystaire said, frowning faintly. "Or if there is, I do not know her. You are welcome all the same. I am Allystaire Stillbright," he added. "Come in peace to Thornhurst." He stepped Ardent to the side, raised a gloved hand and gestured towards the open gate.

"Don't remember any villages out here having walls and gates, to be honest," Rohrich said as he grasped his reins. "Then it's been a fair few years since I've driven this way," he admitted.

"You will find it much changed," Allystaire said. "You will still find this track leading straight through to the green, where folk are beginning to celebrate the snowmelt." Rohrich gave his reins a flick and his team perked up, began dragging the long, low, covered wagon along behind them.

Allystaire watched the wagon pass, then the men trailing the peddler's wagon. Only one of them was openly armed in a meaningful way, with a heavy flanged mace dangling from his belt, and a crossbow cased against his saddle.

He cleared his throat and flung out a hand, called to the guard, "Goodman!" His voice snapped through the air, turning everyone's head. He pointed towards the bow. "I will be collecting that while you stay in Thornhurst."

"Collectin' what?" The man grinned faintly, showing gaps in his teeth.

"The crossbow. Maces and the like, knives, swords even, you may keep. The crossbow will be given back when you leave."

"Doesn't seem like part o'the Baron's law," the man said.

"Baroness," Allystaire corrected. "And if you wish to ask her, you may," Allystaire said. "Just keep following the road. Unless I miss my guess she will suggest that you do as I have asked. And frankly, friend, it is not the Baroness's law that matters inside these walls. I meant it when I said you are all welcome. Crossbows, though," Allystaire shook his head, "those I do not welcome. Please hand it to my associate, who will take excellent care of it. Harrys."

At the sound of his name, the old soldier and new squire gave his horse a nudge and rode forward to take the bow from the saddle of the unconvinced guardsman.

"C'mon now, Myron," Rohrich called back, twisting in his seat. "We're plenty safe among these folk. Give it o'er."

Myron unhooked the strap that held it over his pommel and held it towards a smiling Harrys, who told him, "No worries now, man. I know how t'take care of a crossbow. I'll keep it dry'n'warm. Y'want it stored unstrung?"

Myron nodded, grimacing, then turned his horse and rode on, with a backwards glance at Allystaire.

Andus Carek, nimbly riding a fleet-looking roan, had let the wagon and the other riders drift past, then pulled up closer to Allystaire. "Are you certain there is no Radys Glythe? I met her just a few months ago and she told me folk here were desperate for music, would pay well. She was from my part of the world. Concordat folk are not so abundant here, especially in winter, that she should go unremarked."

"Why did you not come then?"

"Well," Carek said, rubbing his chin with one thickly gloved hand. "Word on the road was keeping most away."

"What does word say now?"

The bard cleared his throat. "Lot of things," he said. "Some of which might make a song if I can hear more."

"Well," Allystaire said, "I have a feeling I know the woman you met, and yes you will find her here. Her name is not Radys Glythe."

The man smiled broadly, crinkling his hard-planed cheeks. "I thought it might not be." Then, tilting his head to a side. "Temple Proclamations were slow to reach towns in the north, but did they speak true?"

"Probably depends on the Temple. If it comes from the Sea Dragon, I am inclined to say no. From Fortune, perhaps."

"Well," Andus Carek said, lifting one hand, palm straight up. "They said the same thing. Just a question of how they said it. The Baron died here. Murdered, said some. Defeated, said others."

"I killed him, if that is what you are asking. But it was no murder."

"Paladin, some stories said." The bard stroked his chin with his gloved fingers, resting his other hand on the pommel of his saddle. "Fair of face and voice, a veritable giant among men."

"Stories lie," Allystaire said flatly.

"They do and they do not," Andus Carek said. "If I might trouble you later for some commentary on said stories, I would be most grateful."

"I have a feeling you are going to trouble me whether I say yes or no. Is that feeling correct?"

Andus Carek grinned, and his dark eyes nearly twinkled. "I suspect it might be."

Allystaire couldn't help but chuckle, then wave a hand. "Go on. You will find the woman you seek if she wishes to be found."

"A curious way of putting it. Might I know her real name?"

"That," Allystaire said, "will be up to her." He nodded to the open gate. "Be welcome in peace."

The bard knew when he'd been dismissed. He tugged the hood back up over his head and lightly touched one heel to the flank of his horse, and it trotted on.

Once they men were all well clear of the gate, Allystaire waved Harrys and Gideon on, but held out a hand to stop Norbert. As Gideon turned to look at him curiously, he thought, *I want you there to keep an eye on everything. Let Idgen Marte, Torvul, and Mol know who comes.*

The boy nodded and turned to go when Allystaire suddenly smiled inwardly. *On second thought—let Torvul and Mol know. Let Idgen Marte learn on her own.*

Gideon's smile when he heard was a match for Allystaire's own, and the boy let his horse run a few paces to catch up to Harrys.

Allystaire then swung his gaze towards Norbert, frowning. Once the squire caught the paladin's look, he winced.

"Draw your bow, Norbert," Allystaire said.

The boy's left hand slide to his side, and his wince deepened into a close-eyed grimace. He then reached to his right side, fumbled, started to draw the weapon free, only to have it suddenly tug on his reins and pull them out of the too-loose grip of his hands. His horse took a couple curious steps to the side, then raised its head and sent an almost mournful look at Allystaire. Meanwhile, Norbert struggled to grab bow and reins both, succeeding only in getting them more thoroughly tangled.

"What have you learned, Norbert?" Allystaire said as he rode over and took hold of the gelding's bridle. The horse snorted, in thanks, Allystaire thought.

"Make sure I put m'bow case on my left side."

"And?"

"To make sure my reins are clear."

"Those are the specifics of the lesson, yes," Allystaire said, assuming the tone of a tutor nearing the end of a vast store of patience. "Now induce to the general."

Norbert thought hard for a moment. "Always be…ready?"

"Close," Allystaire said. "Be *certain* that nothing you can control comes between you and the means to do your duty. You can control the placement of your weapon, your reins, the movement of your horse. None of those things should ever impede you. It is not enough to assume that they will not. Be certain of it."

"And things I can't control?"

"Those are usually the things you will want to put arrows in. But there are others, of course," Allystaire said. As Norbert finally untangled weapon and reins and grasped one firmly in each hand, he let go of the gelding's bridle and the two of them began riding, side by side, back into the village. "You cannot control what other men, those with you, or those against you, might do. But you *must* always control what you do."

"I'm sorry, Arm," Norbert said. "I will work harder."

"Not today, no," Allystaire said, cutting him off with a hand slashing through the air. "Today, the snow is melting on the green, as they say, and even squires are given the liberty of the day. Do you as you wish this day. Take joy in the celebration. Now, give that horse its head and let us have a run back to the green, eh?"

Without waiting for a response, Allystaire gave Ardent a flick of his heel and the grey's muscles bunched and gathered beneath him, then set them rocketing down the track, churning cold mud into the air. Norbert did the same with his gelding, who joined the run with spirit, though it had no hope of catching the warhorse.

Though the air still stung with cold, the quality of the light held a promise of spring. As they often were in the Baronies, the season of the new would be brief and quickly give way to the pounding heat of summer. But at least on the day that winter officially ended in the minds of the people under their care, Sir Allystaire Stillbright and his squire Norbert briefly filled the air with laughter at the joy of a simple race.

CHAPTER 19

The Peddler and the Bard

By the time Allystaire and Norbert pulled up their mounts at the edge of Thornhurst's oval green, Timmar had prised the lid off a barrel, and foaming mugs were being passed around the crowd, with no special care paid to who was given one and no links changing hands. A few of the children who weren't curious enough or thirsty enough were busy packing snow and slush into missiles and hurling them at each other, but in large part they had the good sense to remain at the edges of the crowd.

Allystaire caught Norbert eyeing the ale line. "Always see to your animal's needs before your own," he said, and the youth nodded wistfully as he and Allystaire led their mounts away.

Across the oval of melting snow and small patches of brownish grass, Rohrich had set chocks behind the wheels of his wagon and was busy pulling the canvas cover down, with his surly guard lingering nearby.

As they led their horses away, Norbert said, "Why'd ya take the crossbow but not his mace?"

"A mace is often the choice of the unskilled, for one," Allystaire said. "And I do not feel right depriving a man of the means to do his job, for another. If he was hired to guard that peddler, he should be able to do it within reason. I doubt anyone will give him much of one. As for the crossbow, well." He shrugged, feeling the weight of the chain shirt he'd been wearing since that morning's run. "That weapon allows the wielder to kill silently, at a distance, and in a moment. With a crossbow, if he had a mind to stir trouble and a steady enough hand, he could kill me, you—maybe any one person in the village, excepting Idgen Marte—before we could react. With a mace? By the time he can work up to serious, permanent mischief, there is a good chance of having to deal with more than he can handle."

"Meanin' you?"

"Or Torvul, or Idgen Marte, or Gideon. Or Harrys. Or, for that matter, you."

"I woulda been no use if it'd come to a fight just now."

"It might have taken you some time to get into the fight, mayhap," Allystaire said. "But you have months of training now. You have gotten faster, more accurate. Most importantly, I know how you react in a crisis. I have known for weeks."

By now they'd reached the stables, and Norbert went ahead to open the doors, leading his gelding in ahead of Ardent. They led them to adjacent stalls and began removing saddles and tack.

"What d'ya mean?" Norbert's voice was muffled as he bent to work at the belly-cinch.

"When the late, unlamented Sir Donals Brinden got hold of a knife and put it to a man's neck, a lot of armed men stood around watching when they should have been drawing weapons," Allystaire said. "Harrys filled his hands with steel. Landen tried to take charge of the moment. But before either of them could act, I heard the sound of a bowstring drawn."

Norbert stood up, sliding the saddle off of his gelding and only just managing to catch it before it hit the ground. "Didn't e'en think really," he muttered. "Arrow was in m'hands 'fore I knew what I was doin'."

"That is how it ought to be," Allystaire said as he lifted his saddle clear of Ardent's back and set it on the edge of the stall. He picked a brush from where it hung on the same wall, began gliding it over the destrier's back, his hands so accustomed to the work he barely thought on it. "Tell me something. If I had told you to loose, could you have hit Brinden?"

"I dunno," Norbert answered after thinking on it a moment. He'd picked up a brush as well, though his hand was stiffer than Allystaire's, the movements slower and less sure.

Allystaire sighed. "Then you have more work to do."

"He had that man in front of 'im. It woulda been a risk."

"I know," Allystaire said. "That moment was a rare exception to the rule I am about to tell you. When you brandish a weapon, it ought not to be to threaten a man, to impress a woman, to reassure yourself, or to bluff. You put steel in your hands for one reason, and one reason only. And that is to kill. Do you understand?"

Norbert lifted his head to look at Allystaire, who'd looked over the stall divider and set the brush back upon its hook. He nodded slowly.

"It may not sound very knightly, putting it that way," Allystaire added, rubbing Ardent's long neck absently with one hand. "Yet there is no sense in hiding from the truth. What is more," Allystaire went on, as he exited Ardent's stall and shut the door closed behind him, "if you are going to aim a lance, cut with a blade, swing a hammer, or loose an arrow, you cannot doubt, you cannot hesitate, you cannot think 'I do not know if this will work.' You must believe that it will."

"Then what'll you do if it don't? I mean, if ya miss."

"You do it again, or you try something else. But your belief must never, ever falter."

They packed their tack away, and pushed back into the bright of the afternoon, out of the heavy reek of horse and hay and into the fresh bite of the air. "Go on, lad. I promised you no more work today, and I have already broken that promise. Go," he said, waving the boy ahead of him. "Drink, dance, sing if you have a mind. I will be along."

Norbert nodded smartly, then trotted off to join the throng gathered on the green. Allystaire could hear the general hubbub, snatches of song, the barking of Rorhrich's patter, the squeals of children as they struck or were struck with balls of wet snow.

He was practically lost in a brief reverie as he strolled aimlessly towards the green, when he was jolted out of it by a thump, and an impact against his chest that momentarily stole his breath.

Allystaire looked down to see the slushy remains of a wet, well-thrown clump of snow splattered across his vest and coat. He looked up, caught sight of Gram, standing several paces away, a guilty grin on his face, hands behind his back.

"Gram!" Allystaire's voice was sharp, his face stone. "You ought to know better."

The boy's face paled, and he stammered, "I'm sorry, Sir All—"

By the time the boy had begun to apologize, Allystaire's face had begun to crack, and he'd bent at the waist to scoop up a handful of the damp snow that melted even as he tried to pack it between his hands.

"Know better than to pick a snow fight with an Oyrwyn man."

The boy was caught wide-eyed as the fistful of slush exploded across his chest, knocking him back a step.

* * *

Rohrich was well and truly into his sales pitch, and Torvul was watching and weighing from a few paces away, arms crossed over his chest.

"Finest cloth a silver link to the hand, two to the pace and five the span," Rohrich was saying, as he arranged bolts of fabrics on a shelf that folded out of his wagon. "Can be dyed to your taste, good women," he added, "for additional weight, but what is cost when you get *precisely* the colors you desire?"

The half-joyful, half-panicked squeals that Gram emitted as Allystaire slung the boy off his shoulder into one of the larger piles of snow cut through the noise and drew some surprised stares.

"Calm, good people," Torvul said, effortlessly pitching his voice to drown out Rohrich's for a moment. "That terrifyin' expression your paladin is wearin' upon his broken husk of a face is meant to be a *smile*. I know, I know," the dwarf said, raising his hands to the air. "It's ghastly. But he's tryin'."

Rohrich shot a glare at the dwarf, with an upturned eyebrow. Torvul grinned and wave a hand as if in surrender. The merchant cleared his throat and continued.

"Pots, iron and copper," he belted out. "Knives, needles, and other assorted domestic ironmongery. Needles, pins, thread of all colors and sizes, soap, salt, pepper, and spices still more exotic and delightful to the palate!"

"Ghastly? Broken husk?" Allystaire crossed his arms as he stood at Torvul's shoulder. Folk had gone back to examining Rohrich's wares, stepping forward to fondle bolts of cloth or hold up pots and knock them on the bottom with a knuckled fist.

"Made 'em stop starin' at you."

"I suppose so. Cold, have I become so dour that people are shocked to see me having a bit of play with a lad?"

Torvul craned his neck to look up at the paladin. "Isn't that a question you ought've asked yourself, oh, half a score of years ago? More?" He went back to contemplating Rorhich's sales pitches. "He's not bad," the dwarf murmured, so only Allystaire would hear. "Not too good, either. So long as he doesn't try pitching any tonics or medicines."

"I think the village folk have the good sense not to buy that sort of thing when they have a resident alchemist whose potions and philtres have something of a potent guarantee, and an agreeable price," Allystaire pointed out.

Torvul hrmphed, and waved his hand to dismiss the notion. "I'm not worried about competition. I've cornered the market, though, of course, it bein' a market with no weight, that's not quite the achievement it sounds like. Just don't want to him t'be a charlatan."

"Have you any reason to believe he is aught but an honest merchant?"

"The most honest merchant in the world is like t'be the poorest," Torvul pointed out. "There's differin' degrees of acceptably crooked, though, and I doubt he'll cross any lines. I just like t'be sure."

Allystaire looked from the dwarf to the peddler, who was now heaving a heavy, locked strongbox to the edge of the wagon.

"Books!" He jingled a ring of keys on his belt, selected a long, heavy one, slid it into the lock and clicked the top open theatrically, sweeping back a heavy cloth covering that shielded perhaps a dozen slim volumes stacked carefully inside the wool-lined wooden box. "Some of them carefully block printed, all the way from the Keersvast Archipelago! In bindings of wood and leather, hand-stitched and clasped with fine metalwork."

Allystaire eyed the case of books, felt a sudden thought bloom. He started to step forward only to realize that he had no purse on his belt, and couldn't, truthfully, account for how much weight in gold, silver, copper, or gemmary he could claim to have.

"Welcome t'the life of the holy man," Torvul muttered, having caught Allystaire's suddenly halted step. Rohrich, with a peddler's sharp eye for custom, had noticed it as well.

"Sir Allystaire," he called out genially, his voice all smiles and warmth and conviviality, "a learned and lettered man, I knew it right away! If you wish to examine my selection of titles privately it can surely be arranged." He set the lockbox down, quickly scanned the crowd for other interested customers and saw, for the moment, none, so quickly locked and stowed it.

Allystaire merely nodded, waved a hand in acknowledgement. "I was wondering if Gideon might want any of the titles," he muttered.

"Wouldn't kill ya t'read them yourself."

"Where will I find the time?"

"Even you have half a turn as you lay down t'sleep if y'want it," Torvul replied. "Stones, I'd like to look at his books myself. Always eager to add t'the library in my wagon."

Allystaire sighed. "In truth, Torvul, I would not mind taking the time to read now and then. What, I do not even know. Some old histories, perhaps. Yet there is so much to manage."

"I know. Time t'get all our guests back where they belong. Off to Wind's Jaw, the Dunes, and the Archioness off to the Vineyard. Not to mention whatever we're going to do with Rede."

Allystaire sighed heavily. "Cold, would you believe I had almost forgotten all about him?"

"I hadn't," Torvul said. "I've kept an eye on him as I could. So has Idgen Marte. He's done a great deal of stayin' out o' your way, I'll say that much. Like a hare that knows just where t'lay up and avoid the hawk altogether. He's made himself useful here n'there, doin' chores. Lot of it where people don't see. Woodpiles stayin' stacked, water barrels full, cowsheds mucked, that sorta thing."

"Mayhap he means it, his repentance," Allystaire said. "The Shadow's Curse seemed a powerful thing."

"Maybe he does and maybe he doesn't," Torvul said, then raised a finger towards Allystaire and spat to one side. "Mark my words, now. You should've killed that cold-eyed bastard."

"I cannot kill him now," Allystaire pointed out. "Unless he gives me reason."

"I could find a reason," Torvul grumbled, then gave his head a quick shake. "Come on. These village folk are canny enough, they don't need me lookin' o'er their shoulders. I've somethin' for ya."

The dwarf set off without another word and Allystaire followed him, curious. For all that his legs were so much longer than Torvul's, it was still a chore to keep up with the dwarf when he put on a determined stride.

Rohrich's patter diminished and was soon gone, swallowed up in the general buzz of shouting, laughter, drinking, and camaraderie that filled the air. Soon even that receded as Torvul led Allystaire towards the armory.

"You did not happen to see a Concordat man with a lute case on his back head into the Inn, did you?" Allystaire asked.

"I believe I did," Torvul replied, "with Gideon taggin' along, studying him careful and gathering up all the questions he means to ask later on." The dwarf held up a hand to call a halt, as they had reached the trio of structures where Torvul spent most of his time: the shed, his wagon, and the house. The dwarf pulled himself up onto the board of his wagon, and disappeared inside it.

* * *

"Radys. Glythe."

It took a moment for Idgen Marte to realize that the words spoken aloud were a name, and that the name referred to her. She was propping up the bar in Timmar's Inn, halfway through a cup of some of the better brandy rather than joining in the ale-quaffing throng outside.

When she turned around, she registered Gideon first, but the boy quickly melted away. Then her eyes were on the minstrel she'd met, seemingly ages ago, in Ashmill Bridge. The finely sculpted cheeks, the warm hazel eyes, the wooden lute case slung behind his cloak and coat. Carefully, like a parent lowering a child into its crib, he slid the instrument off his back and set it down by his foot, let it lean against his hip.

He smiled and gave a very small bow from the waist. "Andus Carek," he said, slipping into their native tongue, "at your service. If only I knew your name, so I could greet you properly."

Idgen Marte set her brandy down and stood. Adjusting the sword at her hip to where it sat just right, so as not to tangle into her legs or drag too heavily at her side, took barely a touch of her hand. She offered a conciliatory smile and

a small shrug. Her voice rasped as she replied, with more than its typical huski-
ness, as the words of her homeland had grown foreign with disuse.

"I am sorry to have deceived you, Andus Carek," she admitted. "It was
necessary."

"I do not doubt you there," the bard replied with a carefree shrug, followed
up with a glance that took in the rustic Inn, its mortar-chinked stone walls and
bare timber beams. "Having seen the place myself, though, regrettably I *do* find
your claims of how much silver the folk of this village would be willing or able
to pay me a bit exaggerated."

"I'm sure you'll be paid and well paid for any music you care to give us,"
she replied carefully. "I would see to it that your box was well salted with silver,
though from what I heard of your lute, it should earn gold."

"I would count your name among the first payments put down upon my
skill," Andus Carek replied, smiling once again in a way that Idgen Marte found
appealing enough to nod, take a deep breath, and answer.

"My name," she said, "is Idgen Marte."

He bowed again, slightly. "It is well to meet you. Truly of Cansebour, as
well? Your accent is of the region, I think. But perhaps it could be Viefaldt?"

She cleared her throat, suppressed the reflex to raise her hand to the scars
along her throat. *Time was no one would've mistaken my voice for a Viefaldt shep-
herd girl.* "No. Cansebour it is."

"It is a common enough name, but you wear it exceptionally well," Andus
Carek said, as he came a few steps closer, leaned his lute case against the bar. "I
recall hearing stories of an Idgen Marte of Cansebour, when I traveled there to
study with the lute masters of the Tower."

She snorted. "It's a common enough name. You said so yourself." She
picked up her brandy, turned her face away from his. "What is it that they say?"

"Many things. Most on the theme of how dangerous it can be to come too
close to the wrath of a Mercator prince," Andus Carek said. "But surely such
men are accustomed to killing the enemies they bother to acknowledge. Coincidence, I'm sure."

She drained the cup, set it down, shrugged. "Agreed." She turned to him,
put on her lopsided grin, tilted her head to shade her eyes a bit. "How long do
you plan to stay?"

"Well," he said, wetting his bottom lip with the tip of his tongue, "there are more things in the world than silver. I've a sense there might be songs waiting to be found here."

"Songs?"

"The battle! The paladin! Someone's got to make songs of it."

Idgen Marte chuckled. "Have you *met* the paladin?"

"At the gate to the village, yes."

"Your impression?"

"That man had the coldest eyes I've ever seen. And yet, I wasn't frightened of him."

"That's good. Means you've no reason to be. Be careful, though," she added, as she stood up, stretching to her full height, and crossed behind the bar to retrieve another cup and the brandy. "You're around him long enough, you'll find yourself hopping to his orders."

"Oh? Why is that?"

"After a time, you just sort of want to follow him." She poured small measures into both her cup and the one she slid in front of the bard.

"Been following him long, then?"

She lifted her cup, tilting it towards him; he mirrored the gesture and they tapped rims with a dull clunk. "The longest."

He smiled as he passed the cup to his lips and sipped. "What is it that you do here, then? Do paladins typically employ swords-at-hire?"

"Mostly I hang about in his shadow," she replied as she downed her own drink. "And, no. That was another—"

"Necessary deception, yes. Well," he finished the rest of his brandy and sat down. "At your convenience I'd like to hear it. *All* of it. From the moment you met him."

She held up a hand to forestall him. "Not that easily, Andus Carek. You're going to have to earn it. And you can start by tuning up and giving them a taste of the music."

"If I play *The Streets of Cansebour,* will you run away again?"

"Nowhere for me to go," she said with a rueful laugh. "But no one else will know the tune."

He slid off his stool and grabbed his lutecase in one hand, the stool in the other, and headed for the hearth, looking about him theatrically. "Well. There's no one else in here, is there? Except the lad over there," he added, pointing to where Gideon had faded into a corner, "who is quiet as a damned mouse."

"I had naught to add to the conversation," Gideon said.

It took both of them a moment to realize he'd responded in the Concordat, and not the Barony, tongue.

"You speak my language, lad?" Andus Carek tilted his head to one side. "Where are you from, then?"

"I don't know," the boy replied. "I was largely raised in Keersvast but I have no idea where I was born. I do speak the Concordat tongue, and three or four of its regional variants."

"How many languages do you speak?"

"Well," Gideon said, "my Islander is little used, but it is simply a rougher edged Keersvasti anyway. Say four Concordat tongues. The Baronies. The Eldest."

That's probably enough, Gideon, Idgen Marte sent the thought quickly.

The boy trailed off with the bard looking at him in wonderment. "Storms, lad. You're a prodigy, to command that many tongues at your age."

The boy shrugged, his bearing neither modest nor confident, though he chose his next words carefully, pausing over them. "I had thorough teachers who believed in negative reinforcement. I learned quickly."

Andus Carek opened his mouth to respond, but Gideon pointed at the lute case. "Are you going to play or keep questioning me?"

The bard sat down upon the stool he'd carried over and shook his head. "Ah, you have me there. It is in my nature to be inquisitive." With that, he unlatched his case and slipped the lute from it into his dark, long fingered hands.

It was as beautiful an instrument as Idgen Marte remembered. Not because of any precious metals or inlays, but because of the wood, the bands of it that gleamed in the soft firelight, carefully waxed, the patina of endless, loving use beaming from every piece of it.

Andus Carek began tuning it, strumming absently at the strings and adjusting pegs, bringing it quickly into line, plucking a chord here, a run there. And Idgen Marte slowly realized that Gideon was watching his hands move on the strings with utter, rapt attention.

* * *

Torvul shut the door of his wagon with a push of his hip, and carefully set down a cloth wrapped bundle on the board, hopped down, took the bundle reverently in both hands, and walked towards Allystaire.

"Seems right, on the day that winter ends," the dwarf said. "Spring is upon us soon, all three turns of it, and summer after it. The sun will hold sway and dominion once more. It's time." He held it up to the paladin, who reached for it, and instantly knew he was holding a hammer made, with greater skill than he had ever known, to his own hands.

Allystaire carefully, slowly pulled the cloth aside. The hammer he held was roughly of a size with the one he'd broken, though the head was more slender, rounded rather than squared. He let the cloth fall to the ground and took it in both hands.

Instead of stout oak, banded in iron and nailed where it had split, the haft was made of bright steel, with the lower half of its two-foot length wrapped in well-cured hide. He turned it over in his hands, marveling at the weight. It was heavier than his old hammer, true, but not so heavy that he could not swing it at need.

The rounded head was slightly darker, duller than the haft. When he looked at the blunt face, he saw something etched into the surface. He peered closer, squinting; it was the same sunburst as on his shield, his cuirass, and his pennant, picked out in golden filigree. Inside the sunburst, he could barely see the plain outline of a hammer.

"Hammer of the Sun," Torvul murmured solemnly. "That is what the Voice says they may call you some day, many years from now. I thought you needed a weapon appropriate to the title."

Allystaire stood back, took it in both hands, wrapping his fingers around the hide-wrapped part of the haft and testing its weight. "Torvul. It is beautiful. How did you manage it?"

"Much is taken from me, Arm," Torvul said, looking solemnly down to the toes of his boots. "Much of the craft I could once have brought to bear is gone. With Stonesong and *mchazchen* I could make you something with true magic in it. Something to call down the fury of the sun itself. But much remains. There is not, I think, a human worker in metal who could do as I have done."

Allystaire took a few steps back, extended his arms, and gave the hammer a slow, sweeping test swing. "There is some give in the haft," he said, wonderingly. "Some sway."

"Aye," Torvul agreed. "When Her Gift is upon yer arm, the force you bring t'bear is too much for wood. But the steel I've wrought will flex as you swing, will deliver the force of your Gift without destroying the weapon in your hands. What's more, it's a match to your armor."

"What does that mean?" Allystaire, smiling broadly, took another slow cut at the air.

"When we dedicated the altar and the Temple," Torvul said, "we had a vision of each other. You were a knight straight out of legend, seven feet tall and clad head to toe in gleaming, mirror-bright steel. Your right hand clutched something as bright and furious as a bolt of lightning. I knew when I saw it, it would fall to me to make that vision true. When your Gift is upon you, and the hammer is in your hand, it will shine like the sun." The dwarf cleared his throat. "Remember, I said it is like the armor. It will shine, but there'll be no fire, no heat, no real power in it aside from your own. Do not mistake me, though," the dwarf said, swiping a hand through the air. "That is as fine a weapon as you'll ever know. We know I am given to boasting, Allystaire, but this is no vain boast. That hammer will stand up to anything. The scales of the Sea Dragon Himself would give beneath it."

Allystaire nodded, lowered the hammer, slid the head down to rest against his fisted left hand. "I understand." His right hand he extended towards Torvul. "You are a master of more crafts than I had known existed, Mourmitnourthru-kachstorvul," he said quietly. "I cannot thank you enough."

"Thanks aren't needed," Torvul said, taking Allystaire's arm in his own, sur-prising the paladin with his strength. "We have our parts to play. Mine is to make the thing. Yours is to swing it."

Allystaire spread his hands on it, held it out to look upon it again. "If what you and Idgen Marte say is true, Torvul, if songs and tales are going to speak of what we do, they ought to speak of all of us. It will be an injustice if they do not. You have done nothing less than I have."

Torvul shook his head. "Well, I haven't been kickin' down death's door quite the way you have."

"But the things you did during the battle probably saved more lives than anything I did," Allystaire said. "You kept the walls from burning. You kept the Battle-Wights from swarming the Temple. You stood up to a sorcerer. More than that, you made him feel *fear*. I heard it in his voice. If there must be songs, Torvul, they must include you, and Idgen Marte."

"Songs lie. At least, your songs do, human songs. None of my folk are likely t'sing of me."

"If songs are to lie, they ought to lie as much about the Wit and the Shadow as they will about the Arm," Allystaire countered.

"They will," the dwarf replied, his knowing smile turning down at the corners of his mouth into an expression of sad resignation. "They'll not mention us." He lifted a hand to forestall Allystaire's protest. "And it doesn't matter, in the end. It's not about credit or accolades and you know it. Folk need somebody to follow, a name t'shout in battle. That'll be you."

"You think it will come to that? Battle, I mean."

"You know it will," Torvul said darkly. "I don't know who with. Braech, another Baron. Oyrwyn, even. Yet it will come."

"Well," Allystaire said, hefting the hammer. "I will be ready for it."

"Aye. And with Idgen Marte watchin' your back, n'me pointin' out the things you don't think of, and Gideon…" Torvul trailed off, then recovered with his grin. "Well, you just might live up to the legends."

"What about Gideon?" Allystaire tilted his head to one side.

Torvul sighed. "Boy's got a plan. Not my place to try'n explain it, because I'm not even sure I understand it. He'll tell ya when it's time. Now for all the gold in a vein, can we go have a damned drink already?"

Allystaire laughed. "Two of them." He slid the hammer onto the ring set into the side of his belt. "Damn," he said, almost sighing. "I missed that. Felt like I had been walking on the side of a hill all winter."

"Why're you so attached to the hammer as a weapon? Seems odd for your folk. Most o'your knights I've known favor the sword above all else." Torvul hitched at his robes and the two started walking back to the green.

"Idgen Marte asked me the same thing once. I told her it was because the hammer makes no false promises. There is no pretty dancing, no dueling, no first blood. You bring a hammer out in a fight and a man knows precisely what you mean to do with it. You are not out to mark his cheek or sweep his blade from his hand with a flourish. The hammer cannot do any of that. I never liked lying, even when I could do it," Allystaire said, pausing for breath. "Not even to a man I was trying to kill. And," he added, his tone brightening, "you can try to carpenter something with it after the battle."

"You've never carpentered anything in your life."

Allystaire laughed and clapped the dwarf's shoulder lightly. "Idgen Marte said exactly the same thing. And I told her the story I will tell you."

* * *

"Cold, you had them crying over *Vale of Kings*," Idgen Marte said. "Most of them weren't even alive for the reign of the Rhidalish Kings, and if they were they oughtn't remember it with fondness."

She lay atop her bed on her bare stomach, sweating in the heat thrown by the fire they'd built up in the hearth inside her room. *To remind us more of home*, Andus Carek had said, as he fed the fire deftly with those clever lutist's hands.

"You know what they teach," he said, the richness of his voice rolling over her flesh. "It's never as much about what you sing as how you sing it. A true bard can wring drama from the life of a cabbage farmer." She was looking away from where he lay on his back, staring at the wall through the curtain of her hair in a fairly happy haze, but she felt the bed shift as he sat up upon his knees.

"Those tears likely tasted of ale, y'know," she muttered, her voice muffled by her cheeks pressed against her arms. And then those strong, calloused fingers were digging into her back, thumbs pressing upwards along either side of her spine, and the words turned into a long, low moan. She stretched herself out against his hands, then turned her head to look up at him.

The room was lit only by the hearth, which glowed steadily if not brightly. He was a shadowed outline, fairly slender, leaning over her. Slender, but well fit; the solitary life on the road demanded that, really, she knew.

"They never tire of hearing songs about knights and paladins around here, do they? I sang every song I knew about Parthalian and his Companions and Reddyn the Redoubtable."

"You sang one song about Parthalian twice. And they prefer the songs callin' him Reddyn of the Red-Hand around here."

"Really? The Red-Hand? He's practically as much butcher as paladin in those."

"Folk in the Baronies take robust view of the work their heroes do," Idgen Marte replied. Then she cleared her throat, and said, "My shoulders are a little sore."

He chuckled and moved his hands slowly up from where he'd been digging the pads of his fingers into her lower back, and began kneading them into the meat of her shoulders. She sighed happily, swept some of her hair well out of the way of his hands.

"And y'can try the cycles of Arentenius and the Argent Blade if you need more o'the type as you play here."

"Don't know them," he said, as his hands continued to work into her skin.

There was a pause as knotted muscle in her shoulders loosened up under his care and her fingers gathered handfuls of the blankets she lay upon.

"I don't suppose there's anyone in the village who could *teach* them to me," he wondered in a carefully studied tone of idle musing.

"No," she said flatly, "there isn't."

"Alas," he murmured. "At least you did not flee when I sang *The Streets of Cansebour.*"

She responded only with a low sigh of satisfaction.

"It truly is the jewel of the south," he went on. "If Viefaldt and its great rivers are the heart of the Concordat, Cansebour must be its soul. The light of sunset in the stained glass in the Twelve Towers of Song—"

"Enough," she muttered. "You've made me long for home enough for one night." She rolled over, slid a hand up along his lean chest and around his neck, half sat up and kissed him, if only to shut him up.

Then she pushed him back to the bed and settled her head on his shoulder. He stretched his legs out, crossed them at the ankle.

"They do speak of an Idgen Marte there at the Towers," Andus Carek offered, his voice a pleasant rumble underneath her cheek. "She is not only a cautionary tale of politics."

He trailed off as her free hand slid down his chest and across his hips.

"You are trying to distract me," he muttered.

"No," Idgen Marte said, as she rolled halfway atop him. "I *am* distracting you."

CHAPTER 20

Spring Departures

Allystaire, Gideon, Harrys, and Norbert returned from their early morning run, only to find Rohrich busy setting up his wagon already, his guard Myron leaning sleepily against it, arms crossed over his broad chest.

"Ah, Sir Stillbright," Rohrich called, waving, as they neared the green. "I see you're a fellow for the morning as well. A lie-in puts no weight in the purse, as they say."

Allystaire chuckled politely. "It is not really the purse we are putting weight on," he said, shifting the stone he carried to his other shoulder.

"I should say not. Once you divest yourself of your burdens come speak with me of books, if you would. It's a fine morning and we're likely to have privacy for some time."

"Seems reasonable," Allystaire admitted. The four of them went to pile their stones by the Inn, and Allystaire looked back to the peddler, who was busy hauling the strongbox full of books out of the wagon. He said, "Harrys, give Norbert work with spear, if you would. I will be along presently."

The old soldier nodded, turning an evil-looking grin on the taller Norbert, who smiled defiantly back. "I'm gettin' faster, old man," he said.

"Not fast enough, unless y'come upon me in m'sleep," Harrys said, and the two walked off together towards Torvul's carefully maintained armory.

Meanwhile, Allystaire mulled the books over in his mind. Beside him, Gideon, typically so hard to read, practically vibrated with hunger for them, he could see. His wide eyes stared hard at the strong box, focused on it to the exclusion of all else. *Cold*, he thought, *it would be nice to have something new to read of an evening. Maybe to discuss with the boy.* But the thought of the cost made him wince.

"Books are very expensive here," Allystaire muttered dutifully to Gideon as they made their way to the wagon. "Most of the folk in the village will not benefit from them, so we must bear that in mind."

"If most here aren't lettered, we ought to be changing that," Gideon said as they neared the peddler. "Teaching them."

"I can teach anyone to ride, hunt, fight, joust, and something of history and geography and heraldry," Allystaire said. "I have no idea how to teach someone to read or cipher."

"Mol probably can. As could I," Gideon said with a shrug. "Torvul has a library, but most of its in Dwarfish marks. There are so few other books in the village."

"Well, I can fix that," Rohrich said, overhearing their conversation and theatrically pulling back the cloth cover of the volumes in his strongbox. "I have another box as well, smaller than this, though," he said. "You'll find here a history of the Baronies compiled by an Urdaran monk, spoken aloud to a scrivener," he began, pulling free a thick volume with a blue cloth cover and wooden bindings holding the leaves together. "Great ones for history and the recordin' of it, the Blind Monks. I've a history of Keersvast and the Islandmen as well. Books of poetry and romance. An herbiary."

As he spoke, the peddler's hands moved deftly among the books, pulling free now the largest of them and untying the leather thongs holding it shut. He turned back to the green-dyed leather of the cover to reveal a beautifully illuminated page identifying a plant, with tiny, closely-set words describing the uses of its leaves, stem, and root. Allystaire would've had to lean close to read it.

"Meant to be read with a glass or a crystal, which I can provide, of course."

Allystaire had been half-listening to Rohrich's words and half-pondering what Gideon had said. The boy stepped forward to look at the herbiary, looking to Rohrich for permission before carefully turning a page.

"Gideon," Allystaire suddenly said, "would you do me a favor? Go to my room in the Inn. My purse will be on the table. Bring it here."

The boy looked reluctantly up from the book, but nodded and dashed off.

"Your son?" Rohrich asked as he carefully closed and tied the herbiary shut and slid it back into the chest.

Allystaire mulled the question a moment, then answered, "Yes," with a faint smile.

"Must favor his mother then," Rohrich offered. "Nothin' meant by it o'course, Sir Allystaire," he quickly added.

Allystaire laughed. "You have no idea how right you are, goodman peddler. If you would be so kind as to let us examine the other chest of books, I would appreciate it."

By the time Rohrich had roused Myron and had him haul forth a similarly sized strongbox of books and bring it forth, Gideon had returned with the pouch. As the peddler was opening the second chest, Allystaire reached in with two fingers and felt them close around a slip of parchment wrapped around two hard ovoid shapes. He pulled it free, unrolled the parchment in the palm of one hand, and held forth the two clear, beautifully faceted topazes that had once adorned the golden mask of the Archioness Cerisia.

Allystaire made sure to let Rohrich see them, moved them about in his palm so they caught the morning sunlight. The merchant's jaw dropped just slightly, but he caught himself and quickly composed his features.

"Two gems, two chests of books. It hardly seems a coincidence, eh?" Allystaire grinned. "We will have the lot."

* * *

Allystaire found Mol expecting the books, practically cooing and giggling over them as he delivered the boxes to the Temple. He had managed a box easily enough. Gideon insisted on carrying the other, straining and puffing by the time they reached the doors and he could set it down without losing face. Mol had opened the door to meet them.

"We will need to find a safe, dry place for them," he was saying, "away from any open flames."

"I will speak with the Wit of how best to safeguard them," Mol said brightly. "He has had a lifetime of doing so, after all. And then I will begin to sort out which books I might use to teach folk their letters."

"Many of those will probably be too difficult for the totally unlettered," Gideon said.

Mol held up a hand to forestall them. "All that will be required is patience and material. I have great reserves of the former and now enough of the latter. It will do. The two of you have work to be about."

Allystaire nodded, thinking for only the barest moment how odd it was to hear a girl of Mol's age speak the way she did, and order him about. And yet it wasn't odd at all.

"She is right, Gideon," he said. "I should be off to practice with Harrys and Norbert. You are welcome."

"That is not what I meant," Mol said. "It is time for our guests to leave. Excepting any that wish to stay, of course. Some will. But it is important that Landen, Chaddin, Garth, and Audreyn all begin their varied ways home. They have parts to play in what is to come and it is time they began."

"In that case," Allystaire said, "I ought to get my armor on. Make it look official."

"You're a paladin with or without the armor," Gideon pointed out.

"I think it is just Torvul rubbing off on him," Mol said, smiling. "He's embracing the showmanship the Wit is always on about." She reached out and plucked at the plain, thick homespun Gideon wore. "It would not harm you to do the same. Wear your robes once in a while. Carry your staff like a proper wizard."

Gideon lifted his chin. "I am *not* a wizard. And staves are props, nothing more."

"A staff is also one of the most versatile of weapons if a man knows what to do with it," Allystaire pointed out. "And wizard or not, Gideon, that is how the folk see you. How they need to see you."

"You underestimate them," Gideon countered.

"The folk you live among are one thing. The folk we meet in the world will be something else entirely. Please," he said, "do as Mol suggested. Meet me at the gate by the Oyrwyn camp in half a turn."

"Thank you for the books," Mol said, but something in how she said it let them know they were both dismissed to other business, and they went without question.

* * *

Andus Carek walked out of the Inn at mid-morning feeling fulfilled. Idgen Marte had been gone when he woke, and in fact, he hadn't heard or seen her leave. Hadn't even stirred, which was odd, for a life on the road practically demanded light sleeping and pert ears.

Even so, he had slept well, if not overly much. He planned to take a turn of the grounds, as it were, the pocket of his hooded, lined cloak stuffed with parchment, ink, and pen. There were songs to be mined here, tales to be metered and given melody, and those would be his tools. Nothing concrete today, just a few words, an image, perhaps a sketch of a run of notes if they occurred to him.

Even the cold of the air couldn't hurt his mood. That these northerners were calling the day spring was no more baffling than anything else about this country made of stone and frozen mud.

He'd taken only a couple steps out of the Inn when a knight of legend stepped out behind him.

The paladin still wasn't a man overly fair to look upon. A certain charm in his jawline once upon a time, perhaps, before it'd been knocked around so much. His nose hadn't had the decency to break in a picturesque way, and the tiny scars around his eyes that one could only see when close didn't add a mystique the way dueling scars back home might. His hair was shot with grey and clumsily hacked at till it was out of his eyes and off his ears and neck, and he was scrupulously clean-shaven when his face could have benefited dramatically from a decent beard. He wasn't even particularly tall; his thick chest and shoulders gave him the aspect of a bear walking around hunched over and angry.

And yet standing there with the sun beaming off his mirrored armor, even as Andus Carek saw and catalogued the faults of the man, soon all he could see was the *Paladin*. Despite his keen eye for detail it was as if such things as the man's height, age, and features eluded him. There was a man in there somewhere, but Andus Carek, for all his worldliness, for all that he knew of song and legend and the often slanted ratios of truth and lie that went into them, could only see the hero.

Momentarily, he was afraid. Andus Carek generally thought of himself as a decent enough person; it didn't pay to steal from the crowds that fed you, and though he carried a knife on his belt and one in his sleeve, and had a cudgel in his bags, he preferred never to employ them. He knew he'd given the paladin no reason to look askance at him, much less to threaten him. And yet for a brief instant he feared the man. It passed with a calm breath and the realization that what he feared was the *possibility* of making this man his enemy.

Andus Carek made a note that, no matter what ends his own moral code might stretch to, he ought never to stretch it too far in front of Allystaire Still-bright.

Then the name and the significance of it in the armor he was now staring at a reflection of himself in dawned on him, and he laughed.

"Are you well, bard?"

The paladin's voice, now that was a thing worthy of the stories, Andus Carek thought, and it was something apart from his face. It was a voice for a more handsome man; a voice equally at home on the battlefield and the court. Probably not musical, but powerful, resonant.

"Pardon me, Sir Stillbright," Andus Carek said, and he bowed low in his best courtly manner. "It is not every day that one is confronted by a walking legend before one has properly broken fast."

"We tend to start our days early, Andus Carek," the paladin said, "which may be why you have not found any food. And a walking legend? I am a man, I assure you."

"The armor and the hammer say differently, Sir Stillbright. And I daresay 'Stillbright' is less a family name and more of an appellation befitting some act of derring-do."

The paladin looked for a moment as though he were about to respond, but thought better of it. "The name is the work of the Mother's Wit, Mourmit-northrukacshtorvul."

"The dwarf? What do you mean by the Wit?"

"The same," Allystaire said, and then smiled. "And surely, Andus Carek, you did not think that the Mother had appointed only an Arm?" The smile faded, and he nodded lightly, never lowering his eyes, excusing himself. "If you will excuse me, I must be off."

Andus Carek cleared his throat. "I hope, Sir Stillbright, you would not object to my following behind you. At a respectable and non-interfering distance, of course."

"What about breaking fast?"

The bard smiled. "When songs beckon, the needs of the flesh must wait."

"It is a free village. Follow me as you will." With that, the paladin turned on a heel and walked on, his armor and the hammer at his side flashing in the sunlight.

When they reached the gate at the southern end of the village's track, the youth with the prodigious talent for languages was waiting for them, only he'd traded his villager's garb for a robe and was carrying a long wooden staff. The robe, Andus Carek thought, was the color of a certain kind of sky as dawn had just begun, almost invisibly, to overtake the dark.

By the time they had walked out the gate, the bard was scribbling furiously on a scrap of parchment folded in his hand, carefully managing both ink bottle and pen in the other.

A paladin and some sort of wizard prodigy. It was, Andus Carek reflected, almost too much.

"What is it that the two of you are out to do today, if I may be so bold as to inquire?"

"Today?" The paladin stopped in his tracks and flexed his hands inside the lobstered steel of his gauntlets—the left example of which left the palm of his hand curiously bare. The bard noted it, reminded himself to inquire, delicately, later. "Today we are trying to end the Succession Strife."

Andus Carek hoped he had brought enough parchment.

* * *

Allystaire and Gideon's entry into the Oyrwyn camp drew a fair share of stares and some muttering. Given that the nights were no longer likely to kill them with cold, most of the Delondeur men had moved back to the now properly equipped tent. The sight of Allystaire armored as he'd been during the Battle of Thornhurst sent a larger ripple among them, with a few dashing quickly out of his path.

By the time they'd reached the central pavilion, Garth and Audreyn had come forward to meet them. The Lord of Highgate wore his own distinct armor, green enameled scales, while Audreyn wore a matching dark green dress, lined with strips of brown fur, and sealskin boots, though she had dispensed with the enormous bear fur she'd been wrapped in during the colder weeks.

"Brother," Audreyn said, her tone bright and yet biting. "To what do we owe this visit? They have been infrequent enough."

Allystaire sighed, lowered his eyes to the ground. "I am sorry, Audreyn," he said. "You are right. There are so many things that need doing I could abandon sleep altogether and still lack for time." In truth, her fairly gentle jibe shamed him, and he felt his cheeks flush a bit. Aside from a few dinners and the odd ride, he'd seen little enough of his sister despite her presence nearby for months.

She stepped forward and laid a gloved hand carefully on a bracer. "Allystaire, I am used to having only the time with you that the wider world allows me."

"I should have gone about changing the world a long time ago, then." He lifted his eyes to hers. "I should have been more present in your life. No child deprived of her parents so young should have been raised by tutors and a brother she saw for less than half a year. I am sorry that I did not see it then. I am sorry that I made war the dominant fact of your existence for so long."

Audreyn stepped forward and slipped her arms up around his neck, awkwardly embracing her brother around his armor. Stiffly and slowly he slid an arm around her back.

"You did not make it that way, brother," she murmured to him, then stepped back. "You could not have changed it."

"I could have tried. I *should* have tried. And I am Cold-damn well going to try now." He slipped his arm from around his sister's back and looked between her and Garth. "The snows are melting, the roads are clearing. It time for everyone to start moving."

Garth nodded, shifted his feet, scales rattling a bit. "I know. I've given orders to start breaking down the camp, preparing the horses and supplies for the return. Be a bit tricky figuring what passes to take."

"I can help with that," Gideon offered. "Before you leave, bring me a map. I will mark upon it what roads and trails are clear. Mol can give you some idea of any weather that might change what I tell you."

"How are you going to do that, lad?" The knight bent down towards the much shorter Gideon, hands resting against his legs. Garth's voice was, for a moment, so patronizing Allystaire felt a surge of anger, but he forced it away with a chuckle.

"My name is Gideon, and I would prefer you call me that," he replied calmly. "And I will do it by projecting myself into the air using the Will I absorbed when I destroyed the sorcerers Iriphet and Gethmasanar. And if you do not believe I am capable of it—as your tone implies you think I am an idiot child— you are welcome to try and stumble home with no more prospect of reaching it than a drunk trying to board a rocking boat on a moonless night. However, for the sake of your wife, whom Allystaire clearly loves even if he will not say so, I strongly recommend that you listen to my advice."

For a moment, the only sound was the furious scratching of Andus Carek's pen on the parchment flat against his palm.

Garth looked too surprised to be angry, while Allystaire and Audreyn shared a laugh at his stunned silence. The pale knight's cheeks colored easily, but Audreyn laid a hand on his armored shoulder and smiled winningly up at him, which seemed to calm him.

"Gideon is the Will of the Mother, Garth," Allystaire said. "He is not bound by the same limitations as you or me. If he tells you can do a thing that sounds impossible it is because he can. Trust me."

"I will," Garth said faintly.

"Now," Allystaire said, with an air of returning to business, "I am not here to try and kick you off the village land. Yet it is time to be leaving, yes. But tonight, come to dinner. I am sure Torvul can be persuaded to prepare something special. And I have some letters I would like to give you. To take to Wind's Jaw."

"Letters for whom?" Garth's brows furrowed.

"We will take them," Audreyn said, offering Allystaire a knowing look, her brows raised, head slightly inclined. "I'll explain later," she muttered to Garth.

Allystaire offered his sister a smile and the pair of them another shallow bow, the kind where he didn't break eye contact, more an inclination of his head than anything else. "Lord and Lady of Highgate, if you will excuse me."

Garth extended his hand, which Allystaire clasped in a clatter of metal on metal. Audreyn rose up to kiss his cheek, a gesture he returned awkwardly, as if he were unused to it.

They parted, Gideon sighing in frustration.

"Patience, son," Allystaire said. "Many people are going to have trouble taking your words literally."

"Where are we headed now?"

"Landen and Chaddin," Allystaire said.

From behind them there was a delicate clearing of a throat. Allystaire turned to find the bard, the fingertips of his parchment-clutching hand pointed upwards, palm out, as if asking permission to speak. Allystaire nodded, looking for a moment at the lines of ink scrawled, neat but too tiny to read.

"If I may, Landen and Chaddin? As in Landen Delondeur?"

"Yes," Allystaire replied. "As in the Baroness Delondeur. And her Lord Magistrate and newly legitimized half-brother."

Andus Carek made a quick dash. "And, ah, Will of the Mother…"

"There are five of us, Andus Carek. She named me her Arm. The Will," he said, pointing to Gideon. "The Voice, the Shadow, and the Wit make up the rest."

"Fascinating. And they are?"

"You will not miss them, I promise you," Allystaire said, smiling faintly. "In fact I believe you are well acquainted with the Shadow already."

The bard lifted his head from the paper, his dark eyes narrowing, crinkling the skin around them. "Idgen Marte?"

"The same," Allystaire replied. "The Voice will be the only child you see going barefoot through the snow. And talking to your horse if she has a mind to. And the Wit, well," Allystaire's smile widened. "He will have plenty to say to you. He has plenty to say to everyone."

"Why those titles? Why those symbols?"

"I am not the man to ask," Allystaire said, then he raised his left hand to forestall the inevitable question he could see the bard forming.

Andus Carek couldn't quite help himself. "Why the bare palm?"

Allystaire's eyes narrowed. "The questions are becoming burdensome."

The bard placed the back of his hand against his lips, nodded firmly.

The paladin set off again, Gideon at his side and the bard two steps behind and silent once more.

Allystaire was a good deal less formal when it came to the Delondeur lords. He stuck his head inside their tent, and called out, "Landen, Chaddin. Dinner this evening in the village, if you would be so kind." Without waiting for a reply, he strode off.

Gideon looked up at him, frowning. "That was decidedly less cordial than how you dealt with the Lord and Lady of Highgate."

"The Baroness Delondeur and the Lord Magistrate are not my sister and her husband, who I have known on his own account since he was seven years old."

"One would imagine that familiarity would encourage you to be less formal."

"I do not want Landen or Chaddin to think that this meeting is optional."

"And you thought if you showed the same attitude to Audreyn and Garth they might bristle?"

"Not merely that," Allystaire said. "I owe both of them debts I am not in a position to repay. The least I can do is show them courtesy."

"We should strive to do more than the least."

"I know, Gideon," Allystaire replied, pausing and lifting a hand to his face. "I know. I left them under difficult circumstances. I have not been able to…" He shook his head with a sigh, and said, "Enough. Let us go collect the rest of our dinner guests."

"Who?"

"The Archioness. And, I think, one more, though I do not know where to find him."

* * *

Cerisia was perhaps anticipating Allystaire's visit, given that the door of the room she'd occupied for the winter was open and she was packing.

She stood, smiled slyly. "Sir Stillbright. I was beginning to think—"

"I had forgotten you. I have not, Archioness, I assure you. Yet there are many demands on my time."

"I know, Allystaire," she said, her smile expanding and warming her features.

"I was hoping you would join me for dinner this evening," Allystaire said. Her eyes widened, just a touch, a careful, optimistic expression. "Along with the rest of the Mother's servants, the Baroness Delondeur and her Lord Magistrate, and the Lord and Lady of Highgate and Coldbourne."

Her expression wavered, but if he hadn't been watching her carefully he probably wouldn't have noticed. It was there, and gone, a flash of some kind of hope appearing in her features and then being shoved aside. He was grateful, in that moment, that he'd asked Gideon and Andus Carek to wait in the taproom below.

"Am I to be shown the road, then?" she asked lightly, her tone making it a jest.

"The snows are melting. If you want to make the Vineyards in good time, the journey is best started soon."

"Am I to go alone?"

"I have some thoughts on that score," Allystaire said. "I think that the warband that helped to defend Thornhurst, the Iron Ravens, could be hired to accompany you, if you wished. I also believe that the Will of the Mother can help to make sure that the way is clear."

"I don't suppose it is possible that the Arm of the Mother might escort me himself," she asked, smiling faintly, her eyes knowing the answer, asking anyway. "Your presence would provide a good deal of negotiating leverage. And it would impress Hamadrian Innadan."

Allystaire shook his head very lightly. "You know I cannot leave Thornhurst now. If we can get the Barons to a peace congress, as I have suggested, I will be there."

She sighed faintly, rested one hand on her white-gowned hip, the jewelry on her fingers catching the silver and gold threads woven into the fabric. "You are a compelling man, Allystaire Stillbright. And a stubborn one."

"You are a compelling woman, and beautiful. I would never deny that. But I am committed elsewhere."

"A goddess is not a lover, Allystaire."

He tried to keep his face blank, impassive, but he felt color rise in his cheeks, hoped the many weeks spent in the morning sunlight had darkened his skin enough to hide it.

Cerisia's suddenly indrawn breath told him it hadn't. "Truly?"

He nodded very slightly, unable to meet her eyes for reasons he couldn't have explained.

"*How?*"

"I am not much of a theologian, Cerisia," he quipped.

She laughed lightly, breaking some of the tension, and he met her eyes again.

"Stop," she said lightly. "I do not want to compete with a Goddess. Not so literally. And it's not as if we are doomed lovers in some ballad, separated by war and politics and blood. We could have dallied."

"I do not think I have ever been a dalliance," Allystaire said. "I should have liked to try it. Alas." He shrugged. "I do know, Cerisia, that Thornhurst and the Mother's folk are in your debt. For what you did in the battle, and for what you will go to do now. If I can repay it, I will."

"There are people in the Baronies who worship Fortune as well, Allystaire. And She has not been kind to them these two score years and more. If I can correct that, I should. As for the battle, it was clear that Lionel had become a monster, even before the sorcerers made him one in the flesh. To not oppose him was to endorse him, and that I could not do."

"Even so," Allystaire said, "you will always have the option of the Mother's refuge and protection. I do not pretend that I can convert you, but Thornhurst and the Temple will never turn you away. In fact," he said, laughing, "you just bought the village the start of a library."

"How did I do that?"

"The gems you left back in the autumn. I traded them for two strongboxes full of books."

"Are there enough lettered folk here to make use of them?"

"There will be once the Voice is done with them," Allystaire said.

She smiled. "The uprising comes on leaves bound in wood and leather. It was much the same in Keersvast once, when the First Captains ruled it like princes. A man or a woman who can read and write is a good deal harder to swindle."

"The Old Baron Oyrwyn insisted that all of his knights knew how to read, write, and cipher," Allystaire said, "for much the same reason, I believe."

"Do you mean to make knights of all the village folk, then?"

"No," Allystaire said, "but knowledge cannot be exclusive to knights."

"So you'll put weapons in their hands and ideas in their heads. Do you not see how this can go wrong?"

Allystaire let out a harsh laugh. "Of course I can. I see almost nothing but the paths that veer into chaos and failure and death. Yet if I did not try to find the one path among them all, no matter how narrow it might be, how shrouded, that leads to something better, then I would be no paladin."

Cerisia sighed and smoothed down the front of her dress, one hand coming to rest on her hip. "And may Fortune favor me, that's probably why I'm letting myself be dragged into this, if I were to be honest. I do want peace, believe me," she said, raising a hand to deflect his protest. "But I have heard other men speak of peace. Hamadrian Innadan wanted a peace congress, years ago."

"I know," Allystaire said. "I was there. For a fortnight we drank his wine, rode at one another with tourney lances instead of real steel for a change, and pretended to listen to what he said."

"My Temple did not even send a delegation," she said. "My predecessor felt it too unlikely to succeed, and that we should not be seen favoring it. The Temple of Braech sent a warlike Marynth and a troop of Dragon Scales simply to let everyone know how thoroughly they disapproved of the idea of *peace*. And this was at a meeting called by one of the most powerful Barons. Certainly the most respected."

"I know," Allystaire repeated, "I was there."

"I am still coming to my point," Cerisia said, a bit sternly. "Which is that the same idea was mooted not long ago by a man of vastly more wealth, influence, and standing than an exiled lord in a village so distant from the Dunes that many folk in Londray don't know where to find it. And yet, you have one Baroness on your side already, you will find Innadan a willing second, and Telmawr will do as Innadan does. The man who is now the most powerful lord in Oyrwyn second to the Baron himself will do whatever you say out of sheer love for you, and he alone might sway Gilrayan Oyrwyn to this cause. *And* you have an Archioness of Fortune's Temple carrying your messages. I'd say you've already done better than he did, with less."

"I have the Mother. I have Torvul, and Idgen Marte, Gideon, Mol."

"And all of that is considerable," Cerisia agreed. "Yet I say all this to point something out, Allystaire. All your life people have wanted to do as you have asked, or ordered them, because there is something in you that they want to follow. And *that* is the most dangerous thing about you. You may be able to start something grand, but I do not know that even you will be able to control it. Please keep that in mind."

"I do not want an uprising, Cerisia. Blood will not be the answer. If I must lead a crusade I will make it a crusade for peace."

"And I fear," Cerisia said, voice low, eyes sad, "that the world will not allow you that." She sighed, gave her head a tiny shake, let her eyes linger on his a moment, and then made a shooing motion with one hand. "Go. I must finish packing. How soon can you have documents ready for me?"

"Tomorrow," Allystaire said.

"That eager to be rid of me?"

"The world has been moving on outside these walls, Cerisia. We must meet it."

"And what are you going to do while I go negotiate your congress into existence?"

"Build the Order of the Arm. Keep the Mother's folk safe. Whatever I have to."

Allystaire bowed to Cerisia then, a deeper and more formal gesture than he had made before. Restricted somewhat by his armor, it was as courtly a gesture as he could manage, and she smiled to see it. She watched him as he backed out the door and closed it, then returned to her careful packing.

CHAPTER 21

Interlude

Symod stepped onto the crudely lashed together dock amidst the scent of rotting fish and wood smoke. The underlying smell of winter didn't just contrast with the noisome stench hanging over the tiny settlement; it cut through it like a sharp axe through soft flesh.

The Choiron took a deep inhalation through flared nostrils, trying to catch more of that scent, to drive the unpleasant odors away from his senses. He turned sea-green eyes critically over the hovels. Fisherman's shacks, smoke rising from crude holes cut in the top, fires built in pits on the dirt floors inside, he was sure. Furs and hides draped over their entrances and likewise over their inhabitants. Despite the crudity of their surroundings, or perhaps because of it, the men who met his boat at the docks were imposing brutes, many of them of a height with Symod himself.

He was accustomed to being the tallest man in a room, usually by a head or more. Nonetheless, when the Islandmen saw the deep blue robes, the rich ermine trimming, and most of all the amulet he wore—sapphire-crusted wave beneath heavy silver dragon head, hanging from a thick silver chain—they sank to a knee. That left standing only himself and the three men who'd rowed him to shore. Despite the late winter cold, all three were bare chested, cloakless, carrying a brace of throwing axes apiece in their belts. All three were tattooed, their torsos covered in images of battle, of ships, of the Sea Dragon Himself.

"People of Braech," he began, his voice booming through the air, thrown back in echo by the water behind him, an inlet providing an open channel straight to the sea. "Loyal children of the Sea Dragon. I am the Choiron Symod and I come to you across the sea's ice through the miracle of Braech Himself. None but one truly blessed by the Father of Waves would dare sail to you as I have done." With an extended hand he indicated the ship that lay moored, visible but distant. "And it is on the Sea Dragon's behalf that I have come."

Symod folded his arms behind his back and swept forward off the dock, his three guardsmen swept up in his wake.

"You are the sons of the great conquerors of Barony Vyndamere," Symod said. "You brought down its lords in their stone halls, its knights in all their pretty steel. You drove them under your heel and took their children, their land, and their chattels. And now," he said, disgust creeping into his voice, and his features, lips peeling back over his teeth, "now look at you. Fishermen. Farmers. Grubbing in the dirt. Toiling with nets instead of driving your ships into the other Baronies. Filling your hands with shovels instead of blades."

One man, older but hearty looking, pushed himself to his feet. "Honored Choiron," he said, "you do us wrong. A man's family can't eat the dirt, nor the spoils of raiding. And the Baron Delondeur keeps a strong border. We've been beaten."

"And yet you live, disappointing Braech, me, your fathers, and the spirits of your home islands. For a true son of Braech is not defeated until he is dead." Symod's voice was utterly calm, but his eyes bulged, his cheeks quivered with a barely contained rage. Holding the older man still with his eyes, he said, "Jorn."

One of the tattooed men behind him whipped a throwing axe from his belt straight into the face of the protesting Islandman. The weapon was hurled with such force it split a gaping hole through his face and into his skull, sending him to the ground with a spray of blood, bone, and brain.

The berzerker swept forward, picked his axe from the old man's remains with a contemptuous swagger. Sweeping his eyes over the kneeling men, he lifted the long, thin blade of the axe to his face and sniffed deeply at the blood, then let out a low growl that hung in the air. The tendons in his bare arms went suddenly rigid, his chest expanding with quick, shallow breaths. He bared his teeth and swept his arm back, till Symod spoke again.

"JORN!" The berzerker lowered the axe, growled again, a sound that seemed foreign from a human throat. "No one else here needs to die if they heed my word. No other men will be dragged inland, far from the sight or sound of the sea, from any running water, and hacked into quarters as this *disappointment* will be if they but listen for Braech's call."

Symod smiled at them, waved Jorn back behind him, and said, "Who is your headman?"

"He was." Pointing at the corpse, a man stood. He was taller even than Symod, and as broad, with arms as well muscled as any of the Dragon Scales looming behind the Choiron. "Now I am."

"By what virtue?" Symod's lips twitched in a smile. A murmur ran among the kneeling men, which caused the new headman to lift his head higher, curl his hands into fists.

"I am the strongest among us, the best warrior." The man's words were cut off suddenly as blood bubbled upon his lips, then poured in a torrent from his open mouth. As he fell to the ground, another man, of similar age but less impressive size, ripped a long knife from his back, the foot-long blade covered in heart's blood.

"And an idiot. Can't think with your arms, Avang," the dagger-wielding man said, as he kicked the twitching man to the ground. He casually bent over and slid the dagger's edge across the man's throat, swatting away his feebly protesting arms, wiped the blade on the dead man's furs, and considered its edge. "And I say I am the headman now." He let his eyes sweep around the kneeling men. None moved, none spoke. He turned to Symod and bent at the waist, but did not go to a knee. "I am Arvid, honored Choiron. And we all stand ready to do as Braech bids."

"I am glad to hear that, Arvid." Symod narrowed his eyes, studied the face of the man standing before him and the dead one twitching on the ground, then lifted them back up. "Kin to you?"

"Brother," Arvid said, with a shrug. "A fool's a fool and I'll not follow one."

"We have much to speak of, Arvid."

While this scene was transpiring, a knot of women and children gathered several paces back of the men who'd come to meet the boat. Arvid turned to them. "Food! Drink! NOW," he barked, his voice suddenly impressive, if a bit forced. "The rest of you, tend the honored Choiron's baggage."

"I haven't any," Symod said, "for I will not tarry. But I will take bread and mead with you while we discuss the purpose of my visit." Symod turned to his berzerker guards, pointed to two of them, and then made an expansive gesture towards the corpses. "Take these as far inland as you can make in the next two turns and dispose of them accordingly."

"As you will, honored Choiron," Arvid said, trying his best not to look too closely at the hulking, tattooed men who were, even now, hauling the corpses to their shoulders and setting off for the wood at a run. If he thought twice of his brother being buried beyond the reach of Braech, he said only, "My hall is this way." Slender for an Islandman, dark haired, dark eyed, but pale-skinned, he led Symod past the damp hovels towards a building that barely qualified as a hall. It was perhaps twice as long as any other building in the village, but would've disappeared in the corridors of the great Temple of Braech in Londray, much less in Keersvast.

When Arvid pushed open the ragged hall door, a woman with braided ropes of grey hair met him at the door.

"Why do you come into Hemond's house, Arvid Gullinburtisson?" Her voice was proud and steady, but Symod heard a quaver beneath it for a moment.

"Hemond is dead, Lirs," Arvid said flatly. "And I have claimed his position."

"Your older brother—"

"Also dead," Arvid interrupted her, rather more brightly.

Lirs put her back up straight. "His body."

"Is being seen to." Symod felt impatience growing in his throat, turning his words into a growl. "You need not concern yourself with it. He is being taken beyond the embrace of the Sea Dragon."

As if only just realizing he was there, the old woman turned old, rheumy, pale blue eyes upon the Choiron, gasped in horror. "You cannot."

"I can and I did," Symod grated. "And Jorn Dragon Scale who accompanies me is eager to let his axe drink further blood. He will not be particular if it is the blood of an old woman if she persists in standing in my way, for that means standing in Braech's way. In fact, since he ended your husband's life, ending yours will provide a sort of symmetry. I imagine it will be lost on Jorn himself, but I will admire it."

Before the Choiron was even done, Lirs was sinking to a knee before him, lowering her head, fighting back tears. In a voice that seemed to retain none of its earlier pride, she said, "Of course, honored Choiron. As you will."

Symod swept past her into the hall. Jorn bared his teeth at her, his eyes bulging in their sockets, as he passed in the Choiron's wake, though she hadn't lifted her eyes. Arvid paused for just a moment to lift her back to her feet. If he wasn't gentle, he wasn't rough, either. "We will need bread and drink," he murmured to her. The newly-made widow only nodded.

The hall was made of rough timbers, full of drafts, without enough hides to keep the warmth inside it. Like the other hovels in the village, a fire pit occupied the center of the room, but this one was large enough for a dozen men or more to gather around. Stumps, stools, and one crude chair made of thin hides slung between poles were clustered around it, with the latter at the far end of the fire. Symod claimed it, and Jorn stood behind him. Arvid grabbed a stool and dragged it near Symod's chair, waving away a curlicue of smoke from the fire that drifted towards him.

"Why do proud Islandmen huddle miserably in a fishing village, Arvid?" Symod didn't wait for any further formalities, or for mead to be served, to begin his questions. Even as he spoke, though, Lirs was approaching with a jug in one hand and three wooden bowls in the other. "Be mindful and humble in your answers."

"We rose when the alliance came sweeping down off the islands to challenge Delondeur," Arvid answered. "That was my father's time. He didn't come back. Uncles neither. All told me I was too young t'take up arms so here I am." He swallowed and gestured at Lirs to pour for the Choiron first, which she did, having set the bowls down upon a stump set near the chair. She filled one, spilling a little, and handed it to the Choiron. Symod drank a sip, observing the formalities. She then offered a bowl to Arvid, who did the same.

As she lifted a bowl to Jorn, he snatched it from her hand, poured it down his mouth at a gulp, and then seized the jar, drinking from it noisily.

Arvid rested his bowl carefully in his hands, laying them against his lap. "What did come back from that fight were knights in steel and soldiers in green. They took any blades we had over so long," he said, spreading his hands a short distance apart. "Any axes they decided were not meant for cutting wood. Any armor, and most of the tools. They told us if they came north again, they'd burn our boats. Can't raid much with wood-axes and knives, not that we didn't try. But that Baron Delondeur was a hard man. He beat us well and truly."

Symod smiled slyly and adjusted himself in the rickety chair. "The Baron Delondeur, who crushed your people so thoroughly, is dead."

Arvid's hands tightened on his bowl, and he sat forward, but said nothing.

"His daughter moves to assume his seat, backed by the very man who killed her father. A man who presents a real threat not only to your folk, but to Braech himself. This, Arvid Gullinburtisson, is why we come seeking the Sea Dragon's true sons and daughters."

"What must we do?"

"You must first earn back your honor in the eyes of the Father of Waves. Go south over the Ash, or take to your boats and sail down into the bay. The men and women who come back with their broadaxes or their skinning knives blooded will be of use to the Sea Dragon." Symod leaned forward, setting his barely-sipped bowl aside. "Do not linger. Raid and vanish. The man who stirs things, the man who killed Lionel Delondeur, is vastly more dangerous than the Baron was. Give him nothing to strike back against."

Arvid nodded eagerly, feeling the song of bloodlust beginning to stir in his veins. "And then what?"

"Those of you who return will join with me on the border of Barony Varshyne," Symod said. "Before the summer is upon us."

"Where on the border?"

"If you cannot find it, you won't deserve the glory Braech will bestow. Nor the swords, the hard mail, the coats of scales, the longaxes that will be waiting. You people should long ago have overcome what remains of that Barony. I intend to begin by correcting that mistake."

"Begin what?"

Symod bared his teeth in a smile that made Arvid uncomfortable, that dimmed the proud song stirring inside him.

"A crusade."

When he saw the uncertainty on Arvid's face, Symod said, "A holy war. Blasphemy stirs to your south, and I mean to make an army that will destroy the man who spreads it."

"What is this man's name, the man who is so dangerous?"

"He calls himself Allystaire Stillbright," Symod said, practically hissing the words. "And he will die for his sins. But not until he sees the blasphemy he has wrought utterly destroyed, and all those under his sway dead before him."

"It will be done, honored Choiron. We will set out as soon as the ice allows us."

"Braech has prepared your way, Arvid. Could ice possibly be an impediment to the Father of Waves, or to those who serve him truly? I cast it aside, melted it, broke it, as I sailed here. Now go, gather your men. Form a plan for them. I do not care what it is," he added hastily. "I want blood flowing in the south. The Sea Dragon demands it." He waved Arvid away and stretched his legs out towards the fire, propping boots that were likely more valuable than this entire village on one of the firepit's stones. "I expect plans to be underway before we sail."

Arvid quickly drank down the rest of his bowl of mead, counting on it to quiet the nerves that fluttered in him. He stood, bowed to the Choiron, then left his new hall wondering how long he might hold it.

Longer than Avang did, anyways, he told himself. As he went to gather the men, he reached behind his back and tugged free the sheathed dagger that had taken his brother's heartsblood, shoved it through the front of his belt. He wanted it in the open now, if only so it would remind everyone what he'd done with it that day, but he couldn't help feeling it too small, too poor a blade to do real service for Braech. But the Choiron had promised blades, and mail, and Arvid, for one, meant to be alive to arm himself like a man should.

* * *

While the Choiron Symod sipped mead and nibbled at a crust of bread for the form of the thing, hundreds of miles distant, Allystaire sipped wine and ate heartily while conversation bubbled and flowed around him.

Two of the longer tables in Timmar's Inn had been dragged together to accommodate everyone: Allystaire, Idgen Marte, Torvul, Mol, and Gideon along one side; Chaddin and Landen on the other, with Cerisia and Rede between them and Garth and Audreyn beside. Two of Mol's huge savory pies sat steaming on the middle of the table, with baskets of breads provided by Torvul flanking them. Bowls of butter and cheese and jugs of wine and beer were scattered anywhere there was room, and by the time they were all gathered, they turned to Allystaire, who set down his wine and the bread and cheese he was eating and stood.

"I will not keep you long from the food," he said. "I do not mean to offer a blessing, or a benediction. There are those here better equipped for that than me, and there are at least three different faiths at this table. Mayhap four," he amended, as his eyes passed over Rede. The man seemed thinner, more intense than when Allystaire had last seen him, practically vibrating with unspent energy. The former Urdaran monk resolutely refused to meet his gaze.

"And perhaps it is fitting that many faiths, and two Baronies long at war are represented here. Tomorrow, all of us will engage in the first step of the most important work we will ever do. We should not go to it on empty stomachs."

There was a general, though muted, rumble of approval, then heaping servings of brown-crusted pie began filling bowls. Allystaire found himself too occupied with venison and turnip in onion gravy to pay much attention to most of what was being said. In fact, between bites he realized that he was hearing his name repeated.

Finally he looked up, swiping at his mouth with the back of his sleeve, to find Audreyn laughing lightly as she looked at him from across the table.

"Brother of mine, you always did pay more attention to your food than to your dinner companions," she needled.

Allystaire laughed at her joke, and shrugged as he reached for his wine. "I apologize, Audreyn, but I protest that I come by it honestly. A man on campaign—"

"Has to eat what's in front of him, while it's hot, and as much as he can," Audreyn said, fairly mimicking his voice and drawing laughter from the table. "You have said precisely the same words every time I needle you about your table manners."

"Well, he is hardly wrong, Audreyn," Garth said quietly.

She frowned at him and he turned back to his food, offering an apologetic shrug to Allystaire, who laughed.

"Ah leave him be," Torvul said as he scooped gravy from his own bowl with a thick end of black bread. "He works twice as hard as any man I've ever known and sleeps half as much. Some sort of character failing, you ask me."

"No," Audreyn said, "it's something he learned from Gerard Oyrwyn. If you want men to follow you, you need to show them you'll work as hard as any of them. You do it with reserve, of course, at a distance." She ate more slowly than Allystaire, more carefully, but not at all delicately.

"I do find myself wondering," Garth said tentatively, "just what the Old Baron would think of all this talk of peace."

"Not much, I think," Landen offered from down the table. "In all the years of the Succession Strife, when did he ever strive for peace? He was as much a warmonger as my father."

"Careful with your words, Baroness Delondeur," Garth put in, setting his spoon down slowly. "I'll not hear ill words spoken of that man."

"Calm yourself, Lord of Highgate," Allystaire said. "The Baroness is not wrong." Garth turned disbelieving eyes to Allystaire, as did Audreyn. Allystaire responded by shaking his head sadly. "I loved Gerard Oyrwyn, but I was blind to his faults. Now I see they were much the same as the faults we have begun to take for granted here in the Baronies. He thought war was a natural thing. Honest, red-blooded sport. If he worried over the cost it took from his weakest folk, it never stopped him from going on campaign come snowmelt." He shook his head. "No. I will not let thoughts of what the Old Baron might have done or not done slow me down or stay my hand when it comes to peace."

"Well spoken, Arm," Mol said, her voice instantly drawing all eyes to her. "Those kinds of allegiances are often accidents of birth, are they not?"

Cerisia frowned, delicately pushing her spoon around in her bowl. "What do you mean, accidents of birth? Do you discount the love of children for father, or of student for mentor, in Allystaire's case?"

Mol chuckled. "I would think you'd had enough of sparring with me over dinner, Archioness. That you loved your Baron," she said, indicating Allystaire and Garth, "or that you loved your father," she went on, turning towards Landen, "is no kind of sin. It never could be. But we cannot let love blind us to fault in our friends or family or lead us to follow them where we ought not to go. The answer," she said, anticipating Cerisia's protest, "is not less love, but *more*. If we recognize that the men our Baron orders us to kill might be as worthy of love as the Baron himself, we find it harder to kill them, do we not?"

"You are a daunting conversation partner, Voice of the Mother," Cerisia said, and though she smiled, the expression didn't seem to reach her eyes. "I would give anything to know the deep connection you seem to have with your Goddess's mind."

"Only a fragment of it," Mol replied. "And no, Archioness, I do not think you would. Even that is sometimes too much. Too loud."

"What do you mean?" Most of the other diners leaned forward to listen as the two priestesses spoke.

Mol bought herself time to answer by carefully chewing a mouthful of venison pie. Finally, she said, "Imagine all the living things you encounter in the village attempting to speak to you, Archioness, and having to sort out the noise and learn how to respond back by yourself. It was not easy, and I was unprepared when it first came upon me."

"I hesitate to question the miracles the five of you claim any longer, for I've seen too many of them, but when you say they speak, you mean literally?"

Mol smiled again, set down her spoon, then closed her eyes. After a moment there was a clattering on the stairs leading to the second floor, and the old hound that had often been at Mol's side throughout the winter suddenly trotted to her chair With two fingers, the girl plucked a morsel of meat from the pie in her bowl and held it to the dog, who took it delicately from the girl's hand and chewed it quickly. Mol's hand settled onto the dog's neck for a moment, and the hound settled at the side of the girl's chair.

"You spoke to the dog?"

Mol nodded. "I asked her to come here. I had previously asked her to stay with Leah, who is upstairs and large with child, and to let me know if she needed for anything. So far she hasn't."

"And you can do this with any animal?"

"Most easily with animals we husband. Dogs, horses, cattle, sheep. The latter haven't much to say. And cats like to make a show of not listening, but are happy enough to be spoken to. With birds, perhaps a little. Truly wild animals like wolves, or deer, though, I do not think so, though I haven't tried. Even if they could hear me it would be very difficult for them to understand." The dog settled under Mol's chair, laying her grizzled old head upon her paws and closing her eyes.

"Fascinating," Cerisia said. "Fortune's servants are granted powers, but they are so much less than what the five of you bear."

"There are a great deal more of you," Gideon noted. "I theorize that the power the gods are able to distribute to their servants is roughly equal, so the more servants power is given to, the less power each must receive."

"This is all getting a bit too scholarly for me," Garth noted.

"Listen to Gideon whenever you get the chance, Lord of Highgate," Allystaire said. "He has done more than anyone else to challenge my own thinking."

"Cold, Ally, if he can challenge you I don't expect he'd much like talking to me," Garth chuckled nervously.

"Perhaps the Lord of Highgate has a point," Torvul rumbled, after setting down his cup from a long pull. "We ought to save the metaphysics and the scholarship and the theorizing about the limits o' divine power."

Chaddin frowned, and spoke for the first time to the table at large. "It seems to me if power is divine it isn't limited."

Allystaire reached for his winecup and drank as they considered the statement. When he set it down, he thought a moment, and said, "She has told me there are rules governing what She may do. And that there are things that are forbidden, even to Her. And," he added, smiling ruefully, "that She cannot tell me what the rules are."

"It is as I said." Gideon sat up straighter, lifted his eyes from the table. "The gods may be vastly more powerful and complex than we are, and yet still limited, or perhaps we can only interact with a part of them in a meaningful way without being overwhelmed. It is an interesting theoretical question, but not a very practical one, such as, say, what is for dessert?"

There was a general chuckle around the table and went back to their dinners. Allystaire in particular found himself shifting a large second piece of pie, hen and leek and mushroom, into his bowl and eating it as quickly as he'd eaten the first.

Torvul eventually provided the answer to Gideon's question by bringing out from the kitchen a huge basket of small, flat discs of hot pastry slathered in honey. "Crispels," he announced, setting them down.

Allystaire grabbed himself a handful and popped one contentedly into his mouth, chewing slowly, washing it down with a sip of wine.

"Does this sort of feast cause any friction within your village? I mean, the servants of the Mother all having a special meal with the noble guests?" Cerisia delicately nibbled on the edge of a crispel after asking her question.

"No," Mol said. "They're staying away out of respect for the business we need t'do, not because they're frighted or unwelcome. There's no one in the village I've not cooked for, excepting those who just arrived, and nothin' on this table not available to everyone."

Allystaire felt a pang as he thought of the six score bottles of wine his sister had brought to him. A shaming regret at having given most of it away, though leavened with some guilt at having kept half a dozen bottles for himself. He consoled himself with a sip of the very same and let his eyes drift nearly closed with the pleasure of it mingling with the tastes of the savory pies and sweet pastries.

"I've not the time to bake every day, but I'd be happy t'show anyone interested how t'make these," Torvul said as he popped a crispel into his mouth. "I've already shown Timmar but he's waiting for new custom t'try 'em out."

"I am curious," Cerisia admitted, "as to how goods are bought and sold here. What will I owe Timmar for having stayed so long, for example, and having eaten so much of his food?"

"That will be up to him," Allystaire said. "Within the village itself." His voice slowed and halted as he considered the disc of pastry cooling in his hands, the honey sticking to his fingers. "I am not sure I know."

"The folk trade what they can spare for what their neighbor can spare, in the main," Mol said. "Or they simply give what is needed where it is needed. I doubt a gold link's worth of silver has changed hands from villager to villager all winter."

"I have doubts about how big such a system can get, or how long it can last," Gideon muttered, as he carefully wiped crumbs away from his mouth, having gone crispel for crispel with Allystaire. "But for now I think it is best. Silver brings evil with it."

"You watch your tongue, boy," Torvul said, garnering a bit of a chuckle from the other diners. "Don't go draggin' silver into all this talk. No evil in the metal herself, only in the men countin' it."

"The same could be said of steel or iron," Allystaire said. "There is nothing evil in the things men make of them, only in the hands that wield them. All the same, the less need we have of any of them, the better."

"I can drink to not needing steel, but never to silver or gold," Cerisia said.

"Even he's not mad enough t'try and drive the weight out o'the world," Torvul grumbled. "The war and the poverty and the despair, maybe. But not the links."

"Is that a challenge, dwarf?"

"I would think that ending a war that's gone on longer than you've been alive would be enough, brother," Audreyn said.

"For now," Allystaire replied, "it will do."

Landen laughed. "Just like that? Ending the bloody work of thousands, or trying to, and if you succeed, 'it will do.'"

Allystaire shrugged. "Hope. Justice. Those were the two tasks She set me, to bring them back into the world. If there is anything more devoutly hoped for than an end to the Strife, I do not know what it is."

"For the sky t'rain spirits and hail silver?" Torvul grinned at Allystaire over his cup, saluted him with it, drank, and the paladin couldn't help but laugh.

"And justice, then?" Chaddin looking at him, setting his hands on the table.

"The same. The glory and the riches have gone too long to the men who need not bear the great burden of dying, son after father after grandfather. The living Barons and their lords and knights may not have made this war, but many of them think—as I did—that it is a fine thing, a high sport, a good test of who they are as men. Bring it to a stop, it does not line up the balances, but it stops it tilting the other way."

Cerisia lifted her cup. "To peace, then? If we are all bound to this crusade, we ought at least to drink to it?"

Everyone at the table stood, lifted their cups and tapped them together, muttering or, in Torvul's case, rumbling, the single word, "Peace."

* * *

Allystaire claimed to need air, and in truth he wanted it, but as he stepped out into the cold night air, he simply moved a few paces away from the Inn's door and waited. In truth he didn't find himself waiting as long as he'd expected, for Rede exited soon after him, lifting his hands.

"I know you're waiting for me, Arm." His voice had gone thin and quavering, like it had been when Allystaire had first seen him, eyeless and fevered.

"Tell me why you are here, Rede."

"I am fulfilling the charge the Shadow laid on me," he replied. "And trying to earn my redemption."

"Why do you think you need to do that here?"

The man stepped closer to Allystaire, still holding his hands out. "Because I can help you, Arm. I already have, once."

"What do you mean?"

Rede's head tilted to one side, and Allystaire had the impression of the man's wide, intense eyes shining in the darkness, not blinking. "Have you not thought on why I brought your sister and her husband here? Or rather, how? How did I know to come to your aid?"

"An army, even a small one, does not cross a Barony the size of Delondeur without news of it spreading," Allystaire said. "I assume you heard the rumors and guessed keenly."

"I was not even in Barony Delondeur when it came to me. I was trying to spread Her word, do my work, north of the Ash, into Barony Vyndamere."

Allystaire crossed his arms over his chest. "You tried to bring word of the Mother to the Islandmen who destroyed Barony Vyndamere, you mean?"

"Exactly that," Rede said, his voice still with that quaver, as if there was too much energy in him that he needed to get into words. "Where better to go? Who better to spread the word among?"

"I am amazed you are still alive, Rede," Allystaire said. "I would think that any village or settlement up there would have killed you just as soon as look at you."

"It is true that I was not welcomed among them," he agreed, bobbing his head. "Not at all. But many thought me beneath killing, and most tossed me out to root in their middens, gave me no work, no chance to offer them any help."

"Poor you," Allystaire said, sneering. "Poor, cursed Rede, forced to spend the night reliving his blindness. Pardon me if my pity does not extend as far as you wish it would."

"Not just my blindness, Arm," Rede said. "In those nights I dreamt of blindness, yes. But my dreams brought back the *gift* my eyes had paid for." The words tumbled out of him in a rush now. "It is weak and it is jumbled. Dark. Hard to parse, or to understand. The dreams are hardly worth it. That is why I knew to seek out your old Hall, your sister. I saw the place, I saw her, I knew that the Mother needed her. And that is what I can offer you, Arm. I can offer you the Inward Eye."

Allystaire swung his arm out and seized Rede by the collar, dragging him away from the front door of the Inn. The man weighed almost nothing, skin stretched across his long bones, and Allystaire felt he could've lifted him clear of the ground with one arm. He swung him around as they went around the side of the building, the former priest offering no resistance, and Allystaire placed his hand around Rede's throat, but lightly.

"Try to lie to me, Rede."

"I haven't spoken a word of a lie to you, Arm," Rede said, his voice maddeningly calm and even. "Not a word."

"Do you truly still see visions in your dreams?"

"I do. They are fragments of what the Inward Eye is meant to be."

"Nothing can hide from it. That is what the old priest told me when you first came here. Is that true?"

"I think Urdaran's monks like to make themselves sound like more than what they are," Rede answered. "Goddess knows I did. But I think they see more than I do in these dreams."

"And why do you want to offer your 'gift' to me?"

"I don't," Rede answered. "I want to offer it in the service of the Goddess. If that means serving you, I'll do it."

"And I am to believe your repentance is real?"

"I can't make you believe anything."

"What else have you seen, then?"

Rede shook his head. "I'm not sure. Men whose very flesh churns with the sights of battle. Claws sprouting from their hands. Flame and war in their wake. All of them coming for you."

Allystaire removed his hand from around Rede's neck. "And what will you do if I refuse your offer? If I banish you from Thornhurst?"

"You won't do either of those things," the man said, the unnerving calm of his voice clashing with the wide wildness in his eyes, huge dark pools in his face, the whites standing out starkly. "You won't banish me because the Voice won't allow it. And you won't refuse my offer because, Allystaire Still-bright, you need to prepare for a war, and you know you can't turn down the advantage of my visions, muddled and hard to understand though they might be."

"Do not presume to tell me what I will or will not do," Allystaire said, anger rising in him and clawing against the growing certainty that Rede was right.

"If you tell me to leave, I'll go to the Wit and tell him. And you know the dwarf will not turn me away. If you can't be practical, he can."

"Why?"

"I told you. I want to serve the Goddess. She gave me back my eyes and saved my life, and then I used it to do horrible things in Her name. I was badly led by the priests of Braech, true, and their hired men."

"There will be no preaching for you, Rede. No rousing the crowds. No forming bands of supporters behind you. If I allow you to stay, it is at my discretion, and you report to me, Torvul, or Idgen Marte. You will still do any work that is asked of you."

"Folk haven't been any too willing to ask," Rede said.

"How often do the visions come upon you?"

"When I sleep. The Shadow's Mercy is no longer upon me, so now it is every night."

"What? How?"

"When next you see me in this life, for good or for ill the Mother will re-tract this mercy," Rede quoted. "Those were her words when she cursed me with it. She was bound to them."

Allystaire let the words hang in the air for a moment along the steam of their breath. "Then the Shadow's Mercy kept the dreams at bay?"

"On the days that I fulfilled the conditions of it, yes."

"And yet I am told you have been helping where and when you were al-lowed since you arrived. I will admit, Rede, I thought you were doing that because of the curse."

"The conditions the Shadow set no longer have any bearing on how I sleep."

"If I worked with Torvul and Gideon, I believe the three of us could remove it entirely. Give you back your own mind, your own dreams."

"No!" Rede shook his head insistently, lifted his hands in protest. "No. Then I would have nothing to offer Her."

"You would have the same as any person in this village. You would have your hands, your spirit, your willingness to work."

"Even with an Inward Eye that sees all in fragments and shadows, I am more use to Her and to you than a strong back. And you know it."

"You put more value on yourself than I ever will, Rede."

"Allystaire! Have you not listened to me? You are in danger."

"From whom? Where?"

Rede's arms and shoulders shook as if he could barely keep the answer contained, finally groaned, "Everywhere," through clenched teeth. Allystaire felt flecks of spittle flown from Rede's mouth land against his cheek, wiped them away in disgust. "I can't…the fire, the death, it is all over. So many places. And yet it is all for you."

"You are babbling, Rede. Do I have enemies in the world? Of course. If that is the best you can tell me, then begone. Go to Torvul if he will have you."

"I only want to help!" Rede shouted, but by then Allystaire was walking away from him. "You need what I can tell you."

"You are telling me nothing more than any fair-day charlatan with a globe of glass and a pack of painted tiles," Allystaire said. "I do not listen to them and I shall not to you."

Behind him he heard a choked, sobbing sound, a thump as Rede fell to the ground, clubbed at it with a fist, then a rush of noise as the man ran off.

Torvul? Allystaire thought.

Inside enjoyin' a smoke and a jot of ikthaumanavit. And I heard all of it.

Allystaire pushed open the door. Mol, Timmar, and Cerisia were busy clearing the table, while Andus Carek had appeared in the taproom and was idly tuning his lute on his stool near the hearth. He seemed far too quiet and too observant for Allystaire's taste, and he offered the bard a frown.

Andus Carek only smiled broadly back.

Torvul was seated right close to the hearth, doing precisely as he said, a silver-fitted pipe clenched in his jaws.

Allystaire took the seat opposite him. "How did you hear?"

Torvul tapped the sleeve of his robe with a thumb, the nail knocking against something concealed inside it. "I took the liberty once I saw him follow you out."

"Will you watch him? See if sense is to be made of his ramblings?"

Torvul thought on it as he puffed at his pipe, then sent a series of perfect smoke rings upwards, uncurling as they reached the ceiling. "Ya know what he says is true, since you used your gift upon him."

"You could not possibly have heard that," Allystaire replied.

"No, but I know you, and I know you'd not take a single word from him without making damn sure it was the truth." Another mouthful of smoke, this time allowed to drift out in a cloud. "You should've killed him, but if he's alive and willing to help, how can we turn him away?" "I think he believes he is having visions, Torvul. Flame and war? Men whose skin writhes with battle and who have claws on their hands? It is babble. Too little to make any sense of."

Andus Carek suddenly let off his lute playing. "Forgive me for intruding," he began, his richly accented voice mild. "Sir Stillbright, have you ever *seen* the Dragon Scale Berzerkers?"

"Big hairy bastards in fur and badly made armor swinging dull iron," Allystaire said. "No different from your average Islandman except in their devotion to Braech."

"Ah," Andus Carek said, shaking his head and raising one hand, palm out. "Ah, no. No, Sir Stillbright. You have *not* seen a true Dragon Scale Berzerker. Not every Islandman warrior who swears himself to Braech and mans a boat to raid in the Sea Dragon's honor is one of them. The Dragon Scales wear no armor but upon their hands. And they mark their flesh with scenes of battle, to honor what they have done and how they hope to die."

Allystaire and Torvul turned their eyes from the bard to each other's, Torvul's pipe drooping in his mouth until he reached up and took the bowl carefully in his fingertips.

In unison, they stood up and raced out the door, Torvul close upon Allystaire's heels. When Allystaire shoved open the door the dwarf suddenly turned back and ran for the small bottle sitting by his chair, made it vanish up his sleeve, and then double-timed back.

CHAPTER 22

A Little Faith

Turns later, with Torvul's unguents granting them sight in the darkness and sharper hearing, Allystaire and Torvul had combed the entire village and much of the remaining wood beyond, only to find no trace of Rede.

"We're no woodsmen." Torvul puffed as they leaned against the trunk of a tree. "He'll turn back up, I'm sure of it, but we'll do no more good stumbling about and scaring the local critters out o'their winter sleep."

Allystaire felt his skin growing clammy as his sweat-soaked shirt pressed against it and pulled the cold air to him. "I may have erred badly, Torvul. If he was truly having visions we need to learn as much as we can of them. I let my dislike of the man endanger us." He stroked the head of his new hammer, already a familiar weight at his side, his thumb tracing the sunburst.

"He'll not go far. He thinks he's bound to us."

"Mayhap he is not wrong about that," Allystaire ventured.

"We will find him," Torvul said. "In fact, if we asked Gideon to search for him, we'd find him tonight."

Allystaire shook his head. "I do not want that he has vanished to spread, nor do I want it known why we seek him."

"And you'd hide that even from Idgen Marte, Gideon, and Mol?"

Allystaire sighed. "It stings wrong."

"Then don't do it. Stones Above, for you of all people that should be easy to understand. More than likely he's just crawled somewhere warm and out o'kickin' range and is holing up till dawn."

Allystaire frowned. "Folk have treated him that way?"

"I meant *you*," Torvul said. "I don't begrudge how you feel about the man. I was ready to put a bolt into him upon first meetin'."

"And it was Idgen Marte that stopped you, not me."

"I recall."

Allystaire crossed his arms over his chest, sighed. "Let me call to her."

Torvul cleared his throat and started to protest. "That's not a good idea just now."

Nonetheless, Allystaire had let his senses reach out to Idgen Marte's mind. Instead of being met with a sleep-hazed grumble, he found heat and pleasure. She was totally unable to respond coherently, but he had sensory pictures of her in the moment. He realized quickly that the bard was in the room with her, on one knee at the foot of the bed, her startled cry aloud surprising both him and Andus Carek who lifted his head, and quickly Allystaire retreated back to his own head.

Man and dwarf looked off into the night, and not at each other.

"She appears occupied," Allystaire ventured, in a slightly hushed voice.

"I tried t'warn you."

Another long pause broken only by a low night wind clacking the leafless branches against one another.

"Pray the poor bastard knows what's he's in for," Torvul offered.

"Hmm." Allystaire crossed his arms over his chest. "Hope he is a bit tougher than he seems."

"Anyone makes their living on the road has t'be."

"You miss the road, Torvul?" Allystaire seized the moment to change the subject and he could feel the tension draining away, heard the dwarf let out a held breath.

"I'm not made for it," the dwarf said, with a shake of his head. "None o'my folk are. Took t'it because we had no choice. The home we take with us in song, the bonds of family, the Loresong, they are the only things that make it bearable."

"Then why were you on it alone?"

"It may shock you to learn, Allystaire, that I was not always the most obedient and respectable member of my caravan."

"You were banished?"

"Aye," Torvul said, "and it's too cold and I'm too sober t'tell you any more of it just now. I'm for bed," the dwarf added, until a rustling and a loud release of breath startled the pair of them. They whirled, hands going for weapons, only to find the village dog that often accompanied Mol standing only a foot or two away, tail swishing, tongue lolling.

They glanced to one another, then back to the dog.

"I think," Torvul said, "that help has arrived."

"Aye."

"Don't suppose you still need me, then?"

"I would prefer you were present when we find him."

Torvul sighed. "Fine." He waved a hand at the dog and said, "Go. Find him."

In response, the dog sat on her haunches and stared at the dwarf.

"On. Mush. Hunt. Find Rede."

The dog licked her chops and showed no signs of obeying the dwarf's commands.

"Are you really at a loss of what to say to a *dog*?" Allystaire took a half step forward and knelt and extended a hand. The dog stretched her neck forward and sniffed his palm, then licked it once, carefully. Allystaire scritched the top of her head, murmured a few quiet words. "Mol sent you, yes?"

The dog made a quiet "whurfle."

"Good," Allystaire said, scratching a bit more vigorously now, with both hands, one under her chin. "Then you know who we need to find. Help us, would you?"

He stood, the dog gave another light "woof" and began trotting away. Allystaire looked to the dwarf.

"A word of this," Torvul said, "and I'll poison you."

* * *

With the dog leading the way, it wasn't long till they found Rede. Wearing only his thin robe, barely shod, wet, and shivering, he was hunched inside the bole of a dead tree.

He didn't seem to notice Allystaire or Torvul approach, though neither made anything like a stealthy approach. The dog looked from Allystaire to the shivering monk, whining.

"Rede," Allystaire said, wincing as he realized how loud and sharp he sounded. "Rede," he tried again, softening and moderating his voice. "I never thought I would say these words, Rede, but I owe you an apology." Allystaire turned to him. "The vision you spoke to me, that I dismissed? The bard clarified it for me. It was not the useless charlatanism I said that it was."

Rede surged to his feet, unsteadily, blinking his eyes rapidly. "What did he tell you?"

"That what you told me matched the description of Braech's Holy Berzerkers, the Dragon Scales. I believed them ordinary Islandmen warriors. That they go bare-chested, their skin marked with images of death and war, into battle. That they wear no armor but upon their hands."

"Men whose skin crawls with battle, whose arms end in claws," Rede muttered, sharply inhaling. "Then I am worthy. My life may yet be lived in value to Her."

"We will take you in, Rede. Feed you, clothe you, shelter you – which we would have done regardless of what you see as your use to us. In return, I ask that you speak of any visions you have to one of us, one of the Five. Will you do that?"

"Anything," Rede said fiercely, his frame once more shaking with the intensity of his answer. "Anything to pay back my sins to Her." He started to drop to one knee. Allystaire caught him and pulled him to his feet.

"Just tell us anything that you see, no matter how little sense it might make. That is all I ask."

Rede nodded vigorously, his movements bordering on convulsion. Allystaire looked hesitantly to Torvul, who was already stepping forward to take the former monk by the arm with one hand and reaching for a bottle in one of his pouches with the other.

"Have a drink of this," Torvul said, lifting the bottle he extracted towards

Rede. "Warm you up. Let's get back to the village, put some food in you, find some dry clothes."

* * *

With Rede safely housed in the warmth of the Temple for the night, Allystaire and Torvul made their way back to the dwarf's wagon over the crunch of cold grass. Allystaire found himself pondering Rede's jumbled visions when Torvul finally spoke up.

"If I were you, when you're back to the Inn, I'd move *real* quiet past Idgen Marte's room."

"I might just sleep outside," Allystaire said. "The fear will keep me warm."

"Disappoint the Archioness, if you don't give her a last chance."

"We have come to an understanding," Allystaire said.

"Tell the truth, she didn't seem the type to go pining for anyone, 'specially a man with your face."

"I think it unlikely she will pine overmuch," Allystaire snorted. "Surely Innadan's court has fairer men to draw her eye."

"Think you can trust her?"

"I do," Allystaire admitted. "If nothing else, her fate, and her Temple's, are tied to us now."

"Has it occurred to you," Torvul said, "that she may still be tryin' to get what she came here for in the first place? Her Ladyship folded into Fortune's Temple, all that rot? Thrown her lot in with us she may have, but there's nothin' stopping the rest of their faith from tryin' t'swallow us up as we go. They can afford t'play a long game here."

Allystaire shrugged. "The longer they wait, the more opportunity we have to grow."

"The more chance they have to work against us."

"Torvul, it may be time we have to show a little faith. There are those besides us who wish for a better world. We cannot afford to cast aside every potential ally that does not serve the Mother."

"I'd feel better if we could keep an eye on her."

"I feel as though Gideon can do just that."

Torvul grunted. They paused where they would part ways, Allystaire to the Inn, Torvul to his wagon. "Sure Rede'll be well?"

"He survived the hardest part of winter and made it to snowmelt without our help," Allystaire said.

"As y'say," the dwarf grumbled. "Remember, move quiet. I spent too much time on her new sword to have it ruined on your skull."

Allystaire clasped the dwarf on the shoulder and made his way slowly back to his room. He did creep carefully past Idgen Marte's room, but the steady sighing of sleeping breath he heard in the otherwise still silence of the Inn gave him no worries on that score. Once inside his own room, he set his hammer down, tugged off his boots and set them carefully beneath the peg he hung his cloak upon. Other garments were carefully folded. He looked from bed, to the wall, and back.

Only a few turns till dawn. A bed'll not kill me, he told himself, as he lowered carefully onto it, stretched out underneath the blankets, and tried to put Rede from his mind.

CHAPTER 23

Partings and Blessings

Cerisia was the first of Thornhurst's many temporary residents preparing to leave the next morning. It dawned bright and cold, but the sun promised to warm the day later. Many of the village folk gathered, along with the Goddess's Five Servants, and the Lord and Lady of Highgate, with the black-mailed Iron Ravens gathered around them. They had avoided Allystaire through the winter, and he'd been content to let them. Now their gap-toothed, foul-mouthed captain Ivar was engaged in conversation with Audreyn.

Deliberately, Allystaire gave them a distance, seated on Ardent's broad back and wearing his armor. He felt in his back the folly of having slept on a soft mattress the night before, and the weight of the armor on his shoulders wasn't helping.

"Stones Above, just heal yerself o'the pain," Torvul said, when Allystaire shifted in the saddle with a sour wince.

"No," he replied, forcing his face into an even calm once more, pushing the pain away. "It is trivial and I will not spend Her Gift on small matters."

"Suit yerself," Torvul grumbled. In truth the dwarf looked much like Allystaire felt, a relic of their late night searching.

For her part, seated on her courser, Idgen Marte seemed well rested and content, but had yet to say a word to either Allystaire or Torvul, which fact Mol and Gideon, sharing Allystaire's palfrey, seemed to find funny and curious, respectively.

Let it remain a mystery, Allystaire thought wearily. Cerisia seemed to have made a personal connection here and there with the folk of the village, including Timmar, in whose hands she left a sizable purse. In one or two cases it seemed she offered a blessing, moving her hands in a circle over someone's clasped hands, speaking a few words he could not hear.

His jaw had started to clench the first time, but Mol was suddenly looking at him. "She does no harm to us by offering a blessing. Besides, Her Goddess cannot reach into this place. The Will saw to that."

Seated behind her on the horse, Gideon shrugged. "That would matter little to Fortune, I think, if She were to concentrate more power in fewer hands. Perhaps great enough need would suffice. Regardless, I do not think what I did could *truly* keep another god from this place if it were determined."

"Boy. It's early for disquisitions on the limits of divine power and your own," Torvul grumbled. "The sooner we get all these folk on their way, the sooner we can be after our own business." He swung a bloodshot eye towards Allystaire. "Which is what, anyway?"

"Preparing the way for peace," Allystaire replied.

"Whatever the Cold that means," Torvul grumbled.

"Gideon, if you would, check on the Cerisia's route to the Vineyards?"

Gideon nodded and slid down from the horse, showing more ease, more familiarity with the task than before. He slipped a parchment from his pocket, opened it to reveal a simple but carefully drawn map, showing Thornhurst, the Ash River to its north, the Thasryach range to its west, the increasingly hilly country to the left that persisted to and across the Innadan border.

The boy knelt to the ground, still holding the map, his eyes rolled back in his head, and the Will of the Mother took to the air as the wispy outline of a dragon. Any who saw the vague form, especially as he gained altitude, would think it nothing more than a flutter in a tailing cloud, perhaps the remnants of some distant trail of smoke.

* * *

From his vantage, the entirety of Barony Delondeur spread out beneath Gideon like a massive quilt bunched haphazardly upon an empty bed. White warred with the pale greens and brown-tinged yellows of the earliest signs of spring. He bore north from the village, to the banks of the Ash, passing Ashmill Bridge, Birchvale, flew well above the High Road as it paralleled the river and passed near or to the towns along its banks.

The Will pushed himself further up into the clouds as he neared the trio of towers that guarded Harlach's close border with Oyrwyn, Innadan, and Delondeur at Standing Guard Pass, over the mountains as they descended into the rocky hills of Barony Innadan.

The change was nearly instantaneous. The mountain ranges that rose up into Oyrwyn and Harlach and walled Innadan away from most of Delondeur were far larger, far grander than the small strip of the Thasryach, and the harsher cold of its neighboring Baronies was largely kept at bay. Once he was well past the mountainous border, well-tended, manicured fields and terraced vineyards spread out over the rolling hills, with the High Road better tended and several smaller tracks and paths branching regularly off of it.

It wasn't long before the projection of Gideon's mind was soaring near the Vineyards itself. Larger, more graceful, but less defensible than the Dunes, more easily reached and assaulted than Wind's Jaw in its remote crag, it was nevertheless an impressive fortress. In contrast to the Dunes, which placed the entire population of the city it purported to guard as a buffer before its walls, the Vineyards was placed in the heart of the Barony that was ruled from it. Once a typical motte and bailey, the castle had grown upwards as well as out, and the hill it sat upon artificially steepened. From a height, Gideon could easily see that every major road in the Barony passed near the Vineyards, and the river Yew passed within sight of its western walls. It was masterfully placed to defend the surrounding Barony, for no army could penetrate far from any direction without needing to pacify it.

Something in him was captivated by the mastery of its construction, by the precise angles of the switchback trails cut into the high hill it sat upon, the delicate-seeming but formidable bridges and towers inside its curtain wall, to learn whatever it was the massive grey edifice could tell him. The towers had several banners and pennants snapping from them, though the only one he recognized was also the most prominent: a red field with a great helm wrapped in green vines.

Gideon felt the pull of Allystaire's mind, a presence that was at once both comforting and demanding. He thought that no matter how far he might fly or how much he might forget himself, he could never again forget that presence. Reluctantly, he reeled his Will back to his physical self, the landscape receding in a blur.

* * *

Little time had truly passed. A few moments at most, but the Gideon's stillness, his seeming vulnerability, bothered Allystaire.

We are going to have to find the boy some guards if we are to face another battle, he thought, sharing it with Torvul and Idgen Marte. *Too dangerous to leave him unattended in a moment like this.*

Keegan's lot, Torvul offered. *They owe their lives to him.*

I will talk with them, Idgen Marte offered.

Gideon's eyes opened wide and suddenly, and he stumbled to his feet, twitching as though unused to his body, the muscles of his legs searching awkwardly for the trick of standing still.

Allystaire's hand was quickly at his shoulder, steadying him, and soon his feet found purchase and he calmed, took a breath.

"As best I can tell there is nothing but road and mountain between here and the Vineyards," the boy said, slowly, the breath heaving in his chest. "No armies on the march, no bandit or brotherhood bands that I could see, and no bad weather or piles of snow or ice. Of course, everything can change between now and the time the Archioness reaches any place much further away than Ashmill Bridge."

"She will have the company of Garth's van further than that," Allystaire replied. "And the lack of armies on the march would make it difficult for any to interpose them between here and there. Ivar will know how to deal with any road agents," Allystaire replied, with brisk confidence. "And it is likely enough that Cerisia does as well. It would take a truly desperate man to attack a high priestess of Fortune."

"You know," Gideon mused, "I think I could carry her there myself." A pause. "Now. Today. With no danger. Well, perhaps some, if priests of Braech were to try to intercept me, but I doubt they are ready for another confrontation."

The eyes of everyone in Gideon's hearing suddenly snapped on him.

"What did you say, boy?" Torvul's words were quiet and careful.

"I said I could carry her there. A simple enough matter if it were just her, her mount, and baggage."

Allystaire's eyes were wide, and he met those of Torvul and Idgen Marte. He knew, instinctively, that all three of them were imagining the implications.

"How many could you move all at once, Gideon?" That was Idgen Marte, finding the words before Allystaire could.

Gideon frowned, thought a long moment, the silence heavy.

"I should think no more than a handful," Gideon finally said, and some part of Allystaire deflated, just a bit, even if most of him believed it to be for the better. "It is possible that more than one at a time might drastically increase the amount of energy I would have to expend, perhaps exponentially, and it will already be considerable. If I were to burn myself out, perhaps six at one time to a very distant place. At risk of my death. Or theirs."

"Yet you could move Cerisia now, at no risk to her or to yourself?" Allystaire's hand had started to clench around the loose hood of Gideon's robe and he'd only just realized it. Gideon hadn't noticed. He forced himself to relax his grip, and Gideon turned to face him.

"A very limited risk."

"How limited?"

Gideon shrugged. "It's possible I could be wrong about the necessary power. It has happened. I am hard pressed to think of an example."

Torvul let out a chuckle, as did Idgen Marte. Allystaire narrowed his eyes in disapproval, though his mouth carried the faint hint of a grin. "Well," he said, "let us find out."

* * *

"Are you *certain*?"

Cerisia only smiled. "Sir Stillbright, are you truly asking a high priestess of Fortune if she wants to miss a chance at something no one living has ever experienced before?"

"That is not entirely true," Gideon put in. "Sorcerers have a limited range of the same kind of power, though they can carry nothing but themselves."

"Hush," Torvul said. "Don't ruin it for the lady."

"Sorry," Gideon said. "I will say again that there is very little danger."

Behind them, the Ravens loitered with Garth and Audreyn, while the Lord of Highgate spoke with some men in leathers, wearing the livery of the towered wall, who nodded sharply at his words and then set off at a trot.

Cerisia, meanwhile, turned to Ivar. "I am afraid, Captain, that it seems I will not require your services. I am sorry that a contract was not drawn up."

The wiry black-mailed woman shrugged. "No matter, Arch'oness. Spring comin' on, there'll be work." She spat to the side, the way she punctuated most sentences.

"When should we leave, Will of the Mother?" Cerisia led her white horse behind her, its grey mane braided and tied with silver chains that jingled lightly and glinted, along with the rest of the silver-and-gold worked into her saddle and tack, in the morning sunlight.

"Now, if you are ready. You may want to cover your animal's eyes."

"I can tell it what to expect," Mol said, letting go the lead of the palfrey she and Gideon had earlier shared. She walked boldly up to Cerisia's mare, laid her hand on the nose it dipped to meet her. Mol and the horse stared into one another's eyes for a few moments, the horse gave its head a shake and whinnied, and Mol stepped back.

"She says a bite of sugar wouldn't go amiss once it's all over, but that she won't panic or bolt on you," the girl said, tilting her head to look up at Cerisia.

"Thank you, Voice. I find I am in your debt," Cerisia said, extending one white-gloved hand to Mol, who took it. It was an odd sight, the grown and mature woman parting with the slip of a girl as equals, though Mol more than matched her for self-possession and presence.

"Without your intervention, who knows what havoc Delondeur crossbows may have wreaked on Thornhurst? There is no debt, Archioness."

They nodded to one another, and Mol stepped away.

"Perhaps," Cerisia said, "it would be best to set me a turn or so's ride from the Vineyards? Dropping me straight into Hamadrian's courtyard might not make exactly the impression we are hoping for."

"As you say," Gideon replied. "Everyone should step back."

Haste was made to give room. He extended a hand to Cerisia, who took it. He stared hard at her and her horse for a moment.

Then woman, horse, and boy all disappeared.

* * *

This, Gideon thought as soon as he could think again, *was a good deal more difficult than I had planned.*

Instead of taking flight as a creature of will and leaving his body behind, Gideon had focused intently upon the physical facts of himself, of Cerisia, and of her mare. He'd fixed all their details in his mind, thought of the ground they were standing on. It was ground he knew well, the ground of Thornhurst, of his home.

Next he thought of what he'd seen of Barony Innadan, the blur of manicured fields, of rows of vines stacked one upon the other, the High Road heading west from the Vineyards and into the other Baronies. He ran the images back in his mind with perfect recall, total clarity. He picked a spot, just off the road, behind gentle curve of the ground and near a stand of trees, and simply thought, very hard, of the three of them being in both places, then only in the latter.

And suddenly they were.

But the strain was far more than he'd anticipated, and Gideon fell to a knee, then over onto all fours, as they arrived.

The horse was the least disturbed of the three, as Cerisia herself leaned against its flank, dizzy and disoriented.

Gideon found himself fighting hard not to fall prone to the ground, which seemed to rush up to meet him, promising a deep well of oblivion if he landed upon it. He focused on his hand, the lines on the back of his light brown skin, the knuckles, clenched it into a fist, digging his fingers into the soft dirt and coming up with a handful of it.

Slowly, on unsteady legs, he pushed himself back to his feet, looked blearily at Cerisia. "That did not go as planned."

"Did it not?" Cerisia had wrapped one hand around the pommel of her saddle. "We appear to be in Barony Innadan."

"True," Gideon admitted, as his feet tried to move out from underneath him, sending his legs swaying after them. "It was simply a good deal more difficult than I expected."

Cerisia slumped against her horse, laughing so hard that she half-choked. "You just performed a miracle unlike any in any song, story, or scripture," she gasped out, "and your reaction is that it was harder than you expected." She pushed herself away from the animal and composed her face quickly, getting her breathing under control. "Wherever did Allystaire *find* you, Will of the Mother?"

"Apprentice to the sorcerer Bhimanzir in the bowels of the Dunes," Gideon answered matter-of-factly. "Though he would probably tell me not to tell you that sort of thing. Or he would have, anyway."

"I know he didn't trust me, Gideon. He was right not to."

"I know," the boy agreed, finally finding his legs agreeable to a more stable relationship with his torso, and standing straight, stretching his arms and legs.

"What was being apprentice to a sorcerer like, Gideon?"

He tilted his head to the side, wide eyes narrowing slightly. "Are you sure that you want to know?"

She nodded, pulled herself up onto the saddle. "Walk with me a bit, if you would, until I gain my bearings."

"The Vineyards are that way," he said pointing east. "The road is just a few dozen paces south of us."

"Walk with me anyway, and perhaps answer my question?"

Gideon shrugged, started walking alongside her horse. "Being apprentice to a sorcerer was a daily trial, life or death, where I was the accused. I was not made aware of what my crime was until I was already being punished for it. The hope of someday, with dedication, being the hand doling out the punishment was to be my reward for survival."

Cerisia was silent as her horse walked a few paces on the slightly damp ground. It was greener here than back in Thornhurst, but not by much, not yet, but the air and the ground both had a slightly wet smell. Gideon breathed it deeply, glad to miss the sharp tang of winter.

"How did you become a sorcerer's apprentice? And where?"

"Sorcerers are careful to guard the secrets of where they hail from. I believe from my features that I was born in the eastern part of the Concordat, where the Knowing are given more sway than in other places. But I cannot tell you where I was taken, for I have no memories of not being Bhimanzir's student."

"Was it truly that young that you were taken to apprentice? As an infant?"

"Allow me to rephrase," Gideon said. "My memories *do not begin* until I am perhaps six or seven summers old. Likely enough I was taken earlier than that, but I have either forgotten or was made to forget."

"How old are you, then?"

"Thirteen or fourteen, I believe."

"What did Bhimanzir try to teach you?"

"The Seeing Dark. Finding, mastering, and focusing my will. The history of the Knowing and the Eldest. Haruspicy."

"Haruspicy?" Cerisia drew her horse to a halt.

"Divining the future by reading entrails."

"I know what it is," she said, her tone remaining patient. "It was, in the past, practiced by Fortune's priests, though it has long since been left behind. It is barbaric and useless."

Gideon shook his head. "It is not useless. Bhimanzir was considered quite gifted at it, and it was his divination that led the Knowing to send him here, to the Baronies. He had, he said, uncovered some threat that needed to be contained."

"He learned that from reading the entrails of, what, sheep?"

"Birds, sheep, goats, rats, cats, dogs, and eventually women."

Cerisia's face paled. "Women?"

"When we came to the Delondeur Baron, his inquiries led him to begin trying to read the entrails of women, yes. Women who were over a certain age, and had borne at least two or three children."

"The Mother," Cerisia said, with a small gasp. "He was learning of Her rise from…"

Gideon nodded. "Yes."

"And you were there? Learning the craft?"

"I was assisting him," Gideon replied, forcing his voice. "Handing him his tools. Telling the guards when he needed one." His eyes swung suddenly down to the ground.

"I am sorry, Gideon. Truly I am." Cerisia swung down off her horse and put an arm on the boy's shoulder. "I had no idea."

"I did not know that what I was doing was wrong," the boy replied. "If anything I was curious. I was eager to learn, eager to please Bhimanzir so that eventually I could best him."

"Gideon, if no one has yet told you this, you were a victim of the sorcerers as surely as the women you speak of."

"No," he replied, shaking his head. "I could've forced Bhimanzir to kill me. I knew I could've said the words that would have made him snap, have forced his hand. I was making a choice."

"And had you done that, where would Bhimanzir be now?"

He thought a moment, then looked up at the priestess. "He would've killed Allystaire. And while I think there is a good chance Idgen Marte could've killed him…"

"You made the better choice, Gideon. Had you been able to change the fate of Bhimanzir's victims in any way, I would say it were different. But you couldn't have, could you? You would only have died along with them. In this, I think no one can fault you. By choosing as you did, you made it possible for Bhimanzir, and others like him, to be destroyed."

"It might be as you say, or I may yet have sins I must pay for. I was not always an unwilling participant, as I said. I was curious, and I wanted to be counted among the Knowing."

"And what changed that?"

"Allystaire did. I had seen Bhimanzir at torture before, but I hadn't seen anyone resist him."

"I am sure that his connection to the Goddess helped."

"No," Gideon said, shaking his head. "While his wounds may mend faster than those of other men—and I say may for I do not know for sure if that is true—what Bhimanzir did to him merely caused pain, not wounds. The Goddess did not come to his aid, for surely I would've felt it. No," he emphasized, shaking his head. "Allystaire resisted Bhimanzir because of who he is, not because of what She made him."

They had reached the road, and Cerisia looked east across the gently rolling countryside, towards the waiting keep and the Baron within. "You think of him as a father, don't you?"

Gideon frowned and turned narrowed eyes upwards at Cerisia as she seized her pommel, prepared to mount her mare again. "Why do you ask? Why are having this conversation?"

"To be honest, Gideon, I ask you questions because you frighten me terribly," Cerisia replied. "You are, I have no doubt, the most powerful being walking the world just now, given all the things I have seen you do. I would be remiss if I did not try to learn about the person behind that power."

Gideon's frowned deepened, but he answered. "He is my father in every way that matters."

"Good," Cerisia said. "I think there is much you can learn from him, and in turn, much you can teach him. There are few men who could offer you a better example, in the main. And yet…" She trailed off.

He didn't reply, only cocked his head.

"Be mindful of the anger within him, Gideon," Cerisia said. "When it comes upon him he is terrifying, and I am afraid it could lead him to ruin. In this, if nothing else, do not emulate him."

"A paladin is meant to be frightening, Archioness," Gideon said. "If you find him terrifying, I would suggest asking yourself why."

Cerisia pulled herself back up onto her horse, sitting side-saddle with practiced ease. "I know that it was just as likely we would become enemies as we have allies, and that he does not trust me completely, nor approve of how my clergy live. Yet the Goddess I serve is the Mistress of Chance, and thus it feels likely to be a divine chance, rather than a simple one. Even so, I will not be blind to his flaws."

"I should be leaving," Gideon said shortly. "Be well, and ride safe to the Vineyards, Archioness."

"Before you go, Gideon, would you accept my blessing?" She extended a hand uncertainly. "I do not know what you think of it, and I would understand if you refused. Yet if our Goddesses must work together then there is no reason we cannot accept one another's benediction. I would accept yours in return, if you were to offer it."

Gideon thought a moment, his face becoming the impassive mask it so often was. "You know that extending any of your power towards me is dangerous, yes? I could seize it, draw so much if through you that it would kill you."

"You won't," Cerisia said, calm certainty in her tone and her features.

"What makes you so sure?"

"Because you said yourself you are Allystaire Stillbright's son."

"I wouldn't do it on purpose. There is much I still don't understand about my Gift."

"Then I am offering you an opportunity to learn. And need I remind you that chance rarely goes against me?"

Gideon shrugged and walked to the side of her saddle, felt her hand lower onto his head.

"May Fortune smile upon you. May all your ways and means be favorable. May the wind be strong in your sail and the rain soft on your field. May chance lay lightly upon your heart and may you fear no risk. Be neither miser nor spendthrift and the Goddess will surely reward you as you deserve."

Gideon felt a small tingling in the air, a gathering of power, though very small. Coalescing within Cerisia, it sank into him, and into the well of power that the Goddess's touch had opened within him, a cup of water tossed onto a half-full bucket.

He cleared his throat and bowed his thanks, then reached up to place his hand on hers, thinking for a moment on the words. "May the Mother find you in sun or in shadow, but never in darkness." He felt again a trickle of power flow through him into the world, into the woman whose hand he touched. She flinched slightly as she felt it, and he stepped away.

"Be well, Archioness. I hope Baron Innadan finds you persuasive."

She smiled, and slipped her mask from an inside pocket of her cloak, tying it with a silk ribbon around her head. While the gems were gone, Cerisia's own eyes provided enough jewel-like glitter in the blank gold of Fortune's face. "He shall, Gideon. Be well."

She gave her horse a gentle kick and rode on. Gideon gathered his Will, closed his eyes, and focused his mind on Thornhurst, on the steps of the Temple, and concentrated on being there, standing upon them, feeling their sun-soaked warmth.

He vanished, and the Archioness of Fortune sped up her horse, carrying with her the first missives of the Mother's Crusade.

* * *

While Cerisia and Gideon came to know and to bless each other hundreds of miles away, Allystaire rode alongside Garth and Audreyn as the first elements of the Oyrwyn encampment began moving through the village on the start of their trek north.

"I sent the scouts ahead this morning," Garth was saying, "while the men broke down the camp and packed. Given their long idleness I thought it best to have men rather than animals bear the weight of tents and gear. I don't expect resistance, or at any rate, not much more than the odd bandit or deserter."

Allystaire raised a hand to cut him off. "Garth, you do not report to me any longer, remember?"

The blond knight sighed, sagged in his saddle. "It is easy to fall into old habits, Ally." He held his gauntlets lightly in one hand, tapped them with metallic clinks against the scale armor that lay across his thigh. "How many times had we done this? Breaking down a camp in the early turns, marching all day, hunting for some Delondeur knights to teach a lesson to, or setting a trap in the mountains for some Harlach bastards. I'd give anything for it to be that way again."

On Garth's other side Allystaire could see Audreyn's face darkening. He raised his hand again, but in her direction, rather than her husband's.

"Garth, have you listened to nothing I have said in all the weeks you have been here?"

"Of course I have," he protested. "Peace and all that. And I know deep down you're right, but damn it all!" Garth slapped his gauntlets against his thigh with a clatter. "It's what I was *made* for, Ally! The riding, the hard living, the hot blood of battle, the glory at the end of it."

Allystaire lowered his head and sighed. "What glory was that? The glory of having killed other men, whose names you did not know, whose widows and children you would never see."

"Damn it! You're the one who made me what I am, Ally. You taught me all of this, made me good at it, made me love it."

"And if you would listen now, I would teach you something else. War is neither glorious nor pretty, Garth, not as we fought it all those years."

"You're still fighting, Allystaire. Your armor and your hammer may be all brightness and glimmer now but I know you've put blood on both of them."

"Aye, and I will again. But only if I must. Tell me one time, on all those campaign mornings you remember with such fondness, that we were driven by necessity to kill the men we sought to kill."

"There were times Harlach were coming over our border."

"Claiming useless mountains, without fertile valleys or veins of iron. Why should men die over bare rock and ice? And more than likely Harlach was coming over our border because we had done the same to them a month or a year or decade before. It must end."

"Then when can a man fight, Allystaire? Must he politely wait for his enemy to arrive and beg his pardon?"

"When he must, Garth. When failing to do so would lead to more death, more ruin." They'd ridden beyond the northern gate now, cresting the gentle rise of land that gave them a view of the timber-walled village behind them, and Allystaire shifted in the saddle and raised a hand to indicate it. "Take Thornhurst. Why did we fight a battle here? Was there glory to be gained? Prizes of ransom or treasure?"

Garth shook his head almost sullenly. Beside him, Audreyn sighed.

"We fought here, and died here, to protect homes, spouses, children, Lives that had been built and rebuilt. Lives that, to men born to what you and I were born to, once seemed so very small. Yet how big or how small a village seems owes much to where a man was born, does it not?"

"What do you mean?" Garth frowned, his long, pale, beard drooping and hiding his mouth.

"Coldbourne Hall and Highgate and Wind's Jaw are grand homes, full of silver plate and gemmary, fine tapestries and furs, and when such a place is sacked, knights and lords the Baronies over weep for its loss and sing of its grandeur. And yet, who loses more? The knight whose hall is lost but still keeps his title, his income, his horses, and arms, or the village man whose life is ruined utterly when a one-room cottage is torched? Do they write songs for the villages we burned in our wake?"

"We were careful to burn only the buildings, Ally. Your orders. We left stock alone unless we bartered for it, and you hung anyone who interfered with the women."

"A pathetic excuse. A thin blanket to warm my soul at night, done for the looks of the thing rather than any real benefit. If I had any courage at all back then Garth, *any*, I would have left every village alone. I would never have led armies that were out for conquest and plunder only."

"I can't believe I'm hearing this," Garth said, disgust in his tone, and he turned his mount, preparing to spur it, until Audreyn reached over and caught his reins. He met her eyes, something passed between man and wife unspoken, and he turned back to Allystaire with a sigh. "What would you ask of me then? I can't renounce who I am. I won't."

"When you return home, speak with the poor folk who answer to High-gate, the farmers and shepherds. Learn how small their dreams are: a harvest not trampled in the field, sheep not stolen and butchered by deserter's brotherhood or another Baron's army or their own Cold-damned knights, a child not pressed or become a camp follower. Then think on the devastation we wreak upon them when those dreams are shattered. Take what you learn to the Young Baron, and convince him to come to the congress."

Garth sighed heavily, began tapping his gauntlets against his hauberk again. "I was never much of a talker, Ally."

"We will both do what we can, brother," Audreyn put in. "But you know Gilrayan Oyrwyn. He has never been a man of peace, and he will not be now unless he can see some advantage in it. We will need other means."

"I will not be part of a revolt unless it is thrust upon me like in Delondeur," Allystaire said, "nor will I be in league with assassins."

"Your imagination remains limited, brother, to think that these are the only ways to influence the Young Baron's decision making. We will do ask you ask, both with our own folk and in Wind's Jaw, and we will do more." Audreyn edged her horse around Garth's and rode it up beside Ardent, whose eye followed her and her mount carefully, though he didn't bite or snap at them. "I would carry the Mother with me, Allystaire, along with your missives of the peace congress. After seeing what She offers—after speaking with Idgen Marte and with Mol—I can no longer pray earnestly in the chapels of Braech, or Fortune, or with an Urdaran monk."

Allystaire smiled broadly, though the expression was ill suited to his blocky, scarred face. "When we can come among the people of Oyrwyn, we will, but until then—"

"I know," Audreyn said. "Mol has give me a scroll of prayers and I have spent lots of time with Idgen Marte this winter. I am no priestess, and I do not mean to be. But I will tell anyone who asks what I know of Her, and I will teach them the prayers the Voice gave me."

"Be careful. Of Braech's priests especially. I think it likely that the next battle I fight will be with them," Allystaire said, and for a moment he was chilled at the thought of bare chested, tattooed berzerkers hurling themselves into battle. For a moment, just a moment, he felt and he saw something else, something huge and fierce and glowing angrily, but it was gone as quickly as it came.

"I've the power to expel them from Highgate lands," Garth said. "Just say the word."

"That is a decision you must make yourself, Lord of Highgate," Allystaire said. "Remember that I am no longer your warlord. I would still be your friend and your mentor if you will let me, though." He extended one arm towards the taller, paler man, who clasped it hard.

"Brother of Battle?" Garth's voice was hopeful.

"Let us try to be brothers in peace as long as we can, Garth," Allystaire said. "And be brothers of battle when we must."

Garth nodded, braids at the side of his head bobbing, and pumped Allystaire's hand twice, then let go.

Audreyn drew closer to him still, leaned out of her saddle, and threw her arm around his neck. "Goodbye, Allystaire. If I can help you bring about this peace, I will."

Allystaire slung an arm around her back, mindful not to pull her from the saddle. He lowered his head against hers and murmured to her. "I am still sorry, Audreyn, for all the months you spent alone. Forgive me for that. I beg you."

"There is nothing to forgive, Ally," she murmured back. "You did the best you could."

"No," he protested, pulling back and shaking his head. "I never did, and I never knew it until now."

"Then you are forgiven, though I don't believe you need to be." Then, clearing her throat, she said, "We have said our goodbyes to our brother, but would the Arm of the Mother offer us his blessing as we leave?"

"Of course," Allystaire said, before he realized it, and he found himself frantically searching for the words. *Please, Goddess,* he thought, slightly hopelessly, then lowered his head and lift a hand out to Garth and Audreyn both. The words rolled from him without much thought.

"May the Mother guide you and keep you. May love be warmth in your hearth and your heart both in equal measure. May you want for nothing but the light of the next day. May the memory of Her sun bring you beyond any darkness."

Allystaire lowered his hand to the pommel of his saddle, and lifted his head. He felt, as much as heard, a chime ring in the air, and he nodded in farewell to his sister and her husband.

"Go with the Mother. And be safe. Audreyn," he called, as the pair started to ride off, "if ever you need me, pray. Think of me, of Mol, of Gideon. We will know of it."

She nodded, then turned and let her horse trot, the animal naturally moving alongside Garth's huge black destrier, equal in size to Ardent. Allystaire watched the column move, the ranks of men marching in time, boots like a rolling drumbeat on the track, the Highgate Towered Wall and the Coldbourne Hawk snapping above ranks of dark green-tabarded men shouldering axes and spears. For a moment, just a moment, he felt the pull of it, the urge to ride to the head of the column, small though it was, and direct it to his will.

But then Allystaire Stillbright looked back to the village that was his home, saw the curved roof of the Temple and caught a glint of sunlight off its windows, and rode back to it.

CHAPTER 24

The Vineyards

Before Cerisia came within shouting distance of the sprawling length of the castle's curtain wall, she had pulled a thin, well-polished wooden pole from where it was strapped across the back of her mare. From her saddlebags, she pulled free the banner of Fortune, the nude form of her Goddess picked out in threads of silver and gold. With fingers that remained nimble, even while gloved, she tied it around the pole and lifted it high. The wind caught it as she rode forward and snapped it taut against the pole, and she knew well that the glittering threads woven along its silk length would catch the sun. Any guard watching the road would know that one of Fortune's Temple rode towards them.

Her mare had a road in front and the huge structure of the Baronial Seat rising before, so the horse knew well what to do, and Cerisia relaxed. She thought of the talking she'd have to do, the forms to be met, when she'd last seen Hamadrian Innadan. She hadn't come this far east for three years, on a grand circuit of the western Baronies when she'd been named Archioness. Whether Barony Innadan fell under her purview was, perhaps, a matter of some debate. Given its central location both the eastern and western Baronies tended to claim Innadan as one of their own. Since Fortune's Archions and Archionesses were reluctant to draw strict lines of influence and responsibility—all the better to allow room for maneuvering and the vagaries of chance—she could certainly claim a degree of power among any of Fortune's clergy she would encounter.

Frowning behind the mask that was quickly growing cold against her skin, Cerisia searched her memory for the names and faces of those assigned to the chapel in the Vineyards and any local temples. She could come up with but two names: Jastin Meer, the senior priest at the Vineyards chapel, and Anlys, one of his assigned bearers. She bit her lip as she tried to recall the girl's last name.

"Baronial lordlings and their ridiculous glut of names," she muttered, unable to come up with it.

She was jolted out of her reverie as she realized that a contingent of riders had left the Vineyards and were making straight for her. She made minor adjustments to her dress, arranged the fur collar of her cloak, readjusted her hand around the banner, and rode to meet them.

Sunlight glinted off their armor, and she could see the red Innadan tabards they wore, and as she drew closer she smiled at the honor being accorded her visit.

The lead rider wore a suit of carefully crafted plate, etched and enameled with green vines bearing plump purple grapes across its arms, and a great helm that matched the huge banners unfurled above the Vineyards, with green vines appearing to wrap around it.

The knight sat tall in the saddle, mastering the dun-colored stallion he rode with his knees and with light flicks of the reins, making the horse appear to bow, lifting one leg and lowering its head.

She pulled her mare to a halt a few yards away, and watched as the knight pulled his vine-covered helm free. She was quite surprised, then, at the youth of the man who'd come riding to meet her, expecting the worn but proud face of his father.

"Welcome to the Vineyards, servant of the Mistress of Wealth," the man called in a clear and courtly voice, a voice to match his looks. Clean-shaven, with a strong jaw and high cheeks, brown eyes and long brown hair carefully but loosely queued at the back of his neck, it took Cerisia a moment to place a face she remembered as much younger.

"Arontis Innadan," she called back, watching carefully for a reaction to his name. "To what do I owe the honor of being greeted by you?"

"You have me at a disadvantage, my lady," Arontis called back. The planes of his cheeks did nothing to reveal any reaction to that. "Yet it is my duty as Castellan of the Vineyards to greet all honored guests. May I ask whom I address?"

"Archioness Cerisia, Lord Castellan Innadan. We met three years prior. You had just been knighted, as I recall," she added.

"Indeed, Archioness. You are most welcome to our seat. May we escort you in the walls?"

She carefully inclined her head and nudged her mare forward. Arontis gently turned his horse so that they rode side by side, the stallion picking up its hooves carefully one by one and flagging its tail, whether at her mare or by some subtle prompting of his rider, she wasn't sure.

A half dozen red-tabarded lancers spread out to surround them, allowing several yards between their own mounts and those of Cerisia and Arontis, a space she was grateful for.

"Baron's Own Heavy Horse?" It was a guess, Cerisia knew, but likely enough to be true. She turned her masked face to the young lord riding along next to her.

The smile he offered was, perhaps, a bit patronizing, but it was pleasant enough to look at that she paid it no mind. The somewhat diffident boy she remembered had grown up a great deal since she had last visited. She found herself wondering just how much even as he answered.

"Here we call them the Thornriders, Archioness, but then, everything must have to do with wine, grapes, or vines in Innadan."

"I see," she said. Then, pitching her voice lower. "Arontis, please be honest with me. I know that it is the Castellan's duty to greet honored guests only if the Baron is unavailable. How is your father?"

His jaw and sharp cheekbones set with fetching determination as he considered her question. "You will see, Archioness."

"That sounds grim. I fervently hope that he is still among the quick."

"As do I, Archioness. This winter was hard on him."

"Please," she murmured, briefly reaching out to touch his armored wrist. "Call me Cerisia."

* * *

Masked in smooth and featureless silver, Jastin Meer, Fortune's Chaplain at the Vineyards, was waiting for Cerisia with a delegation of priests just inside the courtyard. At his right hand, bearing the banner, was the girl she remembered, still a slip of a thing, but lovely in the pristine white dress, silver threads, white wool cloak; at his left, a boy barely old enough to apprentice, dressed in rags and covered in a dirt that seemed all too real to her, carried the wheel.

Arontis had swiftly dismounted and extended his hands towards her, one knee bent, to help her from the saddle. She grinned, glad of the mask's concealment, sure that if he could see her face he'd find it patronizing. Still, she reasoned, a gesture of chivalry that was unnecessary was no less welcome. She slid one foot down into his couched hands, and then dropped carefully to the ground.

Had the Innadan heir not been armored as thoroughly as he was, Cerisia might have allowed herself to fall against him slightly. *It's not blades alone armor was made to repel,* she thought, still grinning. She smoothed her dress and held her own banner straight in her hand, with Arontis holding out a mailed elbow. Behind her, the Thornriders had taken her horse towards the long stone-walled stables built into the very side of the inner wall, and dispersed to whatever tasks occupied fighting men when at home.

In fact, there were rather more fighting men in evidence than she had expected. In a distant part of the courtyard another troop of red-tabarded lancers were mounted, moving out through the gatehouse, down the three-turned path through the outer curtain and to maneuvers in the fields and the road beyond.

Finally, Jastin found his courage and came forward, attendants in his wake. "Archioness, to what do we mere chaplains owe the honor of your visit?" He had tried for booming authority, found something just short of hoarse yelling.

Cerisia took in his clothing with distaste. From a distance, he passed, but up close his vestments were spotted and stained, the hem of his robes trailed on the ground, and the silver fittings of his belt were tarnished. Unforgivably, his mask had lost the patina of polish and was starting to dim and darken as well.

"It is Baron Hamadrian Innadan I have come to visit, Chaplain Meer," Cerisia intoned calmly, the authority in her voice always easy to find. "I will have time to meet with you later."

"Even so," the man insisted, his voice just this side of a whine, "had we received notice of your visit we could have arranged proper quarters."

"Leave that to me, Chaplain Meer," Arontis said, his voice as smooth as the skin stretched taut over his cheekbones. "It is, after all, my castle to look after. Come, Archioness," he said, turning his head to indicate that the chaplain and his party were dismissed, from his notice at least, "let me bring you to my father."

Instead of being led to the great hall as she was expected, Cerisia found herself climbing a stairway ahead of Arontis. She struggled to recall what she remembered of the layout of the inner keep, and felt likely she was being taken towards the Innadan family apartments.

She had little time to marvel at the marble floors, the vine-carved columns. In truth, the vines covering everything all began to blur together, and while the tapestries hung along the walls at regular intervals were dutifully impressive, Cerisia had always found that tapestries made her think of the drudgery required to produce them.

Finally, Arontis led her up another stair, two turns down corridors that all looked the same, and to a door flanked by two knights in full armor, naked greatswords resting point-down upon the stone floor. They wore tabards of their own sigils, halved with the Vined Great Helm of Innadan.

Arontis rapped hard upon the door, and a strong, yet tired voice responded. "Enter."

He swung the door open. The heat inside was practically suffocating, and Cerisia swept in before Arontis, who swung the door closed behind them. The room was both a sitting room and a study, with richly cushioned and heavily carved chairs scattered before a sizable fireplace. A writing case with a canted red leather surface and silver fittings sat on a high table near a window, its glass stained with the Innadan crest. Nearby shelves held scrolls, bound books both large in small with leather, wood, or even worked metal covers, and fine pens and pots of ink lay scattered about.

Standing straight, if not tall, wrapped in a long fur mantle, Baron Hamadrian Innadan looked worse than Cerisia had imagined. Even three years ago, he'd been on the verge of being an old man, but there had been a fierce intelligence in his eyes and a hard resignation about his compact person.

Now he seemed smaller than he ever had. Instead of a circlet or a helm, a simple cap of maintenance rested on a pate gone entirely bald. A week's growth of lifelessly grey whiskers covered his cheeks and chin and a neck that, though he was thin, hung in a long fold like a turkey's wattle. One blue eye had gone milky, but Cerisia was happy to see that the other shone as fiercely bright as ever.

Though he looked frail, the Baron stepped forward to greet her with arms outstretched.

"Cerisia," he said, embracing her, though his thin arms couldn't manage much of a squeeze. "Indulge an old man and have that mask off. I would look upon the real beauty of a woman, not the sterile lies of your Goddess."

She felt herself smiling at the compliment, and soon she had tugged the mask free, though she found him pointing at it, his hand trembling slightly as he raised it.

"What happened to your eyes, eh?"

She cleared her throat, allowed a delicate blush to creep up her neck. "I pried them loose and gave them away."

"To a man? What lucky bastard must I duel, then?" His voice quavered, and she pretended not to notice.

"To a cause, as much as to a man. And that cause is why I'm here, my Lord Baron."

"A cause?" He snorted. "Sounds expensive. And call me familiar, damn it all."

"A cause near and dear to you, Hamadrian," Cerisia said, smiling. "Peace." She reached inside her cloak to a long pocket sewn into it, and drew forth a handful of rolled parchments sealed in blue wax.

"Give them to my lad there," he said, pointing to Arontis with a hand that trembled slightly less than it had.

The Castellan and heir reached out to take them, immediately turning them to inspect the seal. "I know not this mark, father," he said, with an armored shrug, lifting his eyes in puzzlement to Cerisia.

"If tales of a paladin have reached over the mountains, Hamadrian, I am here to confirm them. The mark is his."

Hamadrian's eyes narrowed, and Cerisia had a sense of being studied carefully for something other than her curves or the twist of her lips. "Fetch us wine, Arontis. This may take some time. And by your own Fortune, woman, have a seat. I'm Freezing well going to."

The Baron's son pulled his gauntlets free and set them down on a side table, moved to a heavy sideboard at the far wall of the room, and busied himself with a thin jug set in a silver cooling bucket and a tray full of goblets. Hamadrian shuffled to one of the chairs facing the fire, and lowered himself into it with exaggerated care. Thin lips pressed tight against his mouth, the only apparent expression of the pain he must've felt.

"I do well standing or sitting," Hamadrian muttered. "It's moving between them that's the trouble. And sitting tends to put me to sleep," he added, but then aimed a smile at Cerisia. "Not, of course, that such would be a problem in view of you, Cerisia."

His eyes slid away from her, though, to the fire, and then he turned his neck to watch his son approach, bearing two goblets—clear glass resting in a wrought-iron nest of leaves and curling vines—full of a deep purple wine.

Cerisia took one goblet, waited for the Baron to take his. He turned his head to study with his good eye, said, "I love my vines as much as the next man," he grumbled, "more, probably, but Cold do I wish we'd learn to decorate with something other than vines and roots, grapes and leaves and thorns. Carve a bird on something."

She lifted her glass, sipped, found it pleasant but unremarkable. The Baron lifted the wine to his nose, didn't bother to smell, had a sip, smacked his lips. "This is rubbish, for now," he muttered. "Give it some time, it may be the greatest my lands have ever produced. I doubt I'll live to see it, so I taste some every day, have my wine steward haul it up from the butt. I hope, every day, that I'll taste some hint of that greatness. And it always disappoints." He carefully set his goblet down on the table in front of them, focused both the bright blue and the milky white eye on Cerisia. "Tell me of this paladin."

"Before I do," she said, folding her hands in her lap with the goblet clutched between them, "allow me to ask what you have heard so far."

"Not much. Some tales drifted over in the fall of someone claiming to be a holy knight stirring up trouble for Lionel, and good for him, I say. Lot of typical nonsense from those stories though, ripping a tree out of the ground to fell a giant, sending gangs of bandits scurrying with his voice alone. There was something new in them. What was it, Arontis?"

"Something about commanding a spirit of air and shadow. Did not sound very holy."

"Ah," Cerisia muttered. "Then the stories are both more correct than I had expected and more wrong. Please," she said, "let his own words speak for him before I do, Hamadrian. Read his first letter."

"Bring it to me, boy," the Baron said, holding out a hand. Arontis swiftly retrieved the bundle of scrolls and brought them forward.

"Which is it?" He held them out to Cerisia, who reached in and plucked free the smallest, most tightly rolled parchment, held it towards the Baron.

He held it close to his good eye to examine the seal. "What is it? A flower?"

"A sunburst," she said.

The Baron picked at the blue wax seal and pried it loose, but gnarled fingers found difficulty in unrolling it. With a grumble, he held it towards Cerisia, who unrolled it and began to read.

My Lord Baron Hamadrian Innadan, Master of the Vineyards,

Before I begin, I must beg your forgiveness. Years ago, you asked of me, and the other Barons and lords, what I am now asking of you. And instead of listening in good faith and trying even to speak of peace, I happily drank your wine and broke lances in front of your walls and thought what a wonderful lark it all was as a break from the real business of war.

To have been so callous in the face of the one man with the courage to ask us all to stop and think about the cost of our madness is but one of many regrets, many sins I will spend the rest of my life paying for.

What I ask is the very same thing you wished for when we were younger men: a congress of peace. I propose to arrange a meeting with you, Unseldt Harlach, Byron Telmawr, Gilrayan Oyrwn, and the newly elevated Landen Delondeur. If you would consent to pass the message further, I would welcome the presences of Damarind, Machoryn, or any others you might reach.

If possible I propose that this congress convene in Standing Guard Pass.

You, Hamadrian, are the first and most important part. If you will agree to meet, I know that Telmawr will follow your lead. Landen Delondeur will come at my request, and I am confident that Oyrwyn can be lured out of sheer curiosity.

I am certain that by now you have had word of my Exile and Divestiture. I count these as but a very small loss. The stakes of the war we have fought for so long were never, in truth, very high for us; lines on a map, titles before our names, the restoration of a line of kings we extinguished while purporting to fight for them. As I have come to live among simpler folk, folk I once would have called lesser, I now understand how much greater the stakes have always been for them. It has become my appointed task to end the war we have so long inflicted upon the people we believed were ours to lead, but if I am to do it peacefully, Baron Innadan, I beg for your name and your influence to make it possible.

Yours, with Respect, Regret, and Hope,

Allystaire Stillbright, formerly Coldbourne, Arm of the Mother

When Cerisia finished and sat back, the Baron drew a sharp breath.

"Do you mean to tell me," he said, "that *Coldbourne*, that bloodthirsty son of a bitch, is this paladin? And that you believe it?"

"He would tell you, Hamadrian, that he is no longer Allystaire Coldbourne. And in truth, he would be right. If nothing else, he cannot speak aught but the truth any longer, and so if he says a thing, it must be true. And I do not simply believe it, Baron. I know it. I have seen miracles performed by his own hands. I have felt the pull of his Goddess's power on my own mind. I have seen him destroy the ensorcelled dead with his own hands, ripping them apart like so much wine-soaked bread. Baron Lionel Delondeur, a trio of sorcerers, and I do not know how many other men have fallen to him and those who follow him, my Lord Baron. The world will rush behind him to change, and if we rush with it, we can see that it changes for the better."

Hamadrian Innadan reached for his wine and had a long gulp of it, nearly draining the glass. He set it down, the metal base of the goblet thunking heavily against the table. "You say that Lionel Delondeur is dead? Truly?"

"I do, my lord," Cerisia replied.

"That news," Baron Innadan said carefully, "does not find me in sorrow's grip."

"There is quite a tale to be made of all of it," Cerisia offered.

"I am less interested in the tale than I am the truth of it."

"And when a paladin walks the world, and other powers with him, the truth and the tale are hard to separate from one another."

Arontis cleared his throat, and his father waved a hand at him. Stepping forward to stand behind Cerisia's chair, he said, "If he has already pulled down one Baron, how do we know he isn't calling for a congress in order to spring a trap?"

The Baron's head rose sharply towards his son, narrowing his eyes in anger. "Arontis, *think*. Whatever he calls himself now, we're talking about Allystaire Coldbourne. I called him bloodthirsty, and he was that—but he was never a murderer, nor was that kind of deceit in his heart. Or, in truth, in his mind. He was an honest man and straightforward. Never subtle."

"He is even more and even less the things you say he once was, Baron Innadan," Cerisia put in. "If I did not know that this peace conference was his true aim, I would never have agreed to carry this message on his behalf."

That sharp blue eye flicked to her. She found it easy to focus on his bright eye, rather than the clouded one, but the Baron made that easier by turning his head so that only his good eye seemed to be focused on her. "That raises yet another question. Why does he not come himself?"

"He has immediate obligations in the village where the Temple of his Goddess has risen."

"Hmm. And this Goddess, what of Her? Tell me. Do you come to me in service to Her?"

"I am still servant to the Mistress of Wealth, and I always shall be," Cerisia replied. "Most of those who do worship with Allystaire call Her the Mother. Some the Lady. They claim the Sun for Her, among other things."

"The Sun," he muttered. "Be honest with me, Cerisia. Is this a revolt in the making? Are all the great folk to be pulled down and made examples? I know my time in this world grows short. That doesn't mean I wish to end it strung out along the walls of my own home like so much red bunting."

"I think that Allystaire fears such a thing as much as you do," she replied. "He wants peace, Hamadrian. Not a revolt."

"What he wants and what he'll get once he starts putting weapons in the hands of peasants are two different things. Especially if they've got the taste for Baronial blood now that Lionel is dead."

"Lionel had gone mad. I saw it with my own eyes. Hamadrian, he raised a small host on the edge of winter and besieged one of his own villages. Sorcerers in his employ raised abominations. He became one himself, wearing armor and carrying a blade crafted from the bones and the blood of his own men. Allystaire and his companions made an army out of a few score farmers, laborers, and craftsman, and they won. And then they went back to living as poor folk do in winter."

"Hmph. And this daughter of Lionel's that is Baroness now, how did that come about?"

"Allystaire let her live," Cerisia said, resisting the urge to massage her temple, "after taking her captive at the conclusion of the battle."

"Who paid her ransom, then?"

"No one, Hamadrian," Cerisia said. "Do not think that such rules apply to Allystaire Stillbright. Doubtless, Landen is on her way to occupying her seat in the Dunes even now, ready to come to the congress in good faith."

"I'll believe a Delondeur wants peace when she's the last so-named person alive," the Baron Innadan spat, then was suddenly seized with a choking cough. Cerisia stood up, moving towards him, but he held up a hand in protest even as his face reddened.

Arontis reacted quickly, pulling some small bottle from a side table and putting it to his father's lips. Hamadrian snatched it in one hand and took a quick sip.

The coughing subsided quickly, but Cerisia took the opportunity to stand.

"Perhaps, my Lord Baron, we should meet again later," she started, but he waved her down and she sank back into her seat.

"A bit of coughing'll not deter me from seeing to business, Cerisia," he said, his voice a bit ragged, cheeks still red beneath grey stubble. "If what you say is true, this is the most important moment of our age. I'll not be deterred from attending to it." He cleared his throat. Arontis hovered over his shoulder, but Hamadrian gave his son a gentle shove away.

"Barony Innadan will not sit idle if there is a chance at peace," the Baron began.

"What gives us any reason to believe Harlach will lay aside its antipathy with us? Or that Delondeur has forgotten theirs simply because Lionel died? Or even that Oyrwyn has remembered our alliance?" Arontis spoke, unaddressed. His fair, smooth-cheeked face quivered with the tension of a rising anger. "If Lionel Delondeur is dead, the daughter will be weak. We could move forward against her with all haste."

Hamadrian's face grew cold, and slowly, the ailing man pushed himself to his feet. Cerisia found herself standing as well.

"Arontis," the Baron began, his tone low, sad, not the barely-checked anger Cerisia had found herself expecting. "You were young when I called for a peace conference all those years ago, still a page, unblooded. You hadn't seen the face of war, and you didn't feel that faint hope that hung in the air. Mayhap I was the only one there who did, but the failure has haunted me. I'm too close to the Cold now to add any new regrets. So I ask you to think of our legacy, boy, as leaders of men. Answer me a question: which takes more courage, to lend a fallen enemy a hand back up, or to plant a boot on his neck?"

Arontis held his father's gaze a moment, then dropped his eyes. Cerisia took a moment to appreciate the sweep of his eyelashes when he did, cataloguing it absently, saving most of her attention for the father.

"Just because you don't like the answer doesn't mean you don't give it, boy."

Arontis sighed, lifted his eyes. "To lift the man up."

"Then that's what we're going to do," Hamadrian said. "It shames us that it's taken an Oyrwyn mountain savage to show us the way. Innadan ought to have led in peace. If we're given a chance to now, then as long as I'm alive, we're going to take it."

Cerisia felt, for perhaps the first time, the seeds of hope sprouting into something more, growing upwards towards a light she couldn't quite see, but sensed.

Baron Innadan turned to her then. "My scribes, birds, and post riders will be placed at your disposal, Archioness. We'll get messages to whoever will listen, including Allystaire in his village. It can't be a far ride, as you've gotten here so soon after snowmelt on the other side of the mountains."

"In point of fact, Baron, there are facts about my passage here that you ought to know of." She smiled faintly and said, "I hope you are prepared to credit things even more fantastic than those which I have already spoken of. Perhaps we ought to be seated again."

CHAPTER 25

The Shape of Things

"First y'were sendin' us away, be gone or be damned." Ivar spat through one of several gaps in her teeth. "Then when we hie back, tails 'tween our legs, chastened by your sister, who, forgivin' me, can be a Cold of a lot more terrifyin' than you, y'want us goin' with that priestess. Now I'll admit, a week or two spent shepherdin' her o'er the mountains had a certain appeal, and Innadan at the end of a journey always does. But now," the black-mailed warband captain said, "now ya've promised us t'this youngling Baroness Delondeur, the very one you were fightin' when we first showed up. I don't unnerstand ya."

"Conditions are fluid, Ivar," Allystaire said, "and we must respond to them as we think best."

Ivar watched Allystaire carefully, both of them armed and armored, horses nearby, watching the Delondeur men pack their gear, provisions, and arms on the few horses they had left.

"And I will not order you anywhere," Allystaire went on. "To order you out of Thornhurst was a mistake, and I regret it; the sanctuary of the Mother's Temple must always be open to anyone. I am *asking* you to consider helping to escort the Baroness Delondeur back to her seat, yes, for it is a long journey, and not one I can make with her."

"Be quite a change, the Iron Ravens servin' the Baroness Delondeur."

"Change is what I am about."

"We'll take a vote, those of us who're left. And in the end we'll vote t'do as y'ask, no matter my words on it," Ivar said. "But I want t'have a say before we go."

"Have away."

Ivar sniffed in one nostril. "Y'think y'can end a war that thousands been fightin' for two score years with a few hundred villagers and yer Goddess, ya've gone daft. You might stop it fer a bit, get a pause fer yer peace congress, but war'll come back. Way this part o'the world is."

"That the task is difficult, perhaps impossible, does not for one moment change the fact that I must do it."

"Yer makin' too many enemies. Someone'll slip a knife in yer back."

"To get a knife into my back, Ivar, an assassin has to get past Idgen Marte."

"Ya didn't let me finish," Ivar said. "They'll slip a knife in yer back, or try, and if she carves up enough o'the bastards with knives, they'll try t'find another way t'get at ya. You try and change the whole world, m'lord, the whole world's gonna line up t'ask ya who the Cold y'think y'are. Together they'll find a way. Come at the folk around ya, if they must. At the poor n'simple people you're so concerned about defendin'."

Allystaire breathed in deep through his nose and rested a hand on his hammer, still getting used to the rounded shape under his hand, rather than the flat top of the maul he was used to.

"Then I say let the whole world know that I am the Arm of the Mother, and that if they wish to draw me out in the way you describe, they will not be ready for what I bring with me."

"Can't fight entire Baronies by yerself, nor all o'Braech's Temple, if it comes to it, or Fortune's."

"Ivar, why the concern?"

"Well, besides the fact that yer lookin' t'drastically reduce m'company's chances o'making good weight in the comin' years? All that's happened," she shrugged, "I still don't want t'see ya dead for bein' foolish."

"I do not think I was ordained a paladin so that I could live safely to my dotage, Ivar."

The mercenary captain sighed and lowered her head a bit. "Just be smart, m'lord."

"I am trying to be," Allystaire said. "That is why I am asking you to go with the Baroness. I need a friend on that journey, Ivar, because much depends upon Landen taking up her seat. I know you do not agree with me on ending the war, and that you have not come to the Mother. I would like to think despite all the missteps we both have made, though, we could still call one another that."

"I s'pose," Ivar muttered grudgingly. "If ya really wanted t'be smart, why not have yer lad just magick us all there."

"Too much for him. He has not returned yet from carrying Cerisia."

"Ya don't sound worried."

"Because I am not," Allystaire said. "If I concentrate, I can feel him. Far away, yes; hundreds of miles beyond Standing Guard Pass, even, within the shadow of the Vineyards. Yet he is well, and unworried, and will return soon."

"That ain't canny," Ivar murmured, spat again, while making a useless warding sign with one hand against her leg and trying to hide it. "The payment her ladyship made to us still ain't been earned, and if there's one thing I'll Cold well hold true with e'en as y'pull the rest o'the world I know down around me, it's that I'll earn my weight when my word is given fer it. We'll go along with this little caravan, and we'll get the Baroness Delondeur safe to her saltwater keep, but after that I promise nothin'. Place could be crawlin' with assassins or pretenders or lords who're takin' their chance, and there ain't much I can do about all o'that."

"I would ask no more of you, Ivar. It is already more than I deserve." Allystaire extended his hand and she took it, started to speak but held back, cutting off the words as they formed.

The captain of the Iron Ravens hauled herself into her saddle and whistled, then yelled, "Ravens. Let's scout along the road. Hup."

The remaining swords-at-hire had broken down their camp and packed their gear with remarkable efficiency. Pack mules laden with tents and other equipment were strung together on a lead behind Rohrich's wagon in a trice, while the handful of black-mailed soldiers moved out on the small, reliable Oyrwyn horses that carried them from one battlefield to another, but rarely within battle itself. Allystaire watched them ride off, then retrieved a sack from his own saddle and walked to where Rohrich and his guard were loading the last of their pile of boxes and baskets.

"Myron?" Allystaire caught the attention of the guard and handed him the sack, stoutly tied about the neck with thick rope. "I am as good as my word. Once you are out of the village, open the sack however you like and retrieve your crossbow."

The guard nodded, took the bag and started to tug at the rope.

"I said outside the walls," Allystaire repeated.

The thick-necked guard tossed the sack in the wagon and gave Allystaire his best hard stare, thick brows knitting together over his dark, deep-set eyes. "Don't seem fair."

"Alas, friend Myron, things rarely are," Allystaire replied dryly. He held the guardsman's eyes, letting his mouth fall into a flat line, letting his eyes go cold.

"What's t'stop me diggin' it out as I please?"

"Myron. Do you think that the hard man act that works on roadside bandits, drunken townsmen, and the occasional surly greenhat is going to work on me?"

Rohrich had stopped to watch, an empty wicker basket in one hand. He came and stood between the paladin and the guard, putting a hand on Myron's chest and shoving him. "You've got work t'be about and if the wagon isn't rollin' in half a turn with the wheels greased, I'll keep half of your silver today."

The man stomped off with an angry backwards look, and the peddler turned towards Allystaire, shrugging apologetically.

"Sorry, m'lord," Rohrich said. "I don't keep him around for his social graces. Your village has done right by us, though, and my wagons will be rolling back this way before summer."

"It is all right," Allystaire said. "I am familiar with that urge to know who the hardest man in the room is. A year ago, mayhap even a few months, he would be picking up his teeth right now. But if I want the rest of the Baronies to overcome those urges, I must do so as well."

"You're so confident you're the harder man, then?"

"No," Allystaire said, but then he raised one gauntleted fist, "just the one wearing steel." Then, something Rohrich had said struck him. "Wagons?"

"Aye," the peddler said, nodding. "Between the profit I got from you for the books and what I got from the good master alchemist for my entire stock of herbs and simples I can see about expanding a bit, as it were. Hire or buy a new team, second wagon, men to run it."

"Glad to be of help, then," Allystaire said. "If you bring more books here, I will buy them."

Rohrich extended his hand, which Allystaire shook, and then the merchant was off, adjusting the contents of his wagon, yelling at Myron and his other hired man.

Allystaire let out a low whistle and Ardent trotted over to his shoulder, tossed his mane, and whinnied lightly. With the horse pacing beside him, he made his way over to the column of Delondeur men preparing to move out with Rohrich, and they parted for him until he met with Landen and Chaddin, both armed and mounted. He walked alongside Ardent, the horse going still as soon as it sensed his intent. One armored boot into the stirrups, he swung up, and said, "Baroness. Lord Magistrate. Allow me to ride a bit with you."

* * *

Perhaps a turn later, out along the western road out of Thornhurst, Allystaire pulled up, turned to face the Baroness and her half-brother.

"I said it once before, but it bears repeating. Your father became a monster. I believe both of you understand that, but power changes a man, and often he ends up wanting more. The price of a father's sin ought not to be repaid by the child, but if I hear word that either of you begin to repeat his mistakes, I will let Gideon shove the Dunes into the sea with you in it. Am I understood?"

They both nodded, their features serious under mail coif and iron cap.

"You know there's a chance that some other lord has seized power in my absence," Landen said.

"I do. But I have given you all the aid that I can. My hope is that a promise of peace, the new order of law, and you and Chaddin coming forward together will get the people behind you. That none of your major lords came forward to support your father could mean that they believed he was weak, or that they knew he had gone mad. My hope is for the latter, but if it is the former, you will have to move quickly."

"I suppose there is always a chance one of my brothers could show up," Landen said. "But then, they are likely dead."

"Odd way to choose a Baron," Allystaire remarked.

"It has worked for the Delondeurs for more than ten score years," Landen said. "The strongest and smartest come back having learned something of the world and themselves. I am probably a better mariner than any Delondeur in generations, for instance."

"And if you wanted to go to war with Keersvast or the Islandmen that would mean something," Allystaire said, wincing as he heard his own words. "I am sorry, Landen. I do not mean to mock you. I have found you a better woman than I hoped. Perhaps the person I once thought your father was."

"For what it's worth," Landen said, "you aren't quite the monster that mothers in Londray use to threaten their children for bad behavior, but I was brought up to hope I would kill you one day. I am glad that no one has."

Chaddin snorted. "This is all very touching, but those of us who were brought up to work would like to get on with it, hrm?"

Allystaire and Landen both laughed, but Allystaire couldn't resist another moment of instruction.

"Look for the messages from Baron Innadan. I believe they will come swiftly, and it is possible once that we may be able to hurry them along, as it were. Be wary of Braech's Temple, and of the Choiron Symod in particular."

"If he laid waste to Bend, he already attacked folk of my Barony. I intend to have him arrested and put on trial," Landen said.

"And I will hang him," Chaddin said. "After a trial, if I must."

Allystaire shook his head. "Do not think to attack on my behalf, or that he will be easy to take or easy to bring under the law. He is a powerful man and dangerous. It might be too much to attempt to take him right away."

"It's my Barony, Sir Stillbright," Landen said. "And I'll deal with its enemies."

"As you will, Baroness Delondeur," Allystaire said. "May the Mother bless as you as you work for peace." *And may She guard you from Braech's reach should you openly move against his Temple.* Though his thought went unvoiced, Allystaire prayed as deeply for it as he did for the simple blessing he offered aloud.

Chaddin and Landen both gave Allystaire a salute, raising their hands palm out to him as they rode off. He watched them go, wheeled Ardent, and rode back for Thornhurst's timber walls.

CHAPTER 26

To Save the World

Back in the room she'd taken to sharing with Andus Carek that evening, Idgen Marte removed her sword from her belt, pausing reverently to hold the scabbarded length for a moment in her hands, when a sight almost caused her to drop it.

Recovering, she set her weapon down carefully, almost apologetically, and stared warily at the case that leaned against the far wall. It was an ordinary lute case, in most ways like the one Andus Carek carried.

Only his was down in the taproom, open at his feet, as he played local folk tunes for the villagers. She'd admired the way he weaved from one into another, marveled at how quickly he picked them up from snatches that were hummed at him, or from someone who played a few scattered and breathy notes upon an old flute.

Now she stared hard at an instrument that shouldn't be there.

"If you want to save the world, Shadow, you have to learn to love it again." Mol's voice startled her, but Idgen Marte retained her composure and turned slowly to face the doorway and the girl standing in it. She resisted the urge to cross her arms and kept her face even.

"What d'you mean," she rasped, trying too hard to keep her voice as even as her features.

"You know what it means," Mol said. "It is a truth that Allystaire has grasped and you have not."

"What of Torvul and Gideon, then? Are ya' preaching to them on things best left alone?" Idgen Marte almost winced at the way the words came out, but the girl only shook her head.

"Torvul has never ceased loving. If anything, his weakness might be that he loves too much, and can be too devastated by loss. Gideon did not know, until we found him, that he could or should love anything. But he is learning. And you could help him."

"I'd do anythin' t'help that boy," Idgen Marte said. "But it's Allystaire who's got the knack of teachin' him."

"And is it riding, running, fighting, and the trades of war and leadership that you believe Gideon truly wishes to learn?"

"I think those are the things he needs t'learn," Idgen Marte said. "I'd add in skulking, general skullduggery, decent swordplay—all Allystaire can teach him there is how t'butcher a pig in armor—and mayhap a bit o'cardplay."

"Isn't there something else? Something you know the boy wishes to learn?" Mol looked meaningfully at the lute case.

"He could ask me his own self if there was somethin' he wanted me t'teach him," she muttered.

"Except you know he will not," Mol said. "For he does not know that you could teach him, and because he is too timid to ask, too conditioned never to display desire or curiosity or weakness."

"Music's not a weakness," Idgen Marte protested.

"Tell that to yourself, Shadow," Mol said solemnly. "I know what was taken from you, Idgen Marte. I know the pain it causes you to be so near it with Andus Carek here. And yet you cannot help but listen, cannot help but draw near."

"You can't know," Idgen Marte said suddenly, sharply, her voice low and harsh. "It was all I'd ever wanted, and—"

"All I'd ever wanted was to be an Innkeeper's daughter, and be an Innkeeper in turn. To learn the brewer's craft and the subtler arts of giving the folk some-one t'turn to, and offering travelers a safe place. I'll never do any of that, and my father was taken from me," Mol said. "Do I love him less? Do I love this place and its people any less, for all that I can no longer be the girl I was, or the woman I intended to be?"

"I had worked at it since I was a child."

"How long do you think Torvul worked at his craft in order to serve the people who banished him? How many years did Allystaire turn men into knights under the approving eyes of the man he adored like a grandfather? The plans all of us made, Shadow, were taken from us. Much was given to us in return, true. But there are things that can be reclaimed out of our old lives, and for the better."

"I can't sing, Mol," Idgen Marte said, almost too quietly to be heard. "I can't. I won't tarnish the memory of the voice I had by trying now."

"Could Allystaire—"

"Don't you think I'd thought o'that? I asked, Mol. I asked Her, when we held our vigil. She told me that some things became a part of us too deeply for Her gifts to change."

"Plenty sing who shouldn't," Mol quipped. "And you don't need your throat t'play the lute."

"I was never as good a lutist as I was a singer," Idgen Marte protested. "Not sure it'd feel right t'do one without the other."

"I cannot make you do it," Mol said, with a shrug. "I contracted with the peddler to purchase the thing; do with it what you will." She turned to go, then paused and turned back, a solemn little figure in her sky blue robe.

"There's going to be dark times coming, Idgen Marte," the girl added. "Hard times. You haven't needed to be urged to take what joy you can find; you've been willing to do that on your own, and I admire you for it. But the injury that was done to you so long ago can only be made fresh, can only continue to hurt you, so long as you let it. Put your hands to strings again, and you may find it a healing grace. Goodnight, Shadow." With that, the girl glided out of the door.

Idgen Marte sat heavily down on the bed and stared at the cased lute.

* * *

"Not a word of a lie," Allystaire was insisting. "My first tourney at Wind's Jaw after being knighted, the pairings drawn by my father, and of course he set me against himself. Broke seven lances with that stubborn bastard, and him aiming for my head or my neck at every pass."

Harrys and Norbert sat at a table with Allystaire, Gideon, and Torvul, the lot of them drinking brandy from small cups. The taproom, filled with the sounds of Andus Carek's gentle strumming, was suffused with the warmth of bodies and fire, and Allystaire could read weariness at the day's work in the lot of them. Gideon, most of all, for the boy kept starting to nod off and fall forward, then jerking awake and pulling himself suddenly straight.

"Buncha stupid Freezin' nonsense," Harrys muttered, "ruinin' perfectly good lances by puttin' blunt tourney heads on 'em in the first place, then breaking them. Not to mention the men and horses that die."

"It has its problems, yes," Allystaire admitted. "But at its most pure, it is the best sport known to man."

"Known to *nobleman*," Harrys grumped. "I'm a better rider and often a better lancer than most, and have I ever been in a tourney?"

"Can't have ya shaming all the knights in front of the lasses they hope to woo," Torvul put in. "Not that our Allystaire here likely ever pitched any woo at a tourney lady."

Allystaire bit back his response by sipping at his brandy, and he spied Mol coming his way. The conversation drifted away from him as she gestured, and he stood to meet her and follow her to the door and then outside.

The night was black as coal, the stars and a sliver of moon were bright, and the air was sharp with cold, if not the bone-lashing cold of winter.

"What is it, lass," Allystaire asked, watching his breath cloud.

"Three days," Mol said. "In three days, make sure your morning exercises take you out along the west road. Far along it."

"How far?"

"You'll know."

"Can you tell me anything more?"

Mol turned to face him, and the night offered just enough brightness to read the sadness in her features. "I would if I could, Arm. Only that we will face a storm, and I can only see its edges."

"Rede saw something as well," Allystaire said. "He spoke—according to

Andus Carek, anyway—of Braech's Dragon Scale berzekers. I thought I had seen them, ordinary men, if strong, but I am told it is not so."

Mol shook her head. "It isn't. I know little of them, and I want to know nothing more."

"Whatever we must, Mol. That is always the answer."

"I thought we did what we could before we did what we must," she teased.

"That, too," Allystaire said, smiling.

She turned to him, and took one of his hands in both of hers. "You will bear any burden," she murmured. "These are the words you have said, about you and your knights. Is it true?"

"Do you even need to ask?"

"No," Mol admitted, as she pulled his arm around her thin back and stepped against him. "It has been that way since you rode into the village and saved me. But those who will follow you…"

"I will not take them if I think they would quail," Allystaire replied.

"Yet they are merely men, and not you."

"I was merely a man when I found you, Mol."

"That it was the Mother, and not Braech, or something worse, that saw greatness in you, is a small miracle."

"There was no greatness in me, then. Only anger and pride."

Mol pulled away from him and let go his hand. "Be proud and wrathful in full measure when you must be. The time will come. Three days. The western road."

"Aye, Mol," Allystaire replied. "I will remember."

* * *

When Allystaire followed Mol outside, Gideon slipped away and dragged himself wearily up the stairs. Though he tried to keep his back straight and his shoulders from slumping it had been a long, wearying day. He could think of nothing but his bed, and hoped against hope that somehow, perhaps Allystaire would forget to wake him in the morning to run and ride and train.

He pushed open the door to the room he occupied, finally allowing himself to truly slump, to lower his head on to his chest. Then he snapped back up, eyes focusing on a far corner.

"You cannot hide from me in shadow, Idgen Marte," he said. "I learned the Seeing Dark, remember?"

She muttered a curse and stepped away from the corner, holding something behind her with one hand, trying to block it from Gideon's sight. "Should you still be using sorcerer's tricks? Seein' only in the light like a proper person?"

"I think it is not a sorcerer's trick exactly," Gideon said, "so much as an ability anyone with power could learn. It is simply about drawing what light is available to the receptors in one's eyes."

"So it's something Allystaire and Torvul could learn?"

"I'd be shocked if seeing in the dark isn't something Torvul could find a way to do anyway, but yes. Should I try to teach—"

"Cold, no!" Idgen Marte stepped closer, her scar-twisted grin tugging at the side of her mouth. "Too much fun making 'em jump by sneaking up."

"I'd be afraid that Allystaire would react to that with violence." Gideon concentrated a moment, and the two lamps set on either wall flared to life, filling the darkened room with weak pools of light.

"Pfft." She waved a hand dismissively. "He's not fast enough t'hit me. And if he got lucky, he'd just heal me."

Gideon tilted his head to one side. "You are remarkably cavalier about our Gifts."

She lifted one eyebrow. "Am I, now? Says the boy who just used them to light his lamps."

"I don't mean it as a criticism. It is refreshing after all of Torvul's self-conscious and self-satisfied myth-making, and Allystaire being so holy and severe. You are more willing to enjoy yourself."

"Aye," Idgen Marte said, sinking onto the narrow, creaking bed. "For all that he's changed since he was Called, Allystaire remains the man he was raised to be. Severe is who he is, but it makes him the man we need. Try t'forgive him for it."

"I know," Gideon said, "and I don't need to. If you think he is severe, it is because you didn't know Bhimanzir."

"Only as well as I want to," Idgen Marte admitted. "It's about enjoyin' yourself that I've come. Are you?"

Gideon went and sat on one of the room's only other pieces of furniture, a small chair that sat by the washstand. "I enjoy learning new things and being set puzzles, and discovering the limits of my Gifts. I did quite a wondrous thing today. I am still thinking on what exactly it all means, but it seems—"

"I don't mean the work, boy. I mean in your own time, are you enjoying yourself? Are you findin' any pleasure in the world?"

Gideon blinked once, slowly, and sat with his hands resting on his knees. "I'm not sure what you mean. I don't have much time to myself, between Allystaire and Torvul."

"Well," Idgen Marte said, "that's the first problem. Learn t'tell them no. Take time for yourself. And I do mean take it, Gideon, because they'll never give it willingly."

"I'm not sure what I would do with such time. Read. Perhaps sleep more."

"Remind me t'make sure you start drinkin' more," Idgen Marte muttered. It didn't seem a serious comment, so he let it pass and she continued. "Listen, is there anything you want to learn that I could teach you?"

Gideon blinked again, silent for a long moment. "Such as?"

"Well, how to talk t'the lasses, for one."

"They're afraid of me," Gideon said. "And rightfully so. I'm not sure what you could teach me that would change that. Nor do I think I wish it to change."

"You'd be surprised." Idgen Marte let that hang a moment, then went on. "What about cards or dice?"

"I can grasp the maths involved in any such game rather quickly. Unless I needed to relieve the other players of their links I'd have no reason to play."

Idgen Marte sighed, and finally dragged forward the item she'd been hiding behind her legs, and Gideon felt a growing excitement as she laid it on the bed. Almost reverently, she undid the clasps holding the case closed and pulled the top back to reveal a lute.

It wasn't of the same quality as that played by Andus Carek. Even Gideon could see that at a glance. And it wasn't new, either, as the wood had a dullness that spoke of long handling. The pegs that held the strings in place were of different ages, different woods, and different colors, and there were no fancy inlays or metalwork.

"I've seen the way you act around music, Gideon," Idgen Marte murmured. When she spoke so quietly, the rasping hitch in her voice was more pronounced. Often it seemed as though her voice was merely husky and deep. When she whispered, he realized, she couldn't hide the fact that it was broken. "I've seen the way you stare at Andus Carek's hands on the strings, like you're amazed anyone could draw such wonders out of wood and gut and air."

"He's astounding." The boy paused. "He is, isn't he? Good, I mean? I've occasionally heard performers before, but none like him."

"There are better," Idgen Marte said carefully. "But they are damned few, and I doubt any of them are in the Baronies. He's a master in the making."

Gideon let out a long, soft breath. "How could anyone be better? It's almost a kind of magic, of power. But I know it isn't. I would feel if it were."

"It is power, and it is magic, just not the kind you understand." Idgen Marte's hands hovered over the lute, then finally, after she took a deep breath, reached into the case and tugged it carefully free. "But I can teach you t'understand, if you're willing."

"But you don't play. Wouldn't Andus be a better teacher?"

"His name is Andus Carek, and he'd be insulted if you shortened it," Idgen Marte reminded him. "And my guess is he'd not teach you. Further, you couldn't afford his tutelage. If he did consent to do it, you and he both would have to head many hundreds of miles to the south, and enroll as master and student at the Towers, and that would be your life from then on. It's unlikely you'd be accepted there because you're far older than any of the other students would be at the start, and so you might make the trip for nothing. And after all that, I'd prefer to keep you around." She took a breath. "Both of you."

"That still doesn't answer how you could teach me. I've never seen you play."

With another deep sigh, Idgen Marte swung the instrument into her lap. She clenched her hands for a moment, and Gideon watched curiously as she lowered her head and bit her lip. Then, finally, her fingers unfolded and one hand reached for the tuning peg, while the other plucked lightly at the strings.

The first sounds that she coaxed from the lute were raw and jangly, but quickly she tamed the strings into something approximating tune, and strummed once or twice at the strings. Then she plucked forth a couple of chords, then individual notes, then, while Gideon sat entranced, a few snatches of a song.

It was something he'd heard Andus Carek play several times since the bard had arrived in Thornhurst. Idgen Marte didn't play it quite as evenly; here and there a note sounded discordantly, or a run up or down the strings caused her to halt a moment.

She stopped suddenly. "That's the first thing I've played in about as long as you've been alive. It was too slow, not quite in tune, and my fretwork and fingering both were despicable. The instrument needs a lot of work and if my old master had heard it, he'd garotte me with the chanterelle, *if* it didn't snap when he tried." She picked warily at the single highest string, wincing at the resulting note. "But did it prove that I could teach you?"

"Yes," Gideon said quickly, leaning forward, eyes wide. "Would you?"

Idgen Marte nodded. "I would. But there'll be conditions."

"Anything."

"It won't be fun at the start. It'll be learning fingerings for single notes, and care of the instrument. Then the odd scale. It'll be a long time, weeks, before you're even playing simple tunes."

"But one day, I'll be able to play that song."

"With practice? Yes."

"What's it called, anyway?"

Idgen Marte set the lute back down in its case, and took her hands away from it reluctantly, fingertips stroking the wood for just a moment. "The Streets of Cansebour."

CHAPTER 27

Meetings

Allystaire had outpaced everyone but Norbert as they ran that morning. That in itself was not unusual, but Allystaire felt keenly that morning just how easy it was for the taller, younger man to keep pace with him.

Allystaire stole a glance sideways at the boy. *Man,* he corrected himself. The rock that had once sat awkwardly, as if it were crushing one side of him, now seemed an afterthought, tucked comfortably into one arm. His legs weren't churning like Allystaire's own were; rather, they glided over the road. Norbert no longer answered to the description of gangly; the work over the winter had put muscle on the young man's neck and shoulders and arms and the rest of him had slowly begun to fill out.

He felt his own lungs starting to burn, and Allystaire glanced back over his shoulder and saw Gideon and Harrys both laboring, so he raised a hand to call a halt.

All of them gratefully dumped their stones from their arms, except for Allystaire, who carefully bent his legs and let it fall gently from his hands.

"I have seen a man shatter his foot that way, lads," Allystaire said, trying to keep the struggle for breath out of his words. "Best be more careful."

"Why're we out this far anyway?" Harrys made no pretense of ease, bent over with his hands upon his knees. "Longest run we've yet made or I've no eye for this country."

"It is," Gideon agreed with him. For all that the boy had lagged a bit behind, he didn't breath as heavily as the old men. Allystaire supposed he might just be limited by the length of his strides. "I am not sure why we've come this way, but I will need to get back soon." As Gideon spoke, he flexed and bent his fingers, then looked away easy, wincing very faintly.

"To be honest, I do not know why we are out here," Allystaire replied. "Mol simply told me we needed to be, and so we are."

"We take orders from her?" Harrys straightened up, moving a hand to rub at his lower back.

"Yes." The answer came in a three-part echo, Allystaire, Gideon and Norbert all replying at the same time, in the same definitive tone.

"Fair enough," Harrys muttered.

Allystaire turned his eyes back to the western road, squinting, looking for any sign. He wished, for a moment, that he'd thought to ask Torvul for the loan of his glass.

"Let us move forward at a walk," Allystaire said. "Leave the stones."

He had thought to tell them all to come armed. For Allystaire, that meant his hammer belted around his waist. Norbert had his short bow cased on his back, arrows thick on his hip. Harrys wore his axe and falchion, and Gideon a simple dagger. So when his own hand fell to his hammer, as it tended to do, Norbert pulled free and quickly strung his bow, Harrys gripped his own hilts, and Gideon simply frowned and continued to flex his fingers.

"Expectin' trouble?" Harrys carefully slid his axe free and let it dangle from his left hand, his fingers loosely gripping the bottom few inches of the haft.

"Always, but not particularly," Allystaire said. "Mol would have told me if it were dangerous." He paused. "I think." He looked back over his shoulder to Gideon once again, said, "Could you take a look ahead, lad?"

Gideon curled his hands into fists and squeezed them for a moment, then nodded. "Aye."

Allystaire frowned at the way the boy kept moving his fingers, but said nothing. Gideon put one knee to the ground and lowered his head, closed his eyes.

Without saying a word, without really thinking on it, the three men moved into a triangle around the boy. Allystaire and Harrys stood in front of him to either side while Norbert stood directly behind him, bow in hand.

* * *

It was the work of a moment for Gideon to take most of his Will into the sky. He left just enough behind to keep his body upright, to sense danger if it approached.

He flew straight upwards, giving himself no perceivable form. The dragon form he'd styled was an affectation, and unworthy of the Mother, he'd decided.

He didn't have to reach a particularly great height before he saw what it was Allystaire was there to find.

A small cart being drawn by a single horse. Two people sat on its board, with a third lying along the back. Three more walked alongside it.

Walked, Gideon realized, as he raced back to his body, was a poor description of it. They didn't walk, exactly, or not like most folk.

They limped.

* * *

Gideon suddenly sat up, taking a quick, sharp breath. His return was so sudden that it startled Harrys and Norbert, who both took a sudden half-step back.

"Forward," Gideon said, "quickly now. It is not a danger. It is people who need help."

The boy took off at a run that left even Norbert falling behind him for the first few span. They hadn't far to run, though, when the cart that trundled towards them came up a slight rise, spattering mud to either side as it went.

Allystaire halted. "Do not want them to think we are bandits out to take them," he said, stowing his hammer and holding his hands up and away from his body, the palms outward. Harrys slid his axe back to its loop, reluctantly, and Norbert unstrung his bow. All four walked steadily forward, showing their hands, Norbert holding his bowstave, the rest empty.

Walking ahead of others, Allystaire strained to recognize the knot of men that walked towards him. *Not a peddler*, he told himself. *Refugees?*

Squinting hard, he saw that the one walking in front was half-dragging one leg behind him, turning at the hip with every step.

Something fell into place in Allystaire's mind and he rushed forward faster, still keeping his hands out.

As he neared them, Allystaire suddenly pulled to a stop. He knew why they'd come. He knew what they wanted.

But there were forms to observe.

"Travelers." His voice cut through the air like a stone loosed by a siege engine, a powerful and commanding sound. A few paces behind him, Norbert started slightly. "Why do you come to Thornhurst?"

"Then are we near it?" The lead man limped a couple of steps further. "We've come seekin' the paladin. Seekin' his healing."

"Then you have found him," Allystaire called back. He lowered his hands. "I am Allystaire Stillbright, the Arm of the Mother, and what aid I can grant you, I will."

* * *

Tibult cried out and tried to run forward as soon as the paladin identified himself, but he tripped and fell to the mud. He pushed himself on his elbows and tried to drag himself back to his feet, only to look up and find the paladin looming over him.

Gods, Tibult thought, *he is an ugly man.* Anyone who looked would see how often his nose had been broken, the scars about his eyes and forehead, the uneven flecking of grey that was starting to come into his hair.

But as strong hands seized his arms and lifted him upwards, Tibult could already feel the warmth flowing into his limbs from where Allystaire's left hand gripped his right forearm.

The days of walking, for Tibult had refused to ride, had brought fresh hell to the hip the paladin had tried to heal. It still wasn't as bad as it had been, but it was growing worse each day.

And now the pain was draining out of him, sluiced away like grime under a bucket of water. There was pain, too, in the healing, sharp and fresh, as the bones realigned themselves, as his leg grew straight once more.

There was more than pain, though. There was compassion. The paladin knew his pain.

There was love. The Goddess that Tibult had begun praying to saw him, and loved him, and eased his burden. But there was a request in that love, if not a demand.

By the time Tibult had found his feet, and stood with almost no pain for the first time in years—there was a trace of still, a flare, that remained, but it was so light as to be almost a memory of joy—he faced the paladin, and then dropped to a knee.

"I am your man, Allystaire Stillbright. For whate'er you can make of a broken soldier such as me. We all of us will be, I think."

The paladin eyed him carefully, narrowing those dark blue eyes beneath their scar-chipped brows.

"I know," he said, in a voice that was as deep and strong as mountains. "I have been waiting for you. Welcome to Thornhurst; welcome to the Order of the Arm."

* * *

Allystaire pulled Tibult to his feet and looked hard into the man's brown eyes. The former soldier was of a height with him, though not as big in the shoulders and through the arms. He could see the wear that years of pain, and of drink and poor food had done to him.

There was some strength in the man yet, though. Allystaire had felt it when he'd healed him. A determination not to let go, a never dead hope of something better.

I have been waiting for them, he told himself, uncertain how he knew. *Mol did,* he reminded himself, *and that's enough for now.*

"What is the Order of the Arm?" Tibult's voice was halting, his legs shaking as he let them bear his weight evenly.

"Knights who will serve the Mother," Allystaire said, "and Her people. Who will stand at the farthest edges of the hearthfire's light, and face the darkness beyond it. Who will bear any burden for the people behind them."

"How? I'm no knight," Tibult said.

"Neither are we," Harrys grunted, as he and Norbert walked forward. "At least, we weren't. 'Cordin' t'him we are, though."

"You are squires until I say otherwise," Allystaire said with a faint grin. Then he turned back to Tibult and said, "Mayhap you were no knight. But I see before me a man who walked from Londray to Thornhurst—in the winter, no less—because he had one taste of the Mother's Gift. And if you had done that by yourself, Tibult, I would consider you a strong and hardy fellow indeed. But you dragged others with you, with old wounds as bad as your own, or worse. I cannot imagine how you kept them alive, much less moving forward, and yet here they are, and at great cost to you. I see a man that I want standing beside me in the darkness."

Allystaire clapped Tibult on the shoulder, and said, "And now, I should see to the rest of you, aye?"

Too dazed to speak, Tibult only stared.

Allystaire headed to the wagon. Tibult shook himself free of his brief confusion and followed quickly after.

* * *

Audreyn accepted the tray of folded papers from a liveried servant and placed them carefully on her desk. Pens, ink, bowls of sand, wax, and stacks of parchment were marshaled into neat, precise ranks upon it, and the new arrivals were quickly shuffled into their proper unit and billeted accordingly.

Time to begin concocting my lies, she thought. A tiny cold ball of fear blossomed in her stomach, but she pushed it down. In truth, the Lady of Coldbourne Moor and Highgate didn't truly believe she was going to need to lie much. The Baronial demands on the treasure and the people of Highgate and Coldbourne was two or three campaigning seasons away from breaking them anyway, she'd decided, after a preliminary look at the weight on hand, and the first hints of what Gilrayan Oyrwyn expected them to provide now that spring was here.

Audreyn reached for one of the sheets she'd already read enough times to have creased it with her fingers.

Forty barrels of arrows

Mounts for 50 lances

Two hundreds of fresh spearmen, able-bodied

Arms, livery, leather jacks for same

She tore her eyes away from the list and set it back down, delicately reached for a pen, when she suddenly had the impression of being watched.

Audreyn looked up, saw the liveried maid who'd brought the tray of fresh letters standing at the door. She'd heard the footsteps and the door close, but never looked up.

She stood in an instant. "What is the meaning of this?"

"Beggin' pardon, m'lady," the woman said. "But I been doin' this for your own good."

"Doing what?" Audreyn found herself thinking of the dagger in one of the slim drawers beneath the desk's writing surface.

"Seein' how long you'd take t'notice me."

Audreyn threw open the drawer and pulled the bare blade free, bringing it up in one hand, but not coming around the side of her desk. She scrutinized the woman carefully. She was young, a bit pretty in a rough way, with large dark eyes and ash-blonde hair. Thin, and ill-fitted by the livery she wore, she did not fit with the surroundings of Highgate.

"I do not know you," Audreyn said through clenched teeth. Fear rose in her stomach again, but she forced it down and stood.

"Nor should ya, m'lady," the girl said, her accent and bearing suddenly all wrong. "I'm here on behalf of a mutual friend."

"What does that mean?" Audreyn came around the desk, the knife held low, blade leading the way.

"It means, m'lady, that, much like you, I agreed t'walk in the shadow, in hopes of one day walkin' in the Mother's light." She held her hands up, palms out. "And I mean you no harm. Far from it. There's nowhere I could run from her, e'en if I'd a mind t'hurt you. And I truly don't."

The girl in the maid's uniform sketched a terrible curtsey. There was grace in her movements but it wasn't trained; it was perfectly raw.

"My name is Shary. And Idgen Marte sent me north with ya. I'm here t'help."

Audreyn lowered her dagger hand, but not all the way. "Help me in what way? Why would I need it?"

"Beggin' your pardon m'lady," the girl repeated, but the smirk on her face didn't seem particularly apologetic, "but ya didn't look twice at me, even though my dress barely fits and ya'd never set eyes on me before. Had I meant ya harm, I could've killed ya three times by now."

"I think you underestimate how hard it is to kill a Coldbourne," Audreyn said, feeling her back stiffening. Despite her standard assumptions of power over a woman in livery, Audreyn suddenly found herself struggling to meet and hold this girl's deep, dark eyes. They held a haunted knowledge that Audreyn didn't want to share.

"If you're at all like your brother, I don't," Shary said. "I saw just how hard it is t'kill him." The girl's eyes got a little softer, a little awed, when she spoke of Allystaire.

"Does everyone go dewey-eyed over my brother these days?" Audreyn's exasperation vented itself in a question she already knew the answer to.

"I stopped gettin' dewey-eyed a long time ago, m'lady, but you didn't see yer brother durin' the battle." The girl shook her head slowly from side to side. "Took a dozen o'those Wights to drag him to the ground, and them piercin' him all o'er with their blades. No other man could'a lived through that."

"Enough of that. Explain yourself, or I may yet use this." Audreyn scolded herself. She'd let the conversation run out of her control. *It shouldn't be a conversation*, she thought.

"I'd hate fer it t'come t'that," Shary said. "As to what help ya need, well, learnin' ya where t'look for threats'd be a start. Beyond that, I can be an extra set o'eyes and ears, I can carry messages and bring ya news, and if it comes to it," the girl shrugged, "I've got a knife, too."

Audreyn blanched for a moment. "Are you suggesting your Goddess would condone assassination?"

The girl shrugged very gently. "I'm not sure about the Mother, but I'm sure about Idgen Marte, and she'll be bringin' me t'account 'fore the Mother does. Like I said," Shary went on with quietly stunning calm, "I'm in *hopes* o'walkin' in Her light. Ain't there yet."

Audreyn sighed and smoothed her dress reflexively, and turned back to her desk, waving for Shary to follow. She deposited her dagger back in the otherwise empty drawer and sat. "It'll look more natural if we speak here, if anyone should happen to come to the door."

Shary followed her and stood a few feet away, shuffling her feet and letting the silver letter tray dangle from one hand. Audreyn frowned meaningfully at it, and Shary followed her eyes down and then back up, but didn't seem to understand what the look meant.

Audreyn *hmphed* quietly and pressed on. "How did you get here?"

"Fell in wi' yer train," Shary said. "Nobody takes a head count o'the followers, only the soldiers. Once we were in the town, t'were easy t'sneak into the Hall, steal a maid's dress."

"Cold, woman. What were you Idgen Marte found you, a spy, a master thief?"

"A whore," Shary answered with the same unashamed calm she'd already displayed. "And then a wife and a priestess, of a kind, and then a widow in short order." The girl smiled faintly. "D'ya think Idgen Marte spent all the winter talkin' t'you and drinkin' with yer brother? She taught me. It isn't e'en that hard, in truth." Her smile vanished. "Nobody looks at women like me, m'lady. If my eyes are down n'I look busy, I can go everywhere and hear everythin'." As if to prove the point, the girl lifted her tray correctly, lowered her eyes to the ground, and seemed to shrink into herself.

Audreyn had to admit that the girl's actions were effective. She suddenly looked like any maid serving here in Coldbourne Hall, like dozens, scores that Audreyn had seen in her life.

Audreyn was suddenly keenly aware of the fact that of those many women, she could name, at best, a little over half a dozen, and she was ashamed. Suddenly something the girl had said grabbed her.

"I'm sorry, Shary that you've been widowed already," Audreyn quietly offered.

"Thanks, m'lady." The girl frowned faintly, worrying at her thin bottom lip with the sharp points of teeth that were whiter than Audreyn would've expected. "Just so it's clear, I'm not the only widow wearin' a maid's dress in this hall. And, in truth, Gend weren't much of a husband."

"Die he die in the war, then?"

"Not so. Killed by greenhats, or Delondeur swords-at-hire at the start o'winter, when they declared the anathemata. Found us havin' a meetin' up in Ashmill Bridge, chased us out o'town. Were it not for Idgen Marte we'd all've burned for heretics. Couple o'men got close anyway, and Gend stayed behind for 'em."

The entire time she told the story, Shary remained as calm, as cool as ever, hands at her sides, posture relaxed.

"You are remarkably calm for a woman who lost her husband."

"He weren't for long and he weren't much for the time we had," Shary said, "and pinin' o'er his bones isn't like to help me help *you*, m'lady. And that's what I'm here for, after all."

Audreyn knew she'd been told to get on with it, so she pursed her lips. "Do you speak with the other servants?"

Shary thought a moment. "I could, but I best not do it often. Word'll get back to who'er hires that there's a new lass and he'll wonder where she came from."

Audreyn smiled. "*She* will wonder." She gestured at the parchments and implements before her with a sweep of her hand. "All I need do is write the appropriate documents, and we have hired a new maid."

"If I'm spendin' m'day haulin' wood and sweepin' ashes and cleanin' pots I can't do what Idgen Marte sent me here t'do, m'lady. I've already got two women t'answer two. A third'd get no answers at all."

"I can also see to it that you are assigned to me, for whatever duties I see fit. I'll think of a reason later. For now, get yourself hidden. I can have all in readiness by the morning."

"As y'wish, m'lady." Shary made another abominable curtsey and walked towards the door. As she reached and opened it, her entire demeanor underwent a swift change. Her shoulders drooped, her head lowered. She took up less space and seemed to lose all of her confidence, all that forthright calm. And then she was gone.

Audreyn frowned as she watched Shary disappear into the hallway. Turning back to the papers piled on her desk, she felt an unsettling thought rise to the top of her suddenly churning mind.

Likely enough, the girl was here to help, just as she'd said. *But*, Audreyn admitted, though not aloud, *she is also here to watch me, and make sure I do as I said I would.* She selected a piece of fresh parchment and the pen she'd meant to take up when the girl had finally revealed herself, had a deep and steadying breath.

"Sorry, Gilrayan," she muttered, as she dipped the silver end of the pen in the ink bottle. "Coldbourne is about to admit its deficiencies as horse country and the poor work of its smiths is going to get poorer given the high cost of iron."

* * *

Cerisia had been given a room among the Vineyards' many-towered splendor that allowed her a good view of the rookery. On an early morning several days into her visit, she found herself at the window, staring hard at the platform outside a slender tower where messenger pigeons would leave or enter the rookery.

Real work had to be done by riders bearing messages, she knew, but a pigeon flapping and cooing outside with a tiny hollow tube on its legs, perhaps a scrap of cloth in Baronial colors affixed to it, would be the first indication of any movement.

The breeze that the open window brought was colder than she liked, or colder than she'd thought she liked. An entire winter spent more or less in the outdoors of winter had, perhaps, adjusted her preferences when it came to such things. She was at least more willing to admit to the beauty of the landscape, the quilt of green and brown she could just see unrolling from the castle walls.

Cerisia was turned from the window by a rustling among the linens on the massive four-poster that had been placed in her chamber. Its posts were carved—with vines and leaves and grapes, of course—and two sets of curtains, light and heavy, were available to draw across the bed at need.

Currently, no curtains were drawn, giving her a view of the smoothly-muscled torso of Arontis Innadan as he stirred in her bed.

She smiled, pushing aside thoughts of the scandal that might arise if a chambermaid were to walk in upon the Castellan and Baronial Heir in the bed of a Priestess of Fortune. Not that Cerisia herself needed fear any such scandal; servants of Fortune were all but expected to seek liaisons with the rich and powerful. Still, for Arontis it could affect marriage prospects.

Only if his future wife's family is full of Urdarite prudes, Cerisia thought, glancing at the door to see that it was locked.

She glided away from the window and sat carefully upon the bed. She stretched one hand out to Arontis's chest, smiled at the hard planes of muscle that lay just beneath the skin.

She studied his face as his eyes flickered open. He had the body of a man—of that she had no more doubt—but in repose his face was still quite young. The boyishness melted away as he awoke and sat, capturing her hand with one of his.

"Do you still look for messages? It'll likely be another day at least," he murmured, his voice a whispered croak.

"I do," she admitted, shrugging rather more broadly than was strictly necessary, and watching how his eyes were drawn to the clinging silk of her nightdress. "It is important work being done, Arontis. It must move forward quickly if there is to be any chance of success."

He let go of her hand and she let it drop to her lap, then placed his arms behind him and stretched. "And what chance of success do you really think it has?"

"With Allystaire Stillbright and Hamadrian Innadan working at the same purpose, I see a great chance of success. I see woe and ruin for those who would oppose them."

"You think quite highly of Stillbright, and of my father."

"As to your father, should I not?"

"I love my father, and honor him as is my place," Arontis said, sitting up and leaning against the headboard. The linens—colored golden in honor of Fortune, Cerisia guessed—were pulled down and pooled around his hips and folded legs. She briefly let her eyes follow the ripple of lean muscle down to the line of golden-yellow linen drawn over his hips. "Yet I think in his age, his hope is starting to overcome his reach."

"There is every reason to hope," Cerisia said. "There is always reason to hope."

"Is it the paladin, then? Is he the reason to hope?"

"Yes," Cerisia said. "And not only him. There are his companions. There is the fact that people will remember who he once was, and respect him for that."

"Tell me about him."

Cerisia fought the urge to frown or scold. *Better to find some way to gently demonstrate the annoyance of interruption*, she told herself, and took a deep breath. "What do you wish to know?"

"Is he as fair as legends would have it? The songs never cease to speak of the beauty of men like Reddyn the Redoubtable or Parthalian."

Cerisia shook her head. "Not at all. His face is large, and years of battering have made it uneven, with a nose broken so often I could hazard no guesses as to what it originally looked like or where it might once have pointed. In other words, Arontis," she said, leaning forward to hover her mouth near his, and sliding her hand from her own lap to his, "he is not half as fair as you."

Cerisia felt strong arms slide around her and pull her against that smoothly-muscled chest, and put Allystaire, the open window, and the slim tower in its view out of her mind.

And while the room grew temporarily warmer than the air gusting into it, neither of its occupants were watching a small grey and white pigeon with a tiny hollow tube tied to its leg. Even if they had been looking, neither could've seen the device carefully painted onto its feathered breast: a light blue field with the paw of a white bear upon it.

* * *

"The White Bear will come!" Hamadrian Innadan was practically shouting as he held the tiny note aloft in one thin, liver-spotted hand. He, Arontis, and Cerisia were gathered once again in the study where she had met him upon her arrival. "Unseldt Harlach says that further arrangements will arrive by riders with drawn banners within the fortnight. He thinks the use of Standing Guard Pass an excellent one. Or so he tells me," he added, gesturing over his shoulder at the scribe who'd had that morning's charge of the rookery. The young man with a scholar's wispy beard and a red skullcap was still carrying the bird itself in a cage made of thin wires.

"And I want the bird knighted," Baron Innadan said in a rush of heated excitement. "With full honors."

"Yes, m'lord," the scribe answered, bowing. The man seemed entirely out of sorts, bewildered at his inclusion in the company.

"It is a Harlach bird, father," Arontis pointed out, failing to hide his smile. "How will Unseldt take it, you knighting one of his own in your name?"

"I'd say I don't care what that old bearded goat would think," the Baron admitted. "Yet I'm afraid that I care a great deal. Unseldt Harlach agreeing to a peace congress headed by Allystaire Coldbourne, the man who carved away nearly a third of his lands over the years, who never failed to at least bloody his nose every time they scrapped, is a wonder I never imagined I'd see."

"Have you considered, father," Arontis began, "that Unseldt Harlach might show up with his knives out, or an army hidden in the mountains, ready to fall upon all of us?"

"In the first place, Standing Guard Pass makes hiding an army almost impossible," the old man grunted. "In the second, I'm not sure how much army Harlach's got left. They stayed in their mountains the past couple of years. Might be because Oyrwyn had driven them right up against it."

"If all the Barons proceed with suspicions," Cerisia offered, "then this process will go nowhere." Privately, she wondered what sorts of things Gideon could do to an army foolish enough to try and hide itself from him in the mountains.

She tried not to let the chill that crept up her back turn into a shiver.

Her composure was unruffled, or at least neither man had noticed it.

"She's right," the Baron rasped. "But then I have rarely known a beautiful woman who wasn't, usually. And consider again the man, lad. Unseldt Harlach's got an old, prickly kind of honor. If he didn't want to attend a peace congress, he'd have Freezing well said so. All the same, we'll have to be careful not to insult him."

"As you say, m'lord," Arontis replied, sketching a light bow.

Hamadrian looked again at the scrap of paper in his fist, and turned to the scribe, scowling. "Why are you still here?"

The scribed bowed low, using his free hand to keep his skullcap from sliding. "You hadn't given me leave, m'lord Baron."

"Then you have it. And you'll have two gold links and a bottle of my reserve brandy for having brought this directly to me, despite the early turn and the warnings of older men with more station and less sense than you have got. Begone then."

Sketching more thankful bows, the scribe made a hasty exit, the bird in its cage fluffing the feathers of its chest, picking at the blue and white design that had been crudely painted upon it. They watched the exit in silence that Arontis finally broke.

"Very generous of you, father."

"If a man can't afford t'be generous at the end of his life, when can he be?"

"Come now, Hamadrian," Cerisia said, crossing to him and taking his hand in her own. To her surprise the tremor in it was tangible even at rest, and the skin was soft and loose. "Surely it is not quite so bad as that."

"It is, Cerisia. There is no point in hiding it or talking around it. Nothing for it but to do what I can in the time that's left."

"Father," Arontis said, "please—"

"Please nothing. You want to play knight for a while longer and avoid the responsibilities of taking up the Seat, eh? Well you've got no brothers left and your nephews are unblooded boys."

"Hamadrian," Cerisia said, "I do not want to give you any false hope, but there is something that might be done for your health."

"Eh? Can your goddess change my chances, then?"

Cerisia's eyes widened and the Baron laughed. "It hadn't occurred to me, but I suppose I could try. No, what I meant is that the paladin, Allystaire—he can close wounds with a touch, heal ills."

"I thought you said he could rip men apart and uproot trees to swing as a club."

"He can," Cerisia answered, matter-of-factly, "though I have never seen him uproot a tree and swing it, I do not doubt that he could. Yet he has also closed the wounds of battle or mishap with a touch. Villagers, both in Thornhurst and in places he's visited, speak of fevers broken, of rot and pox disappearing. An entire village will tell you, with the light of honest belief behind their eyes, that he took into his hands an infant who could not breathe, and that when he handed him back to his mother, the lad cried louder and longer than any baby they'd ever seen."

She watched the Baron swallow, could see his throat visibly working, the bobbing apple beneath the thin and blue-veined skin. "I am not a boy to be easily entranced by tales, and to think they hold the solution to all my ills."

"I do not know if he could heal you, Hamadrian. I know that he can heal."

"Well," the Baron said, drawing his slightly drooping shoulders up. "All the more reason to make it to the congress then, eh?" He took a deep breath, moved to one of the chairs in the room, and steadied himself against it. "We all have work to do, I am sure. Archioness, if you would excuse me and my son so that we could speak on matters that would surely bore you."

Cerisia held her tongue and let the implied insult in the words—that the details of statecraft would bore her—roll off of her. Hamadrian knew better; he wanted to speak to Arontis alone.

She leaned forward and kiss the old man's whiskery cheek, then turned and left the room. She cut one eye up at Arontis as she passed him, and let her hips have an extra swing in them as she walked, the white silk of her dress flicking lightly behind her.

* * *

Father and son both watched Cerisia leave, and both realized that the other was watching at about the same time. They shared a quiet laugh, then looked away from one another for a moment of awkward silence.

"Son," Hamadrian began finally, lifting his head to look his heir in the eye, "be discreet."

Arontis colored easily, his father noted, smiling inwardly at the prickliness of youth. "I am not sure what you mean, m'lord."

"You only m'lord me when you think you're saying what I want to hear." The Baron cut him off and walked around the chair he was leaning on, sank into it slowly. "I know exactly what is going on with you and the Archioness."

"I'm sorry, m'lord—"

He cut his son's words off by slicing a hand through the air. "If you think I disapprove, you aren't paying enough attention. If I were ten years younger—Cold, maybe five—I'd be competing with you. I'd lose, but I'd make it a race, damn it all. She's a fine woman, smart and well educated. You don't find many people who are all three in this part of the world, which makes her all the more rare, the more to be valued. She is probably teaching you a great deal, and not just what to do with the sword the gods gave you when you were made."

Arontis colored even more deeply, lowered his eyes to the floor.

"Let go of your shame, son," Hamadrian said with a gentle sigh. "I don't mean to scold you. I just want you to be careful. For all that Cerisia is a companion any man should treasure, in or out of bed, she will also serve her own agenda. It is not our task to help her do that."

"I tell her nothing, father," Arontis replied quietly. "It is a dalliance for the both of us."

Hamadrian laughed, a dry sound that rattled in his old, thin chest. "So you think. Likely you have already told her more than you realize. But it's to be expected. Cold, an affair with one from Fortune's Temple is practically expected of a Baron's child. Just be mindful of your future as Baron. You don't want Fortune's Temple able to interfere too much."

Arontis was silent a moment. "Father, what of this Mother's Temple? The Goddess who has lifted up this paladin."

"What about it? Not much of a Temple yet, as far as I understand."

"What if we invited them to make a chapel here?"

"Why would we do that?"

"To hear Cerisia tell it, Braech is likely to be an enemy of any peace congress. Fortune will work for it, if not wholeheartedly. The Mother, though?"

"Is worshipped by a few score farmers and tradesmen, and one exiled nobleman."

"And his companions. She will not say much of them, but she seems to think there are those more powerful than the paladin himself. And then there are his knights."

"Oh, he has knights now, does he?" Baron Innadan shook his head, muttering. "Making knights out of peasants. The White Bear will be thrilled to hear that."

"And yet he defeated Baron Lionel Delondeur," Arontis said. "Something we could never do, not even when working with Gerard Oyrwyn."

Hamadrian thought on that a moment. Lionel had indeed been a fierce figure, performer of daring deeds in his youth, the captain who beat the Islandmen back even after they'd conquered Vyndamere and cut Varshyne off. "No small feat, I admit," the Baron finally said. "Still, it doesn't recommend itself as a reason to endorse a new faith. Kill a Baron, earn a chapel in the Vineyards? Sets a bad precedent, my boy. Very grim."

Arontis sighed and folded himself into one of the other chairs, set his hands on his knees. Hamadrian peeked a look at his son. *More of his mother in him than me,* he thought, looking at the large brown eyes under their long lashes, the finely-cut cheekbones. *And better luck to him for it.* He could see, could sense the boy struggling with something. It fell into place in his mind.

"Arontis, no," the Baron said.

"Father, I haven't even said anything."

"Listen to me, boy. You want to run off and join this paladin's knights. I can read it in your face plain as the sunrise. It isn't possible. Out of the question."

Arontis lifted his head. "It might be a chance to do something truly great."

"You'll have that chance as Baron. More of it." Age and illness had chipped away at Hamadrian Innadan's presence and his voice, but if he'd once known how to make it crack like a whip, he knew now how to draw the words out so as to discourage dissent.

His son was silent a moment. "You have grandchildren."

"Enough!" The Baron's voice rattled in his chest as he raised it, sitting as straight in his chair as he could manage. "I have but one son remaining to me. As luck would have it for me, for your people and home, you are the best of them. Ethrin was a good hand with a sword, but an idiot, and he died for it at Aldacren. Dessen, gods love him, wasn't born with the strength to live enough winters to know much of what he could've been."

Hamadrian Innadan's voice flagged a bit. He paused to swallow, to press the back of a hand to his mouth. "No man should be able to name two dead sons," he muttered. "And too many can."

The Baron blinked a few times, and turned his eyes, one clear, one milky, towards his remaining son. "It is true that I have grandchildren. But none of them, Arontis Innadan, are *you*." He took another deep breath. "I will not stop you from playing a man's part in what's to come. But neither will I allow you to throw aside all the good you could do in my seat for a moment's boyish impulse. I will hear no more of it. That is my command as your father and your Baron. Am I understood?"

"Yes, m'lord," Arontis said. Hamadrian could hear how half-hearted the reply was, how unconvinced his son remained.

"The lives of thousands could depend on an Innadan occupying the Vineyards, Arontis. Thousands. You can do more with a circlet and a proclamation than you'll ever do with a sword."

Arontis nodded and stood to go, leaving his eyes lowered, asking permission to leave. The Baron waved a hand in assent. His son paused just before the door.

"It was neither circlet nor proclamation that ended Lionel Delondeur," he murmured quietly, then slipped out the door.

Hamadrian let him go, sank into his chair, folded his hands together in his lap to keep them from trembling. They shook anyway.

CHAPTER 28

A Fight Before the Dunes

"The winter appears to have done us a favor." Landen offered this observation to Chaddin as they rode at the head of their small column through the nearly empty streets of Londray.

There'd been no problem with the guards at the outer or the inner gate. Of the four guards to examine them, one had taken in the pair of them riding together and hurriedly raised the gate, one had simply bowed at sight of the ring on Landen's finger, a third had peered long but surreptitiously at the resemblance in the cut of their jawlines, and the fourth had run off ahead of them, swinging a handbell and yelling, "The Baroness returns! The Baroness Landen Delondeur returns!"

"What do you mean?"

The streets were empty, and though it was early, they were too empty. No prentice boys were running errands or beginning their morning tasks. Bakeries and inns they passed were not pouring the smoke of oven fires from their chimneys.

"The folk are expecting a fight. Strife in the streets. A scramble for the Dunes and the seat. The winter kept it at bay for this long," Landen said. "With each day that passes, they grow more wary, hide inside their homes, ignore their trades. Probably hoarding food."

Chaddin sighed heavily. "What can we do?"

"Pray that we've gotten here fast enough and that our letters will buy us time."

When they passed a cross street where the signs were carved with the image of a shallow bowl, Landen called forward two of the knights that had ridden with them back from Thornhurst and turned to dig into a saddlebag. Chaddin looked at the armored men a moment, and leaned towards his half-sister, murmuring, "Send the warband men." He dropped his voice to an even lower whisper. "They'll not go looking for any other friends."

Landen thought a moment, nodded. To the two knights, she said, "Ride ahead to the Dunes, then back, quick as you can manage." They spurred off, and after a moment, Landen brought forward the letters she'd been digging for. She pulled free a rolled-up parchment tied with white silk and sealed with white wax with the impression of Fortune's wheel. "Ivar."

The remaining men of the Iron Ravens filed along behind their gap-toothed captain as she approached Landen. Before coming within sight of the walls, Landen had talked Ivar into striking their banner, but their black mail still stood out, as did their horses. The short, shaggy ponies they rode were far more common in Oyrwyn or Harlach than Delondeur.

Landen held out the scroll to the warband captain, who took it in a black-gloved hand. As it moved, a tiny remnant of the perfume worn by the woman who'd written and sealed it wafted into the air.

"Y'sure the Arch'oness isn't damnin' ya w'this?" Ivar raised the scroll doubtfully.

"As sure as I can be, not having broken her seal," Landen said. "I expect it to arrive at Fortune's Temple intact."

"Aye." The mercenary started to turn her horse.

"Captain," Chaddin suddenly said, "there's a silver link for your company for every additional armed man accompanying you to meet us at the Dunes."

Ivar saluted with the scroll, her smile offering brown teeth where it had any at all, and her men and their ponies shuffled off into the drawn gloom.

"Where are you getting those links, brother?" Landen looked towards Chaddin with an arched blonde eyebrow.

"I assume the office of the Lord Magistrate will have an official purse," Chaddin replied calmly. "And the best way to keep the streets free of blood is to have more armed men behind us than in front of us."

"I can't fault your logic," Landen said, "and I suppose you will need funds. Yet you have probably just spent them all."

"How many men can Ivar possibly round up?" Chaddin shrugged and set his horse moving.

* * *

The answer, as it turned out, was the entire available guard of Fortune's Temple: three score men in white surcoats, spiked bronze helmets, and matching enameled mail. They marched in ranks, gleaming dully in the early morning light.

Landen and Chaddin watched them with critical eyes and turned to each other. "Their lines are ragged," Chaddin pointed out. "Bad at marching, bad at fighting."

"We don't want them to have to fight," Landen said.

"I'll wager half of them don't know more than what end of the sword to hold."

As the guards came to a slow stop, with many collisions in the ranks, Ivar came riding to their head, smiling widely and crookedly. "That's if ya have anything left t'wager with, m'lord," the mercenary captain drawled. "I'll happily take payment in gold links if ya've not enough silver."

"We have a castle to occupy first," Chaddin pointed out. "But I will give you a down payment now." He turned in the saddle and started to dig in a saddlebag, but Ivar waved him off.

"We can work it out later," she said, then that ugly smile widened even further. "W'reas'n'ble interest, o'course." The black-mailed woman on the shaggy little horse guffawed at her own wit, then spat on the cobbles and rode back towards the Temple Guards, eyeing them disapprovingly.

One of the guardsmen approached the mounted half-siblings and bowed. He carried no spear and his surcoat bore a wheel embroidered in silver thread. "Guard Captain Sanglais," he said in a mellifluous accent. "I am bid by Archioness Cerisia to place my entire detachment in your hands, Lady Baroness, and Lord Magistrate," he added, sketching a second bow, and then a third—slightly smaller than the first two—to Landen and Chaddin in turn.

"Thank you, Captain," Landen said. She tilted her head. "Keersvasti?"

"Aye, m'lady Baroness," the man replied. "I understand you spent some time among the jeweled islands last summer."

"Aye," Landen replied. Pursing her lips a moment, she spoke again in a more lyrical tongue. Chaddin and the rest of the men around him turned quizzical eyes on her. "I spent most of my time chasing Keersvasti pirates," she said in his language carefully, slowly, "and less among jeweled isles."

Sanglais chuckled lightly and laid a hand against his chest as if lightly wounded. "Any man who violates the sanctity of the sea is no true son of the archipelago."

"There are many islands on all that water," Landen replied. "Not all are as a string of emeralds. Some are merely rock, and full of places for a pirate to hide."

"That may be, but when they come near the archipelago, my lady, we kill them," Sanglais replied. "Pirates would clutter our very lifesblood and see us slowly die."

Chaddin cleared his throat, and Landen lifted a hand to him in apology, switching back to the Barony tongue. "I am sorry, Lord Magistrate. We must cease being rude, captain—and we have business to attend to."

"That we do, m'lady Baroness. To the Dunes, I assume?" When Landen nodded, Sanglais bowed once more and returned to his troops, calling out orders to them. They lurched forward unevenly, a few men butting into the ranks in front of him.

There was no need to give directions. The tall, sand-colored walls loomed over the city in its extreme northwest corner. They reflected the light of the rising sun like a beacon mirror guiding ships to shore in darkness or mist, and Landen felt keenly their pull.

By now folk had started to tail along after the mounted train, and whispers scurried along the lanes and streets. Boys and young men, running the news ahead of them, found themselves getting yanked indoors by prudent parents or cautious wives. Many a door-bar could be heard falling, many shutters drawn tight, and yet a crowd still drew alongside them.

A few cheered raggedly, and Landen felt the pressure growing, a spot in the center of her back that expanded until it became a weight upon her shoulders and the back of her neck. *What,* she thought, *would my father have done?*

Talked them all into taking up arms and marching ahead of him. Even as the thought formed she saw the cold, easily-angered face of Allystaire Stillbright swim in her vision.

She called a halt and stood in her stirrups, cleared her throat. "Good people of Londray. I hope that this day is as bloodless as Snow's Melt or a Harvest Fest."

Silence. A lot of stares that weighed her carefully. Her horse whinnied quietly, stomped at the cobbles.

"However," she went on, "if blood is to be spilled, let it be our blood. Go to your homes. Pray that we can put the winter behind us in peace and plenty. My brother and I have buried any enmity that was between us, and there will no longer be factions plotting in their halls and then fighting in your streets. Please," she added, raising her hands up, palms out. "Please go to your homes. See to the safety of yourselves, your children, your trades."

Landen sighed as she sat back into the saddle. Perhaps half the crowd, dozens of folk that had gathered by then, dispersed back into the streets. The rest milled around. When Landen swung her small and motley column back into motion, they followed, though at a distance.

The Baroness sighed, which her brother heard. "We can't all inspire them to defeat armies like he can, Landen," Chaddin murmured.

"I'd settle for them doing as I asked and heading for safety. No matter what happens, Londray will need them safe and working, fishing, trading, selling, smithing."

"What is it you expect to happen? Another brother? Ennithstide or Lamaliere to have taken the Dunes and named himself Baron?"

"It is not about what I expect," Landen said, "it is about what can happen."

They rode on in silence, but didn't need to wait long, for the pair of riders Landen had sent ahead came thundering back. They pulled their mounts up dramatically; one threw sparks from a cobble with its shoes.

"My lady Baroness," one reported loudly, "there are no banners flying above the Dunes save that of the Barony itself. There are men drawn across our path, though. Armed, but only a score."

"They're under Braech's banner," said the other. "Led by a priest, a young man I don't recognize. Not the Choiron nor the Marynth of Londray's Temple." The man cleared his throat, looked as if he had more to say.

"Go on, Urbin," Landen urged him. "I would have a full report, and truthful, always."

"Very well, m'lady. Among them, flanking the priest? There's two men not wearing armor, aside from gauntlets. Bare from the waist."

Landen suppressed a shiver by tightening her hands around the reins of her horse. "Was their skin marked?"

"Aye."

There was silence save for the sound of horse's hooves shuffling on the stone-lined streets, of the clank of gear and creaking sway of harness.

Chaddin looked from his sister to the reporting knight, frowning. "What? An unarmored man is a fool, and we have them three to one if they mean to force a fight."

"An unarmored man is a fool," Landen agreed, "but sometimes a fool is the most dangerous kind of man to fight. Have we any bows?" She looked back over his shoulder at their ragged train, but the hope in her words was futile; in her sinking gut she knew the truth. "Cold," she cursed quietly as he saw only their horsemen, with their swords, their horseman's axes, or flails dangling from wrists. Behind them, Sanglais's gleaming ranks of bronze and white carried short, stabbing spears and swords. Not a bow or a crossbow in evidence.

"What is it?" said Chaddin. "Will twenty stand and fight sixty?"

"How many men did Allystaire Stillbright have to stand and face three hundred, because he had the will of a Goddess behind him? If the rest of the Islandmen abandon them, which I doubt, the two that Urbin saw would stand and fight if we were six hundred. I have seen them, in the islands, in Keersvast. Urbin," she said, "ride back to the Captain of Fortune's Temple guards and tell him to prepare his men to face a pair of Dragon Scale Berzerkers."

* * *

Landen and Chaddin rode to the fore, spreading the horsemen out in a thin line, flying the Tower of Delondeur in their midst. Ivar and the Ravens had dismounted, mingling with Sanglais's men in hope of stiffening them. While the walls of the Dunes gleaming promisingly, a thin line of men blocked the approach to the main gate.

The men barring their path looked huge, leaning on the gigantic axes and massive, broad swords Islandmen favored. Armor was mismatched or barely visible beneath the their furs, bristling to match the long braids they wore in hair and beard. A blue-robed priest stood in their midst, the berzerkers flanking him.

All eyes were drawn to them. Even among so many grim, hard-looking men, they seemed composed of violence, ready to unleash it like a part of themselves.

At a long distance, Landen stood in her stirrups and called out. "Men of the Sea Dragon! Why do you block the path of the Baroness Landen Delondeur and her brother, Lord Magistrate Chaddin?" Landen had decided it couldn't hurt to trumpet that last bit as often as possible in case any former mutineers were in shouting distance.

The blue-robed priest, who seemed tall and yet somehow insubstantial next to the bare-chested men flanking him, had started to speak, but one of the Dragon Scales threw his head back and roared.

Even from dozens of yards away, the sound boxed Landen's ears like a pair of closed fists. It *hurt* to hear it; it was unearthly and it echoed off the buildings that lined the street.

A pair of horses panicked, screaming and rearing up. One threw its rider and bolted. Some of Sanglais's men started to back away. A few were quickly struck back into line by the butt-end of a black-clad Raven's spear, but a handful turned and ran.

Nothing for it now, Landen thought. Her ears rang and she couldn't hear herself, but she thought that standing straight in her stirrups, raising his sword to catch the sun, and spurring her horse forward would be sign enough.

She could feel, rather than hear, the rumble of the mounted men charging along beside her. She wished they'd had lances. Lances were a distant second to good bowmen when it came to killing Braech's Holy Berzerkers, but a damn sight better than swords and axes.

True to their reputation, the Islandmen charged out to meet the horsemen, but not before unleashing a volley of throwing axes. Most clattered harmlessly to the stones, deflected off of a raised shield, or poorly thrown.

Each of the berzerkers had thrown as well. One of their slim-bladed weapons buried in a horse's skull, sending the poor animal toppling in a boneless heap, the rider thrown forward like a bundle of rags. The other carried off the upraised sword-hand of another rider, blade and gauntlet clattering to the ground, leaving the man to gawp at the stump of his arm as his horse bore him heedlessly forward.

Grimly, Landen lowered her sword and aimed her horse into the mass of fur-clad men.

Islandmen strategy for dealing with horsemen was brutal, but effective; they attacked the horses. Landen knew this, and so when one bent low and held his axe out to sweep at her mount's legs, she waited till the last moment to turn the beast so that it bore down on the Islandman with its weight.

Over a hundred stone of horse and rider barreled straight over the man, crushing him to the street. The horse, trained well, put one iron-shod hoof into the man's head as it swept over him.

Landen let the horse run on, shouted madly at the walls of the Dunes, hoping men inside might hear her, see her, recognize her voice. She started her horse into a turn, describing a wide arc back towards the men. Most of her horsemen had pierced the line, but there were empty saddles and men on foot being surrounded and hacked to pieces.

Sanglais had his guards double-timing, spears leveled. They'd make short work of the ordinary Islandmen warriors, she thought, for all their inexperience. But she searched frantically for the Dragon Scales.

One had leapt upon the man unhorsed when his mount had taken the throwing axe. His scale-gauntleted hands were around the dazed man's throat, twisting.

Even through the ringing in her ears, Landen heard the panicked shriek, suddenly and sickeningly cut off. Mercifully, she was too dazed or too far away to hear the snap.

But she could see it plainly when the berzerker lifted the head clear of the dead man's body, showed his grisly trophy to the sky, and then hurled it into the melee.

The second had run clear of the horsemen and his compatriots and instead flung himself into the midst of Sanglais's guardsmen, clearing their leveled spears with a leap that seemed effortless. Two shocked guardsmen fell to axe and gauntlet in as many moments. A handful more broke and ran.

"My Barony for a decent length of ash and steel," Landen muttered, even as she spurred her stallion towards the nearer of the two berzekers, the images graven upon his bare back making at inviting target.

She sensed movement at her side, spared a glance, saw Chaddin joining her. Together they lowered their swords and spread out, Landen switching her grip to her left hand, so that they'd bracket their target. They risked a dreadful cost, but the half-siblings moved as if they'd trained together from childhood.

The berzerker they bore down on had dragged another Delondeur knight from his saddle. To his credit, the armored figure never stopped swinging his axe, but the force of the fall took some of his strength, and the bare-chested man contemptuously knocked the axe aside with one gauntleted hand. Meanwhile his other hand, curled into a razored fist, crashed into the knight's helm, staving it in on the second blow.

The third sent spurting streams of blood through the mangled slits. Feebly, the knight swung his axe again. The Dragon Scale, kneeling atop his foe, snatched the weapon, clutched it with both hands and pressed the blade against the already ruined helm. He leaned forward, arms rippling.

The axe punched through steel, flesh, and bone, and the knight twitched and bled and died on the street.

As the Dragon Scale stood, Landen and Chaddin's swords, with the speed and mass of well-trained warhorses behind their points, sank home.

Landen felt far more resistance than any bare skin should've offered. It was like striking with the point against steel plate. For a moment she thought her blade might break, but it endured. Both points entered the berzerker's back and punched through the front of his chest; both swords were ripped from the hands of their wielders.

Fumbling to get her flail into her hand from where it dangled on her wrist, Landen turned to watch the berzerker. He still stood, blood pouring freely down his chest and from his mouth, the three streams merging into one over the muscles of his belly. Only when another Delondeur knight rode past, swinging a heavy flanged mace into his skull, did the Dragon Scale fall to his knees.

Still, he looked towards the fighting, eyes restless, smiling beatifically as he bled, joy plain on his features as he slowly died.

Leaving him to it, Landen turned her horse back towards Sanglais's men. The Islandmen were dead or scattering, but a ring had formed around the second Dragon Scale, a ring of black-clad men holding long spears, darting them at him as he hopped and leapt and spun to avoid them.

It was a taut, tense game, and as Landen rode towards it uncertainly, she saw one of the Iron Ravens suddenly seize a chance, step forward, and thrust his spear straight into the berzerker's lower back. It was surely a deadly wound, erupting in blood, piercing a kidney and the bowels. Or it would have, if the berzerker's hands hadn't closed around the shaft and pulled it free, taking the weapon into his own hands and turning on the now unarmed Raven.

The professionalism of his Brothers of Battle saved him, for all three surged forward and caught the Dragon Scale with their spears, pinning him between them.

Grimly, the crazed holy man gripped the shaft of one of the spears, buried in his navel, and started pulling it—and the Raven on the end of it, Ivar herself—closer. *Through* him, Landen realized, with horror. More of the weapon's head, and then its dark wooden shaft, was protruding through his back, just having missed his spine. The other two spearmen leaned into their weapons, but the Dragon Scale ignored their efforts.

Suddenly a white-cloaked figure dashed behind the berzerker, lashing out with a lightly curved blade. Sanglais himself, Landen realized, moving with speed and flair and, above all, calm.

Hamstrung, the berzerker unleashed another, weaker roar—men still flinched away—and fell to the ground.

Smiling even as blood began to seep through his teeth, the Dragon Scale threw back his head and unleashed a yelling ululation in the Islandman tongue.

"Sea Dragon bless my death. Sea Dragon bless this battle. Sea Dragon bless all battles. Sea Dragon bless my foes and the man who killed me with the strength of his arm. Sea Dragon curse the man who killed me his cunning. Sea Dragon take my soul and guard it among His glittering hoard until His waters rise to claim the world."

With the strange, chanting words still filling the air, the berzerker fell forward and died. Like the first, his face was as joyful as any Landen had ever seen.

* * *

When the berzerkers died, the fight went out of the rest of those still standing, and the remaining five Islandmen and the priest of Braech were taken as sullen prisoners. In truth, the priest, a young man with a downy beard who'd never taken his mace from his belt, seemed entirely dazed by what had happened, and allowed himself to be led away mutely.

Shortly after the fight was safely over, the gates of the Dunes rattled open and a detachment of a dozen horsemen rode out, splendid in bright armor and gleaming green surcoats.

Landen found herself staring at the sharp steel tips at the end of their twelve-foot-long ashwood lances, and grew angrier and angrier, but she willed the fury down into a tight, hot ball, let it feed her words and actions, but slowly.

She ignored the lancers and the streaming pennants as she sought out Chaddin, Sanglais, and Ivar. The latter was staring hard at the spear-pricked corpse of the Holy Berzerker. She spat a stream of bloody saliva out of the side of her mouth. "Mighty high butcher's bill in a fight wi' odds three t'one t'us," she said, probing experimentally at her jaw with one finger, wincing faintly as she pressed one spot over and over.

"Aye," Landen agreed. "How many did we lose, Chaddin?"

"Eight," her brother answered wearily. Chaddin was holding one arm awkwardly against his side, but seemed otherwise unhurt.

Sanglais's white surcoat was spattered with crisscrossing lines of blood. "A dozen dead, at least. And many wounded. That berzerker…" He shook his head slowly, eyes in an unfocused stare. "I had heard tales. Seen them at a distance. Never close, never in a fight."

"You," Landen said, raising the sword she'd pulled free from the first berzerker's body at the dazed priest. "What is your name and what was your purpose here?"

"Hissop," the priest sputtered, his eyes suddenly drawn to a focus by the bloodstained sword pointed at his chest. "Hissop. I did not mean to give battle, m'lady, only to seek out your purpose." His voice quavered and he raised his hands. "The Scales. They wouldn't listen. T'wasn't me, m'lady."

Landen's sword hand twitched. She longed to bury the blade in the tall, blond-bearded fool in front of her, but she steadied herself. "They wouldn't listen to a priest of Braech?"

"They are hard to control, m'lady. I tried to bend my will upon them. It was like trying to make a rope fast to a wave. It wasn't possible."

"Who sent them to you in the first place?"

"The Choiron Sy—"

"Symod. Where is he?"

The man shook his head, his skin growing more pallid. "I don't know."

Landen raised his sword again. "Answer me!"

As the priest was shaking his head, Landen felt certain she would run him through, until Chaddin stepped to her side and pressed one hand to the flat of her blade, gently pushing it towards the ground. "No, m'lady. Not in the street." Chaddin flicked his eyes and Landen followed them; a crowd was gathering once more, gawping at the bodies and the wounded.

"You are correct, Lord Magistrate," Landen muttered. She sheathed her sword, heedless of the blood that coated it, and grabbed the priest's arm in her fist, swung the man roughly around.

The troop of lancers had wheeled smartly, ranks gleaming under the risen sun. Landen finally read the sigil on their tabards, lances crossed behind the familiar tower. Baron's Own.

That they seemed to be reporting to her was a good sign, she thought.

"Captain!"

The first man in line, seated on a tall bay warhorse, cantered it forward, snapping the wood of his lance pole against his breastplate in salute. "Detail men to take the remaining enemies to the dungeon," she said, "and to arrange for the street to be cleared, our wounded to be taken to the chirurgeons. Then you report back to me."

Another salute, an "Aye, m'lady" muffled by his helm, and the man rode back to his line, barking orders. One of the riders dashed away towards the gate, with the balance smartly surrounding the remaining Islandmen and Hissop.

Landen and Chaddin had pulled themselves wearily back into their saddles by the time the lancer captain rejoined them.

Steeling her face and working hard to keep her voice calm despite the anger she felt, Landen stole another look at the lance. At the foot of steel it was capped with.

"Why did it take so long to ride out, Captain?" Landen's tone was more clipped than she intended.

"Had to wait for orders to raise the gate, m'lady."

"And who was giving those orders?"

"Sir Kelten had command of the gate, m'lord, as given by the Castellan Lord Sundegar."

"I am not familiar with Sir Kelten."

"He was but lately knighted, m'lady, by his cousin Sir Leoben, before leaving in command of the Salt Spears."

"Bring Sir Kelten to me. In the Great Hall."

By now their horses were carrying them through the gates and into the safety inside the walls. Landen felt herself relax, felt muscles begin to unclench. But she forced herself to think of the carnage on the street just beyond the keep, and the anger knotted up again.

* * *

Landen hadn't bothered to shed her armor, except to remove helm and gauntlets, when she strode into the Great Hall and walked straight up to the seat. She didn't stop to take in the trophies: the banners of defeated lords, the prized Purple Mare of the former Barony Tarynth, or the Gravekmir skull that hung directly above the seat.

With Chaddin at her side, she walked straight to the chair, turned, drew her sword, and sat with a heavy clank. Servants, courtiers, knights, and clerks all rushed in her wake, whispering and murmuring to each other.

Silence fell over them like a wave as she sat.

"I am Landen Delondeur," she said, voice raspy, one ear still ringing. "Fifteenth of my line. Lady of Barony Delondeur. If anyone would contest this, come forward now. For those of you who would swear fealty, take a knee."

Chaddin, standing at the foot of the dais on which the chair sat, was the first to sink to one knee.

The assembled men quickly did the same. Landen stood, descended the stairs, and reached down to take Chaddin by the shoulders and pull him to his feet.

"My half-brother Chaddin, natural son of Baron Lionel Delondeur, I name my full brother, my heir until I continue our line, and Lord Magistrate of Barony Delondeur." She paused to let that sink in, saw more than one raised head, more than one curious look. "There are going to be changes," she added slowly, finding a pair of upraised eyes and staring hard until they dropped. "We have not the time for individual oaths, but know that we are marking every person in this room. You have sworn your fealty to me on your knees. Loyalty, honesty, and courage I will reward. Now," she added, as she ascended back to the seat and sank gratefully into it, "someone fetch my brother a seat. And bring forward any clergy of Braech within the keep."

As Landen settled into her chair she surveyed the crowd that had gathered. Her eye was drawn to a young man, clean shaven, fair-headed, dashingly dressed with a uselessly thin-looking mail shirt polished to a high sheen, a slender sword worn on his hip, a silver spur ringing melodically on one boot, and a half-cloak of crushed red silk hanging over one shoulder.

"You," she said, raising one hand to point at the youth, "what is your name?"

"Sir Kelten, my lady." Though the youth had a slight frame, the voice that issued from it was strong, proud, and clear. "I had command of the gate this morning," he went on, striding forward—strutting, really, Landen thought—and dramatically bowing. "I sent forth a squadron of the Baron's Own to secure your safety, m'lady."

Landen sighed and sat back, flicked her eyes away as a pair of liveried servants hustled into the hall with a chair. Though not so large nor as ornate as the one she sat upon, the wood was well-worked, and showed the gleaming patina of years of polished care. They set it at the foot of the dais, placing Chaddin a span or so below her in height; her half-brother sat carefully, his back blade-straight, awkwardly managing the sword at his side.

"There are three things wrong with what you have just said," Landen spoke up, as she turned her eyes back towards Kelten. She thought, for a moment, of the intensity with which Allystaire Coldbourne had looked at her when trying to impart some message or, as he often did, imply a threat. *Stillbright,* she reminded herself.

Landen doubted her ability to replicate the force of the paladin's gaze, but she had years of training and generations of Baronial breeding behind her eyes, and she narrowed them, tilted her head slightly. "First, it was not a squadron, it was a troop. No man is fit to command who does not know such basic terms. Second, it was not my safety that you secured with your orders, but the death of my men by your lack of haste."

As Landen spoke, the young knight's face grew paler. He licked his lips, blinked, but remained silent.

"Lastly, Kelten, you are no knight. I strip you of that rank and all of its attendant privilege until you prove yourself worthy of it."

A collective gasp went up in the room, followed by the silence of the crowd holding its breath. Chaddin looked back over his shoulder warily. Landen gritted her teeth to keep her chin firm and her eyes locked on Kelten's.

Finally, the fop spoke up, hand falling dramatically to his sword. "My lady! You cannot—"

"Do not presume to tell me what I cannot do, Kelten." Landen twisted the name, making obvious the honorific it lacked. "Whether cowardice, game-playing, or simply incompetence, had the Baron's Own ridden forth the instant our path was blocked, lives could've been saved. Instead they were thrown away while you did what, tested the air with a wet finger to learn the direction of the wind?"

Kelten drew himself up to his full height, which was not terribly impressive. "I am no coward, my lady. And my patron, Sir Leoben, will take it ill that you would disregard his judgment so recklessly."

"Do you see Sir Leoben here?"

"I take it he returned in your train," Kelten answered, though hesitantly.

"Sir Leoben died outside the walls of Thornhurst, engaging in my father's last and most monstrous folly," Landen said.

"Then I demand the right to seek satisfaction against the man who killed him. Tell me who it was."

Landen looked to Chaddin. "Lord Magistrate, can you help the young man direct his ire?"

"I believe I can, m'lady," Chaddin began airily. "It was a dwarfish alchemist, in point of fact, not a man. He resides in Thornhurst, which is many days ride to the east, over or around the Thasryach. Once there, ask for the Wit. Though, be warned, he is a deadly hand with a crossbow, as your Sir Leoben learned."

"A crossbow is weapon of peasants and cowards!"

"I promise you, Torvul is neither of those things," Chaddin said. "And should you make it so far as Thornhurst in some mad attempt to kill him, he will see you coming from miles away. And should he find it expedient, he will put a crossbow bolt through your neck and proceed with whatever more useful work he was about before you showed up. Or, perhaps, he might seek a bit more of a challenge and simply talk you to death. Either way, I can't recommend you go seeking revenge."

"Kelten," Landen said, "you may still serve a purpose here, and earn back the spur you will now remove. Or you may flee the keep and seek what you will of the world—but if you harbor any hope of serving as a Delondeur knight again, you will do as I say and do it now."

Rage and shock warred on his features before settling on confusion. Petulantly, Kelten knelt and stripped the spur off his boot. He hefted it for a moment, eyeing Landen as though he might throw it. Chaddin rose quickly, hand on his sword, but Kelten dropped it sullenly to the ground, where it fell with a jaunty, out-of-place ring.

"Let this be a lesson and a warning both," Landen called out. "I will not tolerate errors that lead to needless death. Act in haste to do the thing you think right in the moment, and I will reward you. Delay to see what benefit you may snatch for yourself, and I will punish you."

Kelten melted back into the crowd and Landen decided to watch him go. She took a deep breath. *Best to get it all out right away,* she thought. "Now bring forward the clergy of Braech. There is an issue of Anathemata that must be rescinded."

CHAPTER 29

The Order of the Arm

Allystaire looked over the squires arrayed before him. They wore new clothes, replacements for the rags they'd arrived in, excepting Harrys and Norbert, who wore their accustomed armor.

So few, he thought, counting them again as if he might come to a figure higher than nine. Harrys, Norbert, Tibult, Mattar, Johonn, Miklas, Gastin, Armel, Teague. He thought on their names as he moved down the line, the last half-dozen still mostly unfamiliar to him.

Unfamiliar, and yet not. All of them had been soldiers, once, and that gave them plenty in common. When he'd healed all of them on the morning that Tibult had brought them, he had come to know their pain, and that was something more. Tibult's hip had been crushed by a scared horse. Mattar's back had been so racked with pain he couldn't lay down or sit, and had slept for years standing against a wall. Johonn's powerful left arm had drawn tight up against itself after a blade had slashed muscle and tendon, shriveling it into a withered and useless claw. Miklas couldn't draw a breath without searing pain in his mangled chest. Gastin's shoulders had been badly broken upon a strapado and never allowed to heal. Armel had an arrowhead grinding in his knee. Teague had been so badly burned by a fire she'd worn rags across her face for years. He'd taken her pain away, but the scars his gift could not touch, it seemed.

And there was still Waltin, whose eyes Allystaire feared were too far gone for too long for his gift to provide any comfort. The last man still lingered in darkness and pain, spending what time he was awake being led to and from the Temple.

Allystaire had thought he'd known pain in his life.

When he'd healed the squires before him, and failed to heal blind Waltin, he'd come to know how wrong he was.

And when he had healed them he had found inside all of them something in common. A stubborn will to live, a refusal to completely let go of hope that life, someday, somehow, would once more be sweet to them. The Goddess had made that hope a truth, through Her Gift to him.

And each healing, he had felt, had come with an obligation. They had all known it, Allystaire had felt in the moment of healing, and taken joy in it. Joy not only in the sudden cessation of pain, but in the knowledge that something redeeming was being offered to them. They were not merely given back life, but purposeful life. Redeeming life.

My brothers of battle, Allystaire thought, as he watched them in the slightly chill of the spring morning. *Or mayhap my cousins, or my children. Whatever they are, they will be Her Knights.*

"The Order of the Arm," he finally said, his words swinging through the air like a hammer descending true upon a nail. "An idea. A vain and foolish hope, I am told, or something out of a story or a bard's song, too pretty to be real."

He smiled. "None of us are pretty like the stories say of Arentenius."

There was a ripple of laughter in the too-thin ranks.

"Neither is the task before us. Together, all of us who serve the Mother—and some who do not, it must be said—are trying to push a boulder up a hill. Up a mountain, even. And strung along it are those who would push it back down upon our heads. At the top of that mountain is peace. I doubt any of us here, save Harrys, remember what it was like to live in a country not at war."

"Boring," Harrys spat. "And t'were still cold."

Another thin chuckle.

Allystaire looked at the faces once more; many were scarred like his, with the mark of fist or blade, or helm hard-struck. The faces were thin or broad, sharp-cheeked or rounded, but all had a certain hardness to them. Even Norbert had it, aided by the scar fading to white on his cheek. The youth's eyes seemed to miss very little now.

"If we ever get this boulder up the summit, it will have been work enough for ten times our number. Though it may seem difficult, impossible, we will put our shoulders to it every moment of every day that remains to us. When others tire, we will keep on. When those around us fall, we will put them on our backs and keep pushing. We will never falter at this task, and when we have done it, we will find another. In peace or in battle, in comforting home or punishing wilderness, we will bear any burden for the Mother and Her people. We will refuse nothing that is asked of us by Her, or by them, no matter the cost. Our arms, our horses, and such personal effects as may fit upon our belts are the only things we reserve for ourselves. If a man has need of my cloak, it will be his. Of my links, his. If any of you wish to leave now, if you think you have not got the mettle for this, step forward, admit it to me and to those around you, put off your arms, and renounce forever the chance that is offered. Those who stay will be my comrades in service to the Goddess."

Allystaire took a discreet breath, watched the two lines. No one moved.

"Good," Allystaire said. "Now we must take such time as we have before the peace congress to become knights in truth. That means training. I will have Torvul let you into the armory to outfit yourselves as you see fit. How many of you aside from Tibult and Harrys were horsemen?"

Only Armel raised his hand.

"The rest of you were foot, then?" They nodded, though Teague—wearing now a fitted leather mask over half of her face, and gloves on both hands—spoke up.

"I was an archer, m'lord. A fine one," she said, her voice hesitant.

"Good. Norbert will see to it that you have a bow, and the two of you will work together every day, every moment. And Teague—call me Allystaire." He looked over the lines again. "Do the rest of you know the rudiments of riding, at least?"

"Never been on a horse in m'life." That was Johonn, who looked too big for any horse to bear.

"We'll find you an ox," Harrys said, turning to face the man, who loomed head and shoulders above him. The big man gave him a wide smile, showing

rough teeth. The years of disuse had shrunk his left arm, the muscles growing thin and weak. Some of the strength had come back to it since Allystaire
had healed him, but it was still smaller and feebler than his right. Even now,
the huge man—not just taller than Allystaire, but broader and more thick-
limbed—clutched a stone in his left hand and squeezed it every so often.

"We will worry about mounts tomorrow. Now, it will be to the armory to see
you outfitted as proper squires. Then we will set about making knights of you."

* * *

When Torvul swung open the doors of the shed housing the armory Allystaire
sighed wistfully.

The dwarf glared up at him, snorted. "What?"

"Just wishing, not for the first time, for the armory at Wind's Jaw. Or even
at Coldbourne Hall," Allystaire answered as the would-be squires filed past
him into the shed, some of them diffidently touching a pile of dusty armor or
searching carefully among a barrel of spears.

"Not a spot of rust there," Allystaire mourned. "It was the nightly duty
of the squires to scour the hauberks. Sword stock waiting to be worked to the
wielder's arm, heavy footman's axes in leather hoods leaning against the wall,
flails and maces."

"Stones Above, lad," Torvul muttered, shaking his head. "Speakin' more
fondly of inferior steel than any woman I've heard ya name."

"Yes, I am sure dwarfish steel never rusts and works itself," Allystaire said,
only to be cut short with another glare.

"Works itself? That'd be an abomination I'd not stand for," the dwarf
grumped. "The ore doesn't know what shape it's suited for, not when it's taken
fresh from the rock. But," he added, "you're wearin' the closest thing t'dwarfish
steel this world's like t'know again." He lifted a finger to point to the hammer
at Allystaire's hip. "I've heard no complaints." The finger lifted threateningly
towards Allystaire's chin. "And I'd best not!"

"I have not had to swing it in anger," Allystaire reminded him. He watched
the men holding chain shirts against their chests; it became apparent that none
were going to fit Johonn.

Torvul sighed and raised his eyes and his hands dramatically. "It's goin' to be up t'me to see that whatever crude iron this ragged lot selects is brought up t'snuff, isn't it?"

"Well," Allystaire said, "I had hoped you might do what you could."

"Lucky for you lot that what I can do, even with slop, is more than what most of your clumsy so-called smiths can do in their dreams."

Many of the men had belted on swords. Johonn had found himself a heavy, double-bitted axe, held it awkwardly in his mismatched arms, searching for a grip. Teague was inspecting the bowstaves, muttering her need for a string, a thick-bladed shortsword on her belt. Miklas, a lanky ginger, and Gaston, olive-skinned and curly-haired, had found spears to their liking. Mattar, second in bulk only to Johonn, had not gone looking for weapons suited to his stature. Instead, he had brace of short-hafted broadaxes shoved them through his belt, and was now searching among the knives and daggers. Armel had found a thin-bladed longsword and was looking among the meager stock of horseman's weapons, finally taking a flail and testing the weight of the pair of spiked balls carefully in the palm of one hand, the chains coiling along his arm.

"We will see what plate we can find once we have made some training progress," Allystaire called out. "For now, if you find yourselves kitted, let us begin."

"I'll need string to make any proper test o'these bows," Teague said, finally drawing free a length of wood and holding it critically in both hands, tilting it and peering carefully from different angles.

"Norbert? Have you to spare?"

The former reaver was already reaching into a pouch and pulling free a waxed coil. "I do," he said, "only it's for the shorter sort o'bow. Not sure it'll work on somethin' that long." He gestured to the curved bow cased on his back.

Teague frowned. "Best not trouble about it, then. It'll just snap, and waste is a sin." She looked to Allystaire, her frown turning contemplative. "Er, is it a sin, for us? I mean, seems that way."

Allystaire chuckled lightly. "I should say that in our Temple, Teague, the only real sin is our failure to love and to aid one another as we can. However," he added, "waste ought to be avoided as much as we might. I know where you can get a long enough string."

The half-masked woman nodded, and glanced at the bow on Norbert's back. "What good is a bow that short, anyway?"

"It's what I know t'shoot," Norbert said with a shrug. "Might know a trick or two already."

"A trick?" Allystaire looked to the tall but no longer gangly youth. "I find I do not much like the sound of it. What do you mean?"

"I'll show you later," Norbert said. "But if it works, I think it'll be useful. Faith."

Allystaire grumbled lightly but said nothing to Norbert. He did address the rest of the Order, such as it was. "Come on, then. I assume that most of you know the rudiments of wrestling and fist-fighting, but that is where we start."

CHAPTER 30

The Will and the Mother

Turns later, Allystaire and his gaggle of squires dragged themselves through the door of the Inn, sore and soaked in sweat. Many moved stiffly, or clutched at their newly-healed limbs or muscles.

For his part, Allystaire felt as if his legs were made of lead, and his left shoulder throbbed in pain where Mattar had managed to throw him, the only one of the squires who did when he had wrestled them one after another. He wanted to reach for it, massage it, even channel Her gift and heal it.

Instead, he directed them to a long table, kept his body stiffly upright and his steps easy, as if nothing troubled him.

"Eat well and sleep fast," Allystaire said. "We will be at it again and again, day after day, for as long as we can."

They sank gratefully onto benches, slumping against the table. Allystaire looked about, saw Idgen Marte and Andus Carek sitting at a table together, talking quietly. Gideon sat with them, watching the bard holding forth about something, moving his hands in the air to demonstrate some point or other. Almost as soon as Allystaire's eyes were upon him, Gideon turned to face him, then back to the pair he sat with, lifting a hand, then standing and looking back to the paladin. The boy gestured towards the hearth and the chairs sat near it.

Allystaire nodded and joined him there, sinking gratefully into a seat, trying not to let his fatigue show. Gideon joined him, slipping into a chair without a sound. He looked into the hearthfire for a moment, his fingers moving curiously against his lap and his stomach, the backs of his hands turned towards Allystaire, wrists curved, fingers moving slowly, concentration on his features.

"What are you doing, lad?"

Gideon looked up, uncharacteristically startled. "Thinking over some of what Andus Carek was telling me."

"And what is that?"

The boy shrugged evasively. "Nothing important."

"Gideon," Allystaire said, "I know you do not do anything that you consider unimportant. I have the memories of many frustrating turns of fighting instruction to show for that. Please," he added, leaning forward, trying to catch the boy's eye. "Do not lie to me."

With a shrug, the boy mumbled an answer. "I'm learning to play the lute."

"Why is that unimportant?"

"It doesn't contribute to the defense of Thornhurst, the Mother's Temple, the peace congress, or advance our aims in any way. It is—"

"Gideon," Allystaire said. "Do you remember what I have said about loving the world?"

"It makes it harder to destroy."

"Yes. And I think that you would not do that even if you never held an instrument. Yet if doing so helps you to love the world all the more, there is no harm in it."

"I think it would," Gideon said. "But it is difficult." He frowned, turned to face Allystaire. "I am not used to finding something so hard."

"Have you not told me that Bhimanzir found you a most intractable apprentice? That you could not learn anything he tried to teach you?"

"True," the boy replied, "but that is not the same thing. He was trying to teach me something that I was born incapable of. When it comes to maths, to puzzles, and in many ways, music is both of those, I am not used to struggling."

"As far as I can tell, Andus Carek ought to be a fine teacher."

The boy shook his head. "He won't teach me. Not directly. That's why neither of us had a lute in our hands. He will explain some points of theory, ideas, show me in the air, but he says to touch the strings without payment and the observance of certain rituals would be to violate certain precepts. He cannot make me his student."

"Then who is teaching you? Or are you trying to learn yourself? And where did you get a lute, anyway?"

"Idgen Marte."

That answer stunned Allystaire for a moment, but he rallied. "To which question?"

"The first and the third both. She is out of practice, as she hasn't played in some time. Years, even. And she is not the most patient of teachers."

Allystaire laughed lightly. "I should think not. I did not even know she played."

Gideon turned to face him, frowning and raising one thin brow. "Sometimes you are as unobservant as she and Torvul claim you are."

"Perhaps," Allystaire said. "Now, I daresay you did not wish to speak to me about your lute lessons. What, then, do you need to say?"

"I have been thinking over some statements the Goddess has made, and things that Cerisia said, and some of my own observations."

"Is this driving to a point?"

"The first god I was ever in contact with was the God of the Caves. He was old, lonely, senile, even. But he cannot always have been that way."

"Yes, and?"

"And the Mother has said the She would not abide what Braech has *become*. Cerisia came to us initially suggesting that the Mother signaled a change in Fortune, not a new temple."

"So gods change?" Allystaire hesitated. "Is that your point?"

"It is a starting point to many other questions. Do all the gods change? Do we change them with our worship? Do they become what we wish them to be, what we believe they are? Or do we become as they wish us to be? You have told me that the Goddess has alluded to things She cannot tell you, things She is not permitted to do."

"That last is not a question."

"No," Gideon said. "But it leads to one. What prevents a goddess, the Mother or otherwise, from doing as they wish?"

Allystaire sat straight up in his chair, the fatigue in the muscles of his back fading as the questions Gideon raised began to eat at his thoughts. He resettled himself, leaning against the wood of the chair, and bit at his lip. "What are you suggesting?"

The boy shook his head. "Nothing. I haven't enough information to make any suggestions, really. The only gods I have direct experience of are the Mother, and the God of the Caves. A bit with Fortune, I suppose, but when I touched the power Joscelyn was drawing it felt very," the boy gestured, searching for a word, "thin. As if it were merely a trickle."

"And to you, the Mother's Gift feels how?"

"Like an ocean I can swim in," the boy replied. "Or at least a lake so large it makes no difference. The God of the Caves was simply a pool. Wide, but not deep, and easily drained." He shook his head. "These metaphors are too easy, too pat. Still too many questions."

"Go on," Allystaire encouraged him. "Think aloud. I find that it helps."

Gideon nodded, was silent a moment. "Have all the gods changed, over time? Where was the Mother in the past? How did Mol's suffering draw Her back to the world, and why? Had She withdrawn from the world on purpose? Why and how did She choose this moment and place?"

The questions hovered in the silence that followed, neither Allystaire nor Gideon breaking it. Finally, Gideon stood and looked straight to Allystaire.

"I have to ask Her."

"She may not answer."

"I know," Gideon replied. "But I have to ask."

"Do you want me with you?"

Gideon thought a moment, then shook his head. "No."

"Then go," Allystaire said. "Learn what you can."

The boy nodded and slipped quietly out of the door. Allystaire watched him go, then stood and walked back to his table of squires. He caught Timmar's eye on the way, and said, "Make sure, goodman, if you have any chores that need doing, to ask any of the men here. They will be happy to help."

* * *

When Gideon ascended the steps of the Temple and opened the door, Mol was at the altar, her back to him. It was dim, but not dark within, despite the failing light outside, and the dimness turned her sky-blue robe to something darker, the color of the sky just before the sun set, perhaps.

Next to her knelt a taller figure, dressed in a long, simple undyed wool robe and a pair of old and worn shoes. Gideon didn't recognize him. As he moved slowly up the aisle, he saw that there was something tied around the man's head, a bandage or a mask.

He waited and watched as Mol held the man's hand and helped him stand. When they turned around, Gideon realized that the man must be the blinded veteran who had lately arrived, for the strip tied around his face covered his eyes. Mol kept a light hand on his arm as he walked slowly forward and found a bench, onto which he slipped, nodding as the priestess spoke to him in a low and soothing murmur.

Mol left him and glided towards Gideon, who walked slowly to meet her. The priestess smiled at him and wound her arm through his to clasp his hand.

Gideon stiffened slightly at the contact, and Mol tilted her head to one side. "What is the matter, brother?"

He shook his head. "Nothing. I am still unused to that."

"Do you want me to stop?"

Again, he shook his head. "No." He leaned against Mol for a moment. Her embrace felt sisterly and, he supposed, maternal at the same time. Then he pulled his hand and arm free, and said, "I have come to ask some questions."

"Anything I can answer, Gideon, I will."

"Not of you, Mol," he said quietly. "Of Her."

Mol looked to the altar, the muted orange, red, and gold bands of the stone oval gleaming softly. "She cannot simply be summoned, Gideon. And She may not answer. She has not spoken to me, not as I am used to, since a week after the Longest Night."

"I must ask, regardless. There is something I think I must do, but before I can I need to at least try and find some answers. I will stay here all night if I have to, and every night until She speaks with me or the world drives me away."

"That sounds like something Allystaire would say," Mol replied with a curious smile.

"I'll take that as praise," Gideon replied, drawing his shoulders back and walking towards the altar with his jaw set firm.

Mol turned to watch him, whispered, "It was." Then she turned back to the blind veteran Waltin and took up his hand, helped him stand. "The Will means to hold a vigil," she murmured. "I will find you a place to sleep. Think on what I have said." The man murmured something in reply.

Gideon heard none of it, for his attention had fallen on the altar. He circled around it, knelt at the Pillar of the Will, placed his hands over the symbol—which had changed three times, from a flame, to a spring of water, to a sunburst, in the short time he'd looked upon it.

Please, Mother, he thought. *Please.*

Those were the only words Gideon put to his thoughts for the moment. He let his mind wander. Snatches of music filled it, of the songs Idgen Marte called forth from the lute. Haltingly, and with much cursing, but it was easy to see the fluency returning to her hands. He envied it, for his were slow and stumbling, and the strings still cut into his fingers. She assured him that with time, callous would grow and the hardest fretwork would feel like second nature.

He thought of the way Mol had embraced him, had taken his hand when he walked in. How he fought the urge to flinch when almost anyone tried to touch him. Bhimanzir had never put a hand upon him except to punish him. An expectation so ingrained was hard to overcome. Why hadn't he tried to explain that to Mol? He wasn't sure he could have, really. And it sounded like whining. He'd not told Allystaire either. Perhaps no one noticed, for though he wanted to flinch, he never did.

Bhimanzir had taught him not to.

He remembered an incident of his youth, early in his training, when the other children taken the same time as him had been discarded. How Bhimanzir had casually lifted a hand to slap him across the face for an incorrect answer, and he'd ducked and covered his head with his hands.

For the next year, every time Bhimanzir made to punish him, he'd found his hands bound to his sides by bands of darkly smoldering red power, his back held stiffly in place.

Gideon started, but did not flinch, when a hand settled onto his shoulder. He was surprised, yes, but the warmth that radiated from the touch was the opposite of Bhimanzir's.

He turned from the altar, and found himself staring face to face with the Goddess, Her skin shed its faint golden radiance, with a single tear suspended from a golden eye, glowing like a drop of water lit by a sunrise.

"I am sorry, Gideon, for how you suffered before you were found."

The boy shook his head. "I will not mourn for the past when it has brought me to this moment," he replied. "Bhimanzir had a hand in making me what I am, and though I might wish it had been otherwise, what I am serves reasonably well."

The Goddess smiled and blinked back Her tear. Gideon felt his heart beat quicken at the sight. "Among My servants, Gideon, you are the most ready to correct Me, and also the most given to understatement about yourself."

"I do not mean to presume, Mother."

"You do not," She replied, reaching out to take one of his hands between both of Hers. It was a contact that he didn't think for a moment of flinching from. "Why do you seek my counsel, My Will?"

The boy lowered his eyes and resisted the urge to squeeze the hands that grasped his. "I am troubled by some implications that have arisen as I have come to know more about the gods, Mother. This is one area where my education at the hands of Bhimanzir sorely lacked. The Knowing do not believe in deities, only in power, and so while I learned of the existence of the temples and their politics, I know nothing of the theology."

"There may be little I can tell you, My Will. I am bound to certain proscriptions."

"That is my first question. How can that *be*, Mother? If your power and knowledge are boundless, how can you be bound?"

She shook Her head slowly. Her totally golden eyes were difficult, even impossible to read, but Gideon thought he felt Her hands withdrawing.

"Wait. Wait. Please, Mother. If you cannot tell me these rules, could you at least tell me when I am asking you to break one?"

"No."

The boy licked his lips and searched Her features. He found it harder to concentrate then, and so dropped his eyes to the floor, which had become indistinct. The Temple was still around him, the warm stone of the altar still in front of him, but all of it had become hazy and indistinct in Her light.

"If I simply speak, without asking questions, you break no rules by not answering."

"This is true, but how does it help you?"

The boy let out a breath, feeling the risk in what he asked. "It all depends on *how* you do not answer, Mother."

Gideon was never sure if the upward lift at the corner of Her mouth was a figment of his imagination, or the merest suggestion of a smile.

He took another deep breath and squeezed Her hand with his own gently. "That there are rules governing your behavior implies that the same rules apply to the other gods. To Braech and Fortune, Urdaran. The elven Green, even."

Something dark passed across Her eyes when the last word passed his lips, and then was gone as quickly as it came. He tacked away from his most pressing questions.

"There is either an agreement among you or something beyond you enforcing these rules. As far as I can tell it does not matter at the moment which is true." A pause. "You must act through intermediaries. Through mortals to whom you grant a path to wield your power."

Her hands, perhaps, squeezed his very lightly.

"There may be hundreds, thousands even, to whom Braech has granted the power to use their will like a crude club, some are granted power over wind and wave, and then there are the Dragon Scales, who seem to worry Allystaire, whose numbers are unknown to me. But a priest of Braech, or even a dozen of them joining their wills together, are no match for me. This is because we number only five; you are able to grant us far *more* power than Braech may them. The amount you grant is somehow limited."

She did not respond; Her features remained frozen in radiant majesty, Her hands around his.

"Yet this is a precarious position because there are so many more of them. The very number of worshippers may be a factor in Braech's overall power, or Fortune's."

He paused to search the Goddess's unchanging features carefully, then dropped his eyes back to his feet and concentrated. "You have told us before that we are not the pawns of fate. That we do our will in Your service. You cannot see all ends. You, like Braech or Fortune, can only grant your Gifts where You believe they will achieve the most good."

"It breaks no rule for me to tell you that is true," She said, tilting Her head curiously to one side. "You are only repeating what I have told you."

"Then I must ask a question, Mother. Why now, why here?"

"Mol's suffering woke me from a long slumber, Gideon. A child, helpless and alone, crying over the death of her kin and praying for aid, for rescue, for justice? Who would answer Her if not me?"

"Yet there are people all over the world who cry out for the same thing, day after day. Orphans and widows are made by the scores in battle, singly by disease, or by murder on the roadside or the city."

"I am keenly aware of all the suffering in the world, My Will." There was, perhaps, just the slightest edge in Her voice, but Gideon moved forward regardless.

"I know. I do not mean to rebuke you, Mother. I swear that I don't." A thin note of desperation crept into Gideon's voice. "There must be something about the place that drew you. I cannot think what it is."

"There is," She admitted. "Look more closely at the place. That is all I can say on that matter."

Gideon nodded his acceptance. "I am forced to wonder where it was that you slumbered, Mother. I will not ask," he hurriedly added, as Her hand started to pull away. "I will continue to speculate. I know that even a god may change, with time. The God of the Caves had grown mad with solitude. He could not conceive of the ways in which life had moved on from His gifts."

"Similarly," the boy went on, "I have looked into some of the history and it seems that Braech has shifted. His worship always praised courage, strength, pride, boldness—and yet it seems only in the last few decades that it has become so wanton, so bloodthirsty."

"Short lives, short memories," she murmured cryptically. "I will not abide what He has become."

"Then there is Urdaran. He has changed as well, I suspect. I have spoken with Rede; his order are taught their history only to a certain point and it is made clear to them to seek no knowledge of anything before that point. There are books and scrolls within their own vaults that are forbidden to them. This is absurd, and yet it is treated as a command from Urdaran Himself. None are known to have violated it."

There was no response. She did not seem to need to blink, and there were no irises in Her eyes to look closely at. Her mouth did not twitch. But Her hands did not leave his. He swung his eyes back to the hazy stones that he could barely feel beneath his feet.

"I cannot speculate upon what Urdaran may have been once, or what He is becoming. Then, there is the Green."

"Mind what you say when you use that word, My Will."

He nodded faintly. "The Green is more ancient than any of you, as elves are far older than humans. Fewer in number as well. But the Green—curiously it is never called he or she, never given a masculine or feminine principle, which even the dwarfs do with their catalogue of ores—the Green seems to have simply withdrawn from the world. Perhaps other gods we have forgotten have done the same. They grow bored with it, or disgusted. Yet if they can change their minds in one direction, they can move in another."

Silence hung heavy in the air.

"Even a god may wish for redemption if they judged their exit from the world to be hasty or ill-timed," Gideon ventured. "I should like a look at the forbidden archives in Rede's monastery sometime. I have theories they might prove or disprove. It is possible that Urdaran was not always spoken of as He."

"Or that Urdaran, when He was other than He is now, had a consort. There are many possibilities." Her reply was something like a whisper. "I have come right to the line of what I may tell you, Gideon. Perhaps over it. I must leave you soon."

"I have no more questions of you, Mother." He lifted his eyes back to Her and reached out to clasp Her with his other hand. "Not of that sort. You know of what I proposed to the Wit, and I am sure you know my mind. Could I do such a thing?"

"You are My Will, Gideon." Even as She answered, Her voice and form were fading. "You may bring almost anything into the world if you but know where and how to bring it forth."

"How seems obvious enough." Gideon felt frustration bleeding into his words, causing his voice to rise. The Goddess's radiance was slowly fading, or the world around him was slowly coming back into focus. It was impossible to say which. "Why does *where* matter?"

"Where always matters, Gideon."

Before he could make sense of the answer, She had faded completely from his sight. He could see as well as feel the stone beneath his feet, make out the walls of the Temple around him, in the shadows past the dim light the altar gave off.

Gideon stepped back from the altar and walked slowly around it. He took in the shape, the Five Pillars. He tried looking upon the symbols, but rarely saw a single one for more than a few seconds before it shifted. The Wit was a mountain, then a flowing river, a coin, a set of balances, a flask. The Shadow was a thin sliver of moon, a sword, a dagger, a pen. The Voice was a sickle, a mouth, a pair of hands opened in supplication. The Arm was the most consistent, wavering between a hammer and a sunburst.

He stepped back, far enough that he couldn't see the symbols or be distracted by their shifting.

"Why five?" He murmured the words, crossing his arms over his chest. Suddenly he shook his head. "Numerology is not significant," he chided himself. "Shadow and Wit are what the poor and the defenseless have always relied upon to shield themselves. A Voice and an Arm are barred to them. This is easy enough to see. Then why a Will?" He shook his head and backed a few more steps away, peering once again at the altar, trying to see it as a whole. An oval of stone, perfectly smooth, unmarked by any tool. Drawn from a pile of loose stones gathered and stacked together by the Arm, the Shadow, and the Voice, then finished when he and Torvul had joined them.

"An oval. Why that shape?"

He stared hard at the altar, tried to fix its measurements and proportions in his mind.

Then he turned on a heel and out of the Temple, throwing the door open a little more forcefully than he'd intended and almost breaking into a run on the steps.

He retained just enough presence of mind not to run into Mol, who was waiting for him just a couple of steps down. He couldn't make out her expression in the darkness, which had become total since he'd entered the Temple, but Gideon felt he could guess that she was smiling. She typically was.

"Gideon, it has been some time," she murmured. "I take it the Mother was receptive to your petitions?"

"She was," he answered distractedly. He started to step around her, then turned back and place a hand upon her arm. "Mol. Would you answer a question for me?"

"Of course."

"How many villages in this region, do you think, at a guess, have an oval-shaped green in their center?"

* * *

"Stones Above, boy, what're you doing out so late?" Torvul had, it seemed, gone out for a stroll, pipe in hand, and stumbled upon Gideon walking carefully, one foot in front of the other, around the village green.

"Trying to get a reasonable measure of the circumference of the green by using my footsteps measured against the common pace." Carefully, the boy set another foot forward.

Torvul took in that answer slowly, puffing a great cloud of smoke from his pipe. "Why in all the seven secret names of gold would you be doing that?"

The boy lifted his head to stare at the dwarf through the darkness. "The seven secret names of gold?"

Torvul waved his free hand dismissively. "Human tongues lack the nuance required for Dwarfish oaths. Pathetic, really," he added. "And you didn't answer my question."

"How many villages in the region have a green that is oval-shaped?"

"Cold's that matter?"

"The altar in the Temple—the altar we raised—is also oval."

Torvul pursed his lips around his pipe stem, shifted the fingers that cradled the huge, rune-carved bowl. "Coincidence?"

"Surely you don't believe quite so much in coincidence, Torvul."

"I suppose I don't see why it matters."

"Think *symbolically* Torvul. You're the Wit, after all. We serve a Goddess, after all."

Torvul puffed away. "Hrm?"

"A feminine principle."

"And?"

"The *Mother*," Gideon said, exasperation bleeding through his words.

"Wha...oh. OH." Torvul lowered his pipe. "Cold, boy, that's no coincidence. But why's it matter now? Civilized folk are after their first sleep."

"She told me that where matters," Gideon replied. "Where is significant. Here, I mean. That She woke to the world here for a reason. I am trying to puzzle out what it is."

"And measuring the green would help you do that?"

"I think it is the same proportions as the altar. I made only a rough measurement by eye, since I've no tapes or compass."

"So it may be the same proportion. Let me ask, and be honest, why does that matter a whit?"

Gideon frowned and tugged at an earlobe thoughtfully with one hand. "It seemed like something to do. Analyze the information in front of me. Measure and quantify."

"Your turn t'think symbolically. If they're both the same symbol it's the idea that matters, not the size o'the thing."

"I suppose that could be true," Gideon admitted grudgingly. "I feel as though the answer is in front of me. Tantalizingly so. The symbol inherent in the shapes. What else about this village sets it apart?"

"I've only lived here as long as you, and I've been rather too busy stopping it from being burnt or razed to have taken in much of the local folklore," Torvul replied dryly. He joined Gideon at the edge of the green, surveyed it in the light of the stars. "Why aren't we asking Mol?"

"I don't think she'd answer any more than the Mother would," Gideon said. "At times I'm not sure there's a clear line between the two of them. I think I have to solve this, to understand something. There are links, inextricable links between this material world, and the world of the will. I think that is what She is trying to teach me. A year ago I would have doubted there is such a thing as a place of power, and yet..."

"You're gettin' a mite philosophical even for me, lad. But frankly I could've told you that places have power any time, for the askin'."

"I wouldn't have believed you, Torvul," Gideon replied. "No matter how I try, sometimes I still think like a sorcerer."

"What d'ya mean?"

"I disconnect everything. The needs of the body separate from the life of the mind. The physical facts of the world separate from how I can exert my will upon it." He bowed his head and rubbed a hand over his eyes.

Torvul clapped a hand on the boy's shoulder. "We dwarfs have a saying, lad. When it's too late t'sleep, it's time t'drink. Let's pop into the Inn and have a brandy. We'll not wake anyone."

"Having a brandy will help me sleep?"

"No," Torvul said. "But it'll make doing without a bit more worthwhile."

Reluctantly, Gideon followed the dwarf into the Inn. The taproom was dark but for the small glow from the banked fire.

For all the seeming heaviness of his steps, and the considerable bulk packed into his round-shouldered frame, Torvul hardly made a sound as he slumped into bench. "You know where the bottle is," he said. "And get a couple of cups, too. Let's drink like civilized folk for once," he murmured.

Gideon had no difficulty seeing in the dark. He walked around the edge of the long wooden bar and plucked the bottle from a shelf behind it. He cast his eyes around, looking for cups, saw none, so he walked around the shelves that stood behind the bar, beyond which lay more storage, and the kitchen.

Still distracted, the boy didn't see the iron ring set into the trap door that guarded the cold well, and his foot brushed against the ring, almost tripping him.

He stopped, stared down at the wood beneath his feat.

"Torvul," he said, straining to keep his voice quiet. "Come here, please."

By the time the dwarf had arrived, Gideon had pried the trap door open and carefully set it back. The hinges creaked for want of grease, and he knelt at the side of it. It was dark inside, though he could see the pool of water sloshing around the keg that floated in it. The sides of it were earthen, not wide, roughly hewn.

"Would your opinion as a dwarf be that this was man made, or natural, Torvul?"

The dwarf peered over the boy's shoulder. "Probably a bit o'both, why?"

"Cults of feminine deities worship at holy springs. And at crossroads," the boy said, his voice suddenly rising. "I read of this. Bhimanzir made me study the trappings of faith so that it could be manipulated at need. Thornhurst has an oval green. At a crossroads. Was it a holy spring?"

He stood, closed the trap door, heedless of how loudly it shut. "Torvul. This entire *village* was once a temple to the Goddess."

"How d'ya figure?"

"It's a place that is sacred to Her. If She was going to return to the world, to wake from whatever sleep a goddess seeks, it was going to be here. There had to be a reason. It wasn't merely Mol's suffering, or Allystaire's passing by—the lives of poor children are snuffed out like candles all over the world, in a thousand ways, a thousand petty cruelties or savage accidents of fate. But that it was happening in a place that had long been sacred to Her? That, She could not ignore."

By now, the sounds of them banging the trap door about had drawn attention from the rest of the Inn. Heavy footsteps pounded on the floor and a weary but powerful voice called out.

"If you are robbers, you have picked the wrong Inn," Allystaire said. "Step out where I can see you."

"Think a moment, ya great daft blunderer," Torvul rumbled, his voice pitched just loudly enough to carry a few feet. "You'll wake the whole damned village."

Gideon and Torvul stepped out from behind the shelves. Gideon still clutched the brandy bottle, and was too absorbed in the rush of thought to say much to Allystaire, who'd rushed down the stairs wearing only short breeches, carrying his hammer.

"Put some clothes on, for decency's sake," Torvul muttered.

Allystaire lowered his hammer so that it rested on the floor, the haft pointing straight up, and rubbed at his eyes with one hand. "If you two were just after a drink, there was hardly any need for such noise." He dropped his hand and peered forward, frowning. "Unless you are drunk."

"Not at all," Gideon replied as he absently set the bottle down upon a table and slid onto the nearest bench. "Torvul, I think I have it."

"Have what?" Allystaire's question beat Torvul to a reply, but dwarf and man both sat down, the latter carefully setting his hammer down on the tabletop.

"The boy's engaging in some theoretical speculation," the dwarf told him. He glanced at Allystaire and then looked away, his face souring. "If not for yourself, for those about ya," he said. "Ya ought to cover all that up," he added, waving a hand, Gideon assumed, at the network of scars that marred Allystaire's torso, rippled white lines and blotches of discolored skin telling the stories of a lifetime spent in battle.

Then he does see in the dark, Gideon noted to himself, thinking back on his talk with Idgen Marte. *Unless he'd taken some potion.*

"You have seen worse, dwarf," Allystaire chided Torvul. He held up his left arm, pointing to a white patch of skin upon it. "Cold, without you, this one would have killed me."

"I only managed the poison, boy, not the wound itself," Torvul said. Then, with a sniff, he added, "Of course, that's by far the more difficult matter. Most chirurgeons are mere tailors, after all, threaded needle in one hand, blade in the other. Not like an alchemist, an apothecary, a master of crafts." Allystaire casually reached for the bottle Gideon had set down and slid it in front of Torvul, who instantly quieted and began tugging at the cork.

Allystaire turned to Gideon. "What is this theoretical speculation?"

The boy tilted his head. "What we spoke of earlier this night. Learning Her rules. Thinking on what I might do next."

"And what is that?"

Gideon caught Torvul's eye while the dwarf was lowering the brandy bottle. He slid it in front of Allystaire, who lifted it for a small sip.

"I don't want to try and explain just yet," Gideon said. "Not entirely. Yet, perhaps if I phrase it this way." He bit his lower lip. "Imagine you had an enormous armory available to you."

"I was dreaming," Allystaire said, "of that very thing."

"Well, imagine it was no dream. Imagine, then, that only a very few select people were ever allowed access to it. You are one of them, but most aren't. If you were, with effort, able to change that—to distribute the weapons within freely, to all folk able to come for them, without dint of training, or even knowing if the arms would ultimately be used for good or evil—but there was a great crisis, and folk needed any chance to defend themselves against it, would you do it? Would you throw open the doors?"

"How great is this crisis? And I could I not simply collect the arms after it had passed?"

Gideon shook his head slowly. "No. This is a one-way decision. You do it or do not. Some of the weapons you distribute might end up in the hands of thieves and blackguards, and some might become forgotten relics. But some might wind up in the hands of folk who would want nothing more than the ability to defend their own. And some, even just a few, who receive the gift you give might seek to follow after you, and to use it in defense of the Goddess and Her people. Could you deny them that chance?"

Silence hung heavy in the otherwise empty room for a moment, till Gideon reached out for the brandy bottle and wetted his lips with a small belt from it. Torvul and Allystaire were quiet. Finally, the dwarf spoke.

"I couldn't deny it t'them," he said quietly but firmly. "That some might do evil with somethin' dangerous doesn't mean it ought t'be barred t'all."

"I am not sure how more swords makes anyone safer," Allystaire said.

"Well," Gideon replied, "the metaphor is not perfect."

"Can you not tell me what you mean to do, son?"

Gideon sighed and lowered his head. "Might I sleep on it? I am weary, and the dawn is coming, and I would prefer to explain it just the once, to everyone." He stood, but kept his eyes lowered.

"Of course," Allystaire said. "To your bed, then. You can have a reprieve from the morning exercises if you wish. I know it is taxing to speak with Her."

Gideon quickly departed, his steps making barely a sound as he ascended the stairs.

"Do you know what he intends, Torvul?" Allystaire's question was barely voiced above a whisper.

"Aye," Torvul answered. "I do."

"Is it necessary?"

"Can't see how it's otherwise. The chance of the good it could do, Allystaire…" Here, he trailed off, sighed. "I haven't got the words. And that's *me* sayin' that."

"Then I will not stand in his way."

"Good. Not that ya could stop him—none of us could—but if ya told him, he'd not do it."

"I know," Allystaire said, as he stood and collected his hammer. "Faith, Torvul. In each other, as well as Her. Goddess knows the boy has shown it in me; time I returned it."

Slowly, wearily, the paladin followed Gideon up the stairs. Torvul thumbed the cork back into the bottle of brandy and stood, wearily, and headed for the door, and the long walk back to his wagon.

"Took the boy long enough t'figure it out," he muttered as he reached for his pipe pouch.

CHAPTER 31

Visions

Allystaire could feel the sweat steaming off of his head as he threw open the door of the Inn. His muscles glowed with the effort of the morning's exercise, though the sun had not been long in the sky.

Weariness and fatigue were trumped by the feeling of turning men into knights once more. At least it was until Rede intercepted him just a few steps through the door.

Much of the village was only just awake. Timmar was handing out small loaves of bread to folk who'd come by for a morning meal, and Rede had one of them in his hand, whole, unbroken, uneaten. Red-rimmed eyes were huge in the man's face, and his cheeks were pallid and lined, his upraised hand twitching with nervous energy. It was that shaking hand he laid upon the paladin's chest, stopping him as he walked.

Unable to stop himself, Allystaire shot Rede a look, hard enough to have the man recoil away from him, lifting his shaking hand in front of his face. With a sigh, Allystaire lifted his own hand, palm out. "Rede. Calm yourself. What is the matter?"

"I have had more visions, Lord Stillbright," he said, suddenly turning his eyes back to Allystaire. The feverish intensity in them was frightening and Allystaire found himself wondering how far, if at all, it was bounded by sanity.

"Rede," he said, lowering his voice, and taking the man's elbow to guide him to a table, "come, speak to me. And there is no need to call me Lord." The former monk sat, folding his long frame and limbs awkwardly.

Allystaire seated himself, ignoring the trickling of sweat through his hair and down his back that sought to remind him of all the effort he'd just expended. "Now," he murmured, "tell me—quietly—of these new visions." After a moment, he added, managing not to grit his teeth, "Please."

"I saw knights winging through the air from stone tower to stone tower," Rede said. "The sun rising from a well. A mountain floating in the air above a mass of men, who begged and pleaded not to be destroyed by it. I saw a great serpent struck in its middle with a spear and writhing upon the ground and wreaking destruction as it died. Vines and other green growing things withering and dying. The sun that had risen from the well falling into the sea and setting it aflame."

"What does any of it mean?"

"I cannot say," Rede replied. "It comes in flashes amidst so much other nonsense that I am lucky to know what I have told you."

"What kind of nonsense?"

"Things I can barely put into words. Men and women who sing in voices made of fire. A knight who struggles for breath. A laughing corpse buried beneath a standing stone. A set of balances weighing gold against air and light." Rede set the loaf of bread he'd clutched upon the table and wove his fingers together, both hands now shaking. "How can I know what any of it means? None of it makes any sense. I have told you the things I could pull out of the dreams that assail me. I can do little else."

Then what Frozen good are you to me? Allystaire didn't give voice to his immediate thought. He forced himself to take a deep and clearing breath. "Perhaps," he suggested, "if you spoke with Torvul, or Gideon, or Mol, they might be able to help you interpret these visions. I have little head for such things. I will not discount them, but I am not the man who can tell you what they mean." He worked hard to keep his voice even and calming. *To no great effect,* he thought, as the blazing fire in the other man's eyes hadn't dimmed even a bit.

"You're the one that has to understand." Rede's hand suddenly shot across the table and seized Allystaire's wrist. His grip was surprisingly strong, his skin feverish, and Allystaire resisted the urge to do something violent with his free hand. "If these things are not to come to pass, you must be the one to stop them," he hissed, leaning forward. "If I am going to redeem myself, I have to serve *you*."

"No. If you wish to serve, you serve the Goddess, and that means serving anyone in need."

Rede's grip tightened. Allystaire felt untrimmed fingernails digging into his flesh, and he was preparing to use his free hand to pry the other man's fingers away, when they suddenly slackened and let go. "You're right," Rede whispered, lowering his eyes and pulling his hands together in his lap. "You're right. I…is there anything in what I said?"

"I do not know. I like the idea of knights winging their way in the sky," he said, trying a light jest. "If I could move an army in the air, I should fear no enemy. And if I could strike from such a height? No wall would ever stop me."

"Your war won't be within walls, Allystaire Stillbright," Rede said, his voice a low hum that slowly rose as he went on. "It will be with the air that is full of mourning and the sea that is full of fury, with the clouds that bear the storm and the earth that drags you down to the corpses interred within it. It will go on long after you are dead."

Allystaire felt a chill work its way down his spine as the man spoke. "What," he said, slowly rising to his feet, his hand falling naturally to his hammer, "was that?"

Rede raised his head, looking dazed. Sudden awareness lit in his eyes, and he started. "What…what did I just say?"

"Rede," Allystaire said, "you had best not be playing some kind of game."

"I swear I am not." The man extended an arm, pulling back the thin robe that covered it to expose the skin, drawn tight over sinew and bone. "Use your Gift. Ask me any question. I know I was speaking. I know not what I said."

"You said," Allystaire murmured, "a number of things. Things I think I want Torvul to hear. Will you walk with me to see him, Rede? He may have something that would grant you some rest."

Rede thought a moment, a wary expression playing over his face, then he nodded shortly and stood.

His legs are shaking, Allystaire thought, and as the man rounded the table, the paladin reached out to take his arm and buoy him up. For all of his height, Rede seemed to weigh nothing, and Allystaire thought he could feel the heat of the man's flesh through the thin and tattered robe.

The former Urdarite fared better once they were outside, a hobbling walk turning into a more comfortable stride. Allystaire was able to let go of Rede's shoulder and let him walk under his own power. They walked in silence, and Allystaire tried to remember the cold, odd pronouncement the other man had made, slowly repeating the words in his mind while they were fresh.

They had just reached Torvul's wagon, parked as always by the house that served as his workshop, when a figure on horseback came pounding up towards them, one long arm waving, shouting. The rider had cut straight across the village, rather than following a road. Allystaire had let his hand fall to his hammer and took a step in front of Rede, but once he picked out the details—the length of the limbs, the color of the horse, the curve of the cased bow peeking over one shoulder—he relaxed.

Norbert pulled up easily, and slid off the back of the horse effortlessly. *He's becoming quite a horseman*, Allystaire thought, as he looked at the slightly lathered dun courser the youth had taken to riding. Not as huge or imposing as Ardent, closer in shape and length to Idgen Marte's horse and as good a runner, it responded easily to the lad's touch and stayed still when he slid from the saddle, nosing at the spring grass.

"Allystaire," Norbert said, and the paladin envied the younger man's easy breathing. "There are men come in the livery of Innadan, bearing messages from the Baron. They say they'll speak only to you."

* * *

Symod bit back his curses, swallowed the anger that rose up and threatened to explode as he looked down at the corpse. Another Islandman—or in truth, the descendant of an Islandman, since this one had lived his short and dirty life on the Barony mainland—lay messily dead before him.

"This one could have served the Sea Dragon in his own way," he said aloud.

"He sought a quarrel with a Dragon Scale." Jorn's voice was unnervingly low and feral, as if it pained him to make the sounds of speech. Symod found himself, as always, straining a bit more than he liked in order to catch each word. "He reaped the ocean's wrath."

"And how did he seek that quarrel? Throwing loaded dice? Finishing a jar of mead?" Symod shook his head. The dead man's innards were spattered over an area the size of a small chamber. The upper right quarter of his body was practically free of the rest, the arm and shoulder all but torn away.

"Matters not. Man was weak. Man is dead. As the Sea Dragon wills."

"As the Sea Dragon wills," Symod echoed. He reminded himself, again, that no man had ever brought so many of the Dragon Scales together. Nearly three hundreds of them, if the count was accurate, and more arriving, awaited his orders, his pleasure, along the upper reaches of the Valdin river valley, the thick ribbon of muddy, slow-moving water the nominal boundary between Fallen Vyndamere and the barely-struggling-on Barony Varshyne.

Three hundred barely-sane, divinely-powered berzerkers full of a blood lust that was only just contained. Meanwhile, they exercised every other kind of lust available to them in camp. The large tents where the camp followers worked were never short of business. Neither were the tents that sold food or drink.

Symod couldn't quite figure out where the folk had come from, but borders tended to be loose places in the Baronies, especially these more lawless and less settled territories. They might be folk up from Delondeur or across from Oyrwyn, or even the remnants of Vyndamere folk, or Varshynners who felt the wind changing.

Regardless, Symod was glad they were here, for he'd given no thought to provisions or stores aside from weapons. Those he had in abundance. He smiled at the thought. *Surely,* he told himself, *an army well armed is an army that will manage to feed itself.*

Army was, he had to admit, perhaps an overstatement. While many of the settler bands he'd sent on their way had begun trickling in, they hadn't come in the numbers he'd expected. Some carried reports of armed peasants providing stiffer resistance than expected, while others seemed simply to have lost the stomach after shedding their first blood. No matter.

Symod had lost himself in thought, and came to realize that Jorn was asking him a question. He turned his upraised brows at the berzerker, who he'd come to think was the chief of his kind.

"The body," Jorn's voice grated. "What to do with it?"

"Bury it by the river. He was trying to do Braech's work, after all."

Jorn nodded, but didn't make any move towards picking the body up. Symod let it pass, knowing well it'd be gone by nightfall.

"Are there any new arrivals to report on?"

"Some bits of paper," Jorn growled. "And one band. Fisherman weaklings. First village we visited."

Symod thought back to the sea ice he'd had a job of breaking up, to all the rotten-smelling villages and worse-smelling people he'd visited with and talked to at winter's end. The tiny villages were all the same, with their pathetic chief's halls in the middle, in pride of place. Any such hall would fit easily in many chambers in the Sea Dragon's Temple in Londray.

"I think I recall. Arvid's band," he finally said, dredging the name up from memory. "Good. I will see to them soon. And once more, Jorn, they are called letters. And they are quite important."

"As you say." The berzerker took a deep breath, expanding his huge, tattooed chest and arching his back slightly. "Why do we not move?"

"We haven't the men yet," Symod said. "And I am waiting word from certain possible allies."

"The Sea Dragon needs no allies. What can stand against the tide?"

"Allystaire *Stillbright*, apparently," Symod replied, his twisting mouth putting acid into the paladin's new surname. "He is a dangerous man, with dangerous allies. We cannot move against him yet."

Jorn snorted. "I fear no soft southerner. I need only meet him. Then he will die and trouble the Sea Dragon no longer."

"I've little doubt of that," Symod lied. *One Dragon Scale isn't likely to trouble the paladin overmuch*, he thought, *if rumors of his strength are not too greatly exaggerated.* Out loud, he went on. "We must be able to crush not only the paladin himself, but the armies that will rise against us. To do that, we must raise a host."

Jorn toed the ruined corpse they still stood over, the body just off the well-worn track between the messy camp of the warriors and the rather more orderly follower's camp, withdrawn a few hundred paces. "Of such men as this, you'll raise no worthy host." He sniffed. "Ought to seek the Gravek that would serve the Sea Dragon. They'll make an army."

Symod turned away from the corpse and began walking back to his tent in the center of camp. "Gravek, you say? And where am I to find them?"

"North."

"How far?"

Jorn thought on this a while. Though heavier and shorter-limbed than Symod, he easily kept pace. The Choiron had the feeling Jorn could outdistance him without effort, and that he walked beside him as a sign of deference.

"Two day's run for a Dragon Scale. Three, could be. Week or more for a lesser man."

"What would we need to convince them?"

"Weapons. Plunder. Same you've offered the weaklings."

"Well, Jorn, it sounds to me as though you've volunteered to lead a delegation to go speak with whatever Gravek you can find. Do you expect Gravekling or Gravekmir?"

Jorn shrugged. For all the bored expression on his weather-burned face changed, Symod might have been assigning him a watch. "Both."

"Very well, then. See to it, Jorn. Bring me back giants and giantkin."

The berzerker shot him a narrow-eyed look. "No. I will bring back giants for the Sea Dragon. Not for you."

Symod's face went cold, and he gathered his will. In his mind he could feel it coiling like a snake, or an arm pulled back and tensed for a blow. He let it hover over Jorn's mind; for all the berzerker's strength, Symod knew, Jorn hadn't the power of the mind necessary to refuse him.

"I am a Choiron, anointed by the Sea Dragon, and I am the architect of His plan for these Baronies," Symod said, drawing himself to his full height and rolling his shoulders back. "I will lead his army and sweep aside the heresy that nestles like poison in the heart of this country, and I will do it for Braech's glory. I need not be reminded whom I serve by one of *my* servants."

Jorn Dragon Scale didn't pale or quiver or let fear show, but Symod felt the other man's will quail under his. The berzerker lowered his eyes. "Apologies, Blessed Choiron. I will bring back Gravek for the Sea Dragon, or I will kill them in His name. Grant me leave to go."

"Be gone. Never question my devotion again."

Jorn nodded, turned, and bounded away. Symod watched him go, watched the sunlight glinting from the clawed gauntlets that swung at Jorn's side as he ran. The Choiron let out his held breath, deflated a little. Jorn had challenged him more brazenly then, but not for the first time. *If he meets his death wooing giantkin to the cause, so much the better.*

He wound his way to his tent, nodding or waving absently at each bow or murmur of "Blessed Choiron" or "Honored Symod."

Inside his tent, casually tossed on the bedding was a pair of folded, wax-sealed pieces of parchment. He picked them up and examined their seals: a report from the Temple in Londray and a letter from the Marynth Evolyn.

He sliced open the latter and quickly scanned it.

Honored Choiron,

Crossed safely to the Archipelago. Keersvasti Dragon Scales are reluctant to sail for the Baronies, as there are rumblings of war with the Concordat, but some should soon be on their way. They are likely to burn and pillage in Londray, though, I warn you.

I have made contact with the man you sent me to meet. He is difficult to read and I do not know what lever might be used to move him. He fears the boy. I have not yet showed him the book. The time has not been right.

I remain your devoted servant,

The Marynth Evolyn Lamaliere

Symod thought over the words. The boy was, indeed, a problem. He needed to give thought to how best to deal with him before moving south.

There was not a great deal in the world that Symod feared, but when he thought back to the power of the will that had destroyed the artifact in the Temple in Keersvast, he had to fight a chill.

Symod turned to the second parchment and flicked it open with a casual stroke of his thumb. The writing was slapdash, hurried, the ink smeared upon the page. There was no honorific at the beginning, no suppliant greeting.

Dragon Scales dead. Hissop hangs from a tower. Other priests taken. The Baroness has besieged the Temple. Wants all clergy complicit in attack. May sack the Temple. Fortune possibly preparing writs. No more time. Marynth Hr

The letters trailed off into a quick, flat line, as if the writer had dashed away in the midst of scrawling them.

Symod resisted the urge to crumple the paper between his hands, which suddenly surged with anger. "The *cheek*," he grated through clenched teeth. "The impudence. To attack the very Temple of the Sea Dragon."

He looked at the words again, forcing his breath to slow, his fists to uncurl. Marynth Hrigan, he presumed, of the unfinished signature. "A useless sot," he muttered. "I hope your guts festoon the walls of the Dunes even now." The man had left so much information unwritten. "Allystaire was a fool to let Lionel's heir go from his clutches. Perhaps I overestimate him. What attack did Hrigan speak of?"

Once again he looked at the letter, found it maddeningly short. He tried to piece together what information he had been given to make a more complete picture. Hissop had taken the two Dragon Scales he left at the Temple—in order to guide any forces Evolyn managed to raise in Keersvast—and done, what? "Something foolish," the Choiron muttered. He'd died for it, but two berzerkers had died as well. "Even two berzerkers could mean the difference against Stillbright. How to turn this?"

A Baroness had attacked a Temple. Symod could only assume she had looted its treasures, at least, if not razed it to the ground. The nobility did not often meddle in Temple politics, but it seemed as if the paladin and their upstart Goddess had crushed the lines between Temple and Baronial matters.

"The Baroness may have overreached," Symod murmured. "Her seat will not be strong, nor her forces consolidated. If we move swiftly on Delondeur once our own host is forged, Braech's faithful will see us as answering this sin." Tossing the letter down upon his bedding and heading for the opening of his tent, Symod smiled.

* * *

Landen, wearing brilliant green enameled plate with the Delondeur Tower etched into the cuirass, helm tucked under her arm, strode the empty halls of Braech's Temple in Londray, Chaddin, Ivar, and two knights trailing. A workman led her through the Temple corridors, the man all but constantly clutching at the cap he wasn't wearing, or at an imaginary forelock on his bald head.

Finally, he led them to the largest chamber Landen had seen. Half of the room, like much of the Temple, was projected out over the crashing surf, sunk on heavy posts. The huge plinth and statue that stood before them—twice as tall as Landen if it was a foot—seemed to stand right at the edge of solid ground.

"Here 'tis, m'lady," the workman said. A few other laborers in rough clothes stood about, tools strewn about them. Hammers, heavy iron bars, chains, chisels, a block and tackle. "We can't make a dent upon it, nor pull it down from the stone. Like it's grown out of it."

"Worked metal does not grow straight from stone, goodman."

"Beggin' your pardon m'lady, but I know. Stone is m'livin, the carvin' and cuttin' of it. We've brought in blacksmiths and fancier metalworkers, and none of 'em know rightly what it is, nor how t'move it."

Landen frowned, turned and handed her helm to one of the attending knights, and pointed to a rock hammer. "May I?"

A mason scrambled to put the tool in her hands. Landen stepped forward, raised it overhead, and swung hard.

The shock reverberated up her arms, stinging them to the shoulders, just this side of painfully. She looked closely; there wasn't a dent on the metal of the statue.

"Have they tried etching liquids?" She held the hammer out towards the workman who'd led them in.

"Aye, m'lady," the man said, taking the hammer carefully back. "We've tried everythin' we can. One brave soul even climbed b'neath the floor. The stone it is built upon grows straight up under the Temple, through the floor. As if th'whole of it t'were built round this statue."

"Well," Landen said, "if we cannot destroy the statue, we can bring the Temple down around it. Carry on your work, goodmen. Thank you for bringing this to me." She pulled free a purse tucked inside one bracer, carefully prised it open, and dumped its contents into the suddenly open palm of the lead laborer. "To split amongst yourselves, for your hard work and initiative." Each man was given a long string of silver links.

There was a good deal more tugging of locks and m'ladys and bowing before Landen could shake her way gracefully free of the knot of masons and metalworkers. Once they were safely gone, Chaddin sidled up to her.

"Is this wise, m'lady? To meddle so boldly with a Temple?"

Landen turned her gazed on Chaddin, adjusting the helm she held under one arm once more. "They plundered our armory under the false seal of Lord Lamaliere. They interdicted our return to the Dunes. Good men died because of the actions of their holy men. I would say that every priest in this Temple declared himself a traitor."

"The priests, perhaps," Chaddin countered. "But the Temple itself? Its riches?"

"We have to rebuild the armory somehow, and we must do it fast. The ironmongers and smiths know of our shortfall, and can dictate prices. Would you rather I seized their stock, thus alienating an entire guild or two, or three, or would you rather I paid them with Braech's money? Fewer folk are hurt this way."

"I don't quibble with the logic. I only wonder about the consequences. There are many adherents to Braech in the city and beyond. And then there is the—"

"Is Braech the Master of Accords, or of theft?" Landen thought on the empty armory she'd found inside the Dunes, began seething all over again.

"And Hissop and the chapel priests paid for that."

"No, they paid for their treachery. The riches of Temple will pay to re-arm the Barony."

"Has it occurred to you that Lord Lamaliere might have been complicit? It was under his seal."

Landen shook her head. "No one I spoke to could place the man in the city all winter. He squatted in Tide's Watch like the rest of the lords did in their halls, and waited to see how my father's madness would shake out."

A silence stretched on for a moment, then became suddenly awkward when Chaddin said, "Our father's madness."

Landen winced slightly and nodded her agreement. By now they had reached their horses, guarded by still more knights, and mounted their saddles. Once they'd put a few streets between themselves and the slowly emptying Temple of Braech, she said, "Perhaps it is time to call them in and feel them out."

"If you wish, but I would prefer to have more men under arms answering directly to us within the walls before inviting the lords and their retinues."

"You have a point. All the more reason to empty the temple quickly, then."

It was Chaddin's turn to wince, though he said nothing. No sooner had they clattered through the portcullis into the large courtyard of the Dunes, than a corpulent figure was making its way towards them. Clad in a voluminous green robe of crushed velvet, belted in gold—more of which looped broadly around his neck—Lord Sundegard, Castellan of the Dunes, waved a tiny roll of paper in one age-spotted thick-fingered hand. He panted out the necessary honorifics, and Landen only caught something about a pigeon, and the word Innadan.

Landen awkwardly took the roll of paper and pried a seal of red wax from it, unrolled it carefully, and held it to the light. She turned to Chaddin, no small bit of shock in her wide eyes.

"The Peace Congress is on. Standing Guard Pass."

Lord Sundegard cleared his throat noisily. "Peace Congress, m'lady?"

"Aye, Lord Castellan," Landen answered him. "A Peace Congress attended by Hamadrian Innadan, Unseldt Harlach, and Byron Telmawr at the least. It says nothing of Gilrayan Oyrwyn, but it does not rule him out."

"It's a trap, my lady," Sundegard ventured, the folds of his neck wobbling indignantly. "Surely you must go in force."

"The Congress will also be attended by Allystaire Stillbright, who is its architect," Landen replied, shaking her head. "I pity the man who tries to spring a trap upon him there."

"This is the so-called paladin who was the death of your own lord father, and yet you would trust him?"

Chaddin leveled hard eyes on the prattling, fat castellan, who ignored him utterly. Landen, however, cut the man off. "As I have no doubt already said in your hearing, my lord," she began coldly, "Allystaire Stillbright is indeed a paladin, and we are indebted to him for our very lives. Surely you have heard the proclamations read that rescinded the Anathemata upon the worship of his Goddess, and the further proclamations expressly allowing said worship throughout Barony Delondeur. So, yes, Lord Sundegard, I trust the man as much as I trust anyone. Now," she said, putting a snap into her voice that even had Chaddin straightening his spine. "You will have preparations to make for the party that will leave for Standing Guard Pass in a fortnight, and messages to send to the Lords of Tide's Watch, Ennithstide, and the Salt Cliffs."

"Of course, my lady," Sundegard panted, bowing. "I'll see to it at once." The man scrambled off, wobbling beneath his robes.

"Oyrwyn had Allystaire as his castellan," Chaddin observed, as he and Landen watched the fat man waddle off. "And we have Sundegard. How did we not lose the war a decade ago?"

Landen laughed lightly. "He is not so bad if you know how to handle him."

"I haven't the strength," Chaddin replied. "What do you think no word from Oyrwyn means?"

"We will find out at Standing Guard Pass," Landen said. "And until then, we will hope that everyone comes in peace."

* * *

If winter had given up its long battle with spring in the Baronies, it was a distant and maligned memory far to the southwest on the Keersvast Archipelago.

Though it was not her first visit, the Marynth Evolyn could hardly take it all in. She cherished the memory of sailing in, though it was two weeks past now. The Guild Pilot who had come aboard took them on a long route. While the Pilot's job was to bring them past the reefs that formed the great city's stoutest and most famed defenses, not all of those routes took a simple thirteen-bench longship beneath bridges that arced high enough to allow for the passage of caravels and thirty-bench sword-ships.

The city had spread out before her, gleaming pink coral and cool blue marble in its oldest sections, exotic Concordat woods mixed into the newer. The Grand Temple of the Sea Dragon that she was now quartered in was a massive blue marble edifice in one of the very oldest sections of the city. The scores of islands that made up the city were linked by bridges and causeways, and the city had, over hundreds of years, organized itself into rings, with the wealth congregating further in. Braech's Temple was located on its own island, separated from the very innermost ring by only a few score span of seawater.

Evolyn stood at one of the windows overlooking this stretch of water, made quiescent by the artifice of Keersvast's builders, the craft of Guild of Reeftenders and Pilots, and the power of the very Temple she stood in.

"Braech is the Father of Waves," she murmured. "Did he mean for men to try to master them like this?" She murmured these thoughts, but should have kept them to herself. *Never know who's listening anymore, or whom they serve.* She paused in her thoughts, watched the tamed sea gently slosh between man-made wonders. *And whom do you serve, Marynth Evolyn?*

The thought took her unaware, as if it hadn't been her own.

Symod, was her first answer. *And Braech.* She had little time to ponder any further, for a Temple Guardsman, dressed in ornate scale armor, came into the room and addressed her with a bow.

"Honored Marynth." An archipelago man, his Barony tongue softly accented, he bowed deeply, in a manner that curled her lip with disgust. "A pilot awaits to convey you to the first circle. Will you require a guard?"

The sly tone of his words, the undisguised lift of an eyebrow. The man hoped to gain favors, whether hers or Braech's or both, she did not much care.

"No," she answered, putting as much ice in the single syllable as she could manage. He turned and walked away, his unctuous bearing hardly becoming a man under arms and sworn to Braech.

Unblooded tradsemen's sons playing at being guardsmen, she thought, as she waited a respectable length of time before exiting the chamber with its view of the captive sea, and going in search of the pilot. She was startled to remember, before she reached the entry hall, that she'd first heard the words from the man she was now working to destroy.

The pilot proved to be both less and more ornamental than the guardsman who'd seen an opportunity in her. Less, because his competence was clear and bracing, and more because he was clearly an elfling of some half or quarter blood, and arrestingly fair. His auburn hair was cut into the scalplock she'd seen many of his sort affecting on the archipelago. By shaving the sides of their heads and exposing the slim points of their ears they seemed all the more exotic to her, though she wasn't sure that was the intention. Many wore tattoos inked into the scalp as well, and this man was no different, with a vividly blue seahorse—complete with saddle and stirrups, though no rider—cunningly inked into the flesh on the left side of his head.

"Kiawan," he'd said as he made a small bow. "And you are the Marynth Evolyn?"

"Aye." She'd extended a hand in a bold, Barony fashion, and when he took it in his, she found his flesh strangely cool, even cold. Despite that she fancied she could feel the pulse of blood beneath his skin. "To what do I owe the visit of a Pilot?" Evolyn could guess, but wasn't quite ready to hope.

"I have been dispatched by a gentleman of means to convey you to a jetty some distance inward." The elfling—his chin was too broad, his cheeks too full, his shoulders too broad to be full blooded elf—smiled as if sharing in some secret knowledge with her. "He was very insistent that the meeting happen immediately. Hinted that a confluence of the stars demanded it."

"Very well," she muttered her reply. She cast about for thoughts to bring color into her cheeks, and settled on the slim but tightly muscled arms and chest of the elfling, well displayed by the simple blue-dyed leather vest he wore. *Let him think it's an assignation,* she told herself. *No reason for anyone to know otherwise.* "I must fetch something first. Where should I meet you?"

He gave her the number of a quay and a jetty and bowed, turned smoothly on one heel and strolled out of the Temple, showing at least a hint of the fabled elven grace he'd apparently inherited.

Evolyn moved off determinedly, though not hastily, to her chambers.

* * *

Soon enough, the Marynth Evolyn Lamaliere was stepping off of Kiawan's slim boat. He lifted a hand to aid her, and she pointedly ignored it. In formal clerical robes and carrying a heavy bundle against her chest with both arms, Evolyn was still, by Braech, the daughter of the Lord of Tideswatch, and had grown up on and around boats.

She stepped nimbly onto the stone steps that led up onto the jetty and then up the proper walkway, mindless of their saltwater slickness. "Wait for me and there is a gold link in it, Kiawan," she tossed back as she took the steps nimbly.

Once upon the street that overlooked the rows of quays that handled the vast amount of boat traffic this deep into Keersvast's center of power, a man stepped forward out of the crowd.

"Marynth Evolyn," he said, his voice curiously lacking inflection. "Do follow me." The man was dressed as a merchant of substance, wearing soft suede boots—a sure sign that he did no work upon the open water—along with hose and an ornate doublet. His chest bore a large device she didn't recognize, a fish capering upon the top of barrel, which she took to be the sign of some merchant house or other. The man had turned swiftly away from her, but in the falling light she thought she'd seen an unusual green that seemed to move in his eyes.

He led her to what passed for a nondescript building for being this far inward, coral faded with the patina of age and salt carried against it on the wind, a few windows of thick, lightly purpling glass of significant age. Thick curtains were drawn behind them, making it impossible to see if the house was lit.

The man who led her to it said nothing else as they walked. Once at the door, the merchant knocked quietly, then turned and shuffled away.

The door swung open noiselessly. Evolyn stood, watching the dark entryway for a moment. Then, with a quick prayer to Braech, she walked in.

The door closed behind her; she could tell only by the rush of air and the slight click as it closed. It left the room entirely dark, and Evolyn felt something like panic rising in her chest.

Two dark points of green light suddenly appeared at eye level a few feet before her.

There was a dry, chuckle, followed by its faint echo.

"I do forget that most of you haven't the Seeing Dark." Each word was followed by a hollow reverberation of itself. Several candlepoints of light flicked into existence at once, all over the interior of the room. She found herself standing in a sparsely-appointed house. Chairs were scattered about, but no tapestries or paintings hung on the walls. Aside from the curtains draped across the windows, scattered tables and chairs, the house was entirely unfurnished.

"Are we to discuss matters standing?"

Evolyn's attention was snapped back to the man—if man he was—standing in front of her. He wore a heavy dark robe that shrouded a frame so thin as to be nearly emaciated. His hands were tucked into opposite sleeves, and beneath the peaked hood of the robe, only his mouth and chin were visible. These, too, were shockingly thin, the skin drawn so tightly over the bones that their outlines were clear.

"As you would, Eldest," she muttered, bowing slightly, the thick, cloth-wrapped bundle in her hands impeding her motion only slightly.

"And what have you brought me? Does a temple think it can buy the power of the Knowing with a book?"

"It is not merely a book, Eldest," she replied, even as chills stroked her spine from the odd, echoing answer each of his words received. By then he had turned and walked deeper into the house, leaving her no choice but to follow. "It describes the most powerful and ancient of Braech's secrets."

"Let me share with you Braech's secret. He does not exist." The sorcerer had turned on her and lifted a hand, the fingers protruding from his sleeve like bones, or the bare branches of a sapling. "There is only power, to be shaped and molded to the ends of those learned enough to see it. That you and your ilk insist on assigning names and principles to the raw force of the world never ceases to be bothersome."

"I am not come to debate theology with you," Evolyn replied, more fiercely than she'd intended. "I am come to discuss our common enemy, and the manner of destroying them."

They'd reached an inner chamber with a single table. The candlepoints had continued to flicker into being as they'd walked, illuminating the way they'd come down a narrow hallway. Papers lay scattered upon it. In the half-light Evolyn thought she saw a well-rendered map of the Baronies, with notations she could not read drawn carefully upon it in two places; one, in the eastern reaches of Barony Delondeur, past the Thasryach; the second, in the middle of Barony Innadan.

"And why would I need common cause with a Temple to see any enemies of the Knowing into the ground?"

"Because Allystaire Stillbright has killed three of your kind," Evolyn said, "according to our reports."

"Then your reports are wrong. This Stillbright has killed but one of us, the weakest and most foolish. Something much greater and more powerful than a mere knight was the downfall of the others." He paused, the words trailing in the air, along with the power that seemed to leak from his eyes and his mouth when he spoke. "The Negation."

"If you mean the boy, then yes, he is quite dangerous. A dozen of my fellow priests engaged him, will to will. And lost."

"A dozen like you would be as stingless gnats to the Negation," the Eldest replied. "Show me this book, these rituals of which you are so proud."

Evolyn laid the book carefully down upon the table, unwrapped it reverently. It was bound in cloth-wrapped wood, with a heavy lock holding it closed. She produced a key from her belt, turned it in the lock, and opened it, her fingers searching for the thin silver bar that served as a mark. She pushed it across the table towards the sorcerer, and was glad when the bilious green of his eyes and mouth turned to it and away from her.

The respite was short-lived. The sorcerer turned his eyes back towards her, and they opened wide and blazing.

"The principle is sound. Reclaim the power and redirect it. Yes," the sorcerer said, and she swore there was an excitement in the echoing voices that she hadn't thought the man, if man he was, capable of. "I will assist you. When do you plan to depart?"

She swallowed hard. "I am trying to round up as many of the Dragon Scales as I can before I set sail. The more Holy Berzerkers I bring to the fight—"

"The better your chances. Yes, yes. It is quite obvious. It also does not answer my question. When do you plan to depart?"

"A fortnight."

"I will meet you in your temple in Londray when you arrive. Be gone."

She started to reach for the book, but the sorcerer placed one claw-like hand upon the cover. Lines of green power pulsed beneath the skin of his hand, which was webbed with cracks like poorly kept leather.

"Is it your temple's custom to offer gifts and then to take them back?"

"It was not a gift. We struck no accord as to its purchase."

"Let me offer you an accord then, Marynth Lady Evolyn Lamaliere," the Eldest said, his hand still perched on the tome she'd first seen on Symod's desk a lifetime ago. "If you do not attempt to take this book, I will not melt the eyes from your head, nor boil the blood in your heart, nor will I rip the weak muscles of your body free from your bones, all the while keeping you alive to experience the most exquisite of pain. Do you accept?"

Accept, said the echo of the voice that emanated from him and yet not from his mouth.

"Yes," she said, and Evolyn wondered how she kept her voice even. "Take the book as a token of Braech's esteem."

"I need not the esteem of a deity that exists only in the deluded minds of idiots and madmen."

"Very well, then. Do we have an accord?"

"There is one more condition. The boy is to be killed at all costs before I will move against the rest of them."

"We have tried assassins before," Evolyn replied. "When it was just Allystaire and the woman. They failed. Now with the dwarf and the boy, I cannot see a path to success that way."

"If assassination failed, send some of your precious berzerkers. The paladin is going to kill them all anyway. Why not see if they may achieve any small success in the time that is left to them?"

"It is possible that they could be drawn out and exposed, under the right circumstances. But how am I to pass the message in time? Even if a messenger set sail tonight, we would have no answer before it was time for me to sail."

"Leave that to me. Where is Symod?"

"Camped along the Valdin river with the army he is building," she said.

"Sketch to me the basics of a plan, and then leave."

"No." The word was out of her mouth before Evolyn knew what she was saying. *If I am damned, then Father of Waves, let me be damned for following you as I know how*, she thought, and pressed on, the Eldest remaining blessedly silent. "I will not, for anyone, design a stratagem by which we hope to murder a boy by skullduggery. Work out a plan with Symod. The time has come to fight our enemy as the Sea Dragon wills, strength against strength. If we are not strong enough to destroy Stillbright and his companions, then we deserve to lose. I will not help you."

"Will you attempt to stand in my way?"

"No," Evolyn replied. "I am not strong enough. Following the Sea Dragon does not make me wish for death like a berzerker who will chant in joy when he is slain."

"It is not often that anyone attempts to gainsay the Knowing," the sorcerer replied, and she sensed a dry chuckling underpinning the words. "It is amusing. Yet you also understand your limitations, and you may yet prove useful. For now, be gone. I must speak with your better."

Evolyn turned and walked from the house with as much speed as she could muster without sacrificing her dignity.

By the time she reached the front door, the rest of the rooms growing dark behind her as she walked, she thought she heard Symod's voice, faintly, answering the Eldest's.

CHAPTER 32

Letters

Allystaire sat alone in his room in the Inn, reading again the message the Innadan couriers brought. He'd found them standing nervously under Harrys's baleful eye, with the rest of the squires standing close. It had struck him then just what a collection of brutish-looking louts he had taken it upon himself to turn into knights, but they had done nothing more to the Innadan messengers than watch.

He'd insisted, once the nature of their arrival had become plain, on turning the day to celebration, calling for wine and music while he'd taken the messengers aside to talk.

Gradually, Torvul, Idgen Marte, Mol, and Gideon had all joined him with the messengers, but most of what had been said and done had passed in a blur from the moment he'd opened the letter, sealed with wax of Innadan red, with the Vined Helm imprinted upon it. The same letter he now read at his bedside.

Allystaire Stillbright,

The Peace Congress you propose will proceed at Standing Guard Pass as soon as all parties arrive. Attending will be Unseldt Harlach, Landen Delondeur, Byron Telmawr, Ruprecht Machoryn, and Loaisa Damarind. I will play host. I propose that the meeting take place at the very juncture of my own lands with Harlach and Oyrwyn so as to remain as neutral as possible. Machoryn and Damarind are far removed from our particular struggle but have an interest in seeing our long-standing squabbles ended and have agreed to attend largely at my request for something resembling a neutral party. I have heard nothing from Varshyne, but I expected to hear nothing from Varshyne. It may well be there are no Varshynes left.

We have no definitive word from Gilrayan Oyrwyn. I, for one, don't trust him and fear that he may see six other Barons as too rich a prize to ignore. Being something of an expert on him, I hope you can share some insight with us when you arrive.

In terms of retinues, I propose that we be modest. Every Baron will want to bring his favored knights. I should put the number at no more than a score, and perhaps twice that many in total lances or other troops. Even at half these numbers we need not fear bandits, but some of us will insist on fearing one another.

I ask that you make haste to Standing Guard Pass, and bring your companions with you. Perhaps wait, if you can, for the young Baroness Delondeur. If you were to arrive with her, it would legitimize her in the eyes of Oyrwyn and Harlach, make them less likely to try and take advantage.

I will not pretend that it might not be dangerous for you here. Unseldt is not likely to forget how many chunks of his lands you sliced away for Gerard Oyrwyn over the years. If young Oyrwyn comes, he may wish to try and enforce some sentence upon you. Byron Telmawr is not likely to forget that you killed his father outside the walls of Aldacren. I will do what I can to keep them in the spirit of the thing, but I will need you to be convincing.

I will see you at Standing Guard Pass, Allystaire. I have long felt that the best thing I could do with my life was to see peace become the rule, rather than the exception. I will not pretend I will see wars done away with in my lifetime, but I am prepared to put all that I can, and all the life that I have left, into ending this one.

Baron Hamadrian Innadan, Keeper of the Vineyards

There had been other letters, copies of the confirmation from other Barons, and one from Cerisia apprising him of Hamadrian's poor health. "I am not going to allow you to die with this work undone, Hamadrian," Allystaire whispered, as he picked up the Archioness's letter once more, scanned it, catching the light floral notes of her scent still upon the thin sheet of paper. "I will need you more than you will need me."

Come as quickly as you are able. Have Gideon bring you, if he can work that miracle again. If you do not hurry, Hamadrian may not be among us any longer.

Allystaire put the letters away and stood, went to his wash basin on its stand, and splashed his face, beginning to think about sleep.

"How long can we wait for Landen?"

He tried not to show the surprise, but it was too sudden and startling. He whirled to the far corner of the room and found Idgen Marte lounging against the wall, arms crossed over her chest, one foot up against the wall and the other thrust out on the floor. He could just make out her grin in the lamplight.

"Will you ever get tired of doing that?"

"Cold, no. Now answer the question."

Allystaire sighed, and pulled his shirt over his head, folding it carefully before setting it on a stool by his bed. "See if Gideon is willing to look in on him from the air, let us know where she is. That will give us an idea of how long we have to wait."

"Could the boy not simply move us all about the way he did Cerisia?"

"I am loathe to ask that of him. Simply moving one woman and her horse, and then himself, drained him badly. How much to move all of us to Landen, or to Standing Guard Pass? Frankly, I am not sure I want anyone else to know he can do that."

"Can't keep hiding the boy forever, Allystaire," Idgen Marte said quietly. "He's goin' to have t'play a part in this, like it or not."

"I know," Allystaire said. "Idgen Marte, of all the ways everything could go wrong, all the ways I could fail, the one that frightens me the most is the possibility that I will lead him the wrong way."

"You're a father t'him, Allystaire. He'll follow you anywhere, do whatever y'ask."

"I know, and that is what terrifies me. What are the limits upon him? Like unto the dawn, Idgen Marte. Those were Her words. And that it was my greatest task to see that he is not a false dawn."

"Are we even bringing him to the congress then?"

"Of course," Allystaire said. "First, he needs to learn how to deal with people of power. Second, if everything goes badly, it is best to be holding the biggest hammer."

"I s'pose." Idgen Marte gestured to the letter Allystaire had recently set aside. "Cerisia? Still pinin' away?"

"No," Allystaire said. "Urging that we make haste."

Idgen Marte said nothing, only raised an eyebrow with an eloquence that most orators would have envied.

Allystaire sighed. "Hamadrian Innadan is dying."

"Why?"

"Why do we all die? He is old, and the world has asked a great deal of him. He is among the last of his generation left. Him, Unseldt Harlach, Joeglan of the Horned Towers, a few other knights, perhaps. Men my father's age, and my father is dead a long time now."

"Is it simply age, or is he ill?"

"Something in the wind, she says. Trouble breathing, a bloody cough."

"Cold," she swore. "Sounds like the consumption. Still, your gift has healed worse."

"It has," he said. "In younger men, or children. I will do everything I can for Hamadrian Innadan if I get to him in time. But I fear there is only so much I will be able to do."

"Enough o'that," Idgen Marte spat. "I hear any more vague presentiments of doom from you and I'll kill you myself. We're on the cusp of doing something grand, Ally. A few months ago you stood on the steps of the Temple and proclaimed that you'd stop a war that'd been going longer than you'd been alive and I told you that was a foolish and impossible thing. And you're doing it anyway."

"No agreement has been signed. No accord has been made."

"Old enemies are sitting down to make one because you asked them."

"Hamadrian Innadan asked them."

"On your behalf," Idgen Marte said. "And they're coming because they fear you. They know that Delondeur opposed you, and they know what happened to him."

"I do not want to start a revolt, Idgen Marte. I have no desire to depose Barons and raise other men in their place. That path is too blood-soaked for our purpose."

"Then what comes after the peace?"

"I do not know," Allystaire said. "Whatever we can make of it."

"Cold," she said, weariness creeping into her voice. "If we effect a peace, can't we take a rest?"

Allystaire smiled faintly. "We gave up on rest when She called us, Idgen Marte."

She snorted. "You did," she said. "Not me."

"Nothing is stopping you from resting right this very minute."

"Nothing except a boy who hungers for music lessons the way a sot does for wine," she said, "and then a bard who'll want to keep me up half the night asking questions."

"Asking questions?" Allystaire's words were flat and deadpan, his eyebrows lifted lightly.

"There isn't the man born who can keep me awake that long any other way," Idgen Marte shot back. "Even if he is young and enthusiastic."

"That," Allystaire said, raising a hand, "is as much as I should hear."

Idgen Marte snickered. "Prude."

"Hardly," Allystaire said. "I just have to be able to look both of you in the eye tomorrow."

"Does it bother you, then?" Idgen Marte's tone turned serious. "He'll not distract me from my charge."

"Throughout these months, Idgen Marte, I have learned that there is little in the world that will distract you from your charge," Allystaire said. "And no, it could never bother me. Take what love and what joy you find, never regret it, never apologize for it. If we are going to change the world, we need to start by loving it as much as we can."

"Love the world in order t'save it," Idgen Marte said. "That's a long way from the man I met in a shanty town tavern, who acted as if he'd just as soon tear it all down. With his bare hands, if he had to."

"And I will, if I must," Allystaire said. "I learned all my life that Oyrwyn men were made of stone and ice, and I have my life trying to make myself live as though it were true. I know now that it is not, but the stone and the ice are part of the reason She ordained me. Knowing that, I cannot let go of them."

"One day, Allystaire," Idgen Marte said, "She'll let you rest. Let you put down the hammer and take off the armor and do as you will. She loves you too much not to give you peace."

"I love Her too much to ask for it," Allystaire said. "Her work will always need to be done. If not here in Thornhurst, then up in Oyrwyn, or in Varshyne, or fallen Vyndamere, or the islands, or Keersvast, or the tundra."

"I'm *not* goin' to the tundra," Idgen Marte teased. "Too much sun for too much of the year, and then not enough. No shadows. Now sleep, or I'll sneak back in here with a club."

"I will," he assured her. She turned as if to leave, and he said, "I do have a question to ask, if I may?"

She turned around, one hand on a hip.

"How does it feel to have taken up the lute again, to make music?"

Even in the dim light thrown by his lamp he could see her eyes close, read the way she breathed. He wasn't surprised then, at her answer.

"Like I have back a piece of myself that was cut away long ago. Not a finger or a toe, not even a hand or an eye. Something far more important."

He nodded and stood. "Then I am glad you have it back."

"Isn't there anything like that for you? Something you gave up, and want back? Something you wanted that was barred to you?"

Allystaire thought a moment. "Only Dorinne," he said finally, quietly. "And she is gone."

"I'm sorry, Ally."

"It is alright," he said. "I have let go of my bitterness and my anger towards my father and Gerard Oyrwyn. They are just as lost to me as her, so to be angry benefits no one. All along I should have been angry at myself. I should have had the courage to listen to love, not to duty."

"Hard way to have to learn that lesson," Idgen Marte said quietly. "I'm still sorry."

He shook his head again. "No. Now, love and duty are one and the same to me. It is not a bad place to have found. Now go to your lessons. Tutor."

Idgen Marte grumbled but vanished from his sight all the same. He looked between the bed and the floor and decided, for once, to choose the bed. He stretched out upon it, crossed his legs at the ankles, and found sleep, with dreams that varied between the glowing and golden skin of the Mother, and the lightly freckled skin of the woman in his memory.

CHAPTER 33

Banners and Pigeons

In Barony Innadan, and all of the Baronies that bordered it, small companies of knights began moving slowly towards Standing Guard Pass, each of them bearing with them the great standard of their Baronies. From an ice-rimmed mountain fastness, the White Bear of Harlach moved south. The Vined Helm of Innadan awaited the Manticore of Damarind, and the Mailed Fist of Machoryn just outside of the Vineyards, and the three planned a stately and congenial progress west. The Fox of Telmawr slipped northwards at the head of a fairly ragged band of war-weary knights.

The Delondeur Tower had the longest journey to make, across the length of the Barony it represented and through the Thasryach mountains into the bargain. Most of the Baroness Landen's train was made up of knights or lords she had not seen in some time, including both Lords of the Tide, as she had come to think of them: Carrinth of Ennithstide and Lamaliere of Tideswatch.

Both of those lords were older than Landen, part of the generation of Delondeur knights who'd come up as squires under her father and had known her as a child. She didn't trust them, and, Landen was fairly certain, they didn't regard her with an overabundance of affection. The tide lords often rode side by side, kept counsel together during the day and, at times, well into the night.

Lord Intarnis of the Salt Cliffs was the last of the major Delondeur liege lords, and closer to Landen's age, and they rode at the head of the column of lances, with the train of servants, baggage, extra mounts, supplies, and footmen behind them. The Thasryach loomed large ahead of them, but at the pace they rode, Landen feared it would be the better part of another day before they reached it.

She gnawed at the thought that this was all taking too long as Vandyr Intarnis was reminiscing with her over some moment from their shared squirehood.

"I didn't know a quintain could hit a lad in the fork," the tall, mail-clad man was saying through his laughter. Landen chuckled along for appearance's sake, tried not to look back at the tide lords.

Vandyr cleared his throat and pulled his horse close to Landen's. "Don't worry over them, m'lady," he muttered, shifting in his saddle in order to bring his mouth closer to Landen's ear. "Just be your father's daughter and they'll fall in line."

"What worries me, Vandyr," Landen muttered back, "is that I cannot be my father's daughter, not as you mean."

"What really happened with your father, then?"

"Everything I told you when I summoned you," Landen said. "He went mad with power and tried to destroy one of our own villages, full of our own people. The paladin killed him. And he deserved to be killed."

"Paladin, eh? Heard the stories. Can hardly credit it. Felling giants with one blow, tearing apart armor with his bare hands."

"They are not stories, Lord Intarnis, or not all of them," Landen replied. "I have seen the man perform feats of strength that would stagger you."

"Well," Vandyr said, "there was Sir Goddard Bainsley. I did see his body when they brought it home."

"What of him?"

"As it is told, Bainsley was pressing in a village and the paladin drove off his entire company. Bainsley challenged him to single combat and the paladin hit him so hard that his own armor warped and cut off his arms."

Landen shuddered slightly. "If you credit the stories, Lord Intarnis, credit the nature of the paladin as well. He is why I cannot be my father's daughter."

"You sound as though you fear him, m'lady."

Landen turned to face Vandyr squarely. "I do," she said. "And before you say anything else, know this. We are going to meet him at this Congress. After you have seen him, spoken to him, looked in his eyes—I want you to tell me if you fear him as well."

* * *

While seven Barons rode towards Standing Guard Pass, drawn by the appearance of a paladin, or of the chance to see their fellow lords face to face, perhaps to steal a march on them, one Baron, many hundreds of miles to their north and west, was living the nightmare in front of him.

Barony Varshyne had never been as renowned as Oyrwyn, its neighbor to the east. Nor had it ever had the size or the prosperity of Delondeur and Tarynth to its south, even before the former had swallowed the latter. When Vyndamere had fallen to rampaging Islandmen it had seemed only a matter of time till Varshyne—often called Vyndamere 's little brother—followed it.

The Islandmen hadn't even truly settled into the infighting that would have produced a leader to threaten them when Lionel Delondeur smashed all the candidates to bits, burned their boats, then retreated back across the Ash to everyone's astonishment.

Brazcek Varshyne had expected the hammer to fall upon his family then, but instead it was Tarynth that bore the brunt of Delondeur's consolidated power. Even so, in the two decades that followed, little pieces of the Barony had been carved away. Gravekmir and Graveklings had taken some. Lack of trade with Vyndamere had ruined their merchants; hunters and trappers began abandoning the taiga and refusing to approach the tundra beyond, warning that the elves had grown more fierce every season.

Brazcek Varshyne had watched as his father allowed it to happen, allowed the Barony to contract around them, year after year. Fewer and fewer messages had been exchanged with other Barons, or even his liege lords. Fewer young men had been knighted. His father had decided that neutrality in the Succession Strife was Varshyne's best policy, claiming that abstaining from the conflict was the only way to avoid being swallowed up by Oyrwyn or Delondeur.

Brazcek had long been of the opinion that their best defense was the fact that Barony Varshyne didn't have anything the Oyrwyns or Delondeurs of the world wanted. Certainly not badly enough to shed blood.

It was no Barony host that ringed his walls now. Pineward's Watch, the last keep of any size that Varshyne men still manned, had been circled in the night by an army that had moved so swiftly and with such deadly purpose that he had been taken entirely by surprise.

The watchtowers on the trails leading through the thin forests to his keep had been left to rot. The boat patrols along the many small rivers all had been abandoned. There had been no weight to pay for them and no one to fight, in any case, except the odd river pirate or troll.

Brazcek cursed all of those decisions as he looked over his walls now. His seneschal, one of his few remaining knights, stood to his left upon the battlement of the central keep. Both men strained, eyes squinting.

"How did they bring towers up so quickly? How did they circle us, Herrin?" Brazcek swallowed hard, rubbing a thin hand through the sandy patches that passed for his beard.

"M'lord," his seneschal, a balding, straight-backed greybeard said, "those aren't towers. They're not moving on sledges or wheels."

He leaned forward, gripping the hard stone of the battlement. Suddenly one of the tall shapes resolved itself.

"Oh Gods. Oh Frozen, stinking, cursed Gods that have abandoned us," he breathed. "I have never seen so many Gravekmir in one place." He took a deep breath, staving off panic. "I didn't know there were so many in the world."

The giants that moved at the periphery of the force numbered in the dozens, at least, twenty to thirty feet of lumbering, dangerous chaos. Hundreds, if not thousands, of men moved among them, weapons and armor flashing in the morning sunlight, but none formed up into ranks, none attacked.

"Will they want to negotiate? Discuss terms under drawn banners?" Brazcek swallowed as he forced himself to stand upright, blinking hard against the glare.

"I don't see any banners, m'lord," Herrin replied. Then, lifting a hand, he pointed. "Wait."

From behind the curtain of giants the seemingly aimless pool of armed men, a wedge of men moving with purpose came forward. These men stood out; they didn't flash under the rising sun. The glint and glimmer of mail didn't rise up as they moved. These men, Brazcek realized, were unarmored. Even in the still bitter cold that lingered before the relative heat of the day could overtake it, they were barely clothed.

In their midst a huge blue banner was lifted up, the surface stretched between two enormous trunk-poles. On its sea-blue length stretched a painted image of a massive dragon, bronze scales tipped in green, its jaws parted in a wordless roar. If it was crudely done, it was all the more terrifying for its raw and bestial power. As the banner rippled in a breeze, the beast seemed almost as if it were coiling, ready to leap from the cloth and into the air.

The roar that lifted up from the men surrounding the banner was all too bestial. It was a sound that was half-man, half-animal, and Brazcek's first impulse was to flee into the halls of Pineward's Watch, to let the stonework shelter him from the awful, awful sound. But before he could, the sound died away, gone as quick as it came.

"Should I order the men to the walls, m'lord?" Herrin stood at his side, still ramrod straight. Brazcek looked over at his old retainer. The man was pale; his voice had trembled, if only slightly. Yet he was still there. The Baron drew some comfort from his presence.

"What else might we do? Are we encircled? Is the river gate open?"

"I doubt they have left the river gate to chance, m'lord," Herrin said, with a certain dull finality to his words.

"Then how many can we put upon the walls?"

"Trained, who know each end of a spear? Five score. I can sort out a few dozen more from the folk who came running in ahead of this horde the past two days." He cleared his throat. "We haven't the food for a long siege, m'lord. A month, mayhap two."

"What of…what of aid? Can we call upon Oyrwyn? Delondeur? It is no Barony army we face."

"We haven't kept up the mews very well, m'lord," Herrin answered slowly. "Hunting birds we have aplenty, but messenger?"

"Rouse the men. Then to the mews." Brazcek startled himself with the speed and certainty of his answer. "Sending any bird is better than sending none."

Baron Varshyne cursed his personal sloth as much as that of his Barony as he finally hauled himself up the last of the stairs to the tall and drafty tower where the castle's birds were kept. Typically, if he wanted to hunt, the falcons were brought to him. He'd had no occasion to come to the mews themselves for quite some time.

The elderly keeper tried to snap to attention when his portly Baron burst through the door, but her bones were too gnarled to allow it, and besides, the Baron himself doubled over on the step, laboring for breath.

By the time the ancient mistress falconer of Pinesward Watch had reached Brazcek's side to aid him, the Baron had straightened up.

"Pigeons," Brazcek stammered. "What have we for pigeons?"

"Pigeons, m'lord? Why the sudden interest in the more mundane birds, in the humble carriers of message?"

"Because we are besieged, woman," Brazcek shouted. "The Islandmen that the peasants fled from, pushing inside the keep, they spoke the truth! It's an army descending upon us, and we are cut off."

"Most of our pigeon stocks died off some time ago," the elderly mistress said as she turned to the far wall of the room, which was floor-to-ceiling stacked with cages, less than half of which were full. "Your father had ordered us to stop communicating with other Baronies, so our pigeons that knew the routes to the Dunes, to Wind's Jaw, are long since gone."

"What do we have?"

"Let me see," she muttered as she hobbled over to the cages. "Well, there is one very old bird. Near fifteen summers, I expect. Then there are those that arrived in the past weeks, fairly old themselves."

"What do you mean, birds that arrived in the past weeks?" Brazcek still struggled to breathe normally, but between heaves of his chest he angrily bit off each word.

"We received birds over the past few weeks. Elderly birds. Mainly from the Vineyards, but one from the Dunes and one even from the Den." The old woman sighed. "Once upon a time these pigeons knit a kingdom together, m'lord, from the Gates of the West to the Vale of Kings."

"That's all very well, mistress Drewica," the Baron said, pulling the old woman's name from the deep recesses of memory. "What birds arrived? What messages did they carry?"

"Oh, I didn't read them. That was never my task. But 'twere your father's orders to ignore all messages from other Baronies, even if they carried the seal of a Baron his own self," Drewica said, shaking her head. "I simply piled them up upon the table."

"My father has been dead for two years, Drewica. Why did you never bring any messages to me?"

"Orders never changed, m'lord. In all things we carried on as under your lord father."

"Bring me the messages, Drewica. Now!"

The old woman's mouth snapped shut with an audible click, and she nodded, offered a mumbled, "m'lord," and shuffled over to a table in front of her meager fire. On it was a small handful of tiny tubes. Some appeared to be ivory, some wooden. Quickly, Brazcek seized one and nearly snapped it in half, so eager was he to read. He tipped the scroll within it into his hand and unrolled it, walked to the large, unbarred, un-shaded window at the far end of the tower. A stone ledge extended beyond it, the perch upon which the Baronial birds had landed for hundreds of years, if not these past dozen. He held the tiny paper to the light.

Baron Brazcek Varsyhnne,

At the behest of the Paladin Allystaire Stillbright, a peace congress commences at Standing Guard Pass. With the aim of ending the Succession Strife, Barons Telmawr, Damarind, Machoryn, Oyrwyn, Delondeur, and Harlach have been invited. Reply by this bird to the Vineyards.

Baron Hamadrian Innadan, Keeper of the Vineyards

He threw the paper down and hurried back to the table, broke open another and then another tube, flattening the scrolls they contained on the palm of his hand. "Paladin? A peace congress? Six Barons confirmed. Cold, woman, how many messages did you receive?"

"Half a dozen or so, m'lord," Drewica stammered. "Orders never changed."

"Have we birds that can fly to the Vineyards?"

"Old birds, m'lord, but yes," Drewica said, "if they'd survive the flight and remember the way."

"Send them. Send them all. Tell them we are besieged. Tell them we agree to any terms if they can hasten to our aid."

"I will need sealing wax and the minor seal, m'lord," Drewic said, but even as she spoke Brazcek was pulling a ring from the smallest finger of his left hand and practically shoving it into her hands.

"By all the gods, Mistress Drewica," Brazcek spoke, "write quickly and legibly and put the birds in the air now. Immediately." He turned and started for the exit from the tower, then stopped and turned back. "Have we birds that will fly to the parts of our own Barony?"

"Aye, m'lord, those we have."

"Where can they go?"

The old woman cleared her throat and turned to the cages. "Crossing. Green Forks. Treeline."

"Send them. Send them all," Brazcek said. "Summon everyone of the Barony who can hold a spear. Cold, ask for those who can't. But do it quickly."

"My hands don't move as fast as they used to, m'lord," Drewica cautioned.

"Fine," Brazcek said, stripping off the mail glove from his left hand. "You've pen and ink and parchment? I will write the messages myself. Bring me a candle."

* * *

Less than a turn later, with a flurry of white and grey wings—many of them a little too frail for Brazcek's taste—and all the birds he had to send were off. He had stayed only long enough to see them go, and then he was hurrying down the tower stairs and out into the courtyard. Troops of spearmen hurried to the walls. He grabbed one by the arm, said, "Herrin?" and was told, "The armory, m'lord."

Off he went, through the receiving hall and down several drafty grey corridors, but soon enough he could simply have followed the noise. There were the bellows of chosen men, the clatter of metal, a murmur of voices. He turned a corner and found a long queue of men, women, and, in truth, boys and girls. Liveried servants, grooms in riding leathers, even two apprentice scribes in robes, lined up to be handed weapons. Spears, mostly, though a few taller folk were given polearms, and as everyone reached the open doors were Herrin stood in full mail, they were asked if they knew the basics of a crossbow. If the barest hint of a yes was offered, they were handed one along with a sheaf of bolts.

When Herrin caught sight of the Baron he stopped what he was doing, snapped his armored heels together, and saluted by smashing his fist against his chest.

Suddenly all eyes turned to him. Brazcek felt the weight of every pair of them, from the smallest kitchen apprentice to the greyest groom.

"How goes the arming, Seneschal?" The Baron tried for confidence, but to his ears it sounded most like he had simply shouted.

"It goes, m'lord," Herrin replied. "We're all game for it, aye?"

He raised a mailed fist as he turned to those who'd queued for weapons they barely knew how to hold, trying to rouse them, and was met with silence.

Brazcek cleared his throat. "It's not about being game," he said. "It's about being…stubborn."

More silence.

"Stubborn, I say." He pressed on, grasping for words. "Stubborn like a badger that doesn't want to be pulled from its warren. Stubborn like a mule that's decided no, it won't move. Stubborn and angry. This is our home and we're going to hold fast to it with everything we've got, all of us."

They looked at him, at each other, at the weapons in their hands. A kitchen-boy, in his apron, looked as though he were about to burst into tears.

"We're outnumbered," one voice muttered. "They have giants," said another. Brazcek caught Herrin's eye. The old knight suddenly stamped his armored boots on the floor.

"Quit that talk, you lot," he bellowed. "We've got walls, well water, plenty o'grain inside the walls."

And suddenly, Brazcek remembered something he'd read on the first missive from Baron Innadan. "And there is a paladin," he shouted.

Suddenly all eyes, Herrin's included, focused on him.

"A paladin, yes. Leading a peace congress in Barony Innadan at Standing Guard Pass. I have sent our birds, all of them, to ask for his aid and for aid from the Barons gathered there. Six of them, all with their armies," he said, the lies growing as he told them. "And birds have gone out across the Barony, and surely they will come to aid us as well," he yelled. "We only need to be stubborn long enough for aid to come. We can surely do that, aye? We'll just keep the Gravek warm until the paladin gets here, what do you say?"

The words set them buzzing. Stories were suddenly being offered, thrown into the air in one great clamor.

"I heard from a peddler he killed a Gravek with his bare hands, crushed his skull," one man yelled, only to have another say, "No, t'was a tree he pulled from the ground and crushed the giant with." There were tales of fighting the risen dead and of destroying sorcerers and Brazcek finally raised his arms for quiet.

"He is not here yet," he admonished. "Get to the walls. Do as Herrin or other knights and chosen men bid you. Remember that this is your home. Our home," he added. "All of us will fight for it. Now get your weapons, then to the walls with all speed."

Brazcek oversaw the rest of the arming, which is to say he stood in the armory and offered encouraging words as Herrin and the professional soldiers who flanked him decided to do.

He looked at the rows of swords, the shelves full of rusting mail shirts, could smell the rot and the mildew in the leather of the arming jackets.

When the last man was armed and moved off, Herrin sought him out. "All that about the paladin. What's the truth of it?"

"The missives said there was a paladin," Brazcek sighed. "Called him Al… Allys something, Bright," he said. "I didn't read carefully."

"Missives?"

Another sigh. "The other western Barons have been meeting in a peace congress. Are meeting. They sent birds here, but the messages were never passed on to me. Apparently the paladin organized it."

"So you were only half-lying," Herrin replied.

"I said what I had to say to get men on the walls," Brazcek replied. "I did send what birds we have. The paladin could come. I asked for all the help I could ask for."

Herrin was silent a moment. "Best we start rolling barrels out to the walls."

Brazcek blinked. "Why? Do we fear them using fire? I saw no engines and there's not lumber here to make them."

"Not water, m'lord," Herrin said. "Mead. Beer. Spirits if we have it. We want to keep these folk on the walls in the face of what's gathering outside, best we keep them a little drunk."

* * *

Cerisia found the heat in Hamadrian's pavilion almost stifling. Though it was a full-throated spring outside, with the lush Barony Innadan showing forth in green, and the chill was all but banished from the air, Hamadrian had asked for no less than three braziers, and demanded they be kept full of hot coals. Cerisia had hoped that he'd take heart from the approaching congress, but every day she found herself hoping she'd see that odd, frighteningly powerful boy appear from the air with Allystaire in tow.

As she looked on the Baron, stick thin and lying in a camp cot piled with cushions and furs, she wondered how he would make it to the Congress. She could hear his breath rattling in his thin chest, see the struggle as it rose and fell. A chirurgeon sat slumped in a nearby chair, with a bag of tools and medicines at his feet, sleeping when the Baron seemed at rest.

At least he isn't killing him, she thought, frowning at herself. *The man is doing the best he can, but I would prefer Allystaire. Even Torvul.*

Cerisia's thoughts were cut off when the pavilion curtains parted and Arontis stuck his head in, taking pains to be quiet. "The banners have been spotted. Machoryn and Damarind are come," he murmured. "Will he be able to receive them?"

Hamadrian's voice, thin, rasping, but remarkable still, came from barely parted lips. "I'm not dead yet, boy. I will rise and meet them on horseback if I have to be tied to the saddle."

Arontis came to his father's bedside and knelt, even as Hamadrian struggled to push himself upright. "You needn't go so far as to ride out to meet them," Arontis said, but his father reached out and struck him a glancing blow on a shoulder, and forced his feet out of his cot with a grimace. He hunched over his thin legs, breathing in a rasp, and slowly pushed himself up.

Arontis rose with him, supporting him with a hand on his arm, despite his father's weak protests.

"I will meet them dressed, armed, and mounted like a Baron," Hamadrian insisted, ripping his arm free of his son's grasp. "Though as much as I would like the Archioness's help in getting dressed," he muttered, "it is probably best that my son stay to help and you await us outside, Cerisia."

She stood, crossed to Baron and son, kissed the former and the cheek and squeezed the arm of the latter, then stepped out into the brightness of the day. While the spring of Barony Innadan was worlds away from the winter at Thornhurst, Cerisia was glad of the breeze that tugged at her dress after the stifling heat of the Baron's tent. She thought of retreating to her own tent to check her dress or dab perspiration from her face, but she changed her mind when a servant approached her with a jug of wine and a tray of cups. Cerisia gladly took one, felt the carvings of vines upon it as the wine poured, gleaming yellow in the sunlight.

An Archioness does not sweat in front of Barons, she thought, *but then, that is why we have masks.* Her free hand went to the mask that hung from her belt, and she took a bigger swallow of her wine than she might typically have done. It had a clean and powerfully floral taste. It reminded her of the scents she favored wearing, but was not as sweet as she might have preferred.

By the time she'd finished it regardless, found a servant to take the empty cup, and begun tying her mask around her head, father and son emerged from the tent. Hamadrian looked a Baron once again, if frail. There was no hiding his age, the milky eye, but his back was straight and his hands were steady enough. There was a sword at his side but the weight of it seemed, to her eyes, like it might drag him down. His cap of maintenance had been traded for a silver circlet worked, of course, in the shape of a vine, set with round-cut rubies hanging as heavy grapes against the spotted skin of his scalp, and he wore a heavy fur mantle over fine robes of red and green silk. He walked upright, but slowly and carefully, as if every step might bring him to ruin. There was still that sense of concentrated determination about him, but it was no longer packed into a compact frame that hummed with energy.

Hamadrian Innadan, Cerisia decided in that moment, was all but spent. *It would be a miracle if he were to make it to Standing Guard Pass,* she thought. Yet even as she did, she saw him force a deep breath into what was left of his lungs and stride more determinedly forward.

"We can probably dispense with the horse," he rasped to Arontis. "Let Ruprecht and Loaisa come to me mounted if they will." Knights materialized around Arontis and Hamadrian, and the son sent them scurrying for a suitable chair of station. In fact, as they walked, the Baron seemed to concentrate on each step, while his son gave orders. Arontis's demands were never snapped or yelled, Cerisia noted. He looked at every person he addressed, man or woman, noble or common, asked for what he wanted, and offered dazzling smiles when his requests were met.

He could be a wonder, she thought as she watched the knights, soldiers, and servants of the camp hurry to meet Arontis Innadan's orders not simply because they were orders, but because something about the man who gave them inspired cheerful service. *But will he be ready to negotiate a peace on his own?*

Soon, an open meadow just outside their camp was rearranged into a reception parlor. Hamadrian was seated in a massive leaf-carved chair, and two chairs of similar size were set nearby. Innadan knights formed a semi-circle behind their Baron, with Arontis standing at his right hand. Cerisia looked behind her, and could see the towers of the Vineyards looming behind them, the massive banner with the Vined Helm rolling with the spring wind. As Innadan's knights gathered around, one held a smaller version of the same banner, rich silk on a silver-capped pole, positioned directly behind the Baron's seat.

Cerisia heard the Baron calling out her name, and, smoothing her white silk with one hand, she glided through the ring of knights and stood at his left. She thought briefly of asking for someone to fetch her own banner, but thought better of it when the Machoryn and Damarind advance parties rode into view. Woven with thread of gold and silver and with gems worked into it or not, Fortune's banner would disappear when the Vined Helm, the Mailed Fist, and the Manticore all stood together. As it was, Baron Machoryn and Baroness Damarind rode side by side, their banners advancing behind them. Ruprecht Machoryn was a thickset man with a face once handsomely aquiline, gone now to jowls. Loaisa Damarind was tall and thin, with long grey-dusted black hair, braided and then pulled into a thick queue down her back. She wore a dress, but with the skirts divided to ride straight, rather than sidesaddle, and wore a slim-bladed, deadly-looking axe stuck through her belt. Both had trains of knights following them, though not many, with the Machoryn knights matching their Baron in dull armor with blue surcoats, and the Damarind wearing black touched with red over lighter mail.

Loaisa Damarind dismounted nimbly and simply dropped the reins of her black courser to the ground; the animal stayed, nosing at the grass. Her bannerman and another figure hurried after her, while Ruprecht Machoryn was slower, needing the help of a quicker knight to find his feet upon the ground.

Loaisa was a handsome woman, Cerisia decided, which had as much to do with her bearing as her form or her lined but high-cheekboned face. She kept her back straight, her chin up, and her wide hazel eyes met everything in front of her with frank aplomb.

"Is all this pomp truly necessary, Hamadrian? Hadn't we best be off on our way to your mountain pass to see this wonder you've promised us?"

"There are forms to these things, Baroness," Innadan rasped. He stood slowly, but his face betrayed none of the signs of pain Cerisia had come to know too well. "As for the wonder, well, I'm just as eager to see this paladin as you. Likely more."

He took a half-step forward. Loaisa extended her hand as if to offer a warrior's shake, but Hamadrian took her fingers with his own hand and raised it to his lips, his good eye twinkling a bit. "I'm too old to go learning a new way to greet a beautiful woman, Baroness," he said as he lowered her hand. "Even one who rides and fights like a man."

"Better than a man," Loaisa insisted, though Cerisia thought she saw a tiny spot of color in the Baroness's cheeks. *He is a charming old coot, no doubt*, she mused.

By then, Ruprecht Machoryn had noisily clomped his way to his fellow rulers. Sweat streamed from his face into bushy side whiskers that had once been deep brown and were now lightly sprinkled with grey and white. "Hamadrian," the Baron said, his voice surprisingly light and clear for a man of his girth, a mailed hand extended. "The years have been kind to your land. It made for a lovely ride."

"The part of my lands that you saw, Ruprecht," Hamadrian said. "Where it touches on Harlach and Delondeur, though?" He shook his head. "Vines untended for months, even whole seasons. Fields laying fallow, herds dead in their fields, and all my young men marching off to their deaths."

"Cold," Ruprecht swore after he shook Innadan's hand delicately. "Your letters were all serious then, and you mean to get right to it."

"I do," Hamadrian said. "I know the eastern Baronies have mostly let it go these past few seasons, save for a small raid or a dagger in the night now and then. Time for all of us to make it official, put it on paper."

"Who's coming?" That was Loaisa, seeing, Cerisia thought, right to the issue that threatened to sink this congress before it began.

"The three of us, Byron Telmawr, Unseldt Harlach, Landen Delondeur. And the paladin who set all this in motion."

"Tales are only just trickling our way," Ruprecht said. "And I don't credit tales. You believe this paladin is the true thing?"

"I do," Hamadrian said, "and I've an eyewitness," he said, extending a hand towards Cerisia.

"Whether you believe in the paladin or not," Loaisa said, "I know I believe in Gilrayan Oyrwyn. And I didn't hear you list his name in the Congress."

"He'll come," Hamadrian said, "if nothing else, he'll come to look the paladin in the eye."

"You sound damn sure of that," Ruprecht said.

"How do we know he won't come with an army at his back? Six Barons lightly guarded in one place may prove too tempting to a grasping bastard like him," Loaisa said.

Hamadrian breathed in with a visible effort, but was suddenly caught with a cough, though not as terrible as many Cerisia had seen. The chirurgeon was at his side, holding a rag damp with some tincture to his mouth. Ruprecht and Machoryn stepped back, until Arontis stepped forward from his father's side.

"Baron, Baroness, if I may speak for the Baron Innadan, we are of one mind on this; there is a risk, but if we can risk our lives to buy peace for our people, instead of asking them to buy land for us with their lives, is that not worth it?"

"And who are you?" Machoryn considered the taller, younger man with a narrowed eye.

"Arontis Innadan," he said, gracefully bowing low enough to be respectful without showing deference. "Heir to my father, and Castellan of the Vineyards."

"Your words are near as pretty as your eyes, boy," Loaisa said. "But I'd rather buy a peace I can enjoy in my old age."

"Then surely we have many years yet to secure it, Baroness Damarind," Arontis said with a light smile.

"You are your father's son, Arontis Innadan," Loaisa said, smiling faintly.

"Surely the both of you are thirsty, and your entourages as well," Arontis said. "Refresh yourselves. Make camp. I'm afraid there is only cold food at the moment, but the carts are even now trundling from the Vineyards to furnish a board appropriate to your stations and your formal arrival in Barony Innadan. In the morning we'll start our progress west."

Ruprecht nodded sharply and turned to plod away, looking like a man who wanted quit of his armor.

Cerisia had moved to Hamadrian's side and saw a smile on his face, hidden though it was by the rag and by his downturned head. The coughing had long since subsided, and Cerisia smiled beneath the cold metal of her mask. The chirurgeon took the rag and led Hamadrian back to his seat, but Cerisia saw the Baron's eyes follow Arontis as servants moved forward, bearing trays of cups of wine and plates of cheese and pastries.

The Innadan heir had been led towards the Damarind entourage by Baroness Loaisa, who was introducing him to a young woman who bore more than a passing resemblance to the Baroness herself. Though her hair was a honeyed blonde, her bearing and figure—and the slim axe at her belt—were all akin to her mother's.

"The boy did just fine," Hamadrian murmured, and Cerisia knew it was for her benefit. She laid a hand on the old Baron's shoulder and he reached up to clasp it for a moment, a ghost of old strength in his fingers for that moment. His hand slipped away, and he craned his neck to turn his good eye up at her. "Promise me, Archioness, that if he has to see this through without me, that he'll have your honest help and counsel."

Her voice somewhat muffled by her mask, Cerisia said, "He shan't need it, my lord. You heard the Baroness Damarind. He is his father's son."

* * *

Allystaire's entire body ached with the fatigue of the work he'd already done that day, the running, the stones, the riding.

Going to do more than ache if you let him get his hands on you, you old fool. The thought was no less true for being unwanted, Allystaire would have to admit. The rest of the Order, gathered together in a circle, watched as he and Johonn circled each other, feet shuffling carefully in the dirt. Allystaire had his hands curled into fists, and his elbows drawn tightly against his body, but the larger man had his hands open, flung out wider, a wrestler's stance opposed to Allystaire's pugilist.

Johonn lunged forward, leading with his right foot, hoping to gather Allystaire into his newly healed and frighteningly strong left arm. The hulking footman was slow enough that Allystaire had time to snap two quick, short punches, with his left hand, into Johonn's face.

He might as well have punched a bull in the snout for all the effect it had. Johonn plowed into him and Allystaire was nearly carried off his feet. A better wrestler would, Allystaire realized too late, have used the bigger man's momentum to toss him over an outthrust leg and onto the ground. Instead, Allystaire planted his toes into the ground and clung on for dear life with his left arm, and pumped his right fist into the other man's lower ribs.

The Order shouted encouragement. Allystaire tried not to dwell on the fact that the only voices he heard yelling his name were likely from Harrys and Norbert.

"Put 'im on 'is back, Johonn!" Allystaire heard, even as Johonn was grunting under the repeated thuds of Allystaire's fist. It was like hitting rock. The question was whether Allystaire's fist or Johonn's ribs would give first.

In fact it was Allystaire's toes dug into the ground that gave. Johonn found new traction and Allystaire felt his knees buckling. He stopped pumping his fist ineffectually into Johonn's rock-like side and let the wrestler's weight bear down on him. Gritting his teeth and dropping to a squat so low that his thighs nearly brushed the ground, Allystaire then sprung upwards, pushing off the grass and trying to throw Johonn, who was so surprised that it nearly worked.

As it was, instead of tumbling to the ground, the former footman only stumbled backwards a few paces. Allystaire felt himself breathing heavily, and they continued to shuffle around one another, more slowly. The circle around them had gone quiet. Allystaire felt his right hand beginning to throb; he saw heavy weals raising on Johonn's ribs. They locked eyes, nodded, and relaxed their stances at once.

There were a few jeers but they turned to cheers when Allystaire and Johonn walked towards each other, hands extended. They clasped arms, and Allystaire placed his left hand over Johonn's right and let the Goddess's Gift trickle through the both of them.

Somehow it was easier healing a man he already knew. The bruises and scrapes that faded had been delivered by Allystaire's own hand, and not in anger; they vanished almost instantly.

I missed the companionship of knights, he thought to himself, even though he knew from drawing on his shared experiences that Johonn didn't think of himself that way. He was a footman, used to carrying a longaxe, rushing walls and formations of spearmen or bowmen.

Doesn't matter, he thought. *He'll be a knight now.*

For his part, Johonn didn't bother putting on a shirt, simply walked back to the line of squires, and crossed his arms over his chest, nodding and silently accepting the backslaps and words of encouragement and congratulation.

Allystaire gathered his shirt and vest, using the time to gather his breath as well. He turned to face them while putting his arms through the vest and tugging it on, studied them for a moment. "Norbert. Teague. Three falls."

The former reaver nodded, and extended a hand towards Teague, who still wore a half mask across her face, long sleeves, and gloves. They shook, and Norbert shed his shirt and walked to the unmarked but respected boundaries of the wrestling green.

Grinning beneath her half mask, Teague said, "I'll spare ya the sight of my back." She did remove the mask, though, tossing it casually towards the men, where it was caught by one of Mattar's surprisingly quick hands. The skin beneath it was still twisted and scarred, much of the flesh having peeled away from her right eye and her mouth. Allystaire had found that, while he could drive Teague's pain away, nothing could bring back the flesh that was so long gone.

Norbert was swinging his arms, limbering up; the months of exercise under Allystaire and Harrys's instruction had changed him from a bean pole to a wiry whipcord.

Allystaire was just about to shout for them to begin when Gideon's voice sounded in his head.

Allystaire, Mol says she must speak to you in the Temple.

The paladin raised a hand. The squires of the Order stopped, all eyes turning to him. He concentrated a moment, felt Gideon's presence rushing past him overhead, though vaguely. Suddenly then he was in the Temple, vivid and present in the world once more.

"Harrys," he said. "Take over. I have business. Try not to hurt each other badly enough to need healing."

"Aye." The old horseman stepped out of the line, thumbs hooked into his swordbelt, spat to the side, and eyed Norbert and Teague. "What're ya waitin' for then? Someone t'wave a flag and sound a horn? To it!"

Allystaire had already begun to stride off, the thudding sound sparring quickly fading.

Gideon was waiting for him on the stairs of the Temple, hands held behind his back, frowning. "Been playing in the dirt, have you?"

The dismissal in the boy's tone, the casual flippancy of it, brought Allystaire up short. He fixed Gideon with a stare and held it till the boy looked to the ground.

"That was unworthy of me," Gideon muttered. "I'm sorry."

Allystaire slowly mounted the stairs and, without saying a word, slipped his arm around the boy's shoulders, for just a moment. "I need to spend more time with you Gideon. I know," he muttered. "Yet I also have to try to make them ready."

"They'll never be ready," Gideon said, "because they aren't you."

"Someone will have to come after me, Gideon. Other men and women will have to do the work."

"And it will be up to the Mother to choose them, or not," the boy replied. "I know you believe in the the Order. I know they are good soldiers and will be faithful to you and to the Mother. But if you mean them to face the same threats you face, in the same way, they are doomed."

"Gideon," Allystaire said, "look at me." He reached out and placed a hand against the Temple door, keeping the boy from opening it. He waited till the boy did as he asked, then took a quiet breath. "I do not know if it is because we have not spent more time together, and you are upset because of that. I do not know if you truly mean the words you have said, or if it is the sting of Renard's death that causes you to disregard them, or if it is something else entirely. It does not matter, because it ends now."

Allystaire kept his voice quiet to take some of the sting out of them. Gideon started to let his eyes slip to the floor and he cleared his throat. The boy's gaze met his once more.

"Tibult guided them across the Barony at the end of winter with every one of them in constant pain," Allystaire said. "Teague was half-mad from her burns; Mattar had hardly been able to lie down in three years; Tibult himself had once grown so desperate he was on the verge of throwing himself into Londray Bay. I healed him that night, but only just enough. On his own, he gathered the rest of them together and shepherded them across the Barony at the end of winter. No weight, no food, no arms. They set out with nothing but their faith and it got them here."

"I am being unjust to them," Gideon said, lowering his head. "I know. But it does not change the fact that trying to keep pace with you in the battles you may face will get them killed."

"We five cannot fight every battle alone," Allystaire replied. "And someone will have to fight them when we are gone. I have touched their very souls, Gideon. They are willing to do what I ask, willing to take the pains of the world into themselves if it means sparing another." He put a hand out to Gideon's shoulder. "If we are to save the world, son, we will do it with souls like theirs."

"If we face armies, I can destroy them myself," Gideon said quietly. "I think."

"No, Gideon," Allystaire said, shaking his head. "I do not mean no, you could not. But I will not let you."

"Why? If it saves lives, why?"

"Because if the powers of the world were to learn that we had among us one who was capable of such a thing, no worshipper of the Mother would be safe anywhere. And because, Gideon, it is one thing to kill a man who is trying to kill you in the hot blood of battle. It is another to condemn a man to death for what he has done, and see him executed on your own word. It is still another to stand remotely and watch hundreds of men die on your commands. What you say would be some awful combination of all three, and there may be men who stand apart from us who are not our enemies. We will kill who we must, and save who we can; there may be those we could save even among an army raised against us. If you had simply destroyed the army Lionel brought against us in the winter, we would be without Harrys, without Landen. Would we be better off then?"

Gideon shook his head silently, taking in Allystaire's words. Finally, Allystaire took his hand from the door and let the boy push it open, asking, "Have you given any thought to finding apprentices of your own? Is such a thing even possible?" He let his hand settle on the boy's shoulder.

Gideon looked up as they walked into the Temple together. "One day," he said, "it will be."

Allystaire was taken aback by the answer, but by then he and Gideon had reached the altar, where Mol awaited them. She was staring at the smooth red stone, frowning faintly.

When the girl turned to face him, her head was tilted oddly, and her eyes had rolled back so only the whites were visible.

"To the north. Just entering the valley. Follow the track and look for them. They come to speak to you, paladin. And they bring answers."

Mol's voice was hardly recognizable, the words distant, soft.

"Come then," he said to Gideon. "We can eat in the saddle."

* * *

Though the entirety of the Order of the Arm, such as it was, had been horsed, few of them were rider enough to keep up with the experienced horsemen. Allystaire, Harrys, Tibult, and Armel, though Norbert and Gideon came closest, with the rest strung out in a line along the road.

Allystaire looked back over his shoulder and saw Mattar and Johonn bringing up the rear, both so wary of being mounted that their horses had picked up on their fear and gotten spooked.

"Johonn," he called out, trying to put some levity into his voice. "You cannot wrestle the horse into minding you."

The huge man didn't seem to take Allystaire's words to heart, tugging hard at the reins with his free right hand, a huge longaxe clutched in his left. *Preposterous weapon for a man to carry in the saddle,* Allystaire thought.

"Ya'd better hope anythin' means t'kill us gives those pair o'walkin' hillocks the time t'fall out o'the saddle," Harrys growled from his left. "More like t'kill themselves on horseback, maybe break a horse's back."

"There is a reason they are on dray horses, Harrys," Allystaire said. "And they do not need to fight from the saddle, but the more practice they get at riding, the better."

"I'll work with them in the evenings," Tibult said, from beyond Harrys. "Mattar was a pioneer and Johonn a footman, and both grew up poor in Londray. I doubt they'd been in a saddle till you put 'em there. Going t'take time."

"What about you, Tibult?" Allystaire shifted in his saddle to look at the man he'd addressed.

"Ah, I grew up with 'em," he said. "My da had a stable just outside Londray, and I did courier riding as a boy. Know horses well. Like 'em better than most folk I've known. They don't lie t'ya and they want nothin' but feed, a combin', and a clean command."

Allystaire nodded, considering. "Had you ridden since your injury?"

He shook his head. "Couldn't get in the saddle, with my hip. Wouldn't have had any right anyway."

"What do you mean by that? Cold, Delondeur had not made riding a noble privilege, had he?"

Tibult shook his blading head. "Not at all. It was that the mount that fell on me, 'twas my fault. I didn't need t'ride him into a river in the middle of a fight, could've held the bank and waited for the enemy t'cross. I wanted the blood, the glory. He paid for it. Good beast, deserved better."

Conversation gave way to the clop of hooves on the track, to the creak and sway of harness. Tibult craned his neck around Harrys and snuck a glance at Ardent. Allystaire caught his look and raised a questioning eyebrow.

"How long've ya had that stallion?"

"Going on three years," Allystaire said. "And his name is Ardent."

The horse blew a huge breath through his nostrils at the sound of his name. Allystaire patted his muscled neck.

"Ought t'stud him," Tibult said. "Somethin' special about that animal."

"Somethin' not *canny*," Harrys put in. "Tried t'take my fingers off, I went t'put a saddle on 'im."

"I should have warned you," Allystaire said. "He is," here he paused, searched for a word, "particular."

"No," Harrys said. "He's some sorta demon taken the form of a horse. Won't let anyone else near 'im, smarter'n some men I've commanded, stronger'n a bullock and I've never seen the beast get lathered. He's no reg'lar horse, I'll tell ya true."

Allystaire laughed faintly at Harrys's words, but something in them rang true. "I think," he said, "that it is possible that even if taken to stud, his traits would not pass on."

"Cold," Tibult said, "it couldn't hurt t'try! I'll see about pickin' out a mare."

The conversation was abruptly ended by a screech from the side of the road that drew the entire column out of their silence or their speech.

A man came careening down the dirt track, yelling, his clothes in tatters. In one hand he clutched a ragged scrap of felt, and even from the distance, Allystaire could see how wide and frightened his eyes were. He pulled Ardent short and slid from the saddle, running forward to meet him.

The man was younger than him, though not by much, and he seemed mad with fear. Blood and grime streaked his face, with the former descending in dried brown rivulets from a wound across his scalp. Allystaire was already reaching his left hand out when the man fell against him, alternating between babbling and screaming. His wide, terrified, bloodshot eyes didn't seem to see the world in front of him.

That changed as soon as Allystaire settled his left hand over the cut on his scalp and reached for the Goddess's Gift; his senses bridged into the man, and he felt almost as if he was running back through his memories. Fire and fear and men with clawed gauntlets on their hands and another, less fierce man, blond and tall, forcing a skin to his lips and pouring salt-water down his throat.

Soon enough the cut that ascended into his hair was closing, and the man's eyes suddenly found focus on Allystaire. His hands locked on Allystaire's shoulders, his arms straightening and tensing.

A trickle of water leaked from the corner of the man's mouth. Allystaire, and now Harrys and Gideon behind him, smelt the faint scent of the sea.

"Paladin," the man said, his voice an eerie croak, the words seeming to emanate from him without truly being formed in his own throat. "North of here, the town built on the bridge over the river, Braech judges others for your heresy. Have you the courage to face his wrath? The man before you did. Now watch him die."

As the man spoke, the trickle of salt water turned into a stream, bringing a bloody froth with it, cascading over his clothing. Allystaire, his left hand still pressed to the man's forehead, searched frantically for the spark of his life as he convulsed and twitched, his throat working as if he was trying, and failing, to breathe.

The tide rolled on, and Allystaire knew he could not stop it. He felt the man pulled away from him as if carried by a wave, felt the panic rise and rise until suddenly it snapped clean away and the man dropped into Allystaire's arms, limp, dead. The paladin slowly lowered him the body to the ground, too stunned to speak.

"What was that?" Tibult said, looking over him, sword half drawn from his scabbard as he scanned the road.

Gideon, coming up on Allystaire's other side, laid a hand on the paladin's shoulder and looked at the body. His other hand, he lifted into the air, peering down at the corpse.

"That," the boy said quietly but firmly, "was Braech trying to lure you into a trap."

"It is not the first time the servants of the Sea Dragon have done so," Allystaire said, lifting his head, his voice as cold and clean as Gideon had ever heard it.

And, the boy knew, as furious.

"It will be the last time I leave any of them alive in the wake of it," he said as he stood, the limp form of the drowned man in his arms.

CHAPTER 34

The Order and the Islandmen

"**I**f you know it's a trap, you can't just go sticking your head in it to see what happens." Idgen Marte was aiming a sharp eye at Allystaire as Torvul helped him get his armor on. Tugging first the left and then the right vambrace firmly into place, he shook his head.

"That is precisely what I can do."

"What's your plan? Ride in and be a target?"

"Well," Allystaire said, "yes. Then kill everyone who tries to take advantage of my being a target."

"It's got a certain simple charm," Torvul said from behind Allystaire as his long and nimble fingers pulled straps taut and buckled them in place. "Not unlike the man himself."

"Dammit, Allystaire," Idgen Marte breathed. "Fine. But I'm comin' with ya."

"I was counting on it," Allystaire said. "You, me, the Order." His eyes flitted to Torvul as he pulled his gauntlets on. "Can you and Gideon manage here?"

"Oh, no," Torvul said, deadpan, his face flat as he stepped in front of Allystaire. "Whatever will we do? However will we defend against any attacker without swords and armor?"

"People have died, dwarf. It is not the time for jokes."

"I know that very well," Torvul shot back. "Between me, the lad, and Mol, we'll have the number of anyone who comes near Thornhurst with ill will on his mind. I'll have a talk with Keegan, too."

"Damn," Allystaire said. "I keep meaning to do that very thing."

"I know," Torvul said. "Ya can't be everywhere. And I think his lot'll do anything if they think Gideon is asking it of them."

"They ought to," Idgen Marte muttered. "Are you sure your, ah, 'squires' are ready?"

"No," Allystaire said, "but if we wait till I am, we will all be dead." He looked from Idgen Marte to Torvul and said, "If you mean to come, best see to your mount. I mean to leave in less than half a turn."

Muttering softly under her breath, she turned on a heel and walked out of the room, rather than disappearing into a shadow. As soon as he felt she was out of earshot, Allystaire looked to Torvul.

"If something does happen, Torvul, watch the boy. Make sure he does not…" Allystaire paused, took a deep breath. "Be certain he does not kill unless it is at utmost need."

Torvul eyed Allystaire from beneath a raised brow. "Can't protect the boy forever."

"It is not about protecting him," Allystaire said. "It is about making sure he becomes the man could be."

"What's him pullin' his blows got t'do with that?"

"Like unto the dawn, Torvul. Her words, at my vigil. And that it was my greatest task to see that he was not a false dawn." He shook his head. "I do not know what it means either. Yet I know that if he learns to value life too cheaply, to take it too swiftly, I would be failing at the charge She set me."

"Ya don't hesitate t'swing a hammer or a sword," Torvul pointed out. "Or hang a man. Ya just spoke of killin' maybe a lot of men, and y'did it rather casually."

"I want Gideon to be a better man than I am," Allystaire said. "And if he comes with me to Ashmill Bridge, and a Braechsworn war party has descended on the place, then yes, I will kill them. And I do not want Gideon with me, not because I do not want him to witness the horror that may await us, but because I do not want to be tempted by his presence. In anger, I do not know what I might ask of him. I am certain, whatever it is, he would do it."

"He would," Torvul said. "And I think you're makin' a mistake, showin' the boy a double set o'rules. But," the dwarf said, raising a hand, palm out, and lowering his eyes. "He's your charge, and I'll not interfere. 'Sides, while you're off riding 'round the country on a chase for raiders who've already left, he and I'll be kicking back and having a drink. Well," the dwarf added, "I'll drink. He'll work on his lute playing."

"We will see. Guard the place well, Torvul," Allystaire said. "I mislike the timing of all this. It bodes ill."

"Boy," Torvul said, "you could see ill omens and bad tidings and danger in a naked woman with a bottle o'brandy in either hand. I'm not sayin' it's not serious. Folk have died and those responsible'll answer for it, and I trust you t'do that. Trust me to guard our home while ya do. Now go," the dwarf said, beckoning for the door.

Allystaire nodded, clapped the dwarf on the shoulder with one mailed hand and headed down the stairs and out of the Inn. Just outside, the Order were drawn up in a row: Tibult, Armel, and Harrys in the front, standing by horses with lances standing in boots next to the saddle. Norbert was fussing with his tack, next to Teague, who once more wore a mask over half of her face. Gaston, Miklas, Mattar, and Johonn all looked more prepared to march than to ride, the former two with their long spears, the pioneer with his broadaxes and the axeman all more comfortable on foot than in the saddle.

Mismatched armor, mostly chainmail only recently scoured clean, didn't gleam in the afternoon sunlight so much as it dully promised violence. Allystaire took a moment, as they all stopped what they were doing as he approached, to marvel at the change of a few weeks. All still bore their scars, body and soul, and yet they were healthy once more, moving with purpose and the reassuring competence of soldiers who knew their lives depended largely on their own preparation. Their transformations were often as much inward as outward, but Johonn, for example, had found his arm as strong as it had ever been only a few weeks after Allystaire's healing.

Allystaire found Ardent at the head of the line, saddled, lance in place, but was surprised to find Gideon holding the bridle, or at least, that the destrier was allowing someone to hold his bridle.

"Gideon," Allystaire said, as he put a hand on the pommel of his saddle and placed one foot in a stirrup.

"I know," the lad said, stepping back. "You don't want me to come with you. And in truth, I am probably more valuable here. I can relay what I see to you from the Temple, along with Mol. But it feels wrong, as if I am hiding from danger."

"Knowledge of the enemy and clear communication wins more battles than any amount of iron and steel ever will," Allystaire said as he swung up and onto Ardent's back. "Working this way, Gideon, you will save lives. That will always be a greater feat than taking them."

The boy nodded and stepped away. Allystaire cleared his throat, and felt the weight of the Order's eyes on him as he turned in the saddle to face them. "We do not know what we are riding into, who is waiting for us, or what they mean to do. There are folk within Ashmill Bridge who worship the Mother, and that makes them our brothers and sisters, our children, our cousins. Remember what the Mother asks of us: any burden."

The response rolled from nine other throats all at once. "Any burden."

* * *

Kormaukr Dragon Scale lay low upon the ground, his sea-green cloak settling over his skin and hiding him in the shadows of the trees. Nearby, he knew that Onundr and Gauk, his brothers in glorious service to Braech, similarly waited.

It galled, to be lying in wait. Men like them were not made for the ambush or the stratagem.

No.

The hot-blooded rush into battle was the glory of Braech's berzerkers, and lying on a forest floor, trying not to move, trying to will themselves into invisible stillness, this was no fit work for men like them.

Even the thought of it, the word "battle" floating across his mind had Kormaukr tightening the muscles of his shoulders, squeezing the earth he laid upon.

Suddenly there was the sound of hooves moving on the road they watched. He crouched, tensing every muscle in his body as men rode into sight.

The lead horse, some huge grey monster. Atop it, in gleaming armor, the paladin. Kormaukr was certain it was him.

He wanted nothing more than to rush forward, then and there, to tackle the man from his saddle and rip the ridiculous armor away, to plunge his gauntleted hands into the soft, weak, southern skin beneath.

But he was bid to wait, and watch, and so he watched the entire column slowly move.Kormaukr only counted eleven horses in the column that passed them. He suppressed the urge to laugh with the Honored Choiron's demand for stealth. Eleven, against the band of Braechsworn Islandmen waiting for them?

He waited until they were long past, then stood, signaling for his brethren to do the same. They popped up, cloaks swirling about their legs. Then Kormaukr let out his laughter, and the other Dragon Scales joined him. Then the three set off at a casual ground-eating lope southward.

The Choiron's commands echoed in his mind again. *Find the boy they call the Will. Kill him, in any way that you can, but be certain he is dead. Fail, and you will be buried beyond the reach of the Sea Dragon forever.*

An eternity on land was a fate not to be contemplated, Kormaukr knew. But after all, with what strength could one weak southern boy hope to meet a trio of Dragon Scales?

* * *

"Most folk are well after their first sleep by now," Torvul said, as he turned the corner on the shelves behind the bar, where Gideon sat on the floor by the cold well, lute in his lap, open case on the floor next to him.

"I do not need as much sleep as they do," the boy said. "And you understand why."

"I s'pose I do," Torvul said, "but I haven't the vigor of youth any longer. Night is lookin' a bit short to me, from here."

"How'd you find me? I was trying to be unobtrusive."

"I might be old," the dwarf replied, then tapped an earlobe with one fingertip, "but I've still got the best ears in this town. I followed the notes. You're gettin' better."

"I am still not much more than a fumbler, or so Idgen Marte tells me."

"You could be well on your way to a legendary career as a lutist and she'd still tell ya that."

"It's true, though," Gideon said, "not just her bluster. She would know. Torvul, I tell you that once upon a time, she saw music the way she now sees a fight."

"What's that mean?"

Gideon sighed. "She can see all the possibilities of a fight. Take Allystaire as a counter example. He sees who his biggest threat is and he attacks it, directly, head on, reasoning that if he can be hit, it means he can hit back, and that he'll win that exchange. But Idgen Marte, and part of this is the Mother's Gift, she sees *all* of the field. Everyone on it, everything that they can do or might do, and where upon it she should move to do the most good. She sees this through the interaction of light and dark to make shadow. When she was a musician, that was how she saw what she did; every place where sound and silence came together to make a song. And she knew exactly where and how she could fit into each piece of it. She can tell when I'm going to blunder up a stretch of a song before I even get to it. And from what she'll tell me, she wasn't accounted nearly as great a lutist as she was a singer."

"She's never talked t'me about any o'this," Torvul remarked.

"I don't think she's talked to anyone about it since she ran away from her home, Torvul. I wouldn't bring it up if I were you." The boy frowned. "I shouldn't even have told you."

"Pay it no mind, boy. I can keep a secret as well as stone itself." Torvul shifted how he stood so that he leaned against the shelf, heard some crockery rattle as he did. "What're you doin'?"

"Practicing, and looking at the well. I know this is the key, Torvul. I just can't figure out how to open it." He paused, and then together, boy and dwarf said, "Then it makes this the lock."

Together, they laughed softly, and Gideon set his lute down in the open case. "Why were you out talking with Keegan today?"

"How'd ya know that?"

Gideon shrugged as he stood up, smoothed his clothing with one flattened hand. "I was following Allystaire's progress up to Ashmill Bridge."

"And how is their progress?"

"Slow, because of the inexperienced riders. They should make the town in another two or three turns. They might not be let in until dawn."

Torvul chuckled quietly at that. "And here I thought you understood Allystaire."

"Allow me amend my statement; the town may not want to let them in until dawn." He frowned. "I thought about taking a look at the town itself, but I felt as if I would be seen, that I would give something away. Once Allystaire is there it does not matter, but until then." Here, the boy shrugged.

"What's he ridin' into? Sorcerer?"

"No," Gideon said, shaking his head. "If it were that, I would go to him, no matter what he said."

"Why haven't they ever simply attacked him openly?"

"Besides needing their games and machinations to stay connected to the world? They're cowards. I think most do not start out as such. It takes a certain courage, after all, to do what they do to themselves in the pursuit of power. But it is a mean, grasping kind of courage, the kind that turns quickly to cowardice once they have the object of their desire. They learned long ago that they could achieve their ends without exposing themselves to danger; why change that now?"

"Fair enough." The dwarf's jaw cracked in a yawn, and as he lowered the hand he covered his mouth with, he said, "We ought to at least be after a nap now. Can be up and after it again when you think Allystaire needs you."

Gideon started to nod his head in agreement, then suddenly looked up sharply. "You never answered my question, Torvul. Why did you go seeking Keegan?"

The dwarf shrugged. "With Allystaire, his band o'knightly thugs, or thuggish knights, whichever ya please, and Idgen Marte gone, this place is a bit short on what ya might call conventional defenders. I wanted t'make sure we could count on them, if it came to it. Besides, Keegan and his lot owe you somethin', and it wouldn't be the worst idea to have a guard around ya when necessary."

Gideon sighed faintly. "I'm not sure that's necessary." He bent down and closed his lute case, pulling the straps through the buckles and closing it firmly, then lifting it carefully in one hand.

"Remember, one of the sorcerers we faced died with an Islandman's axe in his back. You can't see everything around you all the time and protect yourself. Besides," he added, putting a hand on Gideon's shoulder, "I doubt it'll matter much. T'bed now."

They had gone only a few steps away from the bar when Mol's voice sounded sharply in their heads. *To the Temple. Now.*

Torvul was just opening his mouth to say something when Gideon slapped a hand on the dwarf's shoulder. Then Torvul had the sensation of dissolving into near nothingness, of the things around them blurring, and moving at an unmeasurable speed. Suddenly the world resolved itself again, with the pair of them standing at the altar along with Mol, whose face was grimly set.

"Braechsworn are going to attack the village," she was saying, and Torvul felt his heart sink for a moment.

The brief temptation towards despair was suddenly replaced with a roaring hot furnace of anger. "They think they can fool me, and find us unprepared? Me?" He was only dimly aware that he had roared the words, or that Mol and Gideon were staring at him oddly, because they had come out in the Dwarfish tongue.

He took a deep breath, and more words rolled out of his barrel chest, crashing like the stamping of huge hammers dropping upon rocks. "The Wit of the Mother and the last student of the last Stonesinger is not to be trifled with in his home," he said, and it was as if the anger within him was the hammer loosing the bright ore from the stones of his words.

* * *

Allystaire sat silent and still on Ardent's back, waiting. Behind him, he knew, were most of the rest of the Order, waiting for some signal. Few of them were as utterly silent as he was. He could hear the movement of their armor or weapons as they breathed or shifted their weight.

Only the horse beneath him closely mimicked Allystaire's stillness.

Cannot wait forever, he told himself as he let a breath out through his nostrils, a bit at a time. *Can't expect the boy to watch the entire time. He has to sleep.*

In fact, Gideon probably was asleep, which was likely why Allystaire hadn't felt his presence hanging over them for some time. It was a time to be asleep, if the town resting quietly along the river was any model. If there were any fires or lamps still throwing light from the windows of Ashmill Bridge at this turn, his eyes couldn't pick them out. There was only the sprawl of buildings, the bridge rising in a graceful arc beyond them, the massive old mill beside it.

Behind him, he heard Harrys drawing breath, ready to ask him a question. He lifted a gauntleted hand, and the grizzled old horseman settled back into silence. He could manage it only a moment, so Allystaire turned to him preemptively.

"We know nothing of the situation," he said, mouthing the words slowly, as quietly as he could manage. "We will wait on the Shadow's return."

Harrys was close enough, and the moon behind the clouds just bright enough, for Allystaire to make out the shape of the other man's mouth closing in a line. And then the sudden shock, eyes flying wide open at something beyond Allystaire, a hand falling to the falchion at his belt.

He startles too easily. Idgen Marte's voice sounded in his head, casual and calm as always.

He rolled his eyes, confident she'd see it. *They have come too far on too little sleep and face a fight against unknown foes. For most of them, their first fight in months, or years.*

Well, she said, *they've no scouts out, so all your careful quiet is for naught. Gather them around and let me speak with 'em.*

Before you tell them, tell me. How is it?

She eyed him as a cloud drifted over the moon. *Grim.*

He nodded, slid down off Ardent's saddle and waved a hand, beckoning the men to him. He made sure to keep a strong hand on the grey destrier's reins as they crowded around, as he could sense as much as see the stallion eyeing them.

Once they'd gathered, Idgen Marte sighed. "Here's how it is. There's at least a dozen Islandmen in there," she began, her voice quiet. "If that's how many I could count on a quick scout, surely there are more. But they've set a trap and I'm not sure how t'trip it without someone gettin' hurt."

"Getting hurt is what I am here for," Allystaire offered.

Idgen Marte shook her head. "I'm afraid that knockin' on the door and killin' them all isn't gonna work this time. There's a sort of square, used for market days and such, near the bridge. That's where they've set up. No good approach to'em without being seen. And they've got captives." She drew her bottom lip up hard. "They're bound, gagged, and tied t'stones. The river's right there, and it runs fast and deep." She let that implication sink in. A smattering of curses came from the men of the Order. Allystaire felt anger rise in him, felt the first stirrings of the music of the Mother in his limbs.

"There's too many for me t'free on my own, I think," she said. "They're watchin' 'em careful, have baffled lanterns. I think I could get t'one or two, but then it'd be a simple thing to shove 'em into the water and watch 'em slip."

"Have they any bows?" Harrys spat after he asked his question.

"None I could see," Idgen Marte said, "doesn't mean there aren't any."

"If I ride in and present a target, would that distract them long enough for you to free the captives?"

"There's nearly a score of folk tied up by the river, Allystaire," Idgen Marte answered. "I can't possibly move fast enough."

"Y'said there's no good approach through the town," Mattar said, taking a step through the ring of men, rolling his big shoulders beneath his hauberk. "What about on the river itself?"

Allystaire turned to look at the big man, whose hands rested on a pair of handaxes stuck through a belt. "What do you have in mind?"

Mattar shrugged lightly. "I know how t'move fast and quiet and I'm a strong swimmer. If I went wide o'the town and got in the river, made m'way down along the bank, I could be up beneath the bridge in a little more'n a turn."

Allystaire looked to Idgen Marte. "You could put yourself along the bank as well?"

"Not in the water, but yes," she allowed. "Still, two of us to deal with a score of folk right by the water…"

"Who else here can swim well? Not just make his way, but truly swim?" Allystaire looked back among the men of the Order, saw Gaston's hand go up.

"I did m'time on the water as a boarder," the curly-headed man said.

"Then you and Mattar had best strip your armor and make for the river," Allystaire said. "Idgen Marte can watch for you and relay to me when you are in place. Go."

The two men began stripping off their mail shirts. Gaston put down his spear and unhooked his scabbard from his belt, setting it aside. Mattar pulled one of his axes free and held it, haft out, to the slighter man. "Better to cut a rope," the pioneer offered.

With a smile, Gaston took it and stuck it through his belt. "Don't I know it."

The two set off at a loping run, going wide around the spread-out clusters of buildings. Allystaire silently blessed the lack of a wall.

Allystaire watched them go for a moment, took a deep breath. "They killed a man to send me a message. If I ride straight in at them—"

"They might have bows ready to fire," Idgen Marte said.

Allystaire shrugged. "I do not see another way. Just because I ride in first does not mean I ride in alone. If Harrys, Tibult, and Armel ride in behind me, Teague and Norbert watch for bowmen, and Miklas and Johonn act as our reserve, I think we make the most of our chances."

"Lot of open ground t'cover."

"Open ground is where horsemen excel," Allystaire said, to approving nods from his fellow lancers and Harrys. "The more I think on it, the more I think that we have every advantage. The best case is that we are dealing with fanatics who are trying to make a statement; the worst, we are dealing with warriors. We will answer them as soldiers. As knights. Warriors rarely have an answer for knights working in concert. And fanatics never will."

* * *

Gideon watched as Torvul strode purposefully out of the Temple, waving a hand behind him. The roll of Dwarfish words rumbling out of him was briefly interrupted for an interjection of the Barony tongue.

"The two o'you stay here," he said. "Till I know what's happenin'."

"I can tell you what is happening, Wit," Mol said sharply. "If you will contain yourself long enough to listen. It is three men—"

By then, Torvul's angry footsteps had carried him to the door and beyond. Mol turned imploringly to Gideon.

"It is only three men, Mol," he said. "Torvul has dealt with worse."

"It is not three ordinary men," she said. "When I laid my touch upon their minds I felt a chaos, a kind of madness, like nothing I have ever known. I could make no sense of them, nor could I speak to them."

Gideon felt his skin grow cold as Mol talked, and one word only tolled like a solemn bell across his thoughts. *Dragon Scales.*

He pushed his Will beyond the limits of his body, felt his form slump against the altar, and rose up above the Temple. As had become his custom, though no one—that he knew of—could see him when he existed purely in the form of his own Will, Gideon thought himself into the shape of a marsh hawk. It allowed him a more directed use of his power, allowed him to guide himself more narrowly. Without that focus, Gideon knew only too well how easy it would be to become lost, and disconnected from the world.

A half moon lit the night brightly enough, despite some cloud cover, for anyone about at the turn to see their way. But the Will of the Mother did not rely upon his eyes; he let other senses loose upon the village below him.

It was easiest to know where Torvul was, to feel him as color, as song, as *idea*. He was a low, resonant note, an echo down a perfectly smooth stone hallway; he was a bar of silver edged in glowing blue flame, moving through a quiet night with angry purpose. Mol, directly below him, was a steady warmth, a note in a high register, clear and pure, an unwavering disc of orange, a sun in miniature that warmed but did not burn.

There were other tiny pricks of will-light scattered around him, calling for his attention, in Thornhurst or near it, but even to him, they were too indistinct, too vague, for him to see clearly.

For just a moment, Gideon was tempted to let his sense wander even farther, to rise higher so that he could take in the entire world, and all of those in whom manifested the minor of what he now felt.

Instead he was drawn to the three presences that seemed to him almost indistinguishable from one another: a harsh grey-blue that throbbed with a pounding like the ocean. They could only be the men Torvul had gone to confront.

Gideon dove back into his own form, found Mol kneeling at his side, and his heart hammering against his chest. He looked into the girl's face, saw the fear written in her eyes.

"Gideon," she said quietly. "I think Torvul has gone to his doom. This is not a challenge for the Wit."

The boy shook his head as he stood up and adjusted his robe with one hand. "Do not underestimate him, Mol. Or me."

He turned and started for the door. Mol stopped him with a hand on his arm. "Gideon, please," she murmured. "Don't."

Slowly, Gideon shook his head. "I do not plan to kill them unless they force me to it," he said quietly. "I do not wish to. Though," he said, a little sadly, "when I am done with them, they may seek their deaths voluntarily."

* * *

Waiting, Allystaire found, was much easier when he did not have a clear idea of what awaited him. Or rather, when the Mother's Gift of Strength did not soar within his limbs, crying out to be released in defense of the innocents tied up along the riverbank. He found that if he closed his eyes and concentrated he could picture them. Not in detail, exactly, but in the moonlight he felt he could see the huddled forms, shivering in the cool spring night but trying to will themselves into stillness and silence. Hands and feet expertly bound with slim cordage, with rocks lashed to their already hobbled ankles. Hoping that the captors would not notice them, when the time came.

When Allystaire thought of the shivering forms, of the amount of rope, the expertise in the knots, he found the anger that began cold in his stomach fanning hot and bright into his arms, and the song rising louder in his mind.

That much rope, that well-tied, spoke of a plan. Of men who came here meaning to do this in order to lure him out.

Beneath him, Ardent, sensing his restlessness, pawed one hoof at the ground. He and the other horsemen were spread out, not in sight of each other, each taking shelter behind buildings as close to the clearing that led to the bridge as they could find. He gave Ardent a gentle squeeze with his knees to calm him; the destrier whickered softly and bent his neck, the long muscles flexing.

He wanted to run, to get on with it, as much as Allystaire did. *How does he know? Does he simply read my mood? And it comes to it, how does he handle my seat with the Goddess's power upon me?*

Allystaire had no time to ponder the question, for then Idgen Marte's voice came to him. *We are in place. There are better than a dozen of them. Maybe a score. They are wearing long cloaks and rags to cover it, but near as I can tell, every one of them is wearing mail, carrying axes and swords. Speaking Island Tongue and drinking. I see no bows.*

What of Mattar and Gaston?

They're here, but you'll need to distract the Islandmen.

Before Idgen Marte could complete the thought, Allystaire nudged his heels into Ardent's flanks, and the huge grey came around the shuttered two-story building he was hidden behind and broke into a trot. Before long, the bridge swam into focus ahead of him, and the figures patrolling the square in front of it in long cloaks came into view. Allystaire nudged the destrier again, and Ardent picked up a bit more speed. Once they were at the edge of the clearing, with the nearest captor perhaps a dozen paces away, Allystaire drew the horse to a halt and swung his lance free from its boot. The square was perhaps a bit wider than the green back in Thornhurst at its narrowest point, which was where the buildings edging it left off. It widened as it approached the bridge, enough for carriages or troops of horsemen to cross. The Ash was fairly thin here, but not fordable in any case, for the banks sloped steeply downward and the river was deep along most of its length. Delondeur watchtowers—unmanned, for this region of the Barony had been left on its own for too long now—rose just within sight beyond the bridge itself, guarding the approach from Oyrwyn to the north.

Allystaire made it nearly a score of men wandering more or less aimlessly around the square, which was hard-packed dirt with grass at its edges, hard by long buildings that he imagined were warehouses or stables. The seeming emptiness of the town was astonishing; they'd seen but few faces at windows when riding in, hadn't been challenged on the street by greenhat or Braechsworn. Nor had they been welcomed.

But, Allystaire had reasoned, common folk always knew when hiding served them best.

"BRAECHSWORN COWARDS," the paladin suddenly bellowed, his voice echoing over the quiet of the night, waking a few slumbering waterfowl and sending them squawking into the night. "YOU SENT A MESSAGE ASKING IF I HAD THE COURAGE TO FACE YOU. NOW ASK YOUR-SELVES IF YOU HAVE THE COURAGE TO FACE ME."

At once, the score or so of men shed long cloaks and came up with weapons: longswords and axes, held confidently in gauntleted hands. Allystaire found one part of himself searching quickly for any bare-chested men, wearing clawed gauntlets. When he saw none, he couldn't decide if he was relieved or disappointed.

"Paladin!" An island-accented voice, flat and harsh, called out and a man taller than most of the others shuffled a few paces forward. He was blond, had a sword in his hand, moonlight reflecting off of the naked blade and the mail hauberk belted at his waist, its edges flowing to the middle of his thighs. "Off the horse. Or town folk go to the water." His words were halting, but his intent clear.

Allystaire believed he could read a smile on the blond-bearded face as the man said, "Plop. To the bottom."

He badly wanted to turn the lance in his hand and throw it through the figure as he advanced, to pin him to the packed dirt of the square.

Time! Idgen Marte's voice sounded in his head again. *Play for it! Try to draw them to you.*

"And what becomes of the horse, then? Will you try to ride it?" Allystaire knew the words sounded ridiculous as he said them, but with the Mother's Song becoming a throb of anger, they were all that came to him.

"Eat it," the blond man said, and the smile on his face was clear. "You are soft here, ride beasts better roasted."

Despite the stakes of it all, Allystaire laughed, and casually, he slid his lance back into place and lifted one foot clear of a stirrup as if he were going to slide out of the saddle. "You are welcome to try," he called out, "but I think my horse is more likely to eat *you*. Tell me your name so that I can tell folk the name of the idiot my horse ate."

"Arvid," the man called out, thumping a fist against his chest.

"Arvid," Allystaire repeated, testing the name. More men closed in, most staying a few paces away. Casually, he dropped his hand to his hammer and turned to eye one man, braver than the rest apparently, sidling up to the horse. Ardent turned to watch him; the Islandman took a half-step back, then another forward.

"Well, Arvid," the paladin said as he watched a shadowy figure appear behind one of the Islandmen guarding a knot of captives along the riverbank and casually drive a curved blade through his chest, then disappear just as fast, "I think we have wasted enough time."

Even as the words left his lips, the Islandman edging close to Ardent made a lunge for the horse's bridle. Allystaire did nothing but let the destrier defend himself.

Ardent's neck darted to the side, and there was a sickening crunch. The Islandman screamed, drawing back a hand that was now short the better part of three fingers. Allystaire kicked the destrier into motion, and slid his foot back into the stirrup. The force of the stallion exploding into a run knocked the men gathering around him clear.

He spared another glance for the riverbank, and saw two more figures emerge from it and immediately make for the captives, lifting axes to hack at the ropes that kept the stones fast.

As he wheeled the mount around and pulled his lance free, he saw Tibult and Armel come riding into the square, lances leveled. Each of them had a target squared up as if it were a day in the practice yard, sinking lance-points through chainmail, flesh, and bone as easy as pushing the point of a knife through cheese. The cries of dying Braechsworn were loud in the night.

He swung his own lance out and leveled it with no more effort than it would've taken to lift a stray hair from the sleeve of a coat. He looked for Arvid but couldn't find the lanky blond figure in the chaos that erupted now that Harrys had exploded into the square on horseback, reins clutched in his teeth, bent low over the neck of his courser, falchion and broadaxe held out at neck height for a man on foot.

He settled on a target anyway, a man holding a longaxe with naked incompetence, as if he were about to chop wood with it.

A part of Allystaire's mind noted the man's hesitation, his uncertainty about the weapon, but it wasn't enough to stay the paladin's hand, not when weighed against the folk tied up along the riverbank, ready to be casually and brutally murdered.

The lancepoint took the man's throat, and with the force of the Arm of the Mother behind it, ripped the Islandman's head raggedly free and sent it tumbling into the night. The body tumbled bonelessly to the ground, blood gurgling from the gaping neck.

He tossed his lance aside and turned Ardent again, getting a good survey of the battlefield, such as it was.

It was more of an organized slaughter than it was a battle. The Islandmen had been armed and armored, yes, but it became clearer and clearer they hadn't any sense of how to fight together, how to engage the men on horseback, or even the basics of how to guard themselves with a sword. They had courage, yes, and they ran forward bravely and gamely, swinging their weapons with abandon and strength and chanted prayers to Braech.

And the Order of the Arm, against nearly twenty, were dispatching them almost casually.

Johonn and Miklas were providing a screen with long-axe and spear, respectively, for Norbert and Teague to loose arrows into the charging Braechsworn, but none even reached their line of two. If they weren't speared by a lance or run down by the fleet-riding Harrys, the whistling counter-pointed song of long-and-shortbow cut them down till only a bare handful remained.

"Drop your weapons," Allystaire called out. He spared a glance over his shoulder. Idgen Marte, Mattar, and Gaston had done their work well and quickly, freeing the captives and herding them away from the sight of a couple of bodies cooling in front of them.

He slid from Ardent's saddle and stalked towards them. Three of them, including Arvid, given his height and the color of his hair in the moonlight, had gathered back to back, swords held out in front of them.

"We can cut you down like dogs," Allystaire said, as he approached, hand falling to the head of his hammer, "or you can put up your swords and speak with us like men."

When he spoke, one of them, not the tall, blond spokesman but a short, stouter man with a rough, thick-browed face raised his sword in both hands and charged forward towards Allystaire, screaming.

Allystaire sprinted forward to meet him. Before the Islandman could even bring his sword down, the paladin had moved within the arc of his too-long swing. He wanted, badly, to simply drive his fist through the man's face, or even through his chest.

Instead, he threw his hands up and caught the man's descending arms, squeezed till he heard the bones snap, and shoved the screaming man to the ground. He bent, picked up the sword the attacked had dropped, hilt in his left hand, blade in his right.

He walked slowly up to the two remaining men and began to exert pressure on the weapon, bending the steel, twisting it in his hand, until finally he had rolled the last foot of the blade up into a coiled ball. He tossed the ruined blade at their feet.

"You can drop your weapons," he said coldly, "or I can crush your hands till you can no longer hold them. Choose."

They tossed the weapons down and raised their hands. Johonn and Miklas handed off their weapons to the archers behind them and rushed forward to secure the captives, putting rough hands on the back of their necks and kicking their legs out from under them, so that both Islandmen fell roughly to their knees.

Allystaire felt the strength leaving his limbs, a familiar ache start to seep in. He strode forward to Arvid, seizing his thin face with his left hand. "You will find that you cannot lie to me, so it would be best if you do not try. Tell me what happened here. All of it."

Arvid tried to wrench his head away from Allystaire's hand, but with Johonn leaning on his shoulders and the paladin's own grip, even without the Mother's Gift, he couldn't. The Islandman clenched his teeth and Allystaire sighed, pressing his senses, his will, against the other man's determination.

"Honored Choiron Symod," Arvid grated out from between still-clenched teeth. "Ordered us to come south, set a trap. Threaten heretics, make one drink the sea-water he gave us, send him to you."

"Symod." Allystaire practically spat the name. Idgen Marte strolled up behind the two men; he could sense her as much as see her. "What sense is there in this trap? You were as much danger to us as a cloud of flies. Surely you can see that."

The Islandman began to laugh, a harsh and ugly sound. "Trap not for paladin. For town, boy, to the south. Dragon Scales left us soon after we took this town."

Allystaire felt a sudden surge of anger, an impulse to snap Arvid's neck. Instead, he squatted to bring his eyes level with the other man's. "What do you mean, trap for a boy to the south?"

Arvid continued laughing, pausing only to launch a gob of spit onto Allystaire's cheek. "Don't know. Honored Choiron's instructions. Boy has to die, so Dragon Scales go to kill him."

Allystaire thrust the man away and straightened his back. He didn't wipe the spittle from his cheek; he barely felt it. His whole body was cold with dread, as he was already measuring the distance back to Thornhurst.

Allystaire, Idgen Marte's voice, in his head. *Torvul is there too. And Mol. And Gideon is the strongest of all of us. Now is not the time to panic.*

"Harrys," Allystaire said. "See the captives back to their homes and let the town know they are free, find out what other damage was done before we came. Truss this one up and bring him back to Thornhurst with you," Allystaire said, pointing at Arvid. He pointed to the other one who'd surrendered. "You. You go north and find your Honored Choiron and tell him that any harm done here, I will revisit upon him tenfold. Remind him that when I turned his god down, I warned him what it meant to make me his enemy. Take that one with you," he said, pointing to the man whose arms he'd broken.

"How d'ya know he'll go, rather than make mischief in the country?" That was Harrys, who'd dismounted, and handled his axe as if he was thinking on its suitability for the headsman's block.

"The Shadow will see to it," Allystaire said, lifting his eyes to find Idgen Marte. She nodded, and though he could not see her face, he thought he sensed worry from her.

"What o'the bodies?" That was Tibult, still in his saddle—the man made any excuse to stay on horseback he could find, now that he could ride again—looming over Allystaire's right shoulder.

"Toss them into the river. Let them find their way back to their god. Let them warn Him that I am coming," Allystaire said as he turned, seeking Ardent, the destrier waiting patiently a few paces away.

As he walked towards the horse, he heard Idgen Marte's thoughts once more. *Allystaire, don't. He's like no horse I've ever seen, but he's still just a horse. Ride him hard all the way back to Thornhurst and you'll kill him.*

The paladin wouldn't have sworn to it, but he thought that perhaps, just perhaps, his mount heard the Shadow's words, for the huge grey destrier reared up, hooves pawing at the air in front of him for a moment, a deep whinny rolling from his barrel chest. The moonlight turned the grey of Ardent's coat, for a moment, into a silver to match the paladin's armor, and Allystaire smiled.

No, he thought. *He is not.* Then he pulled himself up into the saddle, let the destrier have his head, and they rumbled south, man and horse of one mind, one purpose, one Calling.

* * *

Torvul was halfway to his wagon when he heard the howl.

It was an ear-splitting sound, rending the night. It was a sound without humanity in it, and yet it wasn't the call of any beast he knew. To his ears, it was the sound of a too-large hammer shattering the delicate instrument it was meant to shape. It tore at his ears and set his hands shaking. He looked at them, holding out the long fingers, the stained and scarred palms, and watched hands that had never once betrayed him trembling in the moonlight.

"I am the Wit of the Mother," he rumbled aloud. "I am the last student of Ochsringuthringolprine, who was himself the last Stonesinger. I will not fear some rotten, stinking god of fish and salt. What is the sea when measured against stone?"

The litany should have calmed him. The very act of speaking should have slowed the hammering of his heart and stilled his traitorous hands, and yet a small voice rose up and said, *What is the stone when measured against the relentless pounding of the waves?*

Torvul shut his eyes and willed himself to continue walking onward towards his wagon, when he heard another voice, and this one was not small, nor did it come from within.

Be calm, Son of the Earth. Remember who you are and what has been granted you. Fear may cause your flesh to tremble, but does fear move stone? Does fear contend with rock?

Torvul dropped his hands to his sides, set his shoulders, and walked on. One of his trembling hands he curled into a fist, while the other he shoved in a pouch on his belt, pulling free a small bottle. He thumbed it open and quickly splashed some against his eyes, hummed a low note deep in his throat. The world around him blazed into brightness as if it were the sun overheard and not half of a moon, and shapes in the darkness resolved themselves into houses, trees, rocks—and people.

Villagers who lived inside the walls were coming out of their homes, eyes wide with fear. A few, remembering their months of militia training, were carrying weapons—spears and bows, mostly. Torvul smiled ruefully. *Renard,* he thought, *from the grave you continue to serve your home well. Too well,* he thought, as he realized the danger.

"People, go to your homes. Bar your doors and fill your hands and do not come out again until one of the Five tells you so," he bellowed.

Almost instantly, yet another voice sounded in his head, this one calming, and, he knew, reaching out to everyone in and around Thornhurst.

Return to your homes, please, for your own good, came Mol's voice, and Torvul thought he could detect the slightest hint of fear behind his sense of her. *Danger comes to us this night, but the Mother will see us safely through it, I swear.*

Torvul watched folk pause and look up at the air and if startled by the words they heard. They started to move back to their homes; then the night was rent by another, all too human scream.

The people around him panicked, and broke in flight. Some for their homes, some away from the scream, and one or two armed folk, towards it.

Torvul cursed and ran for his wagon, and the tools he left within it.

Lass, he thought, hoping Mol would hear him, *can you get ahold of Keegan's lot?*

They've already tried to stop them, she answered, and he could feel the grief in her voice. *Torvul, you must hurry to intercept them before Gideon. I don't know what he means to do but I fear it is something dire. Hurry.*

Torvul rarely ran, but he found his legs churning now. His strides didn't eat much ground, but he churned his legs as best he could, though soon his breath was puffing out of his lungs like a bellows-organ of the Homes. He cursed the size of the village, though it wasn't large; he cursed his age, though as dwarfs went, he wasn't elderly yet; mostly he cursed knowing that, for all he jeered at Allystaire's relentless exertions, the Arm would have been to his wagon and back already.

Well, the Arm isn't here, he told himself. *You are. The boy is. We'll do.*

When Torvul did finally reach his door, he was sucking great lungfuls of air, or trying. He fumbled open the lock and darted inside.

He blessed his organized habits. A half step in the door, there was his jerkin. Another step as he shrugged into it, the potion bottles and other oddments clipped to it jingling, and there was his crossbow, a sheaf of bolts. He patted the pockets clipped to the rings on his thick leather jerkin, his fingertips reading the runes inscribed on the hardened leather.

Signal. Woundclot. Nighteye. Echoes. He thought briefly of the ingredients scattered about the wagon. He'd once told Allystaire he didn't use poison out of professional pride, but he knew well how quickly a poison could be wrought from the materials he had. But there was no time; once more he fingered the four pouches he had, and threw open his door, one hand already sliding a bolt home in his crossbow.

Thirty paces from his wagon's door, two figures were moving in, one of them dragging a limp form behind him.

Torvul snapped the crossbow up and fired off a shot. It was pure instinct, and he was no sharpshooter, not by dwarf standards. But it was bright as day to his eyes, the bow was well-made, and at thirty paces, it was an easy shot. As he fired, he registered that the men coming towards him were both not only unarmored, but indeed bare-chested. He felt himself smiling as the bolt loosed.

Except the man he aimed for knocked the bolt aside with one sweep of a heavily gauntleted arm. Laughing.

"Put the toy down, little man," the one who'd knocked his bolt aside laughed. The other, who dragged a limp and bloodied form behind him, laughed along with him. Their mirth was a harsh and grating thing. It was easy to imagine the howl from before coming from men like them.

"You're the brewer," the other said, through his laughter. "You give us a drink, eh. Maybe you live longer." He shrugged. "Take it anyway once you're dead."

"I'll give you some of my best," the dwarf said. "Give ya more if ya like it," he added, putting a plaintive whine in his voice. "Let me go and I'll show ya the Temple treasury. Ya can have all the folk o'the village," he added, taking a half-step back. He unhooked a pouch, the one that read *Nighteye*, and tossed it towards the berzerker.

Thank you, Lady, he thought, *for not layin' the same rules upon me as you did Allystaire.* He studied the body that the Dragon Scale dropped casually on the grass. Torvul couldn't identify the villager, but he lay limp, bloodied. His chest didn't rise, not that the dwarf could see. Then he turned his eyes to the berzerker, who'd ripped open the leather pouch and tossed it aside, and was now eyeing the glass bottle distrustfully.

The other, apparently grown impatient, came to him and ripped it from his hands, jabbering at him in their own tongue.

Torvul slipped a thumb over another pouch and opened it, palming the bottle inside.

The berzerker held the bottle he'd tossed them up in the moonlight, studying it. In one motion, Torvul slipped a bolt into his bow, raised, fired.

The berzerkers were fast, but they were concerned about their own flesh— not the delicate glass bottle one held up, framed in the light.

Torvul's bolt shattered it. The moment passed slowly. Torvul felt he could see the individual droplets as they burst into the air. The berzerkers were pelted with broken glass, drawing tiny dots of blood on their hard features.

Droplets of the *Nighteye* potion the bottle had contained splattered all over their faces—and their eyes.

Torvul threw down the bottle he'd palmed, the one marked *Signal,* then ducked his head behind his arm, eyes squeezed tightly closed.

The night lit up as brightly as the sun itself, even behind closed eyelids and a shielding arm. There was no heat to it, but the brightness left white lines in his vision, blurred it as he hopped from his wagon and sprinted away.

* * *

Many miles away to the north, bent over Ardent's neck, Allystaire saw the brief red flash in the night, the flare rising up and disappearing as quickly as it came. He pulled the destrier to a stop, peered at where he'd seen it, as if he could divine anything from the vague impression the red flare had left on his night vision.

Sweat streamed down his face, a fact he only noticed now that he'd stopped. "Time to let you walk anyway," he muttered, patting the horse on the side of the neck.

Ardent's chest was puffing like a bellows, breath pouring into and then out of him in great gusts. Allystaire started to ease his feet from the stirrups, but the horse gave his great neck a hard shake, struck a hoof at the road so sharply that a spark flashed in the night.

Allystaire nudged the war horse with one heel, and the great grey surged forward again, and paladin and mount were off once more.

Allystaire kept turning his head to where he thought he'd seen the flare, wondering what it could have signaled.

* * *

Torvul ran for all he was worth, which, when it came to sprinting, wasn't much. Another howl rent the air behind him, but it was the cry of a wounded animal.

An angry wounded animal, Torvul thought, as he ran. His course took him back towards the cluster of buildings around the village green. Finally, his legs burning and his chest aching with the effort of drawing breath, he pulled to a stop and checked his pockets again, thumb scattering over the runes. *Woundclot. Echoes.*

He pulled open the former pouch and pulled out the bottle. "Forgive me, Your Ladyship, for the sin of waste." He flicked it open, while he pulled free a handful of crossbow bolts, and began splashing the liquid onto the broad, flat heads. He shoved them, head-up, back into the sheaf at his hip and slotted one into the bow.

He brought the weapon up, flipped up one of the sighting rings, and began scanning his horizon, looking for targets.

Then he heard the laughter. He whirled to face it, saw a third man—Mol had said there were three. This one was dressed similarly to the others: loose trousers, no shirt, heavy gauntlets that covered his hands from fingertip to elbow. They were well-wrought; Torvul found himself noticing the details as the man laughed, spread his arms wide. They were etched, patterned like the scales of some great bronze wyrm, the fingers ending in sharply clawed tips. His torso was covered in a massive tattoo of a wave threatening to swallow a long-keeled boat; on the prow of it stood the crude figure of a man with his arms raised, his mouth open. Whether he welcomed the destruction and uttered a cry of praise, or roared defiance back at the sea, Torvul couldn't tell. And he didn't care; the tattoo made a target. He shot.

This Dragon Scale lowered one arm, trying, Torvul thought, to catch his bolt. He didn't, not quite.

But he did slow it. It only just penetrated his skin, instead of punching clean through him and tearing into his vitals.

The huge man—he was easily a head taller than Allystaire, and built just as broadly—laughed again, slowly sauntering forward towards the dwarf.

"Did you think you could run from the Father of Waves, little trickster? Even if you bested my brothers, no brewer of poisons is the match of Kormaukr Dragon Scale. Bring me the boy," the man said, "or I will kill every family in this village. Starting with the children."

Torvul quickly slipped another bolt into the crossbow and raised it. By the time he fired, Kormaukr had nearly closed the distance. The bolt skittered away into the night, deflected by a gauntleted hand.

The berzerker sent the dwarf tumbling with a casual, backhanded blow. Crossbow bolts skittered out of the sheaf; he only held to the bow because of the sling over his shoulder.

Kormaukr was on him again, lifting him from the ground. Torvul fumbled for a bolt from his pouch, jammed it hard into the berzerker's torso.

It was like trying to push the bolt through rock. It was possible, but only just. It made no more of an impression than the one he'd fired.

The berzerker laughed again, and threw Torvul in a high arc. The dwarf landed roughly, felt one of his shoulders go numb after a loud pop, found himself looking up at the stars. The potion in his eyes had begun to fade, so the sky was becoming that of a spring night once again, with a strange distortion hovering between it and the dwarf's eyes; Torvul almost lifted a hand to feel for the damage.

The berzerker laughed and drew forth the bolt Torvul had stabbed him with, held it up to his eye. "Your poisons are nothing to the Dragon's Scale, dwarf. Our blood is as the sea itself; can you poison the sea?"

"No. But the sea can freeze, and the will of man can direct it where and how he chooses."

The strange hovering cloud become the slim figure of a bald boy clad in bright blue robes, a plain wooden staff in one hand, standing between Torvul and the berzerker.

Gideon raised his free hand, lightly, almost casually. "What happens if your blood freezes, Kormaukr Dragon Scale?"

The berzerker suddenly stopped, one arm outstretched, inches from Gideon's unprotected neck. Torvul watched in shock, and not a little horror, as ice crystals formed on the outside of the gauntlet that reached for the boy's throat. The metal of the gauntlet cracked, shattered, fell away from the arm beneath it.

The berzerker's hand itself was, Torvul thought, scaled and clawed in the same way the gauntlet had been. And now cracks were moving up along his arm, to his neck, to the wide, terrified animal's eyes that rolled in fear.

"Gideon," Torvul whispered, pain shot through his usually strong voice. "No."

"How much would I truly love the world, Torvul," Gideon said, "if I did not save it from men like this?" The boy did not turn to look down at the wounded dwarf; he stared hard at Kormaukr Dragon Scale, and shook his head. "A man who has traded all that makes him a man for the power to bring terror, the strength to rend the flesh of anything unlucky enough to come within his reach? No," the boy said, and if his voice was sad, it was also firm, as if he had made a decision.

Gideon closed his open hand, and Torvul watched as the towering Kormaukr Dragon Scale was suddenly sheathed to his very eyeballs in ice that rose up from underneath his skin. Cracks appeared, starting at the tip of his clawed, outstretched fingers.

Then the Will opened his palm, splaying his fingers, shoving at the air with his wide opened hand. And the frozen berzerker, his eyes still wide and rolling with fear, *shattered*.

Torvul awkwardly shifted his weight to one side, leaned close to the ground so he could push himself up with his good arm, but before he'd even gotten halfway, Gideon was standing over him and helping him up. The boy's arms had a surprising strength in them, the dwarf thought.

What was more surprising was the light that blazed briefly in Gideon's eyes as Torvul met them. For just a moment, they were a hard-edged gold without iris or pupil, then they were once again soft and brown. "Where are the others?"

"Blinded," Torvul said. "Perhaps forever. That way," he added, pointing. "What do you mean to do with them?"

"Make what use of them I can before sending them on their way," Gideon said. Torvul clutched at the boy's robe with his good arm, but Gideon disappeared through his grasp, vanishing like smoke.

* * *

The world may have gone dark for Onundr Dragon Scale, but that did not mean he or his brother Gauk were dead or beaten.

Onundr's thoughts were wordless rage. He had one arm wrapped around Gauk's ankle, while the other Braechsworn crawled ahead of him, his nose bent to the ground.

That Dragon Scales were reduced to sniffing their prey like hounds was a disgrace. It would not last, he was sure, but even with their eyes taken from them for now, Onundr and Gauk would see the Sea Dragon's work done. Their eyes may have betrayed them, but the strength of their arms had not, their skin was still as hard as fine mail, their throats still full of bloodlust and rage and if they had to sniff his enemies out, they would.

No dwarf was going to best them. Onundr knew that as certainly as he knew that the sun would rise, that the oceans would roll against the beach, that Braech's waters would some day rise and claim the world.

Already, the berzerker thought, his eyes were starting to clear, and the dark of the night was beginning to move in on the edges of his vision.

"You should be able to see what happens next." The voice came from nowhere, and the berzerkers recoiled in surprise, if not fear, for neither had heard nor smelled this man until the moment he spoke.

Then Onundr's vision suddenly cleared, filling with the mud and grass of the ground close beneath him; he saw the dirt crusting the etched scales of his gauntlets and recoiled in anger.

Dragon Scales did not crawl.

Onundur tried to bring his feet under him and stand, only to find himself suddenly lifted from the ground. He cast his eyes towards Gauk, saw that his brother was similarly being pulled into the air, bound in bands of bright golden fire. He looked down at himself and saw the same flames, binding but not burning, then heard the voice again as he was turned in the air, until he found himself facing a mere stripling, a thin, bald wisp of a boy in a robe.

"If it is any comfort to you," the boy was saying, "for the first time in your lives, the power that resides within you is going to be used for the good of the world."

Onundr knew in that moment that it was the boy whom he'd been sent to kill who had trapped him, trussed him like a pig going on the spit. What was more, he knew now how foolish, how vain that goal had been, because the power that spoke through the boy was an ancient thing, and vast.

"You will have your lives, when I am done," the boy said calmly. "If you want them."

The boy turned and started walking calmly, casually, and Onundr found himself floating helplessly in the air behind. He opened his mouth, tried to pull the air into his lungs to roar, and found that he could not; something the boy had done had robbed him of that as surely as it had robbed him of everything else.

"Men like you do not even realize what you have become, do you?" The boy spoke slowly, chidingly, as if trying to correct the missteps of a child. "You have no idea of what you have lost in pursuit of the power you have. It could be that what I mean to do will remind you, and that will not be a kindness."

The boy suddenly stopped and turned to look at them, coming close, first to Gauk, and then to Onundr, peering closely at his brother's face, then at his.

The boy himself was bald, his hair shaved carefully away, and his eyes were wide, brown and oddly shaped to Onundr's eye. He was from somewhere far from where they now stood, he was sure.

"He draws from you even as you draw from Him," the boy murmured, almost curiously. "Surely on some level even you understand that."

Then the boy turned and walked again. Onundr imagined they were being taken to the local Temple, to be cut apart and sacrificed to their heathen goddess, so he found himself shocked to find himself floating to rest upon his feet on a bed of soft green grass, facing a tall building with a stone face and a high peaked roof, covered in tiles rather than the thatch that the rest of the village showed.

The boy turned and looked at the two berzerkers and then lowered his head, extending both hands towards them, fingers splayed open.

Almost instantly, Onundr felt a pull deep within him. His mouth filled with the taste of brine, his ears echoed with the roll of the waves.

And something began to issue forth from him, slowly, inexorably.

In each of the boy's hands, small blue-grey balls of light began to grow.

As they did, Onundr felt the strength Braech granted him waning. Already, the gauntlets formed around his hands were growing too heavy, too large, the claws no longer fitting snugly around his fingers.

Slowly, the claws slid from his hands and hit the ground with a heavy thud. Panic rose in him, and he looked to his brother. Gauk's claws slid to the ground slowly as well, slipping away from arms grown thinner.

Onundr watched as his brother's chest seemed to draw in on itself, slowly collapsing, till the huge, muscled berzerker was hardly recognizable. He turned his eyes down to his own body, saw the pact he'd made with Braech vanishing before his eyes.

He hit the ground with a thud, the bands of light that had held him fast vanishing into the air. Gauk tumbled to the ground with him, and the boy joined his hands together, pressing the globes of blue light together into one, the size of a large stone, resting weightlessly in the boy's arms.

Onundr struggled to stand, but all his will, all his strength had been sapped. He got as far as one knee till his legs turned watery beneath him and he fell back to the cool grass.

"It is not a great deal of power that is given to you," the boy opined as he studied the ethereal thing he held. "And yet you do not even realize that. The ability to take whatever you wish—or be given it out of fear—is the only measure of strength you know. It is time that men like you learned to fear a different kind of strength."

With that the boy turned and walked away, the globe of what he'd taken from them, of Braech's broken trust with them, lighting his steps as he disappeared into the door of the tall building in front of them.

CHAPTER 35

The Barrier

Torvul could feel the building pressure all around him, like the feel of the air before a storm against his skin, or the press of an ache against the eyes, the throb of a loud harmony in his throat. It was all of these at once, and yet it also spoke to his inner senses, to his connection to the earth itself, the power of his craft and link with the Mother.

And he knew that whatever it was, it originated with Gideon and it was happening near the Inn.

Wincing in pain, as his broken arm throbbed with every step, Torvul labored towards the green. It was a long and a painful walk, but finally the center of the village hove into his view. Gideon stood in the midst of it, glowing balls of power coalescing in his hands. The two Dragon Scales Torvul had blinded floated in the air, but their bodies were twisting and mutating before his eyes.

He stumped his way up closer, hugging his arm tightly against his side. He sucked in a deep lungful of air. Trying to breathe was difficult, not only from the pain, but from whatever Gideon was doing.

"Gideon! Gideon, stop! Whatever it is you are doing, wait."

"You know what I'm doing, Torvul," Gideon said. "You know what I have meant to do all these months."

"You don't have to do it tonight, Gideon. You can't change the world in one night!"

Gideon turned his eyes to Torvul and once more they flashed that golden color, just for a moment. "Yes, Torvul. I can," the boy said, and though the words were simple and his voice was calm, they resounded with thunder.

"You could hurt yourself. Or the folk around ya. They've already been hurt enough."

"No, Torvul. No hurt will come to them. And I will not let you talk me into delay," the boy said through clenched teeth. He let the moaning berzerkers drop to the ground; they lay unmoving, but Torvul thought they still breathed.

Gideon looked down at them, holding what he'd taken from them in his hands, and shook his head. "Power in the hands of men like them is power in the hands of a dog in foaming madness. When they are made to serve the ends of a man like Symod, of a god as mad with bloodlust as Braech has become, *it never ends*. It will never end so long as the great masses of people haven't the means to defend themselves. I mean to give it to them, Torvul. My solution is not perfect. It will be dangerous. But it will be a step."

Torvul took an involuntary step backwards, chastened by the anger in Gideon's words, by the power that radiated from him, as if he was drawing it from the air.

"Think, boy," the dwarf said. "Just think. Wait for Allystaire. You're tryin' t'do too much."

"No," Gideon said, shaking his head. "He told me once that the most important quality for a leader to be is decisive. Make a decision now, he said, for if you wait for the perfect moment, the clearer picture, you've only made it harder. No. It happens now. Tonight."

"I'll stop you if I have to, boy," Torvul said, taking a step forward, trying to plant his feet more firmly than his voice.

"No, Torvul," Gideon said as he turned his back and walked towards the Inn. "You won't. You can't."

Torvul watched the Will walk away from him, fearful and shamed, for he knew his words to be true.

* * *

Gideon was already inside the Inn and moving past a crowd of frightened on-lookers, including Timmar, who clutched a woodaxe determinedly in both hands, and Giarud's daughter Lenoir, holding one of her father's rock-hammers, before he realized they were all staring silently.

Mouths agape, they watched hushed and fearful as he kicked open the door and took a few steps inside. Finally, he gathered himself. "Try not to be alarmed," he said, though it was difficult to concentrate on forming the words, on keeping his voice calm and even. "There is no longer any danger; the attackers have been dealt with. Two of them are outside on the green, but are no more threat. See to them if you wish."

He stood there, watching their faces, finding himself envious of Allystaire's easy way with command. *A gentle word from him and they're all moving. A loud word and they're running,* he thought.

"I, ah, have business in the storage behind the bar. In the cold well. If someone would be so kind as to open it."

Timmar cleared his throat and lowered the axe to rest the blade beside his foot. "What'll ya need from the cold well? I just put a fresh barrel in there."

"I am afraid the barrel may be a total loss, goodman Timmar," Giden said, his teeth clenched, a dribble of sweat running from his scalp and over his cheek. "But what I have to do is quite vital."

Still no one moved. Timmar tapped his foot against the axe. "Expensive barrel. It was just fired. Good ale, too. What'll ya need ta do?"

Finally, Gideon's patience fraying, he snapped. "I haven't the time to explain to anyone, so no questions please, but the well you use to keep beer at cellar temperatures is a holy spring that was once dedicated to the Mother, in Her last incarnation in this world, in a time lost to our historians. This would go a great length towards explaining why there was rarely even simple violence in this place until the reavers brought it here, and why that act and Mol's refuge in it awoke Her, but I haven't the time to give an extensive lecture on the metaphysics or the theology of it all, so if you could *please* just take my Freezing word for it, move out of my way, and open the trap door, I would be very much obliged."

Gideon's throat was a bit raw by the time he shouted out the final words, but the intensity had the desired effect. Timmar finally moved, quickly, stepping behind the bar and around the shelves.

The boy followed the Innkeep, conscious of the stares upon him, but he heard the telltale creak of the door being lifted open.

He came around the corner finding Timmar quickly pulling down the rope that threaded through a pulley on the ceiling. The rope's end was threaded through the eye at the end of a heavy metal hook, and Timmar quickly lowered that towards the well, pulling up a handful of chain affixed to the top of the barrel.

"Happy t'help, young master," Timmar was saying, as he secured the chain against the hook and then took up the rope and began hauling the barrel out. "No sense wastin' the barrel or the ale," he muttered.

Gideon felt his arms trembling, his body starting to fatigue with the effort of holding the power he'd ripped from the Dragon Scales in his hands, without letting it escape him or drawing it into himself. Some force was trying to tug it free, and his own Gift was reaching for it hungrily.

"You may want to leave the room, and get the others out in case I am wrong," Gideon warned him, before stepping forward and plunging into the cold well the moment the barrel was clear.

His robe instantly waterlogged and clung against him, and he felt the cold seeping into his skin. He plunged his hands into the water and extended his senses, flexing his Will to try and push the coalesced power away from himself, away from the world he knew, and into the world beyond.

It was, in a physical sense, like trying to push a tiny sliver of steel through a castle wall. The ache of the force he expended soon outweighed the shock of the cold water, but soon enough, the facts of his physical existence faded.

A blur of sensation hit him all at once. There was the feeling of being trapped within this well with the heat of a fire raging outside, the foreign sounds of violence and the screams of pain and death. Cold, and hunger, and then a voice that held within all the warmth of the world. There was a long, slow, black silence. A great anger and an overpowering sadness. A vast and incoherent music that he thought, if he could only listen to it closely enough, would resolve itself. It was tempting, so very tempting, to lose himself in the attempt.

His ability to form language, to understand the *idea* of what he was feeling as language, was becoming too small for the concepts assailing him. Gideon found himself losing consciousness. He shook himself, reached a hand up out of the water to slap his cheek.

He pushed all that threatened to close in on him away and focused on that sharp sliver of steel in his hand and pushed with all his might at the wall in front of him. Though he had no steel and there was no wall, he could feel it resisting, feel it looming over him and threatening to tumble atop him and bury him under all of its weight.

There is no wall, Gideon told himself. *There is only strength and weakness. I will be strong enough.*

The point of his sliver seemed to dig a little further, but he had scratched away only a few grains.

If there is no wall, the Will thought, *then there is no tiny bit of steel in my hand. There is whatever I wish.*

And suddenly it was a hammer in one hand, and a chisel in the other. The hammer, he knew without thinking, looked like the one Allystaire had broken against the Battle-Wights, but smaller, fitted to his own hand.

He set the chisel and swung, focusing his own Will upon the point of the power he'd ripped from the Braechsworn.

Stone flaked at the first blow.

He swung again.

It chipped and slid away in a heavy rain of pebbles, but he felt them disappearing and melting away to nothingness as they passed.

It is not stone. The piece in front of me is not stone. It is loose earth. It is damp mud, Gideon thought.

And it was so; the stone crumbled, and he abandoned his tools, digging with his hands.

I do not need to destroy the wall, he told himself. *I need only push through it here, in one place, and in time it will crumble on its own.*

Gideon dug furiously, leaning into a hole in the stone now, crawling in, shoveling the earth behind him like a beast.

The exertion left him all but untethered to his body now. On some level he felt the cold of the water, felt his legs sinking underneath him, his arms trembling, his breath coming shallow.

But his whole being was invested into the action of his Will, and if tearing a hole between two worlds was going to kill him, then it would be a worthy death.

Gideon knew now that all his worrying, his planning, all his fear had been for nothing. This act, this moment, was what his Gift was meant for, what the Mother had hoped all along he would do with the power She had unlocked in him.

He felt a smile play upon his face as he realized what he needed to be willing to do.

Gideon felt his body slump down into the water, the breath driven from his lungs, as he let go of his hold upon his body. He needed to be anchored to the world, yes, but if he loved it enough to die for it, then he did not need to waste any of his Will in propping himself up. It was a small thing, but it was everything.

When he let go, his arms reached for more of the Barrier to move aside and found nothing.

His senses touched a pure flowing stream of power, and he extended himself to it. Gideon knew he could absorb it, could draw it into himself and make himself more powerful than ever he had been, even when he drew into himself the remnant of the God of the Caves.

Instead, he let himself be a channel, a conduit, for the power did not flow through the breach like water through a broken damn. It moved slowly, like an animal being forced into a strange place. He had to reach into it, grab it, and pull.

Once it found purchase within—and then through—Gideon himself, it began to move. Slowly, yes, and Gideon could not imagine how much lay behind the barrier he had bored through, but it was a beginning. The sheer weight of power Gideon felt pressing forward was overwhelming.

It was done; raw magic was seeping into the world. Gideon imagined he could see it, little globes of bright energy in every color, in colors he couldn't name, floating into the night, invisible to any eyes but his own.

He smiled as weariness overcame him. He imagined opening his mouth to mutter some prayer to the Mother, felt cold water seep in to fill it.

It did not matter; his task was done. If he drowned here, he had done the Mother's work. Both his inner and his outer vision clouded.

Gideon was letting himself slip from the world entirely when strong, familiar hands seized his shoulders and hauled him up and out of the cold well.

It was not, Gideon knew, before consciousness left him, the first time that Allystaire had found him adrift and pulled him back to life, back to the world.

In some place in his soul, Gideon had known that he would.

* * *

Gideon awoke in darkness. Opening his eyes was an act of supreme physical exertion; sitting up proved beyond him. He was warm, though, and dry, and despite the darkness of the room around him he could feel another presence.

"How did you know to come back?" The voice that emerged from his throat surprised him. It was barely more than a whisper.

"Took a prisoner in Ashmill Bridge. The whole thing was a trap, attacking there so we would respond, exposing the village, and you."

"It wasn't very well designed," Gideon wheezed. "How would they know you'd leave me behind?"

"They did not," Allystaire said. "I suppose if we had left Thornhurst and the Temple entirely undefended, they would have come into the village and taken prisoners, tried to exchange them. But you were definitely their target."

"How did you get back so fast?"

"Ardent."

Gideon thought on the distance from Ashmill Bridge to Thornhurst, that the destrier would've traveled it one way already in a short time. "Did it kill him?"

"Hardly," Allystaire said. "Torvul and I have both had a look at him. He labored, yes, but he is as healthy as ever."

"Perhaps," Gideon mused, "you were not the only one Gifted by the Mother outside of Bend."

"Speculate at another time," Allystaire said. "For now, you need the kind of healing I cannot give you. Only sleep can."

"Did Torvul tell you what I did?"

"No," Allystaire said. "Says he is uncertain he could explain it so that I could understand."

"I will," Gideon said, even as he felt weariness overtaking him. "Later. You and Mol and Idgen Marte all need to know. But…had t'be done. Had to be," he muttered, trailing off.

* * *

Allystaire listened to Gideon's deep, steady breathing for several long moments until he was certain that sleep had well and truly claimed the boy. He stood, feeling the exertion of the long ride, and his long stay at Gideon's bedside trying to turn his legs to lead. A yawn threatened to crack open his jaw, but he stifled it until he could slip outside the door of Gideon's room and close it as quietly as possible.

Once in the hallway, he let the yawn out, startled by the exhaustion that seized him; he found himself starting to lean against the wall, then stiffened his back and walked down the stairs, keeping his hands defiantly at his side.

The mood in the taproom was somber. Most of the village folk gathered at the tables and chairs, and Torvul and Andus Carek sat by the hearth, though the bard was without his lute and Torvul sat silent and glum.

Allystaire drifted towards them. The dwarf looked up to him, those deep dark eyes all but unreadable.

"He awake?"

"Briefly," Allystaire said.

"What'd ya speak of?"

"Very little," Allystaire answered as he sank gratefully into a chair, sighing. "I do not think he knows about Chals or Morgen."

"Will he be awake for the buryin'?"

"I do not know," Allystaire replied. "It did not seem prudent to press him when he nearly killed himself, Torvul."

"Has he told you what it was he did?"

"No," Allystaire said, letting his voice fall like a clenched fist. "And I will wait until he is ready."

"He did somethin' dangerous, Allystaire. Somethin' that needed more time t'consider," Torvul said, leaning forward, scowling. "Not to mention what he did to that berzerker."

"Faith, Torvul," Allystaire muttered, lowering his voice, conscious of the peering eyes of the crowd around him. *And let us not argue here,* he added.

He killed him like it was nothin', Allystaire. Froze him and then shattered him with a wave of his hand. It was terrifying. Torvul stared hard at him, the anger clear. He stared right back, matching the dwarf's gaze evenly, so it was easy to read the shock when he replied.

Good, Allystaire thought. *If any men want killing, it is these berzerkers.*

To shatter a man like an icicle?

I am not particular about the manner of their deaths.

You're a cold man, Allystaire Stillbright, Torvul replied, as he sat back in his chair, looking away.

I wish I could spare the lad the need to do it, Allystaire offered. *Yet there cannot always be mercy for men as far gone as them.*

Then what'll you do with the others? Hang 'em?

No, Allystaire thought. *They are coming with us to the peace congress.*

"You two are speaking to one another in your minds," Andus Carek suddenly said. The bard had been sitting with them in silence the entire time, eyes flitting from one to the other. "Don't look so shocked," he muttered, when both turned to glare at him. "Idgen Marte has told me of it. It is disconcerting. Even a bit rude," he added.

"She ought t'know what t'keep t'herself," Torvul muttered.

Andus Carek shrugged. "How am I to write the songs or pen the tales if I do not know the whole truth?"

"The day you get the whole truth from the dwarf, do let me know," Allystaire said. "I will want to mark it with a celebration."

Torvul sniffed. "I pride myself on keepin' you confused. Not that y'make it difficult."

"The two of you," Andus Carek said, "are more like brothers than any pair of men I've ever known. One minute you're staring daggers at one another, the next, scoring points with jests like formal duelists. Think on that," the bard said as he stood up, "while you sleep. Which you both ought to do, if you're planning on doing as much in the next few day as I imagine you are."

"And what do you imagine—" Allystaire began, but the bard began ticking his fingers as he cut Allystaire off.

"Holding a funeral. Dealing with any other prisoners or faithful the Order and Idgen Marte bring back from Ashmill Bridge. Preparing to leave for the peace congress while also seeing about the defense of the town. How are my guesses?"

"Not bad for a nosey, two-link singer," Torvul muttered.

"I will admit to being one of those, Master Alchemist," Andus Carek replied, grinning faintly. "And I will simply accept the other as praise from someone whose musical culture is rather different to my own," he added.

Allystaire sighed and stood, offering a light nod towards the minstrel. "You are right, Andus Carek. Sleep is something all of us need badly, I would wager."

The minstrel bowed lightly, and glided up the stairs almost soundlessly. Torvul was doing his best to mimic Andus Carek's quiet steps, and was halfway to the door before Allystaire realized it. If Torvul hurried, Allystaire couldn't see it, but the dwarf was out the door several moments before he was. Allystaire had to hasten to catch up.

Outside, Torvul was waiting for him, looking at the night sky. "He frightened me, Allystaire. That's why it all bothers me so much. I do not frighten easily, and the boy scared me. Even he doesn't truly understand what he's capable of, or what it was he did last eve."

"What did he do? You and he keep dancing around it."

"He dragged magic into the world like a man tearing down a dike to let water flood a field. That's what he did."

"Dragged magic into the world?"

"Remember I told you long ago to think of it like a vast underground river?"

"That the sorcerers leave half of themselves in, aye."

"He dragged it here, or…or punched a hole in the dam, or tore the whole thing down. I don't know. I could only feel the edges of it, and yet it was the most frighteningly powerful thing I've ever known. More so than the sorcerers, or priests of Braech, or the time I sang the Stonesong. I told him I'd stop him, that he needed t'wait. He told me I couldn't stop him, and Allystaire, so help me, he was right. I'd be as helpless as a babe if he turned on me. We all would."

"He will not turn on us, Torvul," Allystaire said calmly.

"That much power in anyone's hands is bound t'corrupt them."

Allystaire shook his head firmly. "Not him. Not ever."

"If you're goin' t'just stand there and say 'Faith, Torvul…'"

"Torvul," Allystaire said. "You do not know what the Goddess hoped for him. Neither do I, truly, but if what you say is true, this may well be it."

"You think She wants t'spread magic around, puttin' power in the hands of anyone?"

"That is exactly what I think She wants. If we could meet power with love and mercy and hope to survive, then we would—but we *cannot*. Yet if power could reside in anyone's hands? Aye, they may use it to gather more unto themselves. Or they might do as we have done, and choose to stand between the hearthfire and the darkness."

Torvul was silent, looked off into the darkened green, his hands hanging limp at his sides. "Having magic too ready to our hands was the downfall of my people, Allystaire. We did wonders with it, yes, and we also wrought sterile beauty, and frivolous toys, and we undid ourselves with the surfeit of it."

Allystaire moved to Torvul's side and laid a hand on the dwarf's shoulder. "Then help guide those who come along now, Torvul," he said. "Could it be that this is part of the Goddess's work for you?"

"I'll have enough work just keepin' you pointin' in the right direction," the dwarf grumbled.

"Moving ahead has never been my problem; it was seeing to my flanks."

"Well, ya've got Idgen Marte for that, and none better." Torvul crossed his arms over his chest. Allystaire could see a disapproving scowl deepening on the dwarf's face.

"Torvul, the night that we kept a vigil, the Mother told me that She called to me, that She put Her Gifts in my hands not—and these are Her words, mind—not to make me a better man, but to draw forth the goodness that was already within me. If you find yourself fearing the weight of the Gift She has settled upon Gideon, then I ask you to think of what goodness She must have seen within him. Think of the life he must have led, the endless, loveless cruelties of it, and then think of how willing he has been to learn, every day, how to be better than those who taught him. And then fear him no more. Gideon is learning to love, learning what he is willing to sacrifice, learning what it means to be *good* as well as great. If any one of us can change this world for the better, if any of us can save it, it will be him."

Allystaire turned and walked wearily off, leaving Torvul staring into the night.

CHAPTER 36

Dragon Scales No More

It was the rare morning that Allystaire found himself asleep on a bed, with real morning light pushing through the shutters instead of the weak pre-dawn grey he always expected when he awoke.

He found it hard to sit up, hard to force his eyes open.

Two forced rides in two days and you're a wreck. Get up, you old fool, he told himself. With a groan of effort, his legs and lower back protesting, he sat up.

"You haven't got time for lying about." Idgen Marte's voice cracked like a whip from a corner of the room, where the light from the window reached only feebly, in thin tendrils. He turned to find her leaning there, half in light, half in shadow, arms crossed over her chest. Her dark blue leathers were grimed with the dust of the road, her knee-high riding boots caked in mud.

"I never do," Allystaire muttered as he stood slowly, forcing his back straight despite its cramping protests. "In fact I should have been awake turns ago." He began hunting out his clothing, the blue trousers and vest a shade lighter than Idgen Marte's. His own dirty riding boots gave him pause; he held one up, frowning at the layers of hardening dirt. "Contemptible," he muttered.

"Need a new squire. Lucky for you I just brought all of them back to you."

"They are squires no longer. They are knights."

"Better tell them that, then," she said. "I brought prisoners, too—and some pilgrims. Folk who turned to worshippin' the Mother along with Shary after we visited back in the autumn."

Allystaire nodded as he dressed, hunted up a rag and a brush to give his boots at least the beginning of a polish. Suddenly he paused and looked back to Idgen Marte. "Where is Shary? I have not seen her in an age."

"She's after her own business," she replied. *A little too quickly*, Allystaire thought, turning to face her.

"Her business, or your business?"

"The Mother's work, then," Idgen Marte said with a shrug. "The less you know, the less you'll bother me about it."

"Idgen Marte."

"Allystaire," she said, raising her hands to cut him of, setting her lips firmly, scars livid against her brown skin. "You don't want t'know the work in the Shadows. Not all of it."

"Fair." He sat down, set one boot on a rag on the ground, and began to work the brush at the stiff flecks of dried mud.

"Why're you botherin'? They'll be dirty again in a turn."

"The first time I let my boots go unbrushed, it becomes easier to do so a second time, and a third. And then it is my armor not scoured, and then it is a weapon not oiled."

"If you didn't take care of your armor and hammer, I think Torvul'd poison you," Idgen Marte opined. "And you really do need a squire t'take care of that."

"They are not squires any longer, and I would ask none of them to brush my boots or curry my horse."

"Speaking of your horse, is he…"

"Ardent is fine," Allystaire said, almost absently, as he concentrated on dragging the stiff boar-bristles across the hard leather of the boot, sending dried mud flaking off in all directions.

"Uncanny. You rode him all night?"

"Aye," Allystaire answered. "You must have ridden pretty hard to get back here yourselves. Not that odd."

"We did it with a day of rest in between." She shrugged. "The Mother's miracles are not endless, but they are many," she muttered. "We did not get much out of the prisoners," she added. "But plenty out of the townsfolk. They came in the night, murdered any who'd resisted, rounded up anyone that said anything about the Mother, or the paladin."

Allystaire's brush stopped moving. The leather of his boot creaked as his hand tightened to a fist around it. "The berzerkers that attacked the village killed Chals, and one of Keegan's men. They meant to do much worse."

"You killed them?"

Allystaire shook his head. "No."

"Torvul, then?"

"Gideon. And he only killed one of them. The other two, he…well, best if you simply come see." Allystaire gave up the boots as a hopeless cause, pulled them on, belted his hammer onto his hip, and led Idgen Marte out the door.

In the hallway, they could hear a faint cascade of notes issuing from Gideon's lute. They were indistinct. Though they sounded fair to Allystaire's ear, Idgen Marte winced and started for the door to the boy's room. Allystaire laid a hand on her arm and shook his head.

"Let him play," he began to say, and she frowned harder.

"He's playin' poorly," she muttered. "And his chanterelle isn't tuned."

"Let him be," Allystaire insisted. "He did something immense the other night, and he needs time."

The music had stopped by then, and Gideon's door swung open. The boy came out carrying his cased lute, eyeing the two of them with disapproval written in his flat lips and lowered brows. "I might as well come with you so I can answer your questions. And look in on the prisoners."

"Takin' Dragon Scale prisoners is no small thing," Idgen Marte muttered. "They don't often stand for it."

"I didn't give them a choice," Gideon said as he hefted the lute case and headed down the stairs. "And, if put to it, they aren't Dragon Scales any longer. Not truly."

Idgen Marte turned a questioning glance at Allystaire, her brows lifted; he shrugged.

At the bottom of the stairs, Rede paced back and forth, muttering to himself. All three of them paused. In the silence of the later morning—most who would patronize the Inn were about their daily work—eventually his mutterings became clear. "Can't contain the sea in the firesongs alone. The singing cannot only be blamed. A rain upon all the world at once. The laughing man still buried. The songs remain to be sung to shape the rain."

Allystaire carefully stepped around Gideon, descended the stairs and put a hand to Rede's shoulder. Through the tattered monk's robe the man wore Allystaire could feel the heat of his skin. "Are you well, Rede?"

"The Eye. It will not stop. I cannot sleep. I cannot think. I haven't a moment."

Before he finished the thought, Idgen Marte was by his side, pressing a hand to the back of his head. "You can," she murmured. "For the next two turns, your mind will be clear and free. Lie down upon the floor, or a bench if you wish, and sleep, Rede. Dreams will not trouble you."

As if in a trance, the former monk nodded. Suddenly his face was cracked by an enormous yawn. As if he were a child hand-led by his mother, he lowered himself to a bench not far from the moderate hearthfire, stretched his length upon it, and was immediately asleep.

Gideon and Allystaire watched in silence. Idgen Marte shook her head as she rejoined them and they walked out into the late morning sunlight.

"It's going t'come to no good," she muttered, "keeping him around. Giving him hope that he'll be one with us."

"He has no hope of that," Allystaire muttered. "Only of providing some service. Despite the hard things the gods have done to that man, he wants to turn his hands to their work, somehow. Even a wretch can be admirable in his persistence."

"You've not forgotten what he did."

"Of course I have not," Allystaire replied. "Yet how much of that was Rede the man, and how much was the work of the Church of Braech?" He shook his head as they followed Gideon across the village green and up along a path past the small, trim houses. "Braech has been our enemy all along, I think. And now we will face the enormity of His rage."

"I'm not sure it's even his," Gideon said. "I think it is as much the men shaping the God as the God guiding the men," the boy said.

"If that's true, then what's to say the Mother doesn't change for us?" Idgen Marte didn't bother trying to hide the doubt in her voice.

"I believe She has," Gideon said. "Who, or what, She is now, is likely not what She was eons ago. May not be what She will be centuries hence."

Before either of them could press him on the implications, Gideon stopped before a shed. Idgen Marte and Allystaire laughed as they recognized it.

"What's funny?" the boy asked, his hand pausing on the lock.

"I spent a sleepless night sitting outside this very shed," Allystaire said, "defending the life of a boy I halfway thought should hang."

"Aye," Idgen Marte added. She pointed to the circling timber wall and said, "And I covered him from a tree that, well," she shrugged, "like as not is part o'that wall now."

"Who?"

"Norbert," Allystaire said. "Cold, it feels like a lifetime ago."

"Well," Gideon said, throwing open the door, "you're welcome to try and convert these two the way you did him. I sense you'll have no luck, though."

The opened door allowed a half circle of light into the cramped toolshed. Inside, two pathetic forms lay huddled upon the ground. Allystaire felt little but pity for them; sunken chests and thin arms that ended in mutilated hands; hollows around their wide and unhappy eyes, and now unreadable ink sketched into their loose skin. One feebly raised his head at the intrusion of light; the other merely threw an arm across his face.

"How were these two a threat?"

"They were Gauk and Onundr Dragon Scale," Gideon said. "Years ago, both men pledged themselves to Braech, swore to do sacred violence in His name. In return, Braech gave them a strength that few men have ever known, and other gifts that I did not have the time to study. They are, or were," he added, with a nod in Allystaire's direction, "the most fearsome holy warriors known to the world. Perhaps the most fearsome entirely. These men have raided Keersvasti ships, fought in wars for Barons, Mercator Princes, and shipping lords, murdered over trifles, and faced danger with a smile, knowing that glorious death would bring them a place at Braech's side, till His waters rise to claim the world, as they say."

"And what happened to them?" Idgen Marte's hand fell to her sword and she walked into the shed, ducking under a long bundle of dried herbs, one of many hanging from the low rafters. "I took all of that away. I drained Braech's

Gifts from them. Like a knife cutting open a wineskin," the boy said calmly. "Only instead of running on the floor I gathered it to me and put it towards another purpose."

"I tired of askin' questions, boy," Idgen Marte said. "So why don't ya say it all at once, to all of us."

"They know what I did," Gideon replied. "And Mol, at least, understands. I hope she approves. I know that Torvul does not, but that is because he is fearful, and I don't believe fear is a good enough reason not to take action."

Idgen Marte raised a hand, forefinger extended, her lips curling angrily.

"To take what action, I know, I know," Gideon said as he turned to peer at the former berzerkers. "I…" He sighed. "I took the power that sorcerers, and thaumaturgists, warlocks, hedge-wizards, and wise women the world over tap into, and I broke open the barrier between it and our world."

"What in the Cold does that mean?"

"It means," Gideon said, "that more folk are going to learn to do what the people I named can do. More are going to be born who can tap into it, and those who already can will do so more easily."

Allystaire, following them with eyes squinted against the sunlight, finally broke his silence. "Are children being born who can breathe fire?"

"Mayhap," Gideon answered. "More likely it means the man who has always felt a presence, something lying just out of sight, perhaps something that beckoned to them in the small turns, or the woman who has heard a glorious note hanging in the air but never a whole song around it—they are going to suddenly know more, learn more."

"Madmen, then?" said Idgen Marte. One of the prisoners lying on the ground reached for her leg. She took a quick half step away, lifting the toe of her other boot as if she was going to launch a kick, but thought better of it.

"Some, perhaps," Gideon said. "It would not be hard to be driven mad by the whisper that would never resolve into words, or to suspect that another world lies within your reach, only to find your hand moving through empty air every time you attempt to grasp it."

"Will they be like you, then?" Allystaire crossed his arms over his chest, tilted his head slightly to look at the boy.

"I do not think my particular gift will occur again, no," Gideon said. "But in the wake of what I have done, who can say? The men and women who come after me could work wonders one day."

"Or horrors," Idgen Marte said. "You don't give a child a knife and hope he teaches himself to use it."

"It is my plan to guide them," Gideon said. "Those that I can find, at least."

"How? When? We've got a peace congress starting to our east, an army to our north, and who Freezing knows what to our south or our west," Idgen Marte said.

"In point of fact, I do know what lies in those directions," Gideon said. "Or I can find out quickly enough. Last I saw, Baron Telmawr was moving north to Standing Guard Pass with his retinue. Landen is doing the same to our west. She is, in fact, not far from here."

"Why aren't you lookin' at Braech's army, then?" Idgen Marte said.

"Because it would give him away," Allystaire put in. "Surely Symod would sense it. We will only have that surprise once, so we had best make it count." He turned back to Gideon then, and said, "What is it you mean about guiding them, though?"

"When the war, or whatever it is that we must do here is done," the boy said calmly, "I have to leave. If I want anyone to follow after me, I cannot wait for them to find me."

"The Order of the Will?" Allystaire knew it was only half a question even as he said it.

Gideon nodded slowly. "I will coerce no one, conscript no one. Those that wish to learn from me shall. If I raise monsters, I believe I can also bring them down."

"Cold, you've a lot of confidence in you, lad," Idgen Marte said. "I suppose that's better than not," she admitted. "But the risk you've taken is immense."

"Something had to change, Idgen Marte," Gideon said. "Someone had to try and set right the balances of power in this world. It is not enough for men like the Dragon Scales that a poor man should always remain poor; he should be hungry and frightened, too. I can't change that there are poor. I can't change that there are hungry. But mayhap I can take away the fear, or I can change who fears whom, and that can lead to the rest," he added.

"What'll we do with them, anyway? They killed—" She caught sight of Allystaire's widened eyes and tried to swallow the words before they tumbled out.

"I know," Gideon said quietly. "They killed Chals. They terrorized his wife and son. They killed one of Keegan's men. One paid with his life. They paid with the strength their oaths had bought."

"If you only took their gifts, what has become of them?" The two thin, pale, sagging-fleshed men had sat up by then, regarding the three of them with open fear and suspicion.

"They had become dependent upon them. Braech gives richly; no longer did their strength need to be of their own doing," Gideon said. "With that gone, they are as you see them."

"I know precisely what we will do with them," Allystaire said. He squatted slowly, till he placed one knee upon the ground, looking at the former berzerkers eye to eye. "I will not hang them. Not yet. If it is death they wish, they will have to earn it."

CHAPTER 37

The Congress

Baron Hamadrian Innadan could barely sit upright. Cerisia knew that, could see it written in the lines of his face. His body was racked with pain from the coughing. Each breath was a searing effort that seemed to take as much life out of him as it brought.

And yet at the head of the table he sat, accorded that honor by the three Barons and two Baronesses who sat with him. Ruprecht Machoryn and Loaisa Damarind sat to his left, dressed in finery with their colors: blue and grey for him, black and red for her. Behind them, bannermen held the Mailed Fist and the Manticore banners, with their swords held fast to their scabbards with curls of brass wire. The eastern Baron and Baroness projected airs of mild disinterest as they studied their western counterparts. Jugs of wine and water were spaced along the table; before every place sat two goblets. Plates of cheese and fruit sat untouched at either end of the long wooden trestle.

"We ought to be on with it, cousin Innadan. The sun is well overhead already, and the day'll be away from us" The deep voice on the far side of the table put the Archioness in mind of old gnarled tree roots, so chewed-upon did the words sound. "Your man'll not show. And what does it matter? He's no Baron, holds no lands and no voice at this congress."

Never did a Baron's banner match the man himself so well, Cerisia thought as her eyes cut towards Unseldt Harlach. When people spoke of the White Bear, no one was ever sure if they meant the Baron or his standard. His beard and hair, long since gone white, were still thick and full, with the former hanging in silver-banded plaits down his broad, scale-armored chest. Eyes dark like temple doors in winter hung beneath a helmet-like shelf of brow. Cerisia hadn't met Unseldt Harlach often. Though her demesne extended within his lands, their remoteness and his hostility to anyone likely to cost him any weight had conspired to keep her and most of her fellow clergy away.

How much of the bear is posturing, and how much is truly himself? It wasn't the first time she'd wondered in the two days she'd spent so far among the camps at Standing Guard Pass. He was all bluff forthrightness, growling out his answers and challenging everyone around him to meet his gaze. *A man absolutely determined to be taken account of.*

Landen Delondeur sat to Harlach's left. If anything, she was more reserved than the eastern Barons that she, Harlach, Innadan, and Telmawr barely knew.

As the youngest and newest to her seat, Cerisia thought. *She is uncertain. Doubly so without Allystaire here.* Indeed, the young fair-haired Baroness's eyes kept trailing to the distant tower that marked the path of the pass that cut from her own lands into the far western reaches of Innadan where they now gathered.

"He'll show," Hamadrian wheezed in reply. "He'll show."

"What makes you so certain?" Byron Telmawr sat at Innadan's immediate right hand. He was a compact, intense man, his face and head both clean-shaven. He fairly vibrated with energy, despite his middle years. He seemed to Cerisia like the kind of man who resented every moment spent idle, or even seated. His fox banner mimicked his restlessness, flapping excitedly in the breeze that whipped around them.

"Because he's *Allystaire. Stillbright.*" Landen, finally, spoke up. "And when that man says he will do a thing, he does it."

Unseldt let out a low, rumbling harrumph. Landen reddened, betrayed by her fair skin and a winter spent indoors.

"I still know him as Allystaire Coldbourne," Harlach growled. "And—"

"And even then," Hamadrian cut him off, his voice rising from its wheeze with a supreme effort as the Baron Innadan leaned forward against the table, "he was a man of his word, Unseldt. You may not have *liked* his words, but he meant them."

Baron Harlach's upper lip curled beneath its heavy white whiskers, though he finally nodded reluctantly.

"Why such reverence for a rival's warlord, Hamadrian?" Though all the Barons sat in simple chairs, unadorned with heraldry or symbol of rank, something about the way Loaisa Damarind sat made hers seem more elegant than the others. *More like a throne*, Cerisia thought. The Baroness brought a grace that the others utterly lacked, her long limbs seemingly always moving at the exact and precise speed she wished: never slow, never hurrying.

"Oyrwyn was not a rival exactly," Hamadrian muttered, his voice dropping to a rasp that the other Barons strained forward to hear. Except for Loaisa, who focused her attention on Innadan's wizened face, concentrating on the words as he formed them. "The Old Baron was a friend at best, an ally at least, and for the last half-score years of his life, Allystaire was his right hand."

"Then why was he Exiled and Divested?" Ruprecht tilted his balding head slightly, reached for a goblet, and swirled the wine within it lazily. "Why would he abandon his liege lord's heir?"

"As much as the Old Baron—and his running dog Coldbourne—cost me, even I can say that Gilrayan Oyrwyn is no fit heir to his father." That was Harlach again, hunched shoulders and folded arms seeming to eclipse the scenery behind the table. His scale armor vest clinked as he spoke; it left his arms bare, and despite his age and the hash of scars that marred them, the bunching of muscles still promised a strength that men in the mountains of Harlach spoke of with reverence. "The Old Baron was my enemy, yes. But here was a foe a man could be *proud* to have. He never took the fight to my folk, never burnt or razed for the sake of the destruction itself, never hanged a man didn't want hanging so far as I know. He was a man, but his son?" Unseldt turned his head and spat on the nearest patch of grass. "Sneaky, thieving bastard. Starts fires at the base of watchtowers and won't accept an honorable surrender. Tries to turn my knights and lords with bribery, the promise of double their lands if they'll stand down to him. The first one who did it, he declared he couldn't trust, and had the man tossed from a cliff."

"If you admired Gerard Oyrwyn so very much, why did you fight him?" Landen raised her eyes from the smooth, polished oak of the table to Unseldt's face. "Many of the things you say about him could be echoes of my father's words to me down the years. Why fight a man you admire? Why not make peace with him? Why not see what you could achieve together, instead of at odds?"

Beneath her mask, Cerisia found herself smiling. *Allystaire got to you, my young Baroness Delondeur.*

"Pfaugh." Unseldt waved a giant hand, sitting back in his chair hard enough to shake the cups upon the table. "What would you know of it, lowlander? These feuds go back before your time. The mountains must be Harlach or Oyrwyn. There's not room for two banners."

Cerisia watched for Landen's reaction; she only just seemed to avoid rolling her eyes, but her fair cheeks did color. She opened her mouth to reply, but then their attention was suddenly drawn by the rapid approach of hooves. As one, the Barons and their advisors and bannermen turned to see two mounts pull up by the ring of knights that guarded the table at a distance of ten paces. Unlike everyone else in sight, these guards didn't have their swords peace-tied to sheaths, but most wore only lighter mail and no helms. They wore a riot of colors mixing the heraldry of their own lines with that of the Barons they served.

The ring of guarding knights parted for the two riders—Arontis, in red surcoat over gleaming mail, and Lurezia Damarind, a younger mirror of her mother—who slid from their mounts, but not before they surrendered their weapons.

"There's a party approaching from the west," Arontis called out, as he came within shouting distance. He was a bit winded, his boots and the lower edges of his surcoat spattered with mud, as were Lurezia's. "I think it may be the paladin."

The Barons all stood up. Cerisia glided to Hamadrian's side and discreetly helped him stand. In his pride, he refused a walking stick or a sedan chair to move about the camp, so for the past few days, the Archioness had been his prop when Arontis hadn't been available, which had been often.

Lurezia Damarind was rarely unescorted around the campsite, and Cerisia had found herself having to temper her own disappointment at the emptiness of her bed with her satisfaction at seeing Arontis coming gracefully into his own.

"Well, let us go have a look at him." Unseldt Harlach's voice was either a growl or a roll of thunder, and this proclamation was the latter; it drowned out the reactions of those around him. "Not that Coldbourne was ever much to look at."

The guarding ring of knights didn't dissipate so much as it expanded as the Barons made their way—slowly, out of deference for Hamadrian—from their central, formal table to the western edge of the camp. The small retinues of soldiers had made neat camps, arranged in a ring around that central hub, with one large flat space of meadow left untouched.

Mountains hemmed the wide plains of this far western corner of Innadan to its north and its west. Standing Guard Pass had gotten its name from the proximity of so many Baronies, and passes through the nearly intersecting ranges that led to this green valley. The spires of watchtowers could be seen by keen eyes on all sides. Delondeur, Oyrwyn, Harlach, and Innadan had, through decades of shifting alliances and nonstop war, been watching each other carefully from this place.

Cerisia was able to slip away from Hamadrian when Arontis glided in to take his father's arm. She let the knot of Barons pass her, trying to observe any pattern of who walked with whom. That Machoryn and Damarind stuck by one another was no surprise to her; they had long since settled any bad blood between their Baronies on the other side of the empty Vale of Kings. Landen Delondeur walked by herself, but eagerly; she was clearly most anticipating Allystaire's arrival. Byron Telmawr stayed as close to the Old Baron Innadan and his son as he could without seeming weak. And then there was Unseldt Harlach, his tree-trunk legs rolling along beneath the great bulk of his chest, all fur and scale armor, muscle and bluster, the proudest to be here on his own and unsupported, the one who seemed like he'd most welcome a fight.

Bored soldiers guarded the outer edge of the camp, and as the party walked up a slight rise she saw a few of them, in Innadan red, peering into the middle distance, spears casually held against one shoulder. She followed the line of their gaze and saw a knot of riders approaching.

Even from afar, Cerisia knew the size and the stride of the great grey destrier at their head, and with the sun straight overhead, there was no mistaking the brightness thrown back by the armor its rider wore.

Watching Allystaire Stillbright ride Ardent at full tilt across the grassy plains of Innadan was a sight Cerisia knew would remain with her for the rest of her days. The brightness of his armor was nearly blinding when the sun caught it right, but if the eye lingered, the sight resolved into something she wasn't sure was natural. A cloud of light haloed around him under the noonday sun, and notes of silvery music seemed to hang in the air. The day grew warmer, brighter, as his party drew nearer, as if the paladin's presence brought the sun itself closer to them. Cerisia spared a glance for the Barons; she found Hamadrian squinting and Landen standing confidently, her back straighter than it had been in the two days since the Congress had started. For the first time since he'd arrived, doubt crept into Unseldt Harlach's face, his easy confidence melting away into wariness, as the lines of age seemed to thicken and deepen on his cheeks and brow. Loaisa Damarind smiled cooly, her eyes narrowing lightly. Byron Telmawr watched Hamadrian's face.

Ruprecht Machoryn took an involuntary half-step backwards, and Cerisia suppressed a laugh.

"Don't challenge them," Hamadrian called out to the soldiers who were stepping forward diffidently, though it didn't seem any had actually intended to. The destrier had pulled ahead of the rest of the party. There seemed to be a half dozen of them all told, but the great grey horse had simply left the rest behind and the paladin was upon them before it even seemed possible.

His armor was dazzling. She heard several breaths drawn and held as the mirrored, silver-bright plate spun rays of sunlight over the eyes of the gathered knights and Barons.

Allystaire slid from his horse and walked forward, passing by the ring of soldiers and never sparing a glance for the knights; his eyes were for the Barons behind them. As he came within a few paces, the dazzling light around him receded, and his hammerblow of a face resolved itself. That was the only word that struck her as appropriate for the violence coded in his features: the oft broken and wayward nose, the scarred brow, the cold and hard eyes beneath them, the battered cheeks and lump of a chin.

If his face was a weapon, though, his voice was a drum and a trumpet together, sounding a charge.

"I am Allystaire Stillbright," he said. "And I bring you word of an army massing in the north. Islandmen, Braechsworn, giantkin, and likely sorcery. They are not out for land, or rights, or succession. They want blood, gold, and glory. If my word will not do, I bring prisoners who will speak to the truth of it.

So I have come not only to ask you for peace, but to lay the question before you: are you man and woman enough—are you *noble* enough—to go to war when the stakes are the lives of your people and not the lines on a map?"

Cerisia felt her breath catch at the boldness of his gambit. Unseldt Harlach bulled his way past Landen and Telmawr to close on the paladin. Allystaire was a big man, with unmistakable presence, but Harlach dwarfed him.

"Watch where your words fall, Coldbourne. The White Bear's taste for battle is second to no man's, but it only goes to war when and where I deem it will." His voice was a throated growl on the breeze.

"I would never insult your taste for war, Unseldt. Your skill at guiding it, mayhap," Allystaire replied coolly.

Harlach's hand fell to an empty loop at the wide, gem-studded belt around his capacious waist, grasping for an axe that wasn't there, but Allystaire simply went on.

"That brings me quick upon my real business here. I will waste no time with subtleties or politics. This threat is real, the army is real, and an army must meet it. In my past life, some of you knew me as an enemy, some as an ally, but I believe that all of you would agree that when it comes to the leading of an army, how to fight in this country, I have some claim of renown. So here, in short, is my offer to you. Put the terms of a peace upon paper. It begins instantly. Raise such men as you can, starting with those you have brought here, and those you all left at your nearest borders. I will put myself at your disposal to direct them in battle, if you will have me." He turned his hard eyes back on Unseldt. "I would never doubt your bravery, my Lord Baron Harlach. Yet every time we met, I won the day. No one standing here can say they ever had the better of me in the field as often as I had it of them. I will put everything I know at the disposal of saving your lands and people from Braech's army."

Cerisia sensed a balance forming, a knife's edge over which the paladin was walking, but she could not yet see the substance of the threat he was negotiating.

Harlach saw it too, as he snorted and waved a huge hand dismissively. "If you've become what the tales say then you'd do as much anyway. Why need we put our names on some treaty on your demand?"

"There is a truth in your words, Baron, yet you do not understand completely. I said I would put myself at your disposal, to lead such men as you will lend me if you compose and sign a treaty that ends, for once and all, the ridiculous wars we have spent our lives fighting. If you do not?" Allystaire shrugged lightly, yet Cerisia felt the weight of the world tilting on his movements. "Then I will raise an army regardless, of all who are willing to flock to the Mother in the name of defending themselves. And when the Braechsworn that threaten us all now are defeated, I will do nothing to stand between them and any Baron whose name is not on a treaty."

There was a moment of near total silence, broken only by the rustling of grass, the spring stirrings of nearby birds. Cerisia felt a shiver sprint down her back; the danger in what Allystaire proposed was frighteningly real.

And, she quickly understood, very close to the fears the Barons had brought with them to this Congress.

"So that's your game at last, Coldbourne!" Harlach's heavy cheeks had gone read beneath the white of his beard. "Threaten us all into laying down arms or you'll raise the peasants and toss us all off our own walls, I don't doubt! I notice that Gilrayan Oyrwyn is nowhere to be seen. Curious that the son of the man who held your leash all these years would be exempt from what you propose. No. I'll not have it, not from Oyrwyn's running dog!"

Landen and Hamadrian both turned to Harlach, opening their mouths in protest, but the White Bear had rolled right over their words with his own. When, finally, he paused to draw breath, it was Allystaire that addressed him.

"My name," he quietly insisted, "is Allystaire Stillbright. But I do not disclaim responsibility for the things I did when you knew me as Coldbourne, Baron Harlach. I did not have it in me then to look truly at the cost of what I did, beyond the death of my own men. All the death, the widows and orphans made. The people displaced. The livelihoods destroyed. The carefully tended farms gone to rot and ruin. I count the cost of my sins every day, Baron Harlach—and in what I have done in the service of the Goddess so far is but the merest sliver of the weight of recompense I still owe. I will be paying for them till I die, and even then I would deserve little more than the eternal Cold. If you wish an apology for the pieces of your Barony I sliced off in Gerard Oywyn's name, I am prepared to make one."

Unseldt Harlach drew himself up, lifting his chin. He drew his words out slowly. "Is that so? How do you figure to make rep—"

Allystaire's lip curled in disgust, and Harlach's softer words were cut off by the sound of the paladin's gauntleted hand curling into a fist.

It was, Cerisia had to admit, one of the more menacing sounds she had ever heard.

"I never said I was prepared to apologize to you," the paladin shot back, cracks finally showing in his composure, his voice rising to a shout. "To your *people*, Unseldt, for it is them I sinned against, not you. Never you. Shrinking the borders of your Barony might have hurt your pride. You can afford to lose some of that. Your people paid with so much more. And I am here, now, offering my recompense to *all* your people," Allystaire said, pivoting away from a fuming Harlach to address the rest of the gathered powers. "Whether I have your signatures on a treaty or not, I will save them from Braech's host. I can do it with your help, lords and ladies. Or I can do it in spite of you. Your people will know which it is. I would say that it is time for all of you to remember what you owe to your people, rather than counting what they owe to you."

Allystaire turned and looked back to where he'd come; the rest of his party pulled up at the edges of the camp. Cerisia was unsurprised to see Torvul sitting atop the board of his boxy, rune-carved wagon home, pipe dangling from his mouth, leading his ponies with the lightest flicks of the reins, nor Gideon riding competently on a small grey palfrey. Idgen Marte seemed uncomfortable to be out in plain sight atop a brown courser. Though she rode expertly, she seemed on edge, her gaze darting endlessly from side to side. The remainder of the company she found somewhat puzzling, like the village youth with the scar on his face.

Three of them had lances booted next to their right-hand stirrups, within easy reach. All three also had a bundle tossed across the haunches of their mounts, which she quickly realized were bound prisoners. One struggled weakly; the other two barely moved. She blanched, glad of the mask that hid her features.

"I must see to a camp for my companions," Allystaire said. "I will come to speak to you again in a turn or so, and you can hear what my prisoners have to say."

"Whatever you tell them to, no doubt!" Harlach seemed to have found his voice again, but this time, the other Barons had had enough, though it was Landen who spoke.

"Enough, Unseldt," the young Delondeur Baroness spoke, exasperation threading through her voice. "I am tired of your bluster, and I am certain the rest of us are as well. The paladin has come to save us from ourselves, if we will but allow him the chance." She turned to Hamadrian. "I will sign whatever document Allystaire draws up. He has extended his trust to me once, and I will do the same for him."

The rest of the Barons began talking over one another in a rush, with Harlach trying to seize the moment again, and Hamadrian all but begging them for silence, but Cerisia's eyes were locked on the paladin as he walked away, nimbused in light.

CHAPTER 38

Limits

"You're not as much of a showman as you think, boy," Torvul said as he and Allystaire were unloading the supplies from one of the pair of pack mules they brought, while Norbert and Harrys worked on the other, and Tibult and Armel set up tents with the bored professionalism of soldiers.

"Well, that is why you are here, Torvul," Allystaire said as he set down a pack-saddle bag. "I have struck at them with such blunt force as my voice can muster. Later, you can speak to them with silk, or with daggers, or…" Allystaire trailed off and waved a hand. "With the metaphor of your choice."

"Might be daggers'd be best for the entire lot," Torvul muttered as he paused to wipe his brow with the sleeve of his jerkin. "Just clear them out and start over."

"Every one of the Barons gathered here has goodness within them, Torvul. If their people are to have a chance, we must find the ways to bring it forth. Otherwise all is lost."

"I wonder if you'd say that if the one who exiled you was here," the dwarf replied as he set down the last bag and unlatched it with a quick flick of his nimble wrist.

"I had left by the time he exiled me," Allystaire answered with a shrug.

"One of these days, we're gonna need the tale of just how that happened." They were both used to Idgen Marte's unexpected appearances, but this time she hadn't jumped into a nearby shadow, but had just sauntered up quietly while they were absorbed in work.

"Simple," Allystaire said with a shrug. "I got on Ardent and rode off to Coldbourne Hall, buried most of the family wealth, packed what I needed, and rode south."

"That's not what I meant," Idgen Marte cut him off sharply, "and you know it. What made you decide to leave?"

"It was an accumulation of things," Allystaire replied with a shrug. He seized and bent the straps of several packs, carried them to the center of camp, making sure all the flaps were pulled wide with the toe of one boot. Inside were thin loaves of twice-baked biscuits, smoked meat, cheese, dried fruit, all wrapped in waxed cloth and bound with twine.

Torvul looked down at their rations and pulled free a flask from his belt. "Why were you so insistent on a humble camp, again?"

"It will send a message. I will not be counted among the Barons," Allystaire said. "I will not be rude to them, but neither will I feast with them."

"Enough o'that," Idgen Marte said with a grimace. "And no changin' the subject. What d'ya mean, an accumulation of things?"

Determined to keep busy, Allystaire walked over to the rough picket line of horses and began unstrapping Ardent's saddle. The horse looked up from the grass as soon as Allystaire approached, whickered softly, nudged his great head against the paladin's.

"As I said, an accumulation of things. Too much hunger for conquest. The boy got his Baronial seat when a brother died, and instead of mourning, he saw it as the stamp of grand destiny. He did not mourn for Ghislain; he reveled, with an eye on a throne, or at least a higher seat, and little scruple about how to get it. The common folk, even the soldiers, were grist for the mill. A knight who dared to speak his mind could face exile and divestiture no matter how long and faithfully he had served the Old Baron." Allystaire shrugged. "The last argument I had with him, I will keep to myself. For now."

"Why?"

"It will have more impact if I tell the story once Gilrayan is here," Allystaire muttered.

"And what makes you so sure this bastard is comin', eh?" Torvul looked speculatively at his flask and held it out to Allystaire, who shook his head, then to Idgen Marte, who took it and swigged.

"He will come," Allystaire said. "In fact," he said, turning to the northwest and gesturing towards the hills that rose into the mountains where Oyrwyn, Harlach, Delondeur, and Innadan all came together, "unless I miss my guess, he is probably up there now, where he can watch us and decide how to make his entrance."

"Didn't answer my question," Torvul replied as he took his flask back from Idgen Marte and tucked it back into its case on his belt.

"He will come because to be excluded from such a gathering would wound his pride. He may come because he has heard my name attached to it. And then there is the chance that he may come with an army in the hopes of catching so many other lords with only a token force about them. Or it may be some combination of all three."

Allystaire looked, as he spoke, to where Gideon was learning how to properly shore up a tent under Harrys's instruction. "And I mean to find out as soon as camp is made."

* * *

There were only a few more needful tasks before their camp was indeed made. Allystaire carried his saddle into the tent he was meant to share with Gideon, only to find the boy and Norbert setting up some camp furniture he hadn't known was to be packed.

A chair and folding desk, a washbasin, a pair of cots, an armor stand and a small rack for weapons had turned what was meant to be a spacious tent into a rather crowded one. Norbert was fussing with the pegs on the folding table when he felt the weight of Allystaire's glare.

"I know you said you wanted a humble camp," Norbert muttered as he tested the table's stability with the flat of his hand. Finding it satisfactory, he stood up, met Allystaire's gaze straight on.

"Go on," Allystaire muttered, while reflecting briefly on the changes the months of training had wrought in Norbert. There was no more hesitancy in him, no halting speech, no fidgeting of gangly limbs. Now he was calm, confident, and never leaking nervous energy. None of his movements were wasted; he was simply *there*, ready, in a way Allystaire had long since known as the mark of a competent man in a fight. The scar on his cheek no longer seemed like something marring his features. His face had grown into it.

"But there's humble, and then there's foolish," Norbert said. "You may'nt need a giant silk pavilion and a bevvy of servants like the Barons, but you need a place to set your arms and to write if you've a need."

"And why can I not stack my arms with the rest of you? Or store my armor in a sack as you will?"

"We're the Order of the Arm," Norbert replied. "You *are* the Arm. It's different." He bore up under Allystaire's hard blue gaze for a moment longer before saying, "N'it was Harrys's idea. He packed it all."

Allystaire sighed faintly and clapped Norbert's shoulder. "Then I absolve you of any blame, if there was any to be given out. If I could have a moment with the Will?"

Gideon sat on his cot, knees drawn up under him, reading a book. Allystaire peered down at it, found it full of unreadable marks that looked as much carved into the paper as printed.

"Dwarven charactery," Gideon said without looking up. "It is advanced grammar and rhetoric. Torvul says I must understand it before I can begin to comprehend the apprentice books of formulae, magical theory, or metaphysics."

"How long have you known Dwarfish charactery?"

Gideon looked up from the book, shrugging and closing it around one finger to keep his place. "I started reading the early primer on the ride from Thornhurst. It classifies the characters by their connections to metallic ores or precious stones, both literally in their descriptions and figuratively in their principles. It is quite fascinating."

Allystaire blinked slowly, lips creasing. "You have moved from beginning the language to advanced grammar and rhetoric in a few days of travel?"

"Since the night back at the holy spring," Gideon said, "everything has come easier since then. It is like the world is unlocking itself for me. Magic runs through all of it, in ways I never expected. If I close my eyes and visualize you standing before me, I can pick out the glamour Torvul laid upon your armor, and the strong bonds he nearly unknowingly put upon the metals in your hammer. I almost fancy I can see the Goddess's own writing upon your throat, condemning you to speak the truth. I can hear the soothing music of Healing in your left hand, and the drum-beat of Her strength in your blood."

"And this facility with language—it is magical, somehow?"

"Language is fundamentally magical," Gideon quickly replied. "That seems obvious. But Dwarfish moreso than most, for magic was such a part of the culture. I am not sure I am explaining very well."

"Consider your audience. I understand these things best as practicalities, Gideon. Explain to me what it is that you can do with this newfound power."

"It is not power. Not in that sense. My Gift is unchanged; I can still take in power and redirect it how I choose. I cannot simply absorb it from the world now that it has leaked out, though at times I swear I see it flowing around me, from the corner of my eye, perhaps. Then I turn to catch it and it vanishes into the air. Even so, I think this change is longer-term than the immediate challenge."

"Fair enough," Allystaire replied. "I need you to take a look into the mountains to our north, northwest, for signs of Baron Oyrwyn. I strongly suspect he is lurking there."

"Where should I look? There is rather a lot of mountain, if you hadn't noticed," Gideon said dryly.

"Well, if I can find parchment and ink I can draw you a map."

"Norbert left a bundle of parchment, a pen, and a pot on his way out, while you weren't looking." Gideon pointed, and Allystaire followed his hand.

"So he did." Carefully, Allystaire eased himself into the camp chair set in front of the table and stripped off his gauntlets, glad, not for the first time, of the cunning adjustments Torvul had made to the straps and buckles of his armor. The gauntlets were off in no time, set aside, and he had soon pulled the cork from the bottle of ink, dipped the pen, and selected a sheet.

Allystaire closed his eyes and visualized Standing Guard Pass. It was a collection of passes, really, where the various mountain ranges let out into the descending hills, then the plains, of Innadan, and the Vale of Kings beyond. So many Baronies jammed together had made it a point of contention during the decades of the Succession Strife, but the narrowness of the mountainous outlets had always made it easy for Innadan to defend it.

With his eyes still closed, his hand started sketching. First an X to mark the camp, then, above it, quick slashes to denote the passes outletting into the mountains north and northwest, then a wider pair for the west. He considered a moment, biting back a feeling of foolishness, as he drew sharp points to denote mountains, filling in the spaces around the slashes. He bit his lower lip, considered them, then put in small circles for watch towers, and drawing lines for trails, three that he knew of that went up into Oyrwyn, two into Harlach.

Gideon came and stood over his shoulder, muttered, "I can see why they have come to call it Standing Guard Pass."

"It was always a rather obvious joke, lad, but you are hardly wrong."

"It seems a vulnerability for Innadan. Why has he never built a keep here, on the border of so many potential enemies?"

"Well," Allystaire said, as he bent low over the parchment as he carefully traced the path of the trails. "It is nearly impossible to get enough men through any one of them fast enough, or in good enough order, to overwhelm any Innadan response. Then there are the watchtowers, and the eyes always watching, ruling out surprise. Innadan usually keeps a strong presence of horse, and fast remounts for messengers to get to the Vineyards, near enough to meet any invader." Allystaire blew over a spot of still wet ink and let his fingertip hover over the pass that led back into Barony Delondeur.

"The western pass is by far the widest, as you have seen. Yet to come through it, Delondeur has to expose a flank to Oyrwyn animosity or Harlach opportunism. Innadan and Oyrwyn have long worked hand in hand, and Harlach was too often busy fighting us—Oyrwyn, I mean." Allystaire corrected himself with a frown. "Too busy fighting Oyrwyn, or dealing with runoff of giantkin, raiding elves, or lawless men on the tundra beyond."

"Men live north of Harlach?"

"Aye," Allystaire said. "Most of them are running or hiding from something, but there are simply those who are born there and know nothing else, do what they can to eke a living from what arable land is left beyond the borders the White Bear cares to keep. Warbands spend quite a bit of time there, coming south when there is work, moving north to defend, or prey upon, the folk there. There are only a few proper towns that far north, and desolate places they are,

I am sure. If we can deal with this army of Braechsworn…" He sighed, letting his words trail off.

Gideon rested a hand on his shoulder, the plates of the armor shifting beneath the boy's touch. "We cannot minister to everyone in the world, all at once. Do what we can, until we do what we must, aye? Well, Symod's threat is the must."

"I know, son," Allystaire muttered. "I know." He squeezed his eyes shut for a moment, then opened them to the parchment. He moved his fingertip over a place where two of the Oyrwyn trails intersected. "Here. There is enough space to stage a small force, it is close enough to Oyrwyn's towers to stay in contact and it could easily be supplied, as it connects straight to the road that leads up to Wind's Jaw."

For a moment, the paladin's finger lingered over the very tip of the trail. In his mind he had a brief glimpse of a tower, a hidden parapet, the grass, and the flowers growing upon it, but he pushed the thought away. "If Oyrwyn is here, that is where I would start looking."

"Anything in particular I should look for?"

"If you have the time and can see close enough, count the tents. That will give us some rough idea of the men he has. The colors they wear, any badges. I will know them."

"As you say," Gideon said. "I will start now, if you like. And Cerisia will be here in a few moments to speak with you."

"How do you know that?"

"I can feel the laws of chance bend around the potential of Fortune's Gift expressed through her will," Gideon said. "It is not a great power as we might account it, but we have seen her use it to good effect. Go outside and meet her so she does not see me, please."

With that, the boy went back to his cot, and stretched out. Allystaire watched for a moment as his prone form relaxed, his breathing slowed. To the casual observer, Gideon appeared lifeless. He went outside to find Norbert standing a few paces away, leaning casually on a spear.

Allystaire clapped him on the shoulder, leaned close, and muttered, "Stay near this tent. Until Gideon comes out, the only folk you let in are me, Torvul, or Idgen Marte. Understood?"

Norbert stood up straighter and nodded sharply. Allystaire returned the nod, then looked up to see Cerisia's golden mask approaching him. He stepped away from Norbert and greeted her with a shallow bow. The Archioness extended her hand, which he briefly took, but did not kiss.

"Sir Stillbright." Her voice was, as always, a bit muffled by the mask she wore, and yet he thought he could hear worry in it. "Would you take a brief walk with me?"

He nodded and bent his elbow. Laughing lightly, she rested her hand upon his armor. Allystaire found himself wishing that he hadn't left his gauntlets upon the table in his tent.

* * *

Gideon was hardly surprised to find Oyrwyn men precisely where Allystaire had said they would be.

He hovered above their encampment, which was cunningly hidden from sightlines along the mountainside, by the means of scrubby bushes dragged into paths, piles of dead wood or rocks that appeared to have fallen.

Quickly, he gave up on counting the tents. There were many—far more than any of the Barons below had gathered with them—and he felt certain there were other camps nearby. But this seemed the primary staging area, for at its center sat a large silken pavilion, grey, shot through with strands of silver thread, with black mountains embroidered upon it. Though it bore no pennant, the plate-armored knights standing before its entrance assured Gideon that he knew who occupied it.

He did manage to study the men moving about. Not the knights, whose heraldry was too varied, and of whom there were at least a dozen, but the men-at-arms. Most seemed to be lightly armored, and wearing a dark grey similar to the pattern on the pavilion, though the device on their chest wasn't a simple black mountain: a coil of grey wound around the mountain itself. Behind the mountain, in red, were implements he didn't recognize, one that looked like a three-pronged hook, and one a thin-bladed axe.

No one in the camp seemed to recognize him or see him moving about above them, though there was one priest of Braech at least, judging by the sea-blue pavilion near the grey one. He felt no music of power from it, no note of the will, no tang of salt air.

Still, Allystaire's suspicions were confirmed and could be reported.

With a flicker of will that, if anyone else could have perceived it, would've looked like a raptor beating its wings to ascend, Gideon did just that. Standing Guard Pass, the camp, and the congress going on within it all receded from his view, and he looked out over a green and living map of the western Baronies.

He strained his senses. It would not be true to say he heard, or tasted, or saw, yet it was somehow all of these things at once, that brought him the knowledge he sought.

The Will of the Mother strained to know the presence of other powers, little flickers of magic. As though he were, with his hands, which were hundreds or thousands of paces below his will, peeling wet pieces of parchment away from one another, he peeled away layers of perception, until he viewed the world as a space featureless but for beacons of power.

There was his own self, but that was easy to ignore. Beneath him were Allystaire, Idgen Marte, Torvul, Cerisia, another minor priest or two scattered throughout the encampment, he thought.

He could see the bright blue vibrancy that was Thornhurst. Perhaps it was Mol; perhaps, when in Thornhurst, the place and the Voice were one and the same.

Distantly, so distantly he was not sure of its physical location, there was something almost overwhelming. Something of primal, a roaring font of power. Yet it was bottled, contained.

Gideon decided he preferred it that way, and sent his senses further. Beyond it, a presence and a power he knew, a sickly and bilious green cloud.

The Eldest.

Almost, he sent a tendril of his consciousness towards that hateful blot. Yet he held back, thinking on what Torvul might say about surprise.

Then he thought on what Allystaire would do, and he reached out anyway.

The contact was brief; he did not want the sorcerer to know his true strength, where he was, or what he could do.

When he pulled his senses together near the Eldest, he knew the being to be on a ship, at sea. There were other powers traveling with him, more Dragon

Scales. Dozens of them, all of them carrying the same power he had taken from the two in the village.

Gideon wanted to smash the boat they rode on to splinters, to pluck it from the waves and hurl it into the air, letting it, and those on it, fall where they may.

Yet there was a crew upon it as well, tending to it, keeping it moving; the Eldest and the Dragon Scales would have no part of such mundane work. So he settled for drawing forth a ray of sun into the cloud of darkness that surrounded the Eldest in the largest cabin on the boat.

He touched the sorcerer's mind for the briefest of moments.

There is nowhere you can go, he said, *where the Sun will not lead me to you. So continue sailing towards me, Eldest. Towards the Negation, and your death. It will be easier for both of us.*

Gideon only felt the merest flicker of the sorcerer's rage, and he outraced easily whatever power the Eldest hurled at him as his Will carried him back to his body, hundreds of miles away.

* * *

No one who was alive at that moment could have seen the bird that was Gideon's will in its speed-of-thought travel. The only few who could have perceived it and known what they were seeing lurked in covens and coteries in distant lands, fearing and fretting over the stirrings of tremendous power they had felt in the past weeks.

Yet as he flickered across the Baronies, here and there, in city, town or village, children—a dozen, maybe a score at most, and all young—suddenly looked towards the sky and then the east, not knowing why.

One infant's tears turned suddenly to laughter as his eyes followed the track of the Will, not comprehending it. Another woke from mid-afternoon sleep crying as something she wanted pulled inexorably away from her, though she could not understand what it was.

A boy just old enough to help with the spring planting, barefoot, carrying a sack nearly as big as himself over one shoulder, let a handful of seeds fall in a pile to the ground as he stared at the sky.

As he darted past, even the Will of the Mother did not quite notice the stares of these children, or the tiny, tiny sparks that were flickering in them even now.

* * *

"You have to go and see Hamadrian, in privacy," Cerisia said urgently as soon as she and Allystaire were out of Norbert's earshot.

"I certainly need to speak to him, but right now?"

"No," the priestess said, her hand clutching hard at his forearm. "You have to heal him. He is dying, Allystaire. It is nearly a miracle that he has lasted so long. The spring air helps, certainly, but his lungs are giving out on him. Every breath is a struggle."

Allystaire paused and lowered his head, only for a moment. He lifted it back up, straightened his shoulders, and said quietly, "Is he with the other Barons?"

"I convinced them to agree to two turn's respite. He will be in his tent."

"Take me to him."

They passed the distance in silence. Red-surcoated guards and knights simply nodded as they passed, with the Archioness serving as Allystaire's pass through any challenge. When they finally reached a great silk pavilion, green vines crawling over its red walls, with the Vined Great Helm fluttering lightly atop it, the two knights outside stepped together to block the entrance.

One, a man a few years younger than Allystaire, with a sandy beard beneath his open helm, gestured to the hammer on the paladin's belt.

"Not armed in the Baron's presence," he said stiffly.

"The Baron has nothing to fear from me," Allystaire replied mildly.

"Is this truly necessary, Sir Gladden?" Cerisia took a half-step towards the knight who barred their way, her voice quiet beneath the mask.

Allystaire sighed, but reached for his hammer and had it halfway from its loop when the tent flaps parted and another red-surcoated knight appeared. Unlike the pair in front of the pavilion, the surcoat over his mail was not quartered with any other symbol. It displayed only the Vined Helm.

"Do not bar the paladin's way, Gladden." Arontis's voice was sure and steady, Allystaire thought, confident in his orders. *Addressing the man familiar, without his title, yet it hardly seems an insult.* Allystaire spared a glance for the guard, who seemed stung, but not angry, acknowledging his orders with a simple nod, and stepping away.

The Innadan heir's back was straight, his shoulders wide, and his face worked to betray nothing. But there were bags under his eyes and he couldn't decide whether to look at Allystaire or Cerisia.

"Come in, paladin," Arontis said, a bit more stiffly than he'd ordered the guard.

The passage from under the afternoon sun into the silk pavilion threatened to dim the world's light. The silken walls held within them a miasma of illness, and far more heat than should've been necessary. In a large central bed, Hamadrian Innadan lay a shivering, wasted form beneath a pile of blankets. Braziers, lit and tended by a pair of liveried valets, made a semi-circle around his resting place.

In a chair by his side sat a man dressed in a long black robe with his sleeves rolled up to the elbow, a large leather case at his feet. He stood up and stepped away from the bed, bowing deeply in Allystaire's direction. The valets did likewise.

Allystaire couldn't keep the frown from his face, though he regretted it when he saw one of the valets take half a step backwards and sink to one knee.

"You need not kneel to me," he muttered. "Any of you. If there is anyone in this camp deserving of your homage, it is the man lying here," he added as he crossed to Hamadrian's bedside with two quick steps.

The chirurgeon's chair was there, and he could've pulled it closer, sunk into it.

Instead, grimacing as the joint took the weight, Allystaire sank to a knee before Hamadrian Innadan and reached out to take his hand.

The skin of the old Baron's left hand was thin, clammy. The pulse beneath it was faint and slow. Allystaire let his senses drift, searched for memories of Innadan. The Baron as a younger, heartier man, in one of Allystaire's first battles outside Aldacren Keep, never hesitant, never cowardly, but always slightly sickened by what he saw. The first attempt at a peace congress outside his own halls seven years ago, vainly, almost plaintively going from Baron to Baron and lord to lord, trying to get them to end their revels, their jousting and gaming and drinking, and talk seriously of peace.

Allystaire found the spark of life within the old, tired, dying man whose hand he grasped. He felt the weakness of the lungs, the disease that attacked them.

The paladin thought on how he'd ignored Hamadrian's pleas for peace those years ago, and he gathered in his left hand as much of the Mother's Gift, as much compassion, as much regretful sorrow as he could, and he poured it through his hand and into the Baron's body.

Hamadrian sat up in his bed and cried out sharply. The chirurgeon rushed to the bedside, loomed over Allystaire's shoulder. Allystaire held tightly to the Baron's hand, listened carefully as the old man drew in a deep breath.

It rattled in his chest and he coughed, the spasm of it racking his chest beneath the dressing gown he wore. The paladin reached out with his gift again, pushing the warm healing music of the Mother into Hamadrian's lungs.

Not every affliction will fall to this gift.

Allystaire heard the words as if for the first time, weighted heavily with sorrow, but he knew that he had heard them before, kneeling beside an oak tree before the Mother on his ride out of Bend.

He let go of Hamadrian's hand, and looked up, meeting one sharp eye and one clouded and milk white.

"What'd you do, lad? Stung like the Cold inside my lungs," Hamadrian rasped, tapping his chest.

"I tried to heal you, my Lord Baron," Allystaire replied.

"What do you mean tried? I feel ready to ride, fight, feast and fu—" He stopped, cleared his throat, eyes having flitted briefly towards Cerisia, then back to the paladin who knelt before him. "I feel better."

"What do you mean tried?" The Archioness's words were only a few moments on the heels of the Baron's, and Allystaire thought he could hear a trace of panic in them.

"I do not doubt that you feel better, my lord," Allystaire said. "For I have…" He paused, clenching his right hand into a fist as he searched for a word. "Fanned the flames of life that still burn within you. For a few turns, perhaps a day, I do not doubt that your wind will be as good as any man your age."

"And when those turns or days are done?"

"Then your disease will return," Allystaire said, meeting Hamadrian's eyes steadily with his own. "The same as it was. Perhaps worse for what I have done."

"Your Goddess hasn't taught you how to soften a blow, has She?" Hamadrian swung his legs over the edge of his bed and stood, holding himself straighter and easier than when Allystaire had seen him leaning on Cerisia's arm half a turn earlier.

"I believe in looking straight at the things we must confront, Hamadrian, no matter how much they frighten us."

"Then stand up and look straight at me already. Cold, the years you've spent at war your knees can't take all that nonsense."

"Not yet, Baron Innadan," Allystaire said, then swallowed hard. "Not until I offer you my apology."

"You told the Bear you didn't intend to apologize to Barons, only to people."

"Baron Harlach never tried to arrange a peace congress before. Never hosted all the western Barons and their lords at his own home, in open welcome. Never despaired while we drank, wenched, broke lances, and mocked him. I do not know if I could have persuaded Gerard Oyrwyn to see the value in what you wanted. I do know that I did not try—and that is a sin against your people, and my own, but also against you. Amongst all of us, Hamadrian, all the lords and great men of the west," Allystaire said, his tone twisting those words to a bitter curse, "you alone had the courage to grasp at peace. You had the courage to be thought weak, to be thought a coward, in the pursuit of something better than glory, and none of us, me least of all, did aught to help to you."

The paladin took a deep breath, and lowered his head. "I will not ask your forgiveness. I only want you to know that I understand, now, what a mistake we all made. How petty we all were. I thank the Goddess for leading me to help you in this task now."

Hamadrian Innadan, his hand steady, reached down to the pauldrons of Allystaire's shoulder and urged him back to his feet. Both settled their hands back at their sides.

"You thought I was a coward?" Hamadrian cocked his head to one side, lips twisted in a faint grimace.

"No," Allystaire said, "a fool, mayhap. Weak, even. I knew better than to think you craven, even blind as I was."

Hamadrian nodded. "You might do to offer an apology to the knights you humiliated in the lists that fortnight, you know."

Allystaire laughed. The solemnity, and the tension it had brought, drained from the tent. "I may still be cursed with pride on that score, Baron," he said. "I do believe the men who jousted against me, that day, any day past my knighting, knew what they were choosing to do."

"At least you never killed anyone in the list," Innadan said.

"I never tried to," Allystaire replied matter-of-factly. "Some men only ever learn how to use a lance to kill."

"Perhaps," Arontis said, clearing his throat and stepping to his father's side, "we ought to organize a small tourney among the knights and lords here. See if your arm still deserves its fame."

Before Hamadrain could respond Allystaire was shaking his head and addressing Arontis. "I will not be a part of it if you do. I know you mean well, Lord Innadan. Give the men something to do, let them test the paladin's strength. It is not a badly-conceived idea, in a way. Yet we do not have the time, and I cannot fight for my own glory."

Arontis opened his mouth to ask a follow-up question, watching Allystaire carefully, but Hamadrian raised a hand and his son fell silent. "Coldbourne—"

Quietly, but firmly, Allystaire interrupted the Baron. "Stillbright."

The old man shrugged and went on. "Stillbright has the right of it. We haven't time for any such nonsense, no matter how much fun it might be to watch him unhorse everyone Harlach brought with him. And while I feel as I do, I am not going to waste any more time abed. Come on, lad, make yourself useful," Hamadrian said, giving Arontis a shove towards the table where the Baron's formal clothes, swordbelt, and circlet lay.

Allystaire turned and strode quickly out of the pavilion. He felt the footsteps following him and turned to find Cerisia. With the jewels gone from her mask he could read some grief in her pale eyes.

"Why can you not heal him?"

Allystaire took a few steps to distance them from the guard, gesturing for Cerisia to follow. "My gift is not without limits," he murmured. "If a wound is new, or the disease new, it can overcome it." He took a deep breath, and went on. "If not? Let me try to explain this way," he suddenly said. "I have tried to heal two blind men, one who had been blinded only days before, and one who had lost his eyes years ago. The first, you know—Rede. His wound was fresh, and he had not accepted it, in body or soul. The second, is a man named Waltin. Having been blind for so long, he had decided it was a part of himself. It was who he was. Perhaps it had been so long that there was no longer any wound there for me to heal. I think it is a mixture of both. In Hamadrian's case?"

The paladin sighed and splayed his hands at his side in a gesture of futility. "He is nearly three-score and ten years old. He is older than Gerard Oyrwyn or my father were when they died. I can prop him up, Archioness. For a time. I cannot make him live past his appointed days."

"He deserves to live to see a peace made," Cerisia said, her voice muffled and yet still almost plaintive behind her mask.

"There are uncounted dead who deserve the same, Cerisia. I cannot save them any more than I can him," Allystaire said. "Yet there are thousands whose days could stretch a long time yet, and who we can save. Hamadrian, barring a greater miracle than my Goddess can deliver, is not fated to leave this place alive. I am sorry."

"Must you be so cruel about it? Can you not find it in yourself to speak comforting words, rather than blunt truths?"

"The truth is the only thing I can speak. If it is blunt, that is no fault of mine."

"You are a hard man, Allystaire Stillbright. A hard man." Cerisia shook her head, sunlight slashing across Allystaire's face as it reflected from the mask she wore, then she turned and headed back towards Hamadrian's pavilion.

Allystaire sighed and marched back to his own camp.

CHAPTER 39

Legacy

Allystaire found Gideon standing outside the tent with Norbert. Neither seemed to feel the need to fill the afternoon quiet with conversation, and in fact, they weren't even facing each other. Gideon was looking off at the mountains looming to the north, while Norbert tried to stay close to the boy without looking like he was trying to.

"What did you see," Allystaire muttered to Gideon as he stood behind the boy. He almost reached out to put a hand upon Gideon's shoulder, but stopped himself.

"That Oyrwyn is precisely where you said he'd be."

Allystaire sighed. "How many men?"

"I don't know," Gideon reported. "It was difficult to count and I was distracted," he admitted.

"How so? Were there priests or sorcerers amongst them?"

"A priest, yes, but I do not think he noticed me. No," Gideon said, turning to face the paladin. "I decided to use the opportunity to look for the results of my handiwork."

Allystaire kept his face composed and his tone calm and even, though he felt a jolt of anger. "I needed to know whatever you could tell me about Oyrwyn men in the mountains, Gideon," he said, and the boy raised a hand, his palm out.

"I know, and you will if you'll let me explain."

Allystaire felt his lips press into a thin line. "Then explain quickly," he muttered.

"I could not count the men at arms because they were well hidden, but I suspect he has more encamped above us than are gathered here. I took note of the badges they wore; the footmen wore the Oyrwyn mountain, with a kind of cord stretched around it, and behind it, crossed, were an axe and a hook, I think."

"Wind's Jaw Mountaineers," Allystaire said, shaking his head. "Good men. Deadly in their own terrain. They would be near useless down here upon the plains, though." He frowned. "What is he thinking?"

"I couldn't answer," Gideon replied. "There were more than a dozen knights, as well, and at least one priest of Braech—but I felt no spark of power from him."

"A dozen knights? Where is he getting them?"

"Should I have read his letters? Listened to his conversations?"

"Did you see Garth? Any men in the same Coldbourne or Highgate colors?"

Gideon shook his head.

"That is something, at least," Allystaire said. "What else was it you saw?"

"The Eldest," Gideon said. "Many hundreds of miles away, upon the sea, with dozens of Dragon Scales. Heading towards Londray, I believe; it is hard to say, exactly."

"The Eldest?" Allystaire wasn't sure why the word put a chill down his spine, even as he tugged at a faint memory of it.

"What the sorcerer in charge of a coterie styles himself," Gideon replied. "The one who gave orders to Bhimanzir, Iriphet, and Gethmasanar."

"How powerful is he?"

"Very," Gideon replied.

"Is he a danger to you?"

"If I am unprepared and overconfident again, yes. If there are ways to bring his power to bear against me without touching me with it directly, then very."

"And you to him?"

Gideon nodded slowly.

"Did he see you? Know you?"

The boy cleared his throat and looked down to the toes of his boots. "I, ah, I may have been bold. I thought to put some fear into him."

"What did you do?"

"I forced the darkness he carries around him to part for a ray of sunlight. I told him I did not fear him, and told him I welcomed him sailing towards me, since it would make his destruction easier on the both of us."

Allystaire tried not to smile, though the spark of pride he felt rising up in his chest was unmistakable. "Why?"

Gideon looked earnestly up at him, and said, "I thought it was what you would have done."

Allystaire smiled and clapped the boy lightly on the shoulder. "I would only ask why you did not simply crush the boat they were upon."

"There were innocent men upon it as well, men who may not know, or have control over, what they are bringing here, or why. I could not be sure of destroying him by something as mundane as drowning him, either. I doubt that he breathes in the sense that you and I do."

Allystaire noted Norbert leaning towards them, his ears all but quivering as he strained to overhear their words. He waved the young man over them. "You might as well hear. This is going to be your war as well, Norbert."

He had the grace to flush a bit, but all the same, he stepped closer. "A year ago I would've said that a boatful of sailors would be a small price to pay for the death of a sorcerer. Or a few Dragon Scales."

"And now?" Allystaire looked at him sidelong.

Norbert took a deep breath. "If the sailors were all Braechsworn, coming to join the fight, they would be making themselves our enemies. But we cannot know that; it would not be…knightly?" His voice rose on the last word he spoke as he looked tentatively over at Allystaire, brows canted.

"No, Norbert. It would not," Allystaire confirmed, nodding his agreement.

Satisfied, he drew himself up taller, straightened his shoulders, looked out over the plains and the mountains beyond. "So, what do we do about Oyrwyn?"

"What do you think we ought to do, Gideon?"

The boy frowned. "Try and divine his purpose, I would think. Gather more information, his numbers, his plans."

Allystaire shook his head. "No. If our numbers could match or exceed his, we might, in order to steal a march or start some kind of maneuver. What we have right now is surprise, initiative—and the biggest weapon in the fight," he said, pointing at Gideon. "We seize the moment; we act, instead of reacting. And we do it where and when the rest of the Barons can see it."

The paladin took a deep breath. "Norbert, if you would, run and fetch Armel, Harrys, and Tibult. Then follow me. Gideon, if you would ask Idgen Marte and Torvul to join us."

"Where?"

"Where the Barons meet," Allystaire said. "And soon, to take advantage of the light. Are you feeling strong, Gideon?"

"That depends," the boy replied, "on what you wish me to do."

* * *

"Stones Above," Torvul cursed. "Do these men never make haste?

"It's almost as if they're accustomed to being the most important person in any gathering," Idgen Marte said.

Torvul spat, and plopped himself into one of the Baronial seats, tossing a heavy boot casually upon their negotiating table. "Then I s'pose we'll have to disabuse them of that notion."

"We are not here to strong-arm them," Allystaire protested. "We need to make them see reason. I do not want to end decades of foolish succession strife only to bring on murderous revolt."

Servants and knights began to mill around the edges of the designated meeting place. The former came up bearing trays with pitchers of water, wine, cups, and food. Torvul lifted a pitcher from a passing tray and sniffed at it cautiously, then tipped it back, taking a hearty gulp of it. Smacking his lips, he set it on the table, but still easily within reach, and said, "Idgen Marte, I'll bet you three links of silver he can't go half a turn without threatening them."

"I know better than to wager with you, dwarf," Idgen Marte shot back.

Allystaire merely scowled, turning his eyes towards the gathering crowd. Baroness Damarind and her daughter were the first to arrive at the table, bringing a small contingent of their black-and-red-clad knights. The Baroness gave

Allystaire a long appraising look with her hazel eyes; he felt the palpable weight of them before they moved on to Torvul and then Idgen Marte.

"Would you introduce me to your attendants, Sir Stillbright?"

"Not my attendants," Allystaire said in a rush, extending a palm towards Torvul, who was already sitting indignantly forward in his chair. "My friends, and fellow servants. They can introduce themselves if they wish, Baroness."

The dwarf hopped out of his chair, sweeping pitcher and a cup into his hands as he stood. He poured as he walked towards the Baroness, and extended the filled cup with a graceful bow that would've done many a courtier proud, and offered her a smile from his cragged face.

"Mourmitnourthrukacshtorvul," he said as she took the cup. "Student of the last true Stonesinger, Alchemist, Craftsman, and Wit of the Mother." With the Baroness holding her winecup, he lifted the now half-emptied pitcher to make a toast. "Among my people it is custom to share a drink upon meeting."

Allystaire could feel Torvul's easy charm taking the Baroness, and the daughter standing behind her, by surprise. She extended her cup and it softly clanked against the edge of Torvul's pitcher.

"Baroness Loaisa Damarind," she said, "Fifteenth of my House, Ruler of the Spines, Eastern Warden of the Vale of Kings."

The dwarf grinned and tipped back his pitcher, gulping what wine remained in it without spilling a drop onto his cheeks. Eyeing him over the rim of her cup, Loaisa did the same, draining it to a drop with a prodigious gulp. Allystaire noticed her daughter's eyes widening as she watched her mother drink, saw her body stiffen.

"Well met, Baroness," Torvul rumbled, as he lowered his now empty pitcher. "Y'can call me Torvul."

"Then I shall," Loaisa said, and stepped forward to set her empty cup down on the table as Torvul stumped off. Her sharp eyes flitted from the dwarf to Idgen Marte. "And you are?"

"Idgen Marte," the warrior rasped, hooking one hand around her swordbelt.

"No titles then? No honorifics?"

She was saved from having to answer that question by the arrival of other Baronial parties. Hamadrian arrived, with Cerisia and Arontis trailing him, walking steadily and without the benefit of anyone's arm. He went straight to the head of the table. Landen arrived quickly on his heels, no delegation with her; Ruprecht Machoryn and Byronn Telmawr practically raced to claim their seats, while both tried to look like they weren't hurrying at all.

In Machoryn's case, Allystaire reflected, with the heavy armor the man now wore, his movements answered too readily to the term waddle.

"We are waiting for Unseldt, aren't we?" Hamadrian's voice still had a rasp to it, but it was stronger than it had been a mere turn before. "Well, we needn't wait dry. Go on and pour the wine, then. I've a feeling what the paladin has to say will be sobering enough that we can afford to take a drop, eh?"

The servants immediately flowed to the table, their movements graceful and unobtrusive as they took up pitchers and poured cups of red and white, distributing them to Barons, knights, and attendants.

One came to offer a cup to Allystaire, but Hamadrian raised a hand, stopping the liveried man in his tracks. He pointed to a decanter set at his place on the table. The servant bowed slightly, plucked the top from the delicate crystal, and poured a stream of dark, purple wine into a cup that, at another time, would've had Allystaire drooling.

Instead, the entire display of servility and power had Allystaire's lip curling, his hands clenching at his sides.

Idgen Marte sensed the tension in him, and he heard her voice come to him silently. *Now is not the time, Allystaire.*

That even good men like Hamadrian Innadan so casually assume so much power—

You can't change it all at once, and you need him on your side. Turning the man's wine-pourers against him isn't the way to do that. Calm yourself and take the cup.

By then the servant had reached him and bowed, eyes lowered. Allystaire reached for the wine but took the moment to study the man: close to his own age, though slight and balding, sweating in dark green trousers and coat with red piping on the seams, collar and cuffs.

Allystaire started to murmur a casual thanks, then impulsively said, "What is your name?"

The servant, his eyes still downcast and his manner still unobtrusive, gave his head a tiny shake.

"I cannot properly thank you, goodman, if I do not know your name."
The man swallowed hard and started to back away.

"You have nothing to fear from me," Allystaire said. "Least of all that I will
try to force you to tell me your name. Thank you for the wine nonetheless."

With that the servant raised his head and muttered, "Willem, m'lord."

"Thank you, Willem," Allystaire said as he raised the cup and inhaled deeply. "Though you need not call me m'lord. My name is Allystaire." He only then
became aware that small talk had stopped, and that the gathered nobility was
staring at his interaction with the servant.

"If you're done scaring my servants, Stillbright," Hamadrian said, "try the
wine. It is my Birth Vintage," he said. "A tradition we have here: a section of that
year's harvest set aside, laid down in good white oak, and only tapped when the
Baron it was laid down for jolly well says so. Most of it has long since been spent:
my weddings, the births of children, their weddings, the birth of their children.
And too many funerals," he added, his face falling, eyes lingering on his own cup.
"In hopes, I had the last barrel breached when we set out for this congress."

Hamadrian took the merest sip of his own, closing his eyes and clearly sa-
voring it. Allystaire mimicked him, taking as small a taste as he could manage.

It was all he could do then to stop from gulping the entire cup. It tasted
of earth and sun, of fruit and clear air and other things he hadn't the words to
describe.

"This," he murmured, after he swallowed, "is a miracle, Hamadrian."

"Thank you, Sir Stillbright," the Baron replied, beaming. "I am proud of it."

"Did you tend the vines? Harvest the fruit? Crush it? Build a barrel for it? Turn
it, care for it, bottle it? It is to the men and women who did that that my com-
pliments are owed," Allystaire quickly added. He could feel Idgen Marte seething
behind him, and Torvul didn't bother to suppress a deep, rumbling chortle.

A shadow of anger passed over Hamadrian's face, his lips tightened, jaw
quivered. A hush fell over the table and heads turned towards them. Arontis,
standing behind his father's seat, pressed his lips hard together and looked from
paladin to Baron and back again.

Then the old man smiled, and raised a barely-shaking finger to point accus-
ingly at the paladin. "I see what you're doing, Allystaire," he said, smiling. "And
damn it all if you aren't right," he added. "It is those people who deserve praise

more than me." He considered his own cup, fingers twined around the stem. "The folk who would've done all the things you said are long since gone to the next world, I should think. Yet doubtless they had sons, and daughters. I will write out instructions to grant them a legacy."

The table had relaxed enough to return to its conversations, though Allystaire felt more eyes than he would've liked lingering upon him, but the cluster of voices, coupled with the setting sun gleaming from Allystaire's armor, had allowed Harlach's delegation to come upon them more or less unawares, and Baron Unseldt announced his presence with the thunderous bombast that was his wont.

"Enough with your talk of wine and peasants," the huge man thundered. "Ale is a man's drink, and I love my folk as much as any other lord but it won't do to go coddling them."

As he heaved his bulk into a nearby chair and folded his huge bare arms across his armored chest, Allystaire noted the axe that had taken back its place upon his belt. Though an inlay of gold glittered upon the head, what he could see of the blade appeared sharp and deadly.

You sure I won't have to kill him? Idgen Marte's voice.

Trust me when I say that you will want him on your side against the Braechsworn, Allystaire answered her. *And he is at least half bluster.*

What is the other half?

Bear.

Harlach reached for and poured himself a generous cup of wine despite his dismissal of it, drained it at a gulp. Hamadrian eyed him with his lips pressed into a thin line, while Loaisa didn't bother to hide the contempt in her eyes for his manners.

"We agreed," she said coldly, "not to come armed to this table."

"Paladin's armed," Unseldt said, nodding towards Allystaire as he reached for a pitcher. "So's the wench behind him. No offense meant to your woman, Coldbourne," he said, "but she doesn't seem like she goes by m'lady."

"Whatever compacts you agreed to regarding this table and what happens at it," Allystaire said, his voice steadily rising, "I was no part of them. I do not care where it is set, how large it is, where anyone sits, how many retainers anyone brings, who drinks what, or what is discussed round it except what gets all of your signatures upon a declaration of peace."

"Sir Stillbright is not wrong, as far as the protocol." Cerisia spoke up, her voice soothing over the anger that was clear in Allystaire's. While she spoke she glided around Hamadrian's chair to face the entire gathered company, resplendent in her gold mask and silver-threaded white silks. "He did not agree to come unarmed to this table. You, Baron Harlach, did."

"Aye, well, that I did, but his being here changes things. I don't trust him and I'll not go unarmed when Oyrwyn's warlord is about and Oyrwyn isn't. Without an Oyrwyn seal on this peace he wants, it doesn't matter anyway," Harlach said, waving a hand dismissively. "So we might as well all set off back home."

"I am no longer Oyrwyn's warlord," Allystaire said, "as I have already said. Yet I do know where he is."

When he paused, he felt all the eyes regarding him. Loaisa Damarind was the first to ask. "Where, then?"

Allystaire raised his hand and pointed to the spur of mountain to the northwest. "Camped along the trailhead just above the pass. Two, mayhap three hundreds of footmen immediately available, a dozen knights at least, a priest of Braech. Surely more camped within easy reach."

"And are we simply to take your word for that, as for so many other things?" Ruprecht Machoryn had, after a couple cups of wine, found his voice. "This Braechsworn army, for instance."

"My men have prisoners that we will present once Gilrayan Oyrwyn has joined us," Allystaire said.

"And some folk they already attacked are in my camp," Landen quickly added. "We came upon them on our way here. They will want to bear witness."

"How do you know Oyrwyn is joining us?" Byron Telmawr spoke for the first time. "Unless you have planned with him."

Allystaire's jaw clenched till his teeth hurt, but he forced a cold smile upon his face. "I do not intend to give him a choice. Follow me. Please."

He raised his arm again, pointing towards the mountains. The late afternoon sun blazed bright from his armor as he thought, *Gideon, now.*

None of the Barons moved but to turn to look where he pointed, shading their eyes with raised arms.

Then a huge voice rolled over the gathered camps like sudden thunder, rattling the cups and pitchers upon the table and causing some to clap their hands over their ears. The very earth beneath their feet seemed to rumble; a few voices raised in fear

"GILRAYAN OYRWYN," it said, "I GIVE YOU THIS ONCE CHANCE. COME FORWARD PEACEFULLY AND ALONE AND NEITHER YOU NOR YOUR MEN WILL BE HARMED. YOU CANNOT HIDE FROM ME, FOR I AM THE WILL OF THE MOTHER, AND YOU DO NOT WISH TO FACE MY WRATH."

Almost as one, the Barons stood, rushing past Allystaire and Idgen Marte, their attending heirs, knights, and advisors swept up in their wake.

Allystaire took a deep breath as they moved past him; even Hamadrian was up and out of his seat more quickly than seemed likely, though Arontis was by his side in a flash. "A horse," the Baron yelled, as he hobbled out of sight.

Cerisia remained behind, fixing Allystaire with her pale green eyes. "What will he do?" she whispered.

"What he can, and then what he must," Allystaire replied. He took a mouthful of wine, decided he could savor it as he walked. As he turned, Idgen Marte stepped around him, into the shadow he cast from the sun to the west, and blinked from sight.

Allystaire walked off with Cerisia, leaving only Torvul. The dwarf sighed, started stumping off, stopped and came back to the table, snatched up a pitcher of wine, and hurried to catch up.

* * *

The mountain air was cool and pleasant in the large silk pavilion where Gilrayan Oyrwyn sat, carefully cleaning a sword with oil and rag. The blade was just shy of a yard long, double-edged, with enough room on the hilt for both hands, if one were inclined, yet it wasn't quite long or heavy enough to demand it. The hilt was wrapped in silver wire, and the pommel was a thick chunk of silver worked into the Oyrwyn Mountain.

The blade, though, was unornamented, sharp, and had the patina of careful regard over long use.

"An excellent blade, of course," the Baron Oyrwyn said, "but my father had no sense of style."

The Baron wore a grey silk surcoat, shot with threads of silver, over a quilted arming jacket, embroidered with black peaks, and a silver circlet with four thin, square-cut emeralds spaced along its length and a sculpted silver mountain that was the match of his blade's pommel.

He stood above a table, and around it were gathered the other four men in the pavilion, three of whom nodded and laughed mirthful agreement. One was a young, bull-necked priest of Braech with a thick black beard, who eschewed his robes for scale armor enameled in rich sea-blue, a heavy flanged mace at his belt. The others wore surcoats of varying colors and device; there was a thickset balding man in dark yellow, with a faded sprig of green leaves and three red berries worked upon it; a younger man, thin-cheeked, grey-eyed and dark-headed, whose surcoat was a plain green.

And towering above all of them, not nodding, was a thin, sinewy man, bald but for a fringe of tightly cropped grey, brown-eyed above a hawk's-beak nose and sharp cheeks. He wore a surcoat of lighter grey than the Baron's; the device upon it was a round tower with the huge, curved horns of a massive bullock sprouting from its battlements.

The Baron himself was the tallest but for this older man, and when Gilrayan looked up at him with some disdain upon his young and handsome face, as if there was some effrontery in one of his lords being taller than he was.

"You do not agree, Lord Naswyn?"

"Your father would have said that style is for dead men," the taller, older man answered.

"Without style, how is the other man supposed to know that you are his better, Joeglan?"

The younger men shared another round of mirthful laughter before Lord Naswyn of the Horned Towers answered, in a voice that had the dry creak of leather about it, "When you defeat him."

Anger flashed across Gilrayan's finely-cut features, for a moment, till it was overtaken by a smile that did not reach his eyes.

"All the easier when you break his spirit first."

"As you say, m'lord." Joeglan Naswyn's voice was flat and even, but the words were the proper form of the thing so the Baron merely nodded and turned back to his more appreciative audience.

"So," the young Baron said. "The coward shows his face and it is time to make our play."

"If I may be bold, m'lord," Joeglan spoke again. "No man who knew Allystaire ever had cause to call him coward."

"Is that so, Lord Naswyn?"

"It is so, my lord," he replied. As he spoke, as he faced the angry glare of the volatile young man before him, Joeglan Naswyn did not move, other than to breathe. He did not fidget with his armor or surcoat, adjust his swordbelt, move his arms, or shuffle his feet. He was simply present in an impressively immovable way, like a fact of the landscape: a barren, nearly leafless tree, exposed to the wind, but too deep in the soil to fear it.

"Then explain why he ran off, Joeglan. Explain why he tried to disappear."

"I don't pretend to know what he was thinking," Joeglan said. "But it was never in him to give in to fear."

Gilrayan smiled, and there was something of the raptor in the way his face contorted when he did. It didn't wear well on him. "It is in every man to give in to fear, Joeglan. Surely you heard my father say as much, aye?" He didn't wait for the Lord of the Horned Towers to nod his assent, only turned back to face his other attendant lords.

"Regardless, he is here, and the prize is before us. Six Barons, lightly defended, and our own exile. Too ripe a prize to let it slip past us."

Joeglan Naswyn felt the effort of biting back his words. *You were invited here peaceably,* he wanted to say. *Your father would have come openly and at least heard his peers out. If he didn't, at the least he would've replied to the pigeons, said that he did not mean to attend. He would not come like a thief in the night,* he thought, but did not say, as Gilrayan expounded on the possibilities of capture, ransom, execution, and kingship that awaited him in the valley below.

"We haven't the men to fight down on open grass," Joeglan finally said, the words coming out in a rasp. Everyone turned to stare at him. Gilrayan's hand tightened on the ostentatious hilt of the still-naked sword. "We don't," he insisted. "Mountaineers with small crossbows and handaxes? Deadly up here. No man in his right mind wants to try and approach Wind's Jaw with them watching his path. Down there, with bad range on the bows, horsemen and archers in the camp, they'll be cut down and scattered."

The words started rushing out of him, his voice growing hoarser as he spoke, but he was never to be sure if anyone in the tent heard him, for the world rumbled, at that moment, with the power of some other, greater voice.

"GILRAYAN OYRWYN," it said, "I GIVE YOU THIS ONE CHANCE. COME FORWARD PEACEFULLY AND ALONE AND NEITHER YOU NOR YOUR MEN WILL BE HARMED. YOU CANNOT HIDE FROM ME, FOR I AM THE WILL OF THE MOTHER, AND YOU DO NOT WISH TO FACE MY WRATH."

There was something in that voice that made Lord Joeglan Naswyn want to throw himself to the ground and huddle in a ball, hoping to be passed over. Gilrayan Oyrwyn was so shocked he dropped his pretty sword, forgot about it as he cast his eyes about, mad and wide, looking for an exit.

Two of the other men in the tent, the plain green surcoat and the older man with the branch and berries, bolted for the exit.

Naswyn drew his sword, and without a word, scooped the Baron's blade from the ground and pressed it into the younger man's trembling hands.

"STEEL WILL NOT AVAIL YOU," the voice thundered, as if it could see them filling their hands. The walls of the pavilion began rattling as if a winter gale suddenly pulled at them. Then as one the ropes holding it taut snapped and the entire thing was torn upwards and tossed into the air, flapping off like a pennant torn loose from a lance.

A giant loomed over the circle the tent had described in the dirt. A giant, but not any kind of Gravek, for Joeglan had fought them in his youth and knew that the tallest Gravekmir would be dwarfed by the huge, luminous thing that stood above them now. Shaped like a man, but seemingly made of soft golden light, the color of a summer sunset, Joeglan almost thought he could see the mountains through this huge monster's chest.

He wanted to scream, to run and flee, but Joeglan Naswyn had learned all his life that the one thing a man could never do was let his fear master him. He turned his fear into a wordless scream, and charged at the giant's descending hand, his sword drawn back over his head in a two handed grip, then describing an arc that would see it cut straight through the giant's fingers, if they could be cut.

For a moment it seemed that Gilrayan Oyrwyn and the priest who'd stayed by his side would stand rooted in place, dumb with fear, but both found weapons in their hands and followed his lead, the priest shouting prayers to the Sea Dragon as he came on.

"I TOLD YOU STEEL WOULD NOT AVAIL YOU," the giant boomed, shaking Joeglan's chest and rattling the campaign furniture that stood around them. Instantly, the giant's hand was wreathed in bright blue flame. It threw no heat that he could feel, yet suddenly the sword he grasped had heated through, the center channel of the blade turning a dark, burnt orange. Without gauntlets, the heat of it traveled into his hands before he could knew it, and he tossed his weapon sizzling to the ground. The priest did the same.

"I WILL HAVE YOUR ANSWER, BARON OYRWYN." The giant's hand closed around Gilrayan, who pushed futilely against its grasp. Joeglan charged to his Baron's aid, only to be flicked away with the giant's other hand.

Joeglan had the sense that the being could have crushed him if it wished, such was the power of it when it touched him. Yet instead of throwing him away like a clod of dirt, to be broken upon the ground, the touch was just enough to send him stumbling away. If he could have credited it, Joeglan might have said that the giant was being careful.

"WATCH WELL, GILRAYAN OYRWYN," the giant boomed, as he lifted the struggling Baron from the ground, dozens of paces into the air. It stepped away from the tent, picking its way through the encampment almost delicately, till it reached the face of a mountainside. "YOU HAVE ONE TURN TO DISMISS ALL BUT TWO-SCORE AND TEN OF YOUR MEN OUT OF SIGHT OF STANDING GUARD PASS AND TO PRESENT YOURSELF, YOUR RETINUE, AND ADVISORS TO THE CAMP BELOW."

The Wind's Jaw Mountaineers that made up the bulk of the forces camped there were professional, hardened veterans. Joeglan silently blessed whatever Bannerman or Sergeant-Major already had them forming a line and raising their crossbows for a volley.

He heard a rough voice bellow "LOOSE" and a bare moment after a couple of dozen bolts went into the air, the sound of the strings twanging in chorus reached him.

The giant swung a hand dismissively, and all the bolts sank straight to the ground. "I WISH NO ONE IN THIS CAMP ILL, BUT IF YOU FORCE MY

HAND MY WRATH WILL BE TERRIBLE," the giant roared. "YOU HAVE ONE TURN, BARON OYRWYN. AND THEN?"

The giant reached into the side of the mountain and lifted a boulder the size of a manor house from it, high into the air, as effortlessly as a man might have lifted a rock he meant to skip across a pond. "I WILL BRING THE MOUNTAINS DOWN UPON ANY ARMED MEN WHO REMAIN HERE TO THREATEN THE PEACE CONGRESS BELOW. ONE. TURN."

Then, carefully, almost solicitously, the giant set Gilrayan Oywryn down, turned about, and vanished.

* * *

Allystaire, Idgen Marte, and Torvul ranged along behind the throng of Barons, knights, and soldiers who rushed to the edge of the trail leading down from the northern face of the mountains. Many were breathing hard, Ruprecht Machoryn especially. A few had thought to grab horses on their way and had gone far afield from the rest of them.

Everyone could hear the booming words Gideon projected across the entire pass. All of them craned their necks when the glowing golden hand of a massive giant appeared along the trail above them, holding aloft a gigantic hunk of rock as it threatened to crush the Oyrwyn encampment.

Allystaire heard gasps of shock and fear, though none became full, fearful wails. Instead of watching the display of power, he studied faces. He found Cerisia eyeing him, could feel the disapproval even through her mask. Loaisa Damarind's face was nearly as serene as it always was, but when he looked close he saw her teeth digging lightly into her bottom lip. Unseldt Harlach was gripping his axe with two hands so hard Allystaire feared for the haft, while Byron Telmawr looked to Hamadrian and tried to copy his air of careful detachment.

It is done. I expect he will come down in the alloted time. Gideon's voice was faint and weak in Allystaire's mind. *If not faster.*

Good. Rest. Tell Harrys and Tibult to bring the prisoners now, please.

By then, Cerisia had glided to his side. "Is he truly capable of that?" Her voice was a quiet hiss, pitched only for him to hear.

He didn't have time to answer, for by then the rest of the Barons had turned to him, Idgen Marte, and Torvul. Landen, Hamadrian, and Loaisa showed no fear, with the latter appraising him cooly with slightly lifted chin. Unseldt was glowering, but the fires of his rage were banked and dimmed, though he still held his axe. Ruprecht had gone even whiter in the face, but it was Byronn Telmawr who, unexpectedly, stepped forward.

"What horror have you wrought?" The trim and compact man seemed to be letting a lifetime of anger out at once, his cheeks turning a mottled red and white. "What foul magic is this? You were always a murderer, but now a sorcerer!"

"Calm yourself, Baron Telmawr." Landen had quickly stepped to Telmawr's side, her voice cool, manner easy. "Sir Stillbright is no sorcerer; neither is the power you just witnessed wielded by one."

"Am I murderer because I killed your father in battle, Byronn?" Allystaire spread his hands. "If so, then everyone here is a murderer. I will be the first to admit that my hands are stained a deep red. That is why we are gathered here."

"Is it? Or is it so your pet demon can demand that we all fall in line?" Unseldt Harlach had slipped his axe halfway back along his hip, but one huge hand still wrapped around the head.

"Demons don't exist," Torvul put in brightly between sips from the jug of wine he'd brought along. "They're a story that sorcerers and warlocks and the like tell to make themselves seem more mysterious. Spirits, now, those're real, but to be inhabited with them a place has got to be good and old or had a lot of magic expended upon it." He assumed the tone of a lecturer until he turned to meet Allystaire's hard stare, to which he shrugged. The dwarf went back to his wine, waving away the pointed stares of the Baronial retinues.

"Your spirit, then!" Telmawr was undaunted.

Torvul swallowed hastily, "You heard the words, but did you understand them?"

"What you have seen is no spirit, nor demon nor sorcerer." Allystaire put the sharp tone of command into his voice. "Baroness Delondeur and the Archioness Cerisia can attest to that fact. He is what he said he was: the Will of the Mother, as I am Her Arm."

"Allystaire speaks truly, as always," Cerisia said. "The Will of the Mother is a most powerful being, as we have all seen."

"I have seen the work of sorcerers, and that evil is not in him," Landen put in. "In his madness my father sought out their hire, and spent vast sums of treasure to bring first one, and then two more of their vile brotherhood to our shores. They would not boast of being able to tear down a mountain; if they could do so, they *would*, even to kill just one man, if they wanted him dead. If the Will were a sorcerer, he would kill all the men in that camp, from ambush, without warning, and then turn their bodies into shambling horrors with which to attack us. I know," she added, the force in her voice growing with every word. "When you have seen what they do, have seen the twisted shadows of men that they become, you will never mistake it."

Landen paused for breath and turned, involuntarily it seemed, towards Allystaire, who nodded very slightly in return. Byronn opened his mouth, raising a hand with one finger extended, till he was cut off.

"Have done, Telmawr," Hamadrian called out. "We all want the same thing here, and this Will of the Mother has given us the means to achieve it. I say we wait here for young Oyrwyn to arrive."

Pressing his lips into a thin line, Telmawr stepped away from Allystaire, lowering his clenched hands to his sides.

"And what if he comes down in strength?" Harlach was not as easily cowed, trying to warily eye Allystaire and Hamadrian simultaneously. "Do we stand here and be slaughtered?"

"Send for your guards if you feel you need them," Hamadrian replied, "but keep them at a distance."

He's coming. Two men with him. His banner is drawn. Even Allystaire hadn't noticed the moment Idgen Marte had slipped away, taking advantage of the gawping crowd's fascination with Gideon's show, but he knew she lingered near the base of the pass, having traveled there from shadow to shadow.

"You will not need them," Allystaire said, raising a hand to point.

As though summoned by yet more magic, three figures on horseback, too distant to see in detail, suddenly came into view at the start of the descent from the mountains.

"Back to the table, then," Hamadrian called out, his voice a shadow of what it had been but a few minutes earlier. "We should not await him standing in a field."

CHAPTER 40

Baron Oyrwyn

*W*hatever *he says or does,* Allystaire thought, *do not let it goad you. Promise me that neither of you will do anything to frighten or provoke him.*

He shared this with Idgen Marte and Torvul. Behind him, the latter drank the last drops of his wine with a faint chuckle, while he could feel the former growing closer by the second.

We've got him good and cowed, Idgen Marte thought. *Why waste the opportunity?*

Because he will be be proud, and looking to save face in light of what happened. And because of all the Barons here, he is most uniquely positioned to ruin what we are attempting to do. He has the most tested, veteran troops, and the best places from which to strike. He will not hold to his father's alliance with Baron Innadan for his father's sake alone, and he will see any other Baron's weakness as his opportunity.

How do you know that about his alliance with Innadan?

Allystaire didn't have time to respond to Idgen Marte's thought, for, as the trio of riders approached, Hamadrian turned to him, his face taut. "Are you and Gilrayan going to be civil?"

"I am not going to kill him, if that is what you mean," Allystaire replied.

"Maybe you should've," the old man offered, causing a general murmur around the cluster of nobles.

"I've no love lost for you, but Hamadrian's right," Unseldt growled. "You'd have been a more fitting son to Gerard Oyrwyn. He had the one bastard," he added, rolling his great shoulders in a shrug. "Sure you weren't one yourself? You act enough like him."

"Positive," Allystaire said, frowning. "My lord Harlach, a year ago I would have considered that the greatest compliment anyone ever paid me."

"Enough." Irritation was thick in Landen's voice. "You all natter on like fishwives and children on mending day. This is not a lark. My people have died this spring. More will, as this Islandman army swells in the north. We should be moving with haste, not looking fondly back on our squiring days."

Heads turned to Landen; eyebrows raised. Harlach's mouth twisted in a dismissive grimace. "I've heard enough out of you, lass. Young rulers need to sit, listen, and learn."

"She is right!" Hamadrian raised his voice to a shout, and it brought the company to a stunned silence. The effort almost immediately cost him, though, as he was suddenly wracked with coughing. Arontis and Cerisia were at his side immediately. Allystaire was half a step away when Hamadrian recovered, raising a hand and speaking in a rasp. "Landen is right, and her urgency shames us all. This congress must end with us moving, in concert, to confront this Braechsworn menace. Anything less is a failure."

He turned to Allystaire then, his face grave, cheeks withdrawn, and good eye dimmed. He looked old once more, much of the vigor the Mother's Healing had given him seeming to recede into the creases of his face, into the sag of his shoulder.

"Tonight, regardless of the outcome of this congress, I will send word to the Vineyards to gather the Thornriders and such knights as can be roused immediately to lead them. And then, Allystaire Stillbright, I will turn them over to your command until you have the head of the man who'd bring the Islandmen and the Dragon Scales down upon us. And if any of the rest of you," he rasped, waving a hand to indicate the gathered Barons, "have an ounce of sense, you'll do the same Cold-damned thing."

Allystaire nodded his thanks and came forward to clasp Hamadrian by the forearm. When he did, he slipped his left hand on the outside of the older man's hand.

Mother, he thought, *the world needs this man for a few days at the least. Please let him live to see his moment of triumph in peace. Please help him find the strength.*

He felt a jolt travel from his hand to Hamadrian's, saw a shiver travel up the older man's body, heard a stale breath wheeze softly from ruined lungs. And then the Baron Innadan stood tall once again, his eye clearing, and Allystaire stepped away as softly and unobtrusively as he could manage.

He's not goin' t'last long, is he? Idgen Marte's thought-voice was resigned, a bit sad.

As long as the Mother gives me the strength to prop him up, Allystaire replied. He turned his back on the group of Barons and retreated a few steps away as they murmured among each other in reaction to Hamadrian's pronouncement. Landen pulled away from them and sidled up to him.

"Allystaire," she said, "you know you have my seal on any peace. And you know you have any men I can raise. Arming them may be a problem."

"Why?"

Landen shook her head, cut his eyes towards the group of Barons behind them, and muttered, "The armory in the Dunes was looted. Emptied of all but the most inferior stuff."

"By whom? How?"

"Under the seal of Lord Lamaliere, though he swears, not by himself. And considering he spent the winter holed up in Tide's Watch, I fail to see how—"

"Evolyn." Allystaire fair spat the word, grimacing. "His daughter, the Lady Lamaliere. The *Marynth* Evolyn Lamaliere," he added, and understanding swept Landen's face.

"My own Barony's arms turned against us," she fumed, her hands clenching into fists. "I will—"

"We haven't the time to go plotting our revenges, no matter how well deserved or exquisite," Torvul muttered, "not to mention how unseemly it is t'speak of such things in the light of day. But," he added, raising a long finger and pointing, "best tend to the arrival of your former liege lord, Ally."

Allystaire felt something—not fear, but a mix of anxiety and regret—spread through his limbs as he turned to face the Baron Oywryn.

Gilrayan looked enough like his father to call Gerard Oyrwyn to mind, Allystaire reflected. *And to suffer by the comparison.* He wore a silver circlet like the one Allystaire had first seen on the Old Baron some thirty years before, but gem studded and overwrought and too large upon his brow. He wore richly enameled black scale armor and a grey silk surcoat with the Oyrwyn mountain outlined in silver thread. He had his father's straight bearing and intense eyes over sharp cheeks, but his hair was closer to blond than the plain brown his father's had been, and he hadn't begun to lose it yet. The young Baron Oyrwyn held his head high and proudly, viewing the table and the seated Barons with cool indifference.

You'd never know he didn't come fashionably late and of his own free will. Idgen Marte shared her thought with him, and he only just stopped himself from nodding agreement.

A stiff back and a flat face. He is not entirely unlike his father.

Behind him walked one knight Allystaire didn't recognize, and another whose appearance made his jaw and fists clench. Standing a full head taller than any other man there, than any man Allystaire had ever seen, Joeglan Naswyn was unmistakable in any crowd. He moved with a kind of moderate stateliness, never hurrying, never slow, and his long frame belied a strength Allystaire knew could be frightening.

He found himself staring hard at the Lord of the Horned Towers, heard his gauntlets creak as his fists clenched.

Allystaire! Idgen Marte's voice was a mental whipcrack. *You can't afford to start a brawl here. And why?*

Her question was cut off as all attention was suddenly drawn to Gilrayan, who raised his hands and spoke.

"Honored Lords and Ladies," he said, "do accept my sincerest apologies for the lateness of Barony Oyrwyn's arrival to these august proceedings. Winter lingers in the mountains," he added.

"We all know of winter, especially in Harlach. Didn't stop me," Unseldt growled.

Gilrayan offered him a smile that spoke of understanding amongst comrades. "The deepest winter knows better than to impede the way of the Great White Bear, as do we all," he said.

Allystaire had to work to breathe, to unclench his jaw, to not press his teeth through the skin of his lips. Gilrayan stood there with his chin up, his eyes bright, hands settled on his empty swordbelt, radiating good cheer and bonho-mie. *The cheek of it,* he thought, *the impudence. To lob friendly words at people he meant to take hostage or kill not two turns ago.*

Meanwhile Baron Oyrwyn was moving slowly around the table, shaking hands. He tried to take Loaisa's hand as if he meant to kiss it, but was quick enough on his feet to simply take her forearm in his and give her the warrior's clasp she demanded.

Seething, Allystaire was not sure how long he could watch, as Gilrayan was careful to ignore him. He caught, from the corner of his eye, Joeglan Naswyn eyeing him, which he tried to ignore.

Stones, all you people ignorin' each other, Torvul thought. *It's like the boys and the girls at their first barn dance, afraid to look at one another.*

Gilrayan had by then clasped hands with Ruprecht, Landen, Loaisa, and tension was growing as he stood before Unseldt Harlach. The Bear had thrown himself out of his seat, and walked halfway around the table to loom ominously over the younger man, with his hand too close to his axe for anyone's comfort.

"Do not put your hand to that weapon, Unseldt." Hamadrian's voice was a dry rasp, but it cut through the cords of tension that were starting to wrap around everyone at the table, fixing them in fearful stillness. "You agreed to come unarmed to this table. You are impugning your own honor and endan-gering our lives with your pettiness."

Alone among the Barons, Harlach and Oyrwyn did not turn to face him. Hamadrian planted his gnarled hands upon the table's edge and pushed himself to his feet. He gathered his breath, only for his words to crumble in the face of a sudden ragged cough.

Arontis was at his father's side, helping him to sit before anyone else could move. Turning a taut jaw and barely concealed anger towards the table, he yelled with all the force his father could not.

"Baron Harlach, you are a guest at my father's Congress, and on his land, un-der the auspices of his hospitality and protection. You have both chosen to flaunt all rules of decency and respect. That ends this instant. You will accord my father the respect he deserves due to his seniority, his age, and the seriousness of the task ahead of us, or I will expel you from this Congress and allow Sir Stillbright to do what he will in regards to you. Baron Oyrwyn, you are welcome here if you come in good faith, but lurking in the mountains with hundreds of men does not speak well of your intentions, and I would have them clarified instantly."

Unseldt was first to respond. "Whelp, I'll not listen to your yelping!"

"No one is impressed with your antics, Unseldt." Loaisa Damarind's voice was acid, etching her words sharply into the air. "If you keep it up, in turn you will threaten everyone here, and yet you've not won a battle since I took my seat. Enough. Be silent and take this last chance to learn from those who know more of statecraft and war than you."

Unseldt was too stunned to respond, but the weight of staring disapproval forced him sullenly into his seat.

Gilrayan had been given the time to find his feet, though. "I did not have much choice but to come here, Lord Innadan. In fact, I would say it seems that I was right to fear for my safety and to bring as many knights and men as I did, given the welcome I was met with. How do I know that you'll not simply let him," with this, he jutted his chin towards Allystaire, "unleash his pet demon or sorcerer upon me now that I am alone and unarmed."

"I will not presume to speak for Sir Stillbright, but I do believe he has only the best interests of the people of the Baronies in his thoughts," Arontis said, turning to Allystaire as he spoke.

With a deep breath, the paladin took a half-step forward. "You have nothing to fear from me, Baron Oyrwyn, or from the Will of the Mother, so long as you do not seek to break the peace of this place."

"*Stillbright*, is it? Sir? And where do you get this title, given the published Writs of Exile and Divestiture?" Gilrayan said. "Did you simply bestow it upon yourself?"

"No," Allystaire said, "but discussion of what titles I bear is not relevant."

"I think that it is," Gilrayan insisted. "Only those with true claim to nobility, or at least to knighthood, have the authority to sit upon a Congress such as this."

"What you know of knighthood, Baron Oyrwyn," Allystaire said, "could not fill a thimble."

"Am I to be threatened and abused by a coward I exiled?"

Allystaire lowered his eyes and clenched his fists. "Enough. Even I am joining in this endless nattering. We are here for a purpose, and that is to arrange a peace so that we can meet the threat massing in fallen Vyndamere."

"And what proof is there of that?" Gilrayan looked around the table as he spoke, and to Allystaire's dismay, found Harlach, Machoryn, and Telmawr nodding their approval.

"Proof?" Torvul's voice creaked with unaccustomed disuse. "Why, I think it's arriving now."

Allystaire turned towards the tramp of feet, and found Norbert approaching, leading the three Braechsworn prisoners, their hands and feet and necks all bound together. Onundr and Gauk seemed barely able to stand, their limbs slack and atrophied, their once fearsome faces fallen and shapeless. Between them, Arvid, who would once have been dwarfed by the two former Dragon Scales, looked brawny and threatening in comparison.

Gasps scattered up and down the table like small gusts of wind as Allystaire seized the rope and hauled them close, pushing them to the ground. Arvid knelt; the other two collapsed in a heap.

Allystaire seized the back of Arvid's neck with the bare skin of his left palm. "Tell them who you are."

"Arvid," he spat. He struggled against the paladin's grasp, more, Allystaire thought, for the form of the thing than any real hope of escape.

"Where did I take you captive, Arvid?"

"A town with a large stone bridge. Largest I had ever seen."

"What had you been doing through the end of winter and the beginning of spring?"

"We come and pillage among the southerners in Braech's holy name."

"How many of you?"

"My band, less than score," he said. "In Braech's name." Here, the blond Islandman smiled. "Many times more on the river to the north. Hundreds of Dragon Scales. Gravek," he said, rolling that last word proudly off his tongue, and sending another ripple of muttered disbelief down either side of the table. "And the Sea Dragon."

Ruprecht Machoryn cradled his forehead in one hand. Landen's hands were fists on the table's smoothly polished surface.

"Who leads them?"

"Honored Choiron Symod," Arvid said.

Allystaire took his hand from Arvid's neck. "If you did not follow, he led a raiding party south into Barony Delondeur as soon as the thaw came. I expect other parties went into Oyrwyn, perhaps slipped through to Harlach. More could be operating. They gather by the Valdin, and I guess that Symod means to cut their teeth against the remnants of Varshyne, if there are any remnants," he added hotly. "And when they have battle in their blood and plunder in their eyes, they will come south, and if a concerted effort does not meet them, they could wreak havoc upon Delondeur's unprotected heart."

"That seems like Delondeur's problem," Gilrayan said with a casual shrug.

"And then it becomes Telmawr's problem, and Oyrwyn's problem, and Innadan's, and Harlach's," Allystaire shouted. "This is no polite battle over map lines. They mean to burn and destroy everything in their wake in the name of their God. The same God many of you keep chapels to in your homes, I add. He would see you swept along a tide of blood, and I come demanding you to no longer do His vile work for Him. Be better men than you have been. Be better *rulers* than you have been."

He paused. The sound of his own breathing was loud in his ears, as the Barons and their advisors regarded him silently. Before any of them could find their voice, he hauled Arvid to his feet again.

"Landen," Allystaire said, "this man pillaged, raided, raped, and enslaved your people. He is yours to judge and punish."

The Baroness Delondeur came to her feet, eyeing the Islandman coldly. "Some of the victims of Symod's raiding are in my camp. He will face their accusations before I decide anything."

"I see how it is, then," Gilrayan Oyrwyn stage-whispered loud enough for the table to hear him, even as he feigned at quiet by laying the back of his hand against his mouth.

"You are tiring me, boy," Hamadrian rasped. "If you've something to say, say it aloud."

"Only that Coldbourne left me to serve my rival. It's as plain as the the break in the coward's nose."

"Allystaire does not serve Barony Delondeur," Landen said through clenched teeth. "If any of you still doubt what happened, let me state the truth of it clear. He killed my father, who deserved killing, something I could not see until he was dead. That I live still is a testament to his mercy, yes, and his faith in me is something I hope to repay. I would offer him a Delondeur title, the richest I could bestow, if I thought for one moment he would take it. In the coming battle, I will stand with him rather than against him. If you have any sense, Gilrayan, you'd rush to do the same."

Baron Oyrwyn sat back in his chair, drumming his fingers along its arms, eyeing Allystaire speculatively. "I see little reason to believe the savage. Perhaps he's been bribed to say what he has. Coached to respond."

"It is clear," Allystaire said, "that my presence at this table is hindering the proceedings. My comrades and I shall withdraw to our camp. The morning after tomorrow, I will leave this place to raise whatever host I can. Be in it if you wish. If you wish to do otherwise, be prepared to explain to your own people why you were not."

With that, Allystaire pulled his small string of prisoners to their feet and turned around sharply. There was a hubbub of protesting voices behind him. Harlach's bass rumble underlaid it all, and he could pick out Gilrayan's faint laughter. After a moment it faded into the noise as he stalked off, sweeping up Idgen Marte, Torvul, the prisoners, and Tibult in his wake.

* * *

"That was not," Torvul said, "the opportune time to leave. Nor was it particu-larly diplomatically done." The dwarf squatted on his stump-thick legs before their fire, fussing with a large pot hung above it on a tripod. From time to time as he stirred, added, or tasted, it released fragrant scents of chicken, onion, or herbs that had Allystaire's stomach rumbling.

"Is it ready yet?"

"You've no sense of timing, is the problem. And about as much tact as a rockslide."

Idgen Marte ceased her pacing behind Allystaire's seat upon a log and said, "He's not wrong, Ally. You didn't make any progress."

"I did not see how I could. I presented them my ultimatum, my prisoners, and then Gilrayan..." He clenched his fists tightly at his sides. "The man knows precisely how to anger me. Had I kept listening, I doubt I could have stayed my hand."

A stray snatch of song floated out from Gideon's tent as all three of them quieted down.

"At least he's not wasting the last of the light," Idgen Marte said. Then, clearing her throat, she called out in her cracked and broken voice. "Scales! Stop tryin' to play songs until the scales are perfect."

"So is that why y'rode away from the life y'knew?" Torvul stood straight, rubbing a fist against the small of his back. "He just angered ya?"

"For three years, Torvul, I tried to make him see sense. I tried to bring out whatever of his father was in him. Finally, his plans, his desires grew to be too much for me to bear. It was leave or kill him, and I had sworn to Gerard Oyrwyn not to do that."

"What was that plan, then? What did he mean t'do?" Idgen Marte swung one leg over the log and sat down at the other end, facing Allystaire.

"Besides bleed his treasury dry? Order his liege lords to raise rents until his people were broken? Knighting swords-at-hire who were little more than assassins? It was an accumulation of things."

"There had t'be somethin'," Toruvl muttered, "and the stew won't be done till ya tell me what it was."

"Fine," Allystaire said, "he was holding a war council. The heat of the summer had reached even up into the mountains and we had broken off a campaign against Harlach when we had made no progress. He then hatched a plan to bring Innadan with us against Harlach. A masterstroke, he called it."

Allystaire sighed deeply. "He wanted us to wear false livery, knights to put on the colors of Harlach knights, our men to put on Harlach tabards, and sack and burn Innadan villages. It was an appalling violation of everything that knighthood and honor could ever mean."

He held up a hand to forestall Idgen Marte's protest. "I know, knighthood and honor do not mean much. Yet I will never forget the look on his face as he laid out his strategy for us, and what he said." He twisted his features and spat out the words, "'Don't stint the rape or the torch.' Those were his words, his plan: to murder the innocents among our *allies*, Idgen Marte. And the hateful way he said it." He shook his head, pounded a balled fist against the log.

"I know," Allystaire went on, staring hard into the fire, "that armies are not easy on the places they conquer, or the people. When I saw it, or heard of it and could prove it, I hung the men who did it. I made reparations when I had the means. And for all these years I pretended that such dumb shows, such carefully maintained distance, absolved me of the sin of it all, the horror wrought upon innocents. That I would hang a man and pay a handful of silver to someone he wronged made me *better* than him, for all that I was part and party to ruinous farce of it all. So I thought. I know that I probably did not hang men who deserved it, or hanged some who did not. My hands are as red as those of any man alive."

Finally he lifted his eyes, first to Torvul, and then he turned to Idgen Marte. "Yet to see those crimes as a weapon? As a lever to move our own ally against a third party with whom he had little quarrel? I could never have lived with that. I could never have been a part of it, and I knew I could not serve the man who proposed it, nor could I kill him. I held my oath to his father, spoken when I was barely six winters old, as the most sacred thing I had ever done."

"You can kill a man who'll propose such a plan and rest easy knowin' you did right that day," Idgen Marte said, following hard on Allystaire's words. "And I never swore any oaths to his father."

"No, Idgen Marte," Allystaire said. "He did not attempt to carry off such a plan; had he done, one of the two of us would now be dead. And yet, if I had killed him then, if one of us did now, what then? He has no heir. It would be a squabble amongst his lords to assume his seat. Perhaps Garth would succeed him, perhaps Naswyn, or perhaps the entire Barony would crack apart as Harlach seized his chance. I could not know then and I do not know now, except for this fact: people would die. Hundreds, at the least."

"He's right, Idgen Marte," Torvul said, after a brief lull where the run of a scale up and then down floated out from Gideon's tent. "We need a united front. He may be despicable, but we can't kill a man solely for the words he spoke."

"If he speaks them to me, he'll die," she replied hoarsely.

"Take your hand off your sword," Allystaire muttered. "We are here to make peace, not fewer Barons. We cannot seem to be threatening them, and we certainly cannot kill any of them unless we have no choice."

"You've already threatened them, Allystaire," Idgen Marte muttered. "You put the threat right in front of them. Revolt."

Allystaire shook his head, hunched over in his seat, and lowered his eyes to the ground. "What other threat could I make? I will march against the Braechsworn, and I will take any man willing, and I needed a way to make them give me the men."

"Why're you so sure they will, anyway? They know where Symod's army is. They could march to meet it themselves." Torvul once again sniffed at the pot, stirred with the wooden spoon that dangled against its side.

"Delondeur and Innadan will want me at the head of whatever force they can muster," Allystaire said. "They have both said as much. When word spreads to Oyrwyn, the men themselves will want me. Telmawr will likely do whatever Innadan says to do. Machoryn and Damarind are far from where Braech's hammer might fall, and will be able to bring little to the campaign, but it does our faith no harm for this to be their introduction to it."

"That leaves Harlach," Idgen Marte said, "and he's too proud to be seen following you."

"All he needs to do is show up on the field," Allystaire said, "and be pointed in the right direction."

Idgen Marte snorted. "If he's so fearsome, why does everyone at the table seem to hold him in contempt?"

Allystaire shook his head. "He is an old-fashioned sort. Too old-fashioned; all he ever understood of battle was to run straight at the other bastard and try to hurt him."

"I've seen you fight," Idgen Marte said flatly, "and that is precisely how I'd describe it."

"One to one? Yes, of course," Allystaire said. "Yet that is no way to lead in battle, when other lives are at stake. Unseldt never met a hill he would not charge, or a false retreat he would not chase after."

"Y'still seem too certain," Idgen Marte muttered, "and I'm not. They'll try to make you break or bend before they agree t'anything."

"Supper is ready," Torvul announced, with a clap of his hands. "If someone'd spread the word."

There was enough light for Allystaire to see Idgen Marte's eyes swing meaningfully to him, so he started off towards the sounds of Gideon's lute practice.

Idgen Marte swung off the log and was by Torvul's side, leaning over the pot with a few steps.

"They'll try to break or bend him," Torvul muttered. "You're right."

"He won't."

"'Course he won't. I'm not worried about him, it's just, d'ya know why you add other ores, or earths, to iron when ya want t'make steel?"

"Holds an edge longer, lighter, more flexible."

"And there it is," Torvul said, pointing a finger towards her. "He's iron, Idgen Marte. Strong and durable, but inflexible, brittle. Easily broken in the right place. You and I, we're what make him steel. D'ya understand?"

Idgen Marte thought a moment, as the rest of the inhabitants of their camp began to converge on their fire. "Dwarf," she said, "the Goddess Herself gave me that task. I need no reminders."

Torvul just smiled as he dipped a ladle into the pot.

* * *

Allystaire sat across the tent from Gideon, who had gone right back to the lute after eating. They boy sat cross-legged on the cot while Allystaire, finally free of the weight of his armor, stretched his legs out from the stool, keeping his hammer on the small table, his right hand only inches from it.

"You are getting better, if you ask me," Allystaire said, when Gideon took his hand from the strings to flex it, curling the fingers and tightening the hand into a fist and then unclenching two or three times.

The boy opened his mouth, then bit his lip, finally spitting out, "Thank you."

Allystaire chuckled. "What did you mean to say?"

"That Idgen Marte's opinion is the one that matters in this," Gideon said sheepishly. "Or that you've said yourself that you have no ear for music."

"I can tell the difference between a note well or badly struck," Allystaire said. "Besides, Idgen Marte could lie to you about what she hears. I cannot."

Gideon nodded, pursing his lips as if he hadn't thought of that. With a sigh, the boy set the lute down on the cot next to him. "Do you think the Baron Oyrwyn will agree to the peace?"

It was Allystaire's turn to sigh. "I cannot make out the workings of that man's mind. I never could, even when he was a lad."

"What was he like, then?"

"Smart, but in a way that cut. Cunning, always looking for a way to promote himself. I suppose he had to be that way, as bastard-born, if he wanted to gain his father's attention. He was never first among his age in the yard—not with Ghislain only a year his elder—but never last, either."

"Ghislain?"

Another, heavier sigh. "Gerard Oyrwyn's only trueborn child. The only one I know of besides Gilrayan."

"How did he die?"

"In battle, eight years past. Delondeur thought he could catch us by surprise by trying a path through Varshyne, what was left of it, circle round the mountains, and come through the taiga. We rushed what we could to meet him, but too many knights were in Harlach when we realized what was happening. Ghislain took charge of the first force to meet him. He was not quite nineteen summers old and he had been knighted a bit less than a year and a half before."

"And he was a better man than Gilrayan?"

"He would have been," Allystaire replied. "Of that I am certain. He was every inch his father. It was easy to see, even in his youth, a man we would all have been happy to follow."

"Why did Gerard Oyrwyn only have one true-born son? And why does it matter so much anyway? And if there was only the one potential heir, why was he not kept out of harm's way?"

"I will answer those questions in reverse," Allystaire said, sitting up and straightening his legs. "Gerard Oyrwyn did not believe that the toll of war should be borne only by the poor. Granted," he said, lifting a palm, "the greater part of the cost always falls to them. Even so, he would never have held his son back from a battle that threatened the very heart of the Barony. Ghislain would never have stood for being left behind, either. He was eager to prove himself, and men were eager to follow him."

He paused for breath, lifted his eyes to Gideon. The boy's dark eyes shone in the lamp light, studying him and his responses in that frank way he had. "To the second, it matters because it always has. A child born to a knight or a lord outside of marriage is only owed whatever the father decides he or she is owed."

"That's despicable," Gideon said flatly. "And to say that it is so because it has always been so is faulty logic."

"I know," Allystaire said, "it is one more thing I never questioned. Though I had reason to."

"You never had any so-called natural children, did you?"

Allystaire shook his head. "None of any kind."

"How certain are you?"

"Certain enough," Allystaire said. "I never married and no woman I, ah… knew…ever claimed to have my child. I like to think they would have done."

"And what would you have done in the event?"

"Are we losing the thread here? This seems irrelevant."

Gideon shook his head. "No. I want to understand."

"Fine," Allystaire said. "I like to think I would have provided all that I could, full rights and recognition. A moot question now, though."

Gideon nodded. "Then what did you mean, you had reason to question it?"

Allystaire swallowed hard. "The only woman I ever wanted to marry, she was the natural daughter of an Oyrwyn lord. He acknowledged her, and she was raised at the fringes of court, but when the time came, he would not grant her his name, nor dower her."

"Could you not have married her despite that?"

"Gideon," Allystaire said, raising the tips of his fingers to his forehead, "I do not wish to speak of it any further."

Silence reigned for a moment. "Then, what about Gerard Oyrwyn? Why did he have only the two children?"

"As I am no chirurgeon, I cannot say," Allystaire replied. "He was married only once, and whether the difficulty in conception was a fault of his or his lady wife's I cannot say. There were rumblings, once, that he should put aside Ismalde once she passed the age, but he would have none of that. Gilrayan's mother was a camp follower."

Gideon *tutted* lightly, his disapproval clear.

"War is a grim and dreary business and those who fight will do anything to distract themselves from the likelihood of their death. I am not proud of it, not defending it exactly, but a camp commander who tries to drive them off, outlaw them, or punish a soldier for visiting them is signing his own death warrant."

"It surprises me to hear you admit this to me," Gideon said. "Then, I suppose you can't lie about it."

"I would not anyway. It is just one more hard fact of the war."

"It is, I would venture to guess, a rather harder fact for those who follow the camps."

"Aye," Allystaire said, "I am sure that it is."

"When we raise an army and march from here," the boy's voice trailed off, "will followers come in our wake?"

"Almost certainly," Allystaire said.

"Then we must make it a point to reach out to them, minister to them," Gideon said.

"Do you mean preach to them?"

"No," Gideon said. "You are right that it is likely unavoidable, and probably a healthier outlet for the soldiers, in some ways, than doing without. Yet it is almost certainly awful for the followers. We must not forget that we will be fighting in their defense as well."

"That is remarkably insightful, Gideon," Allystaire said. "In the coming days, I want you to draw up a list of rules you would suggest for their treatment, and we will see if we cannot make it a policy."

The boy nodded, then switched topics quickly and decisively. "Where will we even get the troops? There are not more than a few hundred men here in the pass, and we cannot know that all of them will join."

"Hamadrian has promised his Thornriders, and Landen whatever men she can spare. Add to that whatever Oyrwyn men are near."

"There is still no guarantee that Gilrayan will sign any peace. From what you've told me, we need to make him see how it is to his advantage to do so."

"I thought not dropping a mountain on his head was a strong argument."

"It was enough to get him to come to the table," Gideon said, "but an argument made using only force is no argument at all. It is merely a threat."

"I am not above threatening Gilrayan Oyrwyn if I must."

"Yet we will need Oyrwyn men, yes?"

"Aye," Allystaire agreed, nodding slowly, crossing his arms over his chest. "It seems as though we will."

"Then again I say we must convince him that it is to his own benefit to agree," Gideon said.

"How do we do that?"

"I haven't the faintest idea," the boy said, "but I suspect that Torvul might. Why not let him represent us?"

"Dwarfs are not the most respected of folk," Allystaire said, "lone dwarfs even less so. Yet he is probably better suited to it than I am."

"Why is Torvul apart from a caravan?"

"I do not know, and he has never offered to say." The last couple of words were cut short by a jaw-cracking yawn. "We will have a long day," Allystaire said, when he recovered, "and we both ought to rest."

Gideon carefully lifted the lute and slid it into its case, closed it, and began fastening it almost reverently. Carefully, he slid it under his cot and stretched out, hooking his feet at the ankles.

Allystaire picked up his hammer and then carefully lowered himself to the other cot, listening to it creak as it took his weight. He leaned his weapon against the cot, laying back and testing the reach of his right arm to it.

"Do you always sleep at the ready?" Gideon asked.

"Usually."

"Are you worried someone in the camp may try to attack us, then?"

"I think they might," Allystaire said, "but I am not worried."

"Why not?"

The paladin closed his eyes and stretched his thoughts. He found Idgen Marte standing by the edges of their dying cookfire. He knew he could not have seen her there, if he'd walked outside the tent to look, but he could feel her all the same.

"Because anyone who tries to sneak into our camp is in more danger than they are likely to understand."

* * *

She tried to remain still. Not because she needed to. No one could see her, folded into the shadows cast by the embers of the fire behind her. She tried to remain still because remaining still was what one did when waiting on the ambush one intended to ambush in turn.

So, she was certain, Allystaire would've said to remain still.

But stillness was never in Idgen Marte. She had too much energy, too many things to do, too many things to think on.

There was Andus Carek in one of the tents to think about. He'd insisted on coming in order to "document the moment," he'd said.

Focus, she told herself. Then, frowning hard, she narrowed her thoughts and sought out Torvul who, she knew, was dozing lightly atop his wagon, crossbow in his lap.

You so sure somebody'll make a play?

Reasonably, he answered drowsily. *If not to kill Allystaire, to get a look at Gideon. They saw the Will of the Mother, but they've not seen him, and it's a curious lot over there.*

You know I could just go threaten them in their sleep. They'd sign that damn document Allystaire wants a great deal faster if they thought their lives depended on it.

He doesn't want to broker peace with the sword, and he's right not to want it.

Idgen Marte frowned, though the dwarf could not see it. *That doesn't tell me whether or not you agree with him.*

I have a more expansive view o'the matter. He's right not to want it, I mean that. Peace'd be as much use as a knife made of unalloyed gold if all that were behind it were threats. And yet.

Threats may be all a man like Unseldt Harlach understands.

I don't think he's likely to send knives in the night anyway, Torvul replied.

They lapsed into silence. Idgen Marte paced around the edges of the fire, toying with the hilt of her sword.

Doesn't seem his style, she admitted. *But what do we know of his advisors?*

Almost nothing, the dwarf admitted. *We ought to have had a sit down with Allystaire t'learn as much about these folk as we could.*

Hold. Someone comes. When the hard moments came, Idgen Marte found stillness easy, and she settled into it entirely. In the right shadow, she would've practically vanished from sight even without benefit of the Goddess's Gifts.

Clinging to the darkness, well beyond the circle of light, where Idgen Marte could not have seen but for her Gift, two men were slowly working their way through the trees. They wore leather, soft-soled boots and had long knives, their blades blacked with ash, held in their hands, lying along their forearms.

They stopped beyond the tent farthest from the fire, the empty one she had insisted upon placing there.

Not amateurs in their craft she thought, as one soundlessly slipped his knife up the slits in order to part any knots holding the flaps closed, while the second remained on watch, *just their thinking.*

Before Torvul could even respond, she had flashed to the side of the one lurking outside the tent, kicked his knee out, and smacked the pommel of her sword into his neck. The first blow staggered him; the second cut off the scream that was gathering in his throat. He went gasping to the ground, stunned, no more threat.

There was still the sound of him falling to the ground, which brought his partner rushing back out of the tent.

Drawn like a fool, she thought to herself, as she flashed to the inside of the tent—shadows cast on its interior by the stars and moon shining through the drawn flap—and pressed the point of her sword to the back of his neck.

"The knife, or your head," she rasped. "One of them is hitting the ground in the next moment. Choose."

He lifted his arms to his sides and opened his hand. The knife fell to the ground with a muffled thump.

"Now," she said, "tell me who sent you, and what you were out to do."

The man didn't say a word. She let pressure build on the tip of her sword, felt it just break the skin.

He leaned forward, away from the sword, and said, "I cannot. I'll…" He stopped talking, swallowed so hard she could hear it, as if he were choking something down.

"What? You'll die? I'm the one with the sword at your neck, you'll do well t'note," she muttered. Then again, that choking-swallowing sound, and then Torvul's thought like a warning bell as he suddenly bolted towards her.

The assassin in Grenthorpe! Do you not remember what the priest of Braech did to him? He's goin' t'die!

ALLYSTAIRE! She screamed for the paladin with her mind, and felt as he awoke all at once. It was something about him she had marveled at since the beginning, and it had nothing to do with the Goddess's gifts. One moment, he was deeply, restfully asleep. The next, he was completely awake, aware, and—in this case—boiling out of the tent carrying his hammer.

He did not move fast, by her standards—by her standards, *nobody* moved fast—but there was always a total singleness of purpose to him. No movement was ever wasted, no foot was put wrong, even if it took him a while to get them moving in the first place. Once he was moving, she knew, as she had known since she saw him in a shantytown tavern a lifetime ago, only a fool would stand in his way.

Idgen Marte would never cease being astonished at how completely he had given himself to his new life. How there was no doubt, no thought for himself, no hesitation at hurling himself into danger. She had called for him, and here he was, nearly naked, weapon in hand, ready to take on an army if need be.

He's choking, Allystaire! Like the assassin who shot you, choking on seawater.

Allystaire ran to the would-be assassin's side, his feet churning in the grass and mud of the campsite. He put his hand to the man's shoulder, who was now hunched over, his retching and gagging sounds now unmistakable.

Torvul had joined them, crossbow dangling across his body from a hook high on his right shoulder.

Almost instantly, Allystaire took his hand away from the dying assassin, as if stung. "I cannot heal him," he said aloud. "It is not a wound, not a disease. It is magic, and I cannot fight it." He stood up, his eyes wide in shock. "I cannot save him. Torvul?"

"Not poison," the dwarf said, even as he knelt by the man, putting his hands to his throat. "I don't know what I can do."

There was a rush of wind, a faint run of notes in her ears, and Gideon was suddenly standing in front of the dying man, extending one hand, a deep golden glow beginning in his palm.

"I can," the boy said. "Step away from him."

Almost at once the sounds of choking stopped, and the glow spread out from Gideon's palm to envelop the man completely. His body went rigid and he came to his feet, and a hard blue light began to seep from him into the soft nimbus that surrounded him.

"Sherdan," Gideon said, "I know that is your name. You entered into a contract with the Sea Dragon. I do not know what your payment was to be, but I do know that the Master of Accords has proven a shrewder negotiator than you.

I need you to reject the terms of it in order to save you. I need you, Sherdan, to give up all hope of the payment you longed for."

The boy tilted his bald head to one side, as if listening for an answer, and shook his head.

"I can keep the magic that is killing you at bay indefinitely, if I wish." He paused. "But I don't. I need an answer very soon, and I think I have shown enough forbearance given that you came here to kill me."

Gideon sighed; there was no sign of exertion in his extended arm. The cloud of gold that flowed around the man from his arm did not waver or dim.

"Of course I can keep you safe. The representative of the Sea Dragon who put you up to this is no threat to me, or to those who surround me. Now, Sherdan, you must consent to give up what you were promised. Or you must prepare your soul to meet Braech. Make your choice."

It seemed to Idgen Marte as if the man nodded. Gideon's hand tightened to a fist, and for the first time, there was a sign of strain.

Not for long, though. The blue drops that had seeped out of Sherdan co-alesced into a small, hard, dark blue ball in the air between him and Gideon. Inexorably, it was drawn to the Will's palm, and when it met Gideon's skin, seemed to sink into him, vanishing. Slowly, Sherdan was lowered back to his feet, and the golden glow that had surrounded him winked out of existence and the would-be assassin fell to the ground in a heap.

Whatever rest he found there was short-lived. Allystaire's hand seized the back of his jerkin and lifted him to his feet.

"We are going to have a long talk, Sherdan." He held the man on his feet with his left arm, almost absentmindedly, as he turned to Idgen Marte, and nodded to the unmoving shape on the ground.

"Did you kill that one?"

She shook her head. "Just put him out. He'll come around."

"Well, then Gideon may have to go through all this again when he wakes."

"Only if we ask him questions," Gideon said. "I think. Simply being cap-tured shouldn't violate the terms of his bargain."

"I do not want to guess when a man's life is at stake. Even if he is not much of a man." Allystaire turned, dragging the deflated Sherdan behind him like a sack of flour. "We might as well rouse our camp," he said. "Sentries and men after a piss or a night's pleasant company will have seen the lights and be coming to investigate."

"Right," Torvul said. "I'll go fetch some shackles for the prisoners." He turned to Idgen Marte. "You can rouse folk the fastest."

She nodded and turned away. Her first stop was her own tent, where Andus Carek lay sleeping upon a pile of blankets. Idgen Marte knelt next to him, waking him by placing her hand upon his bare chest.

"Awake," she said, wincing as she heard her rasping voice saw at the sounds of their shared native tongue, when it should have been nearly sung. She switched to the Barony tongue; it was ugly enough on its own that she didn't hate the sound of her own voice speaking it.

"You're going to want to see what comes," she murmured, then turned and made for the tent shared by Norbert, Harrys, and Tibult.

* * *

Allystaire took a deep breath.

Despite that, his hand still closed into a fist, and he heard his knuckles crack.

No time for putting on armor, he reminded himself, even as he looked longingly at it on the stand, gleaming softly in the dim light of lantern Torvul had sparked to life when he came to shackle the prisoner.

When Allystaire thought of the man again, knife in hand, skin darkened, attempting to creep into the tents, targeting Gideon, he wanted, quite simply, to rush outside and kill someone.

He felt a twinge in his right hand as he recalled smashing the head of a reaver captain against a wall with his fists, one blow after another, until there was almost nothing left of it.

Allystaire wanted a wall, and his iron-banded gloves, and Sherdan's head between them. He closed his eyes and took another deep breath, went back to looking for his shirt and trousers.

Gideon slipped in the back of the tent, took a long look at Allystaire. "I was in no danger," the boy said quietly.

"Not the point," Allystaire replied, and he was surprised at the extent to which his anger seeped into his voice. He pulled his dark blue tunic over his head, finding it difficult to unclench his fists.

"Does it occur to you that if you now go and attack the Oyrwyn camp, the Congress could disintegrate, and perhaps that is all that the Sea Dragon's priest was attempting to do?"

"I am not going to attack the Oyrwyn camp," Allystaire said. "I am going to expel Braech's priest, though. It will be up to him whether he leaves under his own power or I drag his body away. Even so, I doubt he acted of his own accord."

"Why not?"

"Sherdan is an Oyrwyn man. He told me as much as I dragged him here," Allystaire said. He tugged his belt around his waist and cinched it closed, reached for the hammer that he'd set on his cot. "A scout. He was detailed to the priest—Winsar Ethrik, he said, and I am not sure which of those is a title."

"The first is," Gideon replied. "Winsars report to Marynths, who serve Choirons. The titles come from Islandman language roots."

"Now is not the time for a linguistics lesson, Gideon," Allystaire replied.

"Gilrayan Oyrwyn didn't bring a priest of Braech with him to the congress, did he? He was attended by two men, neither of whom wore Braech's vestments."

"Aye," Allystaire agreed. "Neither did."

"Then why are you—"

Allystaire slipped his hammer through the loop on his belt and strode out of the tent, taking the lantern as he went. "It would take too long to explain. Just follow."

* * *

Outside their tent, the rest of the Mother's encampment was moving into action. Idgen Marte had rousted the three men of the Order and Andus Carek, with the former coming armed and the latter bearing a writing case under one arm. Torvul had his lantern out and between the powerful illumination of the dwarf's handiwork and Allystaire's more mundane lamp, they had enough light to see by.

"We had assassins in the camp," Allystaire explained, immediately pressing on over the sudden questions from Harrys, Norbert, and Tibult. "They have been subdued, but we are off to subdue their masters. No one bares a blade or nocks an arrow unless I do, or at the need of saving your life or someone else's. Understood?"

The three men nodded. Idgen Marte stood unmoving to one side with her hand on the hilt of the long curve of her blade.

"Idgen Marte?"

She sighed. "I think you need to kill the lot of them. The Baron Oyrwyn and his advisors, and put Garth and Audreyn in his place."

"We are not here to start a revolt," Allystaire quietly insisted. "It must not come to that."

She spat to one side, then nodded, but her hand never left her sword.

"Good," Allystaire said. "Torvul, once we are at the Oyrwyn camp, such as it is, would you be so kind as to wake the rest of the camp for us."

The dwarf pursed his lips, then thumbed the runes stamped into the leather of the pouches hooked to his jerkin. "I think I can manage," he rumbled.

"Good. Idgen Marte, if you would be so kind as to scout for us?"

She lifted a hand and pointed. "They gave him space in the Innadan camp, to put some distance, and some friendly knights between him and Harlach."

"Well, then," Allystaire said, lifting his lantern. "Let us be off."

"Sure you don't want your armor, boy?" Torvul had already plucked a vial from a pouch with one hand, held it up to the light his lantern cast.

"Want it, yes," Allystaire said. "Yet we cannot spare the time, and if it comes to blood, they will not be armored—and I will give no man a reason to say that I took advantage of that." He turned and led them on, with the Shadow of the Mother, an invisible spot in the darkness just beyond him, the Will and the Wit close behind, and three men of the Order of the Arm, grim-faced, spread out behind them.

Lagging behind them all was the bard Andus Carek, who had already dragged parchment from his writing case, and was struggling to manage pen and ink both in one hand.

* * *

The Goddess's Gift of Strength was not upon the Arm of the Mother, only an anger that was as clean and pure as on the day he had assaulted a warehouse full of slavers. He'd had no gift then.

Anger would serve.

Idgen Marte identified the tent for him. It was a spacious pavilion in Innadan colors, though not so large or ornate as those occupied by the Baron or his heir. With his hammer still hanging from his belt, he started for the tent, only to find Idgen Marte's hand on his shoulders.

"Let Torvul announce us," she muttered.

Allystaire turned to the dwarf and extended a hand. Torvul nodded, took a tiny sip of the bottle he'd palmed, smacked his lips, and then unleashed a bellow that set Allystaire's ears ringing.

"ASSASSINS IN THE CAMP. MURDER! TREACHERY! ASSASSINS! TO THE INNADAN CAMP!"

The words rolled out over the slumbering camps like a wave threatening to swallow a seaside village.

The dwarf, his voice returned nearly to normal, cut through the ringing in his ears with a rumble. "Cover your eyes."

As Allystaire raised his arm he caught sight of the dwarf slipping something free of a pouch and raising his arm to hurl it to the ground.

Even with his eyes hidden in the crook of his arm he felt the heat and had a flash of the bright green flare that lit up the sky around them.

He turned to face the tent when the impression passed, hand hanging on his hammer. His ears cleared quickly, and he could already hear the sounds of frantic scramble inside the tent, strained for the telltale whisk of steel on leather.

Soon enough, three men came boiling out of it, wearing gambesons or arming jackets, weapons in hand. Joeglan Naswyn came first, stooping, holding a scabbarded sword with the belt wrapped around the sheath. Gilrayan Oyrwyn followed, and even his gambeson, Allystaire noted, was embroidered in silk, with the Oyrwyn Mountain picked out in silver, with silver buttons on the cuffs. He carried his hand-and-a-half sword with the heavy silver pommel. Last was the unknown knight, a man of a size with Allystaire, though younger, with a dark beard, carrying a heavy mace in his right hand.

The paladin stared hard at the third man a moment, focusing on the gleam of metal around his neck.

Blinking before lanterns and armed men, they half-heartedly raised their weapons.

"Winsar Ethrik!" Torvul's voice rang out quick and clear before they had their wits about them.

The bearded knight's head swung towards the dwarf, his mouth half open, raising his mace.

"What is the meaning of this?" Lord Naswyn was the first to finally gather himself, his voice as somber and stately as his bearing. He had wrapped his hand around the hilt of his sword but hadn't started to draw it free. "Why are we accosted in our beds when we came with banners drawn?"

"Because you brought a priest of Braech to this place and attempted to hide him from me," Allystaire said, the anger that had been roiling in his stomach starting to rise to his throat. "Because that priest brought assassins into the camp, and they tried. To kill. My SON."

His hammer was half out of its loop before he knew it. Joeglan bared a foot of steel. Gilrayan Oyrwyn tossed the scabbard of his own blade well away, and lantern light played along its length as he held it across his body.

For just a moment, Allystaire felt a tinge of regretful pride. *You have not forgotten everything I taught you*, he thought. *Just the most important parts.*

Behind him, Allystaire heard a rustling as Harrys and Tibult likewise bared steel, and the telltale creak of a bowstring. In his peripheral vision he could see Norbert stepping to the side, his nocked arrow moving from one Oyrwyn man to the other. Idgen Marte's sword was a sliver of bright, deadly moon hanging in the air. He had neither seen nor heard her draw; he guessed that no one else had, either.

"You come armed in the night when you would demand peace! Now you show your true colors, traitor!" Gilrayan Oyrwyn finally found his tongue.

"I am not the one who brought assassins with me, boy," Allystaire spat back. "I will have the Sea Dragon's priest expelled."

"You make strong accusations that want proof," Joeglan said.

"The Mother allows no man to speak a lie to me," Allystaire said. "Your assassins named you, Winsar Ethrik, and I will wager you worked at the bidding of the Baron, or the Choiron Symod, or both."

"Say nothing!" Gilrayan's command rang out sharply. "He is a liar and commands a warlock, or is one himself! Do not give in to him."

"What is the meaning of this?" The voice that rang out over them was commanding in tone, and too rich and powerful to have come from the ailing Hamadrian Innadan.

Arontis Innadan, sword in hand, a robe thrown over his shoulders and worn loose over his chest and underclothes, was the first of the trail of knights, nobles, and Barons to arrive. The Archioness Cerisia trailed in his wake.

"We will not have bloodshed in the camp, Sir Stillbright," Arontis said. Boldly, lowering his own sword, he walked straight between the drawn weapons, putting his own flesh between the weapons of the three Oyrwyn men and the paladin.

"They brought assassins, Lord Innadan," Allystaire growled. He lifted his left hand off the hammer and pointed. "That man is no knight of Oyrwyn, but a Winsar, a priest of Braech come in secret. Two subdued men in my camp will attest to the magic he worked upon them and the accord he made for them to assassinate one of us."

"Lies and slander," Gilrayan yelled. "An exile who consorts with witches and sorcerers impugns the honor of a Baron. He should answer for it."

Allystaire felt a wordless growl rising up in his throat. Before he or Arontis could speak, Joeglan Naswyn stepped forward, straightening up to his full height. Necks craned.

"I will make him, my lord," Joeglan droned. "Allystaire, once Lord of Coldbourne. You have accused the Baron Oyrwyn and his retainer of serious crimes. You have slandered my lord's name. I will defend it honorably, though you are no longer my peer. Do you accept my challenge?"

Allystaire lowered his hammer and stared hard at the man before him. "No longer your peer, Lord Naswyn?"

Behind him he heard a faint gasp from Idgen Marte as she heard him say the man's name.

"Once upon a time, Joeglan, all I wanted in this world was to be counted your peer, and my father's, as knight in service to Gerard Oyrwyn. I could imagine nothing finer when I was seven years old. The day I was knighted by Gerard Oyrwyn and welcomed by men like you into that company was the finest of my life. And now you would say I am not your peer?" Allystaire sneered. "Good. To be your *peer* is to be dross, Lord of the Horned Towers. It is rot. I should have aspired to be a *better* man than you."

"Enough nonsense," Gilrayan shouted. "Do you or—"

"QUIET, BOY." Allystaire's voice rang out like a drillyard master's, and he never took his eyes from Naswyn's. "The men are talking."

Gilrayan lapsed into a stunned silence while Allystaire continued.

"You are part of a knighthood that values accidents of birth above all else, Joeglan Naswyn. Knighthood should mean nobility of spirit, not birth. Willingness to sacrifice instead of the desire to gain," Allystaire said. "You," he said, his voice dripping anger, "who would value the circumstances of birth above even your own blood's happiness are not *my* peer." Shocked murmuring ran through the gathering crowd. Allystaire heard whispers as the news was relayed to those who could not see or hear.

"I have wanted to send you to the Cold you deserve for fifteen years," Allystaire said, choking back his anger and letting the words hang in the air.

He heard a voice, Cerisia's, he thought, saying, "Allystaire, no!"

Then he slammed his hammer back into its ring, and said, "I do not recognize your right to challenge me, Joeglan Naswyn. Nor will I call you lord, or sir. I serve a Goddess now, and though I have *dreamt* of killing you, it would not serve the Mother."

Allystaire tore his eyes from Joeglan Naswyn and looked to Arontis. "I will not shed the blood of any Barony man here under drawn banners." He raised a hand to point to Ethrik, who had stayed silent. "Yet he is no Barony man. Him I will have."

A cacophony of voices, Gilrayan's shrill in protest, Idgen Marte's warning blaring in his mind, Torvul rumbling his displeasure.

Allystaire heard none of them. There was only the roaring of his blood, the need to bring his hammer down on that hateful, rounded face.

Finally, Arontis shouted everyone into silence, turning a hard, sober look at Allystaire. "Do you have proof of this, Sir Stillbright?"

"I have two prisoners in my camp who will tell you they made a bargain with this man, and know him as the Winsar." More shouting. Allystaire summoned his battlefield voice, the one that could pitch itself above any din. "Yet we need not even ask them," he bellowed. "Ask that man there to show us what he wears about his neck." He pointed, and Arontis's head turned.

Behind him, Torvul's lantern suddenly projected a bright white beam straight at the burly man's face and neck, catching the unmistakable glint of silver.

"Why would that matter?" Arontis's question was for Allystaire, but he was watching Ethrik closely as he spoke.

Cerisia stepped into the beam of Torvul's lantern, her white robe sparkling where it caught the light. "Because such things are ranks among the Sea Dragon's clergy, as masks are to Fortune's," she said. "Colors, robes, and vestments may come and go and the faithful adopt many symbols. The wheel, the banner, those might be put in a house to bring good luck, carried at festivals, or brought to Temples for a blessing. Yet the mask is given only to those of us who serve Fortune directly. Braech's amulet is the same."

Silence reigned. The bearded man—Ethrik, Allystaire was certain of it—froze, mace in the hand that he lowered to his side.

"I need do nothing," he finally stammered.

"If you came to this camp under false banner, color, or name," Arontis said, "then you are not subject to guest right, nor are you under the protection of Barony Innadan."

"He came under my banner," Gilrayan shouted, imperious to the last. "Are you suggesting it is false?"

"If he serves the Sea Dragon then it is the Sea Dragon's banner he must arrive beneath," Arontis said. "The Archioness Cerisia is advising my father, yet she traveled under Fortune's Silken Lady, not the Vined Great Helm."

"Show us, Ethrik," Allystaire said. "Surely not all of Braech's servants are as cowardly as I have come to expect. Hiring assassins. Hiding from me. Choosing others to fight their battles."

"Show," Torvul rumbled, "or repudiate Braech. If you don't serve him, surely y'don't fear to deny him."

Arontis' had taken half a step back from the man and cleared a foot of his sword, slowly, deliberately. "Show, or be convicted for your failure, man."

Tilting his chin defiantly, the priest reached a large, heavy-knuckled fist beneath his nightshirt and lifted up the fine links of silver around his neck. He pulled the amulet free of his neck and then let it hang, Torvul's lantern framing it for all to see.

The bright white of the alchemist's lantern beam washed out the colors some, but there was no mistaking the blue lapis that tipped the waves, nor the bronze scales of the crude, fierce dragon's head that sat atop them.

"I am the Winsar Ethrik," the man said, his voice desperately searching for stability. "And I come as the advisor of Baron Gilrayan Oyrwyn, claiming—"

"It is too late to claim anything unless my father chooses to grant it," Arontis said, cutting him off quickly. "Baron Oyrwyn already introduced you as his retainer, which you are not. You will surrender your weapon and come with me," he went on, "or I will let Sir Stillbright do with you as he pleases."

"I will not have him squirreled away from me, Arontis," Allystaire called out. "He sent assassins to my camp, at Oyrwyn's bidding. I will have a trial at arms."

"You will if my father grants it," Arontis shot back. "And I will not rouse him from his bed till the sun rises."

"He has admitted he came under a false banner," Allystaire spat. "Do you doubt my word on the rest of it?"

"If the Father of Waves had sent men to kill you and they failed, they would not live to speak of it," Ethrik shouted, a triumphant smile spreading across his bearded face. "The Master of Accords does not bargain so poorly as that."

Allystaire smiled at him. "The Father of Waves chose a poor servant to contend with the Will of the Mother. They live, Ethrik—and you have as much as admitted now that you sent them. I want my trial at arms, Arontis. I will have it at sunrise."

"If my father grants it," Arontis cautioned.

"He will," Allystaire said, "Take him where you will. And the rest of you, if you would cross this boy," he shouted, gesturing with one hand at Gilrayan—who stood white-faced with anger—"then keep a close watch on your tents." He turned the full force of his glare on Arontis, knowing that Torvul would follow him with the lantern, which he did.

"At dawn," he grated, through a clenched jaw. "Do not try to deny me."

Allystaire turned and started through the crowd that had gathered, his men and the other Ordained falling in behind him.

Torvul's lantern seemed to cut a path through the bodies, with no one willing to step in its way. Or not, at least, willing to step in Allystaire's way once the light revealed the set of his jaw, his clenched fists, the anger that radiated from him.

One figure did hurry to his side, clutching her silk robe about her tightly.

"Allystaire," Cerisia hissed, "this threatens the entire process. You cannot jeopardize the congress for bloodlust."

He whirled on her, ignoring the crowd around them. "It is not bloodlust, Archioness. Consider it an announcement that my patience with politics is at an end, and that I will not speak niceties at men like Gilrayan Oyrwyn or Unseldt Harlach any longer. Nor will I tolerate the presence of Braech's clergy. I need not have been an enemy to them all, but they will allow me to be nothing else. So be it. In my sight, a priest of Braech armed is a dead man until I have broken their Choiron upon my hammer. They have chosen to worship power and strength, Cerisia," Allystaire said, softening his voice somewhat. "I will pay them in the wages they deserve."

"The same could be said of the Barons. Will you do the same to them?"

"If they leave me no choice."

Allystaire turned then and stalked away before she could answer.

* * *

"When I kill the paladin," Ethrik boasted, "I will do so in the armor of my God, not in your Barony plate."

The Winsar stood with Gilrayan Oyrwyn and Joeglan Naswyn, putting on the coat of blue-green scale armor and fastening tight against his thickly-muscled body. In the absence of squires, the Baron and his liege lord were helping the priest arm with the sun already threatening to rise over the Vineyards to their east.

"You would be better off in plate," Gilrayan cautioned.

"Strength is in the arm, not in iron or steel," Ethrik shot back.

Joeglan took a deep breath through his long hawkish nose, and said, "Movement may suit you better than going slow in plate."

"Why would you say that?" Gilrayan raised an eyebrow at the taller man.

"Because if two men in plate stand next to one another trading blows with blunt weapons, and one of them is Allystaire, then I know who wins the combat," Naswyn said. "If you walk out there with the mace you wear, Winsar, and thus allow him to bring his hammer, you could save us all the trouble by slitting your own throat now."

Gilrayan snorted, but Ethrik looked at Joeglan curiously, tilting his head to one side. "What do you mean? What ought I challenge him with?"

"I mean that when it comes to the battering of mace and hammer, no man I've known can contend with the man you'll face today."

"He's not some giant of legend," Gilrayan said mockingly. "And he's older now than when he squired for you, if you hadn't noticed."

"With respect, m'lord Baron, the stories about the paladin have him ripping men in half with his bare hands," Joeglan replied. "Yet that is not what I mean. It's not a question of strength, but a question of how much of a beating a man will take. I've rarely known a man his age who'll take less than he would've fifteen years before."

"What is it between the two of you, anyway? All that nonsense about having wanted to kill you all these years."

"He has his reasons, m'lord Baron," Joeglan answered slowly. "It was before your time at Wind's Jaw. I would not wish to burden you with a story."

"Surely he isn't all that you make of him," Ethrik said dubiously. Having affixed his belt, he lifted his flanged mace and guided it slowly in the air with one thick arm, then another.

"Simply put, Winsar, if you wish to conduct this combat by getting close enough to hit him with that, he will be close enough to hit you in turn. That is always how Allystaire has fought man-to-man, and he is still here."

To forestall their protest, Joeglan raised a palm. "However, he is not a flawless combatant. He was never more than an indifferent swordsman; he was not wearing one today. Blade to blade, a truly gifted swordsman could cut him apart at leisure, if he is forced to fight the same way."

"I don't wear a sword either," Ethrik said, "and I would not call myself a gifted swordsman."

"No," Joeglan said, "but you are younger, and in lighter armor, may move faster. Put reach on your side, and you have a better chance."

"Perhaps I ought to challenge him myself," Gilrayan mused, "I favor the sword, after all."

"Ah, m'lord Baron, the protocol must be followed," Joeglan pointed out. "Allystaire issued the challenge, so the man he challenged has the right to name the weapons. If you were to issue a new challenge, he would be free to fight as he saw fit. Or, worse, to make it a joust."

Some part of Joeglan Naswyn had to fight very hard not to smile when he saw the brief, panicked look that crossed his Lord Baron's face when he said that. But neither could he help but respect the young man when he nodded slowly.

"For all that his exile has cost me," Gilrayan said, "I must admit that no man I've known or seen could hit with a lance like he could."

Joeglan nodded. "Aye. He was to the lance what his grandfather was to the sword. Uncanny."

"Do you think perhaps," Gilrayan suddenly mused, "he could be lured back to the Barony's service? Not as Lord Coldbourne, of course, but some position could be found."

"I'm going to kill him," Ethrik said, almost plaintively, as if willing himself to believe it. "So do not go handing him another fiefdom yet."

Joeglan looked long at the priest. "Even if he should survive, m'lord Baron, no. There is nothing you could do to persuade him. Regardless of what lay between you, he is not a man moved to change his mind."

"Cold," Gilrayan spat, "I am tired of hearing how much you admire a man who admits to wishing you dead, Joeglan. Someday you'll have to explain it all to me. For now—"

The Baron's words trailed off and he unbuckled his swordbelt, holding the scabbarded blade out towards Ethrik. "Here. Best take the advice of the Lord of the Horned Towers, since he knows the man so well. This is the longest blade available to us. Take what time you have to familiarize yourself with it."

"I've not used a sword in some time, m'lord," the priest admitted as he took the silver-inlaid scabbard, wrapping one hand cautiously around the hilt. "Are you certain this is the best course?"

"Yes," Gilrayan said. "And besides, I rather like the idea of him dying on the end of my father's sword. Allystaire was my father's war hound for so long, let my father's weapon send him to the Cold."

"If I may say, m'lord, your father would have never wanted this. If we could avoid it, we should."

Gilrayan cut Joeglan off with a wave of one hand. "Cold, man! Have done with it. You speak of him like a son. Go on, Winsar—go bring glory to Braech. We'll be along."

Almost, almost, Joeglan allowed himself to think the words, *He should have been.* But he banished the thought, buried them with memories of the daughter whose face he couldn't recall, and followed the priest and the Baron out of the tent.

* * *

The Barons and their advisors had gathered about an empty field, arranged more or less in a ring. The combatants would have yards of space to every side to conduct their business.

Hamadrian Innadan was conspicuous in his absence. Since the edict allowing the combat, and declaring the Winsar Ethrik to have come to the camp under a false banner and thus undeserving of hospitality or protection, no word had come from him.

Arontis stood in his place, armored and red-surcoated, at the top of the circle, facing south. Allystaire stood on the western side, and the Oyrwyn party emerged from the eastern.

Allystaire was resplendent once more in his armor, helm under his right arm, shield in his left hand, hammer on his belt. The mirrored steel seemed to gather all the light of the morning to it. The brightness of it seemed to cloud his face, blurring his features to all who stood more than a few paces away.

He walked to the center of the field, meeting Arontis and Ethrik there. If he was surprised to see the latter carrying a sword, or to hear him declare that he accepted the challenge, and that it would be fought with blades alone, neither could detect it; he had simply asked for the loan of a sword.

Arontis had unbuckled his belt and handed over his own blade, scabbarded.

Now, a few moments later, as Arontis spoke formal words that he did not hear, Allystaire looked at the sword in his hands, finely wrought. Three feet of straight, doubled-edged, well-hammered steel. No fancy etching, no ornate hilt or precious golden or silver wire, one deep red gem set on the pommel.

And for that, it cost more weight to make and to own than most men will ever command in a lifetime, Allystaire thought. His mind lingered on the value of the weapon after seeing the Baron Oyrwyn's blade in Ethrik's hands, with its new gems and a rich man's weight of silver in the new hilt. The weight was odd; the weapon was made for a man taller than him, with a longer reach, to be used one-handed. If he had to use a sword, he preferred space for both hands on the hilt.

Finally, he heard someone calling his name, and looked up to Arontis.

"Sir Stillbright, what do you ask if you win? Winsar Ethrik has demanded your arms, armor, and the expulsion of your party from this congress," the Innadan heir said. His tone was purely formal, his bearing sober, dignified.

"What do I ask?" Allystaire thought on the question as he looked again at the sword. "When I win," he called out, "I demand a document of peace delivered by midday. I demand that all priests of Braech are expelled from the keep chapels of every Baron who is a signatory to it unless they repudiate Choiron Symod and all who follow him. I demand that one fifth of all value in weight, goods, and wealth of every said chapel, and every Temple to the Sea Dragon in the Baronies, be seized and redistributed as alms."

Absolute silence reigned in the wake of his pronouncement. Even Arontis stared at him, his jaw hanging wide, if only for a moment. When he gathered his voice, he said, "I cannot promise all of that, Sir Stillbright. It is not up to me alone."

"If I have to sack the chapels myself, I will not stop at one fifth," Allystaire called out. "Now let us begin. The Winsar Ethrik needs to go meet his god."

"The paladin is mad!" Winsar Ethrik seized on the moment to preach, throwing his arms up in supplication, exhorting the crowd. "What more proof do you need that his goddess is a fraud? He demands the wealth of Braech! The weak making demands of the strong is blasphemy itself!"

Allystaire stopped listening as he stared at the sword. He had spent turns with a blade in the winter, swinging one at a makeshift quintain, longer and heavier than the one he now held, and he found in the moment that he had no feel left for the weapon, no taste.

It was the weapon of a knight, or was supposed to be. *No,* he corrected himself. *It is the weapon of a* lord. *The weapon of a* knight *is his own willingness to die.* He nodded faintly, to himself, heard the priest of Braech's voice trailing off, hoarse from his preaching.

Suddenly, Allystaire raised his head, narrowed his eyes to focus on the priest, and called out, "Make peace with your fish-rotten god." Then, knowing that he'd drawn the crowd's attention, he took the sword in his right hand, point downwards, and let it drop. The point stuck in the earth, the blade gave a ripple, and Allystaire stepped forward, away from it.

"Sir Stillbright, what are you doing?" Arontis paused with one hand lifted in the air, ready to signal the start of combat.

"I understand the rules," Allystaire called back. "I simply do not need your sword, Lord Innadan."

"You are forbidden other weapons."

He settled his helm on his head, grimacing as the tightly fitted cheek and nose guards settled over his face. "You cannot forbid me my hands, Arontis. They are all I will need."

What're you doing, Allystaire? Idgen Marte's voice came into his mind, angry and fearful.

Refusing their rules, he thought back. He shut out her angry replies and curled his hands into fists, started stalking forward over the grass.

He saw eagerness in the Winsar Ethrik's face, too much of it, at first. *Then again,* a small part of Allystaire's mind wondered, *who would not be eager and confident facing a man who has discarded his only weapon?*

Ethrik brought his hand-and-a-half sword up in a cross defense, but his left foot half-stepped forward, as if he were fighting his own impulses. They were twelve paces apart, then ten, then eight, Allystaire's strides slow and confident, when Ethrik dispensed with caution and broke into a short, halting run. He lifted the sword up as he came, the blade a diagonal line over his right shoulder, held in both hands, poised for a mighty sweep.

Allystaire's pace quickened. There wasn't enough distance for him to reach a full run, or as much as he could manage in his plate, but even so, it was enough for him to raise his left arm to knock away Ethrik's blow.

The priest was young and strong, but swinging with all the might he could bring to bear. He was no swordsman, though. Instead of paralleling the flat of the blade to the ground, he held it at an angle.

Allystaire's vambrace intercepted the flat with a startlingly loud clash. He knocked the blade aside, but not without feeling the shock of impact up his arm and into his shoulder. His left arm numbed dangerously.

He had two arms. The other, his hand curled into a fist, drove straight into the other man's unprotected face. Ethrik wore an iron-banded cap around his head, but it didn't offer anything to his nose or cheeks. Allystaire had been hoping to smash his nose, hoping for the seconds of blindness that kind of pain brought, but the bull-necked priest had turned against the blow just enough to take it on his cheek.

His gauntleted fist tore open the skin and sent trickles of blood into the man's thick black beard.

When his punch landed, Allystaire was already tightening the muscles of his neck and chest, rearing back, and striking with his helmeted forehead straight at Ethrik's nose.

He hit, heard a solid crunch, the other man cry out and curse. He'd gone too high, though—the lowest band of iron around Ethrik's head had clanged hard against his helmed and added to the impact, for a moment, Allystaire saw bright spots in his vision.

The priest flailed blindly with his sword, sending ringing but harmless blows glancing off Allystaire's left pauldron, and staggered backwards. The paladin let him back away, blinking his eyes against the spots, willing away the ringing in his skull.

His vision cleared just in time to see a bleeding, broken-nose, enraged Ethrik charging straight at him, the sword straight out, like a spear meant to impale him. He waited as long as he dared, then half-stepped to his right, leaving his left leg thrown out far enough to tangle into his enemy's. He felt the blade clatter against his cuirass, Ethrik having left himself no time to adjust. The Winsar was too strong on his feet to be thrown simply and quickly over a leg as Allystaire had hoped. They came together with a clatter, the paladin throwing his left hand towards the blade, trying to keep it out of play.

Ethrik still held it with both hands, refusing to free up even one of them. Effectively this trapped his left between his chest and Allystaire's while they wrestled over the hilt, Ethrik trying to bring the blade back into play, Allystaire simply trying to keep it distant. Meanwhile, it left the paladin a free hand. He couldn't deliver overhand blows towards Ethrik's face, but he had free play against the man's body.

Driving his fist into scale armor hurt exactly as much as he expected, and he noticed as much as he cared to, which was not at all. Inside his gauntlet he could feel his hand already swelling with the force of the blows, but smiled as each was rewarded by a louder grunt of pain.

Finally Ethrik twisted his hips and shoved the paladin away. The priest wasted no time now in bringing both hands to the sword hilt and sweeping the blade down in a sharp and savage arc.

Allystaire had no choice but to bring his arm up, to try and turn the blade with his vambrace and send it skirling up and off his pauldron with his left side.

Instead, the edge of the Winsar's borrowed blade found a seam in the paladin's armor, and bit deep. The wound ran red channels along the blade, but where Allystaire's blood touched his armor, it left no trace on the mirrored surface.

Allystaire half-swallowed the scream that came from feeling the sword lodged in his arm. Already he was losing strength in his left hand.

He felt a horrible, painful tug, realized it was Ethrik trying to free his blade. It had lodged, stuck in the seam in his armor and the bone it had cleaved into.

The paladin gritted his teeth, swallowed the pain, pushed it down to meet the cold anger swirling in his stomach. He used it to bank those fires, to build up the rage he'd felt that morning.

If Ethrik couldn't get his sword free, then Ethrik couldn't get out of his reach.

His right hand shot out, another punch delivered straight over an eye. The struggling priest was too focused, or perhaps too surprised that Allystaire was indeed still coming for him with a sword stuck in his arm, to stop it.

He tried to stagger away but the blade was stuck and he wouldn't let it go. Allystaire howled in pain as Ethrik tugged again.

Again he shot his right hand forward, but not balled into a fist. He dug his fingers into the cut, swollen, bleeding flesh of the priest and squeezed, digging in, dragging the man's face closer to his.

By the time Ethrik abandoned his quest to free his bonestuck sword—the feeling of it dangling from his arm was an all-new and horrible kind of pain— Allystaire had an armored thumb wedged inside his mouth, and had just felt the pop of the priest's left eye as his index finger had pushed through it.

Ethrik screamed, a horrible wet and muffled sound, ground his teeth against Allystaire's armored hand.

He threw himself backwards. Allystaire let him go. He reached to the blade that dangled from his arm and took a deep breath, wrapping his fully armored right hand around the blade and giving a sharp, short pull.

He came very near to passing out when he dropped the blade to the grass; he did fall to one knee.

Allystaire reached up with his right hand and tugged his helmet free, tossing it aside. Ethrik writhed, babbled, screamed upon the grass a few feet away. Wrapping his right hand around his left wrist, he pulled the unarmored palm of his left against to the side of his neck, and called upon the Mother's Healing Gift.

He felt the warmth of healing flow into his own skin, screamed as the fractured, nearly-rent-in-two bone of his left arm snapped back into place.

Then he stood, his armor still gleaming in the sunlight, and advanced on the priest of Braech who was crawling away, his hands covering his broken eye.

He seized the back of his armor and rolled him over to his front.

"Once again I wonder how proud Braech must be of his warriors and priests," Allystaire shouted. "You are not the first of your faith to try and crawl away from me."

The paladin knelt down, placing a hand around Ethrik's neck. The priest flailed his arms, beating his fists ineffectually against the armor that threw blinding sunlight into his remaining eye.

"Is there any man here who will seek blood gold of this man? Any who will speak as to why he should not die?"

"HOLD!" A voice rang over the crowd, one that Allystaire was surprised to hear.

Gideon's.

He looked up and saw the boy pointing, saw every eye following him.

"A rider from the Vineyards, and not sparing his horse," the boy yelled.

The crowd stirred, unsure of where to focus its attention: Allystaire and the flailing, gibbering Ethrik, or the man that was now pulling up on the outskirts of the share Baronial camp, slipping off a lathered horse.

Arontis pushed his way out of the circle and rushed to meet the livery-rider. As it tended to wherever the Innadan heir went, attention followed him.

The brief pause cooled Allystaire's blood by some small measure. He looked at the beaten man before him, bleeding on the grass, struggling to escape him.

This is not knightly.

Allystaire couldn't have said where that thought came from. The Goddess, his own confused rage, his conscience, his memories of his father or Gerard

Oyrwyn or the man he'd tried to be to scores of Oyrwyn boys for ten years and more.

But it was like a bucket of icy water dumped on the furnace in his stomach and roaring in his ears.

As Arontis exchanged words with the rider and took something small from the man's hand, Allystaire hauled Ethrik to his feet and grasped his jaw with his left hand.

Ethrik's cheek and nose were broken by Allystaire's fist. His eye was missing. He flailed weakly against Allystaire's grasp.

Gritting his teeth against it—wanting instead to just crush the man's throat—he reached out through that haze of pain and fear and poured the Goddess's healing into his defeated enemy.

He was not gentle, nor was he complete. He staunched the bleeding from Ethrik's empty socket but stopped short of the eye. He knit the broken bones, but not so that pain wouldn't linger. Then he threw the babbling man to the ground.

Arontis had come back into the circle by then, apprehension written in lines on his handsome features.

"Is there anyone here who will claim this man?" Allystaire surveyed the crowd, settled his gaze on Gilrayan Oyrwyn. "Baron Oyrwyn? No? A few turns ago this man was your retainer. Is this how you value them?"

Gilrayan Oyrwyn's blue eyes were narrowed, his mouth drawn into a thin line. He did not look away, but neither did he speak up.

Allystaire switched his gaze to Arontis, who raised his right hand, clutching a scrap of paper.

"The Vineyards had a pigeon from Pinesward Watch. Brazcek Varshyne is besieged by Islandmen and Gravek marching together beneath the Sea Dragon's banner." Arontis's voice was calm and clear. A light spring breeze tugged at both his hair and the scrap in his hand. "He begs for whatever aid we can send him. You can check the seals yourselves, my lords and ladies, if you still doubt Sir Stillbright's words. I do not."

Quickly, Arontis turned to Allystaire, and gestured towards the priest who lay defeated and unmoving at the paladin's feet.

"That man, I will need," Arontis said, clearly and powerfully. "We may need hostages. He is defeated."

"He is," Allystaire says, "but I demand the peace accord, by midday. Such an army as can be gathered will march tomorrow, and no later. Go now and see to it. You will bargain with Torvul now, not with me. I am done bargaining, done pleading, done playing. I will lead the people in a crusade against Braech on my own if I must, but if I do, I will not stop with your chapels."

CHAPTER 41

The Miracle Has Found You

"**I**t is not like you," Idgen Marte said, "to change your mind about killing a man." She had crowded into the tent with Allystaire and Gideon, helping the former remove his armor.

"He wanted killing," Allystaire said. As Idgen Marte helped to unbuckle the plates along his left arm, he looked down at the rent and bloodied gambeson, picking a finger past the drying stain and against the scar that had already formed on his arm. "I am not sure why I stopped."

"Probably," she said, "but if you'd done it, they'd have decided you wouldn't stop with him."

"Mayhap I should not," he rumbled, as he probed the new fissure of hard, white flesh on his arm.

"If you want to do the lot, every Winsar, Marynth, and the entire Choironate. I'll float corpses in every river from here to Londray Bay. I'll make it so we could walk from the coast to the Keersvast Archipelago without getting wet. But it's not them I mean, Allystaire," she said, as she ran her fingers along the upper cannon of the left vambrace.

"Damn that dwarf, too clever by half," she muttered. "Can't Freezing see where it's taken any damage. Just got t'feel for it."

"I am sure he has a way of seeing it." Allystaire bent and twisted his left arm, flexed the muscle, winced, and grunted as a jolt of pain traveled up his arm. "I will need to ask him to repair it."

"If he has time after he spends all day trying to mend what you've broken," Idgen Marte shot back. "Do you not see the fear you've put in them?"

"They could do with some fear," he said as he began working the straps along his right arm, freeing the gauntlet and the upper and lower cannons of the vambrace. "They have long forgotten what it feels like."

"They need to fear Braech's army," Idgen Marte hissed. "They need to fear for what it could do. They don't need to fear us!"

"Yes, they do," Allystaire said. "Look at how they act, or how they do not. We show them proof of Symod's intentions, they quibble. Gideon demonstrates his power to them, and what happens? Assassins in the night. We come with proof of that, and what do they do to the Baron who brought him? Feed him, ply him with wine, accord him respect, negotiate to secure his participation. They will secure their own power first, shore themselves up on all sides, then they will worry about the people Symod will crush. I will not have it anymore. I am no longer of their class. I never should have been. I will no longer pretend to respect it."

"That's why you threw the sword away." Gideon's voice was quiet, but his assertion was powerful enough to draw them both to silence. "It was your way of affirming that to yourself."

"Sounds like a lot of rot, boy," Idgen Marte rasped.

"I don't think it is," he countered, tilting his bald head, drumming the fingers of one hand on his thigh. "In this part of the world, the sword is the weapon of the rich man, the nobleman, the knight. Glory and honor are won with it; common men are expected to fight with common weapons, aye? Flails. Axes. Hammers. What are they?" Gideon leaned forward, folding his hands together. "*Tools.* They can be weapons, yes, but they are tools as well, something any crofter might have. Yet a sword is, in the main, for knights and lords alone, and it has but the one purpose."

Idgen Marte's hand went self-consciously to the weapon at her belt. "So then what'll you do? Kill every man who's rich enough to own one?"

"Of course not," Allystaire replied.

"Just the Barons, then? And the lords?"

"We can't destroy the system unless we have something to replace it with," Gideon said matter-of-factly.

"I do not want to destroy anything," Allystaire said, tossing his vambrace and gauntlet to the bed. "Yet what choice are they giving me? These Barons will fritter and delay and play against each other and they will let each other die if they think it strengthens their own position."

"Frighten them too much, and you don't know what they'll do," Idgen Marte said.

"I know precisely what they will do," Allystaire said. "Delondeur and Innadan will support us. Harlach will go his own way. Telmawr will offer weak-hearted support to Innadan, but always they will be too few, too far from the field. Oyrwyn will search out the method to turn things to his own gain. And it will all be the same mess even if we do defeat Symod's army."

"You can't frighten them into following you," Idgen Marte said. "And even if you did, they'd turn on you as soon as Symod was defeated."

"Then they need someone else to follow," Gideon said. "They need a king. Isn't this what the Succession Strife was about in the first place?"

Idgen Marte and Allystaire both turned stunned eyes to Gideon, and in unison, the same name fell from their lips.

* * *

Torvul was waiting, his boots propped upon the table and legs crossed at the ankle, as the Barons and Baronesses joined him. Blinking and knuckling their weariness away from their eyes, they gravitated towards the pitchers of wine and platters of bread and cheese at either end of the table.

Unseldt Harlach fixed an icy glare at the dwarf as he heaved himself into a chair. "Are we to treat with peddlers, tinkers, and thieves now?"

"Peddlers, tinkers, and thieves are too honest for this lot," the dwarf replied, swinging his legs to the ground and sitting up straight in his chair. "And I would be more honored to be counted among their company than this, in the main."

"Then why are you here, dwarf? To hurl petty insults?" The huge Baron curled his arm and slopped a mouthful of wine down his throat with a gargling laugh. "You'll have to do better than that," he roared, setting his cup down. "You can't hope to mingle freely with folk of quality, with great names—"

"My name," the dwarf said, his voice instantly cutting through Harlach's, "is Mourmitnourthrukacshtorvul. I am the Wit of the Mother, the last student of the last Stonesinger Ochsringuthringolprine, and I have titles, names, appellations and honorifics you could not understand even if I were to try and translate them into your poor excuse for a language." Torvul's voice rose in volume but sank in pitch as he spoke; it was a voice that summoned attention and held it. "And you *will* treat with me if you wish to save yourselves, because there is one angry Cold-damned paladin in our camp, and may my tunnels collapse if I don't just want to let him take your heads and be done with it!"

Torvul heard the whispers, the indrawn breath, could imagine the race in their minds to summon replies of suitably high dudgeon.

As if any of them could beat him to the necessary word.

"But I won't," Torvul said calmly. "I won't because it would not serve the Mother, and he knows it as well. Yet the longer you wait, the more you cost us all, and the closer you bring yourselves to the moment where it *might* serve the Mother. Face this fact, gentlemen and ladies: we are here to save your people from a marauding army. That some of you," he said, turning his eyes at Gilrayan Oyrwyn, who stood smirking on the other side of the table, "would like to believe this army doesn't exist, I want you to think very deeply about what wagering on that would entail. Very. Deeply."

The dwarf's voice assumed a slow, hypnotic tone. "Think of Gravekmir at your gates," he said, and he stood up in his chair, drawing all the eyes to him as the Barons sank down into their own seats. "Your walls may have held strong against men, but what of giants?"

"Giants have broken themselves on Wind's Jaw before," Gilrayan protested.

"Probably when Allystaire resided there to lead the defense, eh? And in what numbers? A dozen at a time? A score? What will you do against a hundred? Two hundred?"

Torvul smiled as all eyes settled on him. And if those eyes were the tiniest bit glazed or distant, well, so much the better.

"In the mountains they're as good as siege engines, and you can't sally out t'set fire to them," the dwarf said. "And that is not to mention the Dragon Scales. Who among you has seen the work of the Sea Dragon's Holy Berzerkers?"

Landen Delondeur raised a hand. "I have. Two of them killed eight of my men before they were brought down. And we had them outnumbered by dozens."

"Symod has gathered hundreds of them. Maybe thousands." Torvul said. "Men who go to battle with skin like steel, arms that can rend rock, and no fear of death."

"They embrace it," Landen said. "It is a holy thing for them, to die doing battle in Braech's name. I've seen them sing praises to him after taking wounds that would've killed any six normal men."

"Your knights and your soldiers haven't a chance against them alone," Torvul said. "For all your puissant skill at arms, you have no hope if you stand alone. You will have ruined keeps, burned towns, and crude altars to the Sea Dragon built upon your bones."

"And that," the dwarf went on, sticking one boot onto the table and leaning forward, "doesn't even take into account the sorcerer they've bargained with. You've not seen the foul magics they can work, raising your own dead into twisted Battle-Wights. Imagine fighting the corpses of your friends, your sons, your daughters. Imagine what it'd do t'your people, even if you did find a miracle and best them somehow."

Torvul cast his eyes around the table. He felt a slight twinge of regret when he saw the open-mouthed horror on Landen's face, but only slight. He looked down at the far end, to where Hamadrian Innadan sat, withered and bent in his great chair, his mouth pulled into a thin line, his good eye flat and cold in the dawn light.

The alchemist noted the decanter at Hamadrian's right hand; cut crystal, rather than metal. Not one that had been at the table before the Baron Innadan had arrived.

Torvul had only a moment, but he thought he saw the ghost of a smile on the old man's lips before he went on.

"Lords and Ladies," the dwarf said, dropping his voice, "the miracle has found *you*. Yes, you hate him. Yes, likely enough he hates you. You'd be happy enough to shorten him by a head, I suspect, but after what you've seen this morning I

Freezing dare ya t'try it. And that, my good gentlefolk, was not him at his worst. Nor his best, depending on what side you look at it from. In the end, you can be with him against a common enemy and live to sort it out later, or you can make him your enemy in the balance and hope the Gravek get to you first.

"Do you want to be with or against the miracle? A paladin walks among you, and he's put himself at your service, but you've decided t'try and make yourselves his enemy. The light of the sun can bathe your walls and your people in warmth and safety, or it can put a hammer into his hand to smash all you hold to rubble while saving them. Put your names to the agreement now," the dwarf finished, "or be destroyed. It's that simple."

He hopped down off the table and reached out a hand. Andus Carek pushed through the guards around the table and stuffed a handful of parchment into the dwarf's hand.

"The agreement, well, I've taken the liberty. It freezes all borders where they are for two years, lays out a timetable for negotiation of redress and remuneration. It binds the lot of you to taking no aggressive action against another Barony for the same two years, and the rest agree to come to the defense of one who is so aggrieved."

The dwarf started passing out sheets of paper; Andus Carek followed in his wake, setting down pens in front of each Baron, their nibs already wet from the inkpot in his hand. The bard then quickly produced a stick of sealing wax, a candle, and one of Torvul's fire-sticks, which he struck against his thumb to light the candle.

Torvul himself carried down one of the sheets to Hamadrian Innadan. He had the grace to offer a sheepish grin as he handed the old man the blank sheet. The dwarf cleared his throat and adopted a conspiratorial whisper.

"I made them a tad more receptive, but they're signin' o their own will." Hamadrian turned to face him with his good eye, and the dwarf shrugged. "Mostly. You fill in the details as I laid 'em out after they've signed, sealed, and collected, and it'll be perfectly legal."

"What'll it cost," Hamadrian wheezed, "to get you to become my chancellor, dwarf?"

"Alas, my Lord Baron," Torvul said with a faint bow, "I am already employed at a wage beyond measure." He smiled, straightened, and said, "I would hurry, though. They're only likely t'be like this for less than a quarter of a turn."

"What'll Allystaire say?"

"There's very little o'what happened here that he'll need t'know," the dwarf said. "The paladin defeated the treacherous priest and in his wisdom, granted mercy. We know that Braech's army exists thanks to Varshyne's word, and the noble Barons have been awed by the righteousness of the cause."

"Is that so?"

"That's what the songs'll say," the dwarf said, nodding towards Andus Carek. "I'll see to it."

CHAPTER 42

Maps

Allystaire had spent the turns since his duel studying what maps he had access to, figuring the routes from Standing Guard Pass to the Valdin River valley, on the border of fallen Vyndamere and nearly-fallen Varshyne.

"I do not envy the Varshynners their position. Caught between the tundra, the Gravek, Delondeur, and Oyrwyn. They were always Vyndamere's weaker, smaller brother at best. When Vyndamere fell, we all assumed they would as well. They just kept withdrawing and withdrawing, leaving their towers without garrisons, the towns undefended. There is something left; we know that now. But what, beyond Pinesward Watch, if anything?"

"I don't know why anyone would want to live in that godforsaken country anyhow," Idgen Marte drawled, leaning over to look at the map. "What can they even grow that far north?"

Allystaire dropped the edge of the map he was holding and glared up at her. "Rocks? Ice?" He took up the edge again and said, "Our most direct route would be to take the trails straight up into Oyrwyn and then across the width of it. Yet the main part of what we can bring to bear now is going to be heavy horse. Might be faster to head back through Thornhurst and up over the Ash."

"You can't go to battle with just the Thornriders," Idgen Marte said. "Two hundred knights in pretty red dresses against an army of Islandmen foot in a country of hills and ice? You'd be mad."

"They are what I know I will have," Allystaire said. "Along with whatever foot the Barons have brought with them."

"Provided they agree to serve."

"Well," Allystaire said, "seeing as how no fires have started and no battles have been joined, I am assuming that Torvul has them well in hand."

Idgen Marte was silent as she studied the map, chewing on her lower lip. "D'you know which route you mean to take?"

"Well, assuming we are heading towards Varshyne, probably both."

She raised a brow. "Split what meager forces you expect to have? That's a nightmare to manage."

Allystaire held up a closed fist, then extended the first finger. "One: we have no supply trains in place, so a larger concentration of men is going to strain the resources of the land they pass through. If we split up, we give the quartermasters a better chance to catch up." The second finger. "Two: we need to gather *more* men. I presume that Hamadrian can send pigeons, as can the other Barons, but the main of our force is going to be what we bring from this congress, and what we can gather in Oyrwyn along the way."

"You're counting on a lot regarding Oyrwyn," Idgen Marte said.

"He will do it or I will throw him off a mountain," Allystaire said. "I tried dealing their way. No longer."

Idgen Marte narrowed her eyes. "I think you'd have t'throw Lord Naswyn, too, but I suspect you'd like a chance t'do that by itself."

"Three," Allystaire said, extending his third finger and ignoring her gibe, "we have a solution to the greatest problem that has affected two-pronged armies since wars began and man could count to two. Communication."

"Gideon?"

Allystaire nodded. "He travels with me and the horse. You travel with the foot. He can carry messages between the two of us."

She shook her head sharply. "No. I'm not leaving your side."

"Idgen Marte, please," Allystaire said. "I will have Gideon, the Order, the Thornriders, and a few dozen other knights with me. If Gilrayan is to travel up into his own country to raise an army, I *need* you watching over his shoulder. There is no one else I can trust to do it."

"My task," she said slowly, "laid upon me by the Mother Herself, is to keep you alive."

"And I am giving you the most dangerous task. Gilrayan is the one most capable of undoing what we have set out to accomplish. You will best keep me safe by watching him. And if all goes according to plan, we will not engage with Symod's forces until we have met back up."

"How often does anything go according to plan?"

"Roughly never," Allystaire admitted with a drawn-out shrug. "Idgen Marte, I cannot trust him alone, and I cannot send Torvul. His cart will never take the mountains from here. And if I understand what Gideon may do correctly, it will be easier for him to speak to one of us than to anyone else."

She sighed. "If some Harlach knight sticks a knife in you while you're riding off to war—"

"Harlach knives have nothing on Oyrwyn steel," Allystaire said, reaching out to rap a knuckle against the mirror of his breastplate. "Especially not after a dwarf has been after it. And Harlach knights were afraid of me before the Goddess found me. I doubt any of them have the stones to try and slip a knife into me now."

She sighed, shaking her head slightly, but muttered, "Fine. I'll keep a close watch on the man as we head north. I've some business north, anyway." She fixed her attention back upon Allystaire. "About Lord Naswyn."

"What of him?" Allystaire paused as he reached for a pen, arm half-extended and still.

"You told me a long time ago you'd let go of all bitterness about her."

"Dorinne. And," he said, finally reached for the pen and wrapping his hand around it, "I believe what I said was that I had let go of all bitterness and anger towards my father, and Gerard Oyrwyn. I said nothing of Joeglan Naswyn."

"Why? Why him so much?"

"Because all it would have taken," Allystaire said, "was a word and a gesture. A silver link pledged to dower her would have sufficed. Then by all right, law, and custom, the Baron and Lord Coldbourne could not have formally objected. They could have tried to pressure me, it is true. They would have, but they would not have threatened exile, or divestiture, or disinheriting me."

Idgen Marte was silent a moment. "Why would he not do it?"

"I do not know, and I have never asked. He acknowledged her, raised her, educated her, but never took that final step. It would have been a small one, and it could have been done without expense."

She nodded. "Knowing you as I do, I'm surprised you didn't throw everything over for her."

He sighed. "I was a younger and more foolish man, Idgen Marte. I was devoted utterly to knighthood, and to Gerard Oyrwyn, in that order. I wanted to be the greatest knight Oyrwyn had ever produced, to make the Coldbourne name celebrated in song. I could not have imagined that I would have been worthy of her had I thrown that all aside. Looking back, I wish I had been more bold, more willing to see past the Old Baron's bluster and bonhomie. Even so," he said with a shrug, "had I run away then with a wife to think of, would I have come upon the Mother? Would I be the man that I am?" He shook his head, the words running dry.

She was silent a moment, then she struck her first upon her thigh. "Dammit, man. It's too much like a Freezing song. The paladin gives up his own happiness t'save the world."

"I was thinking nothing of saving the world when that happened. I was one-and-twenty summers old and besotted twice over, with knighthood and with her. We know which one I ultimately chose."

"If she hadn't caught the flux—"

"She did," Allystaire said. "And that is that. I should have married her. Of course I should have. I should have let love rule over glory. I did not."

Idgen Marte sighed, and looked out the lightly parted tent flap. "You should go find Gideon, ask him t'scout the Braechsworn army. And then go meet the Barons t'see if Torvul's worked us a miracle."

"Aye," Allystaire said, standing, carefully folding up the maps that were spread on his table, and setting the pen he still held atop the pile of parchment. "Come with me?"

She shook her head. "I have to pack. If I'm to set off into Oyrwyn, I'll do it tonight. I can move ahead of Oyrwyn and his lot to rouse the people, then hop back to him."

"That sounds exhausting."

"It will be," she said, throwing open the flap. She started to leave, but turned back to face him once more. "Allystaire, for whatever it's worth, you did become what you said you wanted to be."

He tilted his head curiously.

"You did become the greatest knight Oyrwyn ever produced."

* * *

"To your chin, lad," Norbert was saying. "Keep your elbow tight. Try'n think of it as pressing the bow open, not just drawing it back."

He stood some distance beyond their cluster of tents, giving instruction to Gideon, who was tentatively drawing back the string of Norbert's shortbow. Allystaire paused to watch.

"Don't let the string loose, now, just relax and let the bow take its shape again," Norbert said after Gideon had drawn the string back as far as it was going, nearly to his chin.

Gideon did as Norbert bid, and handed the bow back. Almost sheepishly, the two turned to find Allystaire watching.

"You might favor a crossbow more," Allystaire said as he approached them.

The boy's cheeks colored faintly. "I can draw the bow. I'm just unused to it."

"Gideon," Allystaire cut him off with a wave of one hand. "I do not suggest that you could not. But the crossbow does not rely on strength the way that does. It relies on seeing the angles and figuring the distance. In other words, I do not mean to hide any weakness. I mean to play to a strength."

Gideon sniffed and cast his eyes to the ground, as if seeking an argument. Behind him, Norbert unstrung the bow and slipped it into the case slung around his back. Finally, Gideon looked up.

"Crossbows rely on more mechanical parts, require more maintenance, and can be disabled more easily because of that."

"Maintenance of a weapon is down to the man who carries it. If it is badly made and bound to fail, it is your own task to learn that before your life depends on it." Allystaire raised a finger towards Gideon. "Why the sudden interest in weapons?"

"We're marching to war, and you don't want me to kill using my gifts unless I absolutely must," Gideon said, "but I want to be able to contribute to any battles."

Allystaire waved a hand to the boy, beckoning him close, then wrapped his arm over Gideon's thin shoulders. "Gideon, what you can contribute so far outweighs the presence of another bowman that I have not the words to describe it."

Allystaire looked over his shoulder and dismissed Norbert with a discreet nod. The lean archer nodded sharply and made for their campfire, likely, Allystaire thought, in search of food.

"What is that?"

"The two greatest problems any army on the march faces aside from how to feed itself," Allystaire said, "are communication and reconnaissance."

"Well, the latter is obvious, but how about the former?"

"You can speak to me and to Idgen Marte across great distances, yes?"

"Easier if I am with Mol at the Temple, but yes," Gideon said. "At the least I can send my Will between the two of you, carrying messages. It will not be instantaneous."

"The fact that it will be even close gives us an enormous advantage."

"I suppose."

"You know I do not disapprove of you choosing to learn a weapon. Basic defense is a skill everyone should know. If you want Norbert to teach you the shortbow, or Idgen Marte the sword, or Torvul the crossbow, or all of them, and anything from me, then you know I will give you the time. Yet there are things I will have to ask of you."

"I know," Gideon said. Then he sighed. "And then there is the lute, which I may have to put aside for now."

Allystaire thought a moment and slipped his arm from the boy's shoulders. "No."

Gideon looked up at him. "What?"

"No. You will not put it aside. It is the only thing I know that gives you joy. If you have to choose between learning a weapon and learning music, choose music."

"That's not the choice you would make."

"No," Allystaire said, "but I do not wish for you to be the kind of man that I am."

"What kind would you have me be, then?"

"Better," Allystaire said suddenly, forcefully. "More joyful. More in love with the world. Less angry and with fewer regrets. Duty is not the only thing in this world, no matter how much I act as though it is."

"Then what is it that gives you joy? What is it in the world that you love?"

Allystaire sighed and ran a hand through his hair, surprised to find it longer than he'd usually left it. *Time to go at it with a knife,* he thought.

"My sister. You, and Mol, and Torvul and Idgen Marte. Ardent. And the Goddess." He shrugged. "It does not seem like much of a list. Mayhap when this war is over, you can help me find things to add to it, eh?"

Gideon nodded. "It is a more full list than you think, but…something to fill your hands that isn't a weapon might not hurt."

Allystaire smiled, but whatever he was about to say was interrupted by a trumpet blast from the center of the camp. Three quick notes, rising: an announcement. He cast his gaze in that direction and said, "It is time, then. I hope Torvul has done his work well. Do you wish to come to see what agreement they have made?"

"I do," Gideon said. "Though I can scarcely credit that they have made one."

"If anyone can work a miracle in words among those men, it's that old dwarf," Allystaire said.

"Should you not put your armor on for this?"

Allystaire looked down at the dark blue tunic he wore, with the sunburst picked out in gold-colored thread on the left breast. "No. I wish to, but no. First, we have no time, but second, if this is to be a moment for peace, I will not go to it attired for war."

"What about the hammer, then?"

"Attired for war is one thing; prepared for disagreement is another," Allystaire said. "Besides, I cannot walk straight without the weight on my hip."

With that, they laughed, then the Will and the Arm of the Mother walked together towards the Barons and their hard-fought peace.

* * *

The Barons stood around the table, saluting each other with goblets of wine. Torvul and Andus Carek were seated on two chairs pulled a short distance away, poring over a long roll of parchment. Even from a distance Allystaire could see the long row of multicolored seals that stood along the bottom of the parchment, beginning in red, then green, blue, grey, black, blue again, and just barely, the tawny red-orange of Telmawr at the very end.

Alone among the Barons, Hamadrian Innadan remained in his chair, folded in upon himself. He hardly seemed to notice the revelry going on around him.

Allystaire could see, even at a distance, the effort every breath was costing him. It was a far cry from the hale and cheerful man of a day past. His skin was grey, and he seemed to struggle to keep his head up, his eye focused on his fellow Barons.

Arontis and Cerisia hovered over him. When Cerisia saw Allystaire her posture straightened. She wore her mask but he thought he could read the pleading in her eyes nonetheless.

He stopped behind Hamadrian's chair and placed his left hand on the old Baron's shoulder, reached for Her Gift of Healing.

The paladin found a heavy wall thrust between him and Hamadrian, one that he had felt before during the Battle of Thornhurst, one that he greatly feared to see.

Mother, I know this man's death is not mine to avert, he silently prayed. *Yet if I can but grant him a few more turns, I beg of you to let it be done. He deserves to live to see this triumph. Please.* The last word almost sprang audibly from him.

The wall did not part, but it weakened, or retreated somehow. Some little trickle of the Mother's Mercy, thinner than Allystaire had ever felt, flowed from his hand into the old, dying man.

Hamadrian took a sharp, audible breath. He sat up, slowly turned his head to bring his good eye to face Allystaire.

"Like drops of water to a dying man in the desert," he muttered. "Have you got a flagon full, by chance?"

Allystaire closed his eyes, grit his teeth, and pushed harder. If the healing warmth that flowed from him grew any stronger, it was by the smallest of margins. He let his hand slip from the other man's shoulder and opened his eyes, gave his head a small shake.

"Ah, well." Hamadrian sat up straighter. "You allowed me to live to see this." His voice rattled in his chest. "I thought I never would." The Baron Innadan reached out for his heavy goblet and tried to strike it against the table to summon attention; he couldn't manage much more than a feeble tap.

Allystaire reached out, seized a pitcher, and slammed it so hard on the table that wine slopped out and onto his hand. Goblets, pitchers, plates, writing implements, and ink pots all clattered enough down the length of polished oak that everyone turned their eyes to them.

"Haven't you the decency to at least be lying in pain and waiting to die of rot?" Baron Harlach's joke was that of a man half-drunk, lifting his mug and beaming almost stupidly as he spoke. "We like the dwarf better anyway!"

Smiling lightly, Allystaire pulled his left sleeve past the elbow, and held up his newly-scarred but otherwise healed arm, turning and moving it in the light. "One of the Mother's Gifts, Unseldt Harlach," he said. The quiet that had followed his pounding on the table was replaced with a taut, palpable hush.

"Is anyone going to tell me the terms of what you have wrought?" Allystaire slipped the sleeve of his shirt back down to his wrist as he lowered his arm.

Torvul stood up, holding the heavy roll of parchment up. "The details would take too long to explain. Suffice it to say that seven Barons have agreed to put their toys away, and t'stop arguin' over borders for two years at a minimum."

"What are the consequences for breaking that peace?"

"The others agree to attack the one who does," Torvul called.

Allystaire nodded, then seized an empty cup and filled it. He lifted it high and said, "To peace. And to Hamadrian Innadan, who wished for this longer and harder than any other. May history record this as *his* peace."

Torvul was quick to seize a drink, a pitcher, and lift it as well. "May it last until the stones of my home are dust."

Those gathered around the table lifted their drinks in unison. Many were already somewhat bleary-eyed. Allystaire studied Torvul's face, but there was as much given away in the heavy brows, deep-set eyes, and blue-stubbled jaw as there would have been in a pile of rocks.

"To Innadan's Peace," Gilrayan Oyrwyn called out.

"Hamadrian!" Other voices joined in, Byronn Telmawr's foremost among them. When every present hand had been lifted and his health drunk, the Baron Innadan pushed himself slowly to his feet. Leaning against the table, he drew a hard breath.

"Signing a document is well and good," he rasped as everyone leaned forward, straining to hear. "Claiming we'll lay down our arms and tend our own fields is a first step, long overdue. But if our peace is to last we'll have to earn it, and an enemy is at our borders."

He paused to cough. Arontis came to his side and took his arm. The Baron openly leaned against his son, making no pretense now of holding himself erect. But when he lifted his head, his good eye was as clear and bright as the spring sky.

"The enemy threatens you first," he said, pointing to Landen, "and you." His wavering finger swerved towards Gilrayan. "It would have a great deal of conquering to do to threaten me. Nonetheless, I will commit my own men, my knights, and household guard—my only living son—to the fight to defend *your* people. Our people. I would ride out myself if the life remained in me. We can all see that it does not," he wheezed. "I urge all of you to do as I have done, and to commend what troops you can into his hands." His hand lifted to point once more, a thin finger extended towards Allystaire.

"Put aside your hatreds and rivalries. Ask yourselves what he has to gain. Paladin or no, he'll be one man in the midst of hundreds, who're loyal first t'you. Then ask yourselves what you have t'lose if you try to fight a Braechsworn army on your own, one by one."

"What of my conditions?" Allystaire's voice rang out louder than Hamadrian's, and he saw more than one face around the table recoil when he spoke. "Need I remind you? Expel the priests of Braech from your keeps unless they repudiate Symod. One-fifth of the wealth of their the temples that refuse is to be seized and distributed to the poorest."

Allystaire could feel Torvul's eyes boring holes into him. *Stop it. STOP it. You're askin' too much and endangering it all!*

"Doing the first only makes sense, if they're to be our enemies," Loaisa Damarind said. "Yet the second will take time to assess, and to implement, if we are to do any more than sack them, which will cost us manpower. I propose we agree to your demands—in truth we have little choice—but that we postpone the second until after the war is won."

That was cunning, Torvul shared. *She's got little to risk, so far from the possible front. Yet she's a point, Allystaire. Defeat Braech before y'destroy his temples, eh?*

"We've venerated the Sea Dragon in Harlach as long as our annals recall," Unseldt said, twisting his mouth and narrowing his eyes. "Why should we go throwing over his temples now?"

"You heard that man Arvid," Allystaire said. "You heard what he said about their army, and what they mean to do. You have it from Varshyne, with his own minor seal upon it. To keep priests of Braech in your keeps is to harbor spies."

"There are no priests of Braech left in Londray," Landen put in. "I made sure of that when they stole the armory out of the Dunes and tried to bar entry to my keep. Their temple there is already sacked, and when this war is done I will distribute all of its wealth to Delondeur folk who've suffered from it, some of whom are already in my camp. If more proof is required of what treachery Braech's faithful can wreak, I can't imagine what it is."

Unseldt still seemed unsettled, sipping at his wine and shaking his head slowly from side to side. Finally, Cerisia spoke.

"Think carefully on this, Unseldt Harlach. Yes, many have worshipped Braech for all the long years of history. Yet I ask you: did your father worship the same God? What happened to the Master of Accords overseeing peaceful trade to enrich seller and buyer both? What happened to the Father of Waves, guiding ships and sailors safely to harbor? They have been swallowed by the Sea Dragon, by the lust for blood, by the pride of strength; blood and battle seem to be the only thing Braech's most devout think of now. When my father was young, there could not have been as many hundreds of Holy Berzerkers in the world as we know have gathered in Varshyne."

As she spoke, Cerisia drew herself up to her full height, lifted her masked face imperiously. "The truth, Barons, is that the Sea Dragon our fathers may have worshipped is not the god we will face in battle. It is often a dark thing, when gods change, or when they come back into our memory. But can it be coincidence that now, when Braechsworn would wipe you from the earth if they could, a new Goddess has seen fit to give you a paladin to oppose Him? Once, I did not believe, but Fortune is nothing if not mutable. Allystaire Stillbright is the man who will save your people, if you will but give him the chance. I will do all that I can to aid you. Fortune and Her Temple, so far as I can speak for them, will stand behind you in this fight."

"I was always," Gilrayan Oyrwyn said slyly, his narrowed eyes leering at the Archioness, "more partial to Fortune than to Braech anyway. I will leave with all haste for the trails north to Wind's Jaw, and there gather my troops to bring them to this war." His smile became less a leer and more a smirk as he turned to Allystaire. "There to work in tandem with your command, of course."

Silence reigned for another moment as eyes fell once more on Allystaire. *Clever,* he thought. *Joins the war without putting his men at my disposal.* He imagined smashing the smirk off the Baron's face with his old leather-banded gloves.

"Arontis," Baron Innadan said, "go now. Ride to the Vineyards and bring forward all the Thornriders that are mustered. Give orders," he wheezed, "to gather spears and bows."

Unseldt Harlach drained off his cup and tossed it haphazardly over one shoulder. "Never let it be said that the White Bear was slow to join battle. I've men camped just beyond the pass," he roared. "Let me go to them and we'll make haste to join you."

"It will take some time for any word to reach Aldacren Keep," Byronn Telmawr said, "but I brought all the knights of my household to this congress."

"I believe," Allystaire said, "that the Will of the Mother can immediately carry whatever word you need brought to your keeps or encampments if you will entrust him with the message."

"Even so," Loaisa said, "it will take weeks for all these troops to assemble. And then plans must be discussed and—"

"No," Allystaire cut her off sharply. "They do not. I will tell you what my plans are and where the men are moving. I may not be able to control how long, especially for you," he said, gesturing first at Loaisa and then at Ruprecht, "given that your lands lie across all the length of Innadan and the Vale of Kings."

"Furthermore," Allystaire said, "I do not plan to wait for a great host of foot to be assembled. I will leave in the morning with my own knights, with the Thornriders of Innadan, and the knights and retainers gathered here. I will make straight through the pass to Delondeur, across the plains to Thornhurst. There I will turn north, cross the Ash, and move into Varshyne to engage the Braechsworn."

"You'll have a little more than three hundred men, unless I miss my guess," Ruprecht Machoryn stammered. "How do you expect to engage them till we've gathered more?"

"More will come," Allystaire said, "when the rest of you march up to Oyrwyn along a separate track. We do not have the luxury of time, so I mean to keep the foot and the horse largely separate in order to retain speed, and we can overcome the traditional difficulties of communication and coordination. The Braechsworn host will be dangerous, and I do not mean to underestimate them. Yet what I can do with three hundred horse against a lot of untrained, uncontrollable warriors in the hills and valleys of Varshyne should not be underestimated either."

"My knights are yours, Allystaire," Landen said, "you know that. I may not have much more to offer, but what I do will be given totally."

"Then we should not waste any more time talking about it," Allystaire said. "We need to break down our camps and ready ourselves to move in the morning, as early as we can manage. Send what messages you need carried to our camp so that they may be carried where you please, and your men will begin moving immediately."

When met with blank looks, Allystaire sighed and waved his hands. "Toasting to the peace you have agreed is all well and good, but now we must do the real work of ensuring it," he all but shouted. "The Braechsworn are not going to defeat themselves."

When he finished, Torvul cleared his throat. "I expect, even now, the berzerkers are tossing bones to apportion your gemmary, your daughters, your sons."

Almost as one the Barons turned and hurried away, fear widening their eyes. Except for Hamadrian, who leaned heavily against the table.

"Peace," he rasped, smiling for just a moment before falling heavily backwards onto his chair.

* * *

Allystaire was once more bent over his map and parchment, pen in hand, marking notes. He put the finishing stroke through a list.

Thornriders, two hundred

Innadan knights, sixteen

Telmawr Knights, eleven

Delondeur knights and lances, two score

Machoryn knights, fourteen

Damarind knights, twelve

The Order, nine

Torvul

Gideon

Me

"No matter how many times ya write it down or add it up, it's not gettin' any longer." Idgen Marte lingered behind him as he wrote, making unasked-for comments and suggestions.

"Between your interruptions and the arrival of messengers bringing word to Gideon, it is a wonder I have even had the chance to write it once," Allystaire said.

Behind them, Gideon lay prostrate on his cot, arms folded on his chest, sleeping as deeply as anyone ever had, it seemed.

Allystaire set his pen down and stood up. "The key," he mused aloud, "will be to not allow them to engage us in too much space. Horse need the ground to move, yes, but terrain and speed will have to be our equalizers."

"Or the boy," Idgen Marte muttered.

Allystaire sighed. "I will not turn him into a weapon."

"He can toss mountains at them. He already is." She turned to look at him. "Why not simply ask him to reach into the Dragon Scales and pull their gifts from them?"

"In twos and threes, he might do exactly that," Allystaire replied. "Yet en masse, he fears that the power he would draw out would be too great for him to channel. He spoke of overrun and blowback and flooding, and I did not understand a word of it any further than knowing that he meant it was dangerous."

A slightly panicked voice drew their attention from outside the closed flaps of the tent. "Sir Stillbright?"

Frowning, Allystaire took a half-step forward and threw the flap open. A red-liveried servant stood with a lantern in his hand. Though night had not yet truly fallen, the lantern was lit behind its shutters, and by the light it cast upwards at the man's face, Allystaire could see the tracks of tears. "M'lord?"

"Yes, goodman?"

"The Archioness asked me to fetch you. It's the Baron, m'lord."

Nodding, Allystaire didn't bother to correct the man's choice of title. "Watch him while I am gone, Idgen Marte, please?"

She nodded, her face grim as she let the tent fall closed.

Before he was out of his own camp, Allystaire heard a faint trickle of music coming from the tent he'd left behind.

As he'd expected, the servant led him straight to the large silk pavilion at the center of the Innadan camp. They walked past rows of hushed and downcast knights, soldiers, and servants. Allystaire was ushered quickly past the guards.

Inside, the number of braziers glowing with fire had increased to half a dozen, and the air was stifling. In the bed that dominated the room, Hamadrian lay a thin and wasted figure beneath a pile of blankets. His chiurgeon paced restlessly. Cerisia sat upon a stool at his side, holding his left hand.

Immediately, Allystaire went to his bedside, going heavily to one knee and taking up Hamadrian's other hand. He found it cold and damp, then heard the awful rattle as the old Baron drew breath.

He closed his eyes and reached for the Goddess's Gift, threaded a tiny bit of the power through his hands into Hamadrian's. Drawing on his memories of the man, the tournament he had won at the first attempt at a peace congress, battles they had fought in together, the siege and fall of Aldacren keep, he tried to revive him, to pour life into his failing lungs.

He found it was like trying to pour water into a broken cup; it could hold only the smallest taste. Hamadrian cried out in pain and Allystaire eased, drawing his senses back from the other man.

With a great effort, Hamadrian lifted his head. Cerisia immediately leaned forward to seize a pillow and place it behind him. He turned to look at Allystaire.

"I know you can't heal me any longer," he rasped. "But I needed to speak to you."

"I can," Allystaire said, "little by little. I can see you through another night."

Gasping, the Baron shook his head. "Not going t'make any difference, and we know it." His voice was a ruined whisper, his face a mask of pain. Behind the grey of his beard all color had left his face, and his clouded eye lay slack and unmoving. "My wind is gone, and life is an agony. If you can ease my passing more than him and his potions," he said, barely lifting a trembling finger to point at the chirurgeon, "do it."

"I can," Allystaire said quietly.

Hamadrian nodded very faintly, then sucked in a deep wheeze of breath that left him unable to speak for several moments. When he finally did, he had fallen back on his pillows and was looking straight up.

"I don't know where the name Stillbright has come from, Allystaire," he said, "but it likes you better than Coldbourne. I always thought you were trying too hard to live up to it. To be a hard man like your grandfather Gideon, or Anthelme."

"It is what I thought I had to be," Allystaire said slowly, uncertainly. Then, he stretched his left hand out over Hamadrian's chest. "Do you at least wish to wait for Arontis?"

"No," the old man said, shaking his head carefully. "I don't want him here for what I've to say t'you. I need you to help him see this through. And not to let him follow a whim."

"What do you mean?"

"The boy has half a mind to throw off his inheritance n'follow you. Join this Order of the Arm."

The tent was silent, but for the gurgle in the Baron's chest. Finally, Allystaire spoke.

"From what I have seen of him, I would be honored to have him," Allystaire said. "And yet."

"He'll do more good as a Baron than as some sort of knight and monk in one," Hamadrian said. "I mean no insult t'you, but no. His head is filled with tales, with the word paladin. But he can't throw it over to follow you."

"I understand. I agree with you, Hamadrian. He is a good man; he is his father's son, and in his father's place he can do more good for more people than in following me."

Hamadrian nodded, then seemed to sink back into his cushions and bedding. His eyes closed, though he still breathed.

"You couldn't…you couldn't have found your goddess seven years ago?"

"I think it was She who found me, Hamadrian," Allystaire murmured. "It will always shame me that it took me this long to see what you already had. They will call this Innadan's Peace, Hamadrian. Generations yet to be born will know that you were the architect."

The old head shook very slightly, side to side. "Paladin was here, that's what they'll remember. Don't care," he muttered. "Peace is peace, whoever's credited." A wet and evil sounding cough racked his body then, and Allystaire took his hand once more.

"Then rest easy knowing what you have done, Hamadrian," he muttered, leaning forward so that the dying man would hear him. He found memories swirling in the man's mind. There were battles there, yes, but they were always a chore of terror and misery. There were vineyards in the sun and the comfort of keeping his people safe and well-fed. There was the sorrow of death: two sons, one barely more than an infant, the other dead in battle before the first congress, eight summers past. There was the Baroness Innadan; Allystaire had known her as a regal and grey-haired matron, but in Hamadrian's memory she was young, blonde, and lissome.

"You have given peace to your part of the world, Hamadrian," Allystaire whispered. "You can leave it now and go into the next, where Ethrin, Dessen, and your Mathilde wait to greet you with their love once more. You have paid a heavy price of grief in this world. There is none in the next."

The Baron Hamadrian Innadan gave a great shudder, exhaled, and then lay still upon the bed. Allystaire searched for the spark of life within him and found none. He lowered his head.

Guide his soul to those he loved and lost, Mother, he silently prayed. *I beg you, let this man know their love again if it is in your power.*

For a moment, Allystaire thought he saw a brief flash in his mind, a younger Hamadrian walking along a path between green vines that bowed heavily with grapes, with a child walking at his side, the father expounding upon some point to the boy, then plucking a grape and handing it to him. It disappeared as quickly as it came; it may have been one of the memories that had come to him at the end of his life, one of the many Allystaire had seen.

He lifted his head and saw Cerisia remove her mask, the corners of her eyes wet. Behind him, the servant who had brought him wept, though he tried to swallow the sounds, to remain unobtrusive.

Allystaire stood and turned to face the man, went to his side. "If any Baron gathered here is worth weeping for," he said, "it was Hamadrian Innadan. Be not ashamed, goodman."

The man nodded, shutting his eyes tightly and knuckling at his mouth with a fist, before he said, "No offense, m'lord, but I didn't need you to tell me that to know it."

Allystaire went from him to Cerisia. "I think," he said, "the body should not wait for Arontis, but I do not want to interfere."

"Are you still that cold of a man, Allystaire? You move so quickly from praying for the man to planning what to do with his remains."

"I am as I have been made, Cerisia," he replied. "The best way to honor him is to make certain that this peace becomes a reality, and to do that, we cannot lose time in grief. He will not be the last good man to die in the the weeks to come."

Cerisia nodded and dabbed at her eyes with her sleeve. "You…you're right, damn you to the Cold," she muttered. "I will see to the body. Arontis should return in a matter of turns. Will you wait for him here?"

"I cannot," Allystaire replied. "There is work to be done. Send for me as soon as he arrives, and I will come."

He watched Cerisia nod, then slip her mask back on. She bent at the waist, swept her hand over Hamadrian's eyes to guide them closed, then started to pull the bedding back from his limbs. She issued quiet commands to both the chirurgeon and the servant. He saw the latter go to a heavy chest set against one wall of the pavilion and begin to pull clothing from it, while the chirurgeon dug into his case. He turned and left, trying to avoid the stares of the men who'd gathered outside, some distance from the pavilion itself.

Almost, Allystaire paused to speak to them, then thought better of it. *Not my place to make an announcement.*

As he walked back to his tent, his own eyes remained dry, despite the tightness in his chest, the grief he felt at the loss.

There is simply, he told himself, *too much to be done, and no time for grief.* His words to Cerisia came back to him.

He will not be the last good man to die in the weeks to come.

CHAPTER 43

Messages

Spring was still bone-chillingly cold at the heights where the Highgate crouched upon the flattened top of a mountain. The massive keep guarded the juncture of the northern and eastern roads in and out of Barony Oyrwyn, and had once been regarded as the last—or first, depending on the direction one traveled—sign of civilization this side of the wild lands that bordered the tundra. Beyond it now lay a few settlements, towns that ruled themselves outside of the reach of Baronial law, but it was still the only true mark of authority, of power, in its part of the world.

The Oyrwyn Mountain flapped listlessly in the cold air as the sun sank, with the Gated Tower of Highgate no livelier beneath it. The Lord of Highgate walked the battlements arm in arm with his wife. Their clothes were a contrast in seasons: his, a simple woolen cloak over black and grey, no hood, light gloves, while she still wore sealskin boots and gloves and had ermine trim and a hooded fur cape draped over her shoulder.

Garth's pale face was drawn continually to the horizon, clouded though it was by the lines of mountains that crossed his homelands.

"If a boy, perhaps my father's name," Garth was saying.

"Ufferth?" Audreyn sniffed. "I think not."

"Well, we're not going to name him Anthelme," Garth protested.

Her aquiline noise wrinkled in distaste. "Certainly not," she agreed. "Besides, it is far too early to know one way or another."

Above them, or perhaps right in front of them, a voice softly but unmistakably spoke. "Hello," it said.

Garth's hand fell to his sword, and he took a half-step to place himself in front of Audreyn. "This wall will be swarming with guards if I but give the word," he said, drawing his sword and holding the blade in a guard across his body, all the while swiveling his head to look for the source.

"Please," the voice said, "do not do that. I mean you no harm. It is Gideon."

"Gideon?" The tip of Garth's sword lowered towards the stones at their feet, but he did not move to sheath it.

"Yes," the voice said. "Gideon. The Will of the Mother."

Audreyn stepped out from behind Garth, placing a hand upon his arm and gently lowering it so that his sword's point lay against the stones. "Gideon?" She looked from side to side. "Perhaps it would help if we had something to speak to."

"Ah." Almost instantly a pigeon seemed to be sitting on the wall in front of them. "Better?"

Garth frowned and carefully slid his sword back into its scabbard. "I suppose," he muttered, "unless anyone sees the Lord of Highgate and his wife speaking to a bird."

The pigeon ruffled its wings. "No one will see or hear. But the longer we spend on these trifles, the more effort this will cost me."

"I presume you're carrying a message for us, then," Audreyn said. "Will we need a scribe?"

"No. The message I bring is twofold. First, the peace congress at Standing Guard Pass has reached an accord, an agreement brokered largely by Hamadrian Innadan, Allystaire, and Torvul."

Audreyn's smile was wider and more welcoming than the look of polaxed astonishment that had Garth's mouth agape.

"How? What are the details?" Audreyn's rush of questions were cut off by the pigeon's sudden flapping of its wings.

"I haven't the time. An army of Braechsworn threatens Barony Varshyne, and once they destroy it, they mean to turn east."

"Braechsworn?" Garth's turn to speak while Audreyn furrowed her brows.

If a bird could look exasperated, this one managed, turning its head to the side to regard Garth with one eye. "Yes. Fanatics. Islandmen armed with Barony steel. Holy Berzerkers. Gravekmir and Graveklings. Many priests of Braech as well, led by the Choiron Symod."

"What? Why? What brings them together?"

"Hatred, bloodlust, greed," the bird said. "I haven't the time to explain the wider ramifications. Please trust me when I say that this message comes from Allystaire, and that it is entirely true."

"We do trust you, Gideon," Audreyn said. "What must we do?"

"I am carrying messages from the Barons to their keeps and commanders to assemble what forces they can bring to bear, immediately, to march west and assemble at the outskirts of Varshyne. I have already carried this message to Wind's Jaw."

"How did you deliver it?"

"I carried a piece of paper," Gideon said, "and delivered it to the scribe in the tower where the pigeons are kept. As at the other keeps I've visited, the scribe was typically too excited by his need to share the news he'd got to notice that the bird delivering it disappeared rather quickly. May we please," the pigeon with Gideon's voice said, hopping from one foot to the other, "dispense with unnecessary questions. This is very taxing."

"Please go on, then," Audreyn said, placing her hand once more on Garth's shoulder, stilling another question that had been forming on his lips.

"Very well. I already delivered Baron Oyrwyn's orders to Wind's Jaw. Nothing was said about men from Coldbourne or Highgate," the pigeon said. "I thought this was information you should know. The Baron himself is going to be moving north towards Wind's Jaw to marshal his men. But I do not trust him; alone among the Barons at Standing Guard, he did not agree to work under Allystaire's command. He said so quite cunningly, but he said it all the same."

"Is Allystaire moving with him?"

"No. Allystaire is moving towards Thornhurst, then north. He is taking charge only of the horsemen, for now, and intends to move up into Varshyne as fast as he can manage in order to engage the Braechsworn there. He is going to send Idgen Marte along with Gilrayan, to look over his shoulder, and I am to coordinate between them."

The bird turned its head to regard Audreyn, who was smiling and opening her mouth. "I know that is an excellent step, but I do not trust him even that far. When it comes to it, Allystaire may be sandwiched between the Braechsworn, and whatever hostile force Gilrayan might choose to seize the moment with."

"And if he sent no orders to me, then he does not want me there," Garth said coldly. "All the more reason that I should be."

"Precisely," the bird said. "The faster you can move, the better."

Garth looked over his shoulder at the fading sunlight. "If I leave tonight, with a string of horses, I can make Coldbourne Hall in a few days."

The pigeon's small head slumped towards the stones for a moment, then lifted slowly. "I do not doubt you are mighty in your own right, Lord of High-gate," Gideon said, "but you alone would be of little use."

"If you leave with all the knights and horsemen you can rouse this night," Audreyn said, "you could be there in a week or so. And it is not so far to the Varshyne border from there."

"He'll need more than just horse," Garth said, frowning darkly. "Though in that country, if he can find the right hills and the right valleys they might be enough."

"Those would be matters to work out with him," the pigeon said. "I am tiring. I wanted to bring you the message, and I did. Now I must go."

And to you, Lady of Coldbourne and Highgate, the Shadow sends her regards, and asks that you continue the work you started after your brother wins this war.

Audreyn was startled, but struggled not to show it, as she quickly realized that the Will's voice was sounding only in her mind. *I have already written to the lady of the Horned Towers, and the wives of several knights with smaller holdings,* she thought back, uncertain if Gideon could hear her. *They were as tired of war as I, and as ready to do what they could to stop it.*

Good. The pigeon faded and then disappeared altogether, and yet she heard his voice one more time. *I could tell you if it is a boy or a girl child, if you like.*

What? How do you? Now Audreyn knew that her expression showed, for Garth turned to her, worry written on his features, hands going to her shoulders.

I can feel it, Lady of Highgate and Coldbourne Hall, Gideon said. *For reasons that do not bear explaining now. I will have to speak to you of it later. In depth. Do you wish to know?*

Audreyn gave her head a slight shake and put her hands to Garth's.

Be well, then. The child will be healthy. I can promise you that much.

Then both the voice and the presence they both realized they could feel was gone. Audreyn turned to her husband, set her shoulders, and placed a hand upon his pale-bearded cheek. "You have work to do," she said quietly.

"Gilrayan will be suspicious," he replied, pulling his mouth into a thin line, "when I arrive unbidden by him."

"But you're going to go anyway," she said.

"I am," he said slowly. Searching her face, he finally said, "I could not do otherwise. Not where Ally is concerned."

"I know," Audreyn replied. She took a deep breath. "Go. I want to watch the sun set, but you have no time to waste."

He leaned forward to kiss her. Not passionately, for guards or other folk might see, but not entirely chastely, either. Audreyn leaned against him a moment. "You will also come home. With all your limbs and bits attached," she said firmly.

"Your brother'll see to that," Garth said. "He already *has*. I know you're tired of hearing it, but he made the finest knights in the Baronies. I do not say that out of simple pride; I mean it. We will flock to him, exile or no, Audreyn. I won't be the only one who'll choose him and even his Goddess over Gilrayan, if it comes to it."

"I know," she said, "and I know you mean that nobly, but a war inside a Barony would be worse than wars on its borders. Promise me," she said, "that you'll do everything you can to avoid that. To avoid open revolt."

"Everything I can," he said, "I do promise—but it may not be enough."

"Make sure that it is," she said, clutching his arms tightly. "We cannot trade one war for another. That's not what Allystaire wants, either."

He nodded slowly, pressed his face against her dark coils of hair for a moment, then pulled himself free of her arms and hurried away towards the nearest tower.

She leaned one arm against the parapet, and draped the other over her stomach, which had the barest hint of swell to it. She watched the sun set, and pondered what it could mean that the Will of the Mother could feel her child.

Audreyn could find no answer that she liked.

* * *

Gideon had been rather drained by the illusion he'd maintained and the conversation he'd had. He found, when he projected his Will in this way, that conversation moved all too slowly for him. It felt like moving through mud, and constantly waiting for everyone to catch up with him to be sure they were not lost.

Even so, he found that as he soared mentally over Barony Oyrwyn, his strength returned much faster than it ever had before.

He paused to concentrate, to draw his senses away from the external world of sights, stilled his Will where it hovered over a wide expanse of moor. Very slowly, he realized, and in small pieces, power was simply flowing towards him, like specks of iron drawn to a lodestone. An impossibly large and powerful lodestone, that drew them from miles away.

The implications, he began to think, then snapped himself back to the task at hand. He forced himself to study the landscape, the lives being led upon it, as he floated over it.

Lives being whittled from it, really, he thought. The light of the day was waning, nearly gone, and yet laborers were out upon the moors digging turf, their spades and mattocks moving in neat strokes to cut blocks of it and load it onto carts or baskets. The end of the day being near, their children and wives had come from their cottages—too small, Gideon thought, to house so many—to haul the loads back to the drying sheds. Many of those outbuildings were in better repair than the cottages themselves, with stouter walls and better roofs.

He moved low. There was no reason to imagine himself quite so high in the air as he typically did, not with the mountains well behind him, and floated close enough to study them.

The men were large, in the same way Allystaire was. Not tall like Joeglan Naswyn, or gracefully muscled like Gilrayan Oyrwyn, but they had stout bodies, broad muscular shoulders, thick hips, tree-trunk legs. The clothes they wore were miserable. Dirty, patched, rough, damp with sweat and mud both. In many cases their shirts were all but shapeless sacks tied around their middles with fraying rope. Many of the children that had come out to haul baskets of turf away were barefoot, though the vapor of their breath could be seen in the air. Some wore little more than pieces of hide wrapped around their feet.

Gideon was studying their sunburned faces, their rough calloused hands, when he realized that a child, a babe worn in a sling around its mother's back, had fixed its blue eyes straight upon him, and was extending a stubby arm, as if pointing.

As he climbed back into the air, Gideon chastised himself.

They are not objects of study, he thought. *It is for these people that I was made. It is for them that my Gifts have been given. And I will see that they have it.*

He soared away, but he fixed the place in his mind, knew that he would remember the newborn child who'd pointed at where his Will had floated invisibly in the air.

Gideon had little time to think on what that had meant—or on what he had felt from Audreyn and Garth's daughter in the womb—because what he saw outside Barony Varsyhnne was a horror in the making.

The keep, the only occupied fortress he'd seen since he crossed the Oyrwyn border, was completely encircled by Braechsworn men. Giants, towering above the others, acted as a ring of watchtowers around their encampments. Crude banners showing devices he was unfamiliar with—crossed axes, ships, and dragons in every possible pose, from flight to recumbent to coiled to pierced with arrows and dying—peppered the camp, but a massive banner of the Sea Dragon, stretched tight between two pine trunks, dominated the central camp.

He fled for Standing Guard Pass before he could make too much sense of it, for he felt power hovering over the camp. Dozens of priests of Braech were gathered there, and he could feel the accretion of their will. If they could gather it together, all of them at once, they could threaten him, he thought.

He knew they could feel his presence. He wanted to confront them, to go amongst them and drive their wills from their bodies, to gather to him whatever sparks of power lay within their mortal shells.

Almost, he turned back, began to form himself into the nearly invisible dragon form he had assumed when he had struggled with priests of Braech before. But deep down he knew that bringing news to Allystaire was more important. He tried to fix in his mind the details of what he had seen as he flew as fast as he could manage—at the speed of thought—to his form on a cot, in a tent, hundreds of miles distant.

* * *

Allystaire had left one flap of his tent open, found a flagon of wine and two cups, and was already pouring when Arontis Innadan arrived after night had fallen. In the light of the lantern, the young man's face was mud-spattered, and he smelled strongly of horse and sweat.

Allystaire held a cup to him, pressed it into his hands when Arontis stared ahead in a daze for a moment. He sank into the other camp chair without a word, and didn't notice the slumbering form of Gideon on the other cot.

"Could you not have healed him?" Arontis's voice was small in the darkness, but it did not waver.

"I did what I could," Allystaire answered gently. "Whatever stories you may have heard, or what folk have told you, or what you hope, there are limits to what the Mother can heal through me."

"To die now, today, at the advent of his great hope. It is a tragedy."

"Forty years of war is the tragedy, Arontis."

Arontis nodded, took a perfunctory sip from the cup Allystaire handed him, slumped in the chair with the cup in both hands.

"Could you have...have kept him till I returned? Could I not have spoken to him?"

"Mayhap I could have," Allystaire said. "Yet every moment would have been an agony."

"Why even tell me that? Why not just say no, you couldn't have?" For all that he was a tired man, slipping into shock and grief, heat crept into Arontis's voice as he sat up straighter, camp chair creaking beneath him.

"I cannot lie, Arontis," Allystaire sighed, "not even if a lie would be a comfort."

The younger man drank his wine, draining the cup off. Wordlessly, Allystaire reached for the jug and filled it. They sat in silence and drank a moment before Allystaire spoke again.

"It is a hard day, the day a man loses his father. Mine died while I was on campaign. I arrived just in time to put him in the family tomb."

"I will not even be able to do that," Arontis said. "If I am to leave in the morning with you."

Allystaire sighed heavily again. "You are going to think I am a hard man, callous, or cruel. But which would your father rather you do?"

"Do you think I haven't already wrestled with that? Of course I'm riding out in the morning. Two hundred Thornriders were mustered outside the Vineyards. I brought all of them, with the remounts, pack horses, grooms. At least it's spring, so we can forage for most of the fodder." He emptied his second cup, shifted in the chair. "Cerisia said she will see to funeral rites, but when this is over, I would ask you to offer whatever rites you can."

Allystaire winced, and hoped Arontis couldn't see his face. "I will do what I can. For what it is worth, Arontis, I was able to ease his passing. He did not die in pain or in fear."

"Passing to what? To the ground? A next world? The Cold?"

"I do not know for sure, but I do not believe it is the first, and certainly not the last of those. I thought I had a vision, at the moment. Of him as a younger man, walking with a child, a young boy, barely a toddler, in an endless vineyard."

"Dessen," Arontis said quietly. "He was born ill, and nothing any chirurgeon could do would change it. He lived only a few years. I barely remember him."

"There was the Baroness, too. Mathilde. Only young and beautiful."

"I don't," Arontis said, lifting one hand, "want to hear anymore. I don't. I have letters to write to my sisters, and my nephews." He stood, holding the cup out to Allystaire, who quickly set it aside. "They should have been here. Alanna especially; she has a better head for all this sort of thing than I do, and her son is the eldest grandson."

Until you marry Landen Delondeur or Lurezia Damarind and produce an heir to two Baronies, Allystaire thought, but chose not to say. "Goddess bless you, Baron Innadan," he said, extending his right hand to Arontis, who took it and shook. His grip remained firm and strong for all that had happened that night.

"That title does not sit well upon me," Arontis replied.

"I disagree. It does. And it will sit better in the days to come. Do what you must, sleep when you can. The border of Barony Varshyne is ten days hence, if we have perfect weather and good riding." *Which we won't.*

He watched Arontis walk off, then turned to find Gideon climbing off his bunk. The boy came into the light, his eyes wide.

"Allystaire." His voice was a hoarse croak after so long spent in disuse. "The keep in Varshyne." He trailed off, his voice dying, reached for the flagon of wine and took a sip, swishing it around his cheeks before swallowing and speaking again.

"It is as the letter said. Besieged. Giants, berzerkers, priests of Braech directing it all. Enough of the last to challenge me, I think."

* * *

As the column of men and horses formed up on the Innadan plain, Allystaire tried to push away the weariness that encroached on his mind. In Ardent's saddle, there was no thought of his limbs failing or betraying him, but a heavy weight lurked just at the edge of his senses.

It had been a long night.

He had decided to let Arontis sleep, but roused Torvul first and looked over the maps with him. The dwarf shooed him away rather quickly, and now slumped on the buckboard of his wagon, with two huge skins bulging on the board beside him.

Allystaire nudged Ardent over towards the wagon and caught the angry gleam of the dwarf's eye. "Is that what we spoke of?"

"No," the dwarf replied sourly. "It's just all the spirit I expect to drink today." He spat over the side of the wagon and grumbled, "Of course it is! Just be careful with it. You'll have them running till they die."

"I do not plan to give it to any of them today," Allystaire said, "or even tomorrow. Best case, we do not even use it until we are on the Varshyne border."

"Then why did I stay up all Freezin' night brewin' it? And outside of Thornhurst my work is harder, you know."

"Because the best case is rarely what we get." Allystaire cut him off and tugged lightly at Ardent's reins, let the destrier trot a few dozen yards down the line. The Thornriders were an impressive sight, he had to admit, in their matching red surcoats, all bearing the Vined Great Helm. The Innadan knights mingled in their vanguard. He squinted at them, trying to make sense of the colors and devices.

Once, and not long ago, you knew all of them by name and reputation, Allystaire told himself. If he thought on it, he could pick them out: Sir Jermin

Vandelar, Sir Uriah Eastin, Sir Malart Dellin. The names sprang to his mind as he scanned three shields, the displayed arms a riot of reds and yellows, of bright greens and flowers.

As he considered them, a trio of other knights rode from up the column towards him, led in their center by Arontis, he quickly realized. The new Baron Innadan's armor was a marvel of craft. Grape-heavy vines, enameled in purple and green, crawled across the steel, and the great helm he wore was the very picture of that on the banner that flapped above his men.

Arontis sat astride a deep chestnut destrier of a size with Ardent, its tail and neck both held high. When the Baron's party drew close—about the length of one of the massive horse's necks—the other destrier lowered its tail and stretched its neck out, drawing back the corners of its mouth and opening its jaw lightly.

Sliding back the visor of his helm to peer down at his mount, and then at Allystaire, Arontis said, "It is not often that Gardener shows deference, Sir Stillbright. I wonder why."

"I would not put too much thought into how your mount acts around Ardent," Allystaire said. "I have long ago stopped questioning it."

"Ardent? I know of no stallions of that line in Oyrwyn."

"I am sure that is not his name in the blood books," Allystaire replied. "And in truth, I have forgotten what it was, something to do with mountains and stones and clouds, no doubt, with a lot of other nonsense appended to it. Ardent is his name." Unbidden by him, the huge horse took a half-step forward; the other knights' mounts took a half step back. Allystaire *tsked* and gave the reins a light tug.

"I see. Do you wish to inspect the Thornriders before we set off?"

Allystaire looked back at the three knights he'd been scrutinizing before Arontis had ridden up. "No. No time for that. I was only reflecting on the differences in arms; here in Innadan they are so much more colorful than in Oyrwyn."

"Well," Arontis ventured, "it's a more colorful country. We're not surrounded by mountains and stones and clouds, after all."

"Or moors," Allystaire added.

"There must be beauty even in them," Arontis countered. "And there are those who would say your own arms are quite striking, the dark blue and gold."

He leaned forward, steadying his great helm with one raised hand. Only then did Allystaire notice the bands of black silk tied tightly around Arontis's vambraces. "How did you get the sunburst emblazoned so lightly and yet so plain? And the polish on it all."

"Magic," Allystaire replied matter-of-factly.

"Ah." A pause. "And what is that inside the sunburst?"

"A hammer." He cleared his throat and Arontis sat straight up in the saddle. "Have you trumpeters to sound the advance?"

"I do," Arontis affirmed. "Are you certain we must leave the grooms and the pack-masters?"

"We need to move as fast as we can, and no room for unarmed men to go into danger. Let the men care for their own animals. It will do them good. Squires can attend to the remounts and pack train, such as it is."

Arontis nodded. He motioned with one hand, and one of the knights beside him turned and let his horse run back down the line. In a few moments, a long blast sounded out over the camp from the back of the column. One sustained note, it rolled across the entire column, and just over three hundred knights and lances, a few dozen squires, three Barons, and two Baronesses rode off to face the Braechsworn, the tip of a spear guided by the Arm, the Will, and the Wit of the Mother.

* * *

While the remaining servants—many of them pages and squires Allystaire had declared too young to ride with his column—broke down the camp, Idgen Marte dogged the steps of the Barons Oyrwyn and Harlach both.

The former insisted upon a leisurely breakfast in the company of his liege-man Naswyn. Idgen Marte left him lingering over shirred eggs served by red-eyed Innadan servants in ramekins sculpted, of course, with vines.

She found the steps being taken by Unseldt Harlach much more acceptable. He and the dozen knights and score of other armsmen who'd accompanied him had packed up their camp quickly, if not efficiently; empty wineskins and broken crockery were notably more plentiful there. The quick dismantling of their hide tents—no silk pavilion even for the Baron—had made shadows to stay hidden in rather scarce.

With a snorted curse, she decided to simply approach the Baron openly, letting herself appear fully in a bright pool of sunlight several paces away. When two of the scale-armored knights clustered around Harlach noticed her, they lifted longaxes in two hands, stepping in front of him.

Idgen Marte raised her hands, the palms out, and rolled her eyes expansively. "I just want t'talk to your Baron. If I wanted t'do anything else, none of you would've seen me."

"I like a woman with a bit of bravado in her," Unseldt Harlach declared as he shouldered past his men, who lowered their longaxes but did not ground them. "What have you t'say?"

"It's best not said in front of your men. It'll only take a moment, but it's in your interest." She affected nonchalance, lowering her hands to her sides, cocking one hip, tilting her head lightly.

"Fine." He waved a hand at his men and they scurried away. "I mean to ride as soon as she's had her say," he roared.

"I don't trust you," she said, "but Allystaire thinks you'll do the decent thing in the end, and I trust him."

"You get right t'hte point, eh, lass?"

She let that slide off of her shoulders. "But I also think you'll do the thing that benefits you. If you ask me, Oyrwyn isn't going to put his full strength into the fight. Not willingly. If you do, the other Barons'll favor you when it's all said and done."

"The White Bear puts its full strength into any fight," Unseldt declared.

"Aye, and what good has it done you this past score o'years? I know what the map looks like now, and what it looked like before. You've lost more land than any living Barony save Telmawr."

"I know every mile of it," Harlach growled. "Every hill and trail."

"I'm not trying to shame you, m'lord. What I'm sayin' is this: if the *people* in those lands you lost see the White Bear fighting harder for them than they do the Oyrwyn Mountain well, maybe they'll start pining a little more keenly to be under the Bear's mantle again."

"Might be somethin' to what you say," Unseldt allowed, lifting a hand to his white-bearded chin. "I left a hundred good men camped a hard day from here because I didn't trust that bastard, and I still don't. Or your man, in truth."

"Yet you've put yourself, and your men, into his hands. So if I were you, I'd ride as hard as I could manage to join up with him."

"I don't right recall how or why I agreed to that," Unseldt rumbled. "But there's no going back on given word. Even so, I've got no good path to make time," he said. "Got to either ride through Oyrwyn, which folk'll take as an invasion, or march back here and then across Delondeur. Lose two days that way, and have got no supplies."

"What if," Idgen Marte said, "I could make the way for you to move through Oyrwyn smooth?"

"What do you mean?"

"Give me the word right now," she said, "and I'll have a message carried to Highgate on the instant. Provide you with remounts, food, and you might be a day behind Allystaire in getting to Varshyne."

"How do we know you're not walking us into an Oyrwyn trap?"

"Because if I had my choice, I'd kill Gilrayan Oyrwyn now," she rasped. "Yet I don't. I'm doing what I can until I do what I must. And what I can do is help make Unseldt Harlach one of the heroes of the songs that'll be written of the weeks t'come. Trust me that far, Baron, and you won't be disappointed."

Harlach watched her a moment, then nodded his great snowy head slowly. "All right. We'll do as you say. Where'll we meet the mounts?"

"Gideon will let you know," she said. "I must say this, Baron, and I hate every word of it—but don't be afraid to kill horses as you cross Oyrwyn country. Gilrayan intends to make a stately progress back to Wind's Jaw, best as I can tell. But even then the time will be close; if he catches wind of you moving through his lands on his mounts…"

"To a Harlach man, the horse is just the thing that gets him to the battle faster," Unseldt said, "so he can fight as men were meant, with his feet on the ground."

"Good," Idgen Marte said. "I'll go make the arrangements."

As she turned away, she took a deep breath in, and thought, *I'm sorry, Mol. I'm sorry Allystaire. Better horses than people.*

She took advantage of a shadow cast by a tent being pulled down, faded into it. The world's colors and light receded into the world of shadows that she had come to know so well, and she began pulling herself through them, dashing from one to the other faster than any eye could've seen.

Even in the colorless world of light and dark that she darted through, Gideon shone like a beacon. She would have been able to find him from across a continent; from across the camp, if she had looked straight at him, she would have feared for her sight.

* * *

Gideon sat Allystaire's palfrey easily, but restlessly. Traveling upon horseback or on foot seemed painfully slow to him now, when he knew he could have had himself outside the walls of Pinesward Watch in a moment's thought.

I could not bring an army with me, though, Gideon reminded himself. Then he closed his eyes and drew in a deep breath, but also drew in the power that seemed to float through the air, dust motes in a shaft of sunlight, and wondered if he could.

He was driven from the reverie by Idgen Marte's sudden appearance at his side.

Gideon. I need you to carry another message to Highgate.

Garth has surely already marched.

Not to Garth. To Audreyn, and to Shary.

What must I say?

Horses. They need to round up as many mounts as they can as fast as they can be brought to a spot—you decide where—to meet up with Harlach's men coming like Cold out of the mountains. They'll need food, too. Haste, haste, haste. The Harlach men need to clear out before Oyrwyn catches word.

Gideon called to mind the map of the Baronies he had seen from high above, picking out the trails from Highgate down into the lower country. Even as he did so, his Will was already moving back to Highgate. As he traveled, he surveyed a spot: an abandoned fort, once on the border between Oyrwyn and Harlach, he surmised. But as the border had been pushed back further, there'd been no need to keep it garrisoned. As he compared the map he looked at now, from the air, drawing a borders along the series of towers, forts, and keeps, he could see that Highgate had once formed a salient into Harlach lands, and the fort he would direct Audreyn and Shary to was thus well south and east of the massive keep, and roughly on a line of march from where Harlach's men were camped above Standing Guard Pass. It would serve.

He didn't bother with illusions or with birds, this time. He found Audreyn awake and at a desk, writing, with Shary pretending to do needlework near the door leading into the room, rather than the window at the other end that would've actually let any light in.

"Audreyn?"

Shary leapt out of her chair, knives both long and slim having appeared in her hands. Audreyn raised her hand from the desk. Though she paled and started at the sound of his voice, obviously she recognized it.

"Calm, Shary," she said, raising one hand to the woman. "It is the Will. What do you need, Gideon?"

"I hate to ask more of you than we already have," he said, trying not to acknowledge the tentative curiosity the child in her womb was exhibiting to his other senses. "But it is desperate and it comes from Idgen Marte."

Only then did Shary's knives disappear, but still the woman didn't take her seat or pick up the frame she'd tossed aside, its dangling threads arrayed across the floor haphazardly.

Audreyn waited patiently. She'd apparently taken to heart what Gideon had said in his previous visit, about brevity and questions.

"Horses. I need you to gather up as many as you can. They do not have to be of quality; they must simply be able to bear riders. Baron Harlach is going to try to steal a quick march to support Allystaire. He and a hundred men are going to ride hard across Oyrwyn, and will need as many remounts as they can."

"If Gilrayan learns of it—"

"If they move quickly enough, he won't. He means to move as slowly as he can. And Idgen Marte will travel with him. If anyone can safely obscure his vision it would be Torvul, but Idgen Marte is a good second."

"Why not just kill him and be done with it?" Shary muttered.

"He is still the Baron of this land by right and law," Audreyn archly reminded her, "and we will not speak of murder."

"It may come to that," Giden said. "Open and direct challenge is not murder, though. But it is better if he can be convinced to serve with us, and we must expend every effort to that end as we can. For now, what we can do is gather horses, and bring them to Baron Harlach."

"If Gilrayan should catch the scent of this" Audreyn murmured, "it will also reveal me as a traitor. Discretion must be our watchword. I can borrow liberally from our own stables, and write to the women of nearby keeps and holds, but the messages will carry danger to all who receive them."

"I will come back to you this evening, and I will carry them instantly wherever you tell me," Gideon said. "They are to be gathered near the disused border fort to the south and east."

"Harlach won't like that," Audreyn fretted, biting her lower lip. "That was the staging area for the first campaign my brother launched against him. He may see it as a slight."

"I am not concerned with whether Unseldt Harlach feels slighted. Allystaire marches on a foe whose numbers we cannot name except to say they are greater than our own. Many among them are empowered by the Sea Dragon, and their resolve will be great, however untested the bulk of the men are. Allystaire needs every knight, every Harlach axe, every spear and bow that can be gathered."

"I understand. I will start writing the messages. I should be able to muster at least threescore mounts. They will not be chargers or destriers. A few coursers at best. I cannot promise tack nor grooms nor sufficient fodder, either."

"Understood. And, Lady of Highgate, I fear to tell you that many of these horses will never return."

"Better the horses than my husband, or my brother. Or any of the husbands or brothers now riding to meet the Braechsworn."

"Good. I will return."

Gideon pulled his Will back to his physical self as fast as he could manage. He was slightly alarmed to see that the column was moving, his palfrey plodding along as part of it; he had missed the setting off. Since no one troubled him, he could only assume that they believed him to be sleeping in the saddle.

He gave the palfrey a nudge with his heels and rode hard to catch up to the van, where he knew Allystaire would be.

CHAPTER 44

The Flower and the Spear

For the last day's ride to Thornhurst, Allystaire had Torvul give the horses the first of his mixture, a few drops sprinkled into the morning water.

A ride that should've gotten them there at sunset—perhaps even just after—had them pulling up outside the walls with the sun still hanging in a slowly purpling sky. Ardent's lungs pumped like a vast bellows beneath him, but the destrier had energy and spirit to spare, he knew. Beside him, Gideon sat on his spare palfrey.

Allystaire hadn't known he'd been expecting Mol to be standing outside the gates—alone but for the herding dog at her side, and the unmistakably huge form of Johonn standing a few paces behind—until he saw her. But then, in that moment, seeing the somber little priestess and the bright and stubborn girl he'd rescued in one, standing in the middle of the track in her sky blue robe and bare feet, he found he could not have imagined coming back home any other way.

He slid off of Ardent's back, but the horse barely came to a stop, plodding after him to greet the Voice of the Mother. The destrier outpaced him and stretched his long neck to place his soft nose against Mol's upraised hand. The priestess laughed and said something Allystaire did not catch, to which the destrier tossed his head and swiveled his ears. Gideon, having ridden beside him, was slower to dismount, unused to so many days in the saddle, and he nearly stumbled when his feet were under him again.

Two impulses warred within Allystaire. The first was to bend down and sweep Mol into his arms in an embrace, though in truth, it hadn't been long since he'd last seen her. The second, which was the one he followed, was to walk forward and sink to one knee.

Though his weight upon the ground send clouds of dust puffing into the air, none of it settled onto his armor. The column behind him was stained by mud and sweat and rust, the fruits of so hard a ride in the saddle, in armor. But at their head, he still flashed in the sun.

Mol extended a hand and settled it onto his uncovered head. "Welcome home, Arm of the Mother." She spoke the words normally to his ears, yet he could also feel the force of her voice moving past him and echoing down the line of men who coiled on the track behind him, spilling onto the grass, disappearing behind a hill and then again, outlined against its crest. He felt Gideon kneel beside him, and almost shot out a hand to steady the boy as he teetered.

Allystaire and Mol both looked sidelong down at him, but the boy lifted his head straight and blinked his bloodshot eyes open. For a moment Allystaire thought he felt or heard the whisper of something spoken between the Voice and the Will, mind to mind, but it quickly passed when the priestess lifted her head. She pushed back her hood and surveyed the column, and her voice rolled over them all.

"And welcome to Thornhurst, Baron Innadan, Baron Telmawr, Baron Machoryn, Baroness Damarind, and all the brave souls who come with you. Welcome back, Baroness Delondeur. I have had food readied on the village green, arranged for space to be made within and without the walls for your horses, laid out fodder, grain, and water. We haven't the room within our walls for all your men and mounts; the bulk of you will have to take your meal outside, but if you ride through in groups of two score or so, we should manage to get you fed quickly enough."

Behind him, Allystaire heard the clatter of metal and the creak of tack as the van—mostly the Barons and their handpicked knights—dismounted and came forward.

He stood and turned to face them. As he'd expected, most of their eyes were drawn to Mol, their faces in varying stages of disbelief or awe.

Allystaire patted her on the shoulder and she leaned against his hand for a moment, but only a moment, then he walked to greet Johonn, extending an arm. The huge footman grasped it and pumped, and for a moment Allystaire regretted it. Then a broad smile split his roughly handsome face and the two shared a moment's laughter.

"Are we away t'war soon then?" Johonn's voice was surprisingly soft for such a giant of a man, with a rough accent, like Mol's had been, but Allystaire felt that he missed very little.

Allystaire nodded simply, which Johonn met with his own nod. "Any burden," the man said, hefting up the longaxe he leaned against.

"It may be a great one, Johonn. We will face something awful," Allystaire said. Behind him, he heard Mol making small talk with the Barons who gathered around her.

Johonn shrugged, a tiny gesture that sent mountainous shoulders rolling. "Mother gave me my arms back, a purpose," he said, nodding, affirming something to himself and to Allystaire. Then, once more, he said, "Any burden."

"Any burden," Allystaire replied, repeating the phrase, feeling something right in it, something that stirred in his chest and sung in his arms. He thought Johonn felt it, too, and they looked back along the column.

"Tibult, Norbert, and Harrys are back with the supply train and Torvul's wagon. A few Delondeur folk who attached themselves to the Baron on her way to the congress. They will not be long, a few turns at most."

"I'll go see t'my gear," Johonn said, shouldering his axe, "unless the Voice finds aught else for me to do." He looked expectantly at Mol, but she was chatting with nobility, and he frowned. "Never thought I'd stand so close to much greatness," he muttered. "I'll fetch the others," he added, as he turned and stomped away, big boots stamping into the dirt on the end of tree-trunk legs.

Allystaire watched the Barons and Baronesses clustered around Mol. Ruprecht Machoryn was the most withdrawn, eyeing the girl with cold distance. Loaisa Damarind and her daughter seemed to be listening to her more closely, while Arontis had tugged one gauntlet off and held his hand out to the herding dog, who was cautiously and thoroughly sniffing it. Byronn Telmawr was standing awkwardly at the taller, younger man's side and seemed uncertain.

Landen had taken her time dismounting and when she approached, Mol looked expectantly up at her. Alone among the nobles who gathered in front of Mol, the Baroness Delondeur knelt, sliding her helm under one arm. Mol's hand settled on the pauldron of her armor and Allystaire shuffled a couple of steps closer, listening intently.

"Voice of the Mother," she murmured, "I have two boons to ask of you, if you would hear me."

Mol nodded and turned to face her squarely, tilting her head lightly to one side and drawing her hands together. "I will hear you, Landen," she softly replied.

"First, there are folk who travel with me who have already suffered the depredations of the Braechsworn. If you would grant them refuge here until we make it safe for them to return to their homes, I will be further in the debt of the Mother."

"Of course," she said quickly. "Honest folk do not need to fear asking for the Mother's refuge. It is theirs if they but wish it. What else would you ask?"

She wet her lips and looked up at Mol, then at Allystaire. "When this war is done, I would ask that you build a new Temple of the Mother in Londray. I will give you whatever support you ask. A building, links, official legal proclamations. I will give you the Temple of Braech to rebuild, if you wish."

"Why do you ask this, Landen Delondeur?"

She squared her shoulders, shifted on the knee that bore her weight upon the ground. "I remember what the Mother did for us when we were defeated here on the Longest Night. By all right of war and justice, you could've killed us. Most would have done so. Instead, you fed us, clothed us, gave us warmth through the winter, and while I cannot speak for all those who were interred here with me, confessing the wrongs I had done to you lightened my heart and cleared my mind. My soul, even. I want all of those mercies available to the folk of my seat and greatest city. I would ask for a chapel in the Dunes, if you would grant it."

"A Temple for the people, yes," Allystaire suddenly put in. "But a chapel in a keep? No. Never." Without even reflecting on the words, he felt them certainly, deeply, utterly.

"It is good that you wish to bring the Mother to your people, for that, after all, is why She has come," Mol said. "But She will not be locked behind high stone walls, or heavy iron gates. The Arm speaks true. We will build up a Temple in Londray, but not a chapel in your keep."

Landen nodded and stood in a single smooth motion. Allystaire envied it, as he started to feel the effects of long days of riding along his thighs and up his back.

"Go, see to your horses, and then to yourselves," Mol said, waving her hands to the knights and lancers who still stood back, the Barons who had stepped away to watch Landen's request. "Our home is open to you, as guests. I must speak with the Arm," she added, turning on one bare heel to walk up to Allystaire and take him by the hand.

Gideon appeared asleep on his feet. Mol looked at the dog at her side, who then wandered and put her head under Gideon's slack hand. He opened his eyes and curled his hand into the dog's fur.

"Go and sleep in your own bed, son," Allystaire said. "It will be an early start in the morning." The boy started shuffling wearily up the road. Mol whistled lightly and Ardent and the palfrey started following her.

Mol came to his side then and took his left hand; her small hand was hard and warm against his unarmored palm. "Must it be?"

"I am afraid so," he answered, squeezing her hand gently. "Pinesward Watch is—"

"I know," the girl said quietly. "I knew before I asked the question. But I wanted to ask, and to hear you answer."

Allystaire laughed lightly. "What do you mean, Mol?"

The girl sighed lightly, then smiled up at him. "I know how you will answer most questions I could put to you now, Allystaire. But there is comfort in hearing the weight of your answers, and the movement of your voice and thoughts as they come round to the blunt truth, as they always have." Her smile turned impish, and her accent became a country girl's once more. "Reminds me of our first days, is all."

Allystaire smiled and squeezed her small hand again. "I thought you were going to drive me mad with your queries then."

WIth her free hand, she patted his gauntlet. "Setting off after a dozen men on your own, with naught but the word of a frighted innkeeper's daughter. The questions just kept ya distracted from how mad y'already were."

Allystaire knew that Landen and Arontis were following them, a few paces behind. They were screened by the horses that plodded along behind him and Mol, without benefit of leads. Ardent suddenly drew to a halt, the palfrey as well. Mol's pace quickened and Allystaire matched it easily, despite the ache in his legs. He heard Gideon laughing faintly, and he looked over at the boy; he saw another hint of a private thought shared between him and Mol.

"I'm sorry I'm so tired, Allystaire. I will be right in the morning," Gideon said, driving the smile from his face.

"Go and sleep, then," Allystaire said, "I will see to your horse."

"No," he said, shaking the weariness out of his eyes, or trying to. He patted the dog that walked by his side on the head and went to the palfrey and collected the leads. "I'll take care of Ardent as well. You haven't the time."

Allystaire almost cried out for him to stop as the boy reached out for the destrier's reins, but stopped, surprised, when the huge grey didn't snap or toss his head.

"Where are we going, Mol?"

"To the Temple or to Leah," she said, "your choice of where to go first."

"Leah? Has she had her child?"

The girl nodded brightly. "Lynn. Just a few days ago. A bit small, but perfectly healthy."

"Does the village have a midwife?" Allystaire felt a flush of shame creep up his cheeks as he asked. "I should know that."

"The village has me."

Nodding, Allystaire asked, "Will she want to see me?"

"Aye. She wants your blessing upon the girl."

"My blessing?"

"Yes." Her flat tone brooked no further discussion of the matter, he felt, so he started reaching for the words he might say.

"Best we go there first," he said.

In silence then, Mol led him to the village green, which was green in truth for the first time that he had seen it. Wildflowers grew in scattered lines along its edges, in rows of white, yellow, and orange.

"How?"

"Torvul," she said, "and me. And you, of course."

"I am nothing to do with that," he said, gesturing, as he walked to the edge of the green and looked down. "I neither planted nor tended."

"Think less literally, Arm," Mol chided him. "Had you not ridden here, drawn by the smoke of the pyre lit on this very green, none of this would be here. I would be dead, having despaired and allowing myself to be drowned in the wreckage of my father's Inn. The rest of our people would've been cut up upon the sorcerer's table, chained to Islandman oars, or sold to brothels in Keersvast. This village would have been slowly reclaimed by the land, its fields overgrown and untended, its flocks scattered and dying, dogs and horses gone wild, if they were lucky."

As she spoke Allystaire bent down and carefully, with the tips of his gauntleted fingers, plucked out a single blanketflower, looking closely at the orange petals for a moment. Behind him, the first squadrons of horsemen had ridden on towards the Temple and the food that had been readied for them. He looked over his shoulder and saw a few, including Landen and Arontis, had stopped to watch him, letting their accompanying knights take their horses onward.

Mol appeared at his shoulder and leaned her arm upon him. "The Temple would not exist," she murmured into his ear, "and I know not how long the Mother would have had to wait for a chance to come to the world again. So yes, Allystaire. You had everything to do with this becoming a green place again, and for the flowers growing upon it. What do you call that one? I just asked for 'em by color," she suddenly said, leaning forward to point at the flower held between two steel-cased fingertips.

"Blanketflower," he said, "and those are beggarticks, and those arrowheads," he said, pointing to the rows of yellow and white, respectively. "Might be some barberrys in amongst them, too," he added, peering with narrowed eyes.

"How does a man who lived his life so dedicated to weapons and war know of flowers?" Mol's question was once more murmured to him alone.

"I knew a woman once who thought very much of them, and taught me something," he said.

"Loved a woman, you mean."

"Aye," Allystaire said. He stood up, face flushed, unsure of what to do with the tiny flower he'd picked. "Where does Leah stay? The Inn, still?"

The girl nodded. He studied her a moment, the serious priestess almost having pushed out the fierce Innkeeper's daughter he'd known. *Almost,* he thought, then impulsively he bent at the waist and carefully tucked the blanketflower he'd picked behind her ear. She giggled, and lost for a moment the somber gravity she wore like an extra garment. She stood on the tips of her toes and kissed his cheek, then settled back on her feet. "I have to go see to our guests," she said. "Go to the girl and then to the Temple. I imagine," she added, "that you'll want some time there to pray."

He stepped away, watched as Landen moved to Mol and offered her arm with courtly grace, despite the mail she wore. Mol had to reach up to take it, but she settled her hand on Landen's vambrace, and with Arontis in tow, they walked off.

The Inn was nearly empty, Timmar busy in one corner with a bucket of soapy water and a scrub brush. Allystaire hailed him as he came in, but he didn't want to burden a busy man with small talk, so he made the stairs and sought out Leah's room.

She was sitting in a chair by the room's only window, its shutters open and oilcloth pinned up, almost dozing, the baby held snugly by her arms beneath a sling tied around one shoulder. From what he could see from the doorway, the bundled child was little more than a scrunched pink face with a tuft or two of straw-colored down atop it.

Leah's eyes suddenly swung open when he shifted his weight, his armor clinking. Almost as suddenly she raised a hand to cover them, murmuring, "Cold but that stuff is bright. Couldn't you throw a cloak over it or something?"

Quickly, Allystaire half-stepped into the room and out of the path of the window's light. "Sorry," he murmured. "I forget."

She smiled faintly and stood slowly, carefully cradling the babe in her arms as she walked to him. "Best piece of looking-glass I ever saw," she said, bending her legs in order to look at her face in the silvery cuirass. She clicked her tongue disapprovingly, and said, "And I look a fright in it."

"Nonsense," Allystaire said. "You look beautiful, Leah. And so does your daughter," he said, looking down at the sleeping babe, whose features, while still muddled to his eye, were peaceful, calming. He found it all too easy to watch the girl simply breathe as she slept.

"Tch," Leah said. "You're just bein' kind."

"I cannot," Allystaire said, "speak a lie. Even to be kind. There have been times these months I wish I could have, but I did not come here to speak of them—I mention it only so that you know, Leah, that if I say you and your girl are beautiful, I must be telling the truth."

She smiled, weakly though, and gave a slightly forced laugh. He took the chance to unbuckle the gauntlet on his left hand, and set it down on a stand next to a washbasin and jug.

He lifted his now bare hand and Leah stepped close, holding the still sleeping babe towards him. He touched the tip of his fingers to her tiny cheek and bent low over her to catch her scent.

Mother, he thought, *it is for this child that a man as brave and plainly good as any I hope to know gave his life. Please give me the words.* For a moment there was only his breathing, and Leah's, and the child's.

"Mother, please turn your gaze on this child. Make Your sun a friend to her, to guard and shelter her always. Let her know peace, and joy, and love above all else. Bless her hands and her eyes and the people and ways she bends them to. Keep her, love her, and guide her."

When he finished, he heard a tiny silvery note in the air. Leah looked up at him as if she'd heard it, too, and Lynn slowly blinked her own blue eyes open. They seemed, Allystaire thought, to focus on his for a moment before the infant closed them and drifted back to sleep.

"Thank you, Allystaire," Leah said. "I'm sure y'have great matters t'attend to," she muttered, stepping away.

"None greater than blessing your daughter," he said. Picking up his gauntlet, he gave mother and child a polite bow—not deep or courtly, for he felt somehow that might have offended her, but enough—and started for the door and the stairs, when Leah called his name after him.

He turned and poked his head back into the room, and she said, "Would y'consider taking Renard's spear with ya? T'the battles, I mean. Even if y'give it t'one o'the other men, just, it'd be like a part o'him was still out there fightin' and as much as I hate the thought, it's what he'd be doin'."

He looked to where it leaned in one corner of the room, a smooth ash pole with three feet of hide wrapped around its middle, dark with long years of use and supple with long years of care. The head had a wooden case slipped over it, but inside he knew it would be razor sharp on both sides, a leaf-shape as wide as his hand until it thinned to a wicked point. There were marks just above the hide grip where metal braces had once projected out of it, serving as a kind of guard, but Renard had apparently preferred it without them. It was a simple weapon, simply made. No bard would find it worthy of song, but there was something about it that glowed all the same.

As he walked to it and wrapped his hand around the hide, Allystaire realized that it was all the greater for having been the simple weapon of a simple man who had, after too many years of using it, found the one use it truly deserved.

"I would be honored to carry it with me," Allystaire said as he hefted it. The balance of it was perfect. "Whoever made this was some craftsman," he murmured. "Thank you, Leah."

"Bring it back," she said as she sat down once again, carefully cradling the babe.

"I will try."

Allystaire carried it down out of the Inn, and started across the remainder of the village to the Temple. He looked at the flower-strewn green. *Could do with some heather*, he thought.

* * *

He left the spear leaning on the inside of Temple's wall, along with his hammer and belt. The Temple itself was empty, but outside many of the village folk and a good deal of the knights and Thornriders had gathered to eat. As best he could tell as he passed, the Barons and lords were being given no preference over the common soldier. The same loaves of bread and bowls of soup were being passed out to all who lined up. The scent of beans and ham rising from the cauldrons as he walked past sent his stomach grumbling, but he felt a different hunger far more keenly.

His steps took him straight to the pillar of the Arm, where he knelt. In fact, he leaned forward till his head was touching the marble-like but warm surface of the pillar. The hammer etched atop it swam in his vision for a moment till his eyes closed.

Mother, he thought, then stopped. *How do I even begin? This is far from the first time I have led men to battle, or even led men to a battle where they will be outnumbered. But never has it meant so much. I have never hesitated, before, to send men to their deaths in battle, men I knew, men I liked, men I respected. Even loved.* He thought then of men like Garth and Skoval, whom he'd trained as boys and bonded with as knights. When Garth had squired for him, he had thought it was a first glance at fatherhood.

I will try to love the world, Mother, he prayed, *if you can help me find the strength to do what I must in the days to come.*

"That strength is not mine to give, My Knight. It is within you already."

Allystaire thrilled to hear Her voice, but had to suppress the tiny surge of disappointment that he still felt stone against his head and hands. He resided in the Temple still, and not with Her.

"I fear the coming battle like none I have ever known," Allystaire said. "Not for myself. No more that than ever. But for Gideon. For Torvul. For Idgen Marte. For Landen, and Arontis, and what their loss might mean to the people of their Baronies."

He took a deep breath and pulled himself upright, shifting his weight on his knee. "I am sorry, Mother. I do not mean to trouble you with my fears. I will not let them consume me, nor will they stop me."

"I know that, Allystaire. I know. That is why you are My Paladin," She said, speaking to him from the air, or within his mind, or from the altar. He could not tell.

"Make no mistake, My Knight," She continued, "this will be the greatest test you face in my service. My brother Braech's power has been turned too long to dark purpose, and what will be unleashed in His name should you fail is more horrid than I can bear."

"I will not fail. Whatever it is that is asked of me, I will do. Yet I would ask one thing only." He paused, and when She did not respond, pressed on. "If it is in your power to see to it that it is asked *only* of me, then I beg you, I beg you to let it be so. Give me some champion to fight, some avatar to slay, and I will do it. Make this burden mine, and mine alone."

"I can no more control what Braech would do than man can control the ocean," She answered. "You know this. You know also that whatever power We may grant, it must be worked through those we grant it to. My Brother has chosen poorly, and you, and the rest of My Ordained, will be the instruments of his education. Remember, My Arm, your own words to the abomination you fought outside this Temple on the Longest Night."

Allystaire thought back to his frenzied battle with Lionel Delondeur, tackling him to the ground and caving in his face, crushing his throat. Screaming defiant words at him. *Your strength is taken from them, Lionel,* he had said.

"Mine is given for them," he murmured aloud.

"Strength is greatest when it is being spent for others, instead of marshaled to ourselves," the Goddess whispered. "Remember that. Carry light into the heart of the storm the Sea Dragon will try to raise. See it clearly; know that your enemies will *not* understand the strength there is in selflessness and sacrifice. You must carry the light of My sun within you through all storm, all darkness. It is a heavy thing, My Knight. I chose you because I know you will carry it."

"There is no burden I would not carry in your name," Allystaire breathed. "Nothing of myself I will not give."

"It is not only your task. The Will shall serve you in all things, My Knight, until this battle is won."

Allystaire paused for a moment. "And then?"

"He will have other tasks," came the very faint answer.

"Has he been the Dawn, then? Was that what he did with the well, and with magic?"

There was no answer this time.

He bowed his head again to the stone. "What if I do fail? What is it that awaits?"

"There is no strength to be found in despair, Allystaire."

This answer was not spoken by the Goddess; it was Mol. Startled, he turned to find her standing on her small bare feet scarcely a pace behind him. He was shocked to look up at the round band of windows in the Temple and find them dark.

"How long?"

"Only a bit more than a turn," the girl answered. "Most of the knights and soldiers have been fed. Their horses are being picketed and seen to."

He stood up, grimacing at the ache of unlocking his knees. "I should eat and find my bed."

"You should," Mol answered. "But someone is here to ask something of you." Allystaire peered into the Temple beyond the priestess. Despite the sun having set, it was never entirely dark inside these walls, and he saw two figures, half in shadow by the doors, their arms wrapped around each other.

One of them he knew, instantly by the way he walked, the spread of newly won muscle along his shoulders and arms. The other, a woman, shorter, with straw-colored hair. He had not met her, but he could put a name to her all the same.

"Norbert," he said, "Lenoir. Why have you come?"

Norbert unwound his arm from around Lenoir's shoulder and stepped forward, more into the light that emanated softly from the altar. The scar along his cheek was a fierce outline, and there was nothing left in him of the youth who'd left his home to take up with reavers.

"Y'know why, Allystaire," he said, just loud enough to be heard. "I know what ya're about to say, about leavin' for war and..." He stopped then, a trace of his old hesitance resurfacing.

"And widow-making," Lenoir finished for him. The mason's daughter had fine and delicate features entirely unlike her father's. "And we don't care to hear it." Her voice was firm above the hint of a quaver.

Not indecision, he thought, *but ready for a fight*. Setting his mouth in a firm line, he shook his head and said, "No."

"No?" Norbert stood to his full height, taking half a step towards the altar. "I can ask Mol t'do it, or Torvul."

"No," Allystaire said. "None of us will marry you tonight." He paused. "Unless her folk, at least, are here to see it."

Lenoir had already stepped forward, raising an extended finger, gathering herself to shout at him, when his words finally settled in. Norbert deflated slightly, laughing, and said, "I'll run and fetch them."

"No need," Mol said. "I have already called to them."

True to her word, they waited scarcely moments before the door opened, and a knot of familiar faces swept in. Giraud, arm in arm with a woman Allystaire knew must be Lenoir's mother, for she was the image of the girl herself, with grey overtaking the blonde in her hair. Henri, and several of the other village militia men Norbert had fought with. Keegan, who'd spent the months of winter teaching Norbert as much of the bow as he could. Finally, the men of the Order of the Arm, all of them silent, still presences who spread out along the back of the curving wall.

Allystaire thought quickly, as Norbert and Lenoir climbed the first two steps of the small dais that led to the altar. He came down to stand one step in front of them. The girl quickly shed the long cloak she'd wrapped around herself to show a dress of bright blue that shone with an air both of newness and hand-made love. She reached up and removed a pin from her hair and let the coils of it fall to her shoulders. Norbert watched her with eyes wide, as her hair seemed somehow to glint in the steady, even light of the altar.

"You were not wrong, Norbert, to assume I would refuse this ceremony, speaking of the dangers you face, of how brief might be your moments of joy. Not so long ago, I would have spoken severely of trading a bride's dress for a widow's. I will do none of that now. If your moments of joy and love are to be brief, then there is all the more reason to embrace them."

He cleared his throat and tried to think back to the first, and so far, the only marriage he had performed, and found, to his shock, the words coming perfectly back to him.

"Lenoir and Norbert. If you would be wed in the sight of the Mother, promise but two things to each other: love and service. Love and serve one another in day and in night; in joy and in grief; in plenty and in want. Know that in the Mother's eyes, love is the greatest and highest of ends. Failure to love is the deepest and darkest of sins. Do you swear your love and service to one another, and to the friends and family gathered here?"

"I do swear," Norbert said, then Lenoir the same, and before Allystaire could say another word they had embraced and pressed their lips together. A cheer went up from the crowd, hands dabbing at eyes—especially Giraud's, who was weeping more openly than anyone else he could see.

A voice, Henri's he thought, called for wine, and another for food and a feast, and before Allystaire could speak up, it was Norbert who raised his hand.

"We'll celebrate proper when we return from the war," he said as the crowd fell silent. "But there's no time nor place for it this night, aye?"

Slowly, the crowd nodded its agreement and deflated, growing silent. The newly-married pair still moved among them, Lenoir being kissed upon the cheeks and Norbert receiving back-pounding hugs—the last and longest from a beaming Henri.

"Once a reaver apprentice and a man who meant to lynch him," Mol whispered to Allystaire, having moved quietly to his side. "And now they are as much father and son as any two in the village." She let that sink in, then seized his hand and squeezed it gently. "Go now and rest, Arm of the Mother. You will need it."

* * *

Allystaire headed for the Inn and climbed the stairs past the empty taproom. He was startled to see a tall and lean figure standing outside his door and almost lowered Renard's spear into position when the form pushed off the wall and came forward.

"Don't spit me on that. It's Keegan."

Glad that the dark would hide the flush on his face, Allystaire shouldered the weapon. "Has a cover over the point anyway," he murmured.

Keegan snorted—a noise that sounded a little more dog-like than it would from most men, Allystaire thought. "You'd probably be able to pin me t'the wall w'it anyhow," he said.

"What brings you here, then?"

"All of us have come in t'do our bit. Ya don't need t'horse or feed us," he added quickly. "We can cover ground just fine, and tend t'our own supplies. Ya'll need scouts, and there's no one here better suited."

"Gideon is the greatest scout the world has ever known, in his way," Allystaire said. "He can see the world from the air. Any part of it."

"I'll not pretend t'know what that means, but I do know that there're men who know how not t'be seen and that includes from above. It'll do ya no harm t'have us movin' on your flanks, and besides, we owe you. And the boy, especially. If nothin' else, we'll be his guards."

"I will not turn that down," Allystaire said, nodding.

"Wasn't goin' t'give you the chance," Keegan said. "We'll do our bit."

Allystaire held the man's gaze for a moment, looking for any vestige of the deserter, or the chimera that had been made by the God of the Caves. He found only dark eyes, sharp and intelligent, and a kind of resolve.

"You do not have to, Keegan. I will not try and order men back into a life that already broke them once."

"That's just it," he said, crossing his arms over his chest. "Ya aren't orderin'. We're goin' of our own accord."

Allystaire nodded and extended his hand. Keegan took it, and then the paladin shuffled past him into the room that had been home for the months since the Longest Night.

Not much of me in it, he reflected as he began to strip his armor off. Just the armorer's dummy Torvul had found for him. Apparently the dwarf had found a place for it on his wagon on the hard ride back from Standing Guard Pass and gotten it back into the room. Carefully, Allystaire began to layer pieces of his armor upon it, after laying his belt and hammer on the bed.

Dawn, he told himself, when he'd climbed free of his gambeson—a large rent still in it where the Winsar Ethrik's sword had sunk into his arm—and began to sit upon the floor, laying his back against the bed. In the starlight his armor reflected from outside, he caught sight of a small bundle on the side table and reached for it. He found a small leather bag, its strings drawn tight. He pulled them open and spilled the contents into his hand: small, hard, and few in number.

"My gemmary," he breathed quietly. He brought the small handful closer to his eyes and moved towards his armor to catch the reflection. There was one tiny fragment of unworked lapis, two men's rings with plain settings, one of dark green tourmaline, one of brown topaz.

"I had no right to take those," he murmured, "and less to keep them."

Finally there was the carnelian, the largest piece, a cameo portrait of a woman worked on it. He ran his fingers over it; the likeness was never very good, but he knew the lines carved into it as well as he'd ever known anything.

He ran his thumb over the carving a few more times, then slid the handful back into the bag and tossed it to the bed. He sat upon the floor, his back propped up by the bed, slid his hammer to his lap, and fell almost instantly asleep.

* * *

"Can't kill him," Idgen Marte reminded herself. She tried to think of just how many times she'd said that today, and realized she had lost count once past five-and-twenty, so she went back to imagining *ways* of killing Gilrayan Oyrwyn.

I could cut the girth strap and let him slide off the saddle to be crushed in a charge, she mused silently. *I could cut the ropes of his pavilion free so that it fell upon him, then light the entire concern ablaze. I could get something from Torvul and poison him. I could cut his head from his neck so fast and clean that it might take him half a turn to realize he was dead and drop to the floor. Or I could just shove him off the side of a trail.* She visualized his body hitting the rocks.

She thought these things as she strolled about the elaborate campsite. Silk pavilions housed the knights, including one for Naswyn and one for his son and heir Eckerl, who was as tall and bald and boring as his father, with an affected strip of tawny mustache and a face full of freckles to boot. One for some Oyrwyn lord named Harding who'd already ridden out after the messages Gideon had passed for the young Baron, and who had brought with him a party of hardy light horsemen, all javelins and flails and magnificent arming jackets in bright blue with yellow slashes, the same colors that loudly announced his pavilion. One for the Baron, of course, the largest.

Between the daily breakdown and then pitching of camp, the slow pace of the footmen and the lack of anyone driving them to move faster, Idgen Marte figured they covered about half as much distance in a day as they should, and it had been three days since they'd left Standing Guard.

Finally she drew herself to a fire, where the younger Naswyn, Lord Harding, and a gaggle of favored knights and armsmen were drinking wine and boasting to one another, while they didn't listen to Andus Carek strum artfully upon his lute. She didn't recognize the song; only belatedly did she realize that it wasn't a song, as such, just an unobtrusive and endless series of runs and trills, not too high an octave, not too loud. Designed not to catch the ear, his playing didn't interrupt conversation or draw their attention to him, just provided a light underpinning to their chat.

Though she wasn't much more than a shadow on the edges of the firelight, she felt his eyes drawn to her. Perhaps he had learned, with time, to recognize when a shadow moved unnaturally.

Don't be an idiot, she told herself.

"Where's the Baron," she heard one of the carousers call.

"With a doxy," some rough voice called back, "showin' her why Oyrwyn girls are bowlegged."

"No, he isn't," called another voice. "Not *yet*. He's talking strategy with the great lords."

There was a general ruffle of laughter, but not a chorus of it.

She wandered away from the fire. Perhaps inevitably, her feet were drawn to that huge silken pavilion at the center of the camp.

Two mailed, surcoated guardsman stood at the entrance, staring ahead, shields at the ready, hands on the hilts of belted swords. They were creditably ignoring the chatter coming from within.

Idgen Marte turned as if to leave when she heard the sudden outbreak of laughter. She listened hard.

"That'll show the lot of them," a voice said. "Soft-headed idiots following a traitor."

Her fingers curled around the hilt of her sword. She took a step to the back of the pavilion, crouched in the shadows there.

A lamp hung from the pole in the center of it. Gilrayan and Joeglan stood over a table, peering down at its surface. The curled edges of a map fell over its sides. She wasn't close enough to read it, but she could see a few wooden blocks positioned atop it.

"All we have to do is take our time," Gilrayan said. "If we arrive at the field and find that the Braechsworn have smashed them, we simply pledge our allegiance to Braech if we can, stop them with the combined might of all Oyrwyn if we cannot. If we find that the traitor has won, then we simply fall upon him with the strength we have gathered. Provided conditions favor it."

Idgen Marte decided to risk a step closer. The amount of furniture scattered around—an armorer's dummy, a sword rack, two trunks of clothes, two folding tables, a washstand with basin—gave her plenty of shadows to slip into.

"And if they do not? If Varshyne surprises us all with something resembling an army? If peasants flock to the Sunburst?" Joeglan Naswyn's voice was a distant rumble in the dark. She stood but a decent lunge away from them both, in the shadows cast by the tent's cot. "The other Barons will well remember that you made a promise and did not live up to it."

"Nonsense. If we are late it was because I was making sure that Oyrwyn, as Varshyne's closest neighbor, could bring enough strength to bear to make the difference."

"What do we make of the reports coming in from the lords and levies that say they will not meet their spring obligations?"

"They always complain. They'll come clean in the end or we'll squeeze it from them."

"If there are no horses to squeeze out of Coldbourne, m'lord, there are no horses."

"Is that what the reports say, then?" There was a shuffling of papers on the desk. "Then why do Harding's light horse, screening our backtrail, tell me that a sizable number of horses are being gathered at an old Harlach guard tower inside Coldbourne's demesne?"

Shit. Idgen Marte's first thought was to draw her sword, paint the inside of the tent in Oyrwyn and Naswyn blood, and then go about her night. *But then this column will be a leaderless mob, and there's no telling what would come of that.*

"I'd say we send a party to investigate. I will lead them," Naswyn said, only to be cut off by a waving hand.

"Send Harding. I need you here." He paused. "Let's give him a fistful of warrants in case anyone who matters needs killing."

The casual way he said that almost ended Gilrayan Oyrwyn's life. *In case anyone who matters needs killing.* Idgen Marte's hand tightened on her sword, but she leapt away to the back of the tent, soundlessly, as Naswyn came to the bedside table and pulled a stack of fresh parchment.

"It is Coldbourne itself that has turned away most requests," Naswyn warned. "Are you sure you wish to issue warrants there?"

"We'll put the sister's name on one. Garth will forgive me, especially if he keeps the fief. Wives are more easily replaced than holdings."

Goddess, he is as awful as Allystaire said he was. Her hand was white-knuckled on her hilt. The first handspan of blade was clear.

Letting it slide carefully back into the sheath was the hardest thing Idgen Marte had done in many a month.

She glided to the back of the tent with silent steps, then went from shadow inside of it to the shadow outside.

* * *

Idgen Marte slipped into the tent she and Andus Carek shared. He was laying atop the bedding spread on the ground, wearing only his pants, arms behind his head, feet crossed at the ankles, asleep.

Even his breathing sounded musical, somehow, a faint trill of notes.

She shook her head to drive away the sentimental rot that threatened to rise up and seize her. She placed a hand on his chest; he awoke instantly, half sitting up.

"Andus," she murmured, adopting their native Concordat tongue. "We have to go. Tonight. Pack up. I'll see t'your horse."

"Why?"

"The Baron is useless. He'll offer no aid to Allystaire. He means to gather all his men, his entire host, and take advantage of whatever greets him on the field once he's good and ready. I can do no more good here aside from killing him."

"Then do it."

"We're inside an Oyrwyn host that's only going to get stronger. We're not up to it. Listen, you're headed north. I'll take you to the trailhead. From there, you follow it till you come to an old border fort. Shouldn't be hard for an old road-hand like you. You may have to ride hard for a day. Wait there. It's t'be a meeting place for Harlach men who'll need remounts."

He sat up, nodding slowly. She started to pull away, but he caught her hand and held it against the bare skin of his chest. She felt the steady drum of his heart for just a moment.

"You'd best not disappear on me before the battles," he murmured, his voice as honeyed and smooth as hers wasn't. "I've got songs of you to write still. And songs for you." He paused a moment, his chest rising with a breath as he added, "Marte."

She stiffened, startled at the presumption of intimacy. "No one has been that familiar to me in more years than I care to count," she murmured, uncertain.

In the darkness, she could still see the maddeningly perfect smile he unleashed at her, knowing full well what it did, and said, "I only followed your lead."

She remembered with a jolt, mere moments ago. Waking him with his single name. She took a deep breath and lowered her eyes from his.

He leaned forward and pressed his head to hers for a moment, just a moment. "So many songs I've yet to sing for you, Marte," he murmured, his lips moving almost against her ear.

Her finger stroked his chest once, then she pulled her hand away. "Then take care of your voice, Andus."

She fled the tent for the picket line. It was the work of a skilled child to unhobble his horse, find his tack, and lead the animal away in silence.

She found him just outside the camp, dressed warmly, lute case on his back, dagger on his belt. She knew there was one more up his sleeve, and what's more, she knew that the edge of the cloak he wore gathered over one shoulder was lined with lead, making it a heavy—and perfectly hidden—cosh.

They didn't speak as she led him onward. At the trailhead, Andus Carek pulled up onto the saddle, then his hand reached out and Idgen Marte's slid snugly into it. Lutist's callus met swordswoman's, and yet she did not find the grip at all unpleasant.

"Come back to me," she rasped, hating the way her native tongue sounded in her mangled voice.

"Where else would the road lead me?"

"Home is the road," she murmured, the old minstrel's phrase forming on her lips before she thought on it.

"And its next bend will surely lead me there," he replied, then he clicked his tongue, setting his horse walking north.

Idgen Marte watched it disappear into the wooded track, then took her time returning to the camp.

* * *

Allystaire greeted the sun already armored. He'd slept for a few turns at most, and hadn't wasted any time since waking in the just lightening dark before the dawn. He had left his bag of gemmary on the counter of the bar in the taproom, scribbled a note hastily on a scrap of parchment, carefully packed his maps in watertight leather cases in his saddlebags. Now with those same bags tossed over his shoulder he was heading for the stables.

A stick-thin figure wrapped in rags awaited his approach. Even from afar

620 – DANIEL M. FORD

Allystaire could see the fevered eyes, huge above cheeks rubbed so raw by wind and cold that the skin was cracked and peeling away.

"Rede," Allystaire said, taking in the sight of the man. "Have you been sheltered, man? Have you been fed?"

As if he hadn't even heard the question, the priest stumbled towards him, reaching out to grasp Allystaire's armored shoulders. "I must accompany you north," he mumbled. "I must. If I don't, disaster. Hosts of wind and air. The awful roaring rage. I must," he pleaded, his hands clutching Allystaire's vambraces with desperate strength.

"It is going to be perilous, Rede," Allystaire said, "and I will be in the midst of the fighting. I will not be able to protect you."

"Don't need you to watch over me," Rede said, his eyes going distant. "You need me to see the things you cannot."

With that, he slumped forward against Allystaire, his eyes rolling back in his head. The exhalation of his breath smelled like rot when Allystaire caught him, and he weighed far too little for a man of his height.

For a moment, Allystaire hadn't any idea what to do. He stood there holding Rede's limp form, weighing whether to heal him or sling him over his shoulder, when a deep and welcome voice rumbled from behind him.

"I'll take the charge of him," Torvul said. "Like as not there's nothin' wrong with him can't be fixed with a loaf of good bread and a jug of small beer."

Allystaire turned and carefully lowered Rede towards Torvul's outstretched arms. With surprising gentleness, the dwarf lowered him to the grass and carefully lifted his eyelids with a fingertip, then held that same finger to the side of Rede's neck.

"How did you know to find me here?" Allystaire knelt as well, watching Rede's now slumbering form.

"Despite my best efforts, you persist in this early rising nonsense. And besides, I've been up all night packing what I'll need and fitting it to the frame of a packhorse. Can't bring my home into battle." He sighed then. "What I wouldn't give for one of the war wagons our larger caravans roll on behind, ballistae mounted fore and aft and wheels o'finest steel."

Allystaire snickered, earning a glare from the alchemist. He was reaching his left hand to Rede's wrist when the man sat bolt upright. Whatever madness had been in his eyes seemed to have cleared, for he looked steadily on, even if his breath remained ragged. He pushed Allystaire's hand away feebly.

"No," he said, shaking his head. "I fear that your healing might drive away whatever gift of foretelling I still have."

"You were divining?" Allystaire tilted his head. "You seem ill, Rede."

"No," he insisted, once again shaking his head. His hair had grown shaggy, unkempt, and matted; this close, he reeked. "I am not ill. I have done what I must do to chase the visions. I will pay you back, Arm. You and the Shadow, and the Voice, and the Mother."

"What were you divinin', then, just now?" Torvul muttered.

Rede looked to Allystaire, who said, "Hosts of wind? Roaring rage? You being able to see things I cannot?"

"I can make no sense of them," Rede said, "but it is not given to me to understand. Only speak. And that is growing harder, receding from me like a tide pulling away from the shore."

"I don't like that talk o'tides n'shores," Torvul muttered. "But hosts of wind? Braech is the Father of Waves, storms, the ocean, wind seems t'me to be a part of that. Perhaps there's some part o'the host we haven't seen yet."

"Rede," Allystaire said, "I will tell you again because I do not know if you heard me the first time. If you accompany us north, I cannot spare myself, or any other man, to protect you. Not until our forces grow. You will be in danger. There is not going to be a rear element or a distant command post to shelter you."

"I am no coward," he protested. "And I will follow you unless you lock me up here, or you kill me. If you did not kill me when I deserved it, you'll not do it now."

"I have not the time to debate this further," Allystaire said, shaking his head. "Follow if you will. Horsed, if one can be found to bear you."

"I'll look after him," Torvul said. "I'm curious to see this puzzle play out. Go on, boy," he said, waving a hand at Allystaire. "Rouse the troops. Catch the sunlight on yer armor. S'why I made it."

Allystaire stood and picked up his saddlebags once more, went into the small stables. Ardent was awake and whickered softly as Allystaire came near.

"As eager to be off as I am?"

The stallion raised his tail and flicked it once. Allystaire opened the stall; before he could enter, the destrier brushed past him gently, but Allystaire reflected that gently for a horse of over a hundred-and-fifty stone weight was essentially undeniable.

The enormous grey walked over towards the shelves that held the tack and saddles, stopped, and looked back over his shoulder at Allystaire.

"Well, then," he said, coming up behind the stallion, making sure to look him in the eye, and running a hand over his densely muscled flank as he walked, "let us get on with it."

* * *

The people of Thornhurst lined either side of the road leading past the Temple and the wooden palisade they called the North Gate, to watch Sir Allystaire Stillbright lead his horse past them, to begin in earnest his defense against the Braechsworn Crusade.

They did it in silence. There were no cheers, no songs, no hymns of praise sung as he rode past them. The pennant they had made for him months ago, the golden sunburst on a blue field, fluttered at the end of his lance. The sun shown brilliantly on the silver of his armor, the golden sunburst on its cuirass.

As he rode, the Order filtered out of the crowd, leading horses, falling into a line. Like him, they had hard faces and rode in silence. They bristled with weapons: swords, axes, a few lances, bows, flails, spears. They didn't look like the knightly companions of a paladin in a story, Allystaire reflected. Dressed in oddments of mismatched armor instead of shining plate, they looked more like a band of robbers than knights. Those who carried shields had applied quick and uneven coats of blue paint to their fronts, and none had any other devices.

The Order of the Arm didn't look, in a word, knightly.

But from their hard faces and grimly-set mouths, from the hands that gripped their melange of weapons like craftsmen clutching the tools of their trade, to the eyes that betrayed nothing, they seemed practically to radiate devotion. To him, perhaps, for what he'd been able to do in healing them. To the Mother, surely.

Devotion was starting them on a long road north to grapple with a larger enemy of unknown strength, to defend people they'd never know, people who'd likely never know them. There was no gold in it, no titles, and, given their looks, probably no fair folk sighing at the sight of them, either.

There was only, for them, the fact that the task needed to be done, that they were suited to it, and that it would mean others could rest easy.

And that, Allystaire thought as he watched them line up behind him, *is precisely what knightly ought to mean.*

The youngest of them, a bow cased on his now broadly-muscled back, a spear in his hand, had to carefully pull himself away from the hard embrace of his new wife. Neither of them shed tears. Not tears for anyone else to see, at least.

The crowd was so quiet that many could hear her fiercely whisper, "Come back to me," as he took his place in the line, and more heard him calmly reply, "Always."

There were nine of them who led their horses behind him when he reached the Temple. He paused then to look towards the doors, thinking on the altar beyond, the field of graves nearby, the mass grave of those massacred by the reavers, Renard's. Too many of them.

He turned to take a look at the village then, at the familiar faces gathered to watch him.

"Look at them," he said to the order lined behind him. "Hold them in your mind as we face the storm. Remember what we are bound to." He placed his foot into a stirrup and swung himself into the saddle, his armor flashing in the sun. "Any burden," he called.

One voice came from nine knight's throats in answer.

"Any burden."

* * *

Andus Carek was lying in the hollow of a wall, scratching notes on a piece of parchment by the early light of dawn.

The abandoned old fort wasn't much account, really, he reflected. A simple stone wall, a couple of towers, a central bailey—if it could be called that. Most of the woodwork had begun to rot away after just a few years of disuse, and much of the stonework, too, was falling away. Still, its location along a north-bending road's intersection with a primary east-west track made it too easy to find for someone used to finding places by feel and instinct in a country with poor roads, irregular post if any, and abominable weather.

Such shoddy work, he reflected, *wouldn't be tolerated in Fen Isiel or Wiefaldt, much less Cansebour.*

The two years he'd spent traveling in the Baronies had done nothing to raise the esteem of their people in Andus Carek's eyes. To someone used to the wide, clean streets of a Concordat city, its spires glittering with stained glass, its gardens tended with near-holy reverence, the Baronies couldn't help but seem barbaric.

And yet, Andus Carek reflected, he'd chosen to come here, bringing his lute and his voice.

Like a missionary carrying his faith and his guilt, I suppose, he told himself. Even so, he had to admit he found the bumbling simplicity of most Barony folk refreshing, in a way. No plots were hidden, or at least not for long, and it seemed as though there was something vital and exciting about the people who lived here. Closer to the realities of war and death than everyone but the most hardened guards and soldiers among the Concordat's patchwork quilt of peoples, their blood ran hotter. Quicker to fight, yes, but quicker to buy drinks when the fight was done, he thought.

He let his thoughts drift while he scribbled with a charcoal stick, trying to let images and rhymes come to him as he always did in the very early stages of composing. They were quickly reeled back when he heard a muffled footfall.

"That's good technique," he called out, from where he still reclined against the missing stones, "but you've not counted on the ears of a southern bard."

With a sigh he set down his barely scrawled-on parchment and his stick and stood, slowly unfolding himself out of the hollow and holding his hands out.

As he'd more or less expected, there was a sudden rush of footsteps, then someone tried to plant a blade at the back of his neck. On the step before the one that would've reached him, he ducked to one side and pivoted away.

"I mean you no harm," he was already saying as he came face to face with his potential assailant, stumbling away from him and trying to get their feet under them, "but I won't have a blade anywhere near my throat."

Finally, his attacker did find her feet, and proved to be a young, whip-thin blonde woman with an intense look about her eyes. She wore men's riding clothes, cut small and sewed close to fit her, and had a dagger with a darkened blade extended from her curled fist. From the way she stood, her feet spread, blade leading, she knew how to use it.

She lowered it, though, as she studied his face. "You're her pet bard," the girl muttered, disappearing the dagger somewhere he didn't pay close enough attention to spot.

"Andus Carek," he replied with a courtly bow and a smile still fixed upon his face, despite how little he liked being called anyone's pet anything. "I assume the her in question is the Shadow of the Mother."

"Aye," the girl confirmed. "That'd be her. What're you doin' here?"

"Enlisting in your cause, I suppose."

"Did she kill him? Oyrwyn, I mean."

"Alas, no," Andus Carek replied with a shrug. "From what little I know of the man, it certainly seems that the world would not miss him. But the Arm of the Mother has forbidden it, so." He shrugged again.

The woman scowled. He reflected that her face, sort of plain and ordinary, was improved by this anger; it went from a mask of disaffection to displaying honest emotion, and he felt he could work with the latter more effectively.

"I'm not sure," she said, "that what the Arm of the Mother wants ought to take precedence over what the Shadow thinks ought to be done."

"She does," the bard replied quickly. "And if you'd spent time around him, you would, too," he added.

"I have. I'm not impressed. Pompous, loud, a fool."

"I think he is definitely loud," Andus Carek said. "And I think you, per-haps, could now save us both some time and effort and tell me your name and your purpose here, since you know mine."

"Shary," the woman said. "And my purpose is to scout this place for the string of mounts being led here, and t'see if I can't help Baron Harlach find the place."

"How far behind you are the mounts?" Andus Carek asked.

"A turn or two at most," she said.

"Listen. How about I take my horse, a note, or flag or emblem of some kind, and go along to the east, see if I can't find Harlach. He's a big loud brute of a fellow, so I doubt he's much for woodcraft or stealth and I imagine the same is true of his knights. The sooner we get him through here, the better, because Gilrayan Oyrwyn knows the horses are coming. I don't know how, but he does."

"Cold, but you use a lot o'words where one or two'd speak jus' fine," the girl drawled, "but ya aren't wrong now. Best we both go. Hurry."

Andus Carek made for his horse.

CHAPTER 45

Foraging Parties

Brazcek Varshyne had not known he could be so tired, or so hungry. He had especially not known he could be both of those things and yet still walking the parapet of Pinesward Watch, crossbow in hand, rallying his men.

He wasn't, in truth, entirely sure what effect rallying was likely to have, or if he was doing it properly. A congratulatory word there on a good shot, a pat on the back there, a casual reminder not to waste either bolts or bread, and the men all smiled and cheered him.

All too often those smiles were underneath eyes that were trying to understand that they were already dead, Brazcek thought.

Upon an empty stretch of wall, he looked out over the enemy encampment and wondered, not for the first time, just what the plan in place was.

A vast body of men without banners, seemingly without much organization, were camped just out of crossbow range along his frontage. Camped behind them, around clusters of blue and green pavilions, were the berzerkers. Small groups, usually led by a pair or so of the bare-chested terrors, would leave every day on foraging parties.

Gravek patrolled beyond them. Thankfully none had come too close to the walls, much less assaulted it, though in one case some horsemen from Greenforks answering their summons, had tried, boldly, to force their way past that outer screen.

From the highest parts of the tower, the Baron Varsyhnne and the seneschal Herrin had been able to watch some of the resulting battle. The thirty or so horsemen had accounted for one Gravekmir with their javelins and horsebows, but then more had fallen on them, cutting off their retreat.

A second Gravekmir had died in the resulting fight among the victors, as they fell out over sharing the remains of a score of men and horses.

Since then, three days prior, no forces had attempted a breakthrough. No banners had even been sighted. Pigeons had come back, confirming that the men of Treeline, Greenforks, and Crossing—the only three holds of any size the Barony had left, it seemed—were on their way. But scraps of parchment tied to a pigeon's leg was all the force they'd seen besides that one company of horsemen.

Lost in the grim math, Brazcek was suddenly startled by Herrin's voice. "Looks like they're coming again, m'lord," the old knight reported.

Wearily, Baron Varshyne looked back out. Sure enough, the mass of men in the first camp were forming themselves into ragged columns.

"Ropes and hooks?"

"Looks that way, m'lord."

"Why do the berzerkers and the giants just sit? They could have rolled over us days ago."

"I've a theory, m'lord," Herrin said, narrowing his eyes and scratching at his bearded chin. "If they're holding back, either they expect something more to come along and test them from behind, or, or we're just for training."

"Training?"

"Aye. The unblooded men they toss at our walls, well, they're learning the hardest lessons of fighting, and they're doing it all at once."

"Cold-dammit," Brazcek growled. He saw the columns starting to lurch forward, driven by pairs of berzerkers shouting at their backs. "Let us get to the lower curtain, then. If we're to give them a lesson, let's get on with it."

* * *

Honored Choiron Symod stood at the head of a clutch of priests of Braech: two Marynths, a handful of Winsars, the rest lacking title due to want of ambition, intelligence, or age. One such young priest, a tall and broad-shouldered young Keersvaster named Theophraste, was vying for his attention as the attack rolled out in front of them. At least a dozen priests always gathered themselves together for each attack at Symod's insistence, though typically it was more.

Dragon Scales ran along behind the lines of Islandmen, swiping at them with clawed gauntlets or aiming kicks at their heels if they didn't move fast enough. The berzerkers shouted and howled in their native tongue. Jorn, erstwhile Dragon Scale headman, stood at a remove of some distance, watching with disdain. Symod ignored him and looked at Theophraste.

"What is it?"

"Honored Choiron," the man began, "the foraging party of two days ago still has not returned. It is an oddity."

"Like as not the men have stripped the lands closest to us and have to range farther," Symod said. "They'll return."

"Even so, Honored Choiron," Theophraste went on, "there are many possibilities we ought to consider. Did they encounter a relieving force? Did they desert our cause?"

Symod turned a frown and a furrowed brow on the man. "Desert the Sea Dragon? Such an idea is not to be borne."

Symod turned to watch the ranks of Islandmen break into a run for the walls. Crossbow bolts came raining down among them, but not as many as had been shot the first day, nor the fifth, nor even the tenth.

"There were two berzerkers among them," Symod suddenly said. "They would not simply run off like cowards. It is not in them."

"No, Honored Choiron, it is not. But there were forty Islandmen. And forty might set upon two in the night, or in darkness. Please, Honored Choiron. Just give me leave to take men to find them. To hunt them down, or to bring their killers the Sea Dragon's vengeance."

Symod frowned as he saw men tossing ropes up at the top of the lower curtain wall. Too few reached their targets and even those that died were all too quickly dislodged. In the rare event that men managed to scramble up a rope, they were easily shoved away at spearpoint.

"You may go, on two conditions. You will return with heads, whether of deserters or attackers. You will discover a good source of lumber. It is time for ladders."

"Yes, Honored Choiron. I will take a hundred of the men."

"And three Dragon Scales," Jorn said, showing evidence that he'd been listening. "They will not carry tools, or cut wood. But they will bring your heads, Honored Choiron." Theophraste bowed low and hurried out of the circle.

A fat Marynth whose name Symod couldn't recall spoke up. "Perhaps it is time we unleashed a few of the Gravekmir? We cannot simply continue spending men."

"An army must be blooded," Symod cooly replied. "This is only the beginning, and we have more than enough men. Once they carry the walls, the berzerkers will gain us the keep."

"We could take the walls, too," Jorn insisted.

"It may come to that. For now, let us watch our army blood itself."

Blood themselves they did. The Islandmen had little enough in the way of training, but courage they did have in abundance. Here and there, singly and in pairs, men would reach the top of the wall only to be thrown off. Men who were halfway up the fastened ropes fell as they were cut, then immediately got up and ran for another descending line. Here and there, particularly brave or hardy souls tried to climb the wall itself, wedging their hands and feet into cracks in the mortar, pulling themselves along by sheer muscle.

We have the men, we have the Gravek keeping relief away, and most of all, we have the Sea Dragon, Symod told himself. *They are doomed.*

* * *

"You have got yourself," Torvul muttered, "about as efficient a band of killers as I've ever known. And believe you me, I have known princes among thugs. Master craftsmen of violence. Adepts at killing men. And this lot just about beats them all."

"They are not thugs, Torvul," Allystaire said. "They are knights."

"Whatever you call 'em, they' cut that batch of Islandmen down like it was a mere day's work on the farm," the dwarf replied. "If anyone sings songs o'that fight they're goin' to be using it t'scare their children to sleep."

He stood, and Allystaire knelt, by the side of their mounts on the slight rise of a hill where they had paused to reconnoiter and rest. The Barons Machoryn and Telmawr and their knights gathered around him, while Landen and Arontis oversaw disposition of their own men, with the Damarinds, mother and daughter, moving along with the young Baron Innadan.

Allystaire had a folded section of map spread out on his bent knee. "If they are sending out regular foraging parties in that strength, they have not got the supplies to maintain a long siege," he mused aloud.

"Or they're just after plunder and food is all they've found," Torvul cautioned.

He looked towards Gideon, who was feigning sleep against his saddle. To all but Allystaire, Torvul, and the two men of Keegan's who stood over him, he might well have been. Those who knew what he was doing for their little army tried to guard the secret as well as they could, for the boy was entirely vulnerable when he projected his Will away from himself.

"We need to get someone close enough to the walls to give us a good count of their numbers," Allystaire said. "If they are few enough, and poorly dispositioned, we might want to strike."

"Gravek," Torvul rumbled. "Got to get past them first."

"I can handle Gravek," Allystaire said.

"Gravekmir, not Graveklings. Though I'd wager you don't see the one without the other. And one or two, yes, I don't doubt you. But the boy said there were dozens."

"Gideon cannot get close enough without revealing himself to the priests," Allystaire said, "and it may well be that they obscure what he can see from afar. In other matters I trust him. In this, I need to be sure."

"Wide open country approachin' that keep. What about—"

They broke off as their talk as a shadow fell over them from behind: Rede. His robes were better tended than when they had left Thornhurst, he'd washed, and food and drink had put at least a bit of flesh back into his cheeks, but he had that same gaunt and fevered look as he held out his hands towards Allystaire and Torvul, carrying a wrapped bundle. The dwarf took it with a nod, and Allystaire thanked him almost absently while the dwarf unwrapped the bread and hard cheese.

Torvul frowned heavily as he bit off a mouthful of the bread, grumbling a few low and gravelly Dwarfish oaths.

Allystaire took his loaf and ate absently. "Keegan might be able to get close," he mused. "He was a scout and he knows how to handle hill country."

"Why not a quick ride close and round," Ruprecht Machoryn called. The Baron walked stiffly towards them, clearly sore from the saddle and trying not to show it.

"Because over open ground and a long enough time, a Gravekmir can out-run a horse," Allystaire said. "We may not fight them often up in Oyrwyn, but we learn that part young. For the tallest of them, this country may as well be flat. A horse will have them in the sprint, but the giant will make up ground as the animal tires. It is a poor bet for the men who do the scouting, and the horses need to be conserved for fighting."

"Rode them awfully hard just to get here in order to save them for battle," Machoryn replied, his cheeks coloring.

"We did what was necessary to get close enough to make a difference," Allystaire replied, standing and slipping the map into the case lashed to his saddle's pommel.

Machoryn opened his mouth again, raising a gauntleted hand, and Torvul stopped him by clearing his throat. "I'll wager you're not a man used t'bein' corrected, your lordship," the dwarf said. "'Less you want continued lessons in it, I'd stop talkin'."

The Baron's thick cheeks colored more fully, and he stomped off awkward and stiff, back straight, taking small steps.

"There's fresh men but a day away," Torvul pointed out. "Boy said the Har-lach banner is that close."

"And if I wait for them to make any decision, might I also not spend pre-cious days rounding up loose Varshyne men? And then hold out just a few more days for Oyrwyn troops to arrive? And then what, it is high summer, we have dug so many ditches and ramparts that a man can walk from here to Pineswatch Ward without laying his eye on a scrap of anything green or growing? No, Tor-vul. I will not fall into that trap. We will work with the men we have until we have more, or less."

Allystaire looked as if he'd come to a decision and tossed a large final bite of cheese into his mouth, chewing fast, when hoofbeats turned him around.

Norbert had come pounding up and swinging off the saddle before his horse had reined in, with the enviable confidence of the young. Keegan, riding double behind him, slid a bit more cautiously.

"Allystaire," the older, bearded man called, "Another foraging party. Larger than the first—much larger. Four, five score."

Allystaire swallowed fast. "Berzerkers?"

Keegan nodded quickly.

"Norbert," Allystaire said, "Round up the Order, get Arontis and Landen. Rest and respite are done."

The young knight nodded quickly and was back in the saddle in a moment.

"What is their line of march?"

"North of here," Keegan, "and moving east along the Pine, following its Needles to any likely looking farmsteads."

"If we could get down into one of those little valleys and start a merry fire," Torvul suggested, "we could draw them down t'meet us."

"No," Allystaire said, "I will trap them, yes. But the same way we trapped the first, with their own lust for blood. To your horses, go. We move in a quarter of a turn. We are going to ride hard to our north and east." He quickly slipped the map he had already tucked away back out, waving Keegan to him. "Show me," he murmured, "and then tell your men to get Gideon up and tie him into the saddle. Then stick next to him, keep his horse moving."

"I'm awake," the boy suddenly said, sitting up. "The Islandmen aren't just plundering or foraging. They're cutting down trees."

"Symod's after ladders, then, or towers." Torvul spat to the muddy grass near his boots. "He'll not have the know-how t'make decent engines, but if he's got over a thousand Islandmen and three hundred berzekers, he can take the place by main force with ladders."

"That it took him this long to realize that is to our benefit," Allystaire said. "Yet it does not take much to make ladders, and they only have to hold for one use. All the more reason to make sure none of them report back."

Keegan held the map out to Allystaire, moving his fingers over it. "This hasn't got all the Pine's Needles marked upon it, hasn't got the one they were nearest, I don't think. But here," he said, stabbing his finger against the parchment at a spot along the unusually straight course of the river in question; small channels spread away from it along most of its length, often supporting such villages as were still inhabited in Varsyhnne.

Keegan's finger pointed to a spot that would be a straight enough ride of a turn or two for the main body of the force. Allystaire nodded and packed the map away again, then offered Gideon a hand. The boy came wearily to his feet.

"Idgen Marte says that Gilrayan hasn't moved from Wind's Jaw yet. He makes excuses, says he's waiting for a force of sufficient size."

Allystaire sighed. "What of Harlach?"

"Still a day out, and running short of mounts."

The paladin nodded. "I will need you to coordinate between me and the men who will be with the other force."

"Other force?"

"I mean to explain only the once," Allystaire replied. "Yet you are going to have to be tied to the saddle again, I expect. I am sorry."

Gideon shook his head. "Do not apologize. This task could be done by no one else."

Allystaire gave Gideon a quick pat on the shoulder, then mounted Ardent. Alone amongst the horses that had made the hard ride of many days north into Varshyne, the huge grey seemed not to have lost any of the shine in his eyes or the strength of his muscles.

Landen, Arontis, Loaisa, and Lurezia Damarind rode up to Allystaire's banner, around which the men of the Order were gathering, leading weary horses.

"Landen, I want you to take your lances, and Loaisa, your riders, and everyone in our midst with a bow, and make a hard line north and west. Arontis, take one half of the Thornriders, and the Telmawr knights forward with me, to the north and east. The balance of our forces will remain reserve should things go sour. We are intercepting another foraging party. This one is also after lumber, and I need not explain what that means for Pinesward. They are moving along the Pine itself, stopping in the Needles. Landen and Loaisa, your job will be to stop their flight if we break them. I expect we will."

"That's confident," Baroness Damarind said with an expression Allystaire couldn't place as a grimace or a smile.

"They are untutored men with an abundance of bravery and no firm hand on their bloodlust. We will be attacking them from higher ground, mounted, with lances. They will break. If you encounter any berzekers, do not try to take them one to one. Spit them on lances, fill them with arrows, hurt them as much as you can before you must come to grips with them. Ride careful for a turn, then stop and walk your horses. Do not mount them again until we come to the Pine, or at need. Go."

Allystaire ignored the face or two that held questions in their expressions, and nudged Ardent into motion. The destrier's hooves found purchase in the muddy grass, churning along at a steady rate. He heard the sounds of other horses scrambling away, turned back to see Norbert, Teague, Gaston, Miklas, and Mattar peel away from his line of men, leaving him with Armel, Harrys, Tibult, and Johonn. He turned to the last, who looked out of place on his horse, like his feet might touch the ground, his longaxe leaned casually against one shoulder.

"Might be more work for you with the other party," Allystaire pointed out.

Johonn shook his head, his jaw jutting out. "Prefer t'stay with you. I'll keep out from under any hooves."

Allystaire nodded. "Stay close to Gideon, then, with the wild men, would you?"

"I'll do it if y'ask," Johonn said warily, "but I'd rather be in the fight."

"This is only our second taste of the Islandmen, Johonn. We will all have our fill before it is done."

* * *

Spring in Varshyne was browner than Allystaire would've liked, but it was still beautiful, in its way. There were patches of green, but in general the entire place seemed to be made of mud; thankfully it wasn't a thick or clinging mud that would work against the horses.

Not yet it isn't, Allystaire told himself. *Another week or two and spring rains find us, then we'll see.*

He stood beside Ardent at the very lip of a hill, prominently displayed against a blue-white sky. Behind him, Harrys held the Mother's Banner, the golden sunburst and blue silk listless in a light breeze that was still enough to stir the smaller pennants on his lance, and on Harrys's, Armel's, and Tibult's.

Below them, in a dip in the earth that was a bit scant to be called a valley, the Pine flowed, a long, straight, brown length. Above it, more hills, more brown.

Crawling along it, well beneath them and highlighted against the brown earth beyond them, was the foraging party. Keegan and his men, with occasional adjustments from Gideon, had led Allystaire's force straight to them.

He hated needing to assume that Landen and Loaisa's party were similarly in place. Gideon was dozens of yards away, with the reserve force, tightly guarded by Johonn and four of Keegan's men.

Only a few yards behind him was the first of the two companies of the Thornriders, the Innadan and Telmawr knights. The small distance would make all the difference to anyone looking up at them from the valley's floor.

All they would see, standing at the very top of the hill above the rise, was the banner, and four knights.

"You're takin' an awful risk," Torvul quietly called from one or two yards behind. In truth Allystaire wasn't sure the dwarf would've been visible even standing next to him, given the angle, but the dwarf had insisted. *For the feel of the thing*, he'd said. *For symmetry*. "They could have bows or crossbows, throwin' axes or spears."

"By the time they are close enough for axes, it will not matter much. As for bows, the bulk of these men have not had the time to learn them well enough to be dangerous. And I would bet my last link that the Dragon Scales eschew bows altogether."

"Have you got any links left? A wager or two might pass the time."

"I think I own nothing but my armor and my hammer," Allystaire replied. "I found the last bit of gemmary I brought with me, rings that belong to the Lord of Coldbourne Hall, a carnelian cameo, and a tiny chip of lapis. Left it at the Inn with a note."

"Cold," Torvul swore. "She didn't make you swear to poverty."

"I tire of this talk. And I tire of waiting," Allystaire said. "Do something to draw their attention, would you?"

"Fine." The dwarf pulled a bolt free from the quarrel on his hip and carefully applied something to it from a bottle, one of the many stuck in pouches affixed to his jerkin. He slotted the bolt, lifted his crossbow high, and fired.

The dwarf had fired casually, aiming at nothing in particular, Allystaire guessed. But when it landed atop a large flat rock, the sound reverberated across the water and sent a huge puff of smoke into the air.

As one, the armed men below them turned towards the sound, and then to Allystaire's bellow carried to them on the breeze, and by the potion Torvul had handed him just before.

"BRAECHSWORN COWARDS. COME AND FACE THE MOTHER'S JUSTICE. COME, AND BE READY TO MEET YOUR GOD."

A yell went up—one of the howling yells from a berzerker at the core of it—and the Braechsworn turned to run across yards and yards of empty mud, brandishing weapons that shone with newness in the sunlight.

"Let them spend their strength," Allystaire cautioned. "Do not even mount yet. We do not fear them."

Tibult was stroking his horse's neck and feeding it a handful of grain. Allystaire had not seen a man bond so deeply, so quickly, with an animal he meant to bring into danger. Every night of the ride, Tibult's horse was fed, brushed, rubbed, watered, and had its hooves checked before its rider had so much as a morsel. Every morning was the same. Harrys was checking his girth strap, with the calm assurance of a master carpenter looking over his tools before setting to work. Armel showed the only sign of nerves, rolling his head around his shoulders, shifting his feet.

"MOUNT," Allystaire yelled, and though it lacked the force of his previous yell, it had enough in it to roll over the men behind them. The sound of over a hundred men in armor mounting their horses was deadly and yet oddly quiet.

The weaker elements of the charging Islandmen began to falter on their run. The strongest, those with the greatest lust for blood and glory, were pulling away from the rest. Allystaire searched the mass of men for the berzerkers, looking for the telltale gauntlets, the bare ink-scrawled chests. He saw one, running at a pace that seemed leisurely. As he searched for the other he saw a priest of Braech wearing an ill-fitting breastplate over his robes, carrying a spiked mace and screaming admonitions at the men as they burst away from him. He was left with no choice but to follow, turning red in the face as he ran after the Islandmen.

When Allystaire judged them past the point where they could easily turn and run, he lifted his lance from its boot, waving the pennant aloft, back and forth, once.

The main body of horsemen started to advance behind him. He waited but a moment more before lifting the lance again and waving it twice.

Then he gave Ardent the spur and the huge muscles beneath him, already bunched and waiting, exploded into movement.

* * *

Theophraste knew, he knew, as soon as he'd heard the sound and then the paladin's yell, what was going to happen.

Even as he was shouting orders at them, yelling for them to form a line and hold it, they broke and rolled forward like a wave towards the shore.

And like all waves, the young priest of Braech told himself, *they're going to smash themselves on the rocks.*

He had no choice but to follow after. As he was running, unlimbering his mace, and looking at the crest of the hill he found himself almost wondering, caught up in the euphoria of the charge, if it really was just four men standing there. And even if one was a paladin, Theophraste would take the odds of four against a hundred.

His hopes were shattered when he saw the two signals given by the paladin's lance. He stopped in his tracks, screaming for the men to stop. A handful, a dozen at most, heard him and stopped. The rest ran fruitlessly on, brandishing their newly-won steel, stolen Delondeur armor flashing in the sun.

Then an answering wave of red-surcoated lancers came pouring over the hill in a wedge formation, their lances a rippling wall of deadly steel moving at the head of thousands of pounds worth of horse and man.

The very tip of their spearhead was the paladin, and the other knights flying the Sunburst.

And they cut through the front-running Islandmen like rays of sunlight through a fog.

* * *

There was something in Allystaire that thrilled to be on Ardent's back, running downhill, his lance leveled. All of his energy, all of the years he had spent training, hardening himself, perfected this moment, this one act.

It had always been this way, from his first tourney joust, to the opening charge of every battle. A thrill, a deepset knowledge that he was doing the thing to which he was best suited, by temperament, inclination, and training.

And yet this time, this charge, while he knew he was doing the Mother's work, there was something in it that sickened him. Islandmen with new weapons and almost no training were crushed into the mud under Ardent's steelshod hooves. The first man he aimed his lance at watched dumbly as it ripped him open and Allystaire had the briefest impression of him clawing feebly at the length of wood as it bore him to the ground.

But then his hammer was in his hand and there was no time to think; there was only the steady rise and fall of his arm, the thud of the hammer into upraised shields, knocking aside blows with his own shield. Always letting Ardent move, guiding him, giving him the spur if the destrier felt for a moment like he was slowing.

He heard and felt the shock from behind when the Thornriders swept down moments after him, the cries of pain and fear as lances met flesh, as horses plowed into and over the men standing in their way.

It was apparent, quickly, that a rout was in the making. Islandmen were tripping in the mud, trying to get their feet back under them to reverse course. A few tossed aside weapons they'd been brandishing only moments before.

"DRIVE THEM WEST," Allystaire bellowed, calling on long experience of yelling orders over the din of death and battle. "DO NOT LET THEM MAKE THE RIVER."

Ardent broke free into a clear patch of ground. Allystaire let his mount slow as he whirled his head side to side, looking for the Dragon Scales. He saw one leave his feet, knocking a Thornrider clear of his saddle, his clawed gauntlets tearing at the man's armor, shredding surcoat and digging into the steel beneath.

Allystaire started to turn Ardent, when suddenly he was knocked from the saddle. The impact felt like a stone thrown from a catapult catching him flush. As he hit the ground he saw Ardent circling, turning his great neck to follow the flight of his rider.

His shield skidded away from him, but he kept a grip on his hammer; whatever or whoever had thrown him free had ridden him to the ground, so

Allystaire used the momentum of the fall, extending his legs to fling the man over his head.

It was the second berzerker, and despite the way Allystaire had thrown him, he landed on his feet.

The paladin was barely back on his feet in time, raising his hammer in a two-handed grip to ward off the swiping claws.

Torvul's steel was up to the task, though it sent a shock reverberating up Allystaire's arms.

The berzerker swiped a few more times, and though the blows were strong, they were artless. Their speed kept Allystaire from counterattacking. Finally, instead of swinging at him, the berzerker tried to hook his claws around the haft of the hammer and pull it from the paladin's grasp.

Allystaire didn't let go, but he did let the other man pull him forward. He stepped into it, snapping the metal haft of the hammer into the berzerker's grimacing face.

It was like swinging a club into a stone wall. But even a stone wall would be chipped by a man with enough force, enough patience, enough knowledge of where to lay the blow. The berzerker's cheek opened and bled freely over his snarling lips and chin.

The berzeker tightened his own grip on the hammer and very nearly pulled Allystaire off his feet. There'd be no more swinging the haft into his face, Allystaire thought. It was all he could do to keep hold of the weapon, and he knew that letting it go, giving a Dragon Scale a way to concentrate all the strength of his arms in one blow, would mean his death.

Allystaire tried twisting, feinting to one side then throwing all his weight to the other. He was convinced that if he was facing a normal opponent it would've thrown the man down, but he wasn't; he was facing a mad, holy warrior with a strength given by the Sea Dragon Himself, and with his own Gift of Strength not responding, he was losing.

He felt the hammer slipping.

Then there was a rush of movement from one side of him, and the berzerker suddenly collapsed, all the strength gone out of him. Allystaire stumbled a few steps backwards, the hammer suddenly free in his hands.

Johonn stood over the fallen berzerker, who was shouting in the Islandman tongue. Allystaire knew enough of it to know it was a prayer, a hymn to his own death in battle.

Half of the Dragon Scale's left leg lay dismembered in the mud; blood pumped in huge torrents from the stump.

Johonn lifted his axe over the fallen form and said, "Take your own advice next time, Arm. Don't take them one to one."

The knight's double-bitted longaxe flashed in the sun as he raised it, and the berzerker's faint screams of prayer trailed to nothing as it descended through his neck.

"Armel, Tibult, and Harrys all pinned the other one with lances. Taking his time dying, though," Johonn said, as he pulled his axe free. "Are ya hurt?"

"You were supposed to be guarding Gideon."

"He came back to himself and ordered me to attend you," Johonn rumbled. "Told me where you'd be."

Allystaire nodded and went to retrieve his shield. Ardent was already trotting back to his side, tossing his head and snorting, his ears flickering, and his tail low.

I think he is embarrassed that I let myself be unhorsed. Aloud, he said to Johonn, "My thanks. We have work yet to do here. There was a priest. Let us find him."

Johonn raised his bloodstained axe in salute and stood at Allystaire's stirrup as he swung back into his saddle. Ardent's height gave him a good vantage. There were red-surcoated men down, horses dead, knights of varying plumage struggling with injuries, yes. Yet for every wounded or unmoving man of his own he could see, they were strewn about with dead, wounded, or surrendered Islandmen.

He turned his horse towards the river; a tall figure in blue was making for it at a dead run.

"Ardent!" Yelling the destrier's name was as good as a command; he took off like an arrow, with the paladin bent low over his neck.

* * *

Landen had strung her knights and lances in a thin line, with several paces between each trooper and horse, trying to cover the entire southern bank of the river with just over two score lances.

She glanced down the line to the Damarind knights. Much like the Baroness and her daughter, they favored a lighter scale armor, and smaller, faster horses. They were somewhere between outriders and heavy horse; the concept intrigued Landen even as it mystified her.

A pair of Allystaire's so-called knights of the Order came running into Landen's view, one a big barrel-chested fellow with handaxes thrust into his belt, while the other, the only woman among his Order, wore a half-mask and carried the stave of a long, unstrung bow, and a quiver that bristled with the fletchings of long arrows.

"They've broken and a few, a dozen or so, are fleeing this way. We're not to let them pass," the larger one said as he slipped the handaxes off his belt. The hafts nearly disappeared into his hands.

"Thank you, Sir…"

"Mattar," the axeman said, "and I'm not particular about the sir. It's not like he knighted us."

Landen didn't need to ask who he was; it seemed as though whenever someone in this little army said 'he', no one needed to clarify. "My thanks then, Mattar. But I do not need reminders of Sir Stillbright's orders." The big man rolled his shoulders in a shrug, and Landen went on. "Did you see any Dragon Scales amongst them?"

"Those bastards're not likely t'retreat," the half-masked archer said. "Not from what I've heard." She had slipped her bowstave between her legs and pulled a long coil of string from a pouch on her belt, tied a loop around the notch on top of the stave.

Landen nodded. "Let's teach the rest of them the wages of cowardice then, eh?" She flushed as soon as he said it, wished she could call the words back to her mouth. The knights of the Order seemed to ignore it, slipping past her horse and moving along her line.

To cover her embarrassment and the flush of her cheeks, Landen pulled her helm down over her head, having slung it by a strap from her pommel. *Freezing stupid. Trying to sound like Allystaire,* she told herself, even as she drew her sword and held it up. She let the sun catch it, and quickly snapped her wrist forward once: advance.

Other knights and lances to her left and right did the same, spreading the order up and down the line quickly without need of a trumpet or drum. She nudged her horse and started it walking.

The line lurched forward unevenly, as some perhaps hadn't been saddled or ready, but only a few needed their mounts to even break into a trot to bring things back into good order.

Good order was not something Landen could say about the oncoming Islandmen. They became visible at quite a distance, a ragged and disunited band. A dozen seemed about the right count. They wore no uniforms or tabards, only unadorned mail, a smattering of helmets, waving new-looking swords and spears as they ran.

Landen held her sword aloft again, then lowered it over her mount's neck, bending low herself, and gave her horse the spur.

That was, in broad daylight, all the signal the men around her needed. Naturally she surged ahead, the knights to her immediate left and right drawing closer.

The Islandmen, fleeing one charge of horsemen straight into another, immediately sought strength in numbers, and drew together in a ragged line. Landen's heart almost sank to see it; it was the worst strategy they could possibly have adopted.

They raised and held their weapons, though without shields, none of them could present much of a defense to the oncoming heavy horse.

It was over in moments. Landen felt the glancing blow of a sword ineffectually swung rebound off her greaves, while her own sword bit deeply.

It took but one charge, when the survivors—now encircled by ranks of riders closing in on them, threw down their weapons. Four of them, pale, bearded, frightened, wearing stolen Delondeur mail. At their feet, nine of their comrades lay dead or dying.

She leveled her bloodied sword at them. It was hard work, keeping her hand level with her blood pumping, with the long expected fight ending so quickly. Hard work, but she managed.

"Do any of you speak Barony tongue, or only Islander?"

One, a man Landen would guess a few years older than herself, with a black beard in a craggy face, looked up. "I do," he grated. "M'mother was Vyndamaran."

"Good. Relay my words to them. You are prisoners now, and you will not be mistreated or killed out of hand. But if you try to escape, no mercy will be shown you. Do you understand?"

The man turned and spoke in the harsh rapid strokes of Islander tongue. Keersvaster, which Landen spoke, was related, but more civilized and regular. Islander was more ancient, closer to wind and stone and sea.

The half-Vyndamaran turned back to Landen, nodding, which the others were doing as well.

"Excellent," Landen said. "We will have to tie your hands, and your arms and armor are forfeit."

Once more she waited while this was relayed. One of the men, younger, fierce-eyed, started shaking his head and answering angrily back.

The others seemed to try to reason with him, but he shouted and swung an arm wildly at one of them, started to back away.

"Lakuv says he won his steel in honest raiding and will give it to no man. He will die first."

"What does honest raiding mean, and why does he think that should matter?"

The half-Vyndamaran cleared his throat. "We raided south and returned to our villages with thralls, to the Choiron w'plunder. For that we were given swords and mail."

"Honest raiding against crofters and herdsman?" Landen felt a shout building in her chest and finally let it out, cutting the interpreter off. Her swordhand had fallen to her side, but she raised it again and flicked droplets of blood from the tip of the blade towards the reluctant Lakuv. "Against children asleep in their beds, and old farmers whose strength is long forgotten? Neither was the steel the Choiron's to give; it was stolen, by subtlety and secrecy, from my keep. Let me have no more talk of honest raiding. Quiet yourselves and hold out your hands. We'll have your mail back later."

The other three held out their hands, tentatively. Lakuv began yelling again, slide-stepping away from Landen, only to find nothing but more horsemen behind him, brandishing more steel. He pointed at all of them, shaking his fist, shouting a challenge.

"Ah, Lakuv says none of you fight like men. On foot, face to face, man to man, without your beasts or arrows."

"If it's an honest fight he wants, I'll give him one." Mattar stepped forward, slipping his bulk between close-gathered horses with ease, palms of his hands resting casually on the heads of the axes belted at his hips. "Clear a space."

"Mattar." The masked archer's voice was muffled, but her annoyance was clear. "We've not the time."

"It won't take long, Teague." He clapped his hands together loudly, then waved them at the horsemen. "Go on. Give him a space. Indulge me, lady Baroness Delondeur," he said to Landen, then turned to the translator. "Go on, my good son of lost Vyndamere. Tell him I'm his man."

While his words were relayed to the young, wild-eyed Islandman, Mattar turned away, flexing his shoulders. Knights and lances looked to Landen, who nodded curtly and turned her horse expertly, with light pressure from her knees.

"Give him whatever weapon he desires," Mattar said, still keeping his back to the man. Landen watched as Lakuv quickly went to the sword he'd thrown down. From this close, Landen could see the smithy mark from the Dunes just above the hilt.

Mattar turned to face the Islandman, as casual and calm as if he were heading to the local taproom, except for his face, his cheeks drawn flat and eyes tight with anger.

"Whenever you're ready, *honest raider*," Mattar said.

The Vyndamaran said something quickly. Yakuv, blond hair streaming behind him in a braid, charged, raising his sword high.

With an indifference that was almost insulting, Mattar plucked an axe from his belt with his fingers wrapped around the blade. He tossed it lightly into the air, caught the haft in a forward grip, stepped his left foot forward, then raised his arm, lowered it quick and threw with a snap.

The axe didn't tumble end-over-end; it sailed straight and true and took Yakuv in the shoulder, dropping him in his tracks and sending the sword tumbling away.

Mattar sauntered over to the Islandman, shaking his head. "Honest raiding. As if there could be such a Freezing thing as honest. RAIDING," he shouted. "What is gained by theft is not yours. Not ever. And when you gain by murder, you forfeit more than the goods. Yet I think I will leave it to the Arm to judge you."

Yakuv reached for the axe in his shoulder, gasping. Mattar knocked his hands aside and seized the haft of his weapon. "Be ready to bind this, someone." He pulled it quickly free, and turned to face the other three, while Yakuv bled, Teague running forward and pulling a bandage free from a pouch at her belt.

"I could arm all of you and kill you as easily as you did unarmed farmers," Mattar spat at the cowed Islandmen. "P'raps I should, for what you say you've done to 'earn' your blades. Yet I won't. I want ya to know what those farm folk felt. I want you to face the Arm of the Mother, and I want you to know the fear of him."

CHAPTER 46

Counsel and Revelation

Night had fallen, and the camp of the small Baronial army was shrouded in darkness on the moors and hills of Barony Varshyne. Just as he'd dispensed with pavilions and long mealtimes, Allystaire had forbidden fires and unshuttered lanterns.

Sentries worked on a volunteer basis with some of Torvul's night-sight potion smeared upon their eyes. When it wore off, other volunteers took their places. The Order of the Arm guarded Allystaire's central position in the camp, where he met with the Barons, and where the growing knot of prisoners were kept.

Landen, Arontis, Ruprecht, Byronn, and Loaisa sat with the paladin around the fractured light of Torvul's shuttered lantern.

Allystaire sat on a folding chair—one of the few concessions to luxury he allowed himself—with his hammer at one foot, listening to the flow of conversation.

"These Islandmen are obviously no account," Ruprecht Machoryn was saying. "We ought to be able to smash them against the walls of Pinesward Watch."

"We haven't an accurate count of their numbers," Byronn Telmawr countered. "Perhaps we could encircle them in turn. Besiege the besiegers, as it were."

Allystaire wanted to lower his head into his hands. Or to scream. Instead, he cleared his throat, and felt all eyes turn to him.

"Arontis," he said, "what do you think of trying a great thrust at their leadership, and breaking them against Pinesward, as the Baron suggests?"

Even in the dim light and the shadows of the lantern, Arontis's face had a handsome nobility that Allystaire found hard to credit. The young Baron took time to think. Finally, looking directly at Allystaire, he spoke.

"As my Lord of Telmawr says, we have no accurate count of the enemy, but we know he outnumbers us at least three to one. Perhaps four. Even if the bulk of those men are unblooded, and even if they have spent themselves somewhat in assaying the walls of Pinesward, should we falter for a moment, should we become bogged down, should competent leadership escape, they would have the numbers to surround and destroy us in detail."

Allystaire nodded affirmatively, feeling inwardly that his confidence was affirmed. "Landen? What of besieging them?"

"Out of the question." The young Baroness, seated at Arontis's right, didn't hesitate in the slightest. "We haven't got the numbers or the supplies for a siege. The very moment we show ourselves in our full strength to what they've gathered around the Baronial seat, we're done for."

"Surely," Byronn Telmawr interrupted, "you're discounting those inside the fortress."

"Of course I am," Landen said. "What role has Barony Varsyhne played on the greater stage these past five years? These past ten, or longer? Vyndamere fell when my father was young, before I was born, and Varshyne has never escaped its shadow in all that time. We don't know who's defending Pineswatch or how many of them there are or how long they can hold. For our own sake, we must discount them."

"Arontis and Landen see the truth of it," Allystaire said. "As things stand, our advantages are mobility and experience. If we try to invest a siege, we lose the first, and if we allow ourselves to be swarmed, we lose the second. As long as Symod is content to send his men out piecemeal, we will keep picking them off. Yet we cannot fight a straight battle when the numbers tilt so far in his favor."

Allystaire let that hang in the air for a moment before going on. "And we have nothing to account for the Gravekmir."

A hush swept over the Barons in the wake of that statement. They looked at him, at each other, and tried, Allystaire thought, not to imagine the prospect of club-wielding giants twice the size of a tall man wading into their midst.

"Damarind horse-archers would make short work of giants," Loaisa said. "Yet they are weeks away, at best."

"We do not have weeks," Allystaire said. "In that time, Pinesward will fall, and Symod will learn how to direct the men he does have. The last thing we can do is fall into the trap of waiting for more men. Even so," he added, "the Will tells me that Baron Harlach should link with us tomorrow. A hundred stout Harlachan longaxes is nothing to sneer at."

"What of Oyrwyn, then? Will Gilrayan ever join us?" Byronn Telmawr hooked his hands on his belt and leaned forward, into the lantern light, to peer at Allystaire.

"I mean to find that out tonight," he answered. "Before I sleep. Which we should all be after. On the morrow, we meet with Unseldt, and then to creep closer to Pinesward, see if we cannot draw out another party."

"What of the Gravek? What if they give chase?" Ruprecht's voice had a slight quaver in it.

"If it comes to that," Allystaire said, "leave the giants to me."

He stood. The crowd of Barons took his hint and started to melt away to their own camps, which were simply mass shapes in the darkness beyond Torvul's lantern light. Allystaire thought of the small knot of prisoners, the priest especially. He'd had enough work healing them, and the wounded of his own forces, that he'd not had the time to question them yet. He saw Arontis and Landen departing, talking quietly to one another, and called softly, "Baron Innadan. Speak with me a moment."

Both of them turned. The taller of the two shapes reached a hand to the other, clasped, and then came forward, the shadows resolving into Arontis's tall form.

Allystaire waited till the others were out of earshot, and said, "Tell me, Arontis, when our campaign is done, what do you see happening to the Baronies?"

"Assuming our campaign is victorious?"

"I can assume nothing else. If we fail, then I am dead, and all my assumptions gone to dust. So answer my question."

Arontis nodded. In the dark, Allystaire couldn't read his features, but he saw the younger man lift a hand to his chin. "With luck, the peace holds. We start sending wine and wool over our borders instead of men and horses."

"And from there?"

"With increased trade, the Baronies grow closer again, or so I'd hope. We re-build proper roads, maintain them through the passes and to every Seat and Keep and town. Start reclaiming the pastures and fields that have been battlefields."

"What about the eastern Baronies? Only Damarind and Machoryn seem interested in our travails."

"Ormandich, Arransay, and Lyrranth? I don't know," Arontis admitted. "Innadan hasn't had contact with them in my lifetime. They're names on a map. I couldn't tell you the names of their sitting Barons. Cold, I couldn't tell if you they still stand, much less."

"What of Rhidalish?"

Arontis stopped cold, turning to stare at the paladin. "What of them? You know as well as I do the line is dead, the Vale empty."

"Their lands are still there. Part of Innadan, part of Machoryn, part of Damarind. No king," Allystaire admitted, "no one occupying the Stone Crown."

"A pile of burnt rock and rotting timbers. Of course no one occupies it."

"My point, Arontis," Allystaire said, "is that there was a time when the Baronies were a country. Not eleven or twelve or fourteen countries fighting over each other's lands, trying to elevate one lord above another. They had a common ruler and a common interest. It might be," Allystaire said, very quietly, very slowly, "that they cannot truly see that they have the latter unless they plainly see that they have the former."

There was a long and pregnant pause.

"What are you telling me, Sir Stillbright?"

"I am not telling you anything. Merely raising a question."

"I would rather be a plain knight errant, and throw over the title I already have, than to seek other, greater titles."

"What we would rather do is rarely of any consequence if we wish to make a better world, Arontis Innadan."

"Would you turn me away, then? When this is over, if I've proved myself in battle, and devoted myself to the Mother, would you turn me away from the Order?" Arontis came a step closer. "I have never wanted my father's seat."

"Which is precisely why you should have it." Allystaire let his words descend like a heavy curtain over Arontis. "Whether you should have more remains to be seen. But Arontis, if this land needs a king, you are uniquely positioned to give it one. Your father gave us a chance at peace, if we can win it. You," he said, reaching out to poke the other man's breastplate, "could make it last."

Allystaire stepped away, dropping his hand to his side. "Just think on it, my Lord Baron. Think on the fact that you could do more good from a seat, or a throne, than you could from the saddle of an itinerant knight."

He left the younger man speechless in his wake, and went to find Gideon and Torvul, scooping up the dwarf's lantern as he went.

He let his eyes close, focused on his memories of them, calling them forth to mind. Gideon, a serious and frightened voice in a dungeon, Torvul a gagged convict about to hang at a roadside. Almost instantly his sense of them intensified, where they were, how they felt—healthy, if tired—and a vague idea of what they were doing.

In the darkness, guided by their presences in his mind, he walked straight to them.

Gideon was leaning against his saddle and bags, legs stretched out before him. It was plain to see, even in the darkness broken only by the shuttered lantern, that the boy was bone tired, barely clinging to consciousness.

Torvul sat next to him on a folding chair so small it seemed barely capable of holding the dwarf's weight, drinking from a skin.

He held it up wordlessly as Allystaire approached. He took it, drank a mouthful of strong dwarfish spirit, and handed it back.

"What news from Idgen Marte?"

Gideon took a deep breath. "Men are trickling in to Wind's Jaw, where he is 'assembling' and 'staging' them. She thinks it's clear that he doesn't mean to move in time to take part in any serious fighting."

Allystaire clenched his teeth and tightened a fist. "What men? Did you see banners or hear names?"

"Lord Harding," Gideon said, "Naswyn."

"Coldbourne? Highgate?"

The boy shook his head.

Allystaire's gauntlet creaked. "It is too late to send them a message that would matter, unless we were to fall back as far as the Oyrwyn border. And even then, asking them to move separately would be to start a war inside the Barony."

"As plans go," Torvul said, "falling back doesn't seem a bad one."

"If this were a typical enemy, another Baron's host, I might agree with you," Allystaire said. "But you know I cannot abandon the Varshynners to their fate. Even if Pinesward was beyond our power to help—"

"It might be," Torvul sharply put in.

"I do not believe that. And even if I did, I have no guarantee that Symod would chase us."

"He would," the alchemist insisted. "You're what he's after. I think he'd turn from the walls of Pinesward if it meant a chance at your head."

"Do you?" Allystaire tilted his head to one side.

"Have you not listened to our prisoners?" Gideon sat up straighter, shook his head to chase away sleep. "That's why he raised this Braechsworn host in the first place. To erase the 'heresy.' To destroy the Mother." The boy leaned forward to emphasize his words. "To kill the paladin."

"Killing me does not destroy Her," Allystaire said.

"It's near enough as makes no difference," Torvul insisted. "If Braechsworn manage to bring you down, how strong do you think this little army remains? How long do Her people hold on?"

"As long as you two, and Mol, and Idgen Marte keep up the fight," Allystaire insisted.

"It doesn't matter," Gideon said, "if Symod *thinks* that killing you destroys Her, that's what does matter."

"Has it occurred to you, Allystaire, that you're doing such a fine job destroyin' his little supply expeditions that he doesn't know we're here," Torvul said. "I bet if we got close to the walls and tweaked his nose, he might figure it out."

"If we get close enough to the walls, they can overrun us with sheer numbers," Allystaire said.

"Not if you don't bring the whole army they can't."

Allystaire frowned and set Torvul's lantern down, crossed his arms over his chest. "Gideon, if need be, could you do something about the Gravekmir?"

"Do you want them destroyed, dispersed, or disoriented?"

Allystaire and Torvul shared a shadowed glance, then both looked back to Gideon. "Dispersed," the paladin said, then went to one knee and dropped his voice to a hush.

* * *

Idgen Marte wandered the halls of Wind's Jaw Keep, her hand wrapping and unwrapping from about the hilt of her sword. She didn't bother flitting from shadow to shadow.

In fact, she rather fancied a fight if one came along. The place was right for it, after all. Oyrwyn was not a Barony of cities or large towns like Delondeur or Innadan. The people were spread out, clustered here and there, guarded by well-placed keeps and towers instead of inside city walls. Wind's Jaw was perhaps the best placed of them all, smack in the middle of the Barony where the moors and hills began to climb into the mountains. Any invader would have to reckon with it, whatever direction they came from, and there was but one approach that could accommodate a large body of men. That particular road passed by a pair of tall towers that offered views in all directions, and towered over the trails leading towards the keep.

Idgen Marte felt, she had to admit, at least a moment of awe as she rode into the place and heard the mountain winds keening as they whipped past those towers. She found herself wondering how even a Concordat host would take this place.

It was, for all its formidable defenses, an ugly pile of rock, though. There was no grace in it, no art, just a heap of stone and mortar raised like a shield over the Barony's heartlands. It was meant to break armies, and it had. The great hall was decorated with the banners of lords and knights who'd spent themselves trying fruitlessly to gain its walls.

Idgen Marte felt like she could break an army herself. The knights, the soldiers, even the servants avoided her almost instinctively, not that many were moving about with night deepening.

To keep herself from wandering to the stables, saddling her courser, and riding away, she took herself to the kitchens. Only then, desiring privacy, did she slip into the shadow beneath a torch in a sconce on the wall, to another, then inside the kitchen. She snagged a heavy pewter mug from a shelf, slipped into the cold pantry—an effect achieved simply by leaving a large gap high up on the wall—and dipped it into an open keg. She took a sip and tried not to spit from the piney taste.

What these people don't know about making beer, she thought, *could perhaps fit into the sea between Londray and Keersvast.*

With her mug, she slid into one of the smaller dining rooms, expecting it to be empty. Instead, she found that someone had her idea first, and slipped in for a quiet drink. Looming tall over the small, glowing remnants of a peat fire in a hearth on the far wall, Joeglan Naswyn sipped out of a twin to the mug she held.

Briefly she wanted to dash the heavy pewter against the back of his skull, or slide up to him with a knife. She knew the thought was unworthy of her, even before a voice told her, *Revenge is no way to honor Allystaire.*

Instead, she sidled up to him, forcing herself out of the shadows. "Lord Naswyn," she rasped.

She was not above smiling when he jumped, one hand falling to his sword-belt, the other pouring sour slop all over the stones of the hearth.

"Cold, woman," he said, his voice as somber and serious as always, "you could give an old man his death that way."

"You're not that old, m'lord." She forced a friendly tone into her voice, fixed a grin in place on her mouth.

"Threescore and three is mighty old for an Oyrwyn man," Joeglan said.

"Is that so?"

He shrugged. "Look around. Do you see any other old men? I think there is a servant roaming around here in the keep, polishes the silver, who's older than me, but he is like to be the only one. I am the last of my time left." He took a sip from his mug, and Idgen Marte noted the way his hand shook.

Not Joeglan's first mug of the evening, she thought.

When he came up for air, he sighed heavily. "Ufferth, Anthelme, Ladislas, me, and Gerard. Squires together, then knights, lords and their Baron," he droned, before he sighed again.

"How did they go?" *Keep him talking,* she told herself. *See what slips out.*

He made a deep chuckling sound as he went back for another pull at his mug. "We all of us die in battle, Shadow. Some of us are just too stubborn to realize it for some time. Ufferth, he died quick of it, a Delondeur arrow in the throat, with Garth no more than a boy just learning to walk. Anthelme took a wound in the leg his last campaign, and the damned thing just would not heal, and old Michar was with the Baron in Harlach."

He paused for another swallow. Idgen Marte dared a sip of her own, fostering a hope that it would grow on her.

It didn't. She set it down on the hearthstones. *Perhaps it's better warm,* she thought, while she waited for Joeglan to pick up the threads again.

"Now, Gerard. Gerard had just taken too many wounds. How Michar even kept him alive through some of them, I'll never know. Dwarfish medicine is a powerful thing, but even Michar died, and then Gerard's wounds just flamed up and took him, slowly and painfully. Ladislas, we lost in the winter and just learned of it now. Trying to break a new mount for the spring campaigning, the old fool. Got thrown and broke his neck. Me? If we ever Freezing march west I am probably too slow and too weak to be of much use against Islandmen anymore."

"What do you mean, if we ever march?"

Joegaln emptied his mug with one last pull and set it down by his foot, moving with the exaggerated care of a drunk. "Gilrayan's not his father's son in the ways that matter. He's cunning and he can plot with the best of them, or the worst, just like Gerard could. But he's not got the same dash. If Gerard said he'd do a thing, by the Cold, he did it. This one needs to wait till it's the moment of most advantage to himself."

He suddenly peered down at Idgen Marte, furrowing his brow under his mostly bald head. "I shouldn't be telling you any of this. Treading close to treason."

"Nonsense," Idgen Marte said. "Every man has the right t'talk rot about his liege lord now and then, so long as no one important is around to hear it." She bent down to pick up her nearly untouched mug and his, carefully pouring from one into the other before holding it out to him.

"Then let me tell you this," Joeglan rumbled, as he stared contemplatively at the beer before him. "You'd best get the Cold out of here and get back to give Allystaire whatever aid you can. Gilrayan will never, ever come riding to join him, no matter what parchment he signed and sealed. He'll wait till Allystaire's dead, or overrun, or till the Braechsworn come much closer to threatening Oyrwyn. He hates that man, hated him since Allystaire trained him, hated him for being everything he never was. I've never seen more hate, or more fear, in a man's eyes than when Allystaire did everything but challenge him to a duel when he walked out of Wind's Jaw. What, has it only been two-thirds of a year now?" Another heavy sip. "I shouldn't be telling you any of this. Gilrayan Oyrwyn is still my Baron. Yet if you can help Allystaire, go to him now. Warn him for me. I owe him that, anyway."

Anger welled up in Idgen Marte and curled her hands into fists. She envisioned smacking the heel of her hand into the mug he lifted to his mouth and smashing it into his teeth. Lips pressed tightly to her teeth, she nearly growled.

"Seems to me you owe him more than that."

"Aye, but that is all the weight I have to pay with."

Idgen Marte turned on her heel and was a mere moment from stepping into shadow when she paused and turned back. "He'll never ask, Lord Naswyn. Never. But he's my friend, so I will. Why'd you refuse?"

He drew himself up to his full height with careful precision. "Refuse what? The dowry?"

"The same," Idgen Marte hissed. "Maybe it would've made no difference. Flux could've carried her off the same. But they'd have had something."

He was silent a long moment, till finally he said, "It was Gerard Oyrwyn's command, not my choice."

Idgen Marte's eyes widened. All she could manage was a whispered, "What?"

"I loved my daughter," he said, "no matter the circumstances of her birth. And I would've welcomed her marriage to the Allystaire Coldbourne I knew. Gerard, though? He did not want Allystaire distracted."

"Distracted?"

"Even then he saw the potential in the man, knew he would be the next Castellan, after Ufferth. He wanted Allystaire focused on making knights and winning wars and nothing else. Said that marriage would be fine and well for him in a few years, to someone of better prospect than Dorinne." He peered at her face, somehow read the disbelief there, even in the dark, and shook his head. "Did I not say he was a cunning man, full of plots?"

"And you took that order?" Idgen Marte was too astonished to keep up her anger, too surprised to respond to his second question.

"I serve the Baron Oyrwyn. I swore an oath more than fifty years ago, I have not broken it yet, and I do not mean to."

"Not every oath is worth keeping," she said almost sadly.

"Well, go and tell him what you will. But go, if you mean to do him any good at all."

"Is there nothing that will move Gilrayan to the battle?"

"Word that Allystaire is dead or taken, or Oyrwyn under threat. Those are the only levers that will chisel him out of his seat, as far as I know the man."

Idgen Marte shook her head. "Deep down, Joeglan Naswyn, only a coward chooses a man they serve over a child they love. Think on that."

Before he could respond, she had taken two quick steps and disappeared.

This time, she headed straight for the stables.

CHAPTER 47

Interlude

Evolyn chafed at hiding.

She hated not wearing her robes, or her armor over them, and hiding her dragon amulet beneath a useless dress she'd been forced to waste silver on. She hated seeing the plundered remnants of the Temple that had once been the greatest shrine to the Sea Dragon in this part of the world.

She seethed when she passed near the walls of the Dunes and saw the bodies of her fellow servants moldering on its walls.

My place, she would tell herself every night as she went to confront the sorcerer, *is at Symod's right hand. I ought to be in the battle with him, directing the Braechsworn, leading these Dragon Scales where they belong.*

She knew that what she felt must be the minor of what the berzerkers did. They had sated themselves with drinking and minor mischief so far, but she'd heard tell of one or two unusual tavern killings and knew if she did not move them soon, the city could turn into a bloodbath.

The Marynth Evolyn rehearsed these things every night, as she had for days now, when late at night she crept into the empty Temple, and begged forgiveness where a beautiful statue had hung above the first altar, open to the lashing of the sea beneath it.

Winter might have given way to spring, but in those halls that rocked like a ship, the wind was still cold, the salt spray stung, and her heart raged for the heresy that had been done. Evolyn drew on the anger that burned in her like a seaside signal fire; she drew on the faith that roared like the ocean in a storm and resolved, each night, to tell the Eldest that she was done, she was leaving with the Dragon Scales.

We are going to face our enemy the way Braech calls us to face them, she would say, *strength against strength, resolve against resolve, and we will let the wind and the storm carry us to victory.*

And every night she would find the sorcerer, a haze of green light flowing from his body, standing near the statue that still stood in what had been the most sacred and secret place in the Temple, and her resolve and her strength would turn to ice-water in her bowels. The huge plinth towered in the darkness of the abandoned Temple, shadows thrown by the sorcerer's sinister light across the drawn-up wings of the dragon that stood atop it.

Since they had made port in Londray, the Eldest had grown somehow more intense, more threatening, and yet also less present. Cracks seemed to open up all along him, showing through whatever tattered robes he covered himself in. No longer did the sickly green light emanate merely from his mouth, his eyes, or his fingers. It surrounded him with a nimbus of nauseating, fearful power that she could smell, taste, and feel as easily as see.

"Why do you come, Marynth Evolyn?"

Come. Evolyn.

The words reverberated around her, hollow and cracked and dry.

She cleared her throat and stiffened her shoulders, but found herself cut off before she could speak.

"Do you think your intent is not clear to the Eldest of the Knowing?"

Intent. Eldest. Knowing.

"You will demand we move. Demand that I let you leave. I will not, for I need you near in order to speak to Symod." *Speak. Symod.*

"You didn't before," she said, the words rushing quickly out of her.

"No. Since we arrived things are changing. Power flows freely into me, but it is harder to…" *Power. Power.*

Evolyn shivered. She'd never heard that echo of the Eldest's voice repeat itself.

"Harder to fix these insects in my mind. Harder to tell one from another." *Another.* "I need to draw your image of him from your mind."

"No." Fear turned to resolve inside Evolyn Lamaliere, as it once had when the paladin loomed over her in her study. "No," she repeated, drawing strength from the assertion. "I will go and face my enemy alongside Symod and the Braechsworn. It is where I belong. I will not skulk and hide in the sight of those who murdered my own any longer." She took a deep breath and tensed herself to give a signal.

"Yes. Call forward your berzerkers. I said I could not tell you apart. One gnat, one stinging fly, is much like any other. But not that I could not tell when more than one of you approached me. Call them, so that I may make use of them. They will serve a grand destiny, Evolyn." *Gnats. Destiny, Evolyn.*

From the dark recesses of the building beyond the reach of the green aura, two men suddenly rushed forward, throwing axes flying from their hands.

The Eldest did not move, nor even turn aside from his contemplation of the statue. The axes dropped in midair as if hitting an invisible wall.

Then, and only then, did he lift a hand from the folds of his robes. The fingers were skeletal, glowing like a green fungus in a dark cave. He spread them and the two Dragon Scales she'd brought with her were lifted off their feet like ragdolls.

"Do you know why the rulers of this—" The Eldest paused, as if searching for a word. "This place left this statue intact?"

"Some small scrap of dignity or fear that caused them to recoil from their blasphemy," she said. Though her insides had turned to icy water once more, Evolyn Lamaliere was not going to let her voice quiver, not even if she was now at the turn of her death.

Silently, she began to pray. *Father of Waves. Master of Accords. Dragon of the Sea. Into your hands—*

"Stop that. It interferes with my work here." *Work.* "They left it because no art they possess could destroy it. The Negation might, of course. Or perhaps the Stonesinger, if indeed he has that art to his hand still." *The Negation. The Negation. Negation.*

Something in that echoed voice repeating itself gave Evolyn pause this time. Not because it frightened her. She was a careful study of men and their habits. And she knew when she heard fear in a voice.

She was hearing it now, in the way it quivered and then the way, on the last repetition of the word, it *babbled.*

What can this thing possibly fear? she asked herself, before the Eldest spoke again.

"The idiot boy does not know what he has done. He has handed me the seeds of his own destruction, gathering so much power into this place of crude being. Nevertheless the work here must be done." He lifted his eyes from the statue and turned, slowly, describing thick green vapor trails in the air as he contemplated the two bare-chested berzerkers that hung helplessly near him.

"You have the honor of a grand destiny." *Destiny. Destiny.* He raised his other hand.

The two berzekers began to scream together, an inhuman sound, an animal cry of fear and pain. Evolyn watched in mounting horror as the flesh melted from them. Horribly, she saw the skull of one revealed in the noxious green light, and yet the mouth was open and the sounds of agony still came raggedly from his throat.

She turned, and she ran, resolving to leave that night, with the berzerkers, to put as much distance between the Eldest and herself as she could.

Symod, she thought, as the screams behind her lapsed into a wet burbling, *Symod, what have you done?*

CHAPTER 48

Any Burden

Allystaire sat his saddle with one hand on Ardent's neck and the other on a basket of light throwing spears tied to the pommel of his saddle.

A thousand of these things for my lance, he thought, then amended, *For a good dozen lances.* He pulled one out of the basket, hefted it, felt the light springiness of the two-foot haft, the hollow steel head. *Meant to shatter,* he thought, as he held it up to his eyes in the faint pre-dawn light, inspecting the mark of some unknown smithy in Barony Damarind.

Around him the Order of the Arm sat their own mounts, many of which nosed for grass in the muddy Varshyne ground. Torvul slumped on his pony, snoring gently. Gideon, surrounded by his guard of wild men who'd once been Chimera, was likewise slumped in his saddle, but for entirely different reasons.

Pinesward Watch wasn't much more than a shape in the darkness, a jumbled heap to the west. The camp of the Braechsworn was entirely lost in the overhanging shadow of the keep. The chill early morning air was silent, tense, charged with the risk they were taking in coming so close to the enemy.

Then a huge angry cry rent the air, and a flame-wreathed giant suddenly sprang into being between them and the castle. It was man-shaped, and easily twice or three times the size of any Gravekmir.

Even to Allystaire, who knew that the boy sitting near him, his brow hunched in concentration, was projecting that image, felt like its bellow was a challenge to everything around it with ears. *Come,* it seemed to say wordlessly, *test my strength. Test your own.*

And then dark shapes, smaller than Gideon's giant but taller than any mounted man, began, singly and in clumps, to disengage themselves from the larger shadows and run towards it, answering it with their own long rumbling yells.

"I'll be dipped in shit," Torvul muttered, having lifted his head when the giant unleashed its cry, "it's working. Stones Above, I never thought it would."

"Let us make use of it, then," Allystaire said. "How long till the sun breaks behind us?"

Torvul sniffed at the air, turned to look to the east. "No more'n a quarter turn," the dwarf said.

"Then let us not waste the time," the paladin said, kicking his heels into the sides of Ardent, then laying low over the destrier's great neck as it shot forward like a bolt loosed from a great engine.

* * *

Symod was shaken into wakefulness. For a moment he thought he was on the deck of a ship that had suddenly pitched on its side, and he scrambled out of his cot. For a terrible moment he flailed in the darkness, finding himself on hands and knees on the cold and muddy ground. Something so loud it had seemed to make the earth shake had awoken him, and he knew it could mean only one thing.

Then he stood, his head brushing the top of his tent, and smiled broadly. He stroked the gold-and-sapphire amulet that lay against his bare chest and closed his eyes in concentration, reaching out to every priest of Braech in the camp.

The paladin shows himself. It is time.

All around the Braechsworn camp, priests suddenly roused themselves, donning robes, hefting maces, hammers, and axes and heading for the center of their camp.

For his part, Symod quickly found his robes and slipped them on. Then he went to a trunk at the foot of his cot and opened it. Inside it sat a large glass bowl and a heavy jug. He lifted the jug out and uncorked it, smiling even wider as the scent of brine filled his senses, expanded into his tent.

"I *have* you, Allystaire," he muttered aloud, and strode from his tent into the darkness before dawn, jug of seawater dangling from one hand, bowl tucked beneath his other arm.

* * *

With the sun coming up behind them, the Arm of the Mother, his Order, the Wit, and the Will reined up on a hill that overlooked the Braechsworn camp. Just barely within range of bowshot, he thought, if the archer was good and the bow was powerful.

Pinesward Watch, it was plain to see, would soon fall. From what Allystaire could glimpse, the defenders had abandoned the outer curtain wall and pulled back to the inner keep. He held out one hand and Torvul tossed his leather-wrapped glass tube into it. Allystaire held it to one eye and saw weary defenders with spears and crossbows trudging along the inner battlements. The front gate and barbican still held, but were no longer defended. He guessed that a pile of earth and wood and whatever was handy had been heaped up behind the gate to reinforce it even as the men who'd paid to guard it had withdrawn.

He trained the glass over the walls of the keep and found his eye drawn to one particular soldier walking the wall who seemed shorter than the others. Allystaire peered forward intently. If the soldier was indeed shorter it was because, he could see, the soldier was a boy. No older than Gideon, certainly. Perhaps twelve or thirteen summers old, clutching a spear that towered over him, wearing a chain shirt that probably covered his knees and a tabard he could, and did, trip on.

"No one that young needs to be taking up arms outside of a courtyard," Allystaire growled. "Torvul," he snapped, unable to keep the anger inside him from bleeding into his voice. "I need the Braechsworn to hear me."

"Then give me my glass back before you snap the Freezing thing. I haven't got yet another, and I've not the time nor tools to make one or repair this one if you break it as well." The dwarf snatched the glass away, and not a moment too soon, for Allystaire heard the faint notes of the song begin in his head. Like the ringing of silver trumpets or a harp striking clear notes before the recitation of great deeds in song, the notes tingled not only in his ears but along his body, filling his limbs with warmth.

And with a terrible strength.

He slid from the saddle, surveying the camp beneath him. Only one cluster of tents amidst hundreds of men sleeping haphazardly around cookfires.

Torvul leaned in his saddle, holding out a delicate crystal bottle. He poured a measure of it onto Allystaire's open mouth.

Then the paladin opened his mouth and yelled, his words carrying across the distance, cutting through the wind, powerful enough to shake the bones of any man who stood in front of him and too near.

"SYYYYMMMMMODDDDDDDDDD." He waited for the echo to roll over him before he continued. "SYMOD, YOU COWARD. COME AND FACE ME. I AM ALLYSTAIRE STILLBRIGHT, THE ARM OF THE MOTHER, AND I DO NOT FEAR YOU. CAN YOU SAY THE SAME?"

Then the paladin slipped one of the javelins from the basket, bent his arm, took a running start, and threw on his fifth step.

The weapon arced high into the air, glinting in the sun as it reached the height of its arc, then descended deadly and gracefully into the Braechsworn camp.

* * *

Brazcek Varsyhne leapt to his feet when the glass of the window behind him rattled in its casement, and a decanter fell from a nearby table. The Baron had been dozing in a chair, in his armor. He smelled of rust and sweat and fear and when the sound jerked him awake, his first thought was that the Braechsworn had somehow found the timber and the time to make engines, and now meant to pound his walls to dust.

With Herrin close on his heels he ran out onto the battlements, finding himself among men who stared gape-mouthed to at hill that overlooked the camp spread out before them, the camp full of the tormentors that had cut their numbers in half since their last struggle for the walls.

Atop that hill, something gleamed brilliantly in the rising sunlight, shone like a diamond against the brown and green of early spring. Behind the figure, too small for Brazcek to make out in detail, a blue banner unfurled in the breeze, a golden sunburst bold in its center.

Another wave of sound rolled over the men on the walls, emanating from the figure on that distant hillside.

"ARE THERE NONE AMONG YOU, BRAECHSWORN COWARDS, WHO WILL COME AND FACE THE ARM OF THE MOTHER?"

Something arced into the air from that figure on the hillside, and Brazcek Varsyhne wanted, in the sunlight of a spring morning, to fall to his knees and weep. Around him, some of his men did the very thing, while others cheered, and others roared wordlessly, their anger renewed, to the camp of enemies below them.

The paladin had come.

For the first time, Brazcek Varshyne had felt something besides despair, something besides the grim resignation of ending his life in a manner the bards would approve of.

He felt hope. If a paladin had come to them, with an army at his back, then his Barony was not at its end. Then the terrified folk huddling in a mass in the keep under his feet were not at an end.

Brazcek Varshyne felt tears in his eyes that were not, for the first time in days, shed in grief and despair.

The paladin had come.

* * *

The dozen most senior priests, Marynths and Winsars, had only just gathered around Symod's table, and the glass bowl of seawater, when the words shouted from the hillside rolled over them in shock. Dragon Scales, including their menacing leader Jorn, gathered close behind the Choiron, snarled and howled.

For his part, the Choiron laughed.

If the gathered servants of the Sea Dragon around him noticed that the laughter had an edge of fear beneath it, none of them said as much.

Neither did any join him in mirth.

Symod gestured them back to the bowl, shouting, "To your task, servants of Braech. Fear not. All is proceeding as the Sea Dragon would have it."

And then something fell from the air, whistling as it came. It struck a priest in the back rank, exploding against the scales of his armor. The priest fell to his knees, screaming, his arm dangling useless and mangled from the shoulder that had been struck. All around him, other priests or Islandman guards suddenly bled from torn cheeks; one placed a hand over an eyesocket that leaked blood and gore.

Even Symod paled at that, but still he called the priests around him. They raised their hands over the bowl and the Choiron leaned low over it, murmuring words no one else could hear. Images began to swim in it.

Then another missile fell from the sky, striking one of the priests who stood near the bowl, taking his raised hand off at the wrist.

A fragment of the javelin scraped across Symod's cheek, and droplets of blood began to scatter in the bowl.

Symod bellowed and oath and snatched up the bowl, tossing the water out and bending beneath the table for the jug.

"Dragon Scales," he bellowed as he straightened up, "to me! Jorn! Shield us as we work!"

He set the bowl back down after wiping spots of blood from it with a sleeve, set it on the table, and sloppily poured seawater back into it.

The headman of the berzerkers had called out in Islandman tongue, and more of his bare-chested, scale-gauntleted kin suddenly gathered around. They climbed atop each other's shoulders, raising a barrier of flesh against the threat of javelins falling from the sky.

One of them who stood on the shoulders of another looked down in disbelief as a javelin sank through his collarbone and settled deep into the meat of his chest. His face frozen beatifically, he fell forward, as another ran to take his place.

"We have the paladin now," Symod muttered, as he leaned back over the bowl, heedless of the men who fell around him, of the fragments of steel that whizzed in the air.

* * *

Rede paced nervously around the camp he'd been relegated to. Around him, knights in their many colors, red-surcoated Innadan lancers, and newly arrived, scale-clad Harlachan axemen slapped backs and shook hands. Arontis Innadan and Unseldt Harlach embraced one another, each one calling the other "Brother of Battle" and laughing.

He heard none of it.

Images blurred in his mind. Around a huge hill of sand, a mist rose. Not a mist. Steam. The anthill boiled and burned and screamed. A green tide rolled over an icy lake and could only be rolled back by those who sang in fire. Immovable stone took form and flew.

The images were suddenly driven from his mind by a blinding pain, his thin and wasted body wracked with coughing. He pressed a balled fist to his mouth, and looked on in horror as it came away speckled with blood.

* * *

Allystaire quickly ran short of javelins. Beside him, Teague raised her great bow and arced arrows into the air after each spear Allystaire threw. Norbert paced behind them in frustration, his bow useless at this range.

Torvul sat on his mount, taking sightings with his glass and calling corrections until Allystaire released his last javelin. The song still boiled in his veins, and Allystaire itched to leap into Ardent's saddle and lift his hammer and charge amongst them.

It would be suicide, he reminded himself, *and yet the men behind me would follow. If they had a fragment of my strength…* He let the thought die.

"Why do they not come?"

"Some are," the dwarf called out. "Finally getting up the gumption. Looks like a Freezing lot o'them too, maybe more than we can handle."

Allystaire peered down into the camp and found that the dwarf spoke true, a group was detaching itself from the main body. Moving aimlessly, without lines or formations, just charging ahead, driven by the shouts and imprecations of a small group of Dragon Scales on their heels.

"A fighting retreat then," Allystaire said. "We are everything these men are not," he yelled, as he sprang onto Ardent's back.

Horses snorted and armor rattled, arms were loosened and readied, leather creaked as his knights shifted in their saddles.

"Norbert, draw them after us," Allystaire commanded. The lean knight nodded, pulled himself back into his saddle, and fitted an arrow to his bow. Gripping his mount just with his legs, he nudged the horse into a canter forward, drawing back his bowstring and loosing high, speculatively, at the oncoming Islandmen.

"Any burden," Allystaire shouted.

"Any burden," they answered back, Norbert too, even as he rode towards the enemy.

Allystaire drew his hammer and let Ardent trot, drawing away from the castle and its besiegers.

Ahead of them, Norbert rode quickly to within bowshot of the outermost rings of men. Expertly drawing his bow and twisting his body, he sent a high arcing shot towards their forces, then another, quickly drawing arrows from thick sheaves of them tied to his saddle.

Gideon sat bolt upright in his saddle, his eyes flying wide. "Allystaire! The Gravekmir. We are deceived!"

Allystaire quickly took Ardent to the top of a small rise, easy to find in the rolling ground, looking to the east, expecting the tall silhouettes of giants to be framed against the sun.

"Not us," Gideon yelled. "The host! The Barons! Symod has set the Gravek on them!"

Despite the song that ran in his veins, Allystaire felt a hard cold ball form in his stomach.

Then it rose to his throat as the Braechsworn camp let loose a roar, and hundreds of Islandmen came boiling in a great mass of steel and rage towards him and his men.

Anger slid down his throat and met that knot of ice in his stomach, pushed it down, shoved it away.

"Gideon," he snapped, "go to them, to Landen and Arontis, tell them to prepare!"

The boy nodded and slumped in his saddle again. One of Keegan's men, bareback on a small shaggy horse, grabbed the boy's reins.

"We fight back to the the camp and hope that Unseldt Harlach has found it. RIDE!"

The knights around him didn't need a second command. Led by Tibult, the best horseman among them, they streamed away. He turned his head and summoned his best battlefield voice, "NORBERT," he bellowed. "FALL BACK."

He turned Ardent yet again and let the huge grey run towards the first oncoming branch of the enemy, and where he'd last seen Norbert loosing arrows.

The archer-knight stood tall in the stirrups of his horse, loosing arrows still at the forward rushing Islandmen. He had let his horse range far ahead, halfway down the hill they crested to show themselves. Even Allystaire watched, no longer could he simply arc arrows into the crowd. He was close enough to pick targets, which he did.

"NORBERT," Allystaire yelled again, as Torvul, Gideon, and the knights distanced themselves, "FALL BACK."

Norbert looked back briefly, nodding, but continued to fire as he nudged his horse in a tight turn, twisting in his saddle, one way and then the other, drawing and firing faster and more smoothly than Allystaire would ever have guessed he could. Finally, with the nearest Islandmen able to haphazardly fling an axe at him, he spurred his horse and rode off, one errant missile striking the mud just a few paces behind him.

The mud. Norbert's mount's hooves churned through it, kicking it up in flecks. It wasn't good footing for fast riding. Allystaire had known that when they'd ridden out in the morning, but as he had learned, and had told many a man worried about his horse, *If you wait for the perfect ground, you will wait forever.*

Still, some part of him was surprised when Norbert's mount floundered and threw him forward out of the saddle. He landed with a heavy sound, and Allystaire knew that the breath had been driven from him. His bow was still in his hand, tightly clutched, but the arrows were on his saddle, which were on his horse, which was screaming in pain, an awful and inhuman sound, and trying to run on three legs, its left foreleg held off the ground.

Allystaire spurred Ardent forward, knowing he could heal the horse, or failing that, the destrier could bear him and Norbert both.

But he knew even as he charged forward, hammer in hand, that he wasn't going to reach his knight before the Islandmen did. Ardent was fast, but he and Allystaire were dozens of yards away, and the Islandmen had all the momentum. Seeing their tormentor down upon the ground seemed to put more speed into their limbs. Two particularly fleet, or particularly eager men, axes in hand, were only steps away as it was.

Norbert came to his feet, wrapping both hands around the bottom of his bowstave. He squared his shoulders, roared wordlessly at the oncoming men, and hefted the bow like a club. He swung it forward as the first one reached him, cracking him so hard across the jaw that the wood of the stave snapped and the Islandman whipped around, flopping lifelessly into the dirt. Norbert scrambled for the axe the man dropped and came up swinging it, putting down the second with a wild blow to his midsection, even as the knight curled away from the Islandman's clumsy swing.

A small trickle of Braechsworn diverted from the main group heading for Norbert, putting themselves between him and Allystaire. The paladin saw his knight overwhelmed, saw the casual butchery of the battlefield as one man took the time to run for Norbert's horse, hacking with wild, amateur abandon at the wounded animal's flanks and finally, mercifully, its neck.

Allystaire swung his hammer with unthinking savagery at the men around him. Islandman heads exploded, showering their companions in blood and bone. Upraised limbs were smashed to bloody pulp. Allystaire, swinging the hammer Torvul had made for him for the first time with the Mother's Strength upon him, felt the way the steel of the haft gave and bent, ever so slightly, with each swing.

Ardent was a weapon unto himself, rearing up to strike with steel-shod hooves and all his weight and strength, or rocking forward in order to rear out with a rear leg, striking forward with his teeth, or simply bowling men over with his hundred-and-fifty-stone weight of muscle.

The men who came for the paladin died, and Allystaire was able to spare a glance for Norbert. The Islandmen had swarmed over him, but they hadn't killed him. Instead they had pummeled him with fist and flat of blade, with axe-handles and sword-pommels, and snatched up his still-struggling form. One of the two Dragon Scales leapt forward, brought his gauntleted fist down on the back of Norbert's head, then seized his limp body and sprang away.

Allystaire turned Ardent towards them. The destrier reared, its front hooves kicking at the air, and the paladin raised his hammer. The Islandmen didn't come on; they closed ranks into a line, raising their weapons. Behind them, the remaining Dragon Scale spread his arms and howled.

The paladin drew back his arm, aiming his hammer to throw. But he saw behind them the great mass of the Islandmen lurching forward.

His arm tensed.

Then he heard Gideon's voice in his head, not panicked, but urgent. *Allystaire! We need you.*

Letting loose a roar, he turned Ardent and let the destrier run with all his strength. The huge grey gained the hillside in a few steps, and Allystaire shut his eyes tight as he left Norbert behind, guided towards Gideon and Torvul by their beaconing presence in his mind.

* * *

Symod laughed as he studied the bowl, laughed as his camp emptied of Islandmen, but for the gathered bulk of the Dragon Scales.

Behind him, he could feel Jorn fuming. Symod turned to face the berzerker headman, whose features composed themselves as soon as the Choiron's gaze passed over him.

"Do you question my judgment, Jorn?"

"Battle is at hand. We should all be fighting it."

Symod shook his head slowly. "No. This will be a great blow, but it will not finish the paladin, nor his heresy. For that, you and your brothers will be needed."

"It would be the blow if we ran to the fight now."

"It would not," Symod said, summoning the authority to his voice that ended the berzerker's questions.

Another of them came bounding forward, pushing through the mob of priests, bearing a limp form on his back.

The berzerker—taller, less muscle-bound than the rest, but with the requisite ink scrawled over his bare chest, the clawed gauntlets over his hands— threw the body down on the ground, which was when Symod realized it was not a body, as the man coughed and started weakly to his feet. The Dragon Scale who'd deposited him launched a kick into his ribs. Symod heard the snap of bone and the man, a tall and leanly-muscled, curled his arms around himself.

"Enough, Eyvindr," Symod yelled as the berzerker made to kick the downed man again. The Choiron swept around the table where he stood, priests parting for him, and went to the side of the prone captive, looking down at him.

Blood from a scalp wound had flowed freely over his face, and on one cheek there was a prominent scar.

"Tell me your name," the Choiron said, letting a trickle of power flow into his voice, directing it towards the will of the man curled up at his feet.

"Norbert," he replied through gritted teeth.

"Stand, Norbert," Symod said. "Simply gaining your feet will not draw you more pain."

Slowly, carefully, the young man drew himself up, first going to all fours, then to his feet. He kept one hand pressed against his cracked ribs. Even with the slight stoop in his pain, Norbert nearly looked Symod in the eye.

"What are you to the paladin, Norbert?" Symod let another trickle of his will into his voice.

"I am of the Order of the Arm."

Symod resisted the urge to laugh. *Such grand names they give themselves*, he thought. Aloud, he said, "Then you are in the paladin's confidence, yes? Tell me of his plans and your pain will be eased."

The Choiron felt his trickle of power, that should've bent the will of any injured and nearly broken man, rebound back upon him.

The grim youth across from him lowered his eyes, shook his head, and mumbled a few words.

"What was that?" Symod took a half-step closer, bringing his will to bear on the man before him again.

"I said," Norbert replied, whipping his head back up and meeting Symod's gaze eye to eye, "that I will bear any burden for the Mother."

Symod bent more of his will upon the boy, but only felt it rebounding back upon him yet again. He had felt that only once before this day, a long time ago in a town he had since destroyed for its ruler's insolence.

Fury rose up in the Choiron, and he nearly drove a balled up fist into the defiant boy's broken rib before his control reasserted itself.

Symod smiled coldly. "If it is burdens you wish to bear, boy, then burdens you will have. Someone find a beam!" The Choiron elevated his voice just enough for that to be an order, and he didn't even look up as he heard someone scurry to the task.

He shoved Norbert backwards with one outstretched hand, into the arms of Eyvindr, who seized his neck in one gauntleted claw.

"Secure the beam to his arms," Symod said, "and put him in the center of the camp. Every day, add a stone to it. Give Norbert of the Order of the Arm all the burden he cares to bear. When he is ready to speak to us, he will. Or he will die, crushed under his own heresy."

The berzerker began dragging him off, which the youth didn't seem to want to fight, his body practically gone limp.

But they quickly realized he was just gathering himself.

Broken rib and all, Norbert had some fight left in him. He pried his arms away from Eyvindr with a quick twist of his elbows and came for Symod. The Choiron froze in shock as the knight broke free. Norbert was long and lean and covered a surprising distance in one lunge.

Norbert put one hand around Symod's throat and started to squeeze before Jorn and Eyvindr both pounced upon him. The combined strength of two Dragon Scales, neither of whom treated him lightly, was too much.

Still, Symod had felt a surprising strength as he stumbled away from the attack. He only just stopped himself from reaching for his throat, half-expecting to find the impressions of Norbert's fingers there.

"Start with two stones," Symod bellowed. "Take him from my sight until he is ready to talk."

"The next time I see you," Norbert shouted as they dragged him away, his heels digging furrows in the soft ground, "will be in the next world, because Allystaire will have killed you."

"Allystaire will fall before I do," Symod shouted back, losing his composure, raising his fisted hands, cheeks turning red with rage. "Braech will grant me that. Braech will grant me victory. I have SEEN it in the waters. I have SEEN IT."

CHAPTER 49

Ill-Suited Spears

L anden knew herself well enough to know envy within her when she felt it. Envy of the way every eye in the company of the Barons was drawn to Arontis Innadan.

Even so, Landen told herself, *the man has a way about him. I must admit that.*

Arontis was in council with all the other Barons: Ruprecht, Loaisa, the recently arrived Unseldt, Byronn, and Landen herself. Though Arontis was the youngest of them, and the most junior in his seat, everyone deferred to him.

"So far it's just been rabble," Arontis was saying, "but we've not faced the berzerkers yet, nor the Gravek."

"The giants are just walking trees," Unseldt boomed, slapping the axe on his belt, "and Harlach makes the best lumber-men for the job. We'll have no fear of them."

"I wouldn't like to bring horses against them unless I had to," Arontis put in. "We've not had the time to train them for it. If we are set upon by them, how many could your men handle?"

Unseldt looked over his shoulder at the scores of scale-armored men who had collapsed into sleeping heaps as soon as they'd arrived and slid out of their saddles. Even now, Innadan and Damarind grooms were moving among their mounts, checking their hooves and shoes, rubbing them down. They'd not been easily treated, Landen could see.

Better that horses should die than men, she told herself, then immediately felt ashamed.

Landen could feel Unseldt considering his answer, rubbing the top of the handaxe at his side with the heel of his right hand.

"Now is the time for honest answers, Baron Harlach," Landen put in. "We are in this fight together. Boasting will avail us nothing."

Unseldt sighed. "I should say no more than half a score at a time, and that is if we know the bastard things are coming. What I wouldn't give for a good company of archers. Where's the Oyrwyn whelp?"

"We've heard nothing," Arontis said. "I think we have to assume," the Baron went on, slowly, "that our three hundreds are as many as we shall have."

"And the paladin," Loaisa said. "And his knights." She pronounced the word with evident distaste.

"As if he can go bestowing that title as he pleases," Ruprecht Machoryn was quick to seize upon Loaisa's sneer. "We shall have to have a talk with him about that when this is all said and done."

She knew it to be undiplomatic, but Landen couldn't stifle the laughter that bubbled out of her. "You, Baron Machoryn, are going to have a talk with Allystaire Stillbright? You're going to set his mind right, are you?"

Machoryn drew himself up stiffly, his puffy cheeks reddening in anger. "And just what do you imply, Delondeur? Newly come to your seat as—"

"I might be newly come to my seat, Ruprecht, but I am not newly come to the acquaintance of Allystaire. Believe me, I meant no insult to you, my lord Machoryn, but you must understand," she said, spreading her hands to indicate the group of Barons, "when I say that he truly does not care what any of us think. You could try to lecture him on the finer points of titles and politics, and he will ignore you, unless there is something he wants you to do. And then he or the dwarf will find a way to get you to do it, and he doesn't give a good Cold-damn if you agree with it."

Landen suddenly went silent, as she heard a voice ringing in her mind. A quick glance around the circle told her that of the others, only Arontis was hearing it as well.

Baron, Baroness, Gideon was telling them, a trace of panic in his voice, *Gravekmir and Gravekling are headed for you. They slipped around us. I thought I was drawing them away but they were directed here. I know not how. Make yourselves ready. We will join you soon as we are able.*

Landen and Arontis shared a brief look, then Landen inclined her head lightly and took half a step back. Arontis gave an almost imperceptible nod in reply, then said, "My lords, my ladies. We are soon to be attacked."

A babble of confused voices died as soon as it rose up when Arontis lifted his hands. "So I am told by the Will of the Mother. Lady Baroness Delondeur was as well. We have no reason to doubt him."

"We should flee," Ruprecht said, "move up into the mountains."

"Do yourself some credit, man, and remember that you are a Baron," Unseldt Harlach spat. "In the mountains Gravek are a worse handful than on the plains. Here we can surround them, and they've no rocks to throw. Add to that, neither a man nor a horse, no matter how fresh or fed, can outrun Gravekmir. Our only chance is t'stand n'fight. Gather your lances. They'll make fine spears. We all of us are footmen this day."

"The Thornriders will be, at any rate," Arontis said, "but Loaisa, if your men would stay mounted, watch our flanks and the rear."

The Baroness and her daughter nodded and ran for their picketed mounts. Harlach turned to his men who lay scattered and exhausted on the field.

"UP, HARLACHAN!" His grizzled old voice was a throaty roar. "GIANTS COME AND WE'LL NOT MEET THEM ON OUR BACKS." The scale-clad men began picking themselves from the ground, cheering, raising their axes and their voices together.

Landen found herself looking to Arontis for orders, even as she realized that Ruprecht and Telmawr were doing the same. "Let us go and tell our men," the Baron Innadan said, "and form ourselves as much of a wall of shields and spears as we might."

Landen extended one hand to Arontis, and the two rulers clasped arms, gauntlet to vambrace. "Let us hope the Mother is with us," Landen murmured.

"She will be," Arontis replied calmly. "Or at least Allystaire will—and that might be enough."

Landen swallowed the fear in her throat and pumped Arontis's hand once more before letting go and turning on a heel to run as best she could for her own camp.

*　*　*

Allystaire let anger, and the stinging of the wind in his face, drive away the tears that came to his eyes. Even so, the image of Norbert being carried off by one of the Dragon Scales stayed with him, at least until he caught up with Torvul, Gideon, and the rest of the Order.

The dwarf turned in his saddle as Ardent pounded up behind them at full gallop. The rest of the horses parted to allow the grey to move to their head.

Norbert? Gideon's voice sounded in Allystaire's head.

Taken, Allystaire replied, gritting his teeth.

Torvul's voice intruded. *That's worse than dead.*

I KNOW.

Allystaire wasn't sure how he shouted without using his voice, but he managed it. There was silence in his mind, and only the sounds of the wind and of horse's hooves pounding at the turf while the landscape blurred past him. He felt his destrier rein himself in. At full gallop the huge grey would've left the other horses behind him just by the length of his stride. Brown and green Varsyhne countryside turned into one continuous smudge around him. He strained his senses inwardly. He still heard the notes of the Mother's song. He hefted his hammer and found it as light as a flower. That the strength was still upon him was not reassuring.

After a few moments, Tibult managed to urge his charger to Ardent's side. "We're going to have to stop and rest them soon," the knight yelled, "or they'll be in no condition to fight."

"We will press on, Tibult," Allystaire yelled back. "The lives of too many depend on it. Between me and Torvul we will do what we must to keep them alive, but we will not slow!"

Allystaire, Gideon said, *I could go ahead of us. I could destroy the Gravekmir. Some, at least. Perhaps all.*

How dire is it?

I will tell you.

* * *

Gideon slumped forward in his saddle again as his Will worked itself free of his body; a portion remained of course, enough to animate the functions of life, to breathe and pump blood. Yet the bulk of himself, and the vastness of the power he commanded, came with his mind.

He swept low over the ground, trading the panorama view for speed, imagining himself as a huge owl winging for its prey. Gideon saw the Gravek, tall shapes looming before him, fifty if there was one. But smaller figures ran amongst them as well. Smaller than true giants, but larger still than any man, even the Dragon Scales.

Graveklings, apparently leading their larger, wilder kin into the fray.

He had no time to study them closely, had only the impression of fierce faces with sloping brows, of limbs wrapped in reeking hides and skin that was tough as boiled leather. The Gravekmir carried rocks or huge clubs, there being no weapons large enough to truly suit their stature, but the Graveklings wore armor and carried longaxes or spears

Gideon thought he saw one of the smaller giantkin wearing the blue scales and dragon pendant of a priest of Braech, but he wasn't certain and he passed too quickly to know.

He put an extra burst into his flight and found Arontis arranging the soldiers and knights in a line three ranks deep beneath their many banners, too many for such a small host.

In the center stood the Bear's Paw over compact lines of scale-armored axemen. To either side the red-surcoated Thornriders stood, their horses being taken behind a hill by grooms sprinting with reins in hand. They held lances awkwardly, and from a distance Gideon could feel their unease. Mingled among them were knights in many colors, beneath the other banners: the Fox, the Mailed Fist, the Tower, the Vined Great Helm. He found the Damarind Manticore borne up by the only knot of figures still mounted, black-clad, lightly armored.

Gideon! He felt Allystaire's voice weakly as the Arm tentatively reached out to him, the distance almost too great for his Will to stretch. *Tell them not to be stable. No lines. A circle, if they must, but take the initiative.*

He climbed higher to gain perspective. Gideon did not have to gain too great a height to see the problem Allystaire's words indicated. Along a line, with no walls and no way to build them, they couldn't hope to protect their flanks from foes that were three or sometimes four times their height, with proportionate reach and stride.

Arontis. For a moment, when Gideon saw a red surcoated figure beneath him clutch at his head and fall to a knee, he feared that his contact had been far too strong, but then he saw the Baron stand, waving away offers of help from men nearby.

Allystaire says not to form a line. Don't be stable, he says, take the initiative. If you're forced to fall back, form a circle, but no lines.

He saw Arontis nod, and begin waving and shouting orders, pushing through the crowd to find Unseldt Harlach, whose great mane of white hair and stature made him easy to spot from Gideon's vantage.

Allystaire, they have only moments! He climbed into the air again and wheeled away, turning back towards the onrushing giants. *You will not reach them in time, even if you do kill your horses. I have to try and delay them.*

He rushed forward, once again envisioning himself as some great bird of prey. But then his wings lengthened and curved outwards, their tips growing razor sharp.

You must save your strength, Gideon. What of the Eldest?

The Eldest fears me, as well he should, Gideon replied as he gathered speed. *You told me I would know when I needed to use my Gifts, Allystaire. I need to use them now.*

He heard Allystaire voice some further protest, but did not listen. Gideon envisioned once more the flaming giant, the burnished golden titan he had first become back in a newly-plowed field outside Thornhurst.

He was the Will of the Mother; what he imagined became true, or as true as he needed it to be. The more real it became, the more of his power it cost him, but what did he have his power for if not this?

He needed a weapon. Something with length to it. A whip came to his hand, its long coils the same color as the rest of him.

He waited as the line approached, then snapped the whip out across the necks of a handful.

When Gideon's weapon struck them, they fell in boneless heaps. They did not bleed or show wounds, they simply collapsed to the ground, tumbling against each other, sending others dropping.

Gideon realized that he had not killed them, not by dealing wounds to their flesh. He had simply ripped what animated them from their physical selves.

He had, he realized in some horror, ripped their souls from their bodies.

From these suddenly-free essences, he felt confusion, fear, panic, outright terror. They hadn't known what they were fighting for, or whom, or why; they had been gathered from their warrens, their mountains, their caves beneath lakes of ice, and told that the glory of the Sea Dragon demanded them.

True, deep within, many harbored anger, resentment over the small men of the walls, or even their smaller kin, but it wasn't deep enough to become hatred, to ignite them into a crusade. They barely worshipped Braech, but they feared his power, feared the symbols of it.

And because a mad priest and a Braechsworn berzerker had cowed them in ones and twos, they'd come boiling forth onto the mud plains of Varshyne to fight.

Even as Gideon digested all of this, the forces he had parted from their bodies, six of them, ceased their panicked, insensate wailing, and vanished. He looked for signs of their passage, but even he could find none.

GIDEON! Allystaire's voice was loud in his mind again, *what have you done?*

I took action, he answered weakly even as he willed himself back, at the speed of thought, to his own body.

He sat back up in his saddle, bouncing on the back of the palfrey at the fullest gallop it could manage. A cold knot was forming in his stomach and working its way to his throat.

What did you do, boy? Even Torvul's mental voice sounded labored. His animal was lathered and inevitably slowing.

The same thing I did to the Braechsworn back in Thornhurst. I thought.

Discuss it later. Allystaire's mental command had the force of a blow. *We are moments away.* He held up his hand and pulled Ardent to a halt.

Alone among the animals, the paladin's destrier seemed ready to continue their mad pace, and he slowed only reluctantly. All around him, the men of the Order slid from the saddles of spent mounts, themselves exhausted. Most gasped for breath.

684 – DANIEL M. FORD

Tibult slid right from his saddle to lift his horse's hooves carefully, tenderly. The rest shamefacedly followed his lead, as Allystaire went from animal to animal, extending his left hand to their lathered necks. "Torvul," he called, "get them fast again."

Tibult glared up at Allystaire from where he squatted next to his bay, shook his head, but said nothing.

Harrys cleared his throat, spat into the grass. "What happened to gettin' to the fight fast?"

"They can hold for a moment," Allystaire replied. "They must." Torvul was moving among the horses with a wide bucket full of water mixed with one of his tinctures. "We will ride as soon as the animals have had what the Wit has prepared for them. And so will we."

Torvul gave Allystaire a sharp look, but whatever expression he found on the paladin's face seemed to cow him, at least a little. He nodded lightly and reached to the side of his belt, pulling free the skin and tossing it to Allystaire.

* * *

"Freezing Gods," a Thornrider next to Arontis gasped, as the line of giants hove into view. A ripple of fear and awe went through his little square of men. The soldiers had given up on the long, thin line under Allystaire's orders, and broken into four blocks, preparing to charge. Arontis had planted their banners on a nearby hillock, and yelled orders he hoped the men had heard—to rally there in a circle if things broke badly.

Not far away, he could hear Unseldt Harlach bellowing. "Wait till the last moment, lads, then move inside the arc of their club! Don't stand and wait, scatter if they throw!"

The Gravek had no organization, but they needed none. There was a huge gap in one half of their line, if that's what it could be called, Arontis noticed, lacking the time to ponder it. Their running feet were a thunder rolling out in shockwaves upon the ground. Their hoarse yells, in a language no man there spoke, were a gale of fear.

He shifted his feet and hefted his lance. The Gravekmir were less than a hundred paces now. The stench of the poorly-cured hides they wore wafted on the breeze, souring his mouth. Some carried heavy rocks in both hands, while others hefted clubs. The Gravekling that ran at their sides or in front, that exhorted them onward, carried iron, and wore it, too. Squinting, Arontis thought he saw that one of them wore the blue scales of the priests.

Arontis had learned all his life that horses needed special training to fight Gravekmir without panicking, that without it, fighting giants from horseback was hopeless. Made a man a bigger target, he'd heard, or made it easier for the giants, with their curiously small eyes set under their sloping brows, to see you, or simply that their hunger for horseflesh made them mad fighters against men in the saddle.

He told himself all this and more, but as the giants closed, Arontis found himself wishing for nothing more than to be astride Gardener.

Unless it's for a hundred longbowmen, he thought.

He looked from side to side at the columns on his flanks: Landen's and Unseldt's. The latter waved his axe and Arontis could barely hear him yell, "Till the last moment! Till the last moment!"

Likewise Arontis raised his lance, hefting it like a spear and leaning forward very slightly, trying to keep his body weight behind the steel at the tip of the nine-foot long pole of ash in his hand. It made an awkward spear, but it would have to serve.

Mother, he thought haltingly, *if you are with us this day, please know that we also are trying to serve, no matter how ill-suited we may be.*

He didn't finish the thought, because he saw the Harlach column break and charge, roaring and lifting their axes. As they ran they separated into clusters of a few men each.

Arontis screamed, lifted his lance, and broke into a run. He felt the weight and the sound of the men behind him doing the same, their lances raised upwards towards the Gravekmir's unarmored legs and bellies.

Some part of his mind wanted nothing more than to throw down the heavy, unwieldy wood and turn and run, but he pressed on towards the lumbering, towering, stinking masses. To his right, Landen's column, two Gravekmir raised and threw their huge stones. Arontis heard the screams of men whose feet were too slow, or whose luck was too poor.

He felt and heard the sweep of a massive club passing over his head. He stabbed upward almost blindly, his helm too big to allow him to lift his head and follow the aim of his lance's steel tip. Even so he felt the resistance of the lance sinking into something, heard a massive roar. The club descended again, smashing into men around him, breaking bodies and sending great clods of earth into the air. Arontis twisted his lance and bent his body against it; it split apart with a loud crack, showered his helm with splinters, and left its last three feet of length dangling from where the point was imbedded in the giant's stomach.

Arontis barely had time to rip his sword from the sheath on his hip and begin swinging huge two-handed cuts against the giant's leg, when something bowled into him from behind. He sprawled out upon the ground, looking up at a Gravekmir as it died. Two other lances besides his were imbedded in it and the huge brute had dropped its club, using its massive hands to try and pull the lances free. When it did, blood only gushed more freely and it began to sink to one side.

He had more immediate problems, though, than that the dying giant might fall upon him, for a Gravekling stood over him with axe and shield, raising the former to end him with one great blow.

Arontis rolled to the side and heard the axe hit the ground. He sprang to his feet, brought his sword in a wide, sweeping cut against the Gravekling's shield. He brought his sword in a wide, sweeping cut against the Gravekling, who intercepted it with its shield.

Arontis Innadan was a tall man, the tallest of his line in living memory, a head over six feet, but the Giantkin he faced was more than a pace higher yet. Even as a part of him marveled at the size of his opponent, Arontis wasted no time attacking. He swung his sword again, in a tighter arc, stepping forward into the blows.

His father had been an indifferent swordsman, a better leader than he had been a fighter. But Arontis had grown up a second son enthralled by stories of the great knights of story and song. Sir Parthalian. Reddyn the Redoutable. But especially Arentenius and the Argent Blade, the sword that would serve only the greatest swordsman living, and could not be lost to theft or coward, only to defeat in single combat.

As a second son, Arontis had grown up believing he needed to excel on the field. That he needed, deep down, to be another Arentenius. He had *lived* his training with the sword.

A half-trained Gravekling raider with a wooden shield and an iron axe was not ready to face a man in the prime of his life who'd spent that much of himself on becoming a swordsman.

Arontis's blade had sheared half of the poorly-made shield away and cut into the Gravekling's arm and one leg before that seemed to dawn upon the foe. The Gravekling tried to throw everything into one last mad swing, raising its axe and stepping forward.

Arontis stepped to one side and drew two feet of edge across the Gravekling's belly, then pivoted away as it fell to the ground to die.

Whatever hot rush he'd felt as the battle had been joined began quickly freezing over when he took a moment to survey the field. Many Gravekmir were down or dying, perhaps a dozen, but for each one of them were two corpses in Delondeur green or Innadan red or Harlach blue. He caught a glimpse of Damarind riders dashing in, some bending low over their horse's necks with axes to harry Gravekling, others throwing short javelins at giants that still swung their clubs.

We'll make a good show of ourselves, Arontis thought, *maybe even drive them off. But we'll be left too weak to make a second fight.*

Withdraw to the hill! Go! Arontis knew he was not the only commander hearing the Will's voice in his head. He raised his voice to scream out the order, saw the banner-bearers on the hillock raising the Baronial flags and waving them, heard other voices take up the call.

"RUN," a voice boomed out above them, "PUT AS MUCH DISTANCE BETWEEN YOURSELVES AND THE GIANTS AS YOU CAN!"

Arontis did as he was told, as did all the other members of the Baronial host.

He looked back over his shoulder just in time to see a wall of bright orange flame spring straight up out of the ground, a dividing line between men and giantkin. Some of the Gravekling were too slow diving to either side and their cries of pain echoed in his ears as their clothes ignited.

The flames climbed higher as the Barony men scrambled for the hill. Loaisa Damarind, holding one arm close against her side, slid from her saddle and was directing men into a circle. Most lances were broken, and there were few spears, but they were raising what they had. Those with intact lances were pushed to the front ranks.

The Damarind riders released their horses and put their reins into the hands of the few grooms that had come with them, who led the lathered animals away from the field as fast as they could still run.

By the time Arontis arrived on the hillock along with the remnants of his column of Thornriders, he looked back over the wall of flame and the confused Gravekmir whose heads still towered above it.

Then the fire ceased, disappearing upwards into the air, and a new thunder rent the air. The thunder of horses running madly, dizzyingly fast, and at their head a huge grey bearing a man in the brightest of silver armor.

The paladin put his lance through the belly of a Gravekmir with a thrust that, to Arontis's eye, should not have cut with the force it did, the way Allystaire raised his arm and angled it upwards. Even so, the steel punched through the back of the giant, bringing viscera and a hunk of the giant's backbone with it. The huge creature tumbled to the ground and the paladin's destrier charged straight over the corpse.

Behind him, three other lancers formed a wedge, and they helped clear a path for the rest of his party. Their weapons struck into the legs of the Gravekmir who barred their way, but didn't hit with the shock or force of Allystaire's.

The paladin drew his hammer, bearing down on a knot of Gravekling who'd chosen that side of the fire barrier. Among them was the giantkin priest in his blue scale, which drew Allystaire like a beacon drew a ship to harbor.

The giantkin's mace, swung with considerable force, rebounded off the shield Allystaire raised, and then the priest's head described an arc in the air, flying dozens of yards, knocked clean by one swing from the hammer.

The Gravekling broke and ran when their priest died, and the paladin and his Order won their way clear to the Barony ranks.

* * *

Between the death of the priest, the blunting of their charge, and the dozen or more of them that lay dead or dying on the field, the Gravekmir seemed, at the moment, to have had enough.

Allystaire watched as the Gravekling moved among them, threatening and imploring, but none of the true giants seemed spoiling for any more of the fight.

"Back to the circle," Allystaire ordered, "tend to the wounded and plot our next course."

He and Ardent both still shook with energy, and once again they outpaced the others. He slid from the saddle and had to put one hand on his mount's neck when they reached the top of the hillock.

The ranks of men formed up were pale-faced, spattered with mud and blood in almost equal measure. No cheer went up at his approach, for the giants were still all too real a presence on the rolling country before them. The Barons, led by Arontis, parted ranks to meet him. The new Baron Innadan was wiping the blade of his sword with a rag. Like the men around him he was filthy, though he appeared unhurt, as did Landen behind him. Unseldt Harlach had a rag bound across his forehead and another around one arm, while Loaisa held her left arm close against her body.

"Form up the wounded," Allystaire ordered, forcing steadiness into a voice that wanted to shake, "and bring them to me for healing."

"There'll be wounded still out along the field," Arontis said. "Should we send a party?"

"Mattar, Miklas, Gaston, Johonn," Allystaire said. "Go. Move as swift as you can. You find a wounded man you can move, bring him to me. If you cannot, call for Gideon. We will need to move them all, fast. The main body of Islandmen is moving this way and we are not prepared to fight them. We will have to retreat into the hills."

Behind him, the men whose names he called jumped from their saddles and scattered out towards the field, running with almost unnatural speed.

Landen counted men and horses, her eyes flitting from saddle to saddle and her head bobbing lightly. She looked suddenly up at Allystaire, brows knitted in worry. "You're short a man. The village lad."

"He is a knight," Allystaire responded quickly, "not a village lad. And we have no time to grieve about it. This should not have happened. They came straight for you, with Gideon trying to lead them astray, and now the weight of Symod's army comes as well. How did they know where you were?"

While he spoke, officers and bannermen were forming wounded men into a line around him. He spared little time to look at them or examine their injuries; he simply held out his hand and placed it against their heads, or arms, wherever skin was exposed. He did not have to dig deep to find the common threads to draw on in order to pour the Mother's Gift into them. They had stood with him in common cause, taken up arms to defend not only their own, but those they did not, and would never know.

It was not at all hard to find what he needed to heal them.

Arontis and the other Barons were looking at one another in confusion over Allystaire's query, none having found the words to answer.

"Is it possible," Loaisa said, "that they have someone that can do as the boy does? Scout ahead?"

"There is no one alive on this world, perhaps no one ever, who can do what I do," Gideon said, "and my name is Gideon, not the boy," he added, almost petulant. "At least," he then said, already chastening himself and lowering his eyes, "I do not think it possible. Priests of Braech have their ways of scrying, but they all involve water. They are not prophets or diviners."

"It is a problem to consider as we move," Allystaire said. "Get to your mounts."

"Surely we're not abandonin' this place," Unseldt protested. "We've repulsed their giantkin, let the rabble of Islandmen come."

"The rabble of Islandmen outnumbers us considerably," Allystaire said, "and that does not count the Dragon Scales, whom Symod seems to be holding back."

"They could be runnin' over that keep as we speak," Torvul ventured.

Allystaire bit off a curse and resisted the urge to ball up a fist and smash it into his own armor. "I do not understand what he is after. Does he want the castle? Me? All of us? He is not acting coherently, not by our standards, but that is because we do not understand his objective."

"Don't need to understand his objective to kill him," Unseldt offered.

"But we do if we are to defeat him," Allystaire replied. "Form up. Get mounted. We need to move off, and fast. If you have foundering or wounded horses, bring them to me; my gift will heal beast as well as man."

The Gravekmir, unable to be coaxed closer to the lances or the strange gouts of fire any longer, had begun retreating out of Teague's bowshot. Allystaire turned to face them, counting their numbers: fewer than thirty, now, with many huge corpses beginning their slow and messy unraveling on the muddy fields that stretched before him.

But from what Allystaire could make out, more than a score of surcoated and armored figures lay dead, perhaps two.

That is an exchange we cannot afford, he thought, choosing not to give the words voice. As if he were listening though, Gideon looked to Allystaire, then away, lowering his eyes. Allystaire didn't press him, instead, getting back in Ardent's saddle and riding towards the string of wounded men his knights were bringing back.

CHAPTER 50

Eyes and Sight

Andus Carek considered himself possessed of a certain practical kind of bravery. Surely, he was no coward; life on the road was no place for the craven.

Still, as he perched on a wooded hillock behind the battle, pen in hand, some part of him felt keenly the possibility that he was more coward than he would like to admit.

He told himself he was a fool, that he had no knowledge of spear, lance, or longaxe, that his songs and his knives were not likely to be of much use against a giant.

Unless, he mused, *one was in the process of swallowing me, in which case I could perhaps cut my way free of it.* He squinted forward, trying to make out the scale of the brutes, and dismissed the idea with a shake of his head.

He scribbled furiously during the battle, filling up two precious sheets of parchment, despite how his lettering had grown smaller and smaller as the days had rolled on, in an act of conservation.

There had been, on the whole, more to write than he'd expected.

Behind him in the little wood, restive horses stamped and whickered. Separated from their riders, and sensing the anxiety of the few men detailed as grooms, the animals could not stay still or quiet, but they'd been brought too far from the battlefield to smell any blood.

Even from a distance, the appearance of Allystaire on the battlefield was impossible to miss, and Gideon before him, of course. Andus Carek even felt he heard the strains of distant music as the powers they wielded were written large on the field below him. The boy was something haunting and evasive, something that changed itself moment by moment. Allystaire was a strong, forthright melody. Almost militaristic, never making excuses for itself, loud, inescapable.

He despaired of capturing them merely on a lute, as opposed to the grand harps of home, or an organistrum, or several instruments together.

Andus Carek felt himself dreaming on the combination of multiple lutes of different sizes and string numbers, when a robed figure hurried past him, fleeing away across the hillside.

It was the former priest, Rede, clutching a hand to his mouth, scurrying away. Instinctively, Andus Carek pushed away from the tree he leaned upon and rushed after. He wasn't sure what to make of the man who was once a monk, and who seemed to have a touch of prophet in him.

Idgen Marte had told him that Rede was a sad and cursed man, but had also said, with pity, that he was their responsibility, hers and Allystaire's. She had spoken of him with a mingling of pity and disgust that seemed to him entirely singular; she was a woman who made her judgments quickly and insightfully and rarely changed them much.

Andus Carek came upon Rede fallen onto all fours on the soft, loamy ground, as if he'd run smack into a tree and collapsed.

"Rede? Are you ill?"

The priest didn't answer. His body heaved and wretched. Andus Carek came to his side and kenlt beside him. "Can I get you water? Wine? Stale bread to settle your stomach?"

The monk turned to look at the bard with one hand clenched around his mouth. Liquid was seeping between the fingers. Enough light filtered down through the pines above them that Andus Carek could see that Rede's hand was spattered with blood, but an inexplicable scent of brine wafted from it.

Rede lowered his hand and stammered out, "I have to go. To run. Don't let him find me. Don't. Not till I've taken my eyes. Got to take them, pluck them. Can't see, can't keep seeing."

He scrambled to his feet, the lower half of his robes and his exposed, stick-thin legs stuck all over with needles. Andus Carek shot after him and seized one arm, finding it dangerously thin. "Come now, man, let there be no talk like that. Come with me."

With a strength Andus Carek would not have credited from the plainly starving frame of the man before him, Rede tore himself free and dashed off.

Faced with the choice of chasing after Rede, or finding Allystaire and Gideon, the bard turned and started making his way hastily down the hillside.

* * *

Allystaire had just finished healing a crushed hand and arm, the man they belonged to lying insensate and barely breathing in Johonn's arms, when he heard shouting from behind him.

When he saw Andus Carek coming at him the best speed he could manage through the column of soldiers and knights who were shuffling up the hill the bard was trying to descend, Allystaire wanted to shout for joy. The paladin hurried towards him, extending his arms wide.

"Oyrwyn has come then, and Idgen Marte? Cold, not a moment too soon."

The confusion that wrinkled the bard's dark brow dampened his enthusiasm.

"Ah. Sir Stillbright, I did not travel here with her, more's the pity. Events necessitated that I, ah, accompany Baron Harlach as he cut across Oyrwyn territory. I have not had word from her. Does Gideon not know when Oyrwyn troops will arrive?"

"They have not moved, according to his last report, which was last eve," Allystaire said. "They were still sitting in Wind's Jaw."

"Damn. That does complicate matters. At any rate, I just noticed the man Rede. He appears the worse for wear."

Allystaire felt a cold knot form at the base of his spine. "What do you mean?"

"I mean he appeared to be coughing up blood. And that he smelt strongly of the sea, of brine, which struck me as odd."

The cold knot flooded up to the top of his scalp, where it became a steady red heat.

"Show me," Allystaire said, running for Ardent and flinging himself into the saddle. He swung Andus Carek up into the saddle behind him, as gently as he might with the Strength still in his arms, though still the man grunted and cursed. "Teague, Mattar," Allystaire yelled, "with me."

Gideon, he mentally called, *find Rede. Tell me where he is.*

He kicked his heels into Ardent's hindquarters and despite the extra burden of Andus Carek, the horse tore up the hill like a bird on the wing.

* * *

Gideon had lost himself in the thought of what he had done, of the awful soundless wailing, the unendurable panic of the Gravekmir whose souls he had ripped away.

He was trudging up the hill along with Torvul and his own silent, wild-eyed guards. The only one that would speak to him was Keegan. Surprised at how automatic the acts of walking, riding, sleeping, and eating had become even in his scant few days on what could be termed a campaign, Gideon was able to let his mind replay the incident, trying to determine how he felt about it and whether he would do it again.

Burning them was, if anything, crueler, he was thinking, when those thoughts were interrupted by the fist-like blow of Allystaire's voice in his mind.

Gideon, find Rede. Tell me where he is.

Sighing, the boy gestured to the guards around him and sat down upon the muddy hillside. Torvul, resting his crossbow over one shoulder and cocking one head to the side, said, "What is it?"

Gideon shook his head and then let it loll forward on his chest, sending only a portion of his essence into the air, taking wing and spiraling upwards over the hillside and the pine woods that stretched along its crest and beyond.

Allystaire and Torvul stood out to him, of course, but he looked for other sources of power, no matter how faint. Rede was easy to pinpoint, running north along the crest of the hill.

But something was wrong.

Gideon swept closer to him, sensing the tiny spark of power that moved within him, the remnants of whatever Gift Urdaran had once bestowed him, if the Inward Eye could be called a gift in truth. How the Will sensed it was something more like taste or scent that it was sight; he'd felt it in the man before, and now it was wrong, it was different.

It was tainted with seawater.

Gideon resisted the urge to reach in with his Will and pluck it out, for he was certain than in so doing, he'd end Rede's life.

Allystaire, he reported as he winged back towards his slumbering body. *He is moving north along the crest of the hill. And he is tainted. Braech's touch is upon him.*

He felt, more than he heard, the rage born of betrayal through his connection to the paladin.

Suddenly he was back in his own body. "Torvul," he gasped as he sat up. "Come with me. Now!"

The dwarf spat to the side of one boot. The column had passed them by. Only they and their horses remained on the gradual ascent.

"Crest of the hill, moving north along it, less than half a mile," Gideon said in a rush as he scrambled for his tired palfrey. "It is Rede. He's how they found us. He's their divining pool."

Torvul's eyes shot open so wide beneath their craggy brows that Gideon half-fancied he could hear them snap. "I'll be Cold-damned. I never thought—"

"Don't think, just ride!" Gideon, with an unexpected horsemanship, had the palfrey winding up into its signature steady canter, forcing the rest to catch up with him.

* * *

Allystaire reined up and let the bard down, slid from the saddle himself, his armored boots sinking slightly into the needle-strewn ground. Even he could read the signs of Rede's footprints and the impressions where the man had fallen to the ground, where Andus Carek had said they'd find him. Now Teague and Mattar rushed before him to follow the track he left.

Apparently it wasn't hard. The archer and the pioneer traced it without a word, though both armed themselves as they walked. Neither made a sound, instinctively knowing where to set their feet down amidst needles, fallen branches, stones, and soft earth.

All their care was for nothing, though, as Allystaire tromped along behind them, making enough noise for five.

Quickly, the two knights led the paladin and the bard on a northeast path, moving to the other side of the long hill. Here it thinned out, its gentle slope disappearing, becoming a kind of ridge. The pine trees fell away until they were walking on a slope of bare rock that led down a hundred paces or so to a dry stone-strewn ravine.

And balanced precariously on one small boulder, bracing himself as if to jump, breeze whipping his robe around his thin legs, was Rede.

"Rede," Allystaire yelled, holding up a hand for the others to stop and trudging forward. "Why? Why betray us?"

"I did not," the man shouted hoarsely, bending at the waist and wrapping one arm around himself. "I did not, not knowingly. When you let me go at Grenthrope, they found me. The woman, the Marynth Evolyn, she took me to Symod and he, he did something, I didn't know what. I had told them I would seek you out again if they ever let me go, that I would make amends, that they'd have to kill me. And instead they did something so much worse," he yelled, raggedly, his voice echoing down the slope.

"They made me their instrument. I did not know. I could not have known." He pleaded now, his voice a screeching wail, his eyes leaking tears across his dirt-smeared cheeks and blood-spotted chin. "You gave me back my eyes, but they gave me back the Inward Eye, knowing how I would try to use it. And now both of them have betrayed you."

"What do you mean, Rede? Explain to me."

"Symod," Rede roared. "He sees through my eyes. He knows what I know. I did not, until now, I did not realize. I am sorry, Arm. I lack the courage to pluck them out again. I cannot go willingly back to a life of darkness. But I can do this."

Once more the man braced himself as if preparing to jump and dash himself on the rocks.

Allystaire shouted wordlessly, took a few running steps towards the precipice, but he was too far, and too slow.

Rede hurled himself into the air, arms and legs flailing as if attempting to keep him aloft, but he plunged downwards.

* * *

Miles away, still in the camp outside Pinesward Watch, Symod stared into his scrying bowl, a dozen other priests of Braech joined together around him in a circle, feeding him the strength of their Will.

In it, he saw the scene unfold through Rede's eyes. Laughed as he saw the paladin plead with him, promise him healing, saw Rede shaking his head, until Allystaire, fool that he was, came on to the rock next to him and took Symod's own scrying tool by the hand and led him away.

Symod laughed, laughed at the foolishness of mercy, the weakness in it.

"Stillbright keeps our man in his camp and likely in his confidence," Symod roared to the assembled men, not working to keep the laughter from his voice, the victorious delight from his features. "We will still know everything that we need to know. Jorn! Send a messenger to your brothers commanding the body of the army. They are not to engage Stillbright, only to keep him bottled up on those hills. Circle around him. We will march out and meet him at our leisure."

"What of this keep behind us? It stands unspoilt. It is an affront to the Sea Dragon."

"We can destroy it once the paladin is dead."

Jorn snorted, but he turned, flicking a gauntleted finger against the blade of one of the axes thrust into his belt.

"Pack this up," Symod said, "pour the water back into the jar. Preserve as much as you can. I have one last bit of business to attend."

He found his own tent with hasty steps, pulled it shut. The fire in the brazier had gone low, but not out, so he seized the short metal poker that leaned against it and stirred it to life, then reached up to stroke the amulet around his neck.

Symod wasn't sure why fire was necessary to contact the Eldest, but he was glad it didn't need to be too well-fed. The peat bricks burning in the iron gave a steady heat, but not much flame.

It was but a moment before he heard that dry voice echoing around him.

"Symod. Have you the paladin?"

"We have him trapped. Cornered like a fox in a hole. Soon he will be laid across my saddle. Yet our task would be easier if you would come to us."

"What of the boy?"

"He doesn't seem to be a factor."

"I can feel the power he expends from here. The boy is too dangerous. He is the Negation. I will not come close enough for him to know me. You must kill him, or contain him."

"We have seen and heard nothing of him. Only the paladin and perhaps the dwarf. Not even the woman."

"What of our plan, then?"

"It may not be necessary," Symod whispered in answer. "We can destroy him in open battle."

"Like all who play at soldiering without knowing war, Symod, you think that victory lies in weapons and numbers. Likely, he sees a greater picture. Do not hesitate if you see the chance. Do not contact me again until the boy is dead or gone."

"As you say." Symod felt the contact break and fancied he felt blood flowing in his arms and hands once more.

The Choiron tried to shake off the Eldest's criticism with a snort. "What more is there in war than weapons and numbers? What is there besides which side has gathered more strength to itself?"

With another, more convinced shake of his head, Symod set out to order the breakdown of his camp.

* * *

Allystaire felt like he was running through a river that was freezing around him, with his hand outstretched towards the falling Rede.

He would never, ever move fast enough.

And then a nimbus of soft golden light surrounded the former monk, stopping him in mid air. It raised him up, carried him back to safety on the hillside, set him gently down.

Allystaire turned to see Gideon riding up on his palfrey, one hand outstretched, and Torvul following along behind on his poor winded pony. The guard of wild men lagged a few paces behind, but came doggedly after.

"I think," Gideon said, through clenched teeth, as he concentrated, "that Symod is seeing what he wants most to see."

Allystaire came to Rede's prostrate side, but Gideon raised a suddenly wordless cry as he reached for the man.

"Don't," the boy said, "don't disturb the illusion. Don't wake him up. Symod will break the contact soon." He waited, bobbing his head lightly, then gave it a sharp confirming nod. "There." He gestured to the dwarf, who ran to Rede's side, producing a tiny sharp instrument and a flask that Allystaire well knew contained *ikthaumaunavit* from his belt.

Rede lay quiet, breathing shallowly, while the dwarf's deft fingers first set aside the flask and then began feeling along his stomach and sides. With the tiny pointed knife, Torvul made a small cut in the man's robes. He opened the flask, poured a tiny drop over the tip of his knife—really just an angle of razor sharp metal at the end of a small wooden rod, no bigger than a pen—and then over Rede's skin.

As delicately as Allystaire had ever seen anyone wield any kind of blade, Torvul made a tiny cut on Rede's thin stomach. Blood welled up, and the dwarf swept his finger over it, sniffed, and then lightly tasted it. He spat, took a sip from his flask, and shook his head.

"They put salt-water in him, aye. I don't know how. Sewed a tiny bladder of it into him, I think, or made him swallow it, mayhap. Enough has leaked into him to damage him, and to serve their purposes, but not to kill him. Could be it was enough to drive him mad."

"It is an abomination," Allystaire said. "We need to cut it out of him."

Gideon cleared his throat, looking at Allystaire cautiously, waiting for permission.

"What is it, lad?"

"I don't think you should. I don't think you understand," Gideon said, "when Symod looks through his eyes again, as he surely will, I can control what he sees."

"How sure are ya of that, boy?" Torvul rose to one knee and then pushed himself up, having held a small cloth with a dab of potion against Rede's tiny cut until it stopped bleeding.

"As sure as I am in the course of the sun," Gideon said. "I will have to watch him, for Symod's presence. But so long as I can do that, showing Symod what I wish him to see is no great challenge. It is just illusion."

"Couldn't ya just fly over Symod's camp and do what'er it was ya did to those Gravek."

"No." Allystaire and Gideon answered Torvul at the same time, the former simply curt, the latter turning pale and wide-eyed.

"I understand what you say, Gideon," Allystaire went on, "but we have not the men to stand up to Symod's force, not the Braechsworn and the Dragon Scales and the Gravek, not all together. We need to fall back and stay alive."

"I can have more men here in two days," Gideon said suddenly.

"How?"

The boy let out a deep breath. "Garth is not far away with two hundred horse, including knights. I can make his route faster. I think. I will find a way. Trust me."

"Garth was not ordered out by Gilrayan."

"No. I asked him," Gideon said plainly. "I knew you wouldn't, because you fear starting a war there, and what will happen. But we need to win this fight, Allystaire, and he has already marched, and we can deal with the consequences later, as we must. But the thing is done."

"You should not have done this without clearing it with me, but you are right," Allystaire said. "It is done. The stone is cast and we will have to manage the fall. Fine. Let us arrange it." He bent down and picked Rede up in his arms. The man stank of brine over unwashed flesh. Mattar came immediately to his side to take charge of the unconscious form.

"You need t'get back," Mattar muttered. "See to the defense. Those Braechsworn were marching when we rode off, aye? Cold knows where they'll be now."

Allystaire nodded and took up Ardent's reins again. Even the huge and uncanny destrier had lowered his head and his ears, bowing in weariness. He stroked the giant neck with his bare left palm before sliding back into the saddle.

Andus Carek, silent all this time, said, "I will walk back, if it's all the same. The horse could do with a rest. Besides," he said, raising his parchment, "I find it easier to make notes on foot than in the saddle."

Torvul took his pony's reins by the hand, cocking his head to one side as if listening for a distant sound, then gave his head a shake. "Why we're carryin'

Symod's own livin' scrying pool back into our own camp, somebody's gonna have to explain t'me. Twice, mayhap."

"I will use small words," Gideon said as he took his palfrey's reins in hand.

CHAPTER 51

Faith in the Road

On the descent from Wind's Jaw, Idgen Marte found herself wishing, more than once, that the Goddess had touched her own courser the way she had Allystaire's monster of a warhorse. She was forced, time after time, to pause and walk her horse instead of riding him. She had to lead him down steep trails, when she wasn't even sure where she was going.

And when she had to stop the first night, when she was restless and full of energy and wanted nothing more than to join with Allystaire again—and hopefully Andus—she had to let him rest, feed him, brush him.

Typically she was not frustrated with these tasks, or with any tasks she turned her hand to. But she wanted Wind's Jaw behind her and an enemy in front of her, not endless mountain trails.

By the light of her small fire, carefully hidden, she read the map she'd stolen from Wind's Jaw before leaving. If she was on the right of these damnable mountain trails she'd be coming down out of the mountains early in the morning and be able to make better time moving across the moors, provided she could find a road.

She looked to her horse, its head lowered where she'd picketed it and faced the unhappy prospect that she might have to sell or trade him.

Her sleep that night was slow and fitful, and she set off the next morning before the sun was well in the sky. Her reading of the map was true and she descended out of the mountains by midday, looking at a broad stretch of moor and bog that was, if anything, less appealing to look upon than the grey sameness of the Oyrwyn mountain ranges.

She saw the smoke of a village in the distance shortly thereafter, having only seen a few clusters of mean peat-digger's huts on the moor so far that day.

At the very least, she thought, *you need to eat and so does the horse.*

"Never named you," she murmured to the courser, as she led him by the reins. "Probably oughtn't to do it now," she added.

She almost stopped and backed away when she saw the green-surcoated men in the village's center, the handful of horses grazing on the green.

Then she saw the Harrier Hawk inscribed on the surcoats they wore over their armor, bands of metal riveted into hard leather, and she practically ran to them.

One of them, lightly bearded, a black armband tied around his upper arm, spoke up as she approached. "We'll 'ave to have that mount," he called out. "M'lord of Highgate and Coldbourne needs remounts. I'm authorized t'pay a fair price in silver, more if it's trained."

Idgen Marte only just stopped herself from rolling her eyes in disgust. "Where is your Lord of Highgate and Coldbourne?"

He merely blinked at her, as if stunned that someone was asking him questions. *No more than nineteen and wearing a Chosen Man's armband,* she thought. *They start 'em young out here.*

"We'll 'ave the horse," he started again, "wi' silver or iron," and this time she shook her head and gave a little laugh, which stopped him cold.

"Chosen boy," she said, "if you lay a finger on me or my horse, you'll only hope you live long enough t'regret it. Now tell me where Garth is so I can catch up to him."

There were gasps from the knot of soldiers, four of them, when she used their lord's name familiar. "Sorry," she muttered, "Garth, Lord of Highgate and Coldbourne. Tell me. Where."

One of them, younger-looking even than his Chosen Man, pointed west. "A half day's hard ride thataway," he said. "Who're you?"

"I am Idgen Marte," she replied, "the Shadow of the Mother."

He nodded slowly. "I thought so. I thought I saw ya in Thornhurst. In the winter. Would ya, when ya get to the Barony men out there, tell 'em Cold-bourne is comin' as fast as we can."

"Then make it faster," Idgen Marte said, when she swung back into her saddle. "Stop harrying these people for their draft animals, which'll be useless in a battle anyway." She waved a hand at the small village, where people in patched laborer's clothes stared at the soldiers with a mix of wonder and fear. "If you want to join up with the Barony host, remember that these're the very folk we're out to defend. Start by leaving them the means to tend their crops and do their work, for the Mother's sake."

The soldiers still gawped at her. The chosen man's beard bristled, or almost so, when he jutted out his chin. "Now see here, we're duly ordered to—"

"And now you're ordered to leave the animals here. And the silver you paid, if you did at all, because these folk need it more. When this battle's over, I'll come back here and check," she said, then lifted one hand to point at the animals they had gathered up. "I better see every one of these beasts here at the plow. If I don't, I'll know who to look for, aye?"

With that she turned and trotted off, only once stealing a quick glance back to see that the village folk were leading their horses away.

She leaned down close to her horse's neck. "A half day's hard ride, and then you rest. I promise you that. Rest and fodder and water." She let it build up slowly to the run, but she intended to let him gallop as long as he might.

* * *

While Idgen Marte raced along the roads of Allystaire's old fief, the paladin himself sat in a hasty camp with Gideon, Torvul, and the Barons, listening to Ruprecht Machoryn try not to yell as he waved his hands and reddened his cheeks.

"A traitor! A dowsing rod for the Braechsworn, and you let him live," Machoryn yelled. "Absurd. He must be tried and hung."

"Ruprecht," Allystaire said, "that man is not a traitor. He is the key to our victory, if you would but be silent and listen."

"I will not be silent!"

"Ruprecht," Arontis snapped, "close. Your. Mouth."

The Machoryn Baron seemed too stunned at the imposition to actually close his mouth, which hung open, but he did stop talking. Allystaire to seized the moment, unfolding the map on his lap and holding it up.

"Here," he said, drawing his finger not upon a hill, but upon an old dry riverbed that snaked out from east of their current position.

* * *

Idgen Marte saw the lagging elements of Garth's force before the sun sank down into the moor. She gave her courser one last run to catch up with them, hailing them with her ragged voice. The men riding on rearguard, wearing the barred gate surcoat that marked them as Garth's men, did not recognize her as had the one in the village, so she gave them no time to protest as a pair of them turned to face her. She handed her reins off to one of them and vanished from their sight before they'd had a chance to so much as ask a question.

She jumped shadow to shadow—past a few supply carts, trudging footmen with heavy mattocks on their shoulders, and a column of knights and riders that was smaller than she'd hoped, but nearly a match to the one Allystaire had ridden away with if she was any judge—till she found the van, and the banners at its head.

Idgen Marte had to admit that Garth was a fairly fine-looking figure in his armor, helmetless, blond braids framing his pale, strong face. She could see what Audreyn saw in him.

She also took some delight in the shock that split his features, widened his eyes, and set his horse briefly rearing when she appeared in front of it. The knights around him drew swords or shook out flails, but were calmed when their lord raised his hand to them and inclined his head to her.

He composes himself quickly, she thought. *Not unlike Allystaire, I suppose.*

"Shadow. To what do we owe your appearance?" His voice was calm, measured, but the tightness she saw around his eyes showed her fear. *He fears awful news,* she thought.

"The fact that your Baron is a coward, a schemer, or both," she said. There were some grumblings at that, a few weapons raised again, one knight who looked barely old enough to shave spouting some nonsense about a challenge.

She merely spat in front of her boots and ignored it, hooked her thumbs on her swordbelt and addressed herself to Garth, as if they were the only two on the road and hundreds of armed men weren't surrounding her.

"Whichever it is," she said, raising her voice with an effort she tried not to think too much on, "he still sits in Wind's Jaw, gathering his swords. Doin' nothin', marchin' nowhere. I saw no further point in sitting around his keep and drinkin' his sour beer."

"What news, then? Have you been in touch with Allystaire?"

She shook her head, trying hard to keep the movement as casual as her posture. "Not since the night. They intended to draw Symod out this mornin'," she said. *And given that was turns ago, I ought to have heard something. Unless… No.* She dismissed the doubt as quickly as she had it, fought the urge to wrap her hand around her sword's hilt for reassurance.

"We need to get a move on, Garth. You've got to abandon your baggage and leave the footmen behind you."

Garth shook his head, the knights behind him mimicking him. "Absolutely not. You cannot go to war unprepared to feed or arm your men and beasts, and horse alone win few battles."

"Cold, it's like I can *hear* Allystaire telling me these things," Idgen Marte said, tossing her head and biting her lip. Then, leveling her eyes at Garth, she said, "And they would be true, if we were going to war, but we're not. We're going to a battle. Mayhap two. Could be it'll become a war, and if it does, the wains and the footmen'll have plenty of time to catch up."

"Even leaving behind the footmen," Garth said, "and the wains, we're still three days away at best."

"If we ride safely," Idgen Marte, "which we can't afford to."

"Shadow, if we ride to a battle, we have to get there in a condition to fight."

"Garth," she snapped, "Allystaire is outmanned. Maybe five-to-one. There are more of Braech's berzerkers arrayed against him than he has men with him. The longer we take, the more certain his defeat becomes. And if he does fall, if Symod is victorious, how many more will flock to him? Could be there are Islandman ships even now heeding the call of war and heading to Delondeur's coast. How many men in Oyrwyn, how many warbands, how many Harlachan revere Braech and will come to his winning banner? Symod will not stop with

Allystaire, or with Thornhurst. The Baronial peace won't last because there won't be any Baronies. Right now his force is a river pushing against a dike that's only just been built to hold it back. And if that one dike breaks, the entire sea will come against us."

She felt the words pouring out of her like wine from a forgotten bottle found in a cabinet. *Not a great vintage and not a beautiful vessel,* she thought, *but it'll do if you want a drunk, I suppose.*

She saw the uncertainty on Garth's fair face; his features hid very little of his thoughts or emotions.

"Garth, Allystaire would tell you to have faith. Faith in the light or the sun or somethin' noble-sounding like that. I'm of the Shadows, not the sun, so I can't. But I know there's no sun, and no shadows, on the very bottom of the sea. And that's where Symod'll put us if he's given the time."

She could see him make the decision moments before he nodded. "Fine." He twisted in the saddle, shouted orders. She barely heard him tell his commanders about separating the mounted men from the foot, about taking what food they could carry and nothing else.

Now how do I get them there any faster? Gideon, boy, you'd better have an idea.

* * *

"And you are certain," Landen said slowly, "this'll work?"

"Seems like cowardice," Unseldt rumbled.

Allystaire pressed his eyelids tightly together. "I tire of answering these questions, Baroness Delondeur and Baron Harlach. Yes, we will need to refrain from giving battle tonight and most of the next day at least. The Will assures me he can help arrange this, and the arrival of fresh troops. Have faith in Gideon and Torvul. In me, and in yourselves," he added. "No go to your camps and inform your men. We have work to do." He stopped short of dismissing them outright, but as he stood, packing the map away in its case, they understood, and trickled away.

Allystaire had spent turns while the sun set going over the plan with the Barons, assuring them it would work, and working out disposition of the men along the top of the hillside, counting their losses: almost fifty, mostly Innadan Thornriders and Harlachan.

After walking amongst the guards that had been set at intervals surrounding their camp, including one man from the Order along every station, Allystaire found Gideon sitting quietly with Torvul, the two of them arguing in lowered voices. The alchemist's small shuttered lantern threw just enough light to make out their forms, Gideon, standing, hands at his sides, the imploring teacher, and Torvul sitting almost dejectedly, chin down on his chest.

"I'm tellin' ya, boy, ya ask the impossible. Not only o'me, but o'yerself."

"It might be that nothing is impossible for me, Torvul," Gideon replied, "and certainly not this. As for you—"

"There's no more song for me t'sing out o'the stones. None. It has passed from this world."

"And I punched through the Barrier, Torvul. Well, I gouged a hole through it with a chisel more than I punched. The metaphor is imperfect," Gideon said hurriedly. "The point is that the power is there for you to shape, if you'll but have the faith to do it."

"Even if it were, I'm but one voice," the dwarf protested more feebly.

"And a man singing into a large enough horn can be heard across mountains," Gideon replied. "There is no larger horn in this world than the one I can give you."

Allystaire remained watching the darkened scene in silence. He did not understand why, exactly, but the words of the Goddess when he'd prayed in the Temple before leaving Thornhurst came back to him then.

You must carry the light of My sun within you through all storm, all darkness. It is a heavy thing, My Knight. I chose you because I know you will carry it.

Looking on them, lit only by the light of the dwarf's lantern, which Torvul stood and collected, Allystaire wondered if this night was what she had meant. The Braechsworn were camped below them, but showed no signs of trying to climb the hill to displace them. He suspected that their numbers had swelled in the night, but without Idgen Marte to venture a closer look, he couldn't know. *Should never have sent her away with Gilrayan,* he told himself.

"Shut up with that word," Torvul finally grumbled, as he shut off his lantern. "We'll try it as y'say. Go on, then. I'll try and make what preparations I can."

The dwarf stood, stumping away in the dark, leaving Allystaire and Gideon alone. The moon was dark, whether under cloud or new, Allystaire couldn't tell offhand. He'd never paid much attention to its phases. Starlight was all there was, and none too much of it, so he supposed it must have been cloud.

"I could just sweep them away," Gideon said suddenly. "I could reach out to them with my Will and tear their essences from their bodies. I did it this morning."

"You could," Allystaire agreed, "but you are not going to."

Gideon was silent a moment, staring straight ahead at nothing in particular. "For a moment I felt their fear, Allystaire. The Gravekmir. We call them brutes and monsters, and that we are set against them in this fight is not something we change tonight. But they were so terrified of me, and in truth, I don't think they know what they were fighting for, or why. I doubt the average Braechsworn is different."

"I do not doubt the truth of that, in a general way," Allystaire said. "The Dragon Scales are another thing altogether. And do not forget that the Braechsworn below us will gladly butcher us all if given the chance, for glory and plunder. They already have burned villages and farms in Delondeur this spring, and taken thralls back to their homes. Whatever misery they live in, it is not the fault of other poor men and women, and when they seek to raise themselves by raiding and pillaging, they become my enemy, Gideon."

The boy raised a hand. "I know that. I am not suggesting we can get them around a table to talk peace. We could barely do that with the Barons, and they had vested interests in it. I am saying that I could end this war now, today, in this moment, if I were willing to."

"You would become a monster, Gideon. I have struggled, and fought, and killed. It has been the work of my life, to my shame," Allystaire said. "I sent men to their deaths and the deaths of others. But I could not bear the weight of the deaths if they happened as you described. The men I have killed have either been trying to kill me or the men under my charge, or they had earned it with their actions. So I hope. But that much death, so indiscriminately? No. I could not do it. I will not ask it of you."

"I know. It would turn our own against us, anyway," Gideon replied. "I would be a monster in their eyes. And in truth. And all the Baronies need ownership in this fight. A common enemy gives them something to unite against, makes them feel like countrymen again. Just like a king would," he added, turning his face towards Allystaire for the first time.

"One crisis at a time," the paladin replied, shaking his head. "Why are you telling me this?"

"I just want it to be clear why I won't do that. And to start thinking about what to do after we win the battle, with the enemies who survive."

"Do not plan too far ahead," Allystaire warned. "We cannot lose sight of the next step. Can you do this? Bring the reinforcements here?"

"Torvul and I together," Gideon replied, "are going to make a road."

"There are roads already."

"We are going to make a road through the mountains," Gideon replied. "Straight through. Instead of snaking through trails and winding under impassable peaks, they'll ride straight to us. The road won't last," he added, "it'll collapse almost as soon as they pass through it. But it will hold." The boy looked straight up, and sniffed at the air. "Braech's priests are going to call the rain, bring the storm. It will only serve our purposes here even better."

Allystaire's mind reeled as the boy went on matter-of-factly about the coming rain. "Road through the mountains? How?"

"Torvul is going to ask the stone to step aside. I am going to make sure it can hear him and respond. It's quite simple really."

"Go to it, then," Allystaire said, "and may the Mother guide you. And Gideon," he added, extending one hand to the boy, "I am more proud of you than I know how to say."

Gideon stepped forward as if to take Allystaire's hand. Then, impulsively, the boy stepped close and threw his arms around Allystaire.

"There is so much I could do to shape the world, Allystaire," Gideon said, his voice a murmur with his face pressed against the paladin's armor, "that it frightens me. How will I know when and where to stop? Promise me that you'll never let me become a monster. If Bhimanzir had had the power open to him that I do, or Gethmasanar—"

"You chose *not* to be them, Gideon. You chose that for yourself even though it looked like throwing power away. I do not have to promise you that, because you will never let it happen. I have faith in you."

The boy hugged himself close to Allystaire for another moment, with one of the paladin's arms around his thin back. When he tugged away, he was entirely composed again, using one hand to smooth the dark blue tunic he wore.

"I must go find Torvul, then," the boy said.

* * *

Torvul was kneeling with his hands sunk deep into the mud of the hilltop, try-ing to get a feel for the earth and the stone here. For its age and how it had been worked, for what had been asked of it and what it had yet to give.

He heard nothing.

His master Ochsringuthringolprine had described the first stirrings of the Stonesong not so much as a distinct note as a buzz, a drone, so deep it was felt more than heard. When Torvul had briefly reached out to the earth through the *mchazchen* crossbow he'd so briefly held, the songs had seemed to explode in a riot of colorful noise, a high thin trickle like those coaxed from a fiddle.

Yet there had been few of them, too few for him to do much more than dis-tract the sorcerer. *I gave the bastard something to think about,* Torvul reminded himself, feeling pride's brief bloom in his chest.

"Torvul," Gideon said, having crept up on him unawares, for which the dwarf inwardly cursed himself, "not here. Come with me."

Before the dwarf could protest, the boy had placed a hand on his shoulder where he knelt, and Torvul felt himself reeling upwards from his body into the vast dark of the sky.

At first he quailed in fear, wanted to revolt against the Will's easy mastery of him, but Torvul grew accustomed more quickly than he could have imagined. Beneath them the earth was nearly featureless in the dark, just shapes of hill and mountain, the valleys and ravines lost in pools of deeper darkness.

Just sing, Torvul. Gideon's voice played in his mind, and the dwarf gradually realized that it was only his mind, his essence that was flying above the moun-tains along the Oyrwyn-Varshyne border, that his body was safely back on the outskirts of the camp, with Gideon's wild-eyed guard of bowmen practically invisible around them.

Sing, and let your own song guide you. I need to speak to Idgen Marte.

Back on the grass of the hillside, Torvul's voice rolled from him as a barely audible rumble in his throat. In the realm of pure Will through which he and Gideon flew, it was the blast of a great horn.

* * *

Idgen Marte chafed at how slow the men and horses moved, even though it was dark. The road was steady and level and the mountains much closer than they had been when she'd found Garth's men in the afternoon, but she was only going to be able to egg them on so much longer. And the mountains, starting tomorrow in late morning, would eat the turns away.

It will be two days at least before we can link with Allystaire, she thought ruefully. *At least. Three, more like.*

She tried once again reaching out for Gideon, having heard nothing from him all the day. A voice of panic, a voice that threatened despair, had long since been bound, gagged, and locked away in her mind, but she fancied she could hear it yelling each time she reached for the boy and found nothing.

And then there he was, not just his voice in her mind, but a vision of him floating in front of her, feet hovering a few inches from the ground, robes that glowed faintly, with his hood pulled mysteriously low over his eyes.

"About time," she muttered under her breath. *Nice trick,* she thought. *What is the situation?*

I am not appearing only to you, Shadow. Gideon's voice had an air of distraction in her mind, which she didn't follow up on, because then his voice was booming audibly for all the gathered men to hear.

"Men of Oyrwyn. Friends to Allystaire. The Arm of the Mother needs you and cannot wait for you to travel the roads men have made. I am going to prepare a way for you. It will be dark, but straight, and at the end of it will be dawn, and the paladin. I need you to have faith in me and I need you to follow it. That you are already on this road is testament to your bravery. I ask only that you maintain it for another few turns. Follow the Shadow; she will guide you."

Gideon, what is happening?

Torvul and I are building a road. Sort of. Just keep going straight. All night.

Another turn or two of straight and we're trying to clamber over the southeastern arm of a mountain.

Actually you'll be going under it. Through it. Or possibly over it. Hard to say. Torvul will decide. Quickly now.

She was conscious of the weight of hundreds of eyes watching her from behind. Garth's pale face was easy to pick out for her eyes, long-since given over to seeing in the darkness almost as easily as the light. "You heard him, then. We'll be the first to take a road built by the Wit and the Will of the Mother themselves," Idgen Marte rasped, raising her voice to a familiar, affectionate shout. "We're a bunch of lucky bastards. What are we waiting for?"

Some residual magic of Gideon's seemed to carry her voice down the line and the men raised a ragged cheer as they heard her words. The ranks rolled forward with renewed vigor.

"I always knew somehow," Garth said behind her, "that if I was ever going to live out some tale, that it would be Allystaire's.

"I think that's how it'll be sung, anyway," she said, twisting her mouth in a wry grin.

* * *

Torvul was so startled when the mountain answered him that he almost stopped singing.

It wasn't the mountain, really, that did the singing. It wasn't one thing, an entity with any kind of consciousness; it was the veins of ore awaiting a hand to work them, the geodes like eggs vibrating with the need to crack open to birth their gems cautiously into the world, the shifting piles of rock that, as such things were measured, seemed only to have been thrust against one another moments ago by the convulsions of the earth.

Torvul felt these respond to his call, to the bone-deep ringing notes of the Stonesong, and on a hillside in Barony Varshyne, tears leaked from the corners of his eyes.

He felt Gideon taking the power his voice projected and widening it, broadening it so that every stone in the mountain could hear. It was as if they began clamoring for his attention, so much so that it was hard, in the end, to simply move it all aside, just high enough for man and horse to pass under, just wide enough for two ride abreast, and to hold each part of it just long enough before letting the stones, the ores, the lattices of crystal and pools of water, reassume the shapes that seemed to them most fitting.

Torvul sang for turns that night, but it felt like mere moments.

* * *

The Oyrwyn men stopped just outside the unnatural, yawning hole in the side of the mountain to light torches.

Once inside, Idgen Marte almost wished they hadn't. It was unnerving to see a long, smooth tunnel etching its way through the stone just a few paces in front of them.

All the night they rode, and well into the morning, and never once did she allow herself to look back. Not after the first time she heard something that sounded like a door shutting behind them.

CHAPTER 52

Battle Joined

Symod smiled grimly. Already he could feel the storms gathering above them, drawn by the prayer and chanting of all the priests he'd gathered working to call the storm all that night and through the morning. The berzerkers would draw strength from it, if only in their minds.

As he'd ordered, the servants had already prepared his scrying bowl. He laughed to himself, a grim triumphant laugh, as he bent over it, as he felt the prayers of tired priests join their will with his.

His laughter became exultant when he felt, through the bowl, that the amulets of seawater planted in his tool were still there. He felt the idiot Rede stir to panicked wakefulness, blinking open his eyes and casting around himself in the dirt.

The paladin hadn't even caged him. His hands and feet were bound, and armed men stood guard around him, but his eyes and his mind remained blessedly intact.

Symod laughed as Rede turned around, giving him a distinct view.

The Barony army had moved camp in the night, dividing itself into threes and taking up positions atop three separate hills. Different banners flew on them: the Golden Sunburst in the center, with the Harlach Bear's Paw. To the left was the Delondeur tower, the Damarind Manticore, the Machoryn Mailed Fist. On the right, the Innadan Helm with the Telmawr Fox.

The men drawn up in ranks of gleaming mail and sharp spears seemed, to Symod, entirely inadequate. Perhaps some pitiful attempt had been made at earthworks or barriers of wood, but his Braechsworn and his berzerkers would swarm over them in torrent like the sea destroying a pathetic wall erected to hold it back.

Symod frowned, then, thinking on the Eldest's words. *Must hold some of them back,* he thought. *Most of them. No sense in wasting their lives, after all.*

"Jorn," Symod called out, letting the scrying contact break, "they are atop three hills to the east. Send a hundred of your brothers to disperse amongst the Islandmen. Tell them to march forward. Take the hills. Leave none alive. When that is done we'll return to your pathetic prize of a keep, and then south to fatter lands. All the banners that dared to rise against the Sea Dragon must be brought to their knees."

Jorn, who was already standing at his side, didn't answer with words, just an angry growl, then dashed off. Symod looked up into the hills, where he could make out the weak panoply of men standing and banners rippling in the wind his priests had called up.

"Arm yourselves, servants of Braech," he bellowed to the hundred or more priests who gathered at the center of their hasty camp, breaking their fast with the food they'd plundered from all the surrounding villages.

By the time he turned away from the distant hilltops and stopped scrying, Symod hadn't noticed that the man standing atop them weren't moving, that the banners rippled the same way regardless of how the breeze changed, that no songs or shouts, no clatter of weapon or armor, could be heard from the top of those hills.

* * *

Symod was not a subtle general. Even Gideon could see that, from above the battlefield, where he had so much to manage. He was weary from projecting Torvul's power through a mountain all night, but the dwarf had set to his second task with renewed vigor and almost childlike glee when they'd returned before dawn with Idgen Marte, Garth, and two hundred weary riders in tow.

And now there was his other projection to prepare, but now that he knew the principle was sound it was easy to make it ready.

Roughly equal companies of Islandmen charged up the hill roaring out prayers to Braech, each disorganized mob of them waving weapons and numbering nearly the entire force Allystaire had brought to the battle a few days past. No longer did the Dragon Scales drive them from behind. Now Braech's Holy Berzerkers, beating and scratching deep bloody lines in their own tattooed chests with their scaled gauntlets, led them, ranging ahead, leaping and howling their eardrum-shattering challenges, their fearful taunts and bloody litanies.

Brave men, Gideon thought, *but stupid.*

It was a matter of moments, thought it felt like turns of the glass, before they reached the top, and halted in confusion as the illusory armies they raced after disappeared into the wind.

Then the three hills they stood upon began to collapse into mud, and their victorious shouts and booming songs of victory died into cries of horror.

* * *

Gideon sat bolt upright in his saddle. "Now," he said, then reached out one arm to lay it on the shoulder of the warrior riding next to him.

Idgen Marte took a deep breath as the boy's hand settled on her, and reached out to grasp the lay of the shadows before them.

She felt Gideon seize on her Gift and expand it, throwing it open for all of the men arrayed behind her and Allystaire. She had carried people with her before as she passed from shadow to shadow, slipping between light and darkness in a world of shrouds. But only ever one or two, never hundreds.

"You heard him," Allystaire said, raising his voice to a roar and standing in his stirrups at the head of the wide front rank of lancers, with Tibult, Armel, and Harrys beside him.

"CHARGE."

He kicked into Ardent's flanks and to no one's surprise the huge grey pulled far ahead, almost so far that Idgen Marte feared losing him from the Will's projection.

But then she felt the unknowably vast power of the quiet boy riding expertly beside her, and almost laughed at herself.

They hopped from shadow to shadow in the lee of the hills while they heard the sounds of men yelling in fear and shock as the hills they were trying to take turned into mudslides. She turned her head to watch as she rode, briefly. Some of the men, especially in the front ranks, were simply buried. She saw more than one scaled, bronzed gauntlet raised futilely above the earth as the berzerker wearing it was dragged under.

She had but a brief glimpse, for then the veil of shadow dropped and a hundred knights and lancers emerged from the shadow of the hill only forty paces from the mass of Dragon Scales Symod had reserved, riding under the wind-whipped banner of the Golden Sunburst. Behind them came another line, and another, and then Harlachan axemen beneath their own White Paw, but led by Johnn, Miklas, Mattar, and Gaston, the four knights of the Order outstripping the mountain men in their haste to reach the enemy.

Idgen Marte freed her sword and slid from her saddle. Her gift was her own to use once again.

Dragon Scales learned to fear shadows that day. Shadows that cut out their legs, and slit their throats, shadows that took their arms off and watched them pour their lifesblood into the ground.

Shadows that promised each man, before he died, that his body would never see the water, that his soul would never find its way to his god.

* * *

Symod stood utterly dumbfounded as he saw his men buried by waves of earth and mud. *Not all dead, surely,* his panicking mind said, *and there are still the Dragon Scales, but.*

He didn't finish the thought, because then, out of a fold of air, the armies that should have been dying on the hill beneath the Braechsworn onslaught were charging at his berzerkers from open ground, not a hundred paces away from where he sat.

"Jorn," he yelled, scrambling to his feet from the camp chair he'd been reclining on, "JORN! Tell your brothers to retreat, we'll retreat south over the river!"

The berzerker headman bristled at the order, and shook his head. Energy and anger vibrated visibly through his muscled arms. Though he and a few of his choicest brethren stood near Symod as his guard, amusing themselves by tossing stones onto the beam that prisoner still wore like a yoke, on his knees and grunting with the effort of it, most of the bulk of them had rushed forward to do battle with the Barony army.

But it was no use ordering berzerkers away from a battle that had come to them, Symod quickly realized. The other priests, arrayed for battle with maces and swords and scale armor, all looked to him. "We will retreat south and salvage what we can," he said suddenly. "Jorn! You and my guard will come with me."

Inwardly, Symod reasserted his control, gradually forced it outward. "We will not run in panic," he shouted, as a few priests had begun to do just that. "We will retire in good order."

Behind him he heard the half-dozen Dragon Scales haul their prisoner to his feet. Priests ran to their tents to fetch the thralls they'd taken as they had their men raid the countryside.

After all, the Choiron Symod told himself, as he fled before the wrath of the Arm of the Mother, claiming a seat on one of the few horses his army possessed, *this only gives the Eldest his chance. And Braech all the glory.*

* * *

Allystaire had broken his lance inside the first Dragon Scale to die in the morning's butchery. Some men, he saw in his peripheral vision, broke their lances against the hardened skin of a berzerker; such unlucky lancers generally didn't live to draw a second weapon.

Still, the impact was devastating. Man to man on an even field, Allystaire reasoned that a Dragon Scale was as fearsome a warrior as inhabited the world.

But warriors met knights that day, and soldiers, who had chosen to spend their strength in defense of people who would not know for days, if ever, of the battle that was fought here.

Strength is greatest when it is being spent for others, instead of marshaled to ourselves, the Goddess had told him in the Temple. And he saw the evidence of it today, as his hammer raised and fell. Saw it as Harrys and Tibult laid about themselves with sword and axe, maneuvering their mounts expertly with just their knees.

He even saw it as a berzerker leapt from the ground and carried Armel out of his saddle, saw the second of his knights to fall, the berzerker crushing Armel's throat even as Armel's dagger opened his.

Allystaire would mourn for Armel in his time. Today there was merely the rise and fall of his hammer.

Beneath every stroke another Dragon Scale fell. Their strength was no match for his. Around him, other men, good men, brave men were falling to that strength. But in the end they would fall to his.

He felt and heard the shock of the second line of lancers hitting before his own had broken well clear.

When he did, he saw lines of blue-clad priests running at speed, or riding from the battlefield.

"SYMOD," he screamed, raising his hammer and standing in his stirrups. Rain lashed against his armor and thunder rumbled overhead, and his rage tore at his throat. "COWARD. FACE ME." He settled back to his saddle and prepared to bolt after the priests when he heard Gideon's voice in his mind.

Allystaire, I am reaching for the power the berzerkers release when they die, and I cannot grasp it. Something is taking it from me. Something is snatching it from my hands and gathering it.

The boy's fear was palpable. Allystaire cursed and turned his mount back to the fray, laying about him with his hammer. Behind him he felt two riders fall into place in his wake. Tibult and Harrys. He didn't even have to turn and look.

Is it the Eldest? Has he shown himself?

His knights didn't even question him as he fought free of the battle and rode back towards the shadows of the hill where their small reserve waited, Gideon and Torvul, Keegan's men, Teague.

No. Gideon's voice was panicked, and Allystaire left Tibult and Harrys behind him as Ardent took long and powerful strides.

When Allystaire found him, the boy was pale and shaking; even Torvul looked fearful.

Gideon turned wide drawn eyes to the paladin and said, "Allystaire. I think it is Braech Himself."

Almost at the moment the boy spoke the words, a long stroke of lightning forked out of the clouds above them and down into the battle.

Allystaire felt dismay rising in him, but then he saw that it had struck among the berzerkers, not his own forces. Then another struck, and another, and thunder rolled deafeningly over the scent of charred flesh, as the storm scoured the Dragon Scales who were still fighting.

CHAPTER 53

The Ocean's Rage

Even the Eldest had to admit surprise at the speed and power with which the event began to happen once he set it in motion.

With so much power floating around the world, flowing freely into him, it had been no great task to stretch his Will across hundreds of miles and begin plucking up the bits of power the berzerkers had released back into the void as they died. Small pieces on their own, but growing larger and larger as the paladin devastated them in his wake.

The Eldest wanted very much to taste the power of the paladin for himself. It would come.

For now he simply harvest power and served as a conduit, pouring it into the artifact in the temple. None of the dying men escaped his touch.

It had taken surprisingly few for the power to be yanked from his hands. But he could feel it, sense it, taste it still happening. The strength, the rage, the howling, leaping, yawping *power* gathered from nearly three hundred terrifying men now all poured into one place. One thing. One being.

Something vastly more powerful than the Eldest himself had taken over and now the power gathering around—gathering in—the statue was even more than he had expected.

"Perhaps," he said to no one, "there are gods."

Then there was a great crack, and the statue disappeared in a mist that suddenly rose from the water beneath his feet.

* * *

Walking the walls of the Dunes every day was beginning to irritate Chaddin. The great battle of their age was being fought, or had been fought, or would be, a hundred leagues or so to the north and east, and he was playing at being a lord in residence, settling disputes, trying to buy from the local armor and swordsmiths in bulk without raising suspicions.

On the whole, the soldier in him would rather have been at war.

On the walls there was solitude, at least. There was the illusion of the security of his old life. Spear in hand, walking the wall, watching the city below. Winter quarters.

It didn't feel at all like winter, of course. The spring afternoon was showing the first promise of summer heat, and the day was clear and bright.

So as he circled the curtain wall of the keep and looked out over Londray Bay, he was utterly baffled when a mist as thick as any he'd ever seen came boiling out over the city.

It rose so fast and so far that something in it terrified him. Unnatural and too warm by half, it caused both a chill on his back and sweat upon his brow, and before he knew it, he could not see over the wall to the bay below him.

In the harbor a few masts still poked above it, but even they were quickly swallowed.

"Oh gods," he muttered, thinking of the bodies of Braech's priests still mouldering on the walls of the keep, and of the looted temple. "What have we done? What have we—"

Chaddin's breath was stolen as an enormous animal roar blasted throughout the city. There was no beast he knew that could make that sound, no bear, no leviathan, nothing. It was deafening, it was a punch to an unarmored chest, it was a hammering blow at his ears.

The sound was the breaking of the world and it sent his heart into his stomach. Shutting his eyes, Chaddin lowered himself against the wall in a ball, covering his face with his arms, and he did not know why.

Then the roar came again and tears sprang to his eyes. He forced them open and looked up into the mist, and in it. Something huge, something twice the size of the biggest ship that had ever harbored in Londray coasted through that mist, and Chaddin feared it more than he had ever feared anything. It was a long and sinuous shape but for the shadows of two vast wings on its sides.

Chaddin knew only one word that even that brief impression could answer to, and he bit at his arm to keep from crying out when he thought of it, lest the Dragon that overflew the Dunes should hear him.

* * *

The storm struck down the Dragon Scales, singly and in pairs until the Baronial army was left facing nothing but their own panicked horses and the driving rain.

Allystaire was watching Gideon, who was a miserable sight, huddled and shivering in the stinging of the rain. In all the times he had seen the boy lie insensate while projecting his Will elsewhere, he had never seen him quake in fear as he did now.

Arontis came riding for him, the other Barons riding in his wake, while men were milling around on the field that had become a charnel house, horses shying away from the smell of lightning-scalded flesh.

"Sir Stillbright," the Baron Innadan yelled, exultant as he put up his visor, "has the Will called this lightning?"

The smile faded from Arontis's face as Allystaire turned grimly to him and shook his head.

Come back to us, Gideon. We must know what it is we might face.

* * *

Gideon no longer even thought about the power he might expend as he took to the air, speeding formlessly towards Londray as pure will. He was following the track of the power that was being gathered and redirected on the battlefield, and while he knew that he traveled towards the Eldest, it was not the centuries-old sorcerer that gave him pause.

Londray was nearly invisible to the naked senses; it was one vast formless fog, a huge and unnatural cloud of mist, as if the entire bay had boiled off at once.

And in it Gideon sensed the most vast and malevolent collection of power he had ever seen, could ever imagine. The Eldest was a sickly green presence in the city below, but Gideon paid him hardly any notice. The hoary old sorcerer would do well to flee from him, much less this thing.

This Dragon.

Gideon realized this was the only word for it, that it flew through the mist it had raised over the city on huge wings. That it was a dragon, the Sea Dragon, in the flesh, an avatar of Braech somehow called into being by the Choiron and the Eldest, and by the deaths of hundreds of Braechsworn and berzerkers.

The mist surrounding it parted enough for him to get a glimpse of its long tail, gleaming scales, blue along the top of its length over bronze on its underside, the huge length of it ending in heavy club of bone.

Reaching his senses towards it he found only rage and insatiable hunger, and then it saw him and roared, beating its massive wings and making straight for him.

Gideon fled from it, back to his body in terror.

* * *

Gideon sat up with a start and a loud cry of fear.

"It's a dragon, Allystaire," he blurted, as rain streamed down his face. "A dragon. They have called a dragon somehow, in Londray. Braech's avatar, in the flesh."

All around him Allystaire heard gasps of breath, saw fear overtaking faces that had been flush with victory.

In himself, he felt only purposeful calm.

"Arontis," he said, "gather all the men together and make for Pinesward. Brazcek should welcome you in his walls. Take everyone in and hole up there, waiting for word. Symod is still alive, and so is a sorcerer in Londray."

"Everyone except the four of us," Idgen Marte suddenly put in, as she stepped out of Shadow behind Allystaire.

The paladin did not answer her. He turned to Gideon, whose eyes were large with a refusal only Allystaire could read.

"Go and round them up," Allystaire said, his voice still icily calm. He dismissed them with a wave of his hand. "Harrys. Tibult. Go with them. Round up the Order and be watchful."

"Should we gather the wounded for you?" Tibult, as always, was checking over his horse's limbs, seeing how it had fared in the battle, more concerned for it than for himself. "You should treat them as best you can," Allystaire said, "but I cannot take the time to heal them. I have another battle yet to fight." He waved his hands, dismissing the Barons and their knights.

"*We* have a battle t'fight, you mean," Idgen Marte growled.

"Andus Carek, take Rede, and Keegan, your men go as well. Give us a moment of privacy."

The bard went quietly, leading the almost catatonic Rede by one sleeve, to a pair of horses standing nearby. Keegan's wild men only walked a few paces away, out of earshot, but not out of sight of Gideon.

The boy turned to them and said, "Go, Keegan. Go. I will see you at Pinesward."

The old scout shook his head but turned to leave, waving his men after them.

In a few moments, Allystaire, Idgen Marte, Torvul, and Gideon were left facing each other in a driving rain, a stinging wind. The lightning seemed to have died, for now at least, though the clouds were not breaking.

"I see it in your face, Allystaire," Idgen Marte rasped, cutting him off before he could speak. "I see what y'mean to say. Don't. I'm coming with you if I have to chase after you all the way to Londray."

"Idgen Marte," Allystaire started to say, "I—"

"I can't carry you both," Gideon cut in. "Not and be of any use against the dragon."

"Then we'll ride," Idgen Marte yelled. "I'm not leaving you again, Allystaire. My task—"

"Does not extend to me alone," Allystaire said plainly, shaking his head. "Gideon and I will do this. We must. This is not an invisible threat, Idgen Marte. This is not something you must protect me from. You have done that;

you brought me to this day. This," he said, fighting down a sudden bolt of fear that shot up from his stomach, "this is mine alone. I prayed for this," he went on, "at the Temple. I asked if there could be a battle for me alone, against some champion, some avatar of Braech, that no one else should need to fight. That prayer has been granted now. Whether by the Mother or by Braech Himself or by a twist of chance, I do not know or care. I asked for this burden. Let me bear it."

He watched Idgen Marte's fists ball up, raised as if to strike him, her face twisting in anger. He could not have said if all of the water streaming down the sides of her face was from the rain that pelted them, and would not have ventured to ask.

"That part of your task is done, Shadow," Allystaire said, extending his right hand to her. "You brought me to this day, to this moment. If I could choose any companion to face Braech Himself with, it would be you. That choice is not mine to make."

She took his hand in a quick, fierce warrior's grip, pumped it once. "Then come back," she growled. "Because we're not Freezin' done yet."

He released her hand, glad of the rain that swiped at his own eyes. "Torvul."

The dwarf raised a huge hand. "Don't, not a word. You've not the tongue for it and I've not the time t'offer correction as ya stumble through it all."

"Then I will merely make a request. Is Renard's spear still among your baggage? I had no place for it on Ardent."

The dwarf nodded and stepped quickly away to his packhorse.

Allystaire heard a whicker behind him, the step of a hoof against wet ground.

Despite the calm that had come over him, despite the certainty of his course, the way it had lifted fear from his shoulders, Allystaire felt his heart sink when he turned to look into the huge eyes of the destrier that had followed or borne him on every step from Wind's Jaw to Thornhurst to Bend, to now.

He reached his left hand to stroke the wet neck; the huge grey almost bowled him over by pressing his head against Allystaire's shoulder. He tangled his fingers into the horse's wet mane, heard its great breath puffing in and out, the muscles of his chest working like a giant bellows.

"You cannot follow me now, Ardent," he murmured into a flicking grey ear.

"Go with Idgen Marte and Torvul. If I do not return, bear Gideon wherever he must go."

He stepped away, stroking the side of the great neck once more, looked again into the huge knowing eyes. "Do you understand?"

There was only another whicker, and the horse took two steps backwards, lowered its nose to the ground. Ardent did not nose upon it for grass or plants. He only bowed his head.

When Allystaire turned back, Torvul was holding out the spear he had taken at Leah's insistence. He'd not found a use for it in the battle; it was no lance, and he feared to break it.

Yet he knew to take it with him now.

"Gideon," Allystaire said.

The boy stood, came to Allystaire's side, and took his hand.

"The Mother will be with you," the paladin said to Torvul and Idgen Marte. "Our work is not done, even if I do not return. Tell Audreyn, tell Garth, tell Mol, I love them all."

Then the Arm and the Will vanished from their sight. Idgen Marte took Ardent's reins in silence, Torvul mounted his pony and took up his packhorse's lead, and they set out to rejoin the Baronial army as it made for Pinesward.

CHAPTER 54

Hammer of the Sun

Allystaire did not allow himself the time or the luxury of marveling at their flight, or whatever it would have been appropriate to call it. There was no impression of soaring for several hundred miles, there was just standing in one place, a kind of twisting, lurching feeling—not unlike being on a ship, he supposed—and then he was standing elsewhere.

His stomach tried to heave itself into his mouth when he suddenly found himself standing in the midst of a thick fog, thicker than any he had seen before. He did not allow himself to feel disoriented, or to go down to a knee to clear his dizziness. He clutched at the hammer at his side, preferring centering himself with the touch of steel.

He held both spear and shield in his left hand, arms through the loops of the shield, hand clutching the smoothly-polished oak shaft of the spear.

"Gideon, we are in Londray, yes?" Allystaire could feel cobbles beneath his feet, but otherwise there was nothing to tell him it was the city.

The boy at his side, whom he could barely see, nodded emphatically. "Yes. I can feel it."

"Where?"

"Towards the harbor. West. It—"

Their ears were suddenly assaulted by a massive roar. Allystaire felt his ears popping as though they'd been boxed. He fell to a knee and lowered his head.

There was something more than animal rage in the roar, Allystaire realized, even as he heard pieces of buildings jarred loose by the force of it, heard the shrieking and sobbing of people within.

It was both challenge and assault. He felt it trying to eat at his courage even while it goaded him onward, felt it tugging at his heart, at his decision.

YOU ARE WRONG, it said. **YOU CANNOT HOPE TO STAND AGAINST ME. EVEN WITH YOUR COMPANIONS, WITH A HUNDRED OF YOUR KNIGHTS, YOU COULD NOT HOPE TO DEFEAT ME.**

Allystaire felt that it whispered and yet the power in the whisper beat at him, tried to pound him into the ground, wave after wave of it crashing against him.

He clenched his jaw and forced himself to his feet. "Gideon," he said, though he could barely make out his own voice. "What can we do about this fog?"

"This," the boy said, taking a step back. He extended one hand towards Allystaire, the fingers of his palm splayed out.

Allystaire felt a sudden warmth upon his chest. He chanced a look down. Where once Gideon had, with only the power of his Will, engraved a golden sunburst upon his cuirass, there now blazed a small golden sun, pouring forth its light in a beam.

And where it touched the fog, it burned it away like fire running across parchment.

The light from his armor burnt a hole through the fog and towards the sky. And after a long moment, he felt the rays of the sun reaching down to meet it.

The mist began to recede in earnest, shriveling and shrinking away.

Another roar, but with the fog receding, this one seemed less powerful. It no longer seemed to come from everywhere at once.

It spoke again, setting Allystaire's head throbbing till he nearly stumbled.

YOU CANNOT HOPE TO MASTER ME. I AM THE RAGE OF THE SEA ITSELF. I AM THE STORM GIVEN LIFE.

Allystaire shouted his answer to the retreating waves of thick grey cloud.

"Every storm gives way to the sun eventually." He followed the voice towards the harbor, unlimbering his hammer, his steps slow and purposeful.

* * *

The Eldest felt the approach of the Negation, felt it falling like a star from the heavens. In truth, he wanted to stay and watch the resulting fight, perhaps see what residual power might flow that he could tap into.

And yet, he knew, from the very evidence that the ritual to raise the Dragon had worked, that the battle in the north had gone poorly.

And if the Negation was no longer there, whatever power was in that place, in the woman, or the impudent dwarf, was his to claim.

With interest, he studied the Negation's method of traveling so far so fast, watching the pattern of his terrifying power tear across the sky of pure will.

Then the Eldest simply seized onto his trail and followed it backwards.

* * *

Everywhere Allystaire and Gideon went, the fog rolled away from them. He felt his right hand growing warm inside his gauntlet. He thought little of it.

Then the fog rolled far back enough, as they crested a rise in the street, that they saw the Dragon spread its wings and take to the air.

It was unexpectedly and terrifyingly beautiful. A long, sloped reptilian snout with rows of teeth, as big as any spear or lance he'd ever seen a man wield, nestling together between its scaled lips. Two huge malevolent eyes the color of the sea before a squall, grey and awful beneath heavy brows plated with armored ridges of bone. The top rows of its scales were blue, ranging from a deep lapis at the very top, lightening and lightening into a near sea green, before reaching ranks and ranks of bronze along its belly. Four legs, each as tall as any two destriers the size of Ardent stacked atop one another, and huge leathern wings that beat the air with the force of a gale. Finally the long tail with the huge club at its base. It flew straight upwards, spreading its wings out, stretching its neck and tail to their full length, showing itself against the sunlight.

Allystaire heard more wailing from the houses around him, saw people transfixed at their shuttered windows, saw others huddling in alleys shielding themselves with their hands.

HAVE YOU COME TO SAVE THESE PATHETIC PEOPLE, PALADIN? WHAT MAKES YOU THINK YOU CAN? WHY DO THEY DESERVE TO BE SAVED? HOW WILL YOU SAVE THEM ALL?

With that, the Sea Dragon dove from the sky, spreading its wings and flying low over a distant quarter of the city. It reared its head, and Allystaire could hear the great lungs fill as it took a deep gulp of air.

Then the head and neck uncoiled like a striking snake, and scalding steam poured forth from the Dragon's mouth. It was not flame, but what it touched ignited, and instantly a long inferno spread along the line of its flight.

Allystaire heard the screams of those immolated, awful liquid sounds, shut his eyes as if that could block them out.

He kept walking, picking up speed. Against the Dragon's voice in his mind he felt the Mother's song, filling his limbs with a strength greater than before. His steps became leaps, became bounds as he started running, Gideon frantic to keep pace at his side.

WHILE YOU RUN TO THEM, PALADIN, WHAT OF THE PEOPLE HERE?

The Dragon finished its low pass over the far northern section of the city, rose up with powerful beats of its wings, sailed straight over Allystaire and Gideon's head and landed in the south of the city, crushing buildings with its legs as it didn't even try to shed momentum before landing.

Its massive tail swept out, lashing down more, crushing those within, destroying lives and livelihoods with a contemptuous sweep.

WHAT ARE THEY TO YOU, THAT YOU WOULD RUN TO SAVE THEM?

Allystaire let out a wordless scream of rage and yelled back, pausing to stare at the Dragon. "What are they to YOU that you kill them? What strength do you prove, Braech? What glory or victory do you gain with the destruction of them? Do you hop from place to place because you fear to face me?"

WHY DO YOU NOT RUN TO SAVE THEM? IS THAT NOT WHAT YOU ARE?

"I do what I can until I do what I must," Allystaire yelled, raising his hammer and pointing it towards the Dragon. The beast's tail swished behind it like a mischievous cat's. With a casual swipe of one huge foreleg it destroyed a city street, crushing wood and stone, thatch and brick like a man might crumple bread.

"And what I MUST do is destroy you," Allystaire went on, roaring out the fury that glowed inside of him. "I would save them if I can, but I will save more when you lie dead and broken. There is nowhere you can go that we will not follow. No place on this earth where you can fly that we will not come on your heels. I will have you, Braech. I will face you unless you fear me too much to risk it, and in that, I would stand victorious. Come and prove yourself against someone who DOES. NOT. FEAR. YOU."

The last four words were not the roar of a dragon, but they were louder than any man's lungs should have been able to make them. Tiles fell from nearby roofs. Pots fell from nearby market shelves and shattered.

FINE THEN, PALADIN. THE HARBOR.

The Dragon sprang up into the air again and beat its wings. Allystaire could feel the heat of them upon his face.

"Gideon," Allystaire said, "when it gets there, can you contain it? Wall it in, keep it from moving too far?"

"Perhaps," the boy said, heaving for breath from having had to run to keep up with him. "I can try. What did you have in mind?"

"Do not let it back into the city. Do not let it out to sea, or under the water," Allystaire said. "But let it climb as high it wishes."

Gideon nodded, and then was once more chasing after Allystaire, who bounded ahead, covering great leaps with nearly every step.

* * *

Idgen Marte sat uneasily in Ardent's saddle, the great beast plodding along at the back of the Baronial column. The destrier was too huge for her, too lacking in grace or subtlety. Over and over, she told herself, *Focus on the road ahead. Get to Pinesward with these men. See to their security. Then if I have to leap in shadows from here to Londray for a solid day to find him…* She sighed and looked over her shoulder at the muddy fields, practically plowed by their passage.

She blinked, drew Ardent to a halt, and yelled, "Gravek!" Behind her, huge shapes were silhouetted against the horizon, loping and shambling along, half a dozen or more.

The Order rode back to her call, Teague the first to hop from her saddle, unlimbering and stringing her bow in movements that were so purposeful, so clean, so graceful, Idgen Marte wanted to applaud.

She had an arrow nocked and raised the bow, sent it spinning into the air. She leaned forward, squinting behind her half mask, straining to see.

"They are not moving normally," she said slowly. "Those don't seem—"

"Dwarf! Your glass!"

Torvul dipped quickly into a pocket and pulled free his leather-bound, brass-fitted tube, uncapping and bringing it to his eye.

"Mother save us all," he breathed. "Battle-Wights. Gravek Battle-Wights."

"What?" Teague turned to him, even as she fit another arrow.

"Your arrows are useless against 'em," Torvul said, "they're…" He pulled the glass back to his eye. "Oh no. Oh Stones Above, no. It's…there's hundreds of them, Idgen Marte, we've got—" The dwarf lowered his glass and yelled towards the column strung out ahead of them. "RUN. RUN AND DON'T SPARE THE BEASTS." He quickly slid off his pony and unlimbered a sack from it, tossing it towards Harrys, who caught it easily. "Give that to any that look like flaggin'. Get to Arontis and the rest of 'em, tell them to run."

Idgen Marte slid off of Ardent's saddle, fingering the sword at her side, pondering what use she could make of it against Battle-Wights, casting about for a length of stout wood.

"What use is a Barony that's all pine," she growled, spitting into the mud.

Meanwhile Torvul was digging at his pack frame, cursing a string in Dwarfish, and Teague had lowered her bow, though an arrow was still nocked.

"I hadn't thought," the dwarf said, "I thought if we faced Wights again it'd be fewer, and smaller. I didn't make enough."

He pulled free a heavy bag and from it produced a wrapped jug.

"Enough of what," Idgen Marte said.

"Enough o'this," the dwarf said. "It's, ah, call it holy water. More like a holy tincture of mustard seed, wolfsbane, a bit of spirit, and—"

"I don't care what's in it, dwarf," Idgen Marte yelled. "What does it do?"

"It can slow them down. It should. Maybe kill some. Put it on your weapons." Torvul said. "But there's so many."

Before he could finish the thought, Teague seized the sheaf of arrows at her hip and dumped them onto the ground, then took a second from her saddle and added it to the pile.

She looked to Torvul, the half of her face they could see utterly calm. "Pour it," she said. "On the heads. Reserve as much as you can, but soak them well."

Idgen Marte looked to the woman, started to open her mouth to protest, but she had anticipated it, and raised her gloved hand, shook her head.

"Any burden," was all she said. Idgen Marte nodded, clasped Teague's arm, remounted. Torvul was carefully dousing her arrowheads with the tincture, and Teague was already taking a handful of them, holding them in her left hand against the bowshaft as she drew and nocked with her right.

The Shadow and the Wit ran on, leaving another knight of the Order of the Arm behind them. Idgen Marte heard the hiss of arrows releasing into the air, looked over her shoulder to see one fall into an oncoming Gravekmir Wight, and saw its arm shatter and fall away in a shower of bone and metal.

When she last looked back at her, Teague was smiling as she drew back her bowstring.

* * *

When they reached the walls of the Dunes, Allystaire saw that more damage had been done in the harbor. Boats had been lifted and tossed into one another. Quays and docks were smashed to splinters. Dockside shacks and shanties smoldered from the Dragon's scalding breath.

And the Dragon itself was hovering above the highest tower of the Dunes, flapping its wings, its huge angry eyes fixed on the comparatively tiny figure of the paladin.

For a moment, just a moment, Allystaire felt overcome by awe, and allowed fear to creep into his heart.

And then he saw the sun glint off his armor. The sun that was bathing the harbor, destroyed though it was, in its rays, and that was dappling the bay beyond it. The sun that had burned through the fog, that was staving off the thunderheads the Dragon seemed to summon with each beat of its massive wings.

"Strength is greatest when it is being spent for others, instead of marshaled to ourselves," Allystaire whispered. "Your enemies will not understand."

Allystaire raised his hammer to point to the high curtain wall of the Dunes. "Gideon," he said, "can you lift me to there? Not the nearest point, but well back along the parapet."

The boy nodded. "I can, but, Allystaire. Please, let me—"

"No. Do as I ask." He turned to look down at the boy. "You are going to be a great man, Gideon. That much was always clear," he added, resettling his grip on the hammer, wondering at the curious warmth in his hand. "Be a good one, too. Better than me."

Gideon lowered his head and raised one hand. Allystaire felt himself being lifted, flung, almost, from the ground into the air. He kept his composure, arms at his sides, clutching hammer, spear, and shield, landed with his knees bent, like jumping from a saddle. Around him he saw a guard or two hiding themselves, curled into balls, with their arms over their faces, fitted beneath the outcroppings of the wall.

The Dragon lifted its head and roared straight up into the sky.

WHAT DO YOU THINK TO DO, PALADIN? RAISE THE CASTLE'S SIEGE ENGINES? RALLY THE COWARDLY DEFENDERS? DO YOU THINK BALLISTAE CAN PIERCE MY HIDE? DO YOU THINK FLUNG STONES CAN TOUCH ME IN THE AIR OR UPON THE WATER?

"No," Allystaire said without shouting. He slid his hammer back into its loop, and took the spear in his right hand. "I do not."

The spear of a man who had willingly given up himself in the defense of his home. The weapon of a simple, honest man in love, given to him by the woman Renard had died for.

Perhaps the glow of it was in his mind, but Allystaire felt it would suffice, in hands suffused with the strength of the sun.

He reversed his grip, raised the spear over his head, and began to run. His other hand joined the first, holding the weapon point forwards in a two-handed grip.

His legs pumped faster than they ever had, the Goddess's Gift filling him with all that it had to give. Stone and wood cracked beneath the force of his steps.

He neared the edge of the parapet, raised his right foot in a higher step, planted it on the edge of the curtain wall, and launched himself into the air, straight at the Dragon.

Those beneath him on the wall felt nearly blinded by the radiance of his armor as the sun caught it.

Most of the folk hiding in the city could see only a ray of light fly from the edge of the Dunes and pierce the Dragon in its side.

The Dragon roared and flew straight up.

* * *

Chaddin and the other soldiers and greenhats on the walls of the Dunes had stayed immobile, frozen in place, as the Sea Dragon's rampage tore the city to splinters and dust around them. In his heart, Chaddin hated himself for those long moments of inaction. People were dying, people he was meant to protect. But nothing, no thought of shame or guilt or self-loathing could move him from where he huddled against the parapet. Every time he thought he found himself again, the Dragon's roar battered him back into the arms of his fear.

Until he heard heavy footfalls along the parapet, just above his head.

He turned his head and had only a brief impression of brightness, of a solid ray of sunlight moving past him.

But it lifted fear from his heart and fog from his eyes.

Chaddin sprang to his feet. Distantly, here and there, other soldiers began to do the same, slowly.

He seized the signal horn he carried, as the current ranking commander of the Dunes, and blew three loud blasts.

Chaddin began running for the nearest tower and the stairs to the court-yard, yelling orders to those he passed.

"Open the gates! Out into the city, everyone. We can't fight the dragon, but we can fight fires, dig up fallen buildings. Out! Pass the word."

Every soldier or greenhat or liveried servant he touched or spoke to snapped out of their fugue and hopped to his command. It wasn't long before they turned out in force on the ruined streets of Londray, even while a battle raged in the sky above them.

* * *

It was a hard flight to Pinesward Watch, with the Gravekmir gaining ground.

Idgen Marte tried not to think of what that meant for Teague, but she knew, when she looked back, that the numbers were less than they had been. She felt it, knew it in her bones.

When the walls of the keep rose up before them, she vaulted out of the saddle, sprinting as soon as she hit the ground. Whatever ground she had lost, she made up when she found a shadow, blurred into it. The world slowed around her; there, an abandoned tent, there a pile of rock, there the lee of a small hillock, the walls of the keep, then inside of them, atop the wall of the inner keep.

She appeared before a squat man she guessed to be about her age. Given the engraving upon his armor she assumed he was the Baron.

"Baron Varshyne?"

From the way his haggard, heavy-bagged eyes widened, she knew she'd guessed well, even as around her swords were being drawn and bolts were settling into crossbows.

She looked back. One enterprising young man was raising a weapon, preparing to pull the lever that would fire the bolt.

Faster than any of them could follow, she stepped to his side and hit the bow upward with one hand, sending the bolt firing in an arc, where it landed in the empty courtyard.

"Baron Varshyne," she said as she stepped away from the startled boy in his too-large armor with his too-large weapon, "I'm the Shadow of the Mother, an ally of the paladin, and I have a Baronial army beating its way to your door, with evil hard on its track. Throw open your gates. I beg you not to ask questions until you open the gate."

She watched him carefully. His mouth worked, tongue darting against dry lips. "Open the gate," he croaked. "Now! Go!"

A tall balding greybeard at his side quickly detailed individuals, who dashed down into the courtyard and began speeding towards the gatehouse.

"I am Brazcek Varshyne," he said, "welcome to Pinesward Watch."

"Idgen Marte," she rasped. "Now let's get that pile of broken furniture out of the way, too," she said, pointing to the hasty barriers erected in front of the gate and portcullis.

He nodded and waved his hand. This time, he led his men down to the courtyard himself.

He might look a fright, Idgen Marte thought, *but Cold, at least he's decisive.*

* * *

Allystaire felt the spear sink deep into the side of the Dragon, heard its roar.

And this time, in the roar there was pain and there was fear, not just the arrogance, the strength, the challenge.

The beast flew straight up, flattening its wings against its body. Allystaire felt the shaft of the spear breaking beneath his weight.

He drew back his left fist and punched it hard into the Dragon's scaled underbelly. Steel, even that worked by the Wit of the Mother, was not in itself strong enough to pierce that hide.

Allystaire felt his gauntlet crack and pain travel in shocks up his arm. He punched again. Knuckles in his hand crunched and cracked.

The Dragon starting spiraling, trying to throw him off. The spear shaft cracked.

He curled up his fist, touching his fingers to the palm of his hand, and healed it, punched again, broke through the scales and took a handhold, albeit slippery with blood, in the Dragon's hide.

Then he drew back his right fist and did the same.

Hurting and healing himself with each blow, he climbed up the side of the Dragon to its neck.

YOU ARE A FOOL. YOU WILL DIE. YOU WILL BE UTTERLY LOST. YOU WILL DIE IN THE SEA AND YOUR SOUL WILL BE MINE. The Dragon reversed its tactic. Its wings stopped beating, the spiral stopped, and the Dragon slowly bent itself in the air and aimed its long snout down at Londray Bay.

Allystaire felt them falling, clung hard to the rough, armor-like scales. Wind rushed against him, tried to tear him free.

What was wind compared to the power of the sun above them?

He smiled when he saw golden bars of light, like the bars of a cage, becoming visible beneath them as the Dragon descended like a falling arrow.

Another scream of rage and hollow, impotent anger, as the Dragon was forced to slow its descent, beating its wings.

It raised one huge forelimb and clawed at its own side and neck. Allystaire gasped in shock as the very tip of a claw rent his armor, shearing his right pauldron and upper guard away in tatters, taking most of the flesh of his arm with it.

He kept his left fist clenched, holding himself against the Dragon's side with his arm tightly bent, called on the Mother's Gift, and healed himself, closing the wounds even as the Dragon opened them.

With every awkward rake, the Dragon tore its own scales away, doing far more damage to itself than it could to the paladin, tearing gaping wounds open along its chest and stomach.

"I am willing to give all of it, Braech. To spend every Gift She has given me to defeat you," he yelled, his voice lost in the wind, but he knew the Dragon heard him. "I do not care if I am lost, Braech. I do not care if I am remembered or if my name is given any glory in song. I care only about defeating you."

The Dragon flew straight up again, its roar becoming a screech.

Allystaire felt the sky darken, felt droplets of rain lash his face. Thunderclouds rolled in, covering the distance of turns in the time it would take for but a few grains of sand to fall through the glass.

Allystaire pulled his right arm free and drew his hammer, held it up to the disappearing rays of sunlight.

Though his armor had been sheared away there, his arm still glittered silver, and the head of the hammer began to glow like the sun itself.

He bashed the hammer against the side of the beast's neck where it met the shoulder and the wing, shattering scales, rocking it in its flight. He heard bones, if indeed it had bones, crack.

Allystaire felt the sunfire crawling down the length of his hammer and into his hand, up his arm. His lower vambrace and gauntlet melted away. His arm became a thing of the sun itself, the hammer but an extension of it, all of it golden fire.

He smashed the hammer into the beast, even as the sun's rays consumed him. His flesh burnt away, his bones and sinew, leaving something of brilliant silver and golden light. He felt it; there was pain, but what was his pain compared to those crushed or seared on the streets beneath him? What was it besides the dead in the fields of Varshyne, or the families they left behind him?

The Arm of the Mother, the Paladin, Allystaire Stillbright pulled himself farther upward along the Dragon's neck, his left hand now simply digging into the scales and ripping at them, until he could wrap his legs around the beast and swing himself around behind its head.

Its scalding breath of boiling steam blew into the air, and then back onto him. The pain was indescribable, but he was utterly beyond pain now.

Once more he lifted his hammer and brought it down onto the base of the Dragon's skull. There was a crack loud enough to split the earth.

Allystaire felt the Dragon go limp beneath him and fall away.

He did not fall with the Dragon. He felt himself rise, felt all of his armor melt away, his body gone to sunfire. His hammer slipped from his hands and fell towards the bay alongside the broken body of the Dragon.

Then Allystaire Stillbright knew nothing more.

* * *

On the street below, Gideon was utterly exhausted. He drew power into himself from the air, from the water, from the ground, trying to keep the beast contained. He felt Allystaire drawing from the sun itself, felt a huge explosion of power flung back into the world far in the air above him.

The Will of the Mother reached tentatively for it. Most slipped from his grasp.

What he did catch overwhelmed him, and he fell forward onto the street, unconscious.

* * *

To the people of Londray, the Dragon had fallen like a star, huge and impossible, into the bay. An enormous wave rolled out from where it hit, swamping what few boats remained undamaged in the harbor, washing over the houses that ringed it.

Cautiously they peeked their heads out from doors or windows. People stepped out of doors, fearfully surveying what damage had been done. In time, greenhats and soldiers and even servants from the Dunes flooded the streets, formed bucket lines, brought shovels and mattocks and axes to dig into the destruction in the hopes of saving some.

In some places in the city, no one stirred. Fires raged. Voices cried out in pain from beneath collapsed buildings.

People wandered out into the streets where the green-clad men and women from the Keep appeared. They formed firelines, carrying water from cisterns and troughs and towers full of rainwater to where fires burned. They rushed with tools to the places where buildings fell, and dug madly for turns to free those trapped within.

And on a street near the harbor, a seamstress and netmender named Yolande found a slim, bald boy lying in the street. He seemed unhurt, breathing steady, but there was no waking him up.

With tender care and the assistance of a man who was running toward one of the fires, she lifted him up and carried him into her shop, a tidy little place with a sign outside of it showing a needle, an awl, a net, and a spool. It had escaped the worst of the damage, only some rattled windows and broken odd-ments to show for the excitement.

CHAPTER 55

The Will and the Eldest

Norbert barely kept to his feet, stumbling along behind the five Dragon Scales who taunted him.

The ache in his back was a more powerful pain than he had ever known. Every breath was an agony of fire. If ever he was freed, he knew, his shoulders and chest and arms were likely ruined. He would never draw a bow again.

Never wrap his arms around Lenoir without pain. If at all.

Still, he smiled to think of her as he shuffled along, one step after the other, nearly bent double under the beam lashed to his wrists and arms. Blood seeped from the ropes, which the berzerkers had tied wet, so that they'd truly tear into his flesh as they dried.

"Any burden," he muttered to himself as he took one more step, then one more, then finally crashed to the ground on his knees, dirt billowing up around him.

The berzerkers gathered around him, one prodding him with toe of a boot. The beat of hooves that had been the beat of his march of misery and pain ceased, and he heard footsteps approaching him.

"What's the matter, sir knight?" Symod's voice rolled heavy and mocking, rich in arrogance. "Not prepared to bear this burden any longer?"

"What's the matter, coward?" Norbert rasped back, from an all too dry throat. "Why do you run from the field of your great victory?"

There was a rush of air and Norbert imagined the priest meant to kick him with one heavy boot, to stave in his skull.

He raised his head, shifting the beam on his back as he did, staring up at Symod. "Do it," he growled, tasting blood in his throat. "You lost, or you would not run. What does my life gain you?"

The priest's lip curled in a sneer, and he stepped away. "Leave him," Symod intoned slowly, drawing the words out. "Let him be crushed under his burden. Let him die in the dust like a dog."

Norbert lowered his head back to the dirt track beneath him. He heard the footsteps moving away from him.

He planted one foot underneath of him, pushed up from that and one knee, raised his head.

"Cowards," he yelled, straightening his back, and breathing deep. "Run! The paladin will find you. The Order will find you."

They all stared at him strangely, the berzerkers exchanging looks with one another, and words in their rough tongue.

It was only then that Norbert realized that he had stood up. That he'd had the strength to stand.

That the beam on his back weighed no more than the shirt he wore.

A ray of sunlight touched his face and he flexed the muscles of his arms, drawing them together in front of him.

The beam snapped. The rocks lashed to it went spilling across the road.

Norbert pulled the broken lengths of wood into his hands, ripping the bindings free from the opposite arms. A broken beam was not an ideal weapon, he supposed, and he did not know where this strength came from.

But they would do.

Norbert turned the broken halves of the beam so that the splintered sides were forward, and he charged. Before the Dragon Scales knew what was among them and could credit it, two lay dead with the beams shoved through their chests.

He seized the third by the sides of his face and twisted his neck till there was a sharp crack, then whipped the body around, felt it absorb the blows of the throwing axes the remaining two had stepped back to throw.

Norbert dropped the body and plucked axes from its back with each hand, threw them without thinking on it.

One sank blade-first into a berzerker's chest and sent him tumbling to the ground. The other tumbled in the air and struck with its back end against the other's face, crushing his nose and cheek.

There'll be time for them, Norbert thought, as he saw Symod pounding down the road atop an already lathered horse.

He seized the remaining throwing axe from the body and hurled it with all the force his newfound strength could muster.

It sailed past Symod and into a bush. He hurled another, plucking it from the dying berzerker, stepping on the man's neck and crushing it for good measure.

It, too, sailed wide, and Norbert screamed raggedly in frustration.

He looked at the dead men around him, at the instrument of his torture lying broken in the road, and then up at the sunlight streaming across his face.

Norbert knew where his strength had come from, and he knelt on the road and wept.

* * *

Idgen Marte had fought tirelessly and endlessly for turns. She had never been more weary, more sick of a fight.

She had never wished more keenly for Allystaire to be by her side.

Teague, she reasoned, must have done a job on the Gravekmir, for but two of the giant Battle-Wights made it to the walls of Pinesward, which were defended now not only by Varshynners run off their feet and half-starved, but by Thornriders of Innadan and Harlachan axemen and knights from Telmawr, Delondeur, Damarind, and Machoryn.

And by the Order of the Arm. Or what was left of it.

None had sold themselves cheaply. While other men dug at the pile of wooden debris before the main gate of the keep, Mattar, Miklas, and Gaston, spears and axes in hand, had put down the two Gravekmir Wights that had made it so far.

But none of the three had survived the wounds. A Wight had taken Miklas's head as he pushed a spear through its exposed knee joint and tried to lever it to the ground. He had destroyed the leg, and the thing crashed to the ground, but in its death throes it crushed Gaston.

That left Mattar and Idgen Marte to deal with the second, while the Barony men tried to get inside the walls. She tried to attract its attention, darting away from it, pestering it with her sword, while he tried to climb it and dash its glittering dark head to pieces with a rock he'd seized.

Finally it reached over its shoulder to pluck him free, throwing him to the ground with a contemptuous twist of one hand, the bones still dotted with rotting flesh, wired together with pieces of unraveled chain mail.

Then Torvul arrived, peppering the thing with crossbow bolts. Where they hit, it exploded in showers of bone and metal, and there it died again, and, she hoped, for good.

They dragged Mattar inside the walls, where his death had been hard to see, knowing that Allystaire could have saved him with a touch. Instead, they watched him wheeze and gasp for breath until his lungs finally filled with blood and it seeped from his mouth.

Now she and Torvul stood along a length of wall with the remaining knights, Harrys, Tibult, and Johonn. All of them carried weapons coated in the last of Torvul's holy tincture.

That, Idgen Marte reasoned, had been the only thing that had kept all of them alive.

That and the calming presence of Arontis Innadan, who never flagged, never showed wear, never seemed to take a wound, whose sword was a marvel, a revelation, even to her. He was all over the wall, wherever the fighting was thickest.

In a word, she admitted to herself, *he's been regal.*

"I have to admit," she told Torvul, as they watched yet another group of Battle-Wights loping towards them, preparing to scramble up the wall, "I never thought I'd die in Barony Varshyne."

"Yer not gonna die here." Torvul said. The dwarf unhooked a flask and handed it to her. She drank, let the spirit burn her throat, handed it back. "Allystaire and Gideon'll return. Faith."

Inwardly, Idgen Marte knew that if she concentrated, she could reach out to Gideon and Allystaire, and even if she couldn't find them, she'd know where in the world they were, or at least in what direction. Yet she didn't, because she feared that she would find nothing.

She lifted her curved sword to the dwarf, who lightly reached out with the cudgel he'd improvised from a chair inside the keep and tapped it.

Battle-Wights swarmed up the wall, using their bladed hands, their axe-head hands, the points of spears imbedded on the end of what had once been arms, to find handholds and haul themselves up like awkward spiders.

Idgen Marte's sword whipped through the glittering grey-black head of the first one to show itself over the wall.

"There any Stonesong t'be had in these walls, dwarf?" she asked as she kicked out at one that suddenly tried to throw itself over the wall.

"Too old, too long worked," Torvul said sadly as he swung his cudgel like a smith swinging a hammer, breathing heavy with the labor of it. "And even those mountains could not have heard me without the boy's aid."

A knot of Wights gained the wall. Behind her she heard cries as more seemed to do the same.

The grey skies above were, at least, mercifully no longer dumping rain on them.

Mother, she silently prayed, as she whipped her sword from one Wight to another, trying to maximize each swing, going for joints, for limbs, for heads when she could. *Mother, at least give me sunlight to die in. I beg you*, she said, *I have walked in your Shadows. Let me walk now in the light.*

As if in answer to her prayer, shafts of light broke through the clouds above them, single fingers of gold.

They did not fall on her, though; they lighted on old Harrys, sneering and screaming defiance at the Wight he was locked in a deadly fight with; on Tibult, who seemed so gentle outside of a fight, who spent every moment worrying about his horse and everyone else's; on Johonn, giant, cheerful, game Johonn, with his enormous axe and quiet laugh.

And each of the Wights those three were fighting died beneath their next strokes.

Around them the fighting paused as the three of them looked at one another, and then at Idgen Marte and Torvul.

The knights nodded to one another, and then went back into the fray, pushing along the wall, Johonn one way, Tibult and Harrys together in the other.

The strength they showed, Idgen Marte knew, could only have come from one place.

She did what she had so feared to do and reached out, looking with the inner senses the Mother had Gifted them all with and yet had never spoken of. Gideon, she knew, was far to the west.

Allystaire was not. He was nowhere.

He was gone.

She did not scream, or cry out, or weep. Instead, the Shadow of the Mother whipped her sword sizzling through the head of another Battle-Wight and went back to the fight with renewed vigor.

There would be a time for mourning and for grief. Idgen Marte emptied herself of those feelings and fought.

* * *

With the Mother's Strength descending upon the remaining knights of the Order of the Arm, the tide quickly turned in favor of the Baronies. In perhaps a quarter of a turn, the field lay clear but for the enormous piles of broken and twisted bones.

And then a sickly green light suffused the battlefield. An amorphous figure, barely clinging to the shape of a man, appeared upon it.

His voice emanated not from the figure on the plain before the keep, but from everywhere, at once.

"Who here has the authority? Who is in command of this rabble?"

The words rolled around, echoing madly about the walls of the castle. Some of them repeated, the edges twisted and bent until the words sounded like other words, in tongues no one there understood.

Idgen Marte was already dashing from her side of the wall to where Arontis Innadan was stepping up atop the parapet and raising his hand. Torvul seized a potion from a pouch upon his chest and hurled it over the wall towards where the sorcerer stood.

The Shadow of the Mother had never moved faster, crossing the courtyard, up atop the opposite wall, diving for Arontis as he called out.

"I am Arontis Innadan, Baron of Innadan and Keeper of the Vineyards, and I—"

Before he finished the thought, and moments before she reached him, a thin flat beam of green light shot from the sorcerer's upraised hand, pierced Arontis in the chest, and blew a hole the size of a large gold link through his back.

His handsome face still open in shock, he pitched forward and fell, dead, over the wall of Pinesward Watch.

Then Idgen Marte let out a cry of rage, of frustration and anger.

She looked over the wall, intending to jump down and try the sorcerer herself, but he had turned away.

All over the field Battle-Wights were rising again, turning from smashed piles of bone into fresh enemies.

Instead of spending her life chasing after the sorcerer, Idgen Marte threw back her head and threw everything that was in her into her ruined voice and called, aloud and with her mind.

"GIDEON!"

The cry was almost unintelligible, rattled and echoed around the keep, and seemed to do nothing but disturb a crow or two that were roosting atop the towers, awaiting the end of the battle.

* * *

GIDEON!

The Will felt the cry in his mind, felt the fear in the Shadow's voice, and sat bolt upright.

He was upon a cot, soft and warm, blankets piled on him. A window was open. The smell of the sea and of a pleasant spring breeze wafted in.

A fire burned merrily in a nearby fireplace, before which sat a woman in a chair, drinking tea from a heavy mug. She stood and came to his bedside.

"Awake, lad? Terrible things that happened, terrible," she muttered, shaking her head. "Don't know where it came from, or what it was sent it back."

"When did it happen? How long ago?" Gideon's questions tumbled out of him as he threw back the blankets and came to his feet. His boots and stockings were gone, and he did not waste time searching for them.

"Only a few turns. What's your name, boy? There's no rush. Stay until you're well."

"I am sorry, good woman. In answer to your questions, it was the Sea Dragon, an avatar of Braech itself. And what killed it was the paladin. Allystaire Stillbright." He swallowed hard past a lump in his throat, but shoved the grief away. "My father. And now I have to go. You have my thanks."

Yolande dropped her mug to the ground when the boy simply disappeared.

"Allystaire," she muttered. "That's familiar," she said to her now empty room. And she remembered a vision of a man standing at a quay wearing glittering silver armor, with an arm that flared like a thunderbolt.

"No," she corrected herself, "like the sun."

* * *

Idgen Marte finally did weep, openly and joyfully, when a column of golden light broke through the clouds over Pinesward Watch and descended to the ground with the force of a blow.

All over the field where they had been rising, Battle-Wights fell to pieces.

Bathed in a nimbus of golden light, the Will of the Mother—a slim boy, barefoot and bald—confronted the Eldest.

"The Negation!" the sorcerer's voice babbled when Gideon appeared. The word repeated itself over and over, echoing and invading every ear.

Negation. Negation. Negation.

It was whispered and screamed and giggled and hurled like a curse.

The sickly-green form of the sorcerer hurled power at the Will. There appeared to be no thought, no plan, just an assault.

Gideon bore it all with an air of curious detachment, raising his hand and simply deflecting the energy the sorcerer threw at him into the ground.

"Why do you struggle?" Gideon said, shaking his head sadly. "You are already dead. You are a husk of nothingness, of empty ambition."

"You are the Negation," the Eldest shrieked, "you will NOT have my power."

The sorcerer raised another hand. Wights started to rise, pulling themselves together, metal shrieking as it bent and twisted to draw bones together. Clumps of shattered skulls and broken steel or iron flowed together into the glittering grey-black skulls that sat atop the animated corpses.

Gideon shook his head and they collapsed back to the mud.

"I don't want it," Gideon said. "I don't need it. You only reveal how little you understand, Eldest. All that I have negated is your stranglehold on power. There is nothing that you can do now, Eldest. Or should I call you Yrining, as you were called by the parents you have long since forgotten? There is nothing you can do that the meanest, poorest farm child might not some day be able to match. And they will do so without sacrificing themselves. Without forgetting their names. Without forgetting love, or music, or each other, or the names of their fathers and mothers."

"You would raise up hundreds of me," the Eldest replied in a dry and rotten laughter. "None can wield power without succumbing to it."

It was Gideon's turn to laugh. "Perhaps I will give the world monsters. But I will *also* give the world the means to destroy them. I will go and find my children, and I will teach them to love the world, not their power. I will teach them to love life itself, and others, and not the thrill of domination, of plots and conspiracy. And wherever a conniving Yrining tries to make himself an *Eldest*," Gideon smiled, "we will teach him how wrong he is."

Gideon seemed to grow taller as he advanced on the sorcerer, who shrank away from him. "Your plotting is done. Your grand design has failed. The Sea Dragon lies dead at the bottom of Londray Bay. If it rises again, it will not be within the span of your years. Realize what you should have many hundreds of years ago, Yrining. Know that you are dead. Accept it."

The Eldest raised a hand once more, summoning a ball of green fire.

Gideon stepped close enough to wave his hand contemptuously through it, and the sorcerer collapsed into the mud in a puff of dust.

Cheers rose up from the walls of Pinesward Watch.

Gideon fell to his knees, put his face in his hands, and wept.

Men rushed to throw open the gates and crank up the portcullis.

Idgen Marte threw herself over the wall and ran to Gideon's side, wrapping her arms around him. She knew, she sensed, that Torvul was running as fast as he could manage for the gate. She picked up the boy and carried him with her in Shadow to where Torvul could join them.

Against the side of the wall of Pinesward Watch, the Wit, the Will, and the Shadow gathered each other together in an embrace. Slowly, others would gather around them; Andus Carek, Rede, Keegan, the Barons. But for a few moments, heedless of who was watching or what they might think, they mourned together for the man who had brought them together, who had been brother, father, mentor, captain, friend. They wept and they held each other, a strange family that would not have been, if not for Allystaire Stilbright.

* * *

Far away in Thornhust, the Voice of the Mother leaned against the Pillar of the Arm in an otherwise empty Temple. Her hands lay against her folded legs, holding in them the carefully preserved blanketflower that Allystaire had tucked behind her ear when last he had set foot in Thornhurst.

She had known, one way or another, every moment of that short visit, that it would be the last time she would see him alive. She had wanted to fling herself into his arms, to warn him, to tell him not to go, but had known that she could not. Such was her burden.

She reached up to run the fingers of one hand over the sigil of the Arm.

It pulsed with sudden warmth beneath her hand, and Mol smiled through the tears that streaked her face.

* * *

The last person the Marynth Evolyn had ever expected to meet upon a bridge that spanned the Ash from Delondeur into fallen Vyndamere was the Choiron Symod.

He was unhorsed, walking in broken boots, coated in dust. His once regal face had a haunted and ragged look. The great grey mane of his beard and hair had grown wild and tangled and his face was streaked with dirt.

Even so, he tried to assume a regal air with her, even if were tinged with a touch of mania.

"Evolyn! Evolyn, in the Sea Dragon's name. What happened? Does the Dragon still rage? Did it quiet after it killed the paladin?"

The Marynth looked upon her escort of Dragon Scales, who regarded Symod with evident disgust. The Choiron pressed past them, clutched at her boot in the stirrup.

"Tell me," he shouted, "what news of Londray? I was pursued by a madman. It was catastrophe. The Eldest, he ruined all our plans. You will have to make amends for having brought him, but he can be managed."

"He is probably dead, you idiot," Evolyn said, coldly, kicking him away from her boot. "As is the Dragon, as anyone in any village for miles seems to know already. I cannot credit how fast it spread, but I can credit how it felt when it happened. Did you feel nothing?"

Symod's face cracked, his eyes widened till the whites bulged. "Dead? The Dragon? But the paladin—"

"Killed it," Evolyn spat. "Destroyed it over the bay. Folk say they were preparing to dive to go looking for remains when the boy showed up. The Will, the one the Eldest called the Negation? They say he brought the paladin's arms and armor—such as was left of it—up from the depths, and told them never to disturb the bones of the Dragon, that he had placed a curse upon them."

"Bones? Bones? But, but surely we can raise it again. We need only the right sacrifice, the right key."

"You are a coward and a fool, Symod. I cannot believe that ever I followed you, that I idolized you. You have ruined our Church. If ever a priest of Braech can raise their head again in the Baronies without it being struck off, it'll be after my death. You have destroyed us." She shook her head, her lip curled in disgust, and she said, rolling the words slowly off her tongue, "Kill him."

Then she rode on, without looking back. Not even when she heard his wet, gurgling screams.

CHAPTER 56

The Mother's Peace

The Barons, even Brazcek, had all agreed to travel together to Barony Innadan, bearing with them the body of Arontis Innadan, preserved by the
arts of the Wit of the Mother.

It was said of him that if his time in the seat was brief, it was distinguished,
and that it ended in a true peace.

But their stately progression found itself grinding to a halt when they came
in sight of Standing Guard Pass to find its towers occupied by armed men, with
the Oyrwyn Peak flying from their tops.

Gideon, Torvul, and Idgen Marte reined up outside of the Oyrwyn encampment. They had ridden a day or so ahead of the returning host, fearing just
such impediments. Gideon had not scouted again, saying that he found himself
too weak. Torvul carried copies of the agreement Gilrayan Oyrwyn had signed
and sealed, and marshaled his arguments.

Idgen Marte carried her sword.

Gideon was quiet, as he had been so often since Varshyne, since the Dragon
and Pinesward.

The pass was stuffed with soldiers. The banners of Naswyn and Harding
flew in the camps.

"This," Torvul said, "does not look promising."

A small party rode out under drawn banners to meet them. Gilrayan Oyrwyn was not in evidence. The party was led by Joeglan Naswyn.

"What is going on, Lord Naswyn?" Idgen Marte kept her hand auspiciously
distant from her sword's hilt. "Where is the Baron?"

"The Baron will not be meeting you," Naswyn said in his quiet and sober
voice. "He does not intend to adhere to a treaty which was signed under the
influence of witchery. Moreover," he added, "you three are to be detained as
hostages in order to secure the behavior of the other Baronies as we begin
rooting out the traitors who sought to undercut Oyrwyn's ability to make
war."

"What are you talking about?"

"We know you conspired to weaken us," Naswyn rumbled. "You will be
asked, and then compelled, to provide a list, so we may begin setting this right."

"You mean war within your own borders," Idgen Marte spat.

"For now, yes," Naswyn said. "If opportunities beyond that present themselves, Baron Oyrwyn intends—."

"I do not care what Baron Oyrwyn intends." Gideon's voice was cold and
exasperated, and the boy trembled as he stared up at Joeglan through knitted
brows. "I do not care what he *wants*. Where. Is. He."

Idgen Marte had to fight not to take half a step away from the boy, while
Torvul went to his side, murmuring words she did not catch.

"Do not be insolent with me, boy," Joeglan said. "You will be well treated so
long as you offer no resistance. But the Baron will not be seeing you until your
weapons are surrendered."

There was a blaze of golden light in Gideon's eyes. He waved his hand,
contemptuously, Idgen Marte thought.

Joeglan Naswyn flew backwards off his horse and landed ten paces away in
a clatter of armor. His horse's eyes rolled white and the animal ran wildly away.

The men around him, some wearing Horned Tower badges, some wearing
their own knightly livery, began to draw their swords.

Light flared in Gideon's eyes again. The swords flared so brightly that Idgen
Marte shielded her eyes, and then the men and knights were flinging them to
the dirt and grasping their scalded hands. She looked down; the blades were
molten rivulets flash-burning the new grass.

"Naswyn isn't dead," the boy said, his voice rising, filling the space around him. "But someone will be if I am not given some answers. Where is Baron Oyrwyn?" He pointed to the tower from which the Oyrwyn Peak fluttered. "There?"

One of the knights, his shield painted with birds perching on barrels in blue and red, half-nodded.

"Thank you," Gideon said, though the words rang hollow in a way that made Idgen Marte sweat. He turned towards the tower. He did not make a gesture, but the force of his concentration was nearly palpable.

The stone crenellations atop the tower exploded, one by one, pelting the men standing atop it with fragments of stone. Idgen Marte could hear them pinging off armor and shields, and a few strangled cries of pain.

"Gideon," she yelled. Torvul echoed her. He ignored them.

"Gilrayan Oyrwyn," he called out, "I will take that tower apart stone by stone until you show yourself. Starting now."

The tower began to unravel. Stones fell away and crashed to the ground. Gideon showed no signs of strain; he barely gestured. Somehow, the wooden floors and ladders that made up the interior stayed in place. Men crept back from the edge, shouting in fear. One teetered, only to be pushed back to his comrades with a flick of Gideon's finger.

Idgen Marte watched as the Oyrwyn delegation backed away. They mumbled fearfully, some making useless warding signs with their hands, until in ones and twos and then as a group, they broke and ran. She gave up on speaking aloud. *Gideon, I'm not sure this is helping.*

He didn't answer. More rocks fell from the tower till it was a trembling stairway standing alone full of terrified men in grey tabards and armor.

"Allystaire died for you, Gilrayan Oyrwyn," the boy said, and though he did not yell, his voice carried throughout the entire pass, reverberated off the mountains. "For all of you. And you would repay his death, and so many more, with treachery and war. With grasping and plotting, and thinking of ways to turn it to your advantage."

The delegation before them broke and ran. Torvul and Idgen Marte shared a fearful look.

Gideon! This is not the way.

He turned towards her, his eyes featureless orbs of gold that shone against the dusky skin of his cheeks. "He will answer me, Idgen Marte."

"Or what?" Torvul muttered, just loud enough for them to hear. "Or you'll murder him and all his men in broad daylight?"

"Hundreds died to grant them peace. They would squander it, for *what?*"

"And how many of them would you kill in turn, boy?" Torvul's voice was quiet, but Idgen Marte saw his hand creeping towards a potion-pouch.

"Do not try and stop me. I will not let you." Gideon slid off the saddle but his feet did not touch the ground. Instead, he hovered a few inches from the mud. He flicked a finger, and a bubble of light of the same color as his eyes surrounded him. Torvul's hand dropped feebly away from his pouch and he looked at Idgen Marte.

For the first time since she had known him, the dwarf seemed not only frightened, but out of ideas.

Gideon raised one arm and clenched his hand into a fist. "Gilrayan Oyrwyn. Answer. Me." The hill the tower sat upon in order to command a broad view of the pass and plain below began to rumble and shake.

"Give me Gilrayan Oyrwyn and the rest of you will live." Gideon's voice rolled like thunder.

Idgen Marte wasted no more time on thinking. She acted.

The light emanating from Gideon's eyes, and from the shield he'd erected, provided plenty of shadow next to him. A cloud passing near the sun gave her what she needed. She reached for her gifts and shifted, just a few feet, so that she was standing directly in front of him. Though he floated off the ground, she could look him directly in the eye.

What she found there terrified her more than all of the berzerkers, sorcerers, and Braechsworn she'd already faced.

Though the light in them was golden, it was of the same intensity and quality as the sorcerers she'd seen. The color radiated thinly through the skin of his cheeks, emphasizing how hollow they'd grown since Allystaire's death. She clamped her arms onto his shoulders and forced him to look at her. She could feel power humming through his skin, the bones of his shoulders poking through the robe.

"Gideon, this is not loving the world. This is not what you said to the Eldest."

"Allystaire *died* for them!" he shouted again. "He asked for nothing but peace. They have broken their own promises." The rumbling became a roar. The tower tottered. Men hung suspended in the air. "They don't *deserve* peace."

"And what would he want of you? We will enforce the peace, Gideon. But is this what Allystaire would want from *you?*"

Something in her words broke the cast of his face. The glow dimmed. His feet touched the ground. Gideon lifted his hands and the tower fell back into place. Stones fell from it, crashing into the spring mud below. A man fell through one of the gaps, his scream cut off as he stopped his descent mere inches from the ground, suspended in the air. Then he fell with a light thud.

The golden glow went out of Gideon's eyes, leaving them a wide, deep brown once more. They were red-lined and wet, and he fell against Idgen Marte's shoulder with a great wracking sob.

There was a rush of Oyrwyn men from the tower, precipitating an exodus of Oyrwyn forces from the pass. They ran, abandoning their camps and stores, cutting their horses free from picket lines in twos and threes, until it became a general rout.

Idgen Marte wanted to go amongst them, slipping into their shadows to search for Gilrayan, then haul him to account before the other Barons. But Gideon clung to her, sobbing until his throat was hoarse, and she would not let the boy go.

* * *

Before the Barons arrived, she found a large tent, with a garish knight's livery sewn upon it, and led Gideon to the large cot inside, a featherbed upon it. He fell into it without a sound. She watched him until she was sure he was asleep, then turned to attend to her horse and her bags and Andus Carek and a thousand other, lesser things that would try to demand her attention.

Then Gideon's voice, small and weak, came from the cot.

"Please don't," he said.

"Don't what?"

"Leave."

She turned and took a seat on a nearby folding stool. "I'll be here when you wake," she said. She reached out for Torvul with her mind. *I need something,* she began.

Already on my way.

* * *

Idgen Marte dozed, for how long she wasn't sure. Gideon showed no signs of waking. *Too much I need to be Freezing doing,* she thought. *Goddess knows what they'll ice up out there without me.*

But still she sat. She was never good at stillness, at being idle. So it wasn't long before she snapped open the lute case Torvul had brought her, revealing the plain lute she'd bought Gideon and taught him with. She pulled it free, set it on her lap, and began tuning it idly. It had fallen woefully out of playing shape; there were no signs of recent use or care.

It wasn't long before an idle strum of notes woke Gideon up.

"How long have I slept?"

She shrugged. "How long since you played this?"

"Since before the battles."

She tsked. "A new hand has to keep at it. The skills aren't ingrained yet. You'll lose them if you aren't careful."

He said nothing as she continued to strum, watching her fingers. For a moment, the only sound in the tent was the notes she plucked out.

"He wanted me to be a better man. Than him."

Idgen Marte lifted her head. "What?"

"You asked me what Allystaire wanted for me. That's what he said. The last thing he said to me. That I would be a great man, but that I should try to be a good one. Better than him."

His eyes glistened again as he spoke, but showed no signs of the earlier outpouring of tears.

"That's why I stopped," he went on. "When you asked…he would've been angry. He would've wanted to attack them, kill Gilrayan Oyrwyn. But he wouldn't have wanted me to do it. Not like that. Not to all of them."

"Probably not," Idgen Marte agreed. She stood up and carried the lute to him, holding it out, giving it a shake until Gideon took it, awkwardly, as if he was no longer sure what to do with it.

"I'm not Allystaire," she said. "I can't try t'be a father to you. But you'll have me around as…your sister or your aunt or whatever you care to call me. And Torvul, though he'll never say it in so many words."

Gideon nodded and settled the lute in his lap, setting his hands on the strings.

"I have things I have t'go see to now."

"I know," Gideon said. "I also know the question you want to ask."

Idgen Marte felt a lump form in her throat.

"There wasn't anything you could've done."

Her hand clenched hard around her swordhilt as she nodded and left.

* * *

"I could challenge him directly," Garth was saying as he stood at the head of an impromptu war council in the open air, enough light still in the sky to read each other's faces, and the maps spread on the table. "I'll not lay siege to Wind's Jaw. That's a fool's game at best."

Idgen Marte was Freezing well sick of looking at maps on tables, so she paced back and forth at a little remove, listening, not watching.

"Go back to your home," Torvul said. "See that it is secure."

"I can't let him continue to gather men to him."

"He's got all the strength of the Barony already," Idgen Marte said. "Challenging him might have some merit, but he'll not answer you. He's nothing to gain by accepting, and too much to lose."

"She's right," Torvul advised. "He'll simply be able to say you're a traitor, unworthy of the honor, and have his archers fill you full of pinholes. Go home," the dwarf repeated.

It took some doing, but Garth was reluctantly persuaded, and ordered his men to stand down but for an ordinary watch. The other Barons and Baronesses retreated singly and in pairs.

That night, Idgen Marte lay in her own tent—her own pavilion, insisted upon by Garth—with Andus Carek. The folding cot was in no way comfortable for two, so they'd spread the bedding and pillows upon the ground, and lay on them with their hands entwined, letting the spring breeze blow in through the lightly tied flaps. "It is better," Idgen Marte said, "for one man to die than for armies to clash. This seems obvious," she murmured.

"Marte," he answered, "if I were you, I would have slit his throat weeks ago, back on the trail to Wind's Jaw. That he still lives is testament to your patience and forbearance."

"And Allystaire's order," she reminded him.

"Allystaire is dead," Andus replied, sitting up on an elbow to look down at her. "I take no joy in saying it, but it remains the truth. Allystaire is dead, and you must carry on, and do as you think best. Sometimes you need a hammer, sometimes a siege engine. He was both. But sometimes you need a knife. That is you."

She nodded and sat up. "He can't have gotten far. I can catch him up if I push myself, and still catch up to this funeral procession at the Vineyards."

"Take Torvul with you. I'll watch Gideon while you're gone. Teach him a new song."

She tilted her head to one side, eyes widening. "You'd teach him? Without payment, without going to the Tower?"

"I'm never going back to the Tower if you aren't," Andus said, shrugging. "As for payment? There is the small matter of the Dragon, of everything he did during the war with the Braechsworn, the sorcerer."

She shrugged and nodded, then stood, dressing quickly and slipping on her swordbelt.

Andus Carek hastily scribbled some notes, then took up his lute case. Once outside, all he had to do was follow the notes to where Gideon strummed his lute.

* * *

As it turned out, it wasn't as easy to catch up to Gilrayan as Idgen Marte had thought. The Oyrwyn troops that surrounded him never camped for long, not even long enough for her to determine if he was traveling with them or not. Worse, they kept their short camps too brightly lit for enough shadows to appear for her to scout well.

She and Torvul were hard after them for two days, the dwarf grumbling all the way, before the camp finally pulled up at a watchtower standing at the head of a trail. It was ordinary enough, but something about it seemed to give the fleeing men pause, as if it was a sign that they were well within their own strength, well away from the Will of the Mother and his power.

What's more, Idgen Marte was close enough to their camp, hidden in thicket and fallen stones, to see Joeglyn Naswyn and an anonymous armored soldier heading inside.

"Oh, that little sack of shit," Torvul grumbled as he peered along her line of sight with his glass. "That's him. Look at the gambeson and the surcoat. Too richly embroidered, and with the Oyrwyn peak in silver thread, no less. He was hiding in plain sight all along."

"Cold," Idgen Marte swore. "One of the oldest tricks. Can't believe he snuck it by us."

"We've had a long spring," the dwarf muttered. "Can you get us both inside?"

"Let's wait till night falls."

"Good," the dwarf said. "I have some documents to draw up."

* * *

The Oyrwyn men were lax that night. Torches were lit along the stairs of the tower, and fires outside, but they didn't blanket the camp in lanterns as they had on the march. It was easy work for Idgen Marte to drag Torvul from shadow to shadow, the dwarf clinging to her arm and claiming dizziness whenever they stopped. Finally, she left him in one of the higher firing positions, not much more than a niche before an arrow-slit, and continued on. He'd come when she needed him; he had that knack.

She made straight for the top. She wasn't sure why, but she did. And it wasn't even in the rooms, but rather on the very top, that she found them.

Naswyn standing. Gilrayan, seated at a table, with heavy candlesticks, tapers burning in them, and a pile of papers.

"Going to be a clean sweep of Coldbourne and Highgate lords, more or less," Gilrayan was saying. Arrayed on the table by the papers and candles were heavy silver knobs. Seals, she realized. And sticks of wax.

"And by the all the Gods who care to listen, I'm going to have that underhang on the walls here dug up, the flowers burned, and the grave emptied while I'm at it."

Idgen Marte's mind raced back to her conversation with Audreyn, a lifetime ago.

You'd never see it unless you knew to look for it, as it sort of hangs off one side of the tower, hidden by the battlements. He kept it planted with her favorite flowers. Mountain veitch and loosestrife, as I recall. He never rode that trail, to or from Wind's Jaw, without stopping, climbing the tower stairs, and slipping down to the graveside. Not once.

Tears threatened her eyes when she realized where she stood, and the desecration Gilrayan Oyrwyn spoke so casually of.

Idgen Marte wouldn't die for a grave; she shared that much with Audreyn.

But for this one, for what it had meant to a man who had been her friend, she might kill.

There was no thought. She sprang. The pommel of her sword cracked into the side of Gilrayan Oyrwyn's skull and sent him sprawling onto the stones of the tower roof. She stomped her boot into his throat, heard him start to gargle, and had the tip of the blade pointed at Naswyn's throat before he had half-drawn his own sword.

"You heard him, Lord Naswyn. You heard his words, and you would still defend him?"

Naswyn's sword lowered back into his sheath. "I don't know what you're talking about, witch," he hissed. "I know you have assaulted my Lord Baron, and for that, you'll—"

"Your own daughter's grave, man! Here, at this tower! That's what he means to dig up."

Naswyn faltered. "She's buried at the Horned Towers. Not in our mausoleum, but on the grounds."

Idgen Marte planted the heel of her boot squarely between the choking Baron Oyrwyn's legs. He began retching. She grabbed Naswyn by the front of his cuirass and dragged him to the edge of the tower.

"There," she hissed, pointing with her sword, not caring if anyone in the camp happened to be looking up at that moment.

There was a ladder, barely visible. An under-hanging battlement, hardly worthy of the name. A blanket of purple flowers. A simple stone with nothing engraved on it.

"Allystaire interred her here. Are you so simple that you did not know?"

Idgen Marte was close enough, despite the failing light, to see Naswyn's face change from the passive mask to a rictus of rage. He tore from her grasp and seized the gasping, retching Gilrayan Oyrwyn in his long arms before Idgen Marte could think to stop him.

"You rapacious child. You fatuous, lying, grasping..." Joeglan hauled Gilrayan to his feet.

Idgen Marte knew she could intervene. Perhaps she should. But she didn't.

"I'm your rightful lord, Naswyn," Gilrayan wheezed, but Naswyn was beyond caring. He gave the Baron Oyrwyn a hard shove, pushing his long arms to their fullest length.

Gilrayan Oyrwyn hit the far side of the tower. He bowed precipitously over the crenellations, flailing his arms weakly, overbalanced, and fell without a sound.

"Well," Toruvl said, as he emerged onto the top of the tower, "good thing you've got me here to write a letter explaining why the Baron Oyrwyn decided to end his life."

"Better," Idgen Marte said, "that we have Lord Naswyn here to witness it."

* * *

On the night Gilrayan Oyrwyn unexpectedly ended his life by hurling himself from a watchtower on the southern approach to Wind's Jaw, he left behind several important orders and correspondences.

The first and most shocking was the note detailing his secret plots to invade Innadan, a staunch Oyrwyn ally, under the guise of Harlach uniforms and banners.

Since most of his closest lords knew the plan to be true, they did not question it.

Other orders dispersed all the troops and knights and lords back to their own fiefs for the entire summer, only to be gathered again in the event of invasion.

Lord Joeglan Naswyn, loyal to a fault and with as much imagination as a stone, saw to it that the orders were obeyed by everyone involved. His own seal and witness upon the documents left no question in any mind.

The most important political consequence was his Declaration of Abdication in favor of Garth of Highgate, who, as the new Baron Oyrwyn, was to distribute his fief of Coldbourne as he saw fit, and to pass Highgate to his nearest blood relative.

Most curious was an order little noticed save by a generation of Oyrwyn men who had been trained by, or grown up with, Allystaire Coldbourne. It made the law of the land not to tamper in any way with one particular watchtower that guarded a southern trail down out of the mountains, and that any irregularities in that tower were to be maintained exactly as they were found. It was to stand as long as Barony Oyrwyn did.

* * *

With the Barons gathered for the funeral of Arontis Innadan, conducted jointly by Mourmitnourthrukacshtorvul, Wit of the Mother, and Cerisia, Archioness of Fortune, at the Vineyards in early summer, gossip had largely been on two subjects.

The first, that was on every lip, was the might have been: of King Arontis Innadan. Even Unseldt Harlach and Ruprecht Machoryn, two men it was hard to please together, were both heard to say that if they had to see a crown on any head, they would have chosen his. Arontis the Uncrowned, people began to call him. The name spread.

The second was the shocking suicide and abdication of Gilrayan Oyrwyn and what it meant for Baronial peace.

The Barons returned to their home keeps in high spirits, under beautiful skies and clear weather. But not without reminders from the Shadow, the Wit, and the Will, to the terms they had agreed about the Temples and Chapels of Braech.

In the coming seasons, the Barons were told, the servants of the Mother would be visiting to see that the terms were adhered to.

* * *

It was late summer, with the sun high in the air and hot, and the fields full of high corn, when Idgen Marte, Torvul, and Gideon finally returned to Thornhurst with Rede, Andus Carek, and the last three knights of the Order of the Arm.

Or so they had thought. Mol, of course, had turned out the town to greet them, and foremost among them was Norbert, standing with Lenoir, grinning widely at his three remaining comrades. Soon they were all soldierly embraces and gentle ribbing.

But that soon abated when the train of saddled but riderless horses came into view.

Gideon rode his old palfrey, Allystaire's old palfrey, rather than Ardent that morning. With the crowd watching silently, the destrier led the line of five other riderless horses, each of them with a dead knight's weapons secured to the saddle, straight towards Mol.

The other horses merely followed the huge grey, but there was something different in the way Allystaire's warhorse walked straight to the girl and lowered his great head till his nose was placed in her cupped hands and his head was pressed to her shoulder.

Mol stroked his cheeks with her fingers and made gentle sounds of reassurance, murmured words no one else heard.

Then the Will, and the Wit, and the Shadow came forward. Mol took Gideon by the hand, and the four of them walked towards the Temple, Ardent following slowly after.

The crowd had been ready to greet them with songs, and wine and cheering, but something about the scene had turned the ready good will to somber reflection.

The doors of the Temple of Thornhurst swung open. Mol entered first, then Idgen Marte, then Torvul. Gideon stopped, ran back down the steps and gathered the hammer he'd recovered from the bottom of Londray Bay. It sat heavily in his hands. He spun it to look at one of the rounded heads at the golden sunburst that glinted in the center, and at the tiny image of a hammer in relief inside.

He hefted it, as if preparing to swing, then shook his head. Gideon took it with both hands and carried it into the Temple to lay it against the altar. The door shut behind him.

The people of Thornhurst remembered that day, the day of the funeral of Sir Allystaire Stillbright, the Arm of the Mother, founder of the Order of the Arm, the Paladin and Prophet of Her Church, as an exceptionally bright and warm summer day, but for one mysterious turn. Despite the brightness of the day, with no clouds in sight, it rained for one turn of the glass. Steady long drops falling straight down upon the village from a cloudless, sun-filled sky.

People came to say that the sun itself was weeping for the death of the paladin.

The end of *The Paladin Trilogy*

Acknowledgments

Thanks are due to so many of you for working alongside me for the seven years this story has taken to finish. To Andrew for believing in it. To Melanie, Gwen, Kyle, and Karen for working hard to shape it with (and sometimes against, to the book's betterment) me. To Rion for sharing an open call for fantasy manuscripts so many years ago. To Yeager, Andy, Caren, Sarah, Jacob, Jason, Stephanie, and Josh for nonstop beta reading and advice and listening to me complain. To everyone who's ever sat down at a table and picked up dice with me, who has seen glimpses of Allystaire or Idgen Marte or Torvul or Norbert in the characters I made with them, because that's where they were all born. And thanks to every reader who's taken the time to email me, to talk to me at a con or an event, who has read the book and given it to friends and family and fellow gamers, who tweeted about it or reviewed or mentioned it. I hope you'll all come back, and bring a friend, when I tell more stories in this world.

About the author

Daniel M. Ford was born and raised near Baltimore, Maryland. He holds an M.A. in Irish Literature from Boston College and an M.F.A. in Creative Writing, concentrating in Poetry, from George Mason University. As a poet, his work has appeared most recently in *Soundings Review*, as well as P*hoebe*, *Floorboard Review*, *The Cossack*, and *Vending Machine Press*. He teaches English at a college prep high school in the northeastern corner of Maryland.

Find him on Twitter @soundingline.